Praise for John Sayles's

A MOMENT IN THE SUN

"[*A Moment in the Sun*'s] true importance lies not in its rearview relevance but in its commitment to recalling in heroic detail a little-known and contradictory historical moment, a sunny time of American pride but also of hubris in sun-beaten locales... Sayles is not a neutral channel, but in his respect for facts both documented and extrapolated, he is devoted to offering us a new understanding of the past."

—Tom LeClair, *New York Times Book Review*

"A brutal picaresque complete with melancholy whores, militaristic robber barons, desperate cutthroat prospectors, and puppet soldiers... His period slang rings dead-on perfect. [Sayles's] great achievement is to illuminate the parallel between imperialism and racism in turn-of-the-century America—indeed, to shine so glaring a light on it that even if we screw our eyes shut, the horror remains."

—William T. Vollmann, *Bookforum*

"Independent filmmaker John Sayles has managed to create a work that is both cinematic and literary in its scope and style—a blend so entrancing that you could polish off its 955 pages in one long weekend. It begins in 1897 during the Yukon gold rush and takes us into the Spanish-American war, the Filipino fight for independence, racial injustice and the plight of working people throughout the United States. Short, powerful chapters follow four unconnected characters to create a mosaic of America as a nascent superpower, underscoring the personal and cultural consequences of its ambitions. If you only read one book this summer, make it *A Moment in the Sun*."

—Lucia Silva, NPR's *Morning Edition*

"Following four major characters and dozens of sharply drawn smaller ones, *Moment* jumps from a horse thief's prison break to a Filipino revolutionary secretly photographing a government execution, creating a story so big that even the larger-than-life characters that Sayles weaves into his narrative are dwarfed by comparison. Pick up McSweeney's gorgeous tome—taking care to lift with your knees—and you'll find that the 950-page book moves far more quickly than its bulk might suggest."

—Sam Adams, *The Onion A.V. Club*

"John Sayles may be better known as a filmmaker (*Lone Star, Eight Men Out*, and my favorite, *Return of the Secaucus 7*) than as a novelist, but this drama spanning five years, and stretching from Cuba to the Philippines, proves him to be a great fiction writer. The conscience that infuses his earlier work is evident in this novel, and if you're looking for a summer reading challenge with a big payoff, this may be your book. Sayles tells a story of American racism and American imperialism at the turn of the century, through a kaleidoscope of imaginary and real-life characters, including Joseph Pulitzer, William Randolph Hearst and Mark Twain."

—Elizabeth Taylor, *Chicago Tribune* (Editor's Choice)

"Sayles is a terrific writer. His breathtaking precision and attention to detail can make E.L. Doctorow's historical novels look puny and slapdash by comparison. His ability to map the intersections of scores of plots and hundreds of fictional and real-life characters is truly stunning." —Adam Langer, *San Francisco Chronicle*

"*A Moment in the Sun*'s moment is now, a strapping 955 pages, a sprawling *USA*-style novel that, something like the John Dos Passos classic, follows a group of characters in parallel tracks as they traverse the America of 1897, taking in the Yukon gold rush, the Spanish-American War in the Philippines, and the advent of movies. Like all Sayles films and novels, it's drenched in a detailed, loving awareness of time and place." —*Philadelphia Inquirer*

"Absolutely vivid... Sayles's creative strengths are on full display." —*Newsweek/The Daily Beast*

"In his most spectacular work of fiction to date, filmmaker Sayles combines wonder and outrage in a vigorous dramatization of overlooked and downright shameful aspects of turn-of-the-nineteenth-century America... Crackling with rare historical details, spiked with caustic humor, and fueled by incandescent wrath over racism, sexism, and serial injustice against working people, Sayles's hard-driving yet penetrating and compassionate saga explicates the 'fever dream' of commerce, the crimes of war, and the dream of redemption." —Donna Seaman, *Booklist* (starred review)

"Though known best as a filmmaker (*Eight Men Out*), Sayles is also an accomplished novelist (*Union Dues*), whose latest will stand among the finest work on his impressive résumé. Weighing in at nearly 1,000 pages, the behemoth recalls E.L. Doctorow's *Ragtime*, Pynchon's *Against the Day*, and Dos Passos's *USA* trilogy, tracking mostly unconnected characters whose collective stories create a vast, kaleidoscopic panorama of the turn of the last century." —*Publishers Weekly* (starred review)

"Sayles's cat-squasher of a book... pulls all his characters onto a huge global stage, setting them into motion as America goes to war against Spain and takes its first giant step toward becoming a world power. The narrative is full of historical lessons of the Howard Zinn/ Studs Terkel radical-revisionist school, but Sayles is too good a writer to be a propagandist; his stories tell their own lessons and many will be surprises... [*A Moment in the Sun* is] a long time in coming, with an ending that's one of the most memorable in recent literature. A superb novel." —*Kirkus* (starred review)

A MOMENT IN THE SUN

A NOVEL *by*

JOHN SAYLES

McSWEENEY'S BOOKS
SAN FRANCISCO

www.mcsweeneys.net

McSweeney's and colophon are registered trademarks of McSweeney's, a privately held company with
wildly fluctuating resources.

ISBN-13: 978-1-936365-58-6

Printed in Michigan by Thomson-Shore.

for Maggie

ANDREW
Best,

John Taylor

TABLE OF CONTENTS

Book One
MANIFEST DESTINY

Book Two

A MOMENT
IN THE SUN

Book Three

THE ELEPHANT

BOOK I
MANIFEST DESTINY

FRONTISPIECE

In the drawing Uncle Sam and Lady Liberty stand side by side on the shore. We see them from behind, but know, by their dress, whose pensive vista we are sharing.

There is a breeze coming in, the flame from the Lady's torch, held tentatively at her hip, blowing toward us slightly. The vast ocean stretches before them, and the sun, rays crepuscular on the rolling waves, is only a sliver above the far horizon. Filling the darkening sky above and dominating the page is a question mark.

We are looking west.

We can't see their faces, of course, can't tell if they are seeking adventure, longing for treasure, anticipating unknown horrors. That will come later.

GOLD FEVER

Hod is the first on deck to see smoke.

"That must be it," he says, pointing ahead to where the mountains rise up and pinch together to close off the channel. "Dyea."

There is a rush then, stampeders running to the fore and jostling for position, climbing onto the bales of cargo lashed to the deck to see over the crush, herding at a rumor as they have since the *Utopia* pulled away from the cheering throngs in Seattle, panicked that someone else might get there first. Store clerks and farmers, teamsters and railroad hands, failed proprietors and adventurous college boys and scheming hucksters and not a few fellow refugees from the underground. Hod has done every donkey job to be had in a mine, timbering, mucking ore with shovel and cart, laying track, single-jacking shoot holes with a hand auger. He knows how to look for colors in a riverbank, knows what is likely worth the sweat of digging out and what isn't. But the look in the eyes of the men crowding him up the gangplank, the press of the hungry, goldstruck mass of them, five days jammed shoulder-to-shoulder at the rail of the steamer dodging hot cinders from the stack, half of them sick and feeding the fish or groaning below in their bunks as the other half watch the islands slide by and share rumors and warnings about a land none have ever set foot on—he understands that it will be luck and not skill that brings fortune in the North.

Though skill might keep you alive through the winter.

"Store clerk outta Missouri, wouldn't know a mineshaft from a hole in the ground, wanders off the trail to relieve himself? Stubs his toe on a nugget big as a turkey egg."

"You pay gold dust for whatever you need up there—won't take no paper money or stamped coin. Every night at closing they sweep the barroom floors, there's twenty, thirty dollars in gold they sift outta the sawdust."

"Canadian Mounties sittin up at the top of the Pass got a weigh station. It's a full ton of provisions, what they think should stand you for a year, or no dice. Couple ounces shy and them red-jacketed sonsabitches'll turn you back."

"Put a little whiskey in your canteen with the water so it don't freeze."

"Hell, put a little whiskey in your bloodstream so *you* don't freeze. Tee-totaller won't make it halfway through September in the Yukon."

"Indins up there been pacified a long time now. It's the *wolves* you need to steer clear of."

"The thing is, brother, if you can hit it and hold on to it, you float up into a whole nother world. Any time you pass an opera house west of the Rockies, the name on it belongs to another clueless pilgrim what stumbled on a jack-pot. This Yukon is the last place on earth the game aint been rigged yet."

If the game isn't rigged in Dyea it is not for lack of trying.

There is no dock at the mouth of the river, greenhorns shouting in pro-test as their provisions are dumped roughly onto lighters from the anchored steamer, shouting more as they leap or are shoved down from the deck to ferry in with the goods and shouting still to see them hurled from the light-ers onto the mudflats that lead back to the raw little camp, deckhands heav-ing sacks and crates and bundles with no regard for ownership or fragility, and then every man for himself to haul his scattered outfit to higher ground before the seawater can ruin it.

"Fifty bucks I give you a hand with that," says a rum-reeking local with tobacco stain in his beard.

"Heard it was twenty." Hod with his arms full, one hand pressed to cover a tear in a sack of flour.

"Outgoing tide it's twenty. When she's rolling in like this—" the local grins, spits red juice onto the wet stones, "—well, it sorter follows the law of supply and de*mand*." Hod takes a moment too long to consider and loses the porter to a huffing Swede who offers fifty-five. Left to his own, he hustles back and forth to build a small mountain of his food and gear on a hummock by a fresh-cut tree stump, crashing into other burdened stampeders in the mad scramble, gulls wheeling noisily overhead in the darkening sky, little channel waves licking his boots on the last trip then three dry steps before he collapses exhausted on his pile.

When he gets his breath back Hod sits up to see where he's landed. There are eagles, not so noble-looking as the ones that spread their wings on the coins and bills of the nation, eagles skulking on the riverbank, eagles thick in the trees back from the mudflats. He has never seen a live one before.

"They'll get into your sowbelly, you leave it out in the open," says the leathery one-eyed Indian who squats by his load.

"I don't plan to."

"Better get a move on, then. That tide don't stay where it is."

The man introduces himself as Joe Raven and is something called a Tlingit and there is no bargaining with him.

"Twelve cents a pound. Healy and Wilson charge you twice that. Be two hundred fifty to pack this whole mess to the base of the Pass. We leave at first light."

It is already late in the season, no time to waste lugging supplies piece-meal from camp to camp when the lakes are near freezing and the goldfields will soon be picked over. All around them Indians and the scruffy-bearded local white men are auctioning their services off to the highest bidder. One stampeder runs frantically from group to group, shouting numbers, looking like he'll pop if he's not the first to get his stake off the beach.

"That's about all the money I got," says Hod.

The Tlingit winks his good eye and begins to pile Hod's goods onto a runnerless sledge. "Hauling this much grub, you won't starve right away." He tosses a stone at an eagle sidling close and it flaps off a few yards, croaking with annoyance, before settling onto the flats again.

"Eat on a dead dog, eat the eyes out of spawn fish, pick through horseshit if it's fresh. Lazy bastards." Joe Raven winks his single eye again. "Just like us Tlingits."

The Indian wakes him well before first light.

"Best get on the trail," he says, "before it jams up with people."

Hod rises stiffly, the night spent sleeping in fits out with his goods, laughter and cursing and a few gunshots drifting over from the jumble of raw wood shanties and smoke-grimed tents that have spread, scabies-like, a few hundred yards in from the riverbank.

"Any chance for breakfast in town?"

"The less you have to do with that mess," says Joe Raven, "the better off you be."

As they head out there are eagles still, filling the trees, sleeping.

The eight miles from Dyea to Canyon City is relatively flat but rough enough, Hod's outfit loaded on the backs of Joe's brothers and wives and cousins and grinning little nephews, a sly-eyed bunch who break out a greasy deck of cards whenever they pause to rest or to let Hod catch up. Fortunes, or at least the day's wages, pass back and forth with much ribbing in a language he can't catch the rhythm of. Hod struggles along with his own unbalanced load, clambering over felled trees and jagged boulders bigger than any he's ever seen, saving ten dollars and raising a crop of angry blisters on his feet as the trail winds through a narrow canyon, skirting the river then wandering away from it.

"Boots 'pear a tad big for you," says Joe Raven.

The way he has to cock his head to focus the one eye on you, Hod can't tell if the Indian is mocking him or not.

"Might be." He is trying not to limp, trying desperately to keep up.

"Don't worry. By tomorrow your feet'll swoll up to fill em."

Canyon City is only another junkheap of tents and baggage near a water-fall. Hod forks over two fresh-minted silver dollars for hot biscuits and a fried egg served on a plate not completely scraped clean of the last man's lunch while the Indians sit on their loads outside and chew on dried moose, taking up the cards again.

"Gamblingest sonsabitches I ever seen," says the grizzled packer sitting by him on the bench in the grub tent. "Worse than Chinamen."

"I'm paying twelve cents a pound," says Hod. The coffee is bitter but hot off the stovetop. "That fair?"

The packer looks him over and Hod flushes, aware of just how new all his clothes are. "What's fair is whatever one fella is willin to pay and another is willin to do the job for at the moment," says the man, biscuit crumbs cling-ing to his stubble. "Three months ago that egg'd cost you five dollars. Just a matter of what you want and how bad you want it."

After Canyon City the trail starts to rise, Hod lagging farther behind the Tlingits and thinking seriously about what he might dump and come back for later. There are discarded goods marking both sides of the path, things people have decided they can survive without in the wilderness beyond, some with price tags still attached.

"We maybe pick these up on the way back," says Joe Raven, lagging to check on Hod's progress. "Sell em to the next boatload of greenhorns come in."

A small, legless piano lays in the crook of a bend in the trail, and Hod can't resist stopping to toe a couple muffled, forlorn notes with his boot.

"Man could haul that over far as Dawson and play it, be worth its weight in gold," says Joe, and then is gone up the trail.

The light begins to fade and the Indians pull far ahead. Whenever Hod thinks he's caught up he finds only another group of trudging pilgrims who report not to have seen them. He staggers on, over and around the deadfall, searching for footprints in the early snow. I'm a fool and a tenderfoot, he thinks, heart sinking. They've stolen it all and I'll be the laugh of the north country. It is dark and steep and slippery, his pack rubbing the skin off his back and his feet screaming with every step when he stumbles into the lot of them, smoking and laughing in a lantern-lit circle around the dog-eared cards.

"Another mile up to Sheep Camp," mutters Joe Raven, barely looking up from the game. "Gonna blow heavy tonight, so we best skedaddle."

If he takes his load off for a moment he'll never be able to hoist it again. "Let me just catch my breath," says Hod, holding on to a sapling to keep himself from sliding back down the incline while the Indians gather the rest of his outfit onto their backs.

"You doing pretty good for a cheechako," Joe tells him, adjusting the deer-hide tumpline across his forehead. "We had one, his heart give out right about this section. Had to pack him back to Dyea, sell his goods to raise the passage home. Somewhere called Iowa, they said his body went."

The night wind catches them halfway up to Sheep Camp, and when the sharper at the entrance asks Hod for two dollars to collapse, still dressed, onto a carpet of spruce boughs covered with canvas in a flapping tent shared with a dozen other men, he hands it over without comment.

In his sleep Hod walks ten miles, uphill and with a load on his back.

"We take you to the Stairs, but we don't climb," says Joe Raven as they dump his goods next to a hundred other piles in the little flat area at the bottom of the big slope. "Too many fresh suckers comin in to Dyea every day to bother with this mess."

The last of the tall spruce and alder dealt out yesterday evening, only a handful of wind-stunted dwarf trees left along the trek from Sheep Camp to the Stairs, and now nothing but a wall of rock and snowfield faces them, near vertical, all the way to the summit. There is a black line of pack-hauling pilgrims already crawling up the steps chopped into the ice, and here on the flat ground an ever-growing mob of adventurers crowded around a pair of freightage scales to weigh their outfits before starting the climb.

"Gonna take you a couple days, maybe twenty trips," says Joe Raven, counting Hod's money.

"When I take a load up, what's to keep folks from stealing the rest of my outfit?"

The Tlingit winks. "Anything you steal down here, you got to carry it up."

"But whatever I leave at the top while I'm hauling the next load—"

"You white fellers don't much trust each other, do you?" the Indian grins, then rousts his tribe of relatives with a whistle.

When Hod puts his outfit on the balance it is scant forty pounds.

"Sell you four sacks of cornmeal, twenty dollars," says one sharper loitering by the scales.

"Sell you this yere case of canned goods, beans and peas, for fifteen," says another.

"I got these rocks here," says a third. "You roll em in your bedding, slip em in with your flour and soda, Mounties won't take no notice. Good clean rocks, ten cent a pound."

"You aint that short, buddy," says another man, a stampeder from the look of him, pale yellow stubble on his face and pale eyes, one blue, one green, and pale skin made raw from the weather. "You can pick up twice that weight from what's been cast away on the trip up."

He says his name is Whitey, just Whitey, and that he's from Missouri and has been waiting here since yesterday, searching for a face he can trust.

"The deal with this Chilkoot," he says, "is you always got to have one man mindin the store while the other carries the next lot up, then you switch off. It's simple mathematics."

Whitey shows Hod his own pile, the same goods bought for the same double prices from the same outfitters in Seattle. "One load comes from your pile, then the next from mine. It don't matter who carries what, we both do the same amount of work and both get to spell ourselves at the top while the other climbs. It gets dark, one of us stays up there with what we've carried and the other down here with what's left. We'll get her done in half the time and won't be wore out for the rest of it."

It sounds good enough to Hod. They help each other load up, making packs with rope and canvas and tying on near seventy pounds apiece for the first trip.

"No matter how weary you get, don't step out of line to rest once you're on them Golden Stairs," says Whitey as they nudge their way into the crowd of men at the base of the footpath. "Takes a good long spell to squeeze back in."

They start up, Whitey climbing a half-dozen men above Hod. The blasting cold air and the hazardous footing and the weight on Hod's back drives all thought away, his whole life tunneling down to the bend of the knees of the man in front of him, left, now right, now left, thigh muscles knotting as he follows in step, keeping count at first, step after slippery step, then giving up when the idea of the thousands more ahead proves unbearable.

The first thing left by the stairs is a huge cook pot, iron rusted a different color on its uphill side, that looks to have been there some while. Then wooden boxes and crates, dozens of them, and who has the energy to stop and look inside as the wind cuts sharp across the face of the slope, and next it is men littering the sides of the line of climbers, some bent over with exhaustion or waiting for a moment's gap to rejoin the file, others splayed out on the mountain face with their heels dug in to keep from sliding, helpless as tipped turtles with their pack harnesses up around their necks, weeping.

This is where you earn it. Of course it is still a gamble, gathering all his life's toil into one stake and chasing after gold. But it isn't a weak man's play like laying it on poker or faro, hoping the numbers will smile on you and shun the rest at the table. The weak ones will falter here, only those with the strength, with the will to pull their burdens over this mountain and then down five hundred miles of raging, ice-choked river, will even get to roll their dice in the Yukon. For the first time since he was herded onto the steamer with the rest of the stampeders, Hod feels truly hopeful, long odds getting shorter with each busted, despairing pilgrim he passes.

I will stomp this mountain flat, he thinks, leaning into the slope and forcing himself not to look up when the trail curves enough to let him see past the men ahead to the distant summit. No use worrying about how far it still is. Afternoon sun and the friction of boots slick the icy gouges, stairs only in a manner of speaking, and though there is a rope you can grab on to it is ice-crusted and unreliable, the great mass above and behind jerking it one way or the other, and Hod vows on his next trip to get one of the alpenstocks they're selling at the bottom. His legs burn, then ache, then go to numb rubber and then suddenly it is over, teetering sideways to flop in the snow next to Whitey and a half-dozen others. Whitey is laughing and wheezing, pointing at the unbroken line of men and yes, a few women, that stretches all the way down Long Hill and ends in a black pool of those waiting to start the climb.

"You figure if God got a sense of humor," he says, "this is a real knee-slapper."

They pick a spot in the middle of the hundreds of caches to unload their packs, then walk together to the edge of the ridge.

"You lookin a might leg-weary, buddy," says Whitey, a shining new shovel slung over his shoulder. "I'd better make the next run."

There are two chutes running down the slope, icy sides polished with the traffic of bodies. Some men have made crude sleds and some just lay on their backs and draw their knees up to their chest, feet pointing downhill, wait a ten count, holler and then let fly, hoping not to stack up if someone catches a bootheel.

"You got to be shittin me," says Hod.

Whitey smiles and sits down on the blade of the shovel, the handle pointing out between his knees. "You give me a nudge and go rest up. We can get us in another couple trips before it's dark."

He is at the bottom in the time it takes Hod to pull his mittens off.

At their pile Hod pulls out the blankets rolled at the top of his pack to make a nest and even sleeps a little, his legs twitching and complaining all the while, then wakes and gets up to stretch. Men huddle around a little fire, burning a smashed packing crate, smoking pipes and telling tales of gold. Hod lays his couple stale biscuits close to the flame till they are blistered on both sides. They are only yards away from the line of stampeders waiting for the final weigh-in and tariff, a red-jacketed Mountie with a 76 Winchester standing guard in front of a little white tent with the Union Jack flapping over it, his fellows weighing and thoroughly examining the outfits. Nobody is getting past them hauling stones.

"They count your damn socks," grumbles a man by the fire. "Bunch of mother hens."

"Man wants to go freeze to death, starve to death, whatever, whilst he's searching for his bonanza, that oughta be his lookout," says another.

"They just after that tariff," says yet another as he roasts a potato on a stick. "Make you truck in all this gear and then tax whatever wasn't boughten in Canada. Well hell, these local Indian boys say they got no idea what's Canada and what's district of Alaska, didn't nobody pay it any mind before the strike at Thirtymile."

"That's the deal right there," says a man with a moustache that drops down past his chin. "Wasn't for them boys in red, how long you think the border would hold? Wherever the hell it is."

The soldiers are noting it all, checking off on their lists the picks and shovels, the cooking pots and utensils, the tents and blankets and lamps and oil and flour and soda and bacon and beans and sets of long underwear, everything down to the shoelaces. If there are firearms they note those too, writing down the make and model, the caliber and amount of ammunition.

"St. Peter made this much fuss at the Golden Gate," barks the sourdough whose goods they are poring over, "there wouldn't be a saint in Heaven."

It is nearly evening when Whitey reaches the summit again. He has Hod's tent and promises to set it up while Hod makes the last climb.

"Be a place to get out of the weather when you get here."

"And you'll go back down?"

"I got mine all fixed at the bottom. I tell you, I feel sorry for these poor folks trying to go it alone."

The shovel deal makes him nervous, so Hod chooses to run the chute on his back, folding his arms in the way Whitey shows him, like a dead man in a coffin. He has to wiggle a little to get going, then picks up speed, tucking his chin to his chest and not realizing he is screaming with exhilaration till he is halfway down and the air whipping tears into his eyes, rolling sideways a bit like he might fly out of the groove but then sliding to a long stop at the bottom and slammed by the whooping pilgrim behind him.

He loads his pack as fast as he can and shoves his way back into the line, but there is no speed to be gained on the Stairs, and after two hours of trudging the light dies. The climbers close up then, each with a hand resting on the small of the back of the man ahead, moving slower, digging in at every foothold. There are a few long halts, somebody fallen most likely but no telling, just minutes of bracing still against the night wind, and then creeping upward again.

There is a cot and a tin cup of lukewarm coffee waiting in the tent Whitey has set up at the top. It makes Hod near want to cry.

"You're not slidin down in the dark?"

"Don't see why in hell not," says Whitey, tying the straps of his hat tight under his chin. "I aint gonna *fall*, am I?"

It is possible only to do three trips each a day, the men trading few words in passing, eager to use every bit of light. Hod hates the Stairs more with every grinding ascent, but as the days pass their pile of goods at the top grows larger than the one at the bottom, and he uses his rest time to learn what he can about what lies ahead.

"It's an easy six miles down to Happy Camp on the Canadian side, then half of that to the edge of Lake Lindeman and the headwaters of the Yukon," they say.

"There's bad rapids between Lindeman and Lake Bennett," say the few men who have been there and more who haven't. "And then more on the river beyond. You got to make a boat and it better be a good one."

"Aint a straight tree left standing for miles around that lake camp, what they say. Whole damn forest been felled and whipsawed into planks and gone floatin down the river."

"You don't beat the ice this season, you got to sit there till May when it breaks up again. Go through half your grub just waiting."

"Been so many lost in them White Horse Rapids," they say, "Mounties make you hire a pilot to run you past em."

"Another goddam robbery."

"You a good swimmer?"

"Hell, I'd drown in a bathtub."

"Lucky you aint never been in one."

Laughter then. They are chasing the same nuggets and know there are not nearly enough for all of them, no matter how big the country, but have been drawn together, at least for the moment, by hardship. Not too many spend the night on the summit, a pair of Mounties left to make sure nobody sneaks across, but even with most of the caches unattended Hod hasn't witnessed any notable thievery. He and Whitey might be playing it too safe, he thinks, both of them could be hauling all day long and double their chances of getting down the river before the freeze.

"Been wondering the same," says Whitey when he staggers up with the morning haul. "Met a fella says he's waiting up here for his partner to come before he crosses over—lemme go find him and we'll work something out, couple dollars to look after our tent, and I'll be right on your tail. I'd sure like to see the last of this damn Chilkoot."

Hod sees it is mostly Whitey's outfit left when he gets to the bottom. He loads up with canned goods, rigging a pair of lanterns to hang over the back that rattle some when he moves but won't fall off. His legs have hardened to the trail. He works the sums as he climbs, a new-bought alpenstock to help his balance—two men hauling over two hundred pounds, each making three trips a day staggered, so even if doubling up means only one more climb a day—but that's counting on good weather, which keeps its own account book, and the Tlingits at the scales are muttering about an early freeze this year. He wonders how to ask Whitey to partner with him on the other side and how that will be, no telling what a man is like till you've gone down the long road with him. Whitey brings up whiskey with every load he hauls, and there is a sentry line of empty pint bottles outside each of the tents, but he is never passed out when Hod gets to the top, has never missed a turn on the Stairs. Hod has relied on other men in the mines, depended on his brother diggers for his life on occasion, but partnering, with no one the boss and no one the worker—

It will be half the treasure if they make a strike, of course, but also half the work. This north country is so big, so empty, the whole flocking mass of them, thousands of stampeders, only an aimless scattering of piss-ants in its white immensity. A man alone, tiny black dot stumbling over its treacherous surface, can disappear without a trace.

"Young fellas like you and me," Whitey likes to say, "they aint no limit to what we could do in times like these. Got a steady man in the White House who understands there are fortunes to be made if the government will just step out of the way and let us *at* em. The world," Whitey likes to say, "is our oyster."

The tent at the summit is gone.

The tent is gone and the goods, all of them, the picks and shovels and lamp oil and bacon and beans and flour and the mackinaw suit and mukluks and the thirty-five-dollar China dog coat he bought in Seattle gone with it, only the half-dozen empty whiskey bottles marking the spot where his cache had been. None of the men around, busy with their own tortured passage, have noticed a thing.

"You mind your stake, brother, and I'll mind mine," they tell him.

His outfit is gone and no matter how quickly he slides to the bottom, he will find the rest of it gone too. He's been taken. Nobody pays attention to his cursing, nobody watches as he circles back again and again to the spot where the tent had been set up, kicking the bottles across the snow. There is gold in the country beyond the Pass and one stampeder less in the race can only be good news. Hod wanders the summit for an hour, howling, the other adventurers turning away from him, embarrassed to be on the same mountain with such an idiot greenhorn, before he remembers he is still strapped to the final load. He slips his tumpline and lets it all thud to the snow, glass in one of the lanterns breaking, and seeks the counsel of the North West Mounted Police.

LIGHTNING

There is some folks say the pine air is good for you but Clarence is not one of them. Nothing but the trees all around, pine and pine and pine till you come to the swamp and get some tupelos, the wood the quarters been built from cut from pine and the boiler fires burning pine and the barrels Old Brumby make out of pine and the smell in your nose while you hack and pull is pine like everything else in the damn turpentine camp they keeping him at.

But this is the day.

Clarence reaches high with his long-handle chipping ax, raking a V-shape into the wood to get the gum bleeding. It's him and Wilbert hacking the old section on ladders with Shiflett, who is a free white peckerwood, cutting sap boxes in the virgin pine off to the left. How stupid you got to be to stay in this gum patch if they don't chain you to the beds at night? All Shiflett got that the turp gang don't is his nasty, stringy-hair wife, who Stewball seen her once and it put him off thinking bout women for a week.

"Sooner stick it in a snappin turtle mouf than in that mess," he say. "Even her own childrens is scairt to look at her."

There is a gang of dippers on the right, collecting the flow from the notches in the young trees. Even further off he hears Crowder, which is another free peckerwood, chopping at the used-up pines for boiler kindling. And here come Reese the woods rider on his little glass-eye pony they call Sunshine, shotgun across his lap, right wherever you don't want him to be.

Thirty mile of swamp and longleaf pine, legs chained for the short-step, they aint afraid you gone to run. Reese just here to re*mind* you.

"Put a little muscle in it, boy," he mumble through all that chaw in his mouth. "You aint nearly scratched the face yet." And he spit.

They all spit, the shotguns, chaw and then spit, but Reese win the turkey every time. Twice as far and right on the bullseye. He sneaky, too, that little pony catfoot up behind you and if Reese don't like how you workin *splat!* it fly right past your ear and hit the tree. Come on a stretch of pines got black juice runnin down longside the white gum it mean Reese been there.

But even with him and all the rest around Clarence know that this the *day*.

Clarence wipes his brow with the back of his sleeve and can't help but touch where he's slipped them into the seam of his county-issue forage cap. He hopes his sweat don't soak into the match head.

When they first brung Clarence in he pick out Brumby straight away cause that old man been in camp the longest, ever since they built it, and the old hands always know how it stacked.

"I was a blacksmith before I learn this here," Brumby say, never looking up from his work. "Back on the Langford plantation. Make you anything you can think of out of metal. Mister Langford always brag on me, '*My Brumby save me five hundred dollars a year*,' he say. Five hundred *doll*ars. And then when he start boilin his own molasses and seen what a barrel bought from up north cost, he send me out to prentice at cooperage."

They give Brumby a half-dozen green convicts to help make his staves, cutting and planing and drying the boards, but he do all the bevel work and the rest by hisself, shaving and sanding and setting the hoops and gouging the croze so the head fit in tight—make you seven, eight straight-stave turp barrels a day if they don't want him for no metal work on the stills. They more than three hundred convicted in the camp and Brumby one of five that don't wear the hobble irons. Once in the winter when it was raining too hard to go out and cut boxes he shown Clarence through the whole deal.

"You a young man yet," he say. "You learn to be a cooper, then you got a trade when they set you loose."

"That's four years left they give me."

Brumby laugh at him. "Four years aint nothin. I was here makin barrels before you was born."

Story is Brumby had him a young wife and she start slippin round on him, take up with a man run a spirits house by the Georgia line. One day this man don't show up there, and nobody think much of it till he found floatin toward Savannah in one of Brumby's barrels.

"Trade or no trade," Clarence let him know, "I aint doing no four more years here."

Come evening when none of the shotguns was near Clarence step into one of the barrels didn't have its insides glued yet and try to squeeze down till he nearly stuck. Brumby think this is funny.

"I know what you thinkin, son, but nobody gone sneak out this camp in a turp barrel."

"But they told me—"

"That nigger was in *pieces*," he say, quiet. "And even then it was a tight fit."

Clarence climbs down, careful not to step on his chain, and moves his ladder around the tree. You got to leave some bark between the cat-face slashes or else the tree gone die on you, but you can fit three or four boxes on a pine this old, hacking higher on the trunk every year. And then one day there just no more point to it, too high to climb for too little gum and they cut it down to burn. Brumby one of the few old ones in camp aint been used up like that, look in their eyes and it's nothin left. Hollow wood.

Clarence sets the ladder again and climbs halfway up and takes a look. They cut the low branches away, so you can see a fair piece. Reese is riding off toward the dippers on the whiteface pony. Reese would be easier to fool but Sunshine is short-legged and night-blind and won't get you out of the county. Clarence is waiting for Musselwhite and his racer.

Musselwhite is the meanest and maybe the smartest of the shotguns, cut you with his eyes and take note of things, and is always bragging how much he won running his Lightning on Saturdays. Lightning is a sorrel quarter-horse and all Clarence need to know about *that* is it can cut fast through the trees and every time Musselwhite ride it past the boiler fires it shies and crow-hops.

"Getting hungry," calls Wilbert from the next tree. Wilbert born hungry and stayed that way ever since, and how he keep so fat on turp-camp food is a wonder. Supper always the same paltry hoecakes and beans, one plate to a man, brought out by the ox team that come to get the morning dip. Another year in this camp, maybe I fit in that barrel, thinks Clarence.

"Be some hours yet," he calls back.

"My stomach set to rumbling."

"An I thought that was the *Carolina Special*, come to carry us away."

Wilbert is just another thief, though he go in for housebreaking instead of livestock like Clarence. Caught wearin a ring he stole, tried it on his finger and couldn't get it off.

"*You don't steal nothin*," Tillis used to say, "*less you already know where you gone sell it*." Tillis had three, four people worked at big stables, happy to buy whatever they led in as long as it wasn't too local.

"I been thinkin bout peach pie," says Wilbert.

"Aint none on that wagon."

"Man needs a dream."

"Not me."

"Yeah? You always sayin how you gone walk right out of here."

"A dream means it aint true," Clarence calls back, digging grooves into the tree. "And it won't be *walk*in."

Only a pair of men have tried to rabbit since Clarence come to the camp, Garvey James who was found after the count tied under the wagon that goes to Socastee every evening and Jimmy Lightfoot who got lost in the swamp till Musselwhite shoot him close with the shotgun and drag what's left back in behind Lightning.

"Horse aint built to carry two," he say when they were called out to take a look. "You boys remember that."

The chipping ax is weighted in the handle and got a reach long enough to knock a man out of the saddle, if that's what it come to.

Clarence's hands are sticky on the rungs as he climbs down. The face below where he's slashed is crusty white with dried gum and come winter them that's left will scrape it down into boxes. Not him. There is needles and twigs and pieces of branch laying around everywhere and wire grass growing in patches wherever it can get hold between the trees. Once a month they spose to send a gang out to rake and do a underburn but it aint happen for a while.

"Musselwhite comin," calls Wilbert from his ladder.

"Which way?"

"Virgin pines. Aint in no hurry."

"Damn."

If this is the day he got to be quick. Got to be *bold*. Clarence pulls his cap off and works the match out first, then the key. The key is not cast, but made from different pieces of metal hammered together.

"It work fine, you'll see," say Brumby. "You just be sure an throw it where

God can't find it when you done. They gone spect me anyhow, but no use handin em the evidence."

"I could come by for you," Clarence tell him then, and meant it, too. Old Brumby as near as he ever got to a father. "They won't think about me headin back to the camp."

Old Brumby shake his head. "Only way I leave this place is in *that*," he say, pointing at the coffin he already built, lid all polished and carved in flowers. Anybody else, unless your family claim you in three days, it's just a trench out back of the tar pit. No box, no nothin. "What I done," say Brumby, "this where I'm spose to die."

Clarence sits so that Wilbert is out of sight on the far side of his tree and tries the key. They are big old Lilly irons, ankle-busters, and when the jaws spring open his heart take a jump. Anything you can think of out of metal, that Brumby can make it. Clarence throws the leg irons over his shoulder, grabs a short branch with some needles left on it and presses it up against the wet gum on the tree. He is careful with the match, holding the head close to his fingers and striking it on the heel of his shoe. Once, twice—the third time it takes fire. He puts it to the branch and then that down into the pile of twigs and scrape gum he has kicked together at the base of the pine, which catches right away. Wilbert leans his big head around the tree.

"What you doing down there?"

"What it look like I'm doing?"

"How you get them irons off you feet?"

Clarence hurries from tree to tree, lighting whatever looks like it will take, flames starting to lick up the faces, wire grass smoldering here and there.

"I *dreamed* em off," he says. "You wait till you can't see me no more, Wilbert, and then you call out to that peckerwood."

He runs. Not so steady at first, legs free to stride for the first time in a year. Even got to sleep in the irons, quarters guard watching while you thread the long chain through, handing it from cot to cot till you all tucked in, just you and your crotch crickets and the twenty-nine other men hooked in your row. He runs a half-acre south and slides down into the old creek bottom and then cuts back toward the virgin pine, bending low, throwing the leg irons under some deadfall and carrying the chipping ax in his right hand. He waits then, squatting and smelling pinesmoke.

He doesn't peek up till he hears Wilbert holler fire. Musselwhite is only just past him. The woods rider slows Lightning to a walk, stands in the stir-rups and pulls his shotgun from the scabbard. The sorrel starts to snort and dance as it smells the smoke. Musselwhite gets off quick and ties the horse short to a pine, just like he spose to. Don't worry bout any man with his ankles chained stealing a horse.

The shotgun walks toward the fire and Clarence counts trees. At twenty trees buckshot can still take you down, forty and you might only need to dig some out of your hide. Clarence waits thirty and then runs for Lightning.

The horse is all lathered and quivery, eyes rolling. He's only rode a couple horses he stole and they don't like it much, strange rider, dark outside. There's no way he can hold this one by hand if he unties it first.

"We wants to get away from that fire, don't we?" he croons to the stamping animal. "You an me both."

It tenses but doesn't buck when Clarence climbs on. The tether knot is pulled too tight to mess with, so he wraps the reins about one hand and chops with the ax—

They are free from the pine. There is no steering the horse at first, Lightning just bolting flat-eared and low away through the virgin trees, Clarence throwing the ax clear and holding tight, thinking how every time he cut a low branch down here he was saving his own life. Somehow the horse don't kill them both running so fast, smashing into trees, and they are gone at least a mile before he hear Musselwhite whistle for Reese to come back and come loaded. Clarence pull back gentle on the reins, crooning more, and the horse eases into a canter. Run this pace all the way to the Waccamaw, then walk him north along it a piece before you let him drink. Dogs won't catch them. There is still the river to cross, and himself hungry and in stripes and by noon the word be on the wire and some riders out. But he knows how to stay clear of the swamp and how to travel by the stars and it is still clear in the sky above the treetops, clear with a little bit of a breeze carrying the piney wood smell that they say is so good for your lungs. Clarence hears himself laughing.

"You do me one thing if you make it," Brumby say. "Don't you waste your life, son. We only get one to live out. Find yourself a trade, somethin that aint stealing."

We see, old man, thinks Clarence as he eases Lightning into a fast trot, heading west. See what they got for a runaway nigger.

FORT MISSOULA

The only part that bothers Royal is when the doctor sits on the stool to stare
into the hole in the head of his pizzle. The doctor is a white man, which
he didn't know it would be but is not too surprised since it is their army.
The rest—showing his teeth, making a muscle, bending his knees up and
down, the mirror bouncing light into his eyes and ears, even the white man's
fingers around his wrist while he counts, silently moving his lips—barely
starts him sweating. Six of them at a time, naked, standing with eyes forward and arms hung loose at their sides as the doctor moves down the row
and the colored boy in the uniform who seems to be his helper slides the
stool along. The floor is cold under Royal's feet.

"Peel em back and hold em at attention," says the little colored boy, who
the doctor calls Earl and the boy keeps answering Private Beckwith. A couple
of the naked men snigger. Royal knows what this is for, he thinks, and does
what they say.

"*This is our only chance,*" Junior has told him, "*so you got to act right.*"

It's not like a dare, exactly, not like when him and his brother Jubal were
little and would get up high in the branches over the creek, way too high and
the water not near deep enough, sick in the stomach like how he feels now,
and if one stepped off the other honor-bound to follow. Wild-ass stupid. But
Junior has made it clear enough that nothing short of this will cause people
to pay heed to Royal Scott, lift him up in their eyes.

In her eyes.

The doctor bends and squints at it. The sweat comes now, rolling down his sides and Royal can't help but give up a shiver. Junior's father, Dr. Lunceford, got an eye that can make you sweat like that, even with all your clothes on.

"Any problem making water?"

"No sir," he says. "Aint never had that."

His own Mama did for Towson Miles with her roots a while back, but she didn't need him to take it out and show it in her face.

"Less you want to be a dribblin idiot by-an-by," she told him, "you got to stew these roots twice a day and drink it all down."

"It taste bad?" Towson wasn't ever up to much good, wore him a path between Sprunt's cotton press and the Manhattan Club, dogging anything in a skirt he met on the way.

"What you got," Royal's Mama told him, "it taste as bad as it *ought* to."

The doctor stands and steps to the side, cocking his head to look at Royal the way the old men in Wilmington do when they're set to swap mules.

"Cough."

Royal doesn't know if they're watching for a strong cough or a weak one, so he pushes one out somewhere in the middle, careful not to blow air on the white man.

"That's enough with these, Earl," says the doctor, crossing to write on some papers at his desk.

"Private Beckwith," corrects the colored boy in the uniform, softly. "Put your clothes on and wait outside," he says to the naked men and they hurry to it, rolling eyes at each other and grinning. Royal doesn't dare smile even though the doctor has his back turned. This little Earl might see and tell the doctor something after.

Junior sits on one of the benches along the wall in the hallway with the other dozen who went before. He shoots Royal an asking look, but there is nothing to tell him. It is up to the white doctor and whatever he wrote down.

"You got to fit the uniform, is what," says one of the men who was naked with him. "That's why the man look at you so careful, cause they already got all their suits and they only want them what fits *in* em."

Royal sits and nobody talks for a while, the sounds drifting in from deep-voiced men calling cadence as they drill. They were a sight all right, just like Junior told him they'd be, colored men of all shades and ages marching in squared-off groups with their blue shirts dazzling in the afternoon sun, tall as pines with their rifles held just so over their shoulders. He thought that there would be a stockade wall, but no, just a huge open rectangle of a parade ground surrounded by wooden buildings, sitting by the river at the base of evergreen-covered mountains.

Fort Missoula.

He pictures himself standing in that blue uniform in the parlor at Junior's house, Dr. Lunceford's hard eye digging into him and her, Jessie, standing behind, seeing him like it's the first time. Not the same Royal.

But only they choose him. If they take Junior and send him away that is all there is to it, go back to Wilmington and press cotton at Sprunt's, forget about Jessie. If they take him and not Junior—but that won't happen.

Another colored soldier steps into the hallway, darker and older than Little Earl who shoved the stool along, this one with more yellow stripes on his arm, standing wide-legged and hands on hips, looking down on them like he owns it all.

"On your feet."

He doesn't shout, doesn't talk loud at all but the men jump up. He reads off a list.

"Hazzard, Drinkwater, Lunceford—" he reads and Royal hears a small gasp of relief from Junior, "—Brewster and Scott, stay here. The rest of you go out that door and get back to where you come from."

It takes a while for the ones they don't want to mumble out, disappointed. Royal wonders if some have come from as far as him, all the way up here where they still got Indians who wear deer hide on their feet, a half-dozen of them smoking and looking you over when you walk through the post gate.

"Lunceford," says the older one.

"Yes sir!"

Junior sings it out. He has had Royal practicing his Yes sir and No sir which is how he says you got to answer everybody above you even if they're not old or a white man.

"Step forward."

Junior steps forward smart and stands with his eyes locked ahead. Junior is not so filled in as the others they picked, chicken-chested with skinny pins, but his clothes are nice and he's lighter complected and carries himself high.

"You been to school, Lunceford." The soldier says it as a fact.

"Yes sir. Hampton Institute and then half this year at Fisk."

"Anything you learn there, you gone have to forget it."

There is something in his friend's eyes Royal has never seen before, hesitating before he speaks.

"Yes sir," says Junior in a quiet voice. "I'll try to do that sir."

"You call me Sergeant."

"Yes Sergeant."

"Get back in line."

Junior steps straight back two steps without looking and ends up square with the other four. Royal wonders if he's practiced that too.

"I am Sergeant Jacks," says the dark man evenly, the man with the stripes on his arm. "And you sorry niggers have the good fortune to be selected to join the 25th Infantry."

Royal jumps off the branch.

IN THE TEMPLE

In the last few years it has been the Italians, *Guglielmo Tell* mostly, or *Un Ballo in Maschera*, or something new by Puccini. Diosdado stands smoking with a group of his classmates outside the Teatro Zorilla, slightly rumpled in their white linen as students are expected to be, positioned to watch the daughters of the wealthy and their *dueñas* alight from their closed carriages, each one opening like a box of *bombones* to reveal the delicacy within, girls in satin and taffeta and silk and the occasional butterfly in a *balintawak*, sleeves like delicate, transparent wings, their hair shining with oil and up in combs, bestowing their glances and smiles like the most precious of gifts. Then the *ilustrados* with their European suits and gold watches endlessly consulted to show them off and the *españoles* with their air of disdain and condescension—yes, they'd rather be in Madrid but duty entails sacrifice and this sort of event, though unavoidably second-rate here in the Colony, is such a good influence on the *indios*—the men all lingering in front of the ornate, circular temple of culture until the orchestra is well into the *overtura*. Diosdado searches over their heads for Scipio, who said to meet him here. But Scipio never makes an entrance—he just *appears*.

"A well-placed infernal device," says Hilario Ibañez, eyeing a phalanx of Spaniards talking rather more loudly than the orchestra within, "would do the nation a great deal of good." Hilario is a poet and given to morbid flights of imagination.

Diosdado shakes his head. "And destroy the best along with the worst?"

He is careful to always seem the conciliator in public, the gradualist in questions of politics. A debater who can argue either side of a question, moderate in opinion and passion. It is a role he is beginning to despise.

Kokoy flicks the butt of his cigarette to the ground, sighs wearily. "We're needed inside, gentlemen."

They move, careful to maintain an air of indifference, to the back of the balcony where the smoke from the oil lamps in the chandeliers collects, with the scattered rainbow of young beauties below them and time for a quick flurry of *tsismis* concerning the romantic lives of the performers, the Italians (or the French, for that matter) eugenically destined for scandal, with the *conduttore* turning to count empty seats and the Manila fire department, opera lovers all, standing at the top of the main aisle, doors flung open behind them with the hose in hand and ready for service. The ushers shoo the little street girls selling roses and gardenias out of the building and the din of Filipino society in full flower begins to abate and then there is applause as the curtain is drawn and the first notes cut the air. Diosdado smiles to himself, thinking of how he loves it all, loves it as only a boy raised on cockfights and the occasional scabrous traveling puppet show can, a *haciendero*'s son from the wild coast of Zambales who spent his first year in the great city pretending he had seen it all, that he was not impressed, that he, provincial imposter, belonged there. And usually at this point, lights dimmed to hide him from his cohorts, he would let his guard down and allow the singers to carry him to Paris or Thessaly or ancient Egypt.

Tonight it is the *Tell*, in a mercifully abridged version, the audience silenced immediately by the stirring overture, lederhosen and dirndls barely able to disguise the uncomfortable parallels with the present situation—a despotic government, an insurrection in the *bundoks*, blood feuds complicating the political situation, love and honor—

But tonight the music is only background to his own drama.

"They want you," said Scipio.

This in the Jesuit library, with the late-day sun slanting through the windows and the other *colegios* absorbed, unsuspecting, in their texts. Diosdado felt the building move a little, as it did during the medium-sized tremors common within the Intramuros.

"Why now?"

Scipio smiled. "Because you're the best liar in Manila."

He had hoped they would need his talents as a linguist. Zambal, Tagalog, Spanish, Latin, English from his year in Hongkong, even a bit of Cantonese, all these valuable as the revolt proceeded through its stages. But lying—

"They want me to be a spy?"

"For now. We each serve in our own way."

Diosdado had guessed for some time that his best friend was a member of the Katipunan, but Scipio would never admit it. "*I am a patriot*," he would say, lifting an eyebrow, whenever Diosdado asked to be sponsored into the Brotherhood, "*but not a suicide.*"

"What do I do?"

"Tonight at the Zorilla," said Scipio, smiling, and then was gone.

But at intermission, the apple successfully bolted from son Walter's head and Tell imprisoned by the haughty Gessler, Scipio has still not appeared. Diosdado shuffles downstairs in the throng, shoulder to shoulder with a butcher of a *militar*, a uniformed *capitán de cazadores* whistling the rousing call to arms that closed the first act.

"*Elíxer para el alma*," says the Spaniard, smiling and catching his eye, and Diosdado muses that if the oppressors do in fact have souls, then music must be good for them.

He follows the university boys across the street for *buñuelos* and *chocolate* and talk of music, theater, women, all the things young irresponsible students should be preoccupied with, the *militares* at the next table laughing a little too loudly as always and both groups pretending to ignore the fact that there is a revolution in progress not so far from Manila, that in a few months, a year at the most, they may be trying to kill those other *hijos de puta*.

"I wonder how many will stay, after it is done?" says Kokoy, careful as always to remain vague, in public places, about the exact nature of *it*.

"The ones from Madrid or Barcelona will go home," says Epifánio Cojuanco, who has spent a year studying piano in Spain. "But some of those places, in the bleak mountains—why would you bother?"

"They'll have to give up their privileges, of course." This from Kokoy, who has a manservant who waits outside the classroom door in case his *dueño* should desire anything.

"I long for the day," says Hilario Ibañez. "To breathe our own sweet air again, to walk unburdened on our own fertile soil, among free men."

They can rhapsodize about independence for hours, his friends, but Kokoy is too rich and Epifánio too timid and Hilario a poet doomed to unwittingly plagiarize Dr. Rizal's literary work, from which he no doubt conjured the image of the infernal machine, for the rest of his days. And he, Diosdado Concepción, is still waiting for the call—

"To a better day," says Epifánio, and they touch their cups together. It is Scipio's favorite toast, Scipio who has not yet appeared, most often invoked at a café table like this one, surrounded by Spanish soldiers, looking like any other group of Filipino dandies in white suits and straw skimmers. "*A un día mejor!*" Scipio will say, raising his glass, and then down the throat, all of them smiling with their secret knowledge.

Until this afternoon it has seemed only naughty.

The bell sounds and they hurry back and stand just inside the doors to witness the re-entrance of the *damas*, their fans fluttering in a myriad of gown-matching colors, the students dizzied by passing waves of perfume, and then there is the dress they are waiting for, the dress that has the great fortune to caress the body of Ninfa Benavides, a whisper of organza the color of ripe *guayaba*, with a border of translucent French lace and a cameo brooch nestled between her artfully displayed twin doves of nubility.

"If the fakirs are correct and one revisits this earth in different forms," sighs Hilario Ibañez, "I would end my life now to come back as that cameo."

Ninfa, whose father is the Policarpio Benavides who supplies fresh beef to the Spanish army and can destroy men's lives with a word in the proper official's ear, whose aunt is the renowned Sister María de la Coronación de Espinas who teaches music and deportment at Santa Isabel, Ninfa carries herself like what she is, a jewel of the nation. There are so many *peninsulares* seeking her hand, or merely her interest, as well as the countless *criollos* and *filipinos ilustrados*, that some nights the crowd under her balcony erupts into terrible rows that warrant the militia being called to action. The rumor, for Diosdado has never been privileged to speak with her, is that she is as intelligent as her father is ruthless, and can puncture a man's soul with a single *flecha irónica*. In his reveries it is Ninfa, stepping regally from her landau and catching his eye to say, with a half-secret smile, "You, *campesino*, belong here. And if you work hard, if you study the minds of men and learn to turn them to your will, you may some day be worthy of me."

"Far too rich for your blood, *muchacho*," says Scipio as she passes. He is there suddenly, watching Ninfa with his own private smile. "Follow me."

The coach ride is not a long one. Diosdado tries to guess at the turns and distances with his eyes covered, Scipio silent beside him. Padre Peregrino, his favorite of the Jesuits, is a firm believer in mystery.

"We have been created to inquire, to reason," he tells his students. "To strive to understand the workings of the Universe. But mystery, doubt, the blind flight into the unknown—*these* are the elements of Faith."

The coach stops. Diosdado can hear water lapping, smell the tang of a filth-choked *estero*. Somewhere near the Pasig, maybe the northern corner of San Nicholas. Scipio takes him by the arm, helps him from the coach, and leads him inside.

"Kneel."

A voice he doesn't recognize. Diosdado kneels.

The blindfold is pulled off and he opens his eyes.

It is a small room with dark mahogany walls. On a low table, providing the only light, flickers a votive candle. Before it are laid a revolver, a bolo knife, and a human skull.

"Who is this," asks the tallest of the hooded men, in Tagalog, "who disturbs the works of the Temple?"

"One who wishes to see the True Light," says Diosdado in what he hopes is a strong, confident voice, "and to be worthy to become a Son of the Country."

"Think well and decide—can you comply with all its duties?"

Diosdado allows the smallest of pauses to signal that he is, in fact, considering the weight of this decision. Padre Peregrino always chides him in the confessional for announcing his remorse too quickly.

"I can."

"In what state was our beloved Fatherland when the Spaniard first trod upon its soil?"

"We were as children," says Diosdado, "free, but living in ignorance." He was the shining light of his First Communion, the Bishop posing the Catechism questions to him in Spanish, and Diosdado, at nine, answering by rote but with a semblance of understanding.

"In what condition do we now live?"

"Now we have the Light of Knowledge, but remain enslaved."

"And what shall be our future?"

"We shall live as free men, equal among the many nations."

His father believes that this is worse than heresy, it is stupidity. "Do you fight the sun?" he will shout during their arguments. "Do you fight the rain? You accept them, you use them, without them your crops will not grow. So it is with the Spanish."

His father who kneels in church every Sunday grinding his teeth while the friar drones on, who drinks imported wine with the governor and hides a third of his earnings at tax time. His father who calls bribes "seed money" and Chinese "yellow monkeys." His father who is a secret Freemason, initiated in a secret rite much like this one, who crippled a man in a duel of honor but will not lift a finger for the Tagalog Republic.

One of the other hooded men takes the bolo and, stepping behind Diosdado, reaches around to hold the sharp blade against the base of his throat. Another lifts the revolver and presses the barrel to his forehead.

"Do you know, Brother, what these arms represent?" asks the tallest man, the *hermano terrible* in the hooded red robe. "These are the arms with which the Society punishes those who betray its secrets. If at this moment the Society should require your life, would you give it?"

"I would," says Diosdado, and is glad he is kneeling. Scipio has rehearsed him in the entire litany, but actually saying the words, knowing that irrevocable actions will follow them, this sends awe tingling through him like the Holy Sacraments never have. A small gong is struck. Candlelight, flickering on the wall behind the small table, illuminates a portrait of the martyred Dr. Rizal. Was he a secret member as well, as the *tsismis* has it, or have they only borrowed his image to add weight to the ceremony?

"The sound of the bell is the sound of you leaving your former life and entering the Society, where you will see the True Light. Your body must be given a visible sign that you are a Brother in the Society—can you endure the hot iron?"

"I can."

The sword and pistol are withdrawn and his shirt pulled open, and the tip of an iron crucifix, searing hot, is pressed to a point on his right breast and held there a moment. He smells burned flesh.

"Reflect that you are no longer Master of your body. It belongs now to the Society."

Educated young men have been leaving the university and taking to the hinterlands. Nothing as important as this will happen again in his lifetime. To not be part of it, to sit idly to one side, uncommitted, is unthinkable.

"This I accept," says Diosdado.

"Then welcome, Brother!" The inductor and others pull down their hoods and step forward to embrace him. Diosdado recognizes the inductor as a young man who was only a year ahead of him at the Ateneo, a young man already a capitán in the rebellion, with famous battles to his name.

"Thank you, Brothers. I will try to be worthy."

"There is only the signing left," says one of the others, in Spanish now. "Your arm, please?"

He holds out his arm and the man cuts a slit in the crook of his elbow, then hands him a quill pen as the other, who Diosdado has seen reporting at charity events for the *Correo de Ultramar*, lays the articles out on the table.

He dips the point of the quill in the pooling blood and writes his name. It takes quite a while, *Diosdado Concepción*. They must not keep these, he thinks—what a bounty for the *guardia* if their agents discovered a pile of initiation documents. He finishes his signature and looks up. He is a member of a secret society, an imposter still, but an imposter for Liberty.

"Have you chosen your code name, Brother?"

Padre Peregrino's lesson that day was the Arcadian story of beautiful Io, so lusted after by Zeus that he transformed her into a cow, hoping to hide her from the jealous wrath of his wife Hera. Hera discovered the ruse and set the hero Argus Panoptes, who possessed at least an extra set of eyes on the back of his head, if not a hundred of them spread over his body, to watch over the herd and warn her if Zeus approached. The Padre is a great lover of mythology, drawing, with his Jesuit wit, moral lessons from the pagan stories.

"Your name, Brother?" asks the tallest of the hooded men, the hero of Paombong. They are all watching Diosdado now, who stands with a thread of blood dripping off his fingertips to the polished floor.

"I am Argus," he tells them. "He who sees all."

SKAGUAY

Hod is working on the wagon road three miles out of Skaguay, felling trees and dragging logs through the mud with a chain rig, when a dude strolls up with the road boss.

"That's the one," says the road boss.

The dude, checked sack suit, street shoes and the only straw boater Hod has seen since coming north, cocks his head and speaks loud enough for Hod to hear over the chopping and whipsawing and cursing of laborers.

"I expected a larger man."

But he continues to watch Hod work, a little dude smile on his face, smoking three cigarettes and dancing out of the way as trees are felled, as logs are dragged and dropped on the corduroy road, and is waiting when the shift ends.

"Niles Manigault," he says, offering a soft hand and smiling. "And you are?"

"Brackenridge."

"Splendid. May I ask, Mr. Brackenridge, if you are a practitioner of the fistic arts?"

The words make no sense at first. Hod rolls his shoulders, feeling the chafe marks where the chain cut in. "I fought a couple guys. In Montana."

"Montana."

"Three fights. With other miners."

Niles Manigault nods, considering, then taps Hod on the chest with his finger. "No matter. The lure of ample recompense should outweigh any lack of experience."

"You offering me a job?"

The young man has a markedly Southern accent and a very neatly brushed moustache. "A business opportunity, yes." He indicates the hodge-podge of felled trees around them. "Something of a step up for you, I would imagine."

"What I have to do?"

They walk back toward town over the roadbed that has already been laid, Hod with his ax over his shoulder, the dude trying not to sink his street shoes too deep in the muck.

"You'll need to absorb a certain amount of punishment," says Niles Manigault, smiling. "And, if able, to deal some out."

An older colored man with a pushed-in face sits in a battered wagon pointed toward town.

"Our barouche," says Manigault, gesturing for Hod to get in. Hod climbs onto the bed while the dude sits up front by the drayman, and they begin to thump home over the logs, passing the other road workers slogging back through the mud, lugging their tools over their shoulders. "This is our new pugilist, Smokey," says the dude. "What do you think?"

The negro casts a quick look back at Hod.

"He gonna beat Choynski," he says, turning his attention to the slat-ribbed nag pulling the wagon, "he best carry that ax into the ring with him."

The new docks have pulled all the action from Dyea here to Skaguay, and the town has more false-fronted wood buildings than tents now, new structures being thrown up on every block of the grid the original claim jumpers laid out, the frozen-mud streets swarming with new arrivals in a hurry to reach the Pass and merchants and buncos hustling to pick them clean before they get there. There are dogs everywhere, dogs too small or stubborn or weak or vicious to be useful pulling sleds on the trail, dogs of all shapes and sizes formed into packs that fight over slops thrown on the street or over territory or just for the mean dog delight of it. A half-dozen of them crowd around barking and snapping as Smokey guides the wagon past the little brewery, then scamper away when it's clear there is nothing worth eating or killing. Hod and Manigault climb down onto the board sidewalk that runs in front of the buildings and tents, weaving around stampeders and drunks and the tame Russian bear doing tricks and a hatless, startle-eyed wild man predicting that the usurers, whoremongers, and worshippers of the Golden Idol who rush about ignoring him will soon be cast into a lake of fire.

"Any idea how much you weigh?" asks Niles Manigault.

"A sight less than when I got here," says Hod, and then the dude pulls him down onto Holly Street.

He has passed Jeff Smith's Parlor several times, but prefers the big dance halls on Broadway or Clancy's on Trail Street. All the resorts are pretty much the same, dedicated to separating a man from what's in his poke as quick as possible, but some do it with a lighter touch. Smith turns out to be another Southerner, a bearded, dark-haired, dark-eyed man in a big-brimmed wide-awake hat, leaning back with elbows propped on the bar and one bootheel hooked over the brass rail.

"You're not a boxer," he says, looking Hod up and down.

"Never claimed to be," Hod tells him. Manigault takes a seat on a stool, the bartender laying a short whiskey in front of him. "I just been in a fight or two."

"And how did you fare?"

"Held my own."

A half-dozen other men drift close around him, watching with apprais-ing eyes. Smith has a soft voice and a friendly manner.

"Take your shirt off," he says. "We'll have a look."

Hod hesitates, then begins to peel the layers, draping his work-grimed clothes over the bar counter. They are paying six a day on the wagon road, good wages on the Outside, but prices in Skaguay leave nothing much to show for it, and on every corner there are a dozen busted stampeders ready to work for coffee and johnnycakes. When Hod is down to his skin, Niles Manigault puts in a word.

"Devereaux says he's the strongest of the lot out there, best stamina, most stubborn—"

Jeff Smith raises a hand to silence him, steps close to lock eyes with Hod.

"Young man," he says, smiling, "how would you like to earn an easy one hundred dollars?"

The fight is only a few hours away, and Niles explains that it will be neces-sary to meet with his opponent first.

"Merely a formality," he says as he and Smith lead Hod, struggling back into his clothes, across the muck on Broadway. "Our previous champion being indisposed—"

"Stiff as a plank," says Smith. "Passed out drunk in a snowdrift last night and froze to death."

"—you are something of a last-moment replacement. They need to be reassured that you're no ringer."

"I never even had gloves on."

"We'll do the talking in here, son," says Smith, stepping into the Pack Train Restaurant.

The manager is an older man with a face like boiled ham. Choynski, trim and curly haired, is sawing at a steak.

"Where'd you get this dub?" says the manager, flicking his eyes over Hod.

"The north country breeds fighting men," answers Niles Manigault. "This lad has bested all comers in the region—"

The fighter sits back to look at Hod. "You ever been in the rope arena, young man?"

"He is neither a seasoned professional nor a mere chopping block," Niles intercedes. "A raw talent, you might say."

The manager is not impressed. "Folks won't be happy paying to see a slaughter."

"You underestimate our boy," says Smith, pulling his wideawake off and holding it over his heart. "As well as the drawing power of your Mr. Choynski."

"An exhibition," says Choynski.

"I expect our citizenry will expect a bit more fireworks than that."

"A lively exhibition. What's your name?"

Niles Manigault begins to speak but Hod beats him to the punch. "Hosea Brackenridge. Always called me Hod, though."

The fighter smiles. "That's too good to have made up." He holds out his hand to shake. Several of the knuckles are misshapen. "If you're anywhere near as tough as this beef, Mr. Brackenridge, we will reward the people of Skaguay with a memorable evening."

"Cocky Jew bastard," drawls Niles Manigault as they step out onto Broadway again. A mulecart is tipped on its side and men are trying to right it, boots sliding in the mud as they push.

"We've already sold the tickets." Jeff Smith steps around the accident, unconcerned. "Add the liquor on top and the wagers, there's a tidy sum to be gathered. My only true concern is what to call our boy Hosea here."

"I concur," says Manigault. "One Jew name in the ring is quite enough."

"It's not Jew," Hod protests. "It's from the Bible."

"Which is nothing but Jews till you reach the end of the Book," says Smith. He stops on the far boardwalk to look Hod over again. "Young McGinty."

Niles laughs.

"That a real person?" Hod knows he's signed on for a beating, and hopes that's all it is.

"I ran an establishment called the Orleans Club in Creede during their bonanza," Smith tells him. "I acquired a statue, a prehistoric man who had been artfully carved out of stone, and kept him in the back room. For the price of one nickel the curious were allowed to take a brief look. We named it McGinty."

"Christened thusly," explains the dude, "because anyone that petrified has *got* to be Irish."

The fight is in the dance hall at the front of the Nugget. The room smells of cigars and spilled beer and the wet woolen clothes of the three hundred men already packed in around the tiny roped square where two windmilling prospectors settle a grudge to cheers and catcalls. Smokey walks Hod around the already drunken throng in the hall, then back through the packed, whiskey-reeking bar into a tiny room screened off by a dirty American flag hung over a narrow doorway. A skinny girl, still in her teens, lies on a cot staring at the ceiling. She sits up to look at them blankly. She wears a sleeveless green chemise and has her red hair pinned up with an emerald-colored brooch.

"Sorry, Miss," says Hod.

She looks at the negro. "Boxin over?"

"Just about to start, the real one." Smokey points to Hod. "He got to change."

She nods and stands, glancing at Hod as she steps out of the crib. "He aint no fighter."

"Nemmine her," says Smokey, tossing a pair of stained trunks onto the cot. He holds up a pair of high-topped leather shoes. "These aint gonna fit you, is they?"

"Don't appear so."

"Put them of yours back on when you ready, then." Smokey watches as Hod strips down, turning away when he peels his long underwear off. There are postcards of naked women stuck all over the walls, naked women holding tennis rackets, astride bicycles, lounging on divans, naked women staring right at you.

"These are big, too," says Hod, holding the waist of the trunks out with his thumbs.

"You put this in there, protect your privates." Smokey hands him a molded triangle with padding stuffed in it. "Then pull them drawstrings tight. You sure you been in the ring?"

Hod wedges the protector into the trunks, then wriggles his hips to get it to sit right. "There wasn't any ropes. The other miners just crowded around in sort of a circle."

Smokey shakes his head. "Makin you toe the line with Chrysanthemum Joe."

"He somebody?"

The colored man snorts. "He put that left hand of his on your chin, you find out quick who he is. Beat Kid McCoy *twice*."

"What you think I ought to do?" Hod is more worried about the crowd, raw-faced and shouting around the ring, of being humiliated, than of the soft-spoken man from the Pack Train Restaurant.

Smokey strikes a pose—arms slightly bent and extended out before him, loose fists held palms toward the ground, left hand and foot slightly forward of the right, right elbow tucked in close to the ribs. "You stand like this," he says, "then you try catch his hits with your gloves or duck your head away from them. With Joe they gonna come in bunches, so stay on your toes, keep movin. This here," he taps the spot between the ribs just below his breast-bone, "this is your *mark*. You let him hit you sharp on that mark, your knees gonna buckle right under you. So you keep this elbow down here ready to block him, throw it across your mark when he try at it."

"That leaves my head open on the right."

Smokey smiles, showing a few missing teeth. "Don't it though? That's what *beau*tiful about the game. Whatever a man do, it open him up to something comin back."

"So if I think he's gonna—"

"Last thing you want to do out there is any *think*in, son. It's all time and distance, time and distance, and then you just got to have a *feel* for it."

"You were a fighter?"

Smokey begins to wrap Hod's left hand in a tight, complicated cross-pattern with a roll of cloth bandage. "Bare-knuckle days. My last bout I went twenny-eight rounds with Peter Jackson when he come over from Australia. Near kilt each other."

Hod looks down at his heavy shoes. "These gonna be all right?"

Smokey nods. "Got a nice tread on em. Wood floor, slicked up with blood—"

Hod feels a little dizzy. He tries to focus on one of the postcards. A naked woman with dimpled knees and a feathered hat poses, chin up and eyes to the heavens, before a backdrop of a distant, smoking volcano.

"Should I try to hit him back?"

"Try to hit him *first* and then get away. Hit him, hold him, wrestle him around. Just don't get him mad at you."

There is a roar from the dance floor as one or both of the prospectors hit the floor.

"I think I better piss first."

Smokey sighs, starts out. "I get you a cuspidor." He pauses with the flag half lifted to look back. "Whenever you think you can't stand no more, you take your dive. And once you in that tank, stay under for a while. Can't nobody hit you with nothing down there."

Three hundred men turn to look, whiskey-ornery, as Smokey brings Hod back into the dance hall. Jeff Smith stands with Niles Manigault and several of the others from the Parlor at the side of the little improvised ring, cargo rope stretched between four cattle stanchions nailed to the floor. The one they call the Sheeny Kid barks out from the center.

"Gentlemen, if I may direct your attention—now entering the squared circle—from the mists of County Cork—European Catchweight Champion and challenger for the Heavyweight crown—the Gaelic Goliath—Young McGiiiiiiiinty!"

Smokey holds the ropes apart and Hod ducks in to more jeers than applause. He stands trying to look above the men's howling faces and sees the red-haired girl from the little room leaning against the far wall with her arms crossed. He wishes she wasn't there.

"Hey Soapy!" cries a man from within the mass of spectators. "Where'd you dig this stiff up?"

Laughter then, overtaken by excited chatter and then cheers as Choynski steps in from the street wrapped in a bearskin, his manager shoving a path clear to the ring. "And his opponent—" cries the Kid, turning to gesture theatrically toward the arriving fighter, "—for the first time in the north country—a battler of great renown—the California Terror—the Hebrew Hercules—Chysanthemum Joe Co-wiiiiinski!"

Wild applause and foot stomping as Smokey pulls Hod over to meet Choynksi and his manager in the center of the ring, each man's second watching the other as the little gloves are pulled on and laced, Hod expecting something heavier with padding in them. These are more to protect your own knuckles than the other man's face.

Choynski half-turns to raise an arm and acknowledge the cheers, while Hod hangdogs down at the tobacco-stained floor.

"This evening we will be witnessing an open-rounded exhibition of the scientific art of self-defense, fought under the Queensbury rules," the Kid continues to some booing by the more vicious element in the crowd. "Rounds of three minutes with a one-minute respite in between, a downed fighter taking a ten-count from the referee—" indicating the character the men in the Parlor called Reverend Bowers, "—shall constitute a knockout and end the bout."

"Just call it now, Reverend, and save the dub a beating!" calls a man by the woodstove at the back. More laughter.

"Gentlemen—a show of appreciation for our two warriors!"

More applause then. "Two," says a man behind Hod's corner.

"He won't survive the first," says another.

"Four ounces."

"Piker."

"All right, eight then."

"You're on. He falls like timber in the first."

There is more betting, none venturing that Hod will last beyond three rounds, and then a sourdough raps a blacksmith's hammer against a hunk of metal pipe hung on a rope and Hod is pushed into battle.

There is no run to this deal. Choynski steps up and *whap! whap!* hits Hod twice in the face before he can cover it with his forearms and elbows and *thump!* delivers a short-armed hook to his ribs that hurts a lot worse. Choynski steps back and begins to casually pick openings, shooting his right fist into Hod—head, body, head, head—Hod turtling in and backstepping to the rope, which stretches too much to hold his weight. He stumbles sideways, loses his balance and tumbles forward to grab the fighter around the neck and hang on. Choynski catches Hod and pulls him in, pressing foreheads. There is already booing, and somebody's shoe whizzes over the rope to thump Hod in the back.

"You better throw some leather, son," Choynski mutters in his ear before pushing him away, "or these people are gonna string us up."

Hod goes after him, left, right, left, right, putting everything he has into each swing, hitting shoulder, arm, hip, and once, painfully, the top of the man's skull.

"You're looping," Choynski tells him as he ducks in and steps past. "Hit in a straight line and corkscrew your wrist—" *Whap! whap!* he demonstrates, snapping Hod's head back with two effortless lefts. "Put some shoulder in it."

Hod brings his elbows in and tries to punch straight, Choynski catching the hits on his glove or flicking his head safely to the side at the last moment. By the time the pipe is rapped and he falls back onto the barstool Smokey sets out, Hod's arms feel like he's been jacking bedrock for a full shift.

Smokey takes a mouthful of water, then sprays it onto Hod's face. "Keep your mouf close," he says. "You like to bite your tongue off."

"I'm just about blown."

"That's cause you holdin your wind every time he hit you or you tries to hit him. Just breathe *through* it. Don't want no air trapped in your lungs for them body punches."

There are men screaming at him over the ropes, telling him he's a faker and a dub, telling him to lay down, telling him to stay on his feet one more round, telling him he couldn't punch a dent in a pat of butter.

The pipe is banged again and the stool pulled from under him. He wades in, his arms held further out in front of him. Choynski leaves off from his outfighting, ducking under and in to pound Hod in the ribs. Hod tries to keep breathing, to block the blows with his elbows. He can feel that the other man isn't putting everything into it, punches landing with no weight behind them. The men around them are booing again and Choynski hits him with a sudden uppercut beneath the chin that staggers him back to the ropes where hands catch him and shove him forward into a shot square in what Smokey called the mark and sure enough Hod's legs go to water and he dives forward to hug Choynski's neck.

"Easy, son," says the battler, bending his knees to support Hod's weight. "You got to last six."

"Six rounds?" The idea seems unbearable.

"Your Mr. Smith has some bets down. It's six or we don't get paid. You ready?"

"I think so."

Choynski pushes him free then and snaps two punches, pulled a little so they only sting, to the right side of his face. Hod staggers back, only half acting, and cheers erupt. He steps back in, throwing straight punches with no kick in them, and Choynski smiles and feints and throws some of the same back at him. It is an exhibition, an exhibition of a scientific art he knows nothing about but is willing to pretend at as long as they stay in the center of the ring away from the blood-thirsty sons of bitches surrounding it. Choynski pops him on the nose with his left, a big blue spark before his eyes, but it triggers Hod's cocked right hooking back over to catch the battler on the side of the jaw.

"Attaboy," grins Choynski, dancing sideways. "Let em fly."

Hod thrashes at him left and right and then the round ends and there are cheers and complaints and paper money and gold dust passing hands as he flops down on the stool straining for wind.

"He says I got to last six rounds to get paid."

"They don't tell me noner that," says Smokey, spreading some kind of grease on Hod's eyebrows and cheekbones with his thumbs. "Can you see out that eye?"

Hod's left eye is swollen, closing to a slit. "Sort of."

Smokey presses a chunk of ice to it, looks over to where Jeff Smith and his crew sit on a board-and-barrel bleacher. "If it six, you need to rest some in the middle of the rounds. Just get in tight and lean on the man. He be happy to lean back."

The pipe gongs and they are on again and the boxing lesson continues, sparring back and forth, Choynski hitting Hod with a flurry of half-strength punches whenever the fanatics beyond the ropes get too restless. Hod's arms are leaden and a couple times he has to backstep, dropping them to his sides to shake them out, Choynski closing but not too fast, before they can go at it again. Hod's nose begins to bleed, dripping down over his chin and smearing into the sweat on his chest, and he has to breathe through his mouth. But he stays up through the third and the fourth, only in danger in the fifth when he catches the eye of the girl in the green, still watching through the cloud of cigar and woodsmoke that fills the room, and Choynski tags him with another uppercut that knocks him back on his keister.

Rev Bowers is over him, waving his arm and counting very deliberately. Hod manages to get to one knee but the muscles in his legs are gone, and when the Reverend gets to a slow seven he looks to Jeff Smith who looks to the sourdough with the hammer and *bong!* the round is ended, bettors stomping and shouting with glee or anger, Smokey coming out to lift Hod under the arms and flop him on the stool. The negro mashes a sponge into his face and Hod tries not to gag as the ammonia shoots up his nose to a spot behind his eyes and burns into the cuts on his face. He pushes the sponge away and the sound of the screaming men comes back in a rush and he is furious, furious at himself and ready to fight again. If only he could feel his legs.

"You doin fine, young man," says Smokey. "You got more heart than head, but you doin fine. Where we at?"

"Nugget."

"And where that?"

"Skaguay."

Smokey takes Hod by the gloves and pulls out on his arms. "You hit the boards this round, just stay down. Peoples got what they paid for."

He is able to stand when the sixth starts, his head clearing, his first two straight lefts landing and then a one-two, bringing his right hard over the top and following with a—

Someone is waving a towel in his face. The breeze is nice. He is sitting on a floor that has tobacco stains on it and blood, blood mixed with sweat on his arms and chest. The fighter from the Pack Train, Choynski, is flapping the towel, smiling and not wearing boxing gloves any more. He leans down and says something, just a noise in Hod's ear but it's not clear, nothing is clear—

He's back in the little room with the French postcards on the wall and there is music and men's voices from outside and the girl in green, the redheaded girl with the scrawny arms, winces in sympathy as she dabs at his cuts with a cloth soaked in something that stings like hell.

"They call me Sparrow," she says. "But my Christian name is Addie Lee."

His shoes and his socks are off, and somebody has pulled the protection out of his trunks and tossed it, stained with blood, onto a chair in one corner. He's never been this undressed this close to a woman, the whores in Butte having only pulled his pants halfway down, and now he has to haul his knees up so this Addie Lee won't see him stiff. When he crosses his arms to cover his nipples up it hurts terrible, his ribs on both sides purple with bruises.

"He laid you out pretty good. Hit the back of your head on the floor."

That, too, hurts terrible, an ache that makes it hard to swallow when she tips his chin and gives him some water. "I go six?"

Addie Lee nods. "Don't know if them ginks tonight were sorer at you or at Mr. Smith. They waitin for you out there."

"Mr. Smith?"

She nods again. "The whole crew of em. Celebratin the haul they made."

It takes a while for him to manage to sit up. Dressing himself is a torture, each move reminding another part of his body how hard it's been pounded. When he shuffles out into the bar there is Smokey carefully sweeping the floor and Jeff Smith with a drink in his fist laughing and shaking his throbbing hand and Niles Manigault calling him Young McGinty and Rev Bowers and the Sheeny Kid and Old Man Triplett and Suds behind the bar and a fella named Red thumping him on the back which makes the ache in his skull jostle around and a little weasely one they call Doc.

"Saw a boy die in the ring one night," says Doc. "Hit the floor just like you did. An insult to the cranium."

"You're an insult to the cranium, Doc," says Rev Bowers. "Suds, lay one out for our scrapper here."

"Don't think I could handle any liquor now," says Hod. "Feels like I ought to keep what wits I got left as clear as I can."

More laughter then and Red Gibbs thumping him some more which makes Hod want to deck him and then Niles is on his feet with a toast.

"To Young McGinty," he says. "As game a warrior as ever stopped a punch."

They drink several more rounds then, laughing, Niles imitating the various suckers they have skinned that night, while Hod props his elbows on the bar and holds his head in his hands. He feels like he might vomit. It's late, only Jeff Smith's party still in the Nugget, the wood stove and the whiskey warming them.

"And the sheeny and his fat Paddy manager," says Rev Bowers, cheeks glowing, "think they've made a killing, tickets paid back to Frisco, when the steamers are so afraid of Jeff it won't cost him a penny."

"We have an arrangement," Jeff Smith corrects him. "An understanding between business parties. Fear has nothing to do with it."

They are halfway to the door, leaving Hod alone on the stool, when he remembers and calls out.

"Mr. Smith?"

They all turn as if they've forgotten he is there.

"A hundred dollars?"

He sees Niles winking to Rev Bowers.

"In trade," says Jeff Smith.

"Trade?"

Smith moves his eyes to Addie Lee, leaning in the doorway of her little crib, watching with no expression. "You'll keep track, won't you Sparrow?"

She shrugs and slips behind the hanging flag.

A SHAVE
AND A HAIRCUT

White folks' hair is easy. Dorsey never stops wondering at the way it just grows out straight from their heads, offering itself up to be trimmed. And the shaving, for the ones like Judge Manigault who don't keep a beard or moustache, you just pull the skin taut and slide with the blade. It never curls back into the pores to make a bump or get infected like his own. If only they would keep their mouths from moving while you try to work.

"Humiliation." The Judge sits in Dorsey's chair, lathered up next to Mr. Turpin who owns the pharmacy, who is getting his trim from Hoke. Old Colonel Waddell waits near the door, his face hidden behind the *Messenger*. "We have attempted to hold on to our heritage, to our custom of living," says the Judge, "and we have failed. So now we must be humbled."

"I don't know, Judge," says Mr. Turpin as Hoke clips out the hair in his ears. Hoke is a good boy, stay on his feet the whole day if needs be, only sometimes he forget and commence to hum while the gentlemen are still talking. "You scratch under the surface just a bit, you'll find somebody making a profit on it. That's what politics is all *about*."

"Russell got sufficiently fat before he was governor. But this appointing of half our aldermen—unprecedented. Another chance to force us to eat crow. I believe the yankees are behind him."

"But our own Supreme Court—"

"Failed in their duty to protect the citizens who maintain it." The Judge is one of those who keeps his own shaving mug here at the shop, has a favorite razor. He won't let Hoke shave him, good as the boy is. Dorsey, of course, is famous at the Orton, and hasn't drawn blood since he was a novice.

"*Lex ita scripta est*," mutters the Colonel, lowering his newspaper a bit. "That was their verdict."

"*The law as it is written*," the Judge scowls, "is not meant to serve scoundrels."

Dorsey cuts the guests at the Orton Hotel—merchants from around the state, politicians, even Governor Russell once when he was still running a dairy across the river—but many of the finest white gentlemen who live in the city come to be trimmed here as well. The Judge is a daily customer, as is Mr. Turpin. Colonel Waddell wears a full gray mane of hair and beard, like he did before the Emancipation, when he was known as a real fire-breather. Looks just like the Jeff Davis statue they put up in Raleigh, and only wants a bit of neatening up once a week. He waxes the tips of his moustache at home.

"They've got the governor and they've got the numbers," says Mr. Turpin. "The way they've got it fixed, it'll take a revolution to push them out." Mr. Turpin is thin on top, and Hoke is carefully spreading what's left with his comb to cover the scalp.

"We must not bow to the tyranny of numbers," says the Judge. "What if tomorrow the Sprunts decide to bring in five thousand Chinamen to bale their cotton? Should we be ruled then by Chinamen? I think not."

Dorsey waits, razor in hand, for the Judge to stop moving his jaw.

"Humiliation, I tell you," the Judge goes on. "Russell and his gang sold the farmers and the illiterate mountainfolk a bill of goods, they bought the colored vote with bribes and favors and white men's positions, and now he means to rub our noses in his success. He means to ruin this city."

Dorsey crosses to put a couple towels into the steamer. When the Judge gets going like this it's best to wait him out. He's been known to jump to his feet and pace, so you have to be careful with the cutting edges.

"The Redeemers have worked wonders in other states," says Turpin, soothingly. "South Carolina, Georgia, Louisiana—"

"Where they've looked the thing in the eye and dealt with it."

"It could happen here, Judge. And very soon." Hoke is whisking the back of the pharmacist's neck. "Somebody's just got to put the thing in motion."

"We've got them on the police force now." The Judge shakes his head violently, ignoring the lather on his face. Dorsey taps a couple drops of witch hazel into his palm, holds it under his nose. Mrs. Scott brews up a batch of it for him and he has Hoke pour it into the store-bought bottles when they get low. The Judge swivels his chair around to face Mr. Turpin, getting himself indignant. "Do you think they'll arrest their own? Not on your *life*. And if they do, they've got the juries packed and the darky walks out free as daylight and twice as bold as he was before."

It is the gentlemen's right to choose their topic, of course, but Dorsey always prefers sport to politics. He's one of the sponsors of the Mutuals, and can hold the floor on the relative merits of every ballplayer in New Hanover County, black and white. He can talk horses, he can talk Bible if there's a man of God in the chair, he can even recite *The Arrow and the Song* if pressed into service. Politics, though, especially the Wilmington variety, make him sweat.

"Plato believed that men should be governed by philosopher kings," Colonel Waddell observes. "I fear we have drifted away from that ideal."

"It wouldn't surprise me," says the Judge, "that if it serves the interests of these Fusioneers or Repopulists or whatever they're labeling themselves now, we'll have women's suffrage thrown into the mix."

"Women, white women, have the sense to listen to their husbands' counsel," says Turpin. "Giving them the vote would be redundant." There is still a separate entrance for ladies at the Orton. Dorsey cannot imagine them in politics—the harangues and heated confrontations, the spitting and swearing. Women are above all that, made to bind up what the men have broken.

The Judge snorts and lather flies. "Well I daresay they wouldn't have given the city over to carpetbaggers and Hottentots."

Mr. Turpin laughs. "That's what the illustrious Mrs. Felton would have us believe."

"A woman who writes," Colonel Waddell muses behind his paper, "is like a singing dog. The fascination is not that she does it well, but that she does it at *all*."

Dorsey always starts around the ears, tiny little strokes to outline the sideburns. The Judge has a large mole on the left side he has to be careful of.

"The key," says the Judge, finger jabbing underneath the cloth to make a point, "is to have some sort of qualification as to who is allowed to vote. That's what the Founders envisaged. Responsible government issues from informed voters."

"You're suggesting a literacy test."

"That is one possibility, yes."

"An awful lot of them can read now. I see them at my store with the— what's it called, Dorsey? Your colored paper?"

"The *Record*, suh." Dorsey advertises in the Manly brothers' paper for his other shop, where they cut colored hair.

"Do you read it?"

"No, suh. Don't have the time."

"Well, there is a group over in Brooklyn got them a bit more leisure," Turpin winks to the Judge in the mirror. "Unless it's to wrap fish in, I see an awful lot of em look like they read it."

"I would not propose that puzzling out the limited vocabulary displayed in a colored daily constitutes literacy," says the Judge. Dorsey can do his neck if he's steady. "If we were to take a section of the state constitution and have the voter demonstrate his competence by explaining its meaning—"

Mr. Turpin laughs. "We're going to do that with every voter in the city?"

"Selectively, yes."

"Selectively." Hoke is bending close to clip out Turpin's nose hairs.

"We administer the test to those whom we—we *suspect* of being illiterate, on a ward-by-ward basis."

"I would *suspect* that half the poor whites in Dry Pond might fail that test, Judge. Including a goodly number of loyal Democrats."

"Well, of course, if there is a tra*di*tion of voting in the family—"

"Record turnout in the last election, Judge—"

"Selling your vote for a glass of whiskey does not qualify as a tradition. What I'm suggesting is that if you can prove your *grand*father was a registered voter—"

"Now we're getting somewhere."

"—you would be passed unchallenged at the polling place."

"The Louisiana clause," adds Colonel Waddell. The old gentleman been in office himself, before Dorsey's day, rumored to be a great one for the oratory. He is always very quiet in the shop, but well-spoken, using words like *impecunious* and *recondite* that Dorsey makes sure to look up in his dictionary when he gets home and then slip into his conversations at Lodge meetings.

"Of course, given the present infestation here and in Raleigh, such an amendment to our statutes would stand no chance."

"I wouldn't give it up so easily, Judge. When his back is pressed to the wall, the true white man is capable of—"

Dorsey catches the Judge's look in the mirror, just a tiny nod of warning to Mr. Turpin. Hoke is rapidly snipping air with his scissors, made nervous by the turn of the conversation.

"What?" says Mr. Turpin. "Dorsey? Dorsey doesn't mix in politics, do you, Dorsey?"

"I try to keep my nose out of em."

Hoke shakes the cloth out and Mr. Turpin stands. "What I tell you? The good ones know enough to steer clear of it."

"Almost all absurdity of conduct," Colonel Waddell observes, "arises from the imitation of those we cannot resemble."

Turpin steps a little closer. Dorsey can feel him over his shoulder, watching him do the Judge's cheeks. "You planning to vote this coming election, Dorsey?"

The Judge cocks his head. Colonel Waddell lays the newspaper in his lap, waiting to hear the answer. Hoke retreats to get the broom. Dorsey always voted, ever since he was old enough, but nobody made any fuss about it till lately.

"No, suh," he lies softly. "Don't suppose I will."

"If the rest of your people show that kind of good sense, it'll stay peaceful in this city." It sounds a bit like a threat, but he can see Mr. Turpin is smiling in the mirror, gently tapping the thin layer at the top of his head with his fingers. "Say, Dorsey, how come a good-looking young fellow like you isn't hitched yet?"

Dorsey flicks lather off the blade, rinses it clean in the pan. "Oh, I been studyin it, Mr. Turpin. Got a gal picked out."

"That's good to hear." The pharmacist winks. Dorsey always hates it when they wink, especially if there's a nasty story coming after. "Before we know it you'll have a whole tribe of pickaninnies to support."

Dorsey turns away, strops the blade hard on the leather. "Whatever you say, Mr. Turpin."

"The tyranny of numbers," grumbles the Judge. "If *we* bred like damned jackrabbits we might stand a chance."

Mr. Turpin leaves two nickels on the counter and turns at the door. "Don't you worry, Judge," he calls. "Plans are being formulated. Prominent citizens are involved." With that he steps out onto the street, setting his hat over his haircut before the breeze can muss it.

Colonel Waddell settles into the next chair as Hoke flaps the cloth out and drapes it around his neck. "If a move to remedy the situation is afoot," he says, frowning, "I have not yet been informed of it."

The Judge seems lost in thought, and the lather has been sitting on his face long enough. Dorsey reaches two fingers under but doesn't quite touch him. "Chin?"

The white man grunts and tilts his head back for the razor.

*   *   *

Miss Loretta envies the colored girl her fingers. Her own were never long enough, never nimble enough to do justice to Chopin, her left hand adequate at tempo but her right fumbling to arpeggiate his harmonies. She had to think too far in advance, worrying about what pitfall lay ahead, and would lose the emotional thread of the music. But this one, Jessie, glides over the keys, rocking back and forth slightly as she plays the nocturne, closing her eyes for the darker passages and talking softly to her teacher, not so much distracted from the music as allowing it to take on the color of her mood.

"I love him *so much*."

She does not mean Chopin.

Miss Loretta does not allow herself to smile. She can recall making much the same statement, in much the same desperate tone, to old Aunt Kizzy while the servant combed her hair out at night. "*Chile*," Kizzy would say, shaking her head, "*you got yo life all in a knot*."

"Being in love is a state to be envied," Miss Loretta responds, flipping through the sheet music in her lap as Jessie lets the final tone decay. "Let's go back to the études—try the Number Three."

The colored girl picks out a single E, hums it, then rocks forward into the *Tristesse*.

She has worked so diligently, this one, advancing between lessons much more than she does during them, working at the purely technical exercises without complaint, listening to criticism and acting upon it gracefully. But there is something more, beyond what application and hours at the bench can achieve. She has the gift.

"This is a stroll through a beautiful wooded glade," Professor Einhorn said once when Miss Loretta, in her own student days, was struggling through one of the lovelier preludes. "You, young lady, are pulling up stumps."

She had been the favorite target of his epigrams, and after each she would press on all the more doggedly with her inadequate digits, clenching her jaw, humiliation roiling within her but never allowing it to color her performance. Not like this one—

"My father will never accept him," says Jessie, shaking her head as if it is a new realization, something the music has just informed her of, and not the recurring *opera seria* that has accompanied every lesson this year.

"That is what fathers are for, I'm afraid."

"If he had any idea of how I feel, he'd lock me in the attic."

Jessie plays the *agitato* departure in the middle of the étude, frowning at the keys. Miss Loretta has never thought of colored living in homes with attics before, but the Luncefords are quality people, Episcopalians, Jessie's father a graduate of a northern medical college and her mother one of the doyennes of what Daddy calls "sepia society." They have a lovely house on Nun Street, keep a carriage and a servant girl.

"You have a well-developed sense of drama, Jessie."

"But I'm serious!"

"I do not doubt that for a moment."

Miss Loretta's father scolded and harangued but never took her seriously. Nor did Professor Einhorn, constantly bemoaning of her lack of *Empfindsamkeit*. Men. Self-important men, towering edifices of consequence. At least now when Daddy interrupts her playing with one of his perambulating tirades she is allowed to continue throughout his aria. Her piece must be slow and unobtrusive, of course—once she accompanied his outburst with the *Heroic Polonaise* and was cursed for mocking him. I am forty years of age, she thinks, and my father treats me like a dim schoolgirl.

Jessie leans back as she begins the return, softening her touch, the notes achingly beautiful, the first pale rays of sunshine after a storm, and looks to Miss Loretta with tears in her eyes. Sometimes it is the composition, sometimes her own sixteen-year-old's romantic anguish—it does not much matter. She is not the singer that little Carrie was and has none of her ambition, but she is a channel for the music the way the truly gifted ones are. A prodigy, yes, though any of the colored girls who can make their way through a classical piece is labeled thus, and the term devalued. With this one Miss Loretta has to concentrate to be of any help, to resist the urge to stop judging and surrender to mere listening. The music is always of a piece when Jessie plays.

"I know you're using them all, Miss Butler," Professor Einhorn said to her once, "but I'm only hearing the white keys."

It is, at times, difficult not to be jealous. The girl coming in at twelve and playing, flawlessly, the *Minute Waltz*, and when her teacher professed amazement saying, innocently, "But Miss Loretta, it's a *song*." And now—

"Idiocy!" thunders Daddy from the next room.

He stalks in waving the *Messenger*. Jessie leaps immediately into the Number Four, *attacca il presto* as Chopin himself suggested, the piece she likes to call "Off to the Races."

"'There is no gain,'" Daddy reads in the voice he uses to quote men he thinks to be fools, "'that may be won through the peaceful machinations of diplomacy and commerce equal to that which is ripped from the enemy in the grisly pursuit of war!' Have you ever heard such rot in your life?"

"I know, Daddy, it's terrible."

The sixteenth notes scurry after each other, Jessie seemingly unaware of the old man's estimable presence in the room. Miss Loretta has heard this piece plagiarized in a particularly vulgar melodrama, underscoring the action as hero and villain chased each other around the stage and heroine wriggled helplessly tied across a railroad track.

"Imbeciles!" he cries, God's angry man. "A pack of yellow dogs! Jingoistic, profiteering, mealy-mouthed—"

The veins are standing out in his neck in the manner that worries her so, Daddy thwacking the rolled newspaper against his thigh to emphasize each new deprecation, and Jessie plays through it all, now politely twisting her head to acknowledge his presence, accustomed to his reports from the editorial page. Roaring Jack Butler, his few living friends call him, and his enemies too, though with an implication that he is not of right mind. That the Union prevailed in the great conflict did nothing to mitigate their opinion of him as a scalawag and heretic, and there are few of Wilmington's great men who will meet his eye in passing.

"—self-serving, sanctimonious—"

"Daddy, I have a student—"

"They want an *empire*!" He crushes the paper in his upraised fist, as if it is the neck of a despised fowl. "*Altruism*, they say, *democratic principles*, they say, *a helping hand to the Cuban patriot*—"

"Hypocrisy is the worst sin, Daddy, as you've told me a thousand—"

"Lies! All lies! They'll be gobbling up territories like darkies at a fish fry!" With a final, indignant thwack he stomps back into his study.

Miss Loretta is not certain whether she is amused by his outbursts after these many years, or only relieved that she is no longer their object. His political views and his insistence on not being "run off his patch" no doubt limited her prospects for marriage when she was of a desirable age, her fate sealed by her own—acquiescence? Cowardice? A widow with an inheritance might hope for suitors at forty, but a woman never married at that same age is past consideration.

"My apologies," she says to Jessie, but the girl has only turned back to face the piano and execute the tumbling descent that ends the piece. It is very sweet of her, really, to choose the old-maid daughter of the city's most eccentric landowner not only as a music instructor but as a confidant.

"I believe I'd give anything to be your age again," Miss Loretta muses out loud. "With a young soldier to pine for. Heartsick, yet eternally hopeful—"

"Did you ever—?" Jessie begins, and then falters on the very last note, as if realizing she may have overstepped her position.

"Ever what?" Miss Loretta asks her, gently. "Have I ever *pined* for somebody?"

The girl lowers her eyes, does not turn to look at her. She plays simple, thoughtful chords for a moment. "Did you?"

"Yes," Miss Loretta says to the colored girl.

"And—?"

"It went a good deal beyond the pining stage, I'm afraid, but he was—unsuitable."

Jessie nods sympathetically, as if she understands, as if she can know anything about it. "He was poor?"

Miss Loretta gives her a tight smile. "He was married."

It is evident that the girl is shocked, looking at the keys now as if they may have been suddenly rearranged.

"Daddy attempted to shoot him on two occasions."

She wonders what they think of her around town, what they say about her. After little Carrie's success at Fisk her services have been in demand, by colored and by white alike, and many of those same men who will not speak to her father are willing to pay to send their daughters into his home for lessons. A strange old bird, she imagines. A spinster eccentric whose constant and public efforts to gain suffrage are regarded as yet another deleterious effect of remaining without husband or child.

But Jessie Lunceford is too sweet-natured to mock or condemn her, and Miss Loretta is surprised to find herself not in the least embarrassed to have shared an intimation of her deepest regret with a student. A colored girl.

"Shall we try the Twenty-Three?"

It is the ballade they have been working on, the one she has suggested for Jessie's Academy audition and thus the locus of some anxiety, but today Miss Loretta only turns the pages when needed and allows her thoughts to drift on the music. The girl wears her hair in short braids that reveal the beautiful back of her neck, wears no ring on her long brown fingers, wears no disappointment, no sense of things that will never be. When she talks of her crush on the soldier and the impediment of her father's propriety the tiniest of vertical lines appears between Jessie's wide-set brows, her mouth turned down in the tiniest of frowns, like a seamstress concentrating to pass thread through a needle. How can anyone so untroubled understand the emotion of the music? Leland had a theory that the masters were only vessels, that the spirits of the great composers, or perhaps God Himself, was speaking through them. He would stroke her fingers, dreamily, as he spoke to her of his spiritual ideas, after they had been making love. She understands about the silences, this Jessie, understands that when there is a return the same notes will have a different feeling, a different meaning because of the thunder that has happened in between. Last week Miss Loretta heard her from the stairway, already seated and playing a strange music, slow and rambling and syncopated to the edge of sounding like a mistake. Jessie said she thought it was a rag, something she had heard from the window of a house she was forbidden to enter. "I know it's suppose to be wicked," she said, "but I think it's just sweet and sad and it's a place I like to go sometimes." Which startled Miss Loretta to hear, precisely the way she herself has always thought of the music, not as a thing or a performance but a place, a refuge she can visit but never live in. She still plays every day—badly, but with great feeling.

"I pride myself now on not being tragic," says Miss Loretta out loud as the final chord sustains, then fades. "Disappointed, perhaps—but never tragic."

Jessie is looking at her now, unsettled. Miss Loretta gives her a rueful smile.

"That was excellent, dear, very powerful. Let us proceed to Mr. Liszt."

COMMERCE

"Here's Soapy's other nigger," says Tommy Kearns as Hod walks into the Palace of Delight.

He is used to it by now. "You got some tables?"

"In the back."

A few customers are sleeping off the night's celebration beneath the elaborate painting on the rear wall, Seven Muses in transparent wisps of gauze dancing in a sylvan glade with a thick-muscled man. Smokey has been shy of stepping in here since the night he was accused of staring at it by a cabin-crazy sourdough and nearly lynched.

"What Jeff need tables for?"

"He doesn't," says Hod, crossing toward the back room. "Ham-Grease Jimmie needs tables and he's got a side of beef going over to the Old Vienna who are sending some empty liquor bottles to the Pantheon where they put whatever it is they mix up there into them."

Tommy Kearns laughs. "And somewhere along the line it ends up in Jeff's pocket."

"Right now we just need the tables."

Smokey is waiting with the wagon in the alleyway. They are halfway loaded when they hear the whistle echoing on the sides of the channel.

"*City of Portland*," says Smokey, who is never wrong. "Made good time."

They quickly empty the wagon and pull it around front and join the rush down to the water. The steamer is pulled up to the Juneau Wharf, just throwing the gangplank down when they arrive. Steering is Hod's least favorite part of the job, but Niles says he was born for it.

A steam whistle blows and the greenhorns come down the chute and immediately men are shouting offers to them, pulling their coats and promoting their resorts, handing out cards and handbills, promising to grease the wheels on the way to paydirt and warning to watch out for their fellow touts. Hod picks out the likeliest mark, a man who pulls an expensive watch out on a gold chain to check the time every few seconds and skitters over to eyeball each bit of his truck when it hits the planks.

"This is *mine*," he says to no one in particular, then hurries over to claim the next sack of meal.

Hod waits till he has his back turned, arguing with a deck ape about being in a hurry, and begins to load the man's goods.

"Whoah! Whoah! Whoah! That's mine!"

Hod and Smokey have a heavy crate in hand. "This here?"

"Yes!"

"You sure?"

"Yes!"

They lay the crate on the ground. "Where you going with it?"

"Over the Pass to the goldfields, goddam it, what do you think?"

Hod rests a foot on the crate and stares at it, scratching his head.

"How you gone get it there?"

The mark gets a shrewd look in his eye. "You men packers?"

"No, but we work for the Merchant Exchange. That's who will set you up with packers."

"That's where we goin," says Smokey, "once we load up some goods offen this boat."

The mark narrows his eyes even more. "How much to haul my lot over there?"

Hod shrugs, grins. *"Our horny-handed sons of toil,"* Niles Manigault is fond of saying, *"possess more guile than is apparent."*

"We goin there anyhow," he says. "Don't spose it's no bother."

They pile the wagon with the mark's whole outfit and four crates of fresh oysters Jeff Smith has promised somebody for a favor and roll up Runnalls Street to Jeff's Merchant Exchange building which also holds the Dominion Telegraph Service where greenhorns send their messages home, five dollars for ten words, on wires that end three yards from the back door. Syd Dixon is working the store.

"You get them oysters to the Golden North?" he says, face buried in a ledger book.

"This fella here going over the Pass."

Dixon jumps to his feet, looking pale but not as shaky as some mornings.

"You're a lucky man, sir, to be spared the riffraff at the wharf. We are a young city, growing every day, and it is much too easy for an honest fortune-seeker like yourself to be—well—taken ad*van*tage of. You've already purchased the necessary equipment, I trust?"

"I—"

"We left it on the boardwalk out front."

"Capital." Dixon makes a shooing gesture with his hand. "Now get those oysters to the hotel before they spoil."

The mark gives Hod a dollar coin for a tip.

"You done all the talkin," says Smokey when Hod offers it to him, riding back to the Palace of Delight for the tables.

"Mr. Smith pays me to pick things up and put em down," says Hod, laying the coin in Smokey's lap. "I don't want any profit from the other."

At least once a week he has to be the Eager Prospector, making a show at the Assay Office in front of some mark who will be inveigled to buy out from under him the worthless claim that he lacks the proper paperwork to file on. Or the Desperate Husband, forced to relinquish promising digs to join his dying wife in Kansas. Or the Assayer, approached to verify that the bar of coated lead Doc is peddling, at a severe financial loss, mind you, is indeed solid gold.

"Men so greedy," Jeff Smith likes to say when he has an audience gathered, "men so ignorant, such men cannot withstand the rigors of the frozen wilderness. We do them a service, skinning them down to their birthday suits before they can put their lives in peril."

They drop off the oysters and haul a crated player piano from the wharf to the Garden of Joy just as the winter sun drops behind the mountain and the dance halls begin to fill up. Smokey leaves Hod outside the Nugget.

"You watch out for them womens," he grins, and turns the nag toward the livery barn.

The floor is shaking under the weight of heavy-footed men and brightly dressed women dancing to band music, Hod fading into a corner to watch Addie Lee work. She twirls with one clomping sourdough or another as the fiddler saws out shortened versions of *Mountain Canary* or *Turkey in the Straw* or *The Irish Washerwoman* at a dollar a go till the girls are breathless and suggest their partners sit out the ballad, sung by Dingle Rafferty, who during the daylight hours removes horseflops from in front of those establishments willing to pay, and there is Addie Lee drinking teawater and the sourdough a two-dollar whiskey, sitting in one of the little boxes partitioned against the north wall—

As I trip across the Dead Horse Trail
With an independent air

—sings little Rafferty from atop a liquor crate next to the piano, chin lifted to the ceiling, eyes closed—

You can hear the girls declare
"He must be a millionaire!"

—Hod watching from his corner as half the men crowd back to the bar for a quick one, Suds dealing out the house mixture and sloppily weighing dust on the scales and the percentage girls who are left with no partner clustering together to steady themselves on each other's shoulders as they adjust shoes and straighten stockings and the ones in the boxes allowing just enough to keep their escorts' pokes open—

You can see them sigh and wish to die
You can see them wink the other eye
At the man who found the mother lode in Dawson!

—Rafferty adding verses till he gets the high sign from somebody in the bar and finishing with a high, sweet, wavering note, men stomping and clapping as he hops off his box with the fiddle skreeking a lead-up to a schottische, the banjo man and tubthumper waiting till negotiations on the floor are settled before joining in and Addie Lee out being hurled around in yet another man's paws.

She is catching her breath near the entrance door during a waltz, Rafferty sentimentally warbling *After the Ball*, when Hod steps in.

"Young McGinty." She likes to tease him with the name, though she knows it isn't his real one.

"I was wondering—later—"

Addie Lee nods. "I got one lined up already, but if you want to wait—"

He doesn't want to wait, but she has expenses to keep up and he is a barter client.

"I'll be here."

"All you men," she says, giving him something like a smile. "Give a girl a big head." And then the band swings into *American Beauty* and she is two-stepped away by a man with a hundred-dollar bill pasted to his sweaty forehead.

The dancing goes on and on, Hod watching the other girls work their marks, easing away from three different fistfights, his reputation in the camp as a fighter now a liability, Rafferty's tenor lifting higher after every drink he takes. They are still dancing, fresh prospectors replacing the ones who are too drunk or tapped out, when Addie Lee crosses back toward the bar with Ox Knudsen staggering after her like a drunken bear. The fiddler apparently knows only five songs and no one seems to care as he repeats them again and again till he is spelled by a professor who bangs out *Coonville Cakewalk* on the ivories, the girls rolling their eyes at each other and giggling as the men, reeking of booze and tobacco and wet wool, gallantly offer their arms to escort them in a wavering parade around the floor.

There is no mystery where she is going with the Swede and what they'll be up to. Hod can't help himself and follows.

Jeff Smith and Niles and big Arizona Charlie and skinny Billy Mizner and Tex Rickard down from Circle City are at a table playing poker and eyeing the marks. Rickard has been setting up fights for the Ox, who works as a blacksmith when he isn't bulldogging startled prospectors in the ring.

"Our young Apollo," notices Niles Manigault, always paying more mind to the room than to his cards. "Mooning over his soiled dove."

Hod finds an empty stool and turns his back to them.

"Make him an eggnog," calls Charlie Meadows. It has become a source of great amusement to them all that he doesn't drink.

"No liquor, no tobacco," says Niles, drawing a pair. "If it wasn't for his fascination with the scarlet sisterhood he'd be a model for our youth."

"Leave the boy alone," says Jeff Smith. "He's in training."

Rickard laughs. "What, with old Smokey?"

"One needs to acquire the fundamentals of the science."

"One needs to render his opponent immediately unconscious," says Billy Mizner, "like our Swede in there. See your twenty and call."

Every day when there is a break from hauling Jeff Smith's goods around they put on what Smokey calls the pillow gloves and go at it, the negro coaching him on footwork and head movement. None of it seems natural.

"That's why it's a science," Smokey tells him, breathing hard after a session in the warehouse on Captain Moore's wharf. "If it come natural, any one of these overgrowed plowboys be the champeen of the world."

He means Knudsen, of course, who has been fighting twice a week at the beer hall, taking all comers for bragging rights and side bets. He is a brawler with cannonballs for fists, known for throwing opponents bodily out of the ring and pounding them to jelly once he has them down.

Smokey steps back and takes up the attack stance. "When they was still throwin baseballs at my head," he says, aiming hooks at Hod's ribs, "I'd take them balls off beforehand and go at em with a mallet, soften em up some. Thas what you do with your body hits, soften a man up."

Hod brings up his guard and goes up on his toes the way Smokey showed him. "I use a mallet?"

"You fight that squarehead it best be a railroad tie. What we do now is I temp to knock you block off, and you gots to keep out the *way* of it."

Smokey comes after him then, wild and hard, and it is all Hod can do to dance and parry away from the negro inside the tiny square he has closed in with packing crates.

"You stop movin, boy, you damn well better be throwin them fists."

There is a trio of busted sourdoughs next to Hod at the bar, veterans of two winters in the interior, doling out their little pouches of dust for whiskey and harmonizing to whoever is within earshot.

"You got four, five, maybe a half-dozen fires going," says one, thick-bearded and bitter, "got to burn off that frost layer before you can dig. And every day it's a longer walk to find wood. There isn't but a couple hours of light so half your digging is by fire or lantern and them wolves get to howling—"

"Indins say it's dead men's souls crying out," says another. "But that's only to make us cheechakos flighty. What it is is just wolves, which is the Satan of the animal kingdom. Waiting to gang up and pull you down while you still got some meat on your bones."

"The nights," says the third, a man Hod has seen down by the wharf trying to sell his claim and his cabin and what gear he's brought back to the greenhorns coming off the steamers, "the nights last forever. Out there in a log coffin with an oil lamp and a partner who's like to go off his nut and murder you if you fall to sleep before he does. You done heard all his life's business three times over and he's heard yours and you're sick of it. Enough to make a man pick up the Bible."

Each of them is missing at least one finger and the one next to Hod still has black scurvy gums and a burn scar that covers half his face.

"The good ground's all been picked over," he grumbles, "or jumped by gun thugs. So you pan and you dig and you freeze your damn toes off for that little speck of yellow, more grit in your teeth of a day than you put in your poke, and God help you if you run out of lard or coffee or beans or if your cabin burns while you're out digging or a bear gets into your stores or you take fever or snap an ankle in the rocks. Out there in them open snowfields, a man don't count for nothin. It's too big."

There is a commotion then and Flapjack Fredericks makes his entrance, a runty, beet-nosed character in a top hat and an oversized Prince Albert coat and a constant cigar in his face, trailed by two girls dressed in identical red outfits, the older not more than fourteen.

"I brought my matched set," he winks, "in case one wears out."

The girls wear no makeup, pink-cheeked and curly haired, eyes vacant as sheep, and stand chewing their lips in the corner where Flapjack plants them while he gladhands around the room.

"Look what the wind blew in," mutters the man with the burned face.

Fredericks claps him on the back. "This round is on me, boys. Compliments of Flapjack Fredericks, Gold King of the Yukon."

"Sluice-robbin son of a bitch that got lucky, is what," says another of the busted sourdoughs. "Probly fell over drunk right on top of it."

"And it could happen to you, boys," he winks. "Just don't never give up the hunt. I was down to boiling tree moss for soup when I chopped into a big, fat vein of the yellow stuff—peed my trousers it was so rich—and now I got a palace on Nob Hill and a boat to sail me round the harbor and I spread caviar on my flapjacks every morning."

"Fish eggs," grunts the third prospector, accepting his free drink from Suds.

"At five dollars an ounce," twinkles the Gold King of the Yukon. "Go through the stuff like it's toilet paper."

"Figured out what that's for, have you?"

"I got the world by the dingus," Flapjack calls to anyone within earshot, "and I don't care who knows it."

"You care to sit in, Claude?" says Jeff Smith, who knew the man when he'd stick his hand in a cuspidor full of swoose if you tossed a silver dollar in it. "We promise to take it easy on you."

"Sorry, me and the girls are headed over to the Music Hall. I bought the house out. They're puttin on *East Lynne* just for the three of us." He winks.

"The girls get shy in big crowds. They're sisters, you know."

"Recently plucked from the orphanage, no doubt," says Mizner, and the girls giggle.

"Just thought I'd pay my respects, let you boys know I'm back in town. Let's go, ladies, we got money to spend!"

"Aint no justice in this world," says the man with the burned face when they are gone.

Arizona Charlie laughs. "He'll hit every saloon in town on the way to that theater, showing his roll and telling his story."

"You see that flasher on his ring finger?" says Niles.

"Diamond big as a gull egg."

"Paste," says Niles, laying his cards face up. "I was there when Jeff sold it to him."

"It once belonged to the Duchess of Mesopotamia," says Jeff Smith, revealing his hand and sweeping the pot. "One acquires the pedigree along with the stone itself."

The men laugh then and Ox Knudsen stumbles out of Addie Lee's room with a red tongue of flannel shirt wagging through his open fly, laughing along though he didn't hear the joke.

"Feel like I just went forty rounds," he says loudly, shouldering in between Hod and the burned sourdough. "Gimme a beer, Suds."

"You couldn't hold your left hand up for forty rounds, much less your pecker," says Tex Rickard, and Ox laughs heartily, carefully spilling beer on Hod as he turns to face the card table.

"If a man got balls between his legs," he says after draining the schooner, "he gets his business over quick. Wouldn't take me no six rounds," raising his voice theatrically, "to put away some nigger's assistant."

Hod can feel Jeff Smith watching him, and the others, but doesn't take the bait.

"Seems to me, he lasted that long with Choynski, there must have been some money bet on the round." Ox insinuating, wiping beer foam from his moustache. Smith's eyes go cold the way they do when the wrong person calls him Soapy or he is crossed or just wants to put you off balance.

"If you could count, Ox," he says, "you could make some money too."

The Swede laughs loud with his mouth, then bumps Hod hard putting his schooner back on the counter, raising his voice enough to be heard beyond the hanging flag as he stomps out of the bar. "I'll take your Yellow-Stain Kid or any other man you can find, got-dammit! You know where to find me."

Rickard waits till Knudsen stomps out, clapping his hands slightly off time to the music from the dance hall, before he asks. "So how bout it, Jeff? Middle of the winter, people getting restless—"

Smith shuffles the cards lightly, eyes meeting Hod's as he turns around on the stool. "It's not when the roosters are ready to fight, Tex. It's when the suckers are ready to *bet*."

They go back to playing then, and Hod drinks a soda water Suds hands him. A man like Flapjack drives his stakes in over the right pile of rocks and he is transformed—ugly, stunted, cross-eyed—into a figure of envy, of legend. He throws money at beautiful young women and they throw themselves back. Ox Knudsen struts around the camp accepting free drinks and the nearest seat to the woodstove because he can pound most everybody he meets into blood paste and lets them know it. And Hod Brackenridge, assistant nigger, waits on a stool for his girl's quim to dry up so he can stand to look at her.

He waits till they are deep in a high-stakes hand, too intent to be watching, and slips behind the American flag.

She is sitting on the cot with a cardboard fan from Peoples the undertaker, wafting the air around her toward the door. "I swear that Ox don't eat nothin but beans."

"You see him a lot?"

"Whenever he's got the mazuma," she shrugs, moving her legs so he can sit down. "You ready?"

Hod nods toward the noise from the bar. "Everybody still out there."

"The Nugget don't ever close."

"Yeah. I already heard all the songs twice."

She smiles. "Listen, we could go back to my room where I sleep. Them drunks in the balconies been throwin gold dust at us tonight—I got to wash my hair and see how much come out."

"You can leave?"

"You come out from here in a few minutes and then I'll come out like I'm going back to dance some more. Won't anybody be wise to it."

They listen to Niles Manigault, only a few feet away on the other side of the curtain, bemoan his luck. "It's as if the cards are punishing me," he says. "I am Fortune's orphan."

Hod sits by her on the cot, touching shoulders, and they are quiet for a while. "So when you've made your pile," he asks finally, "what you going to do with the money?"

She looks away from him then, frowning. "I swear I don't know where it all goes. This and that, you know? But I'm gonna start saving."

"That would be good."

"If I had enough right now, right here, what I'd do is stop this box-rustlin and buy some chickens, have a house built for em with a stove set in the middle of it to keep the chicks warm. You know what an egg sells for right now? And if you can get them over the Pass—"

"You'd make more money."

"Most of the girls think they're gonna hook on to one of these bonanza kings. Only that type don't stay in Skaguay very long."

He counts the forty-five stars in the hanging flag a couple times, pulls his shirt out of his belt, kisses her on the cheek and steps out. The men at the poker table are all smirking.

"Our Apollo has unburdened himself," says Niles.

"He who loves last, loves best," adds Billy Mizner. "Though it can get a little slippery."

Hod waits for her outside in the cold, lamplight spilling from every resort on Broadway, noise from within swirling in the wind off the channel, the camp always loudest at this hour as if they can fiddle or sing or laugh away the endless, howling Yukon nights. Addie Lee steps out and Hod drapes his parka with the hood over her and they walk to the Princess Hotel together, her dancing shoes no match for the snowdrifts.

Her room is small, but there is a rug on the floor and a window to the street and it is warm, twice as warm as the drafty bathhouse with bunks Hod has been staying in, his only decoration the advertisement Smokey gave him to paste on the wall, Jake Kilrane in a fighting stance.

LOSE WEIGHT

it says—

AND ENHANCE YOUR MANHOOD

Smokey doesn't read, and Hod can only think it can be a reminder of proper boxing posture.

Addie Lee washes her hair out into a metal pan and saves the water to pick through later. She takes her dancing shoes off and lies back on the bed and before Hod can get his pants off has fallen asleep. He takes his wool socks off and puts them in the farthest part of the room and lies next to her. Later, when she wakes, she sits up and stares at him for a long moment as if trying to remember who he is. Then she smiles.

"You," she says, and they start in, with the lamp on the little table by the bed still on and smelling strong of coal oil and she doesn't look away once while he is on her.

"How many times you think it will be," he asks when he is finished and they are lying next to each other again, "to make up a hundred dollars?"

"I'll let you know."

Light comes in the window and the wild dogs start to snarl on the street, and then there are loud voices as the next room starts to fill up.

"That's Babe hosting the spillover," she says, rising to pull her stockings off. Her legs look even skinnier without them on. "She's gonna be over to get me if we don't go out."

She puts on two sweaters and oversized men's pants and her mukluks and Hod scouts the stairway so they can hit the street unnoticed. With Hod's parka on her and the hood up Addie Lee gets barely a glance from the stunned-looking celebrants emerging from the saloons and dance halls, though a bob-tailed mastiff trails close, sniffing at her till Hod chases him away. They walk north of town, avoiding the wagon road, until Skaguay is only a hundred columns of woodsmoke in the sky behind them.

She plays at blowing puffs of breath into the air, turning in a circle to look up at the treetops, then stops and stares into his face. "McGinty aint really your name, is it?"

"No."

"Most of the percentage girls, they got a different moniker up here than what they were born with. A lot of the men too, hidin from the law or their wives or whatever. Like there aint no rules cause it's not really America."

"There's rules," says Hod. "It's just different people in charge of them."

They start to climb, circling around the boulders and felled trees, the sharp air feeling good in Hod's chest. Inside there is smoke everywhere, cigars and pipes and woodsmoke and his clothes all smell like smoke but here, where the stampeders have never been, there is only clean wind shaking the tops of the spruce trees.

There are women in the camp who aren't for rent, not the way Addie Lee is, who do laundry and cook and wash pots and sell goods or run boarding houses, but they dress against the cold and wear big shoes and none of them, not a one, shows the least bit of interest in Soapy's other nigger. It was the same in Butte, the same in every mining camp he's ever worked in. He climbs slightly ahead when it gets steeper and reaches back to pull her up.

"I suppose you come here for the gold," she says.

"Me and fifty thousand other halfwits."

"So what happened?"

"I got to the top," says Hod, "but I never got over."

He motions for her to stop, taps his mitt against his lips.

There is a bear coming down the slope.

It is immense, dark brown flecked with gray, swinging its head and grunting now and then as it rubs its flanks hard against the tree trunks.

Hod feels Addie Lee slip her arm into his and pull tight, so little that is actually *her* inside the layers of clothing, a thrill shooting through him, and then the bear sees them or smells them, stopping to stand, steadying itself with a massive arm against a spruce tree, its tiny, stupid eyes trying to comprehend.

"We'll get out of your way," says Hod in as steady a voice as he can muster, then pulls Addie Lee sideways, neither of them taking their eyes off the beast.

It makes something between a bark and a grunt and drops back onto all fours, pawprints dwarfing the tracks of their feet as it descends on the path they took up. They watch till it is lost in the trees. Addie Lee has tears running down her face but doesn't seem scared.

"To think there's such a thing in this world," she says.

They climb up a ways farther, not talking much, angling sideways so they won't surprise the bear on the way down. Where there is enough snow she tries to slide down on her back, but it's too powdery.

"There's never a crust on the snow here," she says. "It's dry as sawdust."

"You don't get a thaw, you don't get a crust."

She is in a dark mood by the time they come back to town, making their way through the badgering merchants and frantic, ignorant stampeders.

"It's just what men turn into when they get up here," she says, studying them, her face mostly hidden by the parka hood. "Or maybe that's what they are all along and they just start to look the part more. All hairy and stinky and grunt and snuffle and climb on you and grunt and snuffle and climb off and go digging in the ground." Smokey waves to Hod in passing from the seat of the wagon, signaling that there is work to be done. Addie Lee doesn't notice. "And every once in a while they get sore and tear each other apart."

Hod walks her up the stairs to her room in the Princess Hotel and leaves her there, panning her washwater for gold dust.

SOJOURNER

Father—

Please forgive the tardiness of my correspondence, but we have been in transitu *of late and the regular mail schedule is not in effect. As you may surmise from the postmark on this missive, I am in St. Louis, part of a specially chosen unit testing a novel mode of military transport.*

Our commander Moss, of whose organizational skills I have written before, has long entertained General Miles with the notion of replacing the temperamental, noxious, and oat-burning horse with a vehicle less expensive in its upkeep and more in tune with our age. Thus was born the Infantry Bicycle Corps. Though the cavalry was afforded the first opportunity to participate in this great experiment, they proved much too fond of their equine cohorts (and, I must say, of the dashing figure they cut mounted upon them) to accept. As the colored troops invariably are saddled (apologies) with whatever duties our paler brethren-in-arms abhor, and as Lt. Moss was the originator of the scheme, the honor of implementation has fallen on the 25th.

Junior kneels, tablet resting on a stump, writing. He has been left to guard the wheels while the rest of the squad are off tom-catting on the east side of the river. He had taken it for a display of trust, the lieutenant recognizing the most responsible of his troopers, till Moss went off with the mayor's party and the others started in about all the high times he would be missing. Telling him to polish their wheels while he was at it, Army humor never subtle or kind.

The Corps has, previous to my enlistment, cycled dispatches about the Bitterroot Valley and taken one longer journey, which I am very sorry to have missed, to the Yellowstone area and its attendant natural wonders. A pair of the lieutenant's stalwart wheelmen having since mustered out of the service, I volunteered myself and Pvt. Scott (who, by the way, sends you and family his warmest regards) to take their places. My own recreational familiarity with the device gave me a leg up, so to speak, on poor Royal, but in no way prepared me for the rigors of extensive cross-country cycling. We pedal our steel-rimmed Ramblers over the roads, such as they are, in these vast, unpeopled spaces of Montana, whenever they are available and in passable condition. Otherwise it is the bumpy course through scrub and sagebrush, flushing rabbit and antelope in our path and deploying rapidly to "hand-over" our metallic steeds when we encounter the occasional stock fence. On these training jaunts we carry only our bedrolls, on a rack bolted in front of the handlebars, and our rifles slung over our shoulders.

Junior kneels before the stump, writing, because he cannot sit, may never, in fact, be able to sit again. There is no glory in his wound, the simple mention of being "saddle sore" drawing the wrath of the former cavalrymen in their party, and he has resolved himself to suffer in silence. He talks to Royal, of course, and Royal seems to listen, but there has been a reserve in his friend lately, an edge of *What have you gotten us into?* Not just the cycling, but the whole idea of joining the 25th in hope of heroic action when there has been little more than monotony and cursing and scutwork of the lowest variety.

It wants a battle.

"The bicycle requires neither water, food, nor rest," General Miles has written, and at times it appears that the same qualities are expected from the colored soldier. Our training at the wheel is additional to our other duties at the fort, so as you may imagine only the most intrepid (some would say "ambitious") of the enlisted men have stepped forward. Lt. Moss's quest this year was a sojourn from Missoula to St. Louis (over 1,000 miles as the crow hobbles) and back, to demonstrate that the only limit to this method of transport is human "spunk" and endurance. We are principally under the tutelage of Sgt. Mingo Sanders, a veteran of some years who has distinguished himself, despite being nearly blind in one eye, in several of the regiment's more trying engagements. Largely uneducated but possessed of an ample reserve of "mother wit," he is a man the younger soldiers look up to—sanguine under pressure, resolute in action, a sympathetic guide to the rawer recruits.

Of these we had the addition, shortly before our departure, of a fellow Royal recognized as a figure of some ill-repute in Wilmington. Cooper (not his real name according to Pvt. Scott) is the devil-may-care type often attracted to the service in search of adventure, or, as I suspect in his case, refuge from legal authorities. Though no shirker when it comes to our daily routines, he is lacking in the esprit de corps one would wish for among fellow rookies, repeatedly suggesting that the bicycle experiment is a ruse designed to humiliate the colored soldier rather than an opportunity for him to stand out from the pack. Our reception, however, has been overwhelmingly enthusiastic and cordial, a seemingly endless celebration, though some disappointment is voiced on the discovery that we do not also play instruments. (Our 25th band is lauded as the finest musical aggregation in western Montana.)

We have passed through mountain, meadow, desert, and prairie on the way, alternately slogging through rain and "gumbo mud" and baking, with insufficient water, for days through the aptly named Badlands, vagabonding in conditions many a cavalryman would not deign to expose his mount to, averaging something less than forty miles a day on vertical terrain and something more than sixty on the horizontal. For this odyssey we carry a full kit including half-tent, rifle slung over the back, and fifty rounds of ammunition in our belts, plus food, water, and cooking gear, but severe rain and hailstorms and the great distances between points of resupply have often forced us to travel on extremely short rations. The mountains require "walking" the bicycle up the slope and a cautious, serpentine descent to avoid loss of control. Where wagon roads do not exist we follow the railroad—our machine is not designed for progress on stone ballast or cross ties, and Lt. Moss imagines a special attachment enabling us to "ride the rails." We camped one night on the Custer battle site, wild roses of various colors growing on the hills that witnessed that great slaughter. Most trying, as it turned out, were the sand hills of Nebraska, the roads unpaved, the temperatures well over 100 degrees each day, and water only available from railroad tanks erected at considerable distance from each other. Despite these deprivations, or perhaps because of them, I shall never forget this trip, particularly Sgt. Sanders's fine tenor cutting through the hail that pelted our faces somewhere in the Great Plains to lead us in a heartfelt chorus of The Girl I Left Behind Me *or* Marching Through Georgia *(humorously replacing "darkies" with "crackers" in the second verse of the latter) or the thousands, yes, thousands of spectators here in St. Louis, black and white, who cheered our drills and demonstrations upon our arrival yesterday at the Cottage in Forrest Park.*

Father, I have seen (and cycled across) the Mississippi River. It is not a disappointment.

There is some talk that we will be returned to Ft. Missoula by rail—whether prompted by recent events in Cuba (or, perhaps, China) or merely that we have made our point to the Dept. of War, I do not know. The people we speak with throughout the country are "spoiling for a fight," especially the youth, and it seems not to matter who the opponent shall be. Our near neighbors at the Fort, the Salish (popularly termed

Flatheads, though their heads are not flat at all), have never developed a taste for the warpath, due either to a congenitally pacific nature or the ministration of the Jesuit worthies in their midst. Their chief, one Charlo, seems if not content at least resigned to their recent removal from the Valley to a reservation farther north, and our Missoula post remains an "open fort" without walls to block our sight of the magnificent vistas nor to shelter us from the punishing winter winds. (I do hope that October affords us the opportunity of battle in sunnier climes.) The tales Sgt. Sanders relates of our regiment's role during the labor troubles haunting the Northern Pacific in Coeur d'Alene and other locales sound more like police work than "Injun fighting," and at times I worry I have chosen the wrong unit in which to prove myself. But a soldier's lot is to keep himself prepared for hazardous duty at all times, and to accept that he has no say in how his services will be employed.

A humbling lesson for Yrs. Truly.

(But if the next war is to be fought on bicycles, the 25th shall be in the van.)

Please share this offering with Mother and Jessie, and let them know they are ever in my thoughts. Do inform me of the latest concerning the "politicking" at home. The other fellows are much entertained by accounts of our little struggles there.

With respect from your wandering son,
Private Aaron Lunceford, Jr.

Junior kneels, as if praying, facing an orderly row of bicycles, and the unit's rifles stacked in pyramids—polished, oiled, unloaded. The celebration continues, a band playing a patriotic air, but it is very far away.

EASTMAN BULLET

The screw is supposed to sever your spine at the base of the neck before you are choked by the collar.

Of course no one has ever survived to report whether this is true, and the official document lists *judicial asphyxiation* as the cause of death. Maybe the man who turns the crossbar, the executioner, knows, standing just behind the condemned—maybe he can hear a crack of bone, perhaps sense the moment when the desperate message from the brain is cut short, sense the sudden slackening of convulsing limbs.

Diosdado files onto the balcony that overlooks the courtyard of the *Cuartel de España* with the others—two *militares*, a choleric *haciendero* over from Mindoro, Benítez the defense lawyer from the Ministry of Justice, and Padre Peregrino. There is another *fraile* waiting in the courtyard below, a round, red-nosed Franciscan, knotted rope taut around his stomach, waiting to deliver the sacrament. Diosdado moves to the extreme left, with the box, hidden under his coat, pressed against the balcony rail. He is sweating as much from nerves as from the heat. When the Committee asked him to do this he agreed at once—he has been among the witnesses before, his political sympathies not yet known to the authorities, and he was able to ask to be invited without arousing suspicion. It was only some hours later, after they had given him the box and made sure he knew how to operate it, that the consequences fully dawned upon him. Once the photograph is copied and distributed there will be no doubt as to who has taken it, and his enviable life in Manila will be ended forever, or at least until a better day.

Men must have felt the same way in '96, when Bonifacio told the crowd to rip their *cédulas* to pieces. With this act, thinks Diosdado, I not only tear free from Spain, but destroy my own identity. The Committee has given him a new, forged *cédula personal* that displays his face with a different name, and have promised to wait till he wires from Hongkong, safe with the other *exiliados*, before they spread copies of the photograph across the country.

"For murderers and thieves we admit the public," says the Comandante to his visitors as they settle in, "but with the *políticos*, these days, a bit of discretion must be observed. No use stirring everybody up for nothing."

"An occasional blood-letting does a body good." The general is a tall, pox-scarred man with an impressive moustache. "Blood that is never spilled can only fester, eh Padre?"

Padre Peregrino frowns. "I have never cared for the public ones," he says. "A dying man should be alone with his God."

"If he has one," grumbles the *haciendero*.

"If he *accepts* his Lord," corrects the padre. "Believers or not, we are all his children."

"I could do without all the *moro-moro*." The *haciendero* is wearing a coat that looks fresh from the tailor, paid for that very morning. He points at the device below with a silver-tipped cane. "Making a solemn ceremony of it, proclamations, witnesses—it lends them a dignity they don't deserve."

"You'd shoot them in the streets like dogs," smiles the Comandante.

"And perhaps leave them lying there a few days, as a lesson to the others."

"We must have law."

"Of course," snorts the *haciendero*. "That's the point of it. Make it against the law to move the body from where it lies for a week."

"And what do you think, young man?" the Jesuit asks.

They are all looking at him. Diosdado has angled his body slightly, better to hide the box when it has to come out, and turns only his head to answer.

"I think we have to balance what is instructive," he says, "with what is sanitary."

The men laugh.

The *condenado* is led out from the holding cell then, and Diosdado is spared their attention. This one has shoes.

The one whose execution he witnessed two years ago had been barefoot, just another young Juan Tamad from Bayombong who had been swept up by the movement, joined the Katipuneros, been captured and then chosen to be executed as an example here in Manila. He was a long-legged boy who before they put the *saco* over his head had worn a tentative expression, looking around as if afraid to betray his ignorance of protocol in the presence of his betters. When the moment came his toes had splayed apart, had curled and clutched like fingers, had clawed a frenetic design into the dust at the foot of the stool.

This one has shoes. Cheap ones, scuffed and lusterless from the weeks of his incarceration, but shoes nonetheless. He is a gambler, the Committee told Diosdado, an *indio* with more audacity than sense who wandered down from the north to match wits with the Chinese, as if anyone can equal them at the dice. Not a patriot at all, really, till he was destitute and willing to risk his life itself for a palmful of gold. Valdevía, operating under a false name, hired him to post the edict throughout Binondo, an exploit requiring stealth and speed but no great intellect. The boy he brought along to carry water and paste managed to escape, though shots were fired. But this one—his name is Magapuna, Fecundo Magapuna—possessed no more luck at subversion than at cards.

He has been interrogated, no doubt, and no doubt tortured when his ignorance of the authors of the edict, of the call for resistance, struck his captors as dissimulation. And when the authorities were satisfied that he knew nothing, or were perhaps merely impatient to get on with it, the brief trial and sentencing had taken place. The Committee, of course, did not provide an advocate, and hapless Fecundo was represented by Benítez here, the aptly nicknamed "butcher's assistant" who has never missed the garroting of one of his clients. He leans over the balcony railing now, eyes bright with excitement.

They've chained the condemned man's ankles very close together, and as he is led, no, pushed toward the device, he shuffles with short hopping steps like a *chino* carrying one end of a pallet on Rosario Street. With him are the *capitán encargado* and two soldiers, and, walking with measured dignity some paces behind them, the stocky executioner.

"This one looks like a pimp," says the *haciendero*.

The condemned man has longish black hair, oiled and combed straight back from a broad forehead. His mouth is twisted in a bilious sneer, as if his last meal has left him disgusted. One of the soldiers turns him by the shoulders and guides him onto the stool as the other stands by with rifle at port-arms. The condemned man, Magapuna, does not resist as the soldier pushes him back flat against the board and fastens the collar. They are on the little raised platform that makes it easier for the public to follow the ceremony, when the public is allowed, and there is noise from the street beyond the wall. The wheels of a *calesa* that need to be oiled, horse hooves on hard dirt, vendors selling mangos and lanzones. Within the cuartel, ringed with barracks and stables built around the remnants of the old Colegio de San Ignacio, only a few off-duty *cazadores* glance out at the preparations, then drift back inside to their card games. Dr. Rizal was tried in here, away from plebian support and a stone's throw from the killing ground. Diosdado eases the box out from under his coat and rests it on the balcony railing, hidden from the others by his body.

"We had one try to break free," says the Comandante, still smiling. "The spectators got quite a show that day. As if there was anywhere for him to go. As if those extra few minutes, running like a chicken before the slaughter, falling over his chain into the dirt and having to be carried back, were worth the bother."

"Every moment is precious to a dying man." The Jesuit is smiling as well, as if he is encouraging a joke in progress.

"Was he making a speech?" asks the *haciendero*. "No matter how ignorant they are, no matter how little of any interest they have to say, put the irons on them and they all become orators."

"He kept shouting '*I don't want to sit down!*'" says Benítez.

They laugh again, all but Diosdado, who uses the noise to mask the click of the shutter. The laughter draws a sharp look from the *capitán encargado* below.

"*Decorum necesita est*," says Padre Peregrino softly, and the men bring their faces to order. Before Diosdado moved on to Santo Tomás, Padre Peregrino was his mentor at the Ateneo, teaching Classics and History. He is a stirring lecturer, passionate about the struggle for Christianity and the martyrs it has produced. His favorite is Saint Perfectus, who was decapitated and hung upside-down for display by the *moros* when they ruled Córdoba.

"*He raised his chin to the sword*," the padre will say, tears gathering in his eyes, "*and cried* 'I come to You, my Lord!'"

Diosdado did not tell the padre he had been a witness before when he requested the invitation. "I've been thinking more about the nature of death," he said, trying to sound more philosophical than pious, because the padre knows him well. "I need to look it in the eye."

"Or at the least peer over its shoulder," the Jesuit replied. Peregrino is the most liberal of the masters at the Ateneo and a fountain of enlightenment compared to any of the Dominicans at Santo Tomás, encouraging the young *ilustrados* to visit Madrid. "So you'll have something interesting to confess," he likes to say. He even admitted once that Dr. Rizal's ideas had some merit, but that he had been criminally irresponsible in disseminating them to the rabble.

He is the best of the enemy, but the enemy nonetheless.

The hood is slipped on, just a white linen sack really, and the portly Franciscan leans close, the scapular hanging out from the rolls of his neck, to intone in the condemned man's ear.

Diosdado's fingers are wet against the leather of the box as he steadies it, winding surreptitiously to the next exposure. The platform and device are far enough away to guarantee they will be in the photograph even if they are not centered perfectly. There are cameras for sale in Madrid with a viewing sight on the top, but this one, an Eastman Bullet, is what the Committee had at hand. Scipio was very thorough, very scientific, pacing off the distance measured and assuring that the focus would be sharp. A new cartridge was inserted. It would be best, Scipio told him, if the condemned man's face is recognizable in the first photograph, best to treat the public to human features, a man with eyes, ears, mouth like their own, rather than just an anonymous form, choking in a sack.

"If we cannot have a Christ," Scipio told Diosdado and the Committee, that tiny pucker of self-love denting his cheeks as his voice rose poetically, "then give us Barabbas. If we cannot have another José Rizal—" and here he indicated the leather-bound cube in Diosdado's hands, the "instrument of emancipation" as he liked to call it, "—then give us Fecundo Magapuna."

"*Qué fragancia*," mutters the general.

The condemned man's bowels discharge the moment the executioner's footsteps ring out on the platform behind him. The Franciscan is several feet away now, lips moving rapidly, Bible opened close under his riotous nose, the soldiers standing at attention on either side of the device, eyes forward, feigning no reaction to the puddle forming between the condemned man's feet. It is a sharp smell that reaches them in the balcony, feces and urine intermingled, and the man's body is trembling now, trembling all over as a dog not trained for hunting will tremble at the blast of a shotgun or a crack of thunder. The links of the chain binding his wrists rattle softly and the capitán looks to the executioner and says "*Ahora.*"

Diosdado forgets to cough as he triggers the shutter and it sounds like a cannon-shot to him but not one of his companions looks over, watching intently, their arms resting on the balcony rail, leaning forward toward the moment.

The *verdugo* has thick, muscular arms, as one would expect, though the task is not a particularly strenuous one. Padre Junípero explained the principle of Mechanical Advantage in class for them, enumerating the use of simple machines in everyday life—the lever, the pulley, the screw. This device is a classic variation on the Spanish Windlass. A combination of the lever and the screw, tightening the collar around the condemned man's neck, the cloth of the sack huffing in and out now as he fights for breath, the executioner's face fixed in concentration like any good craftsman at his work. The *verdugos* are always condemned men themselves, murderers, who have agreed to do the government's killing in exchange for a pardon and sixteen pesos per neck.

"Watch him dance," says the *haciendero*, louder now that the ceremony has entered its active phase.

And dance he does, Fecundo Magapuna, the cheap shoes stomping and scraping, digging in at the heel then kicking out as far as the shackles will allow, twisting at impossible angles till one works its way off the man's foot entirely, lying still on the platform while Diosdado snaps and winds, no worry now of the others hearing, caught up as they are in the buckings and writhings of the man's torso, body thrashing like a panicked goose clutched at the neck and the *verdugo* turning the crossbar slowly, stolidly, a man adjusting a valve. The condemned man's legs might come out a blur, thinks Diosdado, but the executioner will be still in the photograph, and the capitán and his two soldiers and the praying Franciscan and even the shrouded head of the condemned Magapuna, cocked at an unnatural angle and cinched to the board by the tightening collar, all frozen together in tableau.

There is an audible *crack!* of the star-nosed bit through the condemned man's vertebra as Diosdado triggers the shutter. The Franciscan raises his voice in supplication, Padre Peregrino softly speaking the Latin words in tandem with him, savoring their weighty euphony, and Diosdado secures the camera under his coat while another man, a doctor, is brought out to verify the act. The executioner, secure of his handiwork, steps down. The doctor lifts the hood from the man's face, places a small mirror under his nose. Blood spreads downward from the nostrils, staining the man's lip and chin, pooling in the cleft of his neck. The doctor removes the mirror, says something to the capitán, then steps quickly out of the sun-baked courtyard. Benítez the lawyer notes the exact time. Diosdado can hear but not see the buzzing flies around the soaked earth at the man's feet. The foot without the shoe on it is clad in a dark blue stocking, three toes protruding obscenely through a hole in its tip.

"I suppose if the *verdugo* kept on turning," says the *haciendero*, "the head would pop right off."

* * *

Diosdado sees the woman waiting as they leave the Cuartel de España and pass through the Royal Gate. She stands at the foot of the bridge across the moat that separates the Intramuros from the Luneta, waiting by a bullcart with a rough wooden casket lying on it, the *chino* porter squatting in its meager shade with his eyes closed. She is small, pretty, dressed in what passes for Sunday finery in the *baryos* up north. She is the widow, he is certain, and if the two officers weren't still just behind him bragging about horses they've owned he would stop and take another photograph. There must still be several exposures left on the roll, and it seems wrong to waste such magical potential, like leaving food on the plate, something his mother ranked even above blasphemy in her catalogue of sins. Diosdado wonders how it would have felt to witness the ceremony with his eye pressed to the sight, to see it through the filter of lens and mirror, to shrink the man's death into that leather-covered box. He looks across to the field of Bagumbayan, where they shot Dr. Rizal. The little man facing the Bay, priests and soldiers on either side, military band trilling through *La Marcha de Cádiz*, then the order and the bark of rifles.

It is not too late. Merely chemicals on a strip of celluloid, not yet a "graven image" as Padre Peregrino would call it, an arrangement of molecules remembered in silver that, if allowed to, will develop into—

He has only to open the box and the sun will do the rest.

Diosdado turns to register the familiar sights—the vendors and the strollers, the frisky carriage ponies of the families making their *paseo* around the beautiful, lamp-lined rectangle of the Luneta as the Govenor General's favorite ensemble plays a sweet *rondalla* in the ornate bandstand, young men not unlike himself staring reflectively, perhaps romantically, over the sea wall, all the color and noise of a Manila afternoon—then adjusts the Eastman Bullet under his arm and walks stiffly toward the safe house in Malate where the Committee is waiting.

Nilda Magapuna waves flies away from her face and stares without seeing at the activity on the green. They say the body will be out soon. She holds a rosary in one hand, fingers slack on the beads.

FIREWORKS

Carnaval was invented by spies. There is no other explanation—an entire week when one is allowed, no, expected, to traverse the city behind a mask, one among thousands of *dizfrazados*, black and white, rich and poor, attending gilded balls or singing in processions or just noisily decorating the streets of La Habana. The gaslights are on now, the breeze blowing ever so slightly out into the Harbor as Quiroga strolls along the Malecón. It is a calm night, waves caressing rather than assaulting the sea wall, and the few lights left burning on the big ships anchored not so far away rise and fall in a gentle rhythm. Quiroga wears a simple domino and his dress suit, only a *lector de fábrica* down from Florida for the holiday. Nobody to worry about. There is tension, yes, and he heard footsteps behind when he left the hotel this morning, but with so much life on the street, so many crowds to lose himself in, Quiroga is certain that his *sombra* has been lost as well.

Individuals have disappeared mysteriously, especially here in the capital, and the arrival of the American armed cruiser has set the always fertile Cuban imagination afire. Quiroga would not ordinarily be needed, parties often transported to and from the island without involving the "sleeping patriots" up in Ybor, but this extraction is more sensitive than the norm. Ambassador de Lôme's missive to Don José Canelejas of *El Heraldo de Madrid*, in which he describes the American president in decidedly undiplomatic terms, has somehow fallen into the eager hands of the *New York Journal*. Unsurprisingly, those worthies have published a copy of the original alongside a translation, and the yellow press are tumescent with outrage to see their leader portrayed as "weak, catering to the rabble—a low politician who desires to leave a door open to himself and to stand well with the jingoes of his party." It is not an inaccurate assessment, mild compared to statements made daily by members of the Cuban Junta in New York or Tampa or even by American interventionists in the editorial pages of the self-same *Journal*. But de Lôme is not a wild-eyed revolutionist or ink-slathered provocateur—he is meant to be the benign, conciliatory face of the Spanish Crown in the United States. Very few persons must be in the position to intercept or purloin the Ambassador's writings, and that nervy fellow, Quiroga assumes, is who he is meant to smuggle out of La Habana.

He pauses by the wall to light a *puro*, cheaper here by a few pennies but considered superior to the product manufactured in Ybor. He is no judge, though, the cigar only part of his contact signal and perhaps the poorest element in the elaborate construct that has been explained to him. Any Spaniard trained in espionage, he believes, will be instantly aware that Quiroga is not a smoker and have his suspicions aroused. Quiroga takes enough of a puff to keep the thing burning, then turns his face out to the placid sea.

There is a sudden thickening of the air, felt more than breathed.

The drums.

A *comparsa*, a twisting, writhing creature of more than a hundred chanting negros, winding down Calzada de Infante toward the Malecón to the racket of a dozen men flailing with their bare hands on what they call a *conga* or *tres golpes*—elongated, barrel-staved drums hung from the shoulder of the player with their bullskin heads just above the man's hip. Barefoot urchins without masks run alongside the aggregation, some dancing wildly to the noise, others leaping and screaming whenever the spirit enters them. Authorities have banned such displays at times, even on the *Día de los Reyes*, fearing, in the not-so-distant epoch of slavery, that the cabildos might use the anonymity afforded by the occasion to perpetrate atrocities upon their masters. But with Emancipation the African societies have lost much of their power, and the Spanish understand that repressing *Carnaval* will engender more mayhem than it will prevent.

As they approach and are illuminated by the gas lamps Quiroga recognizes the celebrants as the *Abakuá*, dancers wearing their colorful, horned *diablito* masks, legs and arms fringed with thick rings of grass and palm fronds, whirling and leaping and shaking their torsos and limbs as if driven epileptic by the music. The secret heart of Cuba, he thinks, beating to an

African pulse. Their sound envelops him before their bodies surround him, the hammering of the *congueros* complex yet insistent, and yes, he thinks, this is the force that drove the great Maceo and his *mambís* into battle. This is the very life-blood of revolt.

Quiroga stands with an unsmoked *puro* in his hand and the Havana moon peeking through the clouds over the Harbor and smiles as the masked tribesmen gyrate, circling, within inches of him. He feels honored rather than mocked. His exile is a voluntary one, merely an economic decision, but an exile nonetheless. Every *canción* he hears in Tampa is a song of longing.

The *comparsa* continues riotously down the Malecón, but one *diablito* stays behind. The mask is Abakuá, but the man wearing it is not even a negro, a man in a white sack suit and mesh-topped spectator shoes. He waits for the thunder of the drums to recede somewhat before he speaks through the mouth-slit cut in the elongated, red-and-black *máscara*.

"These clouds," he says, looking out over the vessels, great and small, that bob in the vast Harbor, "portend a storm from the North."

Quiroga has always disliked the passwords, the codes and secret hand-shakes, smacking of boys at play, and contends that they are as likely to entrap one as to mollify fellow conspirators. But it is a formality that must be honored.

"We could do with a stiff wind," he says, "to clear the air."

They stand side-by-side, looking out over the water. Quiroga thinks he may recognize the voice behind the mask.

"You have the documents?"

"Not on my person," Quiroga answers, annoyed. "I have been at this since Martí was in Guatemala. I am not feckless."

"I was not inferring that. I merely—"

And then the night erupts before them.

Quiroga's *puro* flies out of his hand and his hat is blown off his head in the initial glass-breaking bang and flash, the concussion thumping him in the chest like the kick of a mule and then a more brilliant display in the sky and at the waterline, each blinding airburst accompanied by a ground-shaking explosion, vessels in the harbor illuminated for a moment so brief that the images are like separate photographs—immense, lucent, terrible. It is the American battleship that is ablaze, the first third of it seemingly gone and the rest tilting into the sea as huge, twisted shards of debris plummet sizzling into the water around it. Between the pop and whine of ammunition set off by the fire he can hear the cries of burning men.

Quiroga smells sulfur.

The man beside him has pulled his mask back to see more clearly—as he suspected it is Camilo Gotay, who taught natural sciences at the University until his sympathies became too well known. Each new volley of detonation splashes red light upon him, eyes glowing, his pox-scarred face more devilish without the mask than when hidden behind it.

"They can't be this stupid," says Quiroga, his mind racing to find an explanation as sirens scream all over the city. The presence of the American gunship has been an insult, yes, and the Spaniards are stupid in their arrogance, but this slaughter, if a deliberate provocation—

"Not even Weyler at his most obdurate—"

"And it can't be us," adds Gotay, though with a note of uncertainty. "I would have been informed."

Men are rushing toward the pier, on foot and in carriages, lanterns lit, boats starting away toward the ship which is quickly settling on the seabed with the tops of its remaining stacks jutting above the waterline. The running lights have been lit on every other vessel in the Harbor.

"This will be good for us," says the professor, tears in his eyes, "won't it?"

Bells are ringing on the *Alfonso XII* now, Spanish sailors rushing to lower their boats and rescue those who have not already perished. There is another airburst, one of the larger shells exploding, and in the quick-fading light Quiroga sees men swimming away from the burning wreck, dozens of tiny bumps on the rolling surface of the water. Cocoanuts, he thinks. At this distance they could be cocoanuts floating with the tide. A pair of *guardia* rush past them on the way to the dock.

De Lôme's letter is nothing now. A hundred thousand Cubans may die, tortured, hanged, shot, starved to death as *reconcentrados*, but give us one apple-cheeked Sailor Jack, one blue-eyed American martyr for the yellow press to canonize—yet how can this chaos, this Hell on the water, be good for anyone?

Quiroga smells sulfur, sulfur and hot metal.

"I see the hand of God," he says, turning his back on the sea wall, on the burning ship, on the desperate swimmers. "But we will blame it on the Spanish."

THE DAILY OUTRAGE

The art of it lies in what first strikes the eye, and what that in turn stimulates in the mind of the reader. A screaming head is just that—information shouted across the track at a railroad station as the train is pulling out, steam blasting, whistle shrieking, with only the most vital, most incendiary of the words understood—

USS MAINE EXPLOSION CAUSED BY
BOMB OR TORPEDO?

If you bother to haul out the brass type it had better cause a sensation—

SPAIN'S WAR
AGAINST THE JOURNAL
CONTINUES; CORRESPONDENTS JAILED, DEPORTED

Heads sell papers. The Editor has a look at everything that goes into it, but reserves the front page, its public face and clarion cry, for himself—

CRISIS AT HAND
CABINET IN SESSION; GROWING BELIEF IN
SPANISH TREACHERY

If the Editor cannot squint his eyes at a front page twenty yards away and feel his heart jump, there is something seriously wrong with the head—

CONJECTURE THAT WARSHIP
MAINE BLOWN TO PIECES BY
ENEMY'S SECRET
INFERNAL MACHINE

The Chief will want to post one of his rewards for this one, no doubt, the engraver already preparing a plate to replicate the check. $10,000 is as high as he has gone in the past, but this wondrous catastrophe would seem to merit a greater offering. The Chief will decide when he arrives from the theater. Information, mostly from the sizable lunatic population of the city, will pour in, and the reward will never be paid. But even symbolic gestures demand proportion—

SPANISH AMBASSADOR
DE LÔME
FLEES COUNTRY
AFTER TENDERING RESIGNATION

The Editor's ultimate test of a split head is to imagine it shouted by one of the pack of newsboys who peddle their wares by the hackney stand where he hires his ride home, particularly the jaundiced little street Arab who bellows every word over 20 points high as if the fate of the world were in balance—

AMERICAN GENERALS WANT
INCREASE IN TROOPS IF WE ARE
TO FIGHT SPAIN

The correspondents will file their copy, succinct narratives peppered (never, they argue, laden) with whatever facts they might stumble upon. Facts, however, are complex, facts are often inconclusive or contradictory. The reader who buys on the street is not looking for information about a crisis, he wants guidance as to how he should *feel* about it—

WAR? SURE!

The facts will take care of themselves.

THE MARCH
OF THE FLAG (I)

A crowd of men have gathered in front of the Mondamin, listening to Jeff
Smith up on a barrel of nails. Hod sees Smokey standing a few feet back from
the throng, nervous.

"Our boys asleep," says Smith. "Defenseless. Then the furtive approach,
the infernal device installed at water level, the fuse ignited—"

"What happened?" Hod whispers.

"Seattle papers come in," says Smokey. "This is bad."

"Then the dormant city shaken by a terrible explosion!" Jeff Smith has his
hat over his heart now, a tear in his voice. "Our brave lads blown to smither-
eens. Dismembered. Horribly burned. Drowned in the unforgiving waters."

"They gone blame this on me," mutters Smokey, shaking his head.

"Bodies float to the surface." Smith is using his soap-selling voice, dark
eyes burning with indignation. "The malefactors feign innocence."

Hod is confused. "What do you have to do with it?"

Smokey looks around at the red-faced men, steam rising from their
mouths and noses, jaws clenched in anger. "Cause I'm the closest thing they
got to a Spaniard in this camp."

"But will Americans countenance this treachery?" Jeff Smith raising a fist
in the air. "Will we quail and run? Will we falter before the swarthy Dago
assassin?" The men shout *No!* to each tremulous query. Smith spreads his arms
wide and smiles. "I knew it in my heart. Our country needs us, gentlemen.
I have wired the Territory requesting commission. Any red-blooded American

among you—" and here he points with his hat toward a tent that has been set up in the middle of the street at Broadway and Seventh, "—may strike a blow for liberty by signing on with the Skaguay Guards! God bless America!"

There is cheering and fist-waving and then the band from the Garden of Joy steps out to play *The Stars and Stripes* and most of the crowd, townsmen and busted stampeders alike, hurries to enlist, loudly describing the beating the wicked Spaniards are about to suffer. Jeff Smith hops down and crosses to Hod and Smokey.

"Most of them are hoping Uncle Sam will provide free passage back to the Outside," he winks. "Let's see how bold that reform outfit been nippin at my heels is when I've got my own army."

"We gone to war?" Hod hasn't looked at a newspaper since he's been in the Yukon. It all seems very far away.

"We will, son, soon enough." He claps Hod on the shoulder. "I'll expect you to join the roll, of course. Sergeant McGinty."

A long line has formed in front of the tent, getting longer every moment.

"I suppose I ought to."

"That's the spirit!" Jeff Smith's eyes are glowing. He hasn't changed from last night's poker game, cigar ash on his pants, whiskey on his breath, the butt of his Navy Colt jutting out from the open front of his otterskin coat. "But first you two must bring me an eagle," he says, and steps back inside the hotel.

"Eagles been gone for months," says Hod.

Smokey is already on the move. "I know who find us some."

They take the wagon out to Alaska Street. Voyageur lives in the last cabin at the end of the Line, the only one without cold-stiffened undergarments hung outside to advertise a woman within. Voyageur is a fisherman and meat hunter who sells his game to the grub tents at White Pass City.

"You lookin for a three-dollar whore you come too far!" he calls when Hod bangs on the door. He is a white-stubbled, sharp-smelling old man who dresses like a Tlingit and is scraping the flesh off a marmot hide as they step in to state their business.

"Birds mostly follow the salmon up into Canada when the spawning peters out," he tells them. "But now that you got this run of fools going over the Pass year-round, why bother?"

He lets them borrow a square of weir netting and tells them the best place to look. "Anywhere there's dead things, you find you some birds."

They leave the wagon at Feero's and travel the Brackett Road, able to skirt past the pack trains and the hapless stampeders trying to haul their own goods. The ice won't break for months but still the greenhorns are in a rush, desperate to add their tents to the cluster at the edge of Lake Lindeman and start eating through their supplies.

"Skaguay got no use for you less you got cash money to spend, and it gone take some of that every day," says Smokey as they pass a party that includes two women dragging a woodstove loaded on a sled over the corduroy road. "Stay here too long, they be nothin left of you."

Hod talks them through the toll, explaining their mission, and they reach the base of the White Pass by noon. Even in the freezing cold it stinks.

"That's some that aint gone yet," says Smokey.

The Gulch is full of carcasses, mostly horses. Some are just bones, or frozen and dried to leather, while a few must have fallen or faltered and been pushed off the trail in the last few days. They lie twisted and broken on the rock, bones ripped through their hides, clusters of eagles picking at their exposed innards while ravens waddle anxiously a few feet away, waiting their turn.

The eagles barely flap out of the path as Hod and Smokey walk through the carnage.

"Let's us turn our backs on this bunch here," says Smokey. "Then when I say three, turn and toss it over em."

The ravens all manage to squawk away before the net lands on two feasting eagles. The men sit on the trunk of a deadfall tree on the side of the slope, covering their noses with their mittens, and wait till the scavengers tire themselves out under the mesh. "Mr. Jeff gone want that big one," says Smokey. "We let the other fly." The bird he points at has blood speckling its white neck feathers and smells of dead horse.

Hod can hear a pack train climbing on the trail above them, can hear a man cursing a mule and a child crying, just crying.

"So how you end up here?" Smokey is the only negro he has seen in Skaguay, the only one he's seen since the deckhands on the steamer to Dyea.

Smokey pokes a stick into the tangle of net and the larger eagle strikes at it. "Too many of them ring battles, twenty, thirty, forty rounds. Livin high on the hog in between—it wear you down. Then there was the bottle." Smokey is quiet for a long moment, drawing patterns in the snow at his feet. Hod has never seen him take a drink. "What it come to, they was a little carnival I hooked on with, takin dives. Pay you a nickel and you hits the bullseye with a baseball, it throw open a trap door and I go in the tank."

"I seen that once."

"And it keeps me in the liquor and they lets me sleep in one of the wagons but that's about all. Livin day to day. Only once we gets up to this north country, figure the people is starved for entertainment, the water in the tank won't stay water, it's always *froze*. So they just cut a hole in a curtain, I sticks my head through it. Hit the nigger on the noggin an you wins a prize." He frowns and gives the eagles another poke. "Then Mr. Jeff see me and offer me a real job workin for him. That very day I took the vow and aint took a drop since." He stands to stretch his legs. "Near about everybody stays in town owe Mr. Jeff *some*thing."

When they carefully disentangle the smaller bird it doesn't fly, just backs away from them stiff-legged, skreeking its raspy cry and holding its wings out, trembling, before flapping over to chase a trio of ravens out of a horse's ravaged belly.

There is already bunting hung, red, white, and blue, from the façade of Jeff Smith's Parlor when they get back.

"The noblest of the scavengers," Jeff says, holding his head eagle-like and staring back down at the bird in the bundle of netting. "And a fitting symbol for our proud nation."

"It looks awful, Jeff," says Syd Dixon.

"Throw a couple buckets of water over him, hang him out in the sun, he'll be good as new. If not, I'll have him stuffed."

They manage to slip a deerskin gold-poke over the eagle's head, pulling the drawstrings to shut off any light, and the bird calms enough that they can cut the net away and put him in a cage that held a bandicoot Jeff Smith bought from Smokey's carnival, displaying it in the corner of the Parlor till a sourdough shot it because he didn't like the way it looked at him.

"Anybody who desecrates the national symbol in my saloon," says Jeff Smith when they have hoisted the cage and its hooded occupant onto the bar counter, "shall be dealt with summarily."

"What you gonna name him, Jeff?" asks Old Man Triplett.

"Liberty," suggests the Sheeny Kid.

"Columbia," counters Niles Manigault. "Proud beacon of freedom, torchbearer to the peoples of the world—"

"I had a buddy in Seattle, used to rock side-to-side on his legs just like he's doing," says Red Gibbs. "We called him Wobbles."

"I christen him Fitzhugh Lee," says Jeff Smith, trying to reach in and snatch the gold-poke off the bird's head. "General of the Confederacy and present American consul to the besieged island of Cuba." He looks sharply to Hod. "If you don't hustle down to that recruiting station, McGinty, you're likely to lose your place."

Despite the dropping temperature there are still dozens of men outside the tent waiting to be processed.

"I seen a drawing of that Havana once," says a busted stampeder, shivering, gloveless, in a tattered mackinaw. "They got palm trees."

"You think they'll send us there?" asks the man in front of him, Gottshalk, who sells sawdust he steals from Captain Billy's mill to the saloons and peddles useless goldfield maps to the greenhorns coming off the steamers.

"Hell, maybe if it really gets cooking we'll go all the way to Spain," says the stampeder. "Tangle with them conquistadors."

"Wherever we fight em," says Gottshalk, "it got to be better than livin in Hell's frozen asshole."

When he gets inside the recruiting tent Hod finds Reverend Bowers sitting behind the table, taking names, with Ox Knudsen standing over his shoulder, picking his teeth with a splinter.

"We only take men with balls between their legs," he says as Hod reaches in to sign the roster.

"You on this list?" asks Hod without looking up.

"Right at the top."

"Since when do squareheads count as Americans?"

And then he is on the ground with the Swede on top trying to throttle him, men shouting and yanking as they roll around, finally pulled away from each other and out of the tent by the legs and somehow Jeff Smith and the boys from the Parlor and Tex Rickard and Billy Mizner and half of Skaguay is there gathered around as Ox shouts threats and nearly lifts the three men holding him clear off their feet.

"Dissension in the ranks will not be tolerated!" Smith steps between them, raising his voice so all can hear. "Not while there is a desperate foe to be defeated, not while the defense of our great Northwest is in the care of the Skaguay Guards!" He turns a full circle, waving his hat, and even Ox Knudsen shuts up to listen to his pitch. "These two gentlemen," he cries, "have agreed to settle their differences in the roped arena, this Friday night."

There is a cheer from the crowd and the men holding Hod in a headlock thump him on the back in encouragement.

"Details of the event may be read in tomorrow's *News*. Volunteers for the Skaguay Guard shall receive a one-dollar discount at the gate."

And with that Hod is released and Ox pulled away by Rickard and Mizner and a couple other men and the recruiting tent closed till morning. The crowd disperses, returning to the beckoning saloons, and Hod hurries to catch up with Smith and the others.

"I'm not really a fighter," he says, joining them on the boardwalk. "Just cause Choynski let me stand up for a while—"

"Nor are any of the hash-slingers in this outpost actually cooks, nor the shylocks who collect quitclaims lawyers, nor the Skaguay sparrows who parade at the Theater Royal dancers or singers," says Jeff Smith, putting an arm around him. "You, my boy, are not a fighter any more than Doc, who has been known to prescribe laudanum for a hangnail, is a physician. In this benighted corner of the globe, however, you will have to do. Smokey has been training you, has he not?"

"How many rounds I got to go?"

Smith raises his eyebrows in something like shock. "Why, as many as you are able, my boy. In an affair such as this there can be no breath of scandal."

"The audience will be almost totally local," Niles Manigault explains before he follows the others into the Parlor. "And it is never wise to defecate where one resides."

"Rickard wants it catch-as-catch-can, but Jeff is holding out for the Marquis of Queensbury," says Frank Clancy in front of the Music Hall. "He says we're not savages here."

"I hear they want a twelve-foot ring," says Billy Saportas from the *Skaguay News*. "Might as well hold the scrap in a piano crate."

"Soapy says it's twenty feet or no go," says Goldberg in his cigar store. "Is this a fight or a bicycle race?"

"No gloves, that's what I heard," says Arizona Charlie, lounging in the Pantheon as Hod and Smokey roll barrels of beer across the floor. "Going back to the true spirit of the game."

"Tell Jeff I'm proud of him," says Tommy Kearns when they lug a new Wurlitzer Orchestrion into the Palace, Smokey trying to keep his back to the naked Muses on the wall. There is as much talk in town of the fight as there is of the developments in Cuba, and somehow the two are connected in people's minds.

"Proud for what?"

"For putting his boy in the scrap right away. This old Granny McKinley, feeding diplomats to the Dagoes—"

"You mean Ox is like the Spanish?"

"I mean if there's bound to be a fight, get on with it! How you feeling, son?"

"I'm fine."

Kearns steps close to look Hod over. "And what do you think, Smokey? I lost a bundle when the Jew let him go past three."

"That's cause you sold him short," says Smokey, carefully laying his side of the crate on the floor. "That Swede can't box."

"Neither can a grizzly bear, but I wouldn't step into a ring with one. Show me your muscle, kid."

Hod puts his end down and, for the third time that morning, flexes his right bicep to be felt and evaluated.

"It's kind of knotty. You don't like to see that knotty kind of muscle on a fighter. It should be big and smooth, like—like the muscle on an ox. Pure power."

"You bet how you gonna bet, Mr. Tommy," says Smokey. "But this boy know what he's *about*."

"He says he's gonna kill you," says Addie Lee as she sits with Hod on her bed behind the flag.

"You've seen him?"

"He sent for me to come to a room up at Dutch Lena's. He thinks Soapy and them are out to do him in, so he had a bunch of his friends waiting downstairs."

Hod feels himself flush, thinking of her in a hotel room with him.

"Look, the *Farallon* is leaving today. You could get out of here—"

"So could you," he says.

"Wherever I am, I be doing the same thing. Right here is where it pays best."

The men out in the bar beyond the flag are trading opinions of how the battle will go. "The thing with Swedes," says one, "they don't feel pain the way a normal white man does. Something about how thick their skulls are."

"So he talks about me?" asks Hod.

Addie Lee shrugs. "We've had a couple chewing matches on the subject."

"He ever hit you?"

"Threatened to once or twice. But he's afraid of Soapy and them, like everybody else."

"And you work for Soapy."

"Half of everything goes to the house, wherever you are," she says. "Who owns the house, that aint always so clear."

He buries his fingers in her hair and kisses her on the mouth and she kisses back.

"This don't matter, you know." She is crying, sort of, tears falling but her face composed and serious. "You're just sucker bait for the gamblers. And I'm just sucker bait for you."

He gently pushes her down on the bed then, and for the first time doesn't care about the men out at the bar.

Niles Manigault sits nursing a bourbon when Hod steps out.

"There is a theory," says the Southerner, "only recently given much credence, that proper training for a fight precludes intimate relations."

Hod looks at him blankly.

"Each visit to the daughters of joy, each frolic with the fairies of the *demimonde*," he elaborates, "further saps the warrior's vitality. Even married men are advised to forfeit their conjugal benefits until the foe is vanquished. Of course, if one lacks hope, there is the phenomenon of the condemned man's last meal—"

Hod leaves him contemplating at the bar.

The Skaguay Guards march on the day of the fight. After two hours of drilling conducted by a defrocked Mountie named Hopgood who Jeff Smith has hired, they form up and strut in a pair of ragged columns down Broadway, to the cheers and jeers of those who haven't joined. Knudsen has been put at the head of the second company, a long-handled shovel over his shoulder, while Hod leads the first, carrying Jeff Smith's Winchester. All the percentage girls come out and wave handkerchiefs and the Garden of Joy band is playing as they march behind the volunteers and the sun is showing itself brighter than it has in weeks and for a tiny moment, stepping along smartly to the beat of *El Capitán*, Hod starts to feel that this is something big, something real, something important in the world and that he is a part of it.

Jeff Smith stands waiting on a wagon at Second, a flag draped like a Roman's toga over his shoulders, with Fitzhugh Lee glaring from the cage at his feet.

"Friends," he declaims when the band has sputtered to a halt and the columns have deployed around the wagon and the civilians crowded in among
them close enough to hear. "Patriots. Americans." He pulls the banner off his
body and holds it out to them in both arms. "I speak to you today concerning
the march of the flag, and of the Almighty's designs for our future."

It is freezing cold despite the sun, the breath of the Guards huffing out
like musket volleys as they stand at attention in their ranks, the unenlisted
allowed to dance in place and bury their hands in their coats. Hod hopes that
Smith has not prepared a stem-winder.

"For it is to Him that we must look for guidance in the approaching
millennium," he continues. "It is a mighty people that He has planted on
this soil, a people sprung from the most masterful blood of history, perpetu-
ally revitalized by the virile, man-producing workingfolk of all the earth. A
people imperial by virtue of their power, by right of their institutions, by
authority of their Heaven-directed purposes. The propagandists," cries Jeff
Smith, "not the misers, of liberty!"

Hod sees the reform contingent, who call themselves the 101 Committee,
watching from the boardwalk, arms crossed in disapproval.

"And it is a glorious history our God has bestowed upon his chosen
people, a history divinely logical, in the process of whose tremendous reasoning we find ourselves today."

The eagle in the cage at Smith's feet begins to croak rhythmically, swaying
back and forth like an agitated parrot. Hod feels the Winchester heavy and
cold on his shoulder. He is ready. Sick of this fool's-gold Yukon and ready to
go off to Cuba or the far islands of the Pacific, to wear a real uniform and fight
and maybe die for the flag that droops from Jeff Smith's outstretched arms.

"Shall we free the oppressed Cuban from the saffron banner of Spain?"

"Yes!" cry the Skaguay Guards.

"Shall we add our blood to that of Christian heroes who blazed their way
across a savage continent?"

"Yes!" cry the sourdoughs and the stampeders, the merchants and the
sure-thing men, the citizens of America's farthest outpost. Hod sees Smokey,
standing alone back in the doorway next to the oaken Sioux at Goldberg's
Cigar Store, watching them all with a vacant look on his face.

"Shall we continue," asks Jeff Smith, holding the flag over his head now,
"our march toward the commercial supremacy of the world? Shall our free
institutions broaden their blessed reign as the children of freedom wax in
strength, until the empire of our principles is established over the hearts of

all mankind? Will we not do what our fathers have done before—to pitch the tents of liberty ever further from our shores and continue the glorious march of the flag?"

Uproarious cheers and men throwing their hats in the air and percentage girls waving little flags on sticks that have been passed out and a crackle of patriotic gunfire that prompts Fitzhugh Lee to lift his tailfeathers and unleash a stream of fish-smelling offal onto the cage floor. Then by some common but unspoken agreement all adjourn for drinks of celebration, all but the dozen who linger to watch Hod and Ox Knudsen staring at each other, ten yards separating them.

"See you tonight," says Hod, holding the Winchester in the crook of his arm.

The Swede lifts the shovel from his shoulder and wiggles it in the air. "I go now and dig you a hole."

Hod wanders off in the other direction, which takes him down to the wharves. Both the *Farallon* and the *Utopia* are in, waiting to leave in the morning. He sits halfway down the Juneau Wharf with his legs hanging over the side and the Winchester across his lap, and is watching the gulls when Smokey finds him.

"Shouldn't ought to be out in this cold. You gone stiffen up."

"I can't listen to them inside the Parlor any more."

The negro sits by him, looks at the ragged, screaming infestation that lights and flies, lights and flies, ganging up on whichever of their number manages to get a scrap of food in its beak.

"Always got one eye on they own bidness, the other on their neighbors'."

"They don't ever rest."

Smokey chuckles and shakes his head. "Naw. Don't ever see no fat gull, neither. They just a appetite with wings."

He leans over the railing and points down to the rocks below. It is a rough day in the little harbor, waves breaking hard and rolling up on the mudflats, making a loud sucking sound as they fall back.

"See them shells stuck onto the rocks?"

"The mussels."

"That's the way to do it. Got food all in that water, even smaller than a speck of gold dust, and ever time it wash in or wash out over the rocks, them shells get a taste. Don't have to go nowhere, just keep they mouths open." Smokey shakes his head admiringly.

They are always doing somebody, Jeff Smith and his crew. Doing the wide-eyed gold pilgrims coming in with their store-bought equipment and the scurvy-gummed sourdoughs coming out with the year's cleanup in their pokes. Jeff and Niles Manigault with their Southern manners and way of talking, Doc with his portmanteau and his lead bricks coated in gold, Rev Bowers with his entreaties to Good Samaritans and Syd Dixon offering to cut the savvy newcomer into a sweet deal, Red Gibbs and Ed Burns and the smash-nosed mug from Seattle they call Yeah Mow lounging about to deal with the ones who come back in claiming they've been cheated. The drinks are always on the house for the Deputy Marshal and an unofficial pharmacy operates over the bar and there are always helpful directions for stampeders to "honest" merchants and hot deals that won't last more than a day and to the exact location of the town's famous Paradise Alley. There is spoiled flour topped off with the good stuff and sold out the back door, interests in sure-thing claims obtained from departing sourdoughs whose mothers have just died, the telegraph messages home that go nowhere. *Received message* comes the inevitable reply. *We are all counting on you. Please send money.* And always, while you are waiting for your bacon or your beans or your paperwork there is the casual poker game, a handful of fellas just passing the time and full of good advice for greenhorns, willing to deal you in if you don't mind playing for Skaguay stakes, so much gold out there waiting to be picked off the ground that a certain inflation has crept into all aspects of manly endeavor. Niles is the master of the cards, friendly, flattering, solemnly warning the greenhorn to be on the lookout for buncos like the notorious Soapy Smith and his gang and ready to commiserate that his own luck at poker seems to be as poor as the greenhorn's, confiding, during a break for bladder relief, the secrets of the Martingale system, where you double your bet with each play and are therefore, given the immutable laws of mathematics, assured of victory.

Hod understands that when he fights tonight, it will be as their man.

"Thank heavens you've found him, Smokey." Niles is at the table in the back room of the Parlor when Hod comes in with Smokey to return the rifle. Jeff Smith sits across from him, with Arizona Charlie and Jake Rice and Dynamite Johnny O'Brien who captains the *Utopia* circled under a haze of cigar smoke. "I was afraid he might be in the clutches of that poke-hunting soubrette."

Hod hangs the Winchester on the nails behind the bar. There is a tension in the room, a lack of joking, a stiffness of posture. The steamer captain, O'Brien, sits behind a pile of currency and gold dust.

"Shit and corruption," says Jeff Smith, staring holes into his cards. "You'll have to accept my note for it, but I'm going to call your bluff."

"Cash only, as agreed upon," winks the captain. "No markers, no trade, no excuses."

Smith looks to Charlie Meadows. "Front me a hundred."

"The bet stands at two," the captain reminds him, steady-eyed. The men have peeled down to their shirtsleeves, Jeff's Navy Colt lying on the bar counter with the other gentlemen's hardware.

Arizona Charlie hesitates, thinking up an excuse, and Smith scowls and pokes Jake Rice. "You front me," he says to Rice, and then points to Smokey, who is tossing sardines from a tin into Fitzhugh Lee's cage and watching the bird snap them up on the fly. "I'll sell you my dinge. You've got plenty to keep him busy at your place."

The men are silent for a moment, only the sound of the eagle's claws clicking on the floor of its cage. Jake squirms in his seat.

"For two hundred?"

"He's worth twice that. The best and only nigger in the Territory."

"But what am I going to do with him?"

"That's your business." Jeff Smith has the look on his face that they all try to avoid.

Jake reluctantly lays two hundreds on the table, then turns to Smokey. "Don't worry," he says. "He'll make it double on the fight tonight and buy you back."

"Is that right?" says Jeff Smith and then Dynamite Johnny turns up a pair of kings and Smith throws his hand on the floor, disgusted, and stomps over to the woodstove to give it a violent kick. He points at Smokey. "I want you out of here," he says, and then points at Fitzhugh Lee. "And I want that bird stuffed."

It has been decided that gloves will be worn but throws allowed, that the bell will be in the hands of one side but the time-piece held by the other, that Joe Boyle, down from Dawson and considered neutral in the affair, will referee. Half-clinches will be allowed and it will be up to the fighters to separate themselves. Smokey puts a towel over Hod's face while he wraps his hands in the back room at Jake Rice's place. "I want you to close your eyes," he says, "and imagine how you gone to beat the man." The wraps feel heavy on his hands, which are already sweating. "But keep your body relax."

Men are hollering and stomping on the other side of the door. When Hod closes his eyes he can imagine only blackness. It is cold in the little room, Hod's bare legs starting to ache with it, and when he opens his eyes again the negro is sitting beside him, head in his hands.

"Mr. Jeff and them been makin their bets," he says.

"Let's get this damn show on the road!" yells somebody from outside, kicking on the door.

"And aint none of em on *you*."

The ring has been set up in the middle of the dance-hall floor, men already drinking for hours after the parade, with the Smith faction on one side of the room and his rivals on the other. Hod notices that they are all heeled, Jeff with his Navy Colt in the special gun pocket lined with buckskin and the Sheeny Kid with his Bulldog a lump under the jacket and Red Gibbs standing by the back with a bungstopper in hand, ready to throw the door open or make sure it stays closed. Introductions are shouted. Ox doesn't look any smaller stripped down than he does with all his layers of clothes on. He is bigger than Choynski, a true heavyweight, a full inch taller than Hod as they glare at each other throughout the referee's instructions. There are wisecracks being made and some laughter, but mostly it is the men on one side snarling about what their champion is going to do to the other.

Hod doesn't feel like anybody's champion standing in his corner, leaning his head close to hear Smokey over the shouting and stomping of the men. He is the veteran of only one real fight, carried by a professional and then given his sleep medicine in the agreed-upon round. His hand-wraps feel too tight and his stomach is up under his throat and his knees are buzzing.

"This man go only in one direction, which is straight ahead." Smokey seems distracted, barely looking at Hod as he speaks. "And you don't want to be anywhere near when he gets there. Just keep movin them feet, movin, movin, couple three rounds, see if you can tire him out."

Addie Lee is not in the room, nor any other woman. Smoke hangs low over the ring and Hod tries to breathe shallowly through his nose while Smokey greases his face. Smith and his crew settle in on a bench by the ropes and there is somebody new, laughing and backslapping with Jeff.

It is Whitey.

Whitey who stole his gear, one-eye-blue one-eye-green Whitey who, most likely, has always been part of the gang. Hod feels dizzy, as if he has already been pounded and is falling, falling—

Smokey is trying to talk to him.

"What?"

"I ask if you ever hunt."

"Rabbits, mostly. On the farm."

"You get mad at them rabbits?"

"That don't do no good."

"Same for a ox as it is for a rabbit. You stay cool and keep your wits about you."

"How many you spose we have to go before this bunch'll let us stop?"

Smokey looks away. "Just don't you be the one they carry out from that ring."

Niles Manigault steps close then, smiling, leaning over the ropes to take a final gander. "He ready?"

"Ready as he gone get," says Smokey, and then the bell rings and Hod is trapped inside the tiny enclosure with Ox Knudsen.

The Swede bullrushes ahead with his right arm cocked and then sledge-hammers it downward, holding his left glove open before him to grab with. Hod catches the first blow on the collarbone and nearly leaves his feet, staggering backward while Ox keeps coming, then dances sideways and snaps his lead left over Knudsen's guard again and again. His hands don't feel right, the wraps on them stiffening, and his eyes sting as sweat runs into them. A cheer goes up each time the Swede charges, followed by a moan of disappointment when Hod sidesteps to escape the blow.

"We come to see a prize fight," calls a man somewhere behind him, "not a goddam waltz!"

Ox charges and Hod feints a move right, then skips left and catches the squarehead flush on the face as he goes by, Ox grabbing the ropes to steady himself and bleeding from the nose when he turns to resume his attack. The crowd, anonymous in their numbers, is almost all pulling against Soapy's fighter.

"Get on him! Get on him, you dumb fuckin Swede!"

"Knock him cold!"

"Get him on the ropes and strangle the son of a bitch!"

Knudsen finally catches up with him near the end of the round, throwing his arm over Hod's neck and hurling him against a corner post. Hod blocks the hammer blow that follows with both gloves, then tries to wrap the Ox's arms, but the Swede butts him over the left eye and brings his knee up, aiming for the privates and getting thigh instead. He is too much stronger, working an arm free and jolting his elbow across Hod's jaw and then the bell and another elbow and Hod jackknifing, rolling out backward through the ropes to get away, men shoving and tugging at him as he pushes through the ringside mob, using up half his minute's rest before Smokey can pull him back into his own corner.

"There's something wrong with the hand wraps." His fingers seem bonded together inside the gloves, his fists like clubs.

"Rolled em in plaster of Paris," says the negro. "Must of set by now."

Hod looks up into his eyes. Smokey jams a chunk of ice against where his brow is split from the head butt.

"You gone need whatever help you can get."

There is blood slicking the floorboards when the second round begins, blood and tobacco juice and no sawdust thrown over it and even with the fighter shoes they've given him Hod feels like he is skating every time he backs up near the corners. Ox Knudsen keeps lurching forward, relentless, chasing Hod around the ring with Hod chopping hard at his ears as Ox swings and misses and goes past with the momentum, Hod bicycling backward as fast as he can till Ox wrestles him into a half-clinch, clamping his left arm over Hod's neck and rubbing his glove laces over the cut eyebrow and smashing Hod's face with his free hand as Hod pounds at the exposed short ribs with left and right the way Smokey has shown him, then launches a blind uppercut that catches Ox under the chin and Hod drops to his knees to yank out of the hold, scrambling away on hands and knees while the crowd jeers but back up dancing on his toes before Joe Boyle can count three. His ears are ringing and vision blurred, Ox charging, Hod just able to throw himself sideways and give the Swede a backhand shove that sends him sprawling across to the far ropes. Hod wipes at his eyes, blood streaming into the left, and backpedals while he fends with outstretched arms against the next rush, running out of ring sooner than he expects and catching an overhand right on the jaw that sends him tumbling back through the ropes.

His head is clear enough and his legs are still with him but there are men all around him screaming into his ears and the Ox waiting just inside the ropes for when Hod ducks to step back through, his right cocked, lips moving in a stream of curses, and Boyle behind him counting to ten and Hod gets up onto his knees with somebody trying to shove him back in and he hates them, hates Jeff Smith and Whitey and the whole sure-thing crew and the men screaming all around him and the one shoving behind, hates them all, rising and turning to smash the shoving man flush on the mouth and then clubbed from behind by Ox in the ring, spinning to land an overhand left on the Swede's nose, feeling it crack, backing him up enough to get through the ropes but immediately grabbed in a bear-hug dance till the Ox pins him up against the corner post and goes at him, elbows and fists, Hod turtling in and crouching and catching the blows as best he can till the bell rings and Ox not stopping till Smokey steps in and blocks the Swede with the wooden stool long enough for Boyle to peel Hod away and get him back to the corner. Men are stomping and screaming, red-faced, nigger this and nigger that, some of them throwing things, bottles and beer steins and a malacca cane, and there is blood smearing Hod's face and arms and chest, blood dripping from his gloves, blood staining the ropes and floor, blood staining Smokey's shirt as he presses a sponge soaked in ammonia water into Hod's face.

"You ain't gone out*run* him, we seen that," he shouts into Hod's ear over the cries of the gamblers and the townsmen and the stampeders, the high rollers and lowlifes who surround them. "Got to make yourself a openin and put him away."

Hod tries to say that the man is too big to knock out but his lips have begun to swell and it doesn't come out right. The negro looks across to Jeff Smith and his crowd, all grins behind a cloud of smoke, then turns back to him.

"You got enough kick in them hands, boy." Smokey's face is a way he has never seen it, like he's set to kill somebody, his fingers digging into Hod's shoulders as he hollers and stares him in the eye. "You just put it on him and don't get off till he's out. And I don't mean down, I mean *out.*"

Smokey blows a mouthful of cold water in his face then and the bell rings and Hod stands from the stool and there is a great whooping cry from the men of Skaguay. It is clear how it will end, what they have all come to see, and it will be the Ox or it will be him. Ox keeps his left foot forward as he gallops across the floor, putting legs and hip and back into his punch, only this time when Hod sidesteps he slams him one-two in the kidney and crosses over hard with his left trying to punch through the man's face to the back of his skull and Ox is spitting blood, thick gouts of it out onto the wet floor and bending his knees, intent on the kill as he lurches forward, Hod ducking his head back away from the roundhouse skinning his nose and the force of it twisting Ox, feet slipping in the blood slick and falling, reaching back with his left to catch himself leaving the opening for Hod's uppercut thrown from the hip and Ox knocked back on his ass with a stunned expression on his square white face in the instant before Hod steps in to clamp his left hand behind the Swede's head and piston the club of his right over and over into it, punching down with all of his weight, cracking Boyle away with the sharp of his elbow when the referee tries to step in then going down on one knee to continue pounding the Swede's face, his head against the hard floor now, pounding left and right till men fill the ring in a cursing wave that sweeps him up and away, pummeled and kicked, Smokey unable to fight through to him with the stool in hand, Hod lifted clear off his feet and carried, trying to cover his face, his privates, forehead cracking against the doorframe and then out into the back alley and yanked to his feet, running panicked behind Niles Manigault out onto an alley full of woodsmoke and a sky that has gone insane.

"Get to O'Brien's ship!" shouts Niles as he turns to help Red Gibbs slow down the lynch-minded throng. "And keep out of sight!"

Hod runs then, sweat steaming in the freezing air, men chasing him across Runnalls and down Broadway and off onto Holly Street, Hod cutting through the open door of Jeff Smith's Parlor and past the squawking eagle and through the card room into the backyard where he throws the latch that opens the secret passage through the board fence he has seen them use so many times to frustrate a skinned stampeder. He comes out into Paradise Alley and steps into the first red-lit crib he sees, startling the Belgian girl inside.

"But what is this?!"

Hod is swallowing blood and fighting for breath, realizing, as the hammering of his heart begins to slow, that he is nearly naked.

"I'm freezing." One of his gloves has been torn off in the melee and he manages to work the other off with his teeth, but his hands are nearly useless in the hardened wrappings. He manages to lower the shade. "I got to get under the covers."

"I will get Bernard—"

"Unless he wears my size," says Hod, climbing into the narrow bed, "forget about your maque. Just relax, make me some coffee. Soapy will pay in the morning."

The woman is wearing a wrapper with a Chinese design on it and mukluks. She pours him coffee from a pot already cooking on the little woodstove in the center of the room.

"You have been in a fight?"

"Something like that." The coffee tastes like metal.

"The other man, he beats you."

"Listen, would you mind coming in here with me?"

The woman has blondined hair and huge breasts. She keeps the wrapper on and plants herself on top of him and it is strange, lying with a woman who isn't Addie Lee, but after twenty minutes he stops shaking. He sends her to the Parlor then, and sits wrapped in blankets on the bed, fire poker in hand in case her Bernard is one of Smith's many enemies and betrays him to the mob.

It is Smokey who finally comes to the door, Smokey with a fresh gash across his nose, wearing a fur hat with side flaps to hide his face and carrying a bundle of clothes and a pair of sheep shears to cut the handwraps away.

"Thought you didn't work for Jeff anymore."

Smokey shrugs. "Guess I been bought back."

"How's the Swede?"

Smokey works the blade of the shears under the stiffened cloth and begins to cut.

"Sheriff Taylor got a warrant out for you."

Hod starts to shiver again. "It was a fight. With a referee—"

"Don't nobody remember boxing aint legal till somebody get killed."

Outside the auroras are still shimmering green above and the wagon sitting in Paradise Alley has PEOPLES' FUNERAL PARLOR painted on the side.

"You gone have to climb in there," says Smokey, indicating a casket loaded on the back. "They still mens out hopin to tie a rope round your neck."

When he pulls the lid off he discovers that the box holds the remains of Fritz Stammerjohn who used to work on the Brackett Road with him, murdered yesterday at the Grotto and now frozen quite stiff.

Smokey, nervous, takes the reins in hand. A pack of Skaguay dogs, terriers and shepherds and collies and retrievers deemed too weak or too flighty to pull a sled, have discovered them and take turns propping themselves up against the wagon on their front paws to sniff. "You and him both headin for Seattle," says Smokey. "Gone have to double up till we gets to the boat."

Hod lays the Belgian whore's blanket over Fritz Stammerjohn and climbs in, lying head to feet, Smokey propping the lid over them with a tiny crack for air. It is a bumpy, uncomfortable ride, angry voices calling out here and there, but the wagon never stops till they are on the Alaska wharf alongside the *Utopia.* Captain O'Brien is out on deck, watching the Northern Lights.

"You start to wonder if there's a God in Heaven," he sighs as Hod helps Smokey lug the casket aboard, "and then He sends you a night like this."

KINDLING

In the drawing there are a half-dozen young men standing aimlessly, many with their hands in their pockets, as if in line for a free lunch. They are placed, however, on a ramp leading into the maw of a huge iron pot atop a roaring fire.

The pot is labeled CUBA.

A leather-aproned Hephaestus-as-blacksmith grins down into the brew, steam curling around his large, boyish face—unmistakably a caricature of the Chief—as he pumps a large hand-bellows to excite the flames. A chute extends from the base of the pot, and marching out on it is a neat row of identical, uniformed soldiers with rifles on their shoulders.

THE CRUCIBLE OF WAR

—reads the caption, and the Cartoonist is hard-pressed to say whether the whole effect is critical or laudatory. The soldiers look manly and forthright, a vast improvement over the loafers they had once been, and the Chief might seem either demonic or merely industrious. Since an equal number of men are seen leaving as are seen entering the crucible, there is no indication that any have been lost within it. The word is that the Chief pinned this one on the wall of his office and called the *Herald* to compliment them on the likeness.

The other drawing portrays him as an old geezer, bent double with age and supporting himself on a crutch labeled WAR WITH SPAIN. A Latin-looking nurse wields an oversized hypodermic, injecting JINGO JUICE into his buttocks while Joe Pulitzer, hands on hips, observes disapprovingly.

GOOD FOR THE CIRCULATION

If anything will improve circulation it is the nurse, one of Templeton's specialties, her dress much more form-fitting than would be allowed on a white woman. Pulitzer's *World* has always been merciless to the Chief, of course, accusing him of having manufactured the Evangelina Cisneros affair and of scuttling any hope of diplomatic solution in Cuba. But Old Jewseph has jumped on the war wagon so wholeheartedly himself that this can only be viewed as a purely personal attack.

So once again the Cartoonist is drawing the Eagle.

He has a knack for birds, better than any of the big salary boys, and the Chief knows it. The trick is to make them express themselves with their feathers. The Chief wants not only to rebuke the Spanish and his competitors, but to remind the readers that we need a good scrap, that this won't be American against American, no—if certain people would just get out of the way we could step out and take our place among the Great Powers.

The Eagle, spear and arrows clutched in its talons, strains its wings as it attempts to soar skyward despite the chain around one leg, with Pulitzer and Senator Hanna and a couple of the other naysayers hauling back on it, heels dragging the ground as the mighty raptor threatens to lift them all away. His Pulitzer needs some work, a decent enough likeness but not sufficiently craven. The Eagle's feathers, if you had to put it into words, are proud but angry. Uncle is there already, speaking to his companion yet to be drawn, President McKinley.

SHE'LL FLY IF YOU LET HER

—Sam is saying. The Chief wants the President to be uncertain but dignified. He also wants to try a small boy, an onlooker, off to one side and very much upset by the spectacle, labeled OUR FUTURE WARRIOR or something similar. The terrible effect of peace-mongering on tender minds. The Eagle is looking with furious concentration at a trio of distant islands, Cuba, Porto Rico, and Guam, each with a palm tree and a Spanish flag sticking up from them. Adding China, though in tune with the ambition of the picture, might be confusing.

And maybe Sam should have a rifle.

SALVATION

Hod rides the *Utopia* back to Seattle with the other beaten men. They are a sorry-looking collection, frostbit sourdoughs with empty eyes and greenhorns fleeced before they even got to the fields, a few who probably made a small pile and blew it in town and can't face another winter freezing their lungs and hacking the ground. The fog, constant up on deck, is a relief. Men appear in it, flick a glance at the state of Hod's face, then turn away without meeting his eye. There is no brotherhood on this ship, each defeated stampeder minding his own troubles.

Hod has been down before, but never this alone. He misses the Army.

It started in Butte with hungry men. First the Gold Trust had their way and repealed the Sherman Act, then Amalgamated tossed Hod and hundreds more like him out of their pits.

"There's a man named Coxey," went the word in Finntown and Dublin Gulch, "gonna make it right. He's got a plan."

FREE SILVER! said the banners at the Union Hall. GOLD AT A PREMIUM, LABOR PAUPERIZED!

"May Day in Washington," said the laborers with gleaming eyes. "Every damn American needs a job gonna tromp on Grover Cleveland's flower bed. That don't wake this government up nothing will."

The plan was that the Government, which was the railroads and the mining outfits and the Rothschild bankers who had lured them out West to build their fortunes then dumped them like a gaggle of Chinamen, that Government, would pay them, the Workers, a decent wage to build roads, to dig canals to water the dry Western states and territories, and everybody would come out the better for it. Hod was younger then, just barely off the farm, but even he knew it was a desperate dream. But it was big, big as the Depression that had one man out of four walking the streets and feeling like shit on a bootheel.

"Coxey plans to leave on Easter," said Bill Hogan, little Bill Hogan who'd never led anything bigger than a mule team but was as straight as they came and when voted General of the Butte Contingent said "Thanks, fellas, I'll try to live up to it." There were a bunch of them there who'd been in the same stope with Hod at the Orphan Girl—Hack Tuttle, Orrin Wheatley, Curly Armstrong—all shouting out and stamping their feet when the resolution to march was passed.

Of course marching to Washington was easy for Coxey and his troops, back east in Massillon almost to the Pennsylvania border. The Butte men could walk Coxey's route twice over and never leave the state. The Northern Pacific said they wouldn't haul a mob of tramps on their road even if every one of them paid full fare. Which neither Hod nor any of the other jobless men in Local Number One possessed.

And so it was that one night in the middle of April a dozen or so of the troops who'd been railroad hands snuck into the yard and convinced the watchman it was only patriotic that they liberate an NP locomotive and six open coal cars, plus a boxcar for supplies, and that he not inform his masters until the sun came over the Hill. The train stopped a quarter mile out of the yard and Hod was one of three hundred Commonweal soldiers to scale the coal-car sides and drop down into the grimy interior. Their cheers echoed off the insides of the car while they gathered steam and began to highball east.

Wild train coming your way, said the telegraph message sent ahead. *Stay clear of our tracks.*

It was cold, without a roof and with the train barreling across the scrublands, but with fifty men crammed together and the thrill of defiance running in their veins the night sped by.

The Union forever! Hurrah, boys, hurrah!
Down with the bosses, up with the stars!

—they sang—

Yes we'll rally round the flag, boys, we'll rally once again
Shouting the battle cry of Silver!

It had been the banks and their tight money that drove his old man off the farm, town people putting an arm around his shoulders and cooing into his ear till he took the loan and then there they were out in the yard with Sheriff White behind them, saying how it was just business and you had to be prudent with your finances. His own father, Esam Brackenridge, working for wages at the granary till it killed him with shame.

My country tis of thee

—they sang—

Once land of liberty
Of thee I sing
Land of the Millionaire
Farmers with pockets bare
Gypped by that cursed snare
The Money Ring

He'd never quite understood how they worked it, no matter how many speeches he heard and meetings he sat through. That was part of the con, of course, making it impossible for a simple toiler to follow, wrapping it in a gauze of words and laws and proclamations and economic ciphers, but somehow he knew somebody was getting rich without lifting a finger, and here they were, honest hardworking American men, without a pot to piss in or a window to toss it from.

We are—joining—Coxey's Army—

—they sang, miners and teamsters and railroad men, tillers of wheat and builders of bridges, Northerners and Southerners and men born, like Hod, in the far West—

We are—marching—on to glory
We will—camp in—Cleveland's backyard
On the first of May!

There must be some good men there, they thought, that flag they sang about must stand for something and if only they could bring the truth to Washington, truth in the flesh of a hundred thousand working men from every corner of the land, it would put the greenback boys on the run and there would be work and bread and pride enough to go around. Hod wasn't sure of their names, but there had to be good men in the East, wizards of finance, who could do *something*.

Wild train coming.

They made Bozeman by daybreak and in the rail yard of the cow town there were a hundred people waiting, cheering as the Commonwealers stood on each other's shoulders and climbed stiff-legged over the sides of the coal cars and cheered back, throats raw from singing, and there they commandeered a fresh engine and loaded up with coal from the NP stockpile and coupled ten beautiful spacious boxcars behind it.

"There's law coming," the telegraph operator told them. "Marshal McDermott just left Butte with an engine and two cabooses. Got him some eighty deputies."

There were jeers from the Commonweal soldiers and from the crowd and much speculation as to the character of anyone who would throw in with the Czars of the Northern Pacific Railroad.

"Must not be a pimp left in Venus Alley," said Jim Harmon as he jumped behind the throttle. "Who wants to go to Washington?"

The boxcars were rolling palaces after the open coal-haulers, and the folks in Bozeman had thrown meat and bread and cheese and even a few pies in with them as the wild train resumed its journey.

"This is still hot," said Curly Armstrong, tears rolling down his cheeks. "Some lady woke up before the sun and baked us a damn pie."

They had barely settled in, filling themselves with the donated food and bragging about what they would do if the Marshal and his deputies should have the misfortune of catching up with them, when the train stopped in the middle of the Bozeman Tunnel.

The men piled out and walked in the dark along the other boxcars and the coughing, dripping engine to find half of Bozeman Hill slid down over the track ahead of them.

"The NP done this," decided Hack Tuttle, though the station agent had said there'd been a hard rain the day before and to watch out. "They called their agents out ahead of us."

"It doesn't matter how it happened," said General Hogan. "We have to clear the track or give up."

It was Hod who found the tools, half-hidden on the downside of the slope, the section gang who abandoned them probably still within shouting distance. There were fifteen shovels and they worked in relays, digging furiously till their arms gave out and then handing it over to the next man. Nobody was singing now, with that deputy train running up behind, and just when the track looked ready to roll on there was another cave-in.

"Damn if I aint doin the railroad's work for free," said one of the men, and that led to joking about the bill for services rendered they should hand over and finally Jim Harmon said the hell with it, jumped up behind the throttle again and got up a little steam and plowed right through the whole mess and out the other side of the tunnel. There were cheers and they loaded up with the shovels in hand in case there were more accidents or company mischief up ahead and Hod had the sudden thrilling idea—*This is ours now.*

Hod's old man always said it was the railroad advertising lured him out West, too many years of making scratch in Kentucky and those handbills looked awfully good. It was the railroad brought him out cheap when he signed on to settle and the railroad dumped him off in Topeka with some hints about where any smart fella ought to stake his claim. The old man listened and went in with a crowd who guessed on the area around old Fort Zarah, which they got a charter for and called Zarah City and commenced to build while the old man bought a quarter section between there and Pawnee Rock and put a crop of sod corn in and waited for the railroad to make his town land worth something.

But that was the year the hoppers flew down and ate everything so he went hunting buffalo along with all the other busted farmers, and when he managed to bring a stinking, tick-infested roll of them in without getting scalped the agents were paying less than a dollar a hide. On account, they said, of the railroad charging so much to ship them back east.

The next season it was hailstorms did the crop, and then somebody paid somebody more than somebody else did so Great Falls got the railhead instead of Zarah City and the town dried up when the drought came in and settled, more or less permanent, for the next ten years. Hod, third of eight, would run to find the old man wherever he was whenever the sky broke, eager-eyed, but the old man would barely look up and say "Hope it don't rot the beans." Then the year him and everybody else around went over to the winter wheat that the Mennonites brought to the country he made forty bushels an acre, but the price dropped out when the railroad upped its rates.

"Everywhere there's a river in this country, there's a railroad alongside it," the old man would intone when the oil lamps were lit and the day's work had bested him again. "A river feeds a man—a railroad bleeds him." In what was left of Zarah City and in Pawnee Rock the other busted men who used to talk of Dull Knife and Little Wolf or the murderous Dalton boys or the wide-open days of Dodge could speak only of the depredations of the Atchison, Topeka, and Santa Fe, spitting bitterly into the Kansas dust and elaborating on the many tentacles of the conspiracy. It wasn't the fellas who worked on the road, no, they were just poor stiffs who risked getting scalded or run over or crushed in a pile-up for their two dollars a day, and it wasn't the trains themselves, which made your heart race every time they came smoking past across the prairie. It was something big and dark and far off that was crushing them down, something that sent orders out that fixed the prices against you, and his father railed on about men in top hats whispering, passing bribes in the halls of power to keep the poor farmer down.

There was the cyclone one year, then that killer frost, then the Great Snow where he lost most of the livestock and always the cornworms and the chinch bugs and the birds eating your seed and the sinking recognition that this land you'd bought would bury you before it would feed you. And Mother falling into a mood the winter where the sun never come out once, barely talking, till they found her one day, Hod and his brother Zeb, or found her from the neck down, and the long stain on the rail it took a month for the passing trains to polish away.

And then the bank called in the note and the Unruhs, who were Mennonites, bought it all at auction for half of what they'd offered their father the year before.

Rupe Heizer, who'd been in that original Kentucky colony, was with the railroad office then and offered Hod's father a section house and a foreman job. Just supervising.

"I slit my own throat fore I work for any railroad," the old man said at the time. They told him he was too old for the salt mine in Hutchinson and he was too proud to work for any of the farmers who would offer him a job, so he signed on at the granary and dried up and died.

The Railroad was out there somewhere, big and dark and not so far off, crushing down on them, but this, this engine, this train, this stretch of track, belonged to Hogan's Army. It was owed to them.

Dynamite Johnny O'Brien finds Hod by the stern rail, staring out into the fog.

"You're well clear of that Yukon mess," says the captain. "It's a suckers' game."

"You let the folks you carry up there in on that?"

O'Brien laughs. "People start thinking gold," he says, "they don't listen to nobody. You got plans?"

Hod shakes his head. "Just enjoying the boat ride."

"Cause I got a little sideline, running guns to them that's willing to pay dear for em. This deal in Cuba is heating up, and you seem like a capable young fella—"

"Not my fight." The captain is a friendly old coot and a hell of a poker player, but not likely to be particular about which side he sells to.

"Well, keep it in mind. Always got room for a boy who don't stall at breakin a few rules."

Wild train from copper country.

They rolled into Livingston in the late afternoon, stopping short so the couple soldiers who had been switchmen could trot ahead and reset the rails. It was certain now that somebody was trying to side-track them, but when they eased into the station there was another crowd cheering and General Hogan begged off that he was too busy and so this young fellow, meaning Hod, would explain their quest to the multitude.

Hod stood on a pallet in front of the roundhouse and looked them over. The NP had an office here, it was their biggest train shop in the state, and he half expected to be shot at. But here were all these people smiling, eager to hear his story.

"We're not tramps and we're not cranks and we're not revolutionists," he told them. "We're just an army of honest toilers gone to tell the government what's right and what's wrong. Our politicians are supposed to do that, but somehow the message gets lost on the trip—" and here there was much joking and laughter, "—or they just plain sell us away." A cheer greeted this and a dozen fellows came up and said they were enlisting for the campaign.

"The Northern Pacific won't carry us," Hod told them, "cause they don't want the truth to be known. The newspapers make fun of us, make us out as deadbeats cause it helps them sell papers. The only ones we got pulling for us," he said, feeling like the light in their eyes would lift him clear off the ground, "is the ordinary Americans like you folks."

More cheers then and men pumping his hand and slapping him on the back and a young girl kissed his cheek and pressed a flag into his arms and then a steam whistle blew, the boys ahold of a fresh engine, and it was time to go.

"Whatever you do, don't stop!" shouted a man who wore the Union pin on his lapel, smiling and steering Hod through the happy, cheering crowd to the snorting Liberty Train. "We got enough men jobless in Livingston already!"

Wild train coming. Step aside and watch our smoke.

They left the station with the new engine and a few more boxcars with red-white-and-blue bunting draped on them, the boxcar doors open and men sitting up on the roofs like a horde of scruffy baronets surveying their domain. They waved their hats to the crowd waiting when they rolled through Big Timber at dusk, then a few miles past had to stop and dig out another section of track, this time a mess of big rocks that must have been dynamited down.

There *were* tramps among them, despite what he'd told the people in Livingston. He'd noticed them before, maybe a dozen or so men who stood in the shadows till the food was passed around and seemed to have their own secret language together, the ones who were off relieving themselves in the bushes or just looking on like spectators as the rest wrestled boulders off the track. You looked them in the eye and could see that they belonged to no place, to no one. Hod was not like them, he thought, not just along for the ride. He was going places. First to Washington, and then—well, wherever they had a road needed building. And somehow, though the exact strategy was unclear in his head, he would make enough jack, save enough, to stop chasing the next piece of bread and make his stand. Find a girl. It wouldn't be farming, though—he'd seen enough of that quagmire—or digging rocks out of a hole. It would be—something else.

There was no liquor allowed on the train and the men had been good about that. Cursing was discouraged. One of the soldiers had been a barber, a Greek named Diomedes, and he gave shaves every morning in the lead boxcar. Hod always climbed forward, only just sprouting whiskers then, to be among the first. He'd seen fear in the eyes of small children more than once when he'd approached a house looking for work. There were dogs trained to attack men like him. The line between a man out of work with nowhere to call home and a tramp out after a handout was thin enough for most people to ignore, and there'd been times when he wanted to just throw it all in and either beg or steal, but he wasn't a thief and he wasn't a tramp.

He was a soldier in Hogan's Army.

The track was cleared and the train rolled forward again, headlight cutting through darkness now, stopping at the jerkwater towns where there was suddenly no water to jerk, the tanks emptied by whoever the company had sent ahead of them, going slower and slower till finally Jim Harmon had to stop the train and uncouple the boxcars.

"Can't make steam without water," he said. "And we're boiling it off fast pulling this load."

Hod joined the twenty men who climbed onto the engine to scout ahead, and it wasn't much more than a mile when they found the next tank, emptied. They piled out then and searched around till Idaho Shorty, who'd been a hoist operator for Amalgamated, found a pond and they set up a bucket brigade, all of them aware of the time lost to the deputy train as the mossy water sloshed from hand to hand. They climbed on again and backed up and recoupled, the men in the boxcars cheering, but now they had to go easy, hoping the boilerful would last them all the way to Billings. Hod stayed in the engine compartment, spelling the fireman, heaving coal into the scorching maw of the furnace.

The deputy train caught up outside Columbus, just where the rail cut over the Yellowstone River, yanking off a series of three short warning whistles maybe a mile behind them. Jim Harmon slowed to a stop, pulled off a long warning burst to tell the boys to stay put, then backed them up so the last boxcar was slap in the middle of the bridge. Hod jumped down, the engine still huffing wetly beside him, the river roaring below, walking to join the others hopping down from the boxcars and moving back to spill out on the bridge behind their train, facing the headlight of the posse's locomotive as it slowed and stopped a hundred yards short.

Men with bayonets climbed out of the cabooses then and walked toward them, backlit, uncertain, seemingly leaderless. Orrin Wheatley had the Stars and Stripes the young girl give Hod and the boys spread it out and they got the Butte Miners' Union flag out as well and began to discourse with the deputies.

"Go ahead and shoot," they called. "We got nothing to shoot back with."

"Man have to be yellow scum to shoot through the American flag."

"Hope you fellas can swim," the armed men called back, "cause we get holt of you it's over the side."

"You step near with them frogstickers, you gone end up sittin on em."

The silhouettes shifted around before them, breaking into tentative knots of men who wavered forward and back, while Bill Hogan lined the boys up in three lines of attack.

"They start to fire, I suppose we'll have to rush them," he said, looking grim and very tired. "What's your name, son?"

He was looking right at Hod. "Hod, sir. Hod Brackenridge."

"Well, Sergeant Brackenridge, I need you to lead this first line."

"Yes, sir."

"But only if they fire."

"Yes sir."

"Surrender!" called one of the silhouettes.

"Surrender to who?" called Hogan after the jeers of his men had died down. Heated discussion in front of the posse's headlight.

"We got a U.S. Marshal here," called another voice.

"There been a federal crime committed?"

More heated discussion.

"There sure as hell been *some*thing committed!"

Mocking laughter now, soldiers calling the men with the bayonets a pack of sorry jailbirds and worse.

"You gone give up?" The first voice again.

"Sure are," called Bill Hogan, stepping out in front. If they started shooting, Hod thought, Hogan would be the first to get it. And he would be the next. "We're gonna turn ourselves in to the government. In *Wash*ington."

A huge cheer from the working men then, and if there'd been rail ballast on the bridge to throw they'd have thrown it, so full of the Army and the rightness of their cause they could burst. There was yet more heated words from next to the deputy train and then the silhouettes began to melt away.

"Go back to Butte and starve to death, you yellow sonsabitches!"

"Dogs know when they're whipped, all right!"

"Tell the NP they can pick up their train in Washington!"

But the posse's engine just sat there blowing steam like the boss bull in a pasture, headlight glaring in their faces.

"Better load up, fellas," said Bill Hogan. "This aint over."

They piled back into the boxcars and called roll and set out, at a snail's pace to conserve on water, followed at a not-so-respectful distance by the deputy train.

"If I known we be going this slow," said Hack Tuttle, glumly watching the moonlit hills crawl by, "I'd of *mailed* myself to Washington."

Hod isn't sure how long the little man has been by his elbow, standing at the back rail of the ship, the little man whose face is a worse sight than his own.

"It was the dogs what done it," says the little man, though Hod hasn't asked. "There was a team carrying us up to Dawson. You seen how they run em—"

"I've seen a bit," says Hod. "But I never traveled with them."

"There's a lead dog and he's the boss. Run em all day for a scrap of salt fish that look like shoe leather. Only what they do is just throw it one piece at a time into the pack after they've unhitched em, and that boss dog he got to bully all the others off it, scarf it down quick without the others getting any, or else he's not the boss dog no more. 'Keeps em *keen*,' says this English fella that runs the teams."

"Dogs'll fight over food," says Hod.

"But it aint just the food," says the little man. Deep scars pucker the side of his face, his lip split in two at the corner, one eye milky white. "It's that they hate that sumbitch boss dog. Got the whip behind em and this dog they want to kill, that they're all afraid of, in front where all they can think about is takin a bite outta his hind end."

"But they run as a pack."

The little man shakes his head. "It's just red murder tied into traces. We was asleep by the fire when these two younger dogs went after the boss—they gang up like that sometimes, kill the old boss and then fight each other—and the scrap brung em right on top of us. I tried to push em away and one turned on me, like to chewed half my face off before I rolled him into the fire."

Hod lets it sit for a long moment.

"Hard life up there," he says finally. There are plenty other guys the little man could have picked to talk to. Like the bunch who brought their whiskey aboard and have stayed below dosing themselves with it ever since the steamer pulled out from Skaguay, the ones you figure in a year will be living from drink to drink. But no, he picked Hod, smelled something on him.

"Them gold fields run me good," muses the little man, his dead eye toward Hod. "But didn't nobody throw me a scrap of *nothing* at the end of it."

The mayor was there with the crowd to greet the Wild Train steaming alone into the yard the next morning. The people had flags and food and there were Kodak bugs taking photographs of the historic moment, the Commonweal soldiers waiting for the mayor to finish his welcome speech. But when he got to the part about how Billings had been named for a fella that was President of the Northern Pacific Railroad somebody started shooting, and a couple deputies who'd snuck forward jumped onto the engine to grab Hogan and

Jim Harmon. There were townspeople screaming and running and a couple hit who fell down and it was Hod, not thinking about what might happen, who led the counterattack. There was plenty lying around to throw—rocks and bricks and iron coupling pins—and with half the men from the town joining them it wasn't long before the deputies give up their hostages and made a run to hole up in the NP roundhouse. The mayor had his sheriff arrest the couple of them that had been snatched by the crowd to keep them from being tore apart and then there was a rush to find another engine, as their last one was a sorry sight from the fusillade. It was like the whole town was in with them, men running home to get their rifles to make sure nobody else chanced in from the deputy train and women bringing a stew and the baker cleaning his shop out of loaves and this was a town that lived off the railroad, a town built by the railroad, and when it was discovered the water tanks here had been emptied too didn't they ring the fire bell and set their pumper company to filling the new engine's empty tender.

"If there were boxcars available," called Bill Hogan just before they pulled out in the early afternoon, "I believe this whole town of Billings would throw in and ride to Washington with us!"

The people cheered and little boys ran alongside the train as long as they could, then flung handfuls of ballast gravel at the deputy train when it skulked after a few minutes later.

They'd lifted some rubber hose from one of the shops in the yard and twice stopped for the men to run out and siphon water, once from the Bighorn River and once from Sarpy Creek, their pursuers stopping back just within sight, going so slow now and carrying such a light load compared to the Liberty Train that their engine was barely thirsty.

"Either they've been ordered to escort us out of the state or they've got somebody waiting ahead," said General Hogan. "You boys be ready for anything."

The engine hauling them now had been waiting to be serviced, its metal parts screaming as they ground together ungreased, and they limped into Forsyth to find another. But the only engine waiting there had the throttle taken out of it and the couple mechanics in their ranks had to work in lantern light to pull the one out of their present ride and switch it over. There was no cheering crowd in the yard.

"Word come through they's government troops on their way from Miles City," said the station agent, watching the mechanics with his hands stuck in his back pockets. "If I was you fellas, I'd make scarce."

But they had stuck together this far and weren't about to be scattered. So when the Federal soldiers shown up and surrounded them, not one man among them tried to run.

"We commandeered this equipment in the name of the American working man," Curly Armstrong announced to the major who stepped forward to demand their surrender. "And we'd appreciate it if you'd peel that mess of scabs and reprobates that's lurking behind off our backs."

But the major only put them under arrest and crowded them back into the boxcars to wait for the engine to be ready to haul them to Fort Keough. Coxey would have to do without them in the nation's capital. Hod sat in the crush of silent, sullen men on the board floor and imagined his name being scribed on a blacklist by every mine super from Butte to Bisbee, and figured to be among those picked to draw a month or two in the Helena slammer. He didn't figure on the three more years of jacking rock and half-dozen borrowed names it took him to put a decent prospector's stake together.

Bill Hogan, feeling betrayed by the flag that hung from the bulkhead wall, attempted to reason with the sergeant guarding the boxcar he'd been locked in with Hod and eighty fellow Commonwealers. "You are aware," he said, "that you are bound to serve the United States government and its citizens, not the Railroad Trust."

"That's an interesting theory," the sergeant replied, picking his nose. "You ought to write a book about it."

Hod waits until all the gold and the body of Fritz Stammerjohn has been unloaded before leaving the steamer. Nobody is waiting for him on the Alaska Dock. He hurries up the steep hill and away from the *Utopia* in the light rain, carrying nothing, trying to mix in with the crowd on the streets. Everything south of the Deadline has been rebuilt in brick since the '89 fire, the box-houses moved into basements, with barkers and brass bands trying to lure stampeders in for one last blowout before they can escape Seattle. Yesler Way, the old skid road, has had cobblestones laid in since he left, but there are still tramps loitering outside the Occidental Hotel, hanging a story on whoever passes by. Hod has a ten-dollar bill in his pocket, his parting gift from Jeff Smith, and both sides of his face are still discolored from the fight.

They are advertising for porters at the Occidental and for an experienced mixologist at Morrison's Saloon and for deck apes on the steamship line, but he is white and doesn't drink liquor and all the steamers are heading for Skaguay where he is wanted for murder. The skid-road palaces have the same music coming out of them and the passing stampeders the same look of bewildered hopefulness as when he left, but there are no dogs running free in Seattle, every stray with four legs under it having been snatched up and sold as a champion sled-puller, and there is a streetcar rolling down Yesler full of women not for rent. Hod is about to turn onto Second Avenue when he runs into a Songster Brigade blasting in the other direction.

Before Jehovah's awful throne
Ye nations bow with sacred joy
Know that the Lord is God alone
He can create, He can destroy

—sing the uniformed marchers, the horns behind them flat and loud, swinging four abreast onto the big street—

His sovereign power, without our aid
Made us of clay, and formed us men
And when, like wandering sheep we strayed
He brought us to the fold again!

A phalanx of no-hopers slump behind the ranks, only a few of them clapping in time with the bass drum. A big olive-skinned man in a long coat and bowler hat brings up the rear, walking with his hands in his pockets. He sees Hod watching.

"Soup, soap, and salvation," he says, nodding forward to the marching Army.

"Don't know about soap or salvation," says Hod, "but I haven't eaten all day."

"They got their barracks just up here, with a kitchen attached. Yesterday it was beef stew."

Hod falls in with the man, an Indian from Wisconsin who says he's called Big Ten.

"I got an Indin name too," he says, and then makes a sound with lots of parts to it.

"What's that mean?"

"Walks Far—" he deadpans, "—But Would Sooner Ride."

Major Tannenbaum, in charge of divine inspiration while they wolf down their day-old bread and Scotch broth, is the scourge of demon rum.

"It is the weakness, the craving for libation that has dragged you to this depth," he booms, striding back and forth in front of the benches in the damp basement commissary. "The hop and the grape are seeds of the Devil, and their essence his liquid fire. Satan is a deceiver who goes by many a name. *Gin* is his name, *whis*key is his name, *beer* is his name—"

"Poor bastard wants a drink so bad he can taste it," mutters Big Ten to Hod as they empty their tins. "Lot of these gospel sharks used to swim in the stuff."

"—*rum* is his name, schnapps is his name—"

"He's getting soused just saying the kinds."

"—and wine—*wine* is his name, present even at the Papist Holy Communion—"

"You trying to get to the goldfields?" asks Hod.

"Hell no. Just trying to keep my head above water. But the only thing I got going in this town is I'm not a Chinaman."

"The Devil floats in on a sea of alcohol," says Major Tannenbaum, "captures your soul, and sails away."

"How bout you?"

Hod can feel the Indian studying the cuts around his eyes, the bruises on his cheeks. The rest of the men enduring the sermon are a beat-looking lot, red-nosed and palsy-handed, the walking wounded slurping barley soup under a smoke-darkened banner that reads JOIN THE RANKS OF THE SAVED. Hard to say just when the older fellas' lives went off the tracks, thinks Hod, but the younger ones don't look much different than him.

Tannenbaum shakes his fist in the air. "He who renounces drink renounces Satan!"

"I'm not a Chinaman either," says Hod, and wipes the bowl clean with the last of his bread.

PERISHABLE

If the coolies are curious about Diosdado they don't show it. There are four of them who have bribed their way on board, squatting around the light of an oil lamp in a tiny clearing in the hanging forest of bananas in the hold, rolling dice on a jute sack and sing-songing in a Cantonese dialect it is nearly impossible for him to make out. Something about what they'll do when back in their villages, what big men they'll be. Diosdado is relieved to note the amounts they are gaming for are small, none of them likely to lose too much of their hard-earned contract pay on the quick voyage home.

The freighter rolls heavily, and Diosdado feels, for the hundredth time on this trip, as if he will be violently ill.

The hold smells of coal dust, ripening bananas, and, he imagines, his own foul stench. Somehow the photographs of the execution appeared in Manila sooner than Scipio had promised and Diosdado was forced to spend a night and a day on the river hiding beneath a pile of *zacate* on a stinking *lancha* till he was finally transferred, stuffed into a packing crate, to the hold of the banana boat. It was dark, of course, and surprisingly cold, and though his muscles cramped and his imagination grew morbid and he wet himself more than once, he obeyed his instructions not to try to break his way out of the crate. Hours in the close air of the wooden tomb before the jolt of the engine as they got under way and then, seemingly, more long hours of sickening pitch and roll.

"Just in time," said the captain, holding his nose when the lid was pried off. "This one's already ripe."

Diosdado sits on his damp, half-filled sack of belongings on the floor of the hold, swallowing constantly to try to control his stomach, which seems to be climbing up into his gorge. The huge stems of pale-green bananas tied to the overhead rails swing in unison with each roll of the freighter. He shuts his eyes tightly and tries to imagine something else, something not pitching or rolling, something planted in the unmoving earth.

It is mango time in Zambales.

By now the first of the crop will be ripe, half the tree bearing each season, or trees bearing on both sides and then "sleeping" for a year. His mother used to put him in shirts that were already stained with the juice to go out and play, the fruit surrendering, stem snapping easily when they were truly ripe and they'd grab some of the drops that had been bruised and compromised by insects and hurl them up into the mass above, trying to catch whatever pristine ones fell before they hit the ground. Insects in the air, sugar bees that hadn't been seen since the clusters of little yellow-brown flowers had clothed the trees, and the harvesters working their *sunkits* from morning to late noon, the sweetest time to pick, probing the long bamboo poles till another plump fruit dropped into the sack fastened at the end. If they were feeling lazy they'd only swipe some from the huge baskets covered with jute cloth where the fruit to be sold locally was left to finish, waving away the bees and grabbing and running, the boys, bellies tight with fruit, always happy to be with Diosdado because his father was king here and they couldn't be punished until later. They'd use their knives to peel the skin back then suck the flesh off all around, down to the *hueso*, fingers sticking together till they were wet with the juice of the next one.

"You see how they grow," Don Nicasio would always point out when they passed a tree where the *carabao* were allowed to ripen on the stem. "See how they are red on the side that faces the sun and yellow on the side that faces the tree?"

"Yes, Father," Diosdado would say, mango-colored at the fingertips and with a *mancha* the shape of Luzon on the front of his shirt. "I see it."

"This is how we must be in life. We must adjust ourselves to what we are facing."

And that is Don Nicasio. A drinker of imported *Madeira*, a backslapper to governors and priests, deferential to anyone with ties to what he reverently toasts as *"nuestra gran Madre al otro lado de las mares,"* though when he crossed those seas to visit the Great Mother they thought he was a *chino* and refused to seat him in fine restaurants unless he was the guest of a *peninsular distinguido*. He has many such patrons, though, Spaniards who he has helped make wealthy in the islands and is helping still, a scientist with crops, a genius at trade—maybe this is the *chino* in him—and an able hand at cards or billiards.

By the time of the Katipunero uprising they were having their arguments—actually only one long argument, interrupted when Diosdado went off to the Ateneo, and resumed whenever he returned on a visit.

"I'm sending you to school to study the Spanish," Don Nicasio would growl, "not to play around with *filibusteros*. If you want to get yourself killed you can do it without wasting my money."

"But our country—"

"Country? What is it called on the map? *Las Filipinas*—a group of islands named after a Spanish king. There was no country before they came and there is not one now, only bands of wild men fighting other wild men for the right to remain ignorant."

He had been Diosdado's hero once, the man who knew things, who moved in the world, the man the poor of San Epifanio and its environs came to for help, meekly, hat brims twisted in their hands as they muttered their requests, barely able to meet his eyes. A generous man, a man who advanced pay to those who needed it, who paid for the most elaborate mass on holy days. The Concepcións had their own pew reserved at the front left of the church, his mother God-struck after her second son, Diosdado's brother, died in infancy, rocking slightly and murmuring the Rosary throughout, the carved ebony beads draped over her fingers, Don Nicasio erect and motionless, watched and admired but seemingly oblivious to the others standing crowded behind him. Diosdado imagined his father's talks with God as hearty affairs over cigars and brandy, ending with Don Nicasio's habitual firm handshake and meeting of the eye.

"So—we understand each other?"

There are boat horns now, distinguishable over the engine thrum and the constant drumming of the pump pistons, and Diosdado hopes it means they are entering the harbor. The coolies roll up their possessions and tie them into bundles, still talking excitedly. Even if they have hundreds of miles yet to travel, they are going home. Diosdado is going only to a certain spot in the foreign city, to wait for someone to come and give him a clue about what the rest of his life will be. The word must have reached Zambales by now, his mother on her knees praying for his safety and his soul, while Don Nicasio paces and curses, asking the heavens to explain how he could have fathered an idiot and a criminal.

"You'll be back in no time," smiled Scipio, helping him throw together his most essential belongings on the evening when the photographs appeared, pasted over government notices and decrees on walls throughout the Intramuros. "Once the Americans declare war—"

"And if they don't?"

"Then you'll have to develop a taste for congee and carp."

It was meant as a joke, but there are men, dozens of them, who have never been able to return, scattered around the world, pleading in their letters for news of progress, for any scrap of hope. And most of these are wealthy, with bank accounts and families who have the means to visit them in exile. Diosdado has only the one good set of clothes in his sack, with letters from the Committee to the Junta, coded in Tagalog, sewn in the lining of the jacket, and the little pile of silver Scipio passed on with the forged *cédula* and verbal contact instructions for his arrival.

The name on the *cédula* is José Corpus—born in Tarlac, four years older than Diosdado. The photo is his, though, cropped to conceal the school fencing uniform he was wearing when it was taken. There will be Spanish agents looking for that face when the passenger ships dock, standing by British authorities keen on preventing troublemakers from entering the Crown Colony. The hum of the engine changes pitch. One of the coolies appears beside him, poking his shoulder, and leads him through a maze of bananas back to the packing crate. He speaks in pidgin Tagalog, indicating that Diosdado has to crawl back in.

José Corpus, he thinks as the lid is placed over and pounded shut. Scipio must have known about this part.

The wooden lid is only inches from Diosdado's nose. He is nobody in here, nothing, a tiny spark of consciousness shut off from the living world. Voices outside, movement, men shouting in Cantonese, and several times his crate is banged by workers hauling stems of bananas away, one even standing on top of it for a moment, the boards creaking. Diosdado tries to breathe evenly, to will his heartbeat slower. He doesn't feel nauseous anymore, he feels—lost.

When the crate is lifted he is smashed onto his left side at first, then his feet go up almost vertically and the top of his head bears all his weight, sides of the crate cracking against the ladder and the hatch. He has been flipped onto his face by the time the crate is dropped roughly on what he guesses is the dock, one elbow twisted awkwardly under his ribs, listening with a mounting sense of terror at the bang of another crate being piled on top of his, then another—

"*Reflect that you are no longer Master of your body,*" he thinks. "*It belongs now to the Society.*" Unless the Society has marked the outside of this crate and are on their way, or whatever is supposed to be inside it is meant to be pulled out very soon, he will die in here. Diosdado has imagined dying for the cause, leading a throng of loyal followers in a charge over a corpse-strewn battlefield, uttering last words that will be engraved in marble, but not this. Not this helpless nothing.

Only time, which is not even time in the dark, nothing to mark its passing. Diosdado manages to wiggle into a slightly more comfortable position, maybe even sleeps. It is hard to tell. What sounds he hears are muffled, distant. He can breathe, for the moment. He tries whispering the Rosary to fill the void, the words coming back in their familiar rhythm—the *Pater Noster* followed by ten *Ave Maria*s and a *Gloria Patri* to complete each decade, then contemplation of one of the Mysteries before launching into the next. There are Joyful Mysteries, Sorrowful Mysteries, and Glorious Mysteries to choose from. Diosdado chooses to contemplate the Presentation of Jesus at the Temple, a Mystery whose fruit is the virtues of purity and obedience.

There were no cigars or brandy when he was off to the Ateneo for his first semester and Don Nicasio wanted him to know about women. Specifically the ones who could be found at Doña Hilaria's parlor, who were clean and honest and well-trained if not well-bred. Diosdado, a priest's boy but no stranger to how animals reproduced on the *hacienda*, fought, cheeks burning, to hide his shock. If his father knew such things, he must have "relieved himself" on his trips alone to Manila, and very likely in similar establishments in Hongkong, Macao, Madrid, and Yokohama before and after he was bound in Holy Matrimony.

"Young men," said Don Nicasio, sending him on his way, "are driven by Nature. Fighting Nature leads to religious fanaticism and nervous disorder. Giving in to it without reservation is decadence. An accommodation must be made."

Doña Hilaria charged four pesos per accommodation and allowed you to amass a debt, within reason, on that and on liquor consumed in her parlor.

"I give all my new boys the same lecture," she explained the first time

Diosdado ventured there, with Romeo Mabayag and Bobong Antuñez. "When you have reached your credit limit, you must pay within the month or my representative will visit your parents with a detailed accounting."

They did not argue much on his few visits home. His grades remained satisfactory—well above average, in fact—and he asked polite questions when Don Nicasio offered insights on the operation of his modest empire. Diosdado allowed Trini, who had served at the table since before he was born, to cut ripe mangos into bite-sized pieces for her beloved Dadong and present them with a dash of lime juice. His mother related to him the plot of the latest Carlota Brame novel she had read and informed him that she prayed daily for his soul, but gave no indication that she knew just what peril it was in.

"Philosophy, languages, the history of ancient Greece—these are all fine things to know, I am certain," said his father, who always claimed to have been educated "at the University of Saint Survival." "But a few more practical subjects would not be unwelcome."

"The Jesuits' aim is to develop the man," Diosdado replied, carefully draining his voice of all irony, "not his ability to become wealthy."

"Easy for a priest to say, with what they get away with."

"*Jesús, María, y José,*" his mother ejaculated, her reflexive response to Don Nicasio's criticism of the church or its minions.

"I'm only saying the Lord has provided very well for them on these islands. The rest of us have to scratch for what we eat."

Diosdado was polite and remote on these visits, and his father, who was not stupid, knew that something had changed between them.

"Now there is a sensible young man," he announced when General Aguinaldo and the Junta accepted the Spaniards' financial inducement to go into exile. "Get the *indios* to die for you, then escape with the treasure."

At the station in Tarlac, after the last visit, he took Diosdado's arm to draw him near and look deep into his eyes. "These are dangerous times, *mi hijo,*" he said. "You must step carefully."

"I know, Father."

"So," said Don Nicasio, laying a thick hand on his shoulder, "we understand each other?"

Scraping and banging of wood above him. Diosdado says another *Ave Maria.* The man who finally flips over the crate and levers it open is Chinese and does not even speak Cantonese, only hissing and flapping his arms for Diosdado to hurry, and then scurrying away into the night.

It is hard for Diosdado to straighten his legs at first, to stand. He is not on the dock but on a barge loaded with similar crates anchored nearly a hundred yards out from the shore, several shabby-looking sampans and junks and smaller boats floating in between. It is very quiet, perhaps a curfew in effect, in which case he has to find a new place to hide very quickly. He looks around for the man who freed him—gone. There are some electric lights lining the Praya, and only a few gas lamps still shining, scattered up the slopes that back the city. It must be very late. Diosdado brings his knees up and down several times to get the blood back into his legs, then ties his sack to the back of his belt and starts for the shore, stepping as carefully as he can from boat to boat, the flimsier craft threatening to slide out from under his feet as he makes each transfer, grabbing on to anything he can for balance and trying to look as if this is his usual route, something normal. He stops, crouching in one very tippy rowboat, to rest and to rehearse his lies, both the ones the Committee has given him and the ones he has invented on the journey. José Corpus, if anybody inquires, is here in the Colony pursuing business opportunities, hoping to find buyers for the iron ore from his home province. He is in between residences at the moment—is there a clean, relatively inexpensive commercial hotel he should know about? And right at the moment he has to get to the dock without drowning.

Diosdado slips the rowboat from its painter and paddles with his hands to bring it bumping gently against the side of a junk, able to stand precariously and grab the higher gunwale with both hands to haul himself up. There are people on the deck, dozens of them, fast asleep. He steps cautiously over and around them, not a one stirring, till he reaches the port side. There is a lower sampan tied next to the junk, only a short jump across and down, but he freezes for a long moment, staring anxiously at the open spot where he wants to land. Someone coughs behind him and he makes the leap, a little too forcefully, his momentum sending him bouncing off the far side of the prow of the smaller boat and into the water, the splash rousing what must be dozens of geese held in cages under the sampan's awning, flapping and honking an alarm that could wake the souls of drowned sailors. Diosdado swims frantically then, dog-paddling from moored boat to moored boat, finally finding the bottom rung of a weed-slimed metal ladder leading up to the wooden dock.

There is no time to sprawl and recover. Diosdado staggers quickly out of the range of the shore lights, the geese still hysterical behind him, finally settling behind a heap of wooden pallets next to a stone warehouse. He looks around, dripping and gasping to catch his breath. He is amazed to find that he recognizes the place—it is the old Pedder's Wharf, where he disembarked with his father the first time Don Nicasio brought him along on a buying trip. They stayed at a beautiful hotel halfway up the slope on Ice House Street, and spent an afternoon at the Cricket Grounds watching Englishmen in white uniforms swat a hard round ball and run between two pegs.

Diosdado pulls his good clothes, soaking, out of the sack and twists the seawater out of them, draping them carefully over sections of pallet to dry. The geese are quiet now. He is in Hongkong, in the deep of the night, with a handful of silver and a head full of lies, and no idea if he'll ever go home again.

By the time the sun is barely peeking over the harbor and Kowloon across the way there are already too many Chinese in Hongkong. The streets are choked with them, shouting, waving their arms, making deals from opposite sides of the street, peddling food from carts, the rickshaw boys swarming like hungry gulls if they see a white man who dares to walk. Diosdado makes his way through it all in his wrinkled, still-damp suit, navigating by memory and the muttered directions of Chinese men in too much of a hurry to look him in the eye.

There are Chinese in Manila, of course, thousands of them, the coolies in Binondo running ducklike under their burdens, the merchants haggling in their shops on the Escolta, the gamblers and opium dealers in Tondo luring the adventurous and weak of mettle into perdition. One of General Aguinaldo's plans, when the Republic is established, is to limit the number of coolies allowed into the country as workers, hoping to leave more jobs open for the dispossessed Filipino *kasamas* who flock in from the provinces hoping to change their lives. It seems a hopeless idea, like building a sea wall capable of stopping a tidal wave. With decent leadership and a shared purpose, thinks Diosdado as he shakes off the trio of fan-tan parlor touts pulling at his arms, these people will rule the world.

Statue Square seems almost deserted by comparison. A broad open ground between the Hongkong Club and the various British administration buildings, narrow walks crossing the immaculately kept lawns, all leading to Victoria Regina's elaborately canopied pavilion and its unobstructed view of the harbor. She is cast in bronze, a portly lady with fierce eyes sitting on an angular throne, ornamented pillars supporting the dome above her head, an outsized replica of the royal scepter sticking up straight from its crest like the spike on a Prussian's helmet. There are no soldiers guarding the pavilion, only a few British clerks strolling past and a man who looks Indian trimming the grass in front of the Hongkong Club. Diosdado sits on the third step of the granite base as he has been instructed, the Queen behind him, and watches the harbor. The traffic in the water is no more orderly than that in the market district, junks and sampans and opium traders barely missing the rickety little fishing boats as they whip past, all in a seemingly random frenzy of activity. He sits below Victoria and watches, feeling his clothes dry out in the morning sun, hungry and tired and hoping he is not a day early or a day late. It is possibly the most exposed position in all of Hongkong. At least, he thinks, if someone is coming he will be easy to find.

Hours pass. Diosdado is able to pick out the Star Ferry boats, crossing to Kowloon and back, from the rest of the floating bedlam in the harbor. He sees the steamer from Manila, the one he is not on, ease up to Blake's Pier and disgorge its passengers. The shadow of the royal scepter begins to lengthen across the Square.

It is Gregorio del Pilar who appears to sit on the step above him in the early afternoon, Goyo sharply dressed in white with a skimmer tilted on his head and a walking stick with an ivory handle.

"How was your voyage?" he asks.

"I survived it."

Del Pilar smiles. "You were supposed to be here before those pictures were released. Somebody didn't follow orders."

Diosdado turns to look at his *hermano terrible*. "Do you know if it made a stir? What did the newspapers say?"

He feels weak to have to ask, but this blind leap, this exile, must have some value.

Del Pilar stands, his face unreadable. "Every act of defiance," he says, "is a nail in the Spaniards' coffin." And then, grinning and nodding to the doughty bronze monarch above them, "Let's be happy we're not fighting *her*. Come on—we'll find a place to put you."

WILMINGTON

If Uncle Wicklow got any second thoughts about being a colored man's colored man, he keeps quiet about it. He's worked for Dr. Lunceford since Royal can remember, driving, keeping Boots fed and stabled, keeping the yard up, hauling coal and ice and doing all the other chores most folks got to do on their own. Not that Royal takes anything away from the doctor.

"*Man like Dr. Lunceford,*" his mother is fond of saying, "*provide a aspiration for you young ones.*"

Wick is wiping clean the dash on a new carriage when Royal steps in. It is a moment before recognition creases his face in a smile.

"Look at you."

"Wick. How you coming, old man?"

"*Look* at you."

There was a crowd at the station, almost all colored, when the troop train pulled in, cheering and waving flags while brass instruments thumped out a welcome, little boys dancing alongside him for blocks calling him Mr. Soldier Man and wanting to touch his uniform.

"They're carrying us down to Georgia," says Royal. "Got a few hours to stretch our legs."

"So Mr. Lunceford Junior be coming by?"

Royal feels a tiny pang at the old man's excitement. Wick is *his* uncle, not Junior's.

"He'll come by shortly."

"You been to your mama?"

"That comes next. I got business here."

Wick shakes his head. "You can shinny up the tree, boy, but you aint getting no peach."

"How is she?"

Wick turns back to his work. "Bout like you'd expect. A fine young lady."

If it was somebody else's daughter the old man would be winking and nudging, calling back on his own adventures to offer a plan of action. But this is his livelihood, and there is a part of him that cringes every time Royal steps into the Luncefords' parlor.

Royal makes a show of inspecting the carriage.

"This is a new one."

The old man's face brightens. "Two-seater Park Phaeton, all the way from Massachusetts." He steps back to indicate the features. "Cut under to the reach, folding top for rain, and the springs—nephew, you roll on these springs you aint riding, you *float*in. I seen Dr. Lunceford fall right to sleep on that seat beside me, coming home from a long day of visitations. Sleep through shell road, cobblestones, pot-holes, you name it."

"It's smooth."

"Like a dream on water. Look here—" Wick runs his hand over the black leather of the front seat. "You ever seen polstry like this? That pattern there, that's diamond-tucked and button-tufted is what that is. That is *qual*ity. Wherever I stop, these other old boys that's driving, don't matter for what kind of white people, they got to shut up and wonder. You know Preston McNary, what they call Pinkeye?"

"Ned McNary's daddy."

"That's the one. He's in livery for Judge Manigault, got more airs than a peacock got feathers, and even he got to say 'Wicklow, that is a fine piece of craftsmanship you settin on. A *fine* piece.'"

Before Royal left the Doctor had an old physician's coupe, beautifully kept by Uncle Wick but a little secondhand box-on-wheels nonetheless. Royal's stomach tightens as he studies the coach. He is climbing, the uniform is emblem of that, but maybe the Luncefords are climbing even faster.

"Now if I was a sporting man," Wick goes on, always one to rhapsodize about his rides, "and Boots was still in his prime, I could make me some pocket silver racing against them young bloods as gets together Saturdays at the river run to match their wagons. Phaeton is built for comfort," he says, patting a fender, "but that don't mean she won't *fly*."

Another soldier steps into the carriage house.

"Uncle Wick."

Junior calls him Uncle too, but in the manner of the white people. It is supposed to be affection, maybe even respect, but it always grates on Royal.

"Mr. Lunceford Junior!" Wick makes a show of wiping his hands clean on the chamois cloth before shaking Junior's hand. "All turned out in blue! What is it now—Lieutenant? Major?"

Junior smiles. "Just a private, like Roy here."

"We don't go past sergeant in the regulars," says Royal. "Commissioned officers are all white men."

"But that will change soon enough." Junior has submitted letters to editors, has solicited the aid of congressmen, has made it abundantly clear he is a New Negro seeking his proper place in the Army's hierarchy. He is not the easiest friend to have in the barracks.

"Mrs. Lunceford gonna throw a fit. You didn't write you was coming."

"Sudden orders," says Junior. "We're moving faster than the mail."

"I heard there was colored troops passing through, but they never said no regiment numbers."

"You're looking well, Uncle." Junior gives the old man a small pat on the arm, ready to move on. He turns to give Royal a once-over.

"Are you prepared for battle, Private?"

Royal does not feel ready, but there is no telling where the Army will take him next and it is only by chance they've stopped in Wilmington on the way.

He tries to avoid Uncle Wicklow's eyes. "I won't say very much."

Junior smiles. He wears his confidence like he wears his clothes, even in Montana with the sergeants chewing you out on the training grounds. There are men in the ranks maybe got more smarts than Junior Lunceford, but none of them carry themselves so high, so sure. If colored officers ever do come in, thinks Royal, Junior be commissioned on the spot.

"Modesty would be prudent," says Junior. "This is only to put a new image of you in their minds. Replace the shoeless boy and stripling dockworker of their memories with a very presentable military gentlemen."

"And Jessie?"

It might be hopeless. *"Aint no lack of colored women in this world,"* his mother likes to say. *"They no sense in sniffin after what you can't have when they plenty at hand do you just fine."* His mother never runs out of sayings, most of them made to ward off disappointment. If she ever hoped for something good in life it is a secret to him.

Junior laughs and puts his hand on Royal's shoulder. "My sister dwells in a romance novel," he says. "She will *swoon*."

The performers fill the stage, strutting and singing, and Niles is late again. Harry has his skimmer on the empty seat, looking back across the crowd in the Thalian, already smiling and clapping their hands. He knows enough never to wait for his brother outside, or to expect he'll have the twenty cents admission on his person, and so has bought the extra ticket and left it at the door.

We's sons of Ham from Alabam
The slickest singin birds what am—

And then there he is, Niles dancing down the aisle fluttering his palms in the air and rolling his eyes and mouthing along with the song—

We's fond o' gin an prone to sin
Now let this minstrel show begin!

Niles is winking and waving to his pals scattered in the house around them as he squeezes into the row, stepping on toes, always one to make a ruckus and be forgiven for it. He stands in front of his seat after Harry pulls his hat off it, waiting for the entertainers to make their semicircle, waiting for the Interlocutor, frock-coated and without blackface makeup, to call the session to order—

"Gentlemen," the Interlocutor calls out in his booming voice, "be seated."

—and Niles hitches his pants to make a show of sitting at once with the minstrels.

A few people in the seats behind them laugh. "I was detained on the steps," he tells his brother, not lowering his voice all that much. "Ran into some of the Judge's politicking comrades coming out from work." The Thalian serves as City Hall as well as Opera House and Music Academy. "They said they'd heard I'd frozen to death."

Niles is one week back from the Yukon with plenty of stories and no gold. The rumors have no doubt originated from the Judge's constant grumble.

"*If my son desires to topple off of a glacier on some fool's pilgrimage,*" he tells all and sundry who inquire of Niles's adventures, "*that is his prerogative.*"

"Mr. Interlocutor! Mr. Interlocutor!" It is Tambo, goggle-eyed in a bright orange checked suit and black fuzzy-wuzzy wig.

"Yes, Brother Tambo?"

"What you gets when you crosses a coon wid a octopus?"

"What would that be, Brother Tambo?"

"Don't know what you calls it, but it sho can pick cotton!"

The audience laughs, Brother Tambo and Brother Bones shake their instruments, and the other minstrels shuffle their feet in appreciation.

"Don't you think that's rather demeaning?" asks the Interlocutor.

"De meanin of what?" pipes in Bones, the other end man, in a yellow swallowtail coat and red-striped trousers.

"Brother Bones, you are a buffoon."

"Nawsuh—I's cullid on *bofe* sides of de fambly."

Another laugh, and a little undertone of discussion among the patrons. Harry wonders how far this group, down from the North, will dare to go.

"Mr. Interlocutor," cries Brother Bones, clacking the ribs together to grab his attention. "Did you hear I gots me a new gal?"

"Excellent news, Brother Bones. What is her name?"

"They calls her Dinah the Drayho'se."

"And why, pray tell, would they call her that?"

"Cause when she move—"

"—she got a waggin behind!" calls Niles along with the minstrel.

Waiting out back in the dark makes Coop feel like a thief again. Not the high, fine feeling when you've cleaned a mark out, when the goods are safe from sight or already sold and you can imagine the rich people faces in the morning, no, but that nagging tug at your insides Tillis used to smoke hemp to be shed of.

"*Dulls the senses a mite*," Tillis would smile before a job, pupils wide as gopher holes, "*but it don't make you* stu*pid*."

These are high-tone niggers all right, the Luncefords, Nun Street swells with white folks living right next door, and Alma don't like him skulking round their house. *Skulking.* She learned all kinds of polite ways to say nasty things since she started working for the Doctor, and made sure none of the family ever set eyes on him. Lunceford has laid hands on Coop more than once, of course, stitching him up at City Jail on his Sunday evening visit, but never looked him in the face.

Alma comes to the door frowning.

"What you want?"

"It's me."

There is no gaslight at the back door. It takes her a long moment to figure it out.

"Lord help me. Clarence."

"Name Henry now. Henry Cooper. Call me Coop."

"Whoever you is, keep your voice down! They all in there—what's that you wearin?"

"What's it look like?"

"You joined up too? I be damn! Mr. Lunceford Junior and Royal Scott in there right now, wearin the same uniform."

"Big-headed darkies gummin up the works for the rest of us."

"Told me you was on the work gang, down South Cahlina."

"Well, I aint there no more."

Alma is round-faced and butterscotch brown, with wide shoulders and a nose that lays flat on her face. She always smells like cinnamon, even when she hasn't been baking.

"You glad to see me?"

Alma cocks her head, looks him over. "Something don't look right, you in that uniform."

"I got as much right to wear it as any man. Hell, on my way from the station I seen old Joe Anderson dressed out like a policeman—"

"He *is* a policeman."

"How the white folks let that be?"

"Cause we won the 'lection. Things took better since you was chased off."

"Didn't nobody chase me nowhere. I had some oppor*tu*nities to look out for down south—"

"Draggin a chain from your ankle—"

"That come after. They really made Joe a police?"

"We got six or seven that's police. We movin up here, Clarence."

"Coop."

Alma smiles. "You done *flew* the coop, I expect."

"Didn't stop to look behind me till I cross that state line. And then the Army, they don't expect no papers from a black man. They likely a good number of men I barracks with who don't go by the name their mama call em."

"You look real nice."

Alma was sweet when she wasn't worried about her people watching over her, had those dimples at the sides of her mouth when she smiled and never scolded too much if a man needed a loan to tide him over. They'd been tight as twine before Wilmington got too hot for him to stay in.

"How bout you step into the carriage house with me, we get back where we left off?"

"Wicklow be out there."

"They aint put him to pasture yet?"

"Besides, they gonna need me, with company and all—"

"We only here till they service the transport, Alma. Aint nobody staying over."

Alma looks back into the house, calculating. "I was spose to be home by now."

"Tell them your sister took sick."

"Reesha moved on to Charlotte, got married."

Alma's sister has a wall-eye and sour disposition. Coop holds his tongue.

"I might could just ask if they need anything else—"

"We spose to get back to the station by ten o'clock," says Coop, catching her eye and holding it. "I been thinking about you all the way from Montana."

"That's where you been?"

"Fort Missoula. Girl, they got some winter there—snow come right up under my arms."

Coop is a medium-tall man, dark skinned, his arms thick from years of wrestling barrels up a gangway.

"I lay up in that cot with the wind screaming past," he keeps on, "and who you think I'm missing? Who you think I wants to have there under that blanket?"

Some of them you can't be too nice with, they get spoiled by the sugar and start acting wifey, but Alma is a regular gal. He *has* thought of her, it is true enough, thought of her nights in the stink of the turp camp, thought of her in the long tramp up north, thought of her in the barracks when the others are snoring and only him and the coyotes are still twitching. Thought bout Alma and Lavinia and Inez Brown and Maude Bledsoe who is married to that railroad man and the little one with the spaces between her teeth he took up with in Greensboro before they caught him coaxing somebody else's mule out of somebody else's barn. He's always had a way with animals, which was why Tillis took him on in the first place. But that one knock-kneed, yellow-eye son of a bitch had the devil in him. Hind legs squatting down, dug in and staring at him, a look in his eye that say *"Your time is up, nigger."*

After the little trial the owner say that mule so ornery he wish somebody *would* steal it. Then they give him more years than he ever expect to live and send him into the pines with an iron ball tween his legs.

"Train pull up in that station," says Coop, leaning in tight, "I head straight for my Alma."

She looks over his shoulder to the carriage house. "Light's out now. Maybe Wicklow gone home."

"I wait for you there, sweet girl."

Alma touches his face with her hand. None of the ones who live outside the fort would ever do that, maybe not even if you paid them.

"I'll look in on my people," says Alma, "and get out there when I can."

Miss Dolly St. Claire appears stage right in a spot, the light dimming on the minstrels behind her. Harry helped put the overhead lighting in here, devising a control box that can be operated from the back of the theater, and is gratified to see it put to use.

The soubrette strolls beneath a parasol in a ruffled lavender dress, a bowler-sporting dandy on her arm, singing in a coy, lilting voice—

Take it back, take it back, take it back, Jack
For gold can never buy me

"Maybe she's a Silverite," quips Niles, cocking his head to appraise her the way he does with new women. Niles is two years younger and has always been the brash one, the one who says what's on his mind and leaps before he looks. A large sum of money went missing from the Judge's safe the day he disappeared without a word, and it was two months before the letter arrived from San Francisco explaining how he was on the treasure quest and meant only to save the Judge the bother of sending him his monthly stipend for the next two years, taking it in advance.

Take it back, take it back, take it back
Promise you'll be true

"I'd promise her anything to get to Heaven." Niles fingers his moustache, cocks his head the other way. Harry thinks the prospecting trip was less a bid for fortune than the consequence of Niles's sudden breaking of engagement with Mae Dupree and her father's vow to "horsewhip the scoundrel." Mae is married now, to a Lassiter, and all that has settled down.

Many of the audience join in on the chorus—

So take it back, take it back, take it back, Jack
Take back your gold!

It is the dandy's turn then, a round-shouldered tenor in a light blue suit, wearing a red carnation in his lapel, neither young nor old. The voice that comes from him, though, is like a separate thing, like a beautiful soaring bird—

A little maiden climbed an old man's knees
Begged for a story: "Do, Uncle, please.
Why are you single, why live alone?
Have you no babies, have you no home?"

Mae had been Harry's first, at least in his heart. He had spent many a night extolling her virtues to his younger brother, asking his advice in matters of strategy, planning how to begin his campaign to win her heart. "It just happened," Niles told him after the first time he'd seen them walking together at Lake Waccamaw. "Of course if you want me to back away, old boy, and give you a clear field—"

It was exactly what he wanted, but then he was cross with Mae for preferring Niles and pretended not to care and then miserably resigned himself to their engagement. And when he went to her house after his brother's abandonment, hoping perhaps to make his own desires known, she had refused to see him.

That's why I'm lonely, no home at all—
I broke her heart, pet—after the ball

He resolved to cold-shoulder his brother on his less than triumphant return, but Niles was deathly pale, coughing like a consumptive, his plucky grin so innocent of malice, his exaggerations so childlike, that they were immediately fast friends again. If Harry envies anything it is not his brother's looks or that he was born with normal legs or even his dalliance with Mae Dupree, but the sheer adventure Niles has experienced at so young an age, traveling up north and out west and to the frozen Yukon while Harry has barely been out of the state. That, he hopes, is about to change.

Harry joins in the chorus with half the audience—

After the ball is over, after the break of morn
After the dancers' leaving, after the stars are gone
Many a heart is aching, if you could read them all
Many the hopes that have vanished—after the ball!

A pair of Hibernians in green checked suits enter now, the orchestra playing *The Irish Washerwoman* as Pat hauls Mike out in a wheelbarrow, both wearing baldpates and flaming red muttonchops. Pat stumbles and dumps Mike in a heap at center stage.

"Ye clumsy Oirish fool, ye've broken me neck!"

"And how can ye tell, Mike?"

"Just lookit it!" Mike stands, his head canted sharply off to the left. "I can't put it sthraight atall."

WHOMP! Pat gives him a wallop with his fist that snaps Mike's head all the way around to the right.

"Now it's stuck on the ither side—"

WHOMP! The cymbalist joins the pit drummer as Pat throws another haymaker, this one knocking Mike's head straight. He wiggles his jaw, checks his nose.

"Ye sh'd be a physician, Pat—ye've got a mother's touch."

"Did she bate ye, the auld woman?"

"Only when she could catch me, Pat. Ah, but she was a lovely woman— she passed into a better world just the other night."

"Me condolences, Mike. Did she say anything before she died?"

"Say anything? She nivver shut her trap fer sixty years!"

The drummer cracks the rim of his snare.

"I hate to tap you again, old man," says Niles without turning his head to Harry, "but I'm afraid that once more I've been caught short."

Harry has managed to save most of his monthly stipend, left from their mother's estate, while Niles was squandering his own "advance" in the Frozen North.

"You're not gambling again?"

Niles flashes his dazzling smile, spreads his hands. "Life. Expenses. I am not the paragon of thrift that my dear brother is—what can I say?"

"I had to send me brother Frank a tellygram to give him the hard tidins. Did ye know they charge ye a nickel a word now? A long-winded feller could cost himself a great deal of the auld spondoolacs."

"And what did ye say?"

"*Ma's dead.*"

"That's it? Yer only livin mother who worked her poor fingers to the nub to provide fer ye, gone to her reward, may the good Lord bless her soul, and all ye can say is 'Ma's dead'?"

"The very thing the tellygraph feller sez. 'See here,' he sez, 'a mother's got a right to a proper hewlogy. I'll give ye three more words, *gratis*.'"

"*Gratis*, is it?"

"That's Latin fer ye don't have to pay."

"I know what it *manes*, ye great flamin eejit. What did ye add to yer tellygram?"

"*Ma's dead. Bed fer sale.*"

A big thunk on the bass drum as Pat gives Mike a roundhouse smack, Mike rolling backward and springing up on his feet to join Pat, singing and jigging as the orchestra backs them with the tune—

Mrs. Murphy had a party
Just about a week ago
Everything was plentiful
The Murphys they're not slow

"What do you say, Brother?" Niles continues hopefully, turning to Harry and looking especially repentant. "You know what a hopeless case I am with finances."

Harry decides to make him work for it a little. "How much?"

"Whatever you can spare."

"Have you talked to the Judge?"

Niles shakes his head, grinning. "No blood coming out of that stone."

The bicycle shop has been doing well for him the last few years, word that he's a wizard with a wheel spreading beyond the city, and he's put quite a pile aside. But Niles—he's seen Niles throw away a twenty-dollar double eagle on a single roll of the dice, throw away more in one sitting than the wheel shop takes in for a month.

"I could part with ten," says Harry.

Niles makes a pained face.

Harry knows that there is no way to gauge what his own expenses will be if he really makes the break and goes up north, how long it might take to get himself situated. He tries to hold firm.

"Ten dollars," he says, "if you promise to pay me back on the first."

McGinty he got roaring drunk
His eyes were bulging out
He jumped on the pianer
And loudly he did shout—

Niles has never paid him back a dime, not on any of the loans over the years, so it is as good as gone. The sky, he knows, is not the limit for Niles. His brother crosses his arms and stares darkly at the stage, sulking.

"Who put the overalls in Mrs. Murphy's chowder?"
Nobody answered, so he shouted all the louder
"It's an Oirish trick it's true
And I'll lick the Mick that threw
The overalls in Mrs. Murphy's chowder!"

"Like our Board of Aldermen," grumbles Niles, "but with more dignity." Before he broke off with Mae, Niles had considered a career in politics.

"Most men step into public life from another profession," the Judge observed when this design was revealed, "with allegiances and rivalries already forged in the world at large. Since you are as yet—*in*nocent of employment," and here he raised his eyebrows the way he does when lecturing a convicted man from the bench, "you will be free to defraud the citizenry without encumbrance."

The lights rise again on the minstrels.

"Brother Tambo!" calls the Interlocutor. "Explain to me why you were tardy for tonight's presentation."

"Well, suh," explains the tambourine man, "I's on my way here when I's accosted by a whole mess a young boys."

"Ruffians."

"Little bitty ones. They was wearin sho't pants."

"You mean knickers?"

"Nawsuh, they was white boys."

This one earns the biggest laugh of the night. Harry looks back up to the left rear balcony and they are laughing too, mostly sports out on the town for the night, a few with their hats still on their heads. He has been to tent shows where the numbers have been reversed, five colored to every white man, but those were with real colored on the stage. It was Niles who dragged him to his first nigger show at the Thalian, sneaking in late and staying in the back in hopes they would not be spotted and reported to the Judge. In the afterpiece one of the actors descended from the ceiling wearing angel wings and Harry had been more fascinated with that, with the mechanics of how it was done, than with any of the jokes or songs or travesties played out on the boards.

"Brother Tambo, how would you like to earn a dollar?"

The end man's eyes bug out even more. "Is it 'lection day awready?"

Righteous applause from the fair-skinned patrons. The sports in Nigger Heaven are not amused.

*   *   *

There is furniture in the room Royal doesn't have a name for. He has never been in a white man's house, rich or poor, but his mother is in them now and then to take the laundry and he has read books. Is that a divan or a credenza? Or maybe a credenza is a kind of piano, like the one Jessie is resting her hand upon, smiling slightly, standing in her white dress like somebody is painting her portrait.

"We've been the first called, I believe," says Junior, "because they think we're immune."

"Immune to what?"

Dr. Lunceford is the most intimidating man Royal has ever met, black or white, despite his soft tone and his manners. Sergeant Jacks with his forehead resting on your own, screaming instruction and insult, breath hot on your face, has got nothing compared to this man's gaze. *Why, exactly, are you in my house?* it asks when he smiles and grips your hand. *You don't really belong here, do you?* it suggests as he inquires about your training and destination.

"To tropical diseases," says Junior.

"That's nonsense."

"A prejudice perhaps, but one that works in our favor. This is a grand opportunity. Fighting for the flag, shoulder to shoulder with our white brothers in arms, freeing the oppressed Cuban from his bondage—"

"You really think it will happen?"

"A foregone conclusion. The explosion in the harbor—"

Dr. Lunceford turns to Royal. "And what do you think?"

Royal is surprised by the sudden question. He glances to Junior, who smiles and nods to him to get on with it.

"I enlisted to follow the flag, sir." He can't quite see Jessie out of the corner of his eye. "If hostilities commence—China, Cuba, the red men straying from their agencies—we will do our duty."

"People look up to the man in uniform," says Junior. Junior has told him of the Doctor's disapproval of his enlistment, shown him the letters full of underlined words. "If we are to take our rightful position in this nation, we must be ready to defend it."

"As a private in the infantry."

"You used to call it Mr. Lincoln's Army."

They are all still standing, all but Mrs. Lunceford, who sits in her chair by the silk-covered whatever it is called, a pleasant smile on her face.

"I think he looks splendid, Aaron," she says. "We should be proud."

"Mr. Lincoln," the Doctor continues, seeming to ignore her, "gone these many years, turned to colored troops only as a desperate measure."

Alma Moultrie steps in with a tray bearing wine and glasses, lays them on a small table that probably has a special name too.

"They both look splendid."

Royal turns to smile at Mrs. Lunceford and sees that Jessie is looking at him, an unwavering gaze much like her father's, but there is no challenge in it. Only what—? Admiration? He feels her in the room even when he can't see her.

"We're regulars, sir," he says. "Professional soldiers. If war is declared, the volunteers, whoever they are, will have to wait their turn."

"So you're spoiling for a fight?" Again the gaze, challenging, unblinking. *And what have you to do with my son's reckless decision, young man?*

"If a fight presents itself, we've been trained to handle it."

The others, the veterans, give the rookies no end of razzing about how green they are, about their lack of experience, their lack of the true stuff, how they will turn tail and run at the first angry shot. Junior, immune to every hint that he should hide his breeding or at least not wave it around in public, is their special target. Royal hopes for a fight, if only to break up the boredom of drill and detail that makes up their days in the regiment.

"Put a little water in Jessie's glass before you pour, Alma," says Dr. Lunceford. "I suppose we have to drink a toast to these young fools."

Junior is beaming. Royal can tell, no matter how stiff and strange these people are, that something has happened between his friend and Dr. Lunceford, an acceptance of some kind. There must be a word for it, a word that means only that thing that has happened and nothing else, but he doesn't know what it is.

Niles remains tight and distant as the minstrels reappear and trade a few more jokes and then exit gaudily, cakewalking out to *There'll Be a Hot Time in the Old Town Tonight*. He holds the pose, never once laughing or commenting during the olios, not when the soubrette reappears in front of the curtain to sing *On the Banks of the Wabash* or the equilibrist and his lovely assistant Rose who tosses Indian clubs for him to juggle while rolling precariously along the edge of the orchestra pit atop a huge medicine ball or the tenor back with a beautiful rendition of *Silver Hairs Among the Gold* that has Harry teary-eyed again or even Gerta Wetzel the Human Pretzel and her grotesque bar act that has the audience wincing and turning their heads away at the most extreme of the contortions or the little fellow in leather breeches and campaign hat who is introduced as the Great Teethadore who Harry supposes is meant to be Roosevelt of New York. The little man's routine, high-stepping in place and singing *If Uncle Sam Goes Marching into Cuba*, is the only one that doesn't draw even polite applause, the local folks not sure if it is meant to be funny or patriotic. Niles is still stewing when Perfessor Scipio Africanus steps out for his lecture.

It is Brother Bones again, only now he is wearing the Interlocutor's frock coat, gripping on to the lapels and striking an orator's pose. "Ladies and gennlemens, extinguished guests," he begins, "the tropic of my discoursation tonight is entitled 'The Enfranchisement of the Lower Orders,' or 'How come we gots to let them Irish vote?'"

Niles snorts a little laugh through his nose.

"It has come to my retention," the Perfessor continues, "that this fair city—" and here he pauses to look up at the sports in the balcony, "—aint near as *fair* as it might be."

The colored sports thinks this is funny, slapping hands on the railing and on each other's backs. *"Doesn't nobody but trash go to those shows,"* Alma used to say when she was still with the family, before the incident with Niles. But maybe she only meant among her own people, for nobody in Wilmington would think of Judge Manigault's boys or the Lassiters or the Bellamys or the de Rossets, all well represented here tonight by their younger generations, as trash. Harry misses Alma—the new one Judge has hired can't cook much and is painful to look at, with some sort of goiter sticking out on her neck.

"Leastways it don't look so fair if you is hangin roun City Hall waitin fo a handout or one a them gummint jobs what used to go to members of the Caucasian Persuasion."

It is maybe too uncomfortably true to get much of a laugh, thinks Harry, but somebody has clearly done their advance work.

"But what I caint unnerstan is how this great big ole city, the largest metropopulist in the Old North State, has got itself one hunnid an sixty-nine saloons and houses of ill dispute—an I been to em *all*, fokes—but only *five* mayors."

This breaks the house up. There are, in fact, at least five distinct slates of mayor and aldermen claiming the reins of the city, including the one the Judge is backing that just suffered defeat in a Raleigh courtroom. The Judge has no use for the bunch declared winners by the governor, and can rant for hours about the hell there will be to pay if they are allowed to serve out the full two years left in their term.

"This yere is a sorrowful state of affairs," says the Perfessor, "an I intends to correctify it by thowin my *own* hat into the ring—as soon as I pawns it back fum Mist' Miller."

Niles starts to giggle. He owes money to Miller, quite a bit, and has made Harry swear never to reveal to the Judge that his son is in debt to a colored man.

"As the sixth or seventh mayor of this fine city, I promises to do my nut-most to put a chicken in every pot—and for them what aint got no pot, we's passin em out down to Repubikin Hindquarters tomorrow mo'nin."

"Ten dollars, then," says Niles, affably, and holds his hand out without taking his eyes off the stage, as if ten dollars is nothing, as if the hundreds before, yes, it must be hundreds now, have been a passing trifle. Harry feels strange, exchanging money in a public place like a carnival tout, but digs out the bill and lays it in his brother's hand.

"An since the Consternation of the United States says how it's the perjor-ity of the people what gets to call the shots, I promises to insinuate Negro Abomination here in Wimminton!"

Boos and hisses now, not all of them good-natured. The Perfessor holds his ground.

"The white fokes has abominated the political spear here in Wimminton long enough, and all they done so far has been to run the jint down to its present state of putrification, their gummint caricatured by pecuniary mis-feasances and gross incontinence. Now it's *our* toin!"

More boos, though a few shout *Amen* from the balcony. Fun is fun, but it is possible to cut too close to the bone.

"I spose they's a good number of you fokes out there considers youself Confederates."

Cheers and rebel yells answer this. Niles looks around with shining eyes as the boys downstairs, most of them his old friends, hoot and stomp their feet. Their daddy, the Judge, fought for the Great Lost Cause, as did any man of his generation with two legs and ballocks hanging between them. The comedian has touched a nerve.

"An I is a former advocate of the Fusionist Party."

Booing again. The Fusionists are the alliance of carpetbagger, nigger-cosseting Republicans and poor white Populists who dominated local poli-tics in the last election.

"So I suggests we jine together an forms a co-lition betwixt the Confederates and the Fusionists—we call it the Confusionist Party."

It is good enough to get most of them back on his side. If people get this het up over a pretend colored politician, Harry thinks, what will they do if a real one appears?

"Cause politics in Wimminton is the con*fu*sinist thing I ever try to wrap my nappy head around!"

Applause now, people conceding the truth of his point.

"If any of you fine peoples," the Perfessor finishes, "care to hear the rest of my perambulation, I can be foun at the Abysinnian Embassy—Fo'th Street, co'ner of Bladen."

The Darktown address gets the Perfessor a nice laugh to part with, the curtain beginning to rise before he is fully into the wings.

There is a battleship upon the stage.

Coop has done it in a carriage before, but never with springs like this. Usually they creak and groan, bringing out a lot of shushing from the gal, as if anybody from the house could hear. White people's carriages. It always give him a little thrill, to think of the Mister and maybe even the white Missus parking their bottoms where his bare black ass been only hours before, busy at what they never want to imagine. Sweet Alma is on him, big warm breasts nestling his cheeks, rolling on him slow and tight and the leather against his ass so soft and warm. And these springs. A quiet ride, that's what it is—if he ever runs into old Wicklow again he'll have to compliment the man. Alma grips the back of the seat and presses close to him, smelling like cinnamon, calling him Clarence, Clarence baby, but that's okay because there's no one else to hear, not even the coach horse like a few times in white folks' barns, grinding their oats without interest only a stall panel away. Maybe that's how he'll do it, he thinks, be Coop with the Indian gals by the Fort or whatever ones you can buy in Cuba if they go, be Coop for the stripes and the brass and the white men and the whole damn world you got to bow down to, and save Clarence, save the real man, for a sweet pretty woman like Alma Moultrie.

"Darlin," he says to her, her big eyes drinking him in, the carriage rocking ever so slightly but with no complaint from the springs, "I been needing this for so long."

*   *   *

The battleship rocks on plasterboard seas, and there is an intake of breath followed by a hum of comment as people recognize it as the *Maine.* It is only scrim, of course, unpainted but with the details somehow projected from behind it. Harry smiles at the relatively crude wave effect at its base, two long cutouts of blue swells that rise and fall rhythmically against each other to create a peaceful, safe-harbor illusion.

The operetta begins with the tenor up on deck in his uniform and Dolly St. Claire below, isolated in a spotlight extreme stage left, trading verses as the light turns golden sunset yellow—

Just a song at twilight, when the lights are low
And the flickering shadows—softly come and go

—the soubrette back home thinking of her loved one as he does the same on board in Havana's harbor.

The *Maine.* Harry has studied the pictures, has read the accounts of witnesses and experts, and entertains the possibility that it was nothing but a boiler bursting to disastrous result, an unsurprising phenomenon given the enormous pressure brought upon rivet and seam in the massive steam-powered vessels. They are floating bombs, as every engineer will agree—but a torpedo in the night and an underhanded foe make for better newspaper circulation.

The soubrette and the tenor, called Aura Lee and Ensign Tom in the program, join in harmony for the last chorus—

Though the heart be weary, sad the day and long
Still to us at twilight comes love's old song
Comes love's old sweet song

"Excuse me, old boy," says Niles, rising. "Got to put out a fire."

It is a joke between them, recalling the first time the Judge took them on a hunt, and to entertain themselves after the day's killing was through and the men had begun drinking they wandered back into the thick pines and Niles started a fire in the underbrush using the magnifying glass he'd got for his birthday and they tried to put it out with their own water. Each had consumed a full canteen of lemonade during the day and felt bloated enough to irrigate a cotton field in July, but the fire had outrun their ability to pee on it and the men had to be called to avoid disaster.

"Boys do what boys do," the Judge had said, leading them deeper into the woods away from the smoke and the mocking hunters, "and men do what men do." They had supposed he was going to cut a switch and have at them with it, choosing an isolated spot either to spare them public humiliation or preclude intervention if he was truly furious, but he only stopped and took his own out and proceeded to relieve himself for what seemed like the better part of an hour. No words were spoken, just the splatter of almost clear liquid onto dry leaves, the Judge staring into the distance with a placid look on his face.

"I would hope you boys have learned something about fire today," he said when he'd led them almost all the way back to camp, "and something about bourbon."

Old Uncle Zip, who had belonged to the Judge's family before the Invasion and still served as guide for the hunting trips, came to them later with some praline candies he'd smuggled along. He sat on a log with them, sharing the candies, chuckling and shaking his head. "Don't you boys worry none," he told them. "The Judge boint down the backhouse at his daddy farm in Delco tryin the same speriment. An he uz years older than either of you."

Harry watches Niles apologize to the last patron in the row and head back up the aisle. It is unlikely he will return, concocting some story about an old friend met in the lobby the next time they see each other, an old friend in some sort of a scrape that called for immediate assistance. The invitation to join him at the show has been a pretense, of course, a maneuver to put Harry in a genial mood and in a spot where raised voices and recriminations would draw the wrong sort of attention. Niles is devious, but so consistent in his ways as to be transparent.

Captain Sigsbee, played by the runt who looks like Roosevelt wearing a white beard and moustache, orders the young officer to undertake a vital and perilous mission—transporting a message from the President of Our Great Nation past the vicious minions of the Butcher Weyler, through the steaming Cuban jungles, and into the hand of the wily insurgent general, brave Calixto García. Captain and Ensign hold their hats over their hearts to sing *The Army of the Free*—

> *For the people of America*
> *We're marching in the van*
> *And will do the work before us*
> *If the bravest sailors can*
> *We will drive the despot's forces*
> *From their strongholds to the sea*
> *And will live and die together*
> *In the Army of the Free—*

It is a yankee war song, of course, but Harry can feel the audience downstairs loosen to it as they hear the altered lyrics. Who does not want to be a part of the Army of the Free? A few of the colored sports in the balcony are singing along, and it is a stirring moment. As he sings, the tenor exchanges his navy jacket for a torn shirt and places a battered sombrero on his head, climbing from deck to floor on a rope ladder. His Captain sings the final verse alone, an audible gasp of amazement from the audience as the massive white hull of the *Maine* suddenly melts into a green and brown tangle of jungle—

We will shield our steadfast brothers
Neath the Flag of Liberty
And will live and die together
In the Army of the Free!

The tenor swings a machete and walks in place as the jungle behind him moves in the opposite direction, creating the illusion of travel, the pianist creeping along suspensefully on the bass keys.

A shot rings out, the tenor beginning to run in place as the orchestra leaps into a breakneck snatch of the overture from Rossini's *William Tell,* the bows seeming to ricochet off the strings, a stirring, galloping chase motif as two Spanish sentries appear from the wings in pursuit. The jungle behind is nearly a blur now and Harry realizes it must be some manner of diapositive projection that can be twirled at varying speeds, operated behind the translucent hull of the "ship." One of the Spaniards raises his rifle and fires again and the tenor, wounded in the leg, drops to the ground.

The jungle scenery jerks to a halt, the sentries catching up to take Ensign Tom prisoner.

"Ay, Señor," says one of the sentries, "soon ju will weesh ju was never born."

Jessie has read all the books. The ones her tutors have insisted on, Miss Alcott and Mrs. Stowe, and the ones Alma gives her that she keeps hidden beneath the mattress—Charlotte Brame, Metta Victor, and her favorite, Laura Jean Libbey. There are no young ladies of color like her in the books, only a few dusky parlor maids meant to portray someone of Alma's station, but as she reads she imagines herself in the position of the heroines and by the end of the tale Nell Lestrange or poor Minnie Taylor or Little Rosebud are no longer so pale.

It is from the books and from Alma's chatter and from the cautionary lectures with which her mother describes the world that Jessie has learned there is but one great adventure open to women.

And that hers has begun.

It was true! What her brother had said was true! He was not above teasing her, despite the moustache he had so recently grown her brother was still a boy in many ways, with a boy's fondness for pranks and mischief. But when he had said of his handsome fellow soldier "He inquires of you constantly," her hopes had been raised, and when the young man stood in their parlor, shy and self-effacing, her pulse had quickened so alarmingly she was afraid it would betray her, that her father, with his physician's skill of diagnosis, would at once sense her infatuation. And she felt a fool, cheeks burning with shame, for at first the young man seemed barely to recognize her presence, exchanging polite conversation with her father, hat at rest in the crook of his arm, stiff with a military bearing that only enhanced his good looks. But his words at their parting—

"I hope to see you again."

He had said that, he really had, looking straight into her eyes when he took her hand and bowed slightly to say goodbye. Junior was worried about missing the transport and Mother was in tears to see her boy go off possibly to war and Father was cramming in every last bit of advice, which gave them, Royal and Jessie—it makes her flush now, lying back on her bed, just to intertwine their names in her thoughts—gave them an almost private moment. He held her hand much longer than you would if she was wrong about it and he squeezed it, he did, she wasn't fooling herself about that. Yes, he was saying with that squeeze, you are right. I am too.

They had been children together, he a few years the elder and wonderful in her eyes, sitting bareback high up on their coach horse Boots while his uncle dealt with the harness straps. He let her play with his jacks and his marbles, and pet the field animals he found and cared for awhile, and never taunted her the way some others did for being female or for her manners or for her abrupt departure from their games when it was time for the day's lesson. And then one day it was over, Mother explaining that she was a young lady now and must learn to dwell in a more prescribed environment, to leave that easy camaraderie of bare feet and imaginary battles behind. Sometimes she would look off from her piano bench, out the window to the side yard, and he would be there, watching her. His clothes were threadbare but always clean, his shoes no doubt several generations removed from their original owner, but there was a dignity in him, calm and kindly, that stirred her in the genteel prison of her parents' fine house.

Junior says he'll send an address as soon as they've got one and that Royal will send his own letters through Alma. Without Alma she would be lost. Father has his ideas of what is right for his daughter and he means the best for her but it is *her* adventure, her only one, and she knows from the books and from Alma's lurid stories what happens to girls who ignore their heart and think only of what is sensible. His chest looked massive in the blue uniform, his arms thick and muscular, his hands—she has always loved his hands, loved to watch them at work. Once he let her help him and his brother Jubal groom Boots after a long day's riding and they had barely spoken, just the sound of the brush on the animal's coat, the smell of horse strong in her nose and them standing close together, hot in the crowded stall and she thought her thumping heart would explode. Jessie thinks of his arms around her and rolls over onto her front and wonders if this is wicked, wonders what it must be like to be Alma, whose life has been so filled with men, so filled with adventure compared to Mother's placid account of her brief season of availability, married at seventeen with not a ripple of excitement between courtship and contract.

When she touches herself, or presses her body hard against the bed, she imagines she is Alma. Alma can do what she pleases, so little is expected of her. But Dr. Lunceford's daughter—

"*Every eye is upon you,*" he has told them, Junior most prominent under his judging gaze but Jessie just behind and included in the statement. "*Your actions reflect on us all.*"

And she knows the "us all" goes beyond the Luncefords, beyond even the proper colored community here in Wilmington. But Alma, when she is Alma she can be every thrilling thing she might imagine.

There will be a war. Her brother is sure of it, all Father's friends look forward to it, the newspapers seem to ache for its commencement. The thought of those brave boys on the field of battle, suffering under the enemy's fire, the thought of many of them never to return—but he will survive, he will return. The mortal danger only deepens her resolve to discover a method, first, to communicate her love to him, and then to win Mother and Father to her design. Or, failing, to throw herself into the hands of Fate.

The melodrama continues.

Ensign Tom, horribly tortured by the cruel Dagoes, is warned of their monstrous plot, then helped to escape by a dusky Cuban girl. The stage is black for a moment, then a spotlight catches the beaten, bloodied tenor crawling to freedom across the ground as a single cello echoes his plight. He reaches the wings and the light fades up again on the *Maine*, a single Jack Tar walking the deck on watch, as below, out of his sight, a sinister pair of Spanish saboteurs row out and attach a device—it looks like a metallic limpet—to the prow of the anchored ship. The sailor does not seem to hear the loud warning from the audience, Harry perhaps loudest of all, nor the call from the bedraggled Ensign who has only just arrived at the shore, does not see the sinister boatmen row away into the wings leaving their infernal machine, does not sense anything but the gentle rocking of the great vessel and the orchestra's sweet lullaby until—

KABOOM!

Harry levitates with the rest of the audience, his bottom lifting completely out of his seat at the shock of the explosion, black smoke filling the stage, the white hull of the great ship suddenly engulfed in leaping red and orange flames! Many have risen to their feet in the audience, a few already bolted into the aisles, before they realize it is only another illusion, powerful stagecraft, the conflagration nothing but colored celluloid and projected light. The waves beneath the ship are churning, faster, higher, and there are at least a dozen poor sailors flailing within them, crying out for help that will not come. Harry thinks of the stage direction at the end of the one theatrical he has had a hand in producing—*Tumult with all.*

The smoke clears, some of it drifting out over the first rows, and the hull of the *Maine* is now a verdant field sown with the white crosses of the dead, the rows trailing off in a forced perspective as the strings in the pit weep. The Ensign, back in uniform, and his sweet Aura Lee have been reunited, each with a black band of mourning on their arm. They stroll solemnly along, regarding the simple stone monuments. A small girl with a bouquet of white gladiolas in hand turns and sees them, and tugs at the arm of the naval man. It is the lovely assistant Rose again, dressed in pinafore and sun hat, and it seems that she can sing as well—

My father was a sailor just like you
My father was a sailor and wore a coat of blue
My father was a sailor and I'll ne'er see him again
My father was a sailor sir, a sailor on the Maine

As always it is the innocents who suffer. Harry feels that his cheeks are wet and is glad that Niles is not here to kid him for being a sap. Handkerchiefs flash among the seats ahead. Captain Sigsbee appears then, beginning to speak to the Ensign and Aura Lee, but then turning to face the audience and address them directly. An offstage chorus softly hums a familiar melody.

"We will not allow these brave men to have died in vain," says the

Captain. "We will snatch up the torch of liberty from their fallen hand and raise it, raise it on high over that poor, benighted island that lies below our southern shore. We will battle the forces of greed and cruelty, we will rout the decadent European from his imperial lair and bring the shining light of freedom into this dark corner of the world—"

Harry recognizes the melody now, as the voices humming it grow louder—it is *The Stars and Stripes Forever* that Sousa has made such a hit with.

"For we are *Americans*—north and south, east and west—and Americans will not long allow the iron boot of tyranny to trample upon their hemisphere! The sacrifice of these brave men shall be repaid in blood a hundred times o'er, heroes arising from all corners of our great land to strike fear into the hearts of despots everywhere! *Cuba Libre*! Down with treachery! REMEMBER THE *MAINE*!"

Every piece in the orchestra is a part of it now, drums pounding, brass blaring proudly, fifes trilling above it all, and the players, all of them, march onstage in uniform, no blackened faces among their ranks, singing out as the cemetery view gives way to their country's banner, enormous, red, white, and blue—

Hurrah for the flag of the free!
May it wave as our standard forever
The gem of the land and the sea
The banner of the Right

Harry is weeping with pride now and can see he's not the only one. Somehow they have done it, have brought all of Thalian Hall to tears by hoisting the yankee flag. Maybe it is a dream the others have kept quiet in their hearts the way he has, that something could bring the sections together, that they could march shoulder to shoulder once more on some gallant quest, could live up to the fine words of their common Fathers and clear the foul stain of contention from their souls. He wishes Niles was here to see this, to *feel* this. People are on their feet on the ground floor and in the balconies, clapping and stomping time and singing along in full voice—

Let despots remember the day
When our fathers with mighty endeavor
Proclaimed as they marched from the fray
That by their might
And by their right
It waves forever!

* * *

Niles is halfway to Dock Street when the pony gig pulls up beside him. It is Bramley Dupree, and he is smiling.

"The reports of your death have been premature."

"Wishful thinking, I suppose," says Niles, looking as penitent as possible. "Hop in."

Bramley is a game one, always up for high times, and probably made those threats purely for the sake of form. One's sister is one's sister, after all, and not to be trifled with. Niles sits next to him and he switches the pony into motion.

"If you're headed to one of the coon houses," says Bramley, "you'll have to direct me."

"*Touché.*" For a time the lads had taken to calling him Nigger Niles because of his predilection, but as it was the kind of thing which would eventually reach the Judge's ears he had curtailed the habit. "Actually, I was just taking a stroll."

"Searching for poor girls to dishonor."

Bramley is still smiling, watching ahead as they turn onto Dock.

"And how is your sister faring?" Niles asks, deepening his voice with concern.

"Extremely married."

"To Horton Lassiter."

"Yes."

"That I am truly sorry for," Niles says as Bramley stops the gig in front of Mitchell Bannion's resort. "Is he as—as *moist* as ever?"

"A veritable swamp of a man. It is no wonder that Mae has been taken with the vapors lately."

"I am a degenerate and bounder. But she is far better off without me."

"No doubt."

"You're stepping in for your medicine?"

"Poker tournament. Quite a few familiar faces."

"No thank you." Niles had, in fact, been heading for the House of All Nations to see if the medium-dark one with the spectacular aftworks was still there. It was all Alma's fault, really, or the Judge's, for having her bathe him till he was old enough for schooling. The way the sweat would run down between her breasts, the sweet fullness of her lips, her voice—

"I've never known Niles Manigault to turn his back on a game of chance," says Bramley.

Niles shrugs as he steps down to the street. "I'm tapped out, old boy. Tried to put the nip on my brother Harry, but he wouldn't hear it."

"And no chest of gold from the Frozen North."

"I'm lucky to return with all my toes."

"Hold out your hand." Bramley digs in his coat pocket, then clinks five Morgan dollars into his palm. "With a touch of moderation, that should last you all night. Or until I win them back from you."

"You would have made an excellent brother-in-law."

"You'd have ruined me, Niles."

Niles slips the coins in next to Harry's bill and follows Bramley into the saloon. The House of All Nations stays open till dawn.

They stand and cheer for many minutes after, Harry sniffing back the water-works, so moved that if he was of whole body he would rush out to find a recruiter and sign on for the fight. The orchestra continues to play as the curtain falls, and finally people begin to file out. Harry waits till the aisle ahead is mostly clear, then grabs his hat and hobbles quickly up to the stage. He tries not to use his cane in public, saving it for occasions that require a great deal of walking.

Peachpit is guarding the steps to backstage.

"Evenin, Mist' Harry. Enjoy the show?"

The old man had smallpox as a boy, his cheeks and neck cratered with scars.

"I thought I might take a look at the apparatus."

Peachpit begins to shake his head. "What they tole me, Suh, is—"

"I won't bother the players. I'd just like to see that ship."

"Well, if that's all it is—" Peachpit steps aside and Harry climbs past him. Going down stairs presents more of a problem for him than going up. "I's awful sorry to hear about your brother."

"What did you hear?"

"Word is he was kilt by one of them polar bears in the gold rush."

"He's still with us, I'm afraid," Harry calls as he steps around the curtain. "He was here tonight."

"Praise the Lord," says the old man, pressing his palms together in thanks. "Snatched from the jaws of perdition."

Backstage, a gang of men slide the enormous scrim that made the ship's hull toward the wings, its frame slotted into a groove set with bearings.

Harry loses his balance trying to keep out of their way and stumbles backward into a small man who seems not to have a task among the swarming stagehands.

Teethadore steadies the fellow and leads him to a safer spot. He recognizes the type—a small-city Reuben dazzled by the footlights.

"I'm afraid that the young ladies aren't receiving visitors," he says. "They'll be rushing off to get their beauty rest."

"I was actually more interested in the device," says the rube. There is something wrong with his legs, the sole of one shoe inches thicker than the other. "Whatever you used to make the background views."

"Ah," smiles Teethadore. "An *aficionado* of the illusory arts. Come with me."

He wears a thicker sole himself, both sides equal, on his street shoes. Stature does not betoken character, of course, but at times the supplementary altitude is most welcome.

"Did you enjoy our little extravaganza?"

"Very much so." The local fellow is still rubbernecking as they make their way through the maze of props and scenery. "Your turn as Roosevelt was striking."

Teethadore beams. They all warned him not a soul in Dixie would grasp the reference. "You're familiar with our former governor?"

"No, actually, I've never been to New York—"

"Never been? What a tragedy."

"I expect I'll be going there soon."

"Bully!" Teethadore presents him with one of his cards. "If we've completed our tour of the southlands by that time, you'll have to look me up."

"*Teethadore the Great,*" reads the young man. "*Actor, songster, and dialectician. Stoddard F. Brisbane—*"

"My given name. Civilians call me Brizz."

"Civilians—?"

"As opposed to thespians." He winks. "We have our own little rituals. A bit like the Masonic Code."

The young man offers his hand. "Harry Manigault."

"A pleasure. And this," he says as they come to the device, "is the font of all our magic."

Harry Manigault bends, hands on knees, to peer at the apparatus. The beam remains fixed, pointing toward the audience, while the turret it is housed in can be cranked around in a complete circle, with a slot in which either a single diapositive can be fixed, like the flag or the cemetery scene, or the continuous vista of jungle made by gluing several views into a strip.

"The coloring was beautifully done," says Harry, giving the crank a little turn.

"You're a Kodak bug, no doubt?"

"I built my own stereopticon when I was twelve."

"Impressive."

Young Harry shrugs. "Merely an application of the principle of binocular vision." He picks up the fan of colored celluloid the stagehands wave in front of the beam to project the fire. "I'm working on a machine now, something like a zoopraxiscope, only—"

"Reinventing the wheel, are we?"

"It's a sound principal. And if you've only got access to normal cameras—"

"I know Dickson."

Harry Manigault lays the color fan down. "Mr. Edison's Dickson?"

Teethadore smiles. "Dickson, Brown, Paley, the whole gang of them over in Jersey. I made a comic view with them—portraying Governor Roosevelt on one of his hunting expeditions. Quite a droll scenario with a shotgun and a small bear in a tree."

"I've never seen the moving ones—"

"We use them for *entr'actes* in our New York performances. But on the road—the equipment is difficult to maintain."

"It's only a kinetoscope, what could be difficult—?"

"You should speak to our stage manager, Mr. Giles."

"I should."

A keen fellow, not at all what he expected to find in this section. Teethadore adjusts the spectacles he has begun to affect, the lenses only clear glass but the resemblance uncanny when he puts them on and flashes his choppers. "I trust that the temperance biddies have held no sway in your city?"

"You'd like a drink?" asks Harry.

"Sir," Teethadore replies, spreading his arms in his *Need you ask?* gesture, "I am an *actor*."

Afterward, when the breeze through her window cools her mind, Jessie lies hugging her pillow in her arms. Alma has left her now, she is Jessie again and she is holding him, just holding.

"Royal," she says out loud, as loud as she dares, and knows that in the saying of it she is forever transformed.

*   *   *

Crows are in the sycamore, already rasping their cries, when the Judge is awakened by banging at his door. The girl, the new one, doesn't come till seven, and he is greatly out of sorts by the time he finds his slippers and makes it down to see what the racket is.

Maxwell stands at the door, looking red-eyed and sheepish.

"Sorry, Judge." Maxwell is a competent clerk, but believes he can still burn the candle at both ends.

"What calamity, may I ask, can possibly merit waking me at this hour?"

"It's your son," he says, not quite meeting the Judge's eyes. "There's a—a situation brewing that I felt you should be informed of."

He knows not to ask which one it is. Even if he hadn't seen Harry drag in late last night with whiskey on his breath and preposterous schemes of northern travel on his mind, he would know it was Niles. Three children and only the daughter with a speck of common sense. "Where is he?"

"One of the resorts on Dock Street. I just happened by on my way to—"

"He's in one piece, I take it?" Maxwell lacks the somber cast of the bearer of truly bad tidings. This is some new embarrassment.

"Presently, yes. But imprecations have been forwarded, ultimatums delivered—it involves a sum of money."

"He's been playing cards."

"Unfortunately. And imbibing, Your Honor, or else I'm sure his judgment would have—"

"Niles hasn't any more judgment than a cat in a fish shack. How much has he lost?"

"Thirty-five dollars. Beyond what he carried to the table."

"These card sharps don't believe I'm good for thirty-five dollars?"

Maxwell looks down at his shoes, which seem to have had something spilled on them. "They don't believe your son is good for his word. Apparently he's mentioned your name in association with gaming debts in the past, and—and failed to inform you—"

"They could have come to me directly."

"Given the nature of some of the debts, of the *loci* in which they were incurred, the gentlemen involved were reticent to bring—to bring an officer of the Court into the conversation."

"There are no 'gentlemen' involved in this business. They are a group of ruffians, holding my son for ransom—"

"They've convinced Niles it would be unwise to depart before matters are settled."

It is a cold morning. The Judge turns back into the parlor. "Thirty-five dollars."

"Cash would be appreciated. Under the circumstances."

He turns back to glare at Maxwell. The man looks as if he has slept in his clothing. There is a stain on his bowler and he is shaking slightly, frightened perhaps of his employer, or merely chilled without an overcoat at this hour.

"I would not have become involved," he says apologetically, "but for the fear of scandal."

"Everybody in Wilmington knows he's a damned fool, Maxwell. Wait while I go up to the safe."

In his dream Harry is sitting by Mae Dupree, holding her hand as they watch the operetta. It is a moving-view of the performance, projected on her parlor wall, the image thrown by a device that Harry operates by cranking it with his free hand. Somehow, and even in the dream he wishes he could stop the presentation to study the workings of it, the device is ganged through a bicycle sprocket and chain to a phonograph machine, the needle riding a wax cylinder to play the duet of the Ensign and the lovely Aura Lee, their words perfectly synchronized with the movement of their lips—

He understands that he has invented this device, understands it without being told, as one does in dreams, and can feel how proud Mae is of him. The show continues on the parlor wall, only now Niles is the Ensign and Mae the soubrette, embracing as they sing.

But the most amazing thing, the Harry in the dream shaking his head in wonder as he sits and cranks, is how someone has perfectly hand-colored every single one of the diapositive frames, and how they've captured the exact reddish-gold of Mae Dupree's beautiful hair.

The Judge sits at breakfast trying to avoid the sight of the new girl's deformity when Niles steps in, treading softly.

"I am so very sorry," he says, gesturing with his hat. Beulah, for that is her name, retreats to the kitchen after a quick glance at the boy's blackened eye and bloodstained shirt front.

"You are sorry you lost," says the Judge, spreading quince jam on his toast, "and you are sorry you couldn't skulk away without settling your losses. Beyond that, you are incorrigible."

The Judge's wife, young and beautiful, almost died giving birth to this boy. Niles was always impervious to instruction, beating him a waste of belt leather, and so far the vagaries of life in the world outside have in no way clipped his wings.

The Judge fixes Niles with a look. "You know my opinion of our governor."

Niles ventures a tiny grin. "Something about a fat, treacherous, nigger-coddling son of a whore, I believe—"

"Then you understand what it will cost me in pride, not to mention political favor, to petition him in your behalf."

"Petition?"

"They're making up the regiment for Cuba. Commissions are being handed out—"

"I'm in the Light Infantry here already."

"We're not discussing a club membership. There is going to be a war. I doubt it will amount to much, as wars go, but there are reputations to be made, mettle to be tested. By God, if a dose of combat won't make a man of you, I don't know what will."

"They'll never leave the state," says Niles. "You know that. It's all a show, a bowl of plums for our corpulent governor to pass out to his cronies."

"You won't serve your country?"

"Half the men in that poker game are set to be in the Regiment. Is that the sort you want me associating with?"

He has an answer for everything, Niles. With a minimum of study he'd make a passable lawyer, of the type who waste the Judge's courtroom hours with showy but ultimately pointless objections and points of order. The Judge pushes his plate away and looks his son in the eye.

"You told me you very nearly struck it rich in the Yukon."

"I found the ore," says Niles, making one of his aggrieved, I-am-but-a-victim faces, "but they jumped my claim."

"Perhaps it's time you gave it another go."

"Prospecting?"

"Yes."

"That field is almost used up. The word coming into San Francisco when I left—"

"Somewhere else, then." The Judge stands, wiping his hands on a napkin. "I'm willing to stake you to the amount it would take to get started, on a modest scale, provided you're willing to commit yourself to the endeavor for some time. Let us say three years."

Niles smiles. His voice, when he speaks, lacks all force, as if he knows that no matter how he plays the hand, whether he passes or calls the bluff, he has lost. "But where?" he asks.

"Anywhere but North Carolina," says the Judge, and leaves his son in the breakfast room, dented hat in hand.

TRAMPS

Hod hacks at the chalky ground as tow-headed Mormon boys crawl beside him. Big Ten is over two rows, backing up as he stabs his shovel down, leaving a jagged rut behind. The older Mormon boys have long-handled hoes, crouching to block out plants from the tangled mat of sugar beet, making them into separate islands of green, while the smaller ones crawl after them, rags wound around their bony knees, chopping each cluster back till only the thickest stem remains. The air is dry heat and flies and fine dust coughing up from the mat like a rug beaten on a line and flies, always flies this time of year, worrying your eyes and nose, frantic in your ear as you hack baked soil into yet more dust. Sweat runs off Hod's face, cutting salty rivulets down his mask of dust and crisping away in the dry oven heat before it can reach the thirsty ground. Other young men, Saints, scrape out irrigation rows off to the right, joking and calling out to each other, keeping a cautious distance from him and the big Indian. Big Ten wears a bowler mashed down on his head and barely sweats, chopping his shovel down as if killing snakes.

Hod's ditch is uneven but the first run of water will smooth it out. Saints got just enough sense to plant their stand near the American Fork, he thinks, and have jiggered all kinds of canals and gates, reservoirs and tanks to bring it close. There is no water at the moment, though, the little boys charged with running buckets making a wide arc around Hod and Big Ten to serve their own people, Hod's tongue a dusty hank of wool stuck to the roof of his mouth. His hands have blistered and cracked and blistered again, the gloves he bought in Reno worn through and tossed away two states ago, and there is sticky blood beneath his palms on the wood of the hoe.

"You been to Chicago?" asks Big Ten.

They're not supposed to talk much, Indians, but this one never heard about it. In the barn at night Hod pretends to snore so he'll shut the mouth-works down.

"Never got that far."

"I tried it a few years back."

"Find a job?"

Their blades fall into rhythm as they chop and shovel, Hod moving forward, Big Ten backing up.

"Oh, there's plenty of work, you got a strong back and a weak mind." He says he's from Wisconsin, that he's Ojibwe and Cree and at least half French. "Only it's too jumbled-up there."

If you don't shift your hands on the shovel, just keep them clamped tight the same way, they won't hurt so much.

"You ever been in these beets through a harvest campaign?"

Hod has bucked barley and wheat, has husked corn and dug potatoes, chopped and picked cotton, loaded melons and cut cane in Texas, even picked strawberries once. "Can't say I have."

"You turn the crop up, it's a big fella—" the Indian works methodically, regular as a steam-hammer, "—slice the tops off for the sheep, knock away the dirt, and you got a nice fat sugar beet. Only sometimes it got the root-crazies. Then it isn't just one taproot, it's dozens of em, hundreds maybe, all twisted over and around each other. Make your stomach feel funny just to look at it."

"I never seen that," says Hod. "I come up, we had turnips, and they'd get the knot gall."

Big Ten shakes his head as he chops. "Chicago they got so many different kind of people living all up against each other, over and under each other—if you know who you are when you get there you bound to forget it pretty damn soon."

"A big city."

"I kilt hogs there." The shovel blade slams down and a chunk of crusted earth breaks free. "In the winter the steam come up from the blood when it'd blow out of em, then it froze hard on the ground. Hogs'd shit, scream, kick, and die. Haul that one away, there's another thousand pressing down the chute to take its place. I come back nights, somebody look at me wrong, I just as well cut their throat too."

There is no anger in the telling, the Indian fixed on the hard ground at his feet, chopping and digging.

"Believe I'll give it a pass then," says Hod.

Big Ten wears huge clodhopper brogan shoes with twine for laces and black pants and a black undertaker coat he never takes off even in the middle of the day with the old dusty bowler crammed down over his ears. He chops the shovel blade into the hard ground the Mormon boys have exposed with their thinning, twists and flicks the soil aside. Hod is slashing with a hoe, the heaviest he could find in the barn, and would be swinging a rock pike if they'd offered him one. He can't recall how many days he's been cutting this ground, can barely remember, in the heat and the dust and the constant flies, how he came to be here.

"Only thing a place like that is good for," says Big Ten, "is if you got to disappear."

Disappearing is not Hod's problem. There is a little piece of mirror glass, a jagged triangle stuck in one of the stall posts in the barn that he can't help but look at least once a day while it is light, and the thought is always the same.

Still here?

"You got a reason to make yourself scarce?" asks Hod. The Indian has hinted before that he is some kind of fugitive.

Big Ten lifts his chin at something behind him. "Garvey comin."

Hod sneaks a look back and there is Elder Garvey wandering through the beet-vacation boys, pretending to be looking over their work. Never good when the boss man steps into a field.

Hod puts his head down, chops at the earth. The stand of plants stretches to the horizon, flat and dusty green. It's best never to look at the work ahead, just punish the little bit of it lying at your feet.

"You two!"

Hod blows flies away from his ear and turns to face the farmer. "I'm just loosenin it up," he says, defensively. "Then I come back through with the shovel and scoop it out."

Elder Garvey looks off past him to the untamed crop. They look you in the eye to holler orders and argue pay, but when they look away—

"I got kin showed up," he says.

Hod has to peel his hands off the shaft of the hoe.

"You want us to finish the day?" asks Big Ten. He is still chopping the blade of his shovel down, still backing up as he digs.

"Figured you'd want time to find something else."

Meaning we're let go, thinks Hod. Meaning off the property by nightfall.

Big Ten drops his shovel in the jagged trench he has dug and starts to walk away.

"If it wasn't kin," mutters Elder Garvey, looking off to the other side of Hod. He told them there was work all the way past the harvest campaign. Back then there was fruit to pick down by Provo, there were shovel jobs for the railroad, but he promised them that this would last through the winter. "Pay you for a half-day," he adds.

Hod nods and steps around the old man, carrying the hoe on his shoulder. The nickel-a-day thinners don't look up as he passes, fixed on their little patch of pain, and the older boys turn their heads away and keep blocking. He drops the tool and catches up with the big Indian.

Grasshoppers and beetles scatter in a frenzy on the ground before them, uncovered by the tow-headed boys, and a flock of lake gulls feast on the insects, rising and falling like a white blanket flapped by the wind.

"Make a white man feel like a nigger," Big Ten grumbles when Hod catches up. Hod chooses not to point out he is the only white man been fired this day, and gingerly pulls his fingers straight.

When they reach the yard, Normal, Garvey's oldest son, has a plow laid upside-down and is sharpening the coulter with a file. "I got your pay," he says without looking up. "Gon' pick up some lumber at the station later, I could run you in."

Big Ten grunts and they step into the barn. There is a family spread out around the bunks along the wall, a hungry-looking bunch with hair bleached near white from the sun and blue eyes so clear that at first Hod thinks they're blind. His little pile of things is already laid out on the floor on a blanket, right beside Big Ten's.

"We had to get settled," says the one who looks like the father, scrawny and unshaven. Some of the anti-Manifesto crowd most likely, the kind where you can't tell if the middling-sized girls are daughters or wives. Near a dozen of them if you count the twins chasing the cat across the floor and the one nursing from his mama on the bottom bunk. "Say if there's anything you're missing."

Big Ten pokes his pile with the toe of his shoe, then wraps the corners of the blanket around it to make a bundle.

"Sorry," says the man.

"Aint none of your fault," says Hod. Scabs back in Montana had this look, hollow-ribbed people with their bodies set tense, staring big-eyed past the militia boys protecting them. They can always find somebody hungrier to replace you.

"We come in just this morning from Tooele," the man says, "and he told us to get settled then get on out there in the field. Sorry to touch your belongins."

Norm has the wagon hitched when they come out with their bundles. They climb onto the bed.

"Met your cousins," says Hod, arranging his bundle so he can sit on it.

"No relations of mine." Norm switches and the bay mare starts ahead. Norm looks like his old man, thin and hard-mouthed, dry as the soil. "It's just you can't be feeding Gentiles when your own turn up needing work."

"I aint a Gentile," says Big Ten, stretching out to lay his head on his own bundle. "I'm a Ward of the State."

The people in Lehi barely poke their heads around the door before they close it again. There is no work for them at the stone works or the rolling mill or from any of the farmers who stop by the lumberyard, and the sugar works won't hire again till harvest. Hod wonders if it would be any different if he wasn't with the Indian, but mostly if they see a lone man knocking they think you're on the bum and pull their pies in from the window. It is late afternoon by the time Hod and Big Ten get themselves hid in the ditch just south of the railyard.

"Eastbound or westbound?"

Big Ten lifts up as if to take in the lay of the land. "How much Utah is there to get through going west?"

"Bout the same as east, only it's all desert."

"Colorado, then."

The tracks above the ditch have three rails, converted from narrow gauge and polished with constant traffic. They duck down and wait while a couple little bobtails hauling local freight and an engine hauling passenger cars pass by.

"When the last time you bought a ticket?"

"Can't say," answers Hod after a moment's thought. "Me and the railroad got an agreement."

"But only you know about it."

The men laugh. Hod has been on the bum too many times, alone and without a job, and it is no good. Bad enough when the other citizens look through you, but when you got to pinch yourself to know you're there—

"Freight coming." Big Ten peeks up over the edge of the ditch. "Pulling a full load."

"What line?"

"Denver and Rio Grande."

Hod grins. *"Through the Rockies, Not Around Them."*

"Don't care how they go, long as we get clear from the Land of Milk and Honey here."

They let the engine pass, sneezing short bursts of hot steam as it picks up speed, then scramble out of the ditch, bundles tied to their arms, and run up the bank to the railbed. This part always makes his heart pound. Big Ten grabs the side ladder at the head of a boxcar and vaults up on the stirrup below it, graceful despite his size, but the train is really rolling now, thousands of rumbling tons, an avalanche on wheels that Hod sprints to keep up with till the best he can do, panicking, is catch the grab irons at the back of the car and swing his legs up off the railbed.

The moment he is borne away he knows it is folly. Unless the train slows again he is stuck, no way up, no way around to the coupling that won't put him under the wheels. Big Ten shoots a doleful look back, then hauls himself up the ladder with one hand, the other holding his hat on his head, and disappears. Hod watches the bank fly past, hoping for a spot soft enough it won't kill him when he lets go. It is all jagged rocks and piles of crossties this close to the yard, and the wind shifts to blow black smoke back on him from the stack, cinders clattering against the boards and stinging his face. Only question now is which and how many of his bones are going to be shattered. Hod's arms are trembling, just about to push away, when a rope made from clothes tied together dangles down above him. He makes a snatch for it and hopes that somewhere the Indian learned how to jerk a decent knot.

Big Ten has to grab Hod's belt to get him over the top. Hod lies on his belly hugging the wood of the roof for a moment, catching his breath.

"Where'd you learn how to nail a rattler?" Big Ten hollers over the wind.

"Haven't tried it for a while."

It is a long train, maybe thirty cars, but the grade is flat and straight and anyone looking ahead from the doghouse cupola will see them. Hod lays his hand on Big Ten's shoulder to steady himself, knees still wobbly, as they cross the roofwalk to the front of the car. The access hatch is open. Hod takes a last look as the engine swings left toward the Wasatch Range looming ahead, then squeezes through and climbs down.

The hold is crammed with jute bags full of grease wool.

"Bit gamey," says Big Ten, "but she'll be a soft ride."

The odor of sheep is rank in the box, which rocks gently on the long turn, rails clicking underneath. There are towns ahead where there may or may not be work. At some point there will be railroad bulls to dodge and it will be cold and Hod has only a hard lump of bread wrapped in a handkerchief and seven dollars and change in his pocket. But for now they are moving, compliments of the D&RG, rolling on company iron to the Wasatch Mountains and Hod feels a warm rush of contentment course through him. Luxury to be neither here nor there but in the neutral embrace of travel.

"Can't beat these side-door Pullmans for comfort."

"Yeah," answers Big Ten, shifting huge bags of fleece to make a bed, "we're a pair of kings."

After dozing a few hours the sheep-stink is too much and Hod climbs the ladder to put his head out through the access hatch. The train is climbing to the top of the world. They are well above the tree line and the mountain air is a sharp jab in his lungs as he hauls out and uses a grab iron to anchor himself and look down off the edge of the boxcar. Far below them there is a river twisting through a canyon, frothing white over rocks and shoals. An eagle drifts halfway between, making a perfect floating cross in the air, the late-day sun glistening on its back.

It has been pleasant enough the few times Hod has ridden the cushions, paying his fare and drowsily rocking in his seat with the countryside rolling past, but it never felt like this—clutching the back of his own great snorting beast, master of it all, the rails opening up ahead of him, opening, always opening. He sits, pasha-like, on the roof of a train climbing to the top of the world till he is chilled to the bone and has to crawl back in.

Big Ten is awake.

"We in Colorado yet?"

"No telling. It's just mountains."

"Never cared for the mountains," says the big Indian, rolling up on an elbow. "We're lake people."

"Paddled your canoes."

Big Ten narrows an eye. "Yeah. We did that."

"*By the shores of Gitche Gumee*," Hod recites, "*By the shining Big-Sea-Water*—"

"Gichi Gami."

"What?"

"In Ojibwe. Gichi Gami. Lake Superior."

"You're shittin me. So the poem—"

"Is a load of manure. You ever try to read it?"

"The whole thing? Hell no—"

"For one thing, Hiawatha was an Iroquois. Got nothing to do with us."

"But your people hunt and fish—"

"Lots of that, yeah—"

"Take some scalps—"

Hod means it as a joke but the Indian doesn't smile. "That's the Sioux. We sent them packing before the white people showed up."

"My brothers and me used to look for arrowheads," says Hod. "When we were supposed to be plowing."

"We did that too. You'd be surprised how many you find laying around where Indin people live."

Hod settles back in on the bags of fleece. "What did you hunt?"

"Whatever was around. Birds paid the best."

"You shot birds." Hod tries to imagine hitting a flying crow with an arrow.

"There was a white fella had a summer house out on Madeline Island," says Big Ten. "Called him Colonel Archibald. Don't know if he was a real colonel, but he lost a leg in the War. Ornery son of a gun. Once or twice a year the wild pigeons would come in and feed, the big flock. Cover the woods halfway to Iron County, branches bust from the weight of em, birdshit up to your ankles on the ground. First time I seen it, I's just a chap, I thought it was the end of the world and run home crying. All them beaks and wings—"

"They come over our farm once," says Hod. "My brother Luke and I kilt a dozen, just throwing rocks up into the air."

"We'd help my father drag the fishnets in, he'd rig em up this way he had—what you do is catch one and tie his leg to a stake in the ground with a mess of grain scattered around. He'll eat a little, flap around a bit, eat a little more—see, a pigeon got no more sense than a farm hand." Big Ten smiles bitterly. "The rest of that flock will see him and come down to get what he's feeding on, and that's when you trip the nets. We'd catch three, four hundred a day like that and we didn't have nothing like the rigs the professional bird men did. Me and my brothers' job was to pull em out one by one and pin their wings so we could bring them out on the ferry to the colonel."

"Alive."

"Of course alive. He wouldn't pay for dead ones."

"What's a man do with that many pigeons?"

"Shot em. He let us watch, sometimes. Him and his friends would get to drinking and then this half-breed fella that worked for him, Petey, would load a bird into the trap and snip their wings free and then the old boy would yell 'Pull!' for Petey to spring that catapult trap and sometimes the pigeon would just flop out with a broken neck, but mostly they would start off on the wing and *bam!* the colonel or one of his friends or all of em shooting together would blow it apart with buckshot." Big Ten frowns at the memory. "They'd kill the whole lot of them we brought between lunch and suppertime."

Hod feels a hard pain just behind his right eye. Air getting thin, he thinks, or just hungry again.

"Any ever get away?"

"The pigeons?" Big Ten shrugs. "Oh, now and then. They're beautiful flyers. Fast. Like what an arrow must of looked like, back when Indins shot arrows. Me and my brothers would holler and cheer when one flew off clear and the colonel would call us a pack of damn ignorant savages and threaten to pepper our hides. We'd run and hide then, wait till they all fallen asleep on the screen porch so we could sneak back and fetch some of the broke-neck ones home to eat. The rest had too much shot in em to bother with."

"They tasted good, pigeons, what I remember."

"Tasted fine."

Hod's stomach does a turn and he tries to remember when he ate last. He has the hunk of yesterday's bread but it isn't so big and half of it will be smaller. He wonders if the birds that got away found another flock or if they just stayed scattered. Lost.

Big Ten stretches, yawns. "Yeah, I was a regular little wild Indin. Went barefoot every summer up until the Sisters of Perpetual Adoration got holt of me." He pauses, listening for a moment. "We going downhill now."

"Feels like it."

It's getting cold in the boxcar. Hod and Big Ten can see their own breath as they divide Hod's bread from the Saints and a tin of sardines the Indian bought in Lehi.

"This Sister Ursula," says Big Ten, "she took a shine to me, figured I could be an example to my people."

Mostly when there is someone in the boxcar with you their story is pretty much the same as yours and poor entertainment. Hard times, low pay, dumb bosses, no hope. Except for the cranks and bughouse escapees, who all have their version of the Big Picture and you'd better stay awake and close to the exit.

"Example of what?" asks Hod.

"That we could talk English instead of just Ojibwe and French like my father. That we could be taught to act civilized enough not to make the white people nervous. That we could cut all our trees down and put up some sorry excuse for a farm."

"She run the school, this Ursula—"

"Your General Custer had some of them Franciscan nuns with him," says Big Ten, "he'd still have his hair. German ladies, mostly. Lift you clear off the ground by your ears."

"You learned to read."

"I learned ever damn thing they wanted me to. That way they never shame you in front of the others."

They have both pulled scraps of raw fleece to wrap themselves in now, wool side turned in. It is dark up top, and it has been a long way since the train last stopped.

"When I learned everthing they had to tell me, Sister Ursula put me on the train to the Industrial School in Pennsylvania."

"Your father let them do that?"

"My father was mostly a white man to look at him, French and Irish, but he lived Indin his whole life. When the government started the allotments in '87 the Agent says Armand, that was his white name, Armand, he says, you don't get no quarter section cause you cain't prove you're an Indin. And that means none of his sons get their forty acres cause even through my mother is a direct line down from old Chief Buffalo that makes us half-breeds, which their status was yet to be figured out."

"He tried to cheat you."

"Tried, nothing, there was folks never even seen that lake before who showed up claiming they was eligible for an allotment, the same ones standing in line with money in their paws when the surplus land got sold off."

"White people."

"All different colors, just like us, but they sure wasn't Ojibwe. Anyhow, my father gone to Père Clochard and asks what can he do, and the Père says well if you had a boy at this Carlisle School he would be qualified for an allotment and the annuity payments from the old treaty and be a Ward of the State, which would make you an Indin *ex post facto* which is Latin for the cat is already out of the bag. I was the youngest and the one he could spare

the easiest and Sister Ursula was champing at the bit for me to go so he borrowed Charlie Whitebird's wagon and team and took me down to Eau Claire
for the train. They put me on a special car and it was all Indin kids, boys
and girls—Blackfeet kids and Gros Ventre kids and Sioux kids and lots more
Ojibwe from Minnesota and then we took on a load of Oneida kids from up
by Green Bay and that's when I first seen Gracie Metoxen." Big Ten shakes
his head. "All the things I went through at that school, the only thing I ever
had on my mind was her."

Hod lets this sit for a moment. The food is gone and he is still hungry.

"I could speak English and been around white people plenty already, but
them horse Indins from out west, they was scared. The first thing when we
got to the Industrial School is they put us through the barbers and cut all our
hair off. The Sioux boys got all upset cause this meant their parents must've
died and then they took our clothes and had us wear these soldier-looking
uniforms. Now an Ojibwe," says Big Ten, wiggling to burrow between two
sacks of fleece, "got about as much to do with a Mohawk or a Crow as a
Dutchman does with a Hawaiian. And every one a them tribes think they
got the direct line to the Great Spirit and all the others is just dogs with two
legs. So you can imagine it wasn't no picnic when they stuck you in a room
where none of the other three boys talked your language."

"So you'd have to speak English."

"That was the idea."

"Seems reasonable."

"I throw you in a room with a Italian, a Swede, and a Polack and say you
got to talk Chinese, how you like it?"

Hod finds a bare patch of floor and stamps his feet a few times. He rode
a gondola car through Idaho once with a bindlestiff who'd had all his toes
frozen off, and ever since is worried when he can't feel his own.

"*To save the man*," says Big Ten, putting his hand over his heart to quote,
"*you got to kill the Indin.* That was the motto of the fella who started up the
School. And they done their level best, believe me. The first day, if you don't
already have a white name you got to go up to a blackboard and point one
off a list. So in my room there was Jeremiah Fox Catcher and Clarence Red
Cloud and Henry Yamutewa and me. Clarence was there mostly like a hostage, to keep his old man and uncles on the reservation with the rest of the
pacified Sioux."

Hod gives Big Ten a once-over. If you didn't notice he never had to
shave he could almost pass for white, Black Irish, with his hair cut short

under that bowler and skin no more burned than Hod's from a month in the fields.

"It was an old fort, see, with barracks, and then the first bunch of students that was prisoners from the Indin Wars put up some other buildings. They had me in the carriage shop. I didn't mind the work none, I always been able to work, but the way you had to muster out to the horn in the morning and keep your bed a certain way and eat your food at the same time and then lights out—you ever been in the Army?"

"No," says Hod. "Not the real one."

"There was a boy my first year, Piegan boy from Montana, got so down he hung himself. That aint no way for an Indin to die." Big Ten has his arms wrapped around himself, rocking slowly as he speaks. "I would have done the same it wasn't for Gracie."

"She was pretty?"

"She had the life spirit. They let the girls keep most of their hair and had them in their own kind of uniform dresses, which wasn't so nice, but whenever I seen her she smiled and it lift me right up off the ground. Boys that age, all I could ever think of to say was 'How are you doing?' and always she would give me that smile and say 'I am getting better every day.' That was the other motto at the School, they had it writ on top of all the blackboards and it was in every other sentence in the newspaper we put out. *We are getting better every day.* You stay in a place four, five years and you get better every day, you get an idea how bad you must have been to start with."

"You were there that long?"

"I aint proud of it," says Big Ten. "It was great for some, they learnt a trade or went on to be lawyers or whatnot at the Dickinson College just down the way. Indins from all these different places, all these different ways of living, they was thrown together and seen what about them was alike. That changes the way you look at the world, you know? But for me—I was just there so my family could keep their land."

Hod feels the train start to slow, no brakes yet but they are on flat ground and the bursts of steam outside are more sighs than snorts. Big Ten doesn't seem to notice.

"The last night I was there, we got to talking in the room and Clarence Red Cloud says how he wants to go home and Fox Catcher says it's the same for him, and then Henry who's from one of them blanket tribes down in the southwest Territories he says he goes all the time. Now Henry is a fella can go months without he says a single word and we know he don't go home even on the vacations they give us, Christian holidays, because he don't have the jack for the train fare and they don't trust him to come back. So we start to ridin him a little, especially Fox Catcher cause his Apaches got a long feud with these Hopis and that's the kind of thing you tease someone at the School with, 'Hey, my grandfather lifted your grandfather's scalp back in '65,' or 'What happened to that dog you was pettin? You didn't eat it, did you?' even though you might really be friends and stick together against the Sioux boys cause there was so many of them, and Henry gets riled and brings out this package his people sent him from the mission P.O. down there. He dumps out these little cactus buttons on his bed and Fox Catcher's eyes get big and he says I know what *those* are. 'You want to go someplace, chew on one of these,' says Henry Yamutewa.

"Well, you know how young fellas is, they get together and someone lays down a dare. There wasn't any spines on these buttons, they'd been pulled up and dried, and I chewed down four or five of em before I felt a thing other than Henry's people must have an awful lot of time on their hands to bother with this nonsense, and then I got sicker than a dog and lay on the floor holding my stomach in. Never lost my chuck, but that made it worse."

"So why do they eat them?"

"For their religion. You're supposed to see things."

"Things."

"Visions. Indin stuff."

"Eagles and snakes."

"Hopi things if you're a Hopi, Navajo things if that's what you are. Me, I just left."

"You ran away?"

"I *flew*."

They are coming to rest, a wave of sound rolling back as the couplings knock together.

"I flew out the window—we were on the second floor—flew across the parade ground. Not flapping my arms or anything, just—your body lifts up and goes wherever you think. So I flew in through the window of the girls' dormitory and Gracie Metoxen was there warm and smiling in her bed, awake while all the other girls were sleeping, waiting for me, smiling that smile, but she was too heavy to carry away so I just lay with her awhile and then right before the sun come up I flew out the window again and never stopped."

Voices pass outside the boxcar. If they start to open the door, thinks Hod, we can burrow down into the sheep's wool.

"You went home?"

Big Ten shakes his head. "First thing they do, they wire the Indin Agent where you live, and he puts the law out on you. If you're a Ward of the State and you leave Carlisle without they let you, you're an outlaw. I just kept going."

Big Ten looks toward the door as if just realizing they have stopped. "We're here."

"Where?"

"It don't matter. Time to get out."

The Indian stands and peels his fleece off.

"The girl," says Hod, getting up as well. "Gracie—"

"I run into an Oneida fella up in Oregon picking apples," says Big Ten, stepping up on the access ladder. "There was a spell of consumption went through the School, it took her and some of the others. They got their own little cemetery out back, the white-people kind with the stones. Probably where she is now."

It is a division yard, big, with lots of other freights on the sidings and lots of car-knockers hurrying to and fro with their lanterns. Hod and Big Ten get down off the side of the boxcar and creep low along the train trying to get their bearings, feet on the crossties so they don't crunch the ballast.

The railroad bull is standing hidden on top of a coupling, with no lantern and a shotgun in his arms.

"Run and I blow your damn heads off."

Hod glances to Big Ten, who turns to stone.

"Where we at, Mister?" asks Hod without turning around.

"You're in my freight yard is where you're at. March."

He brings them to the switchman's shed that is lit up and has a sheriff's deputy and another fella wearing some sort of badge inside, both drinking from a pint bottle and in a playful mood.

"What we got here?" says the deputy, feet up on the desk.

"Got this broke-nosed tramp here," says the railroad bull, "and the Last of the Mohicans. Or maybe the Next to Last."

"You come in on that freight?" asks the deputy.

"You know, it did cross our mind to jump on it," says Hod. It is always a negotiation with the bulls. If you're too scared they walk all over you and if you're too bold they crack your skull. "But we had second thoughts."

"You trespassing on railroad property. That's a crime."

The other one stands up then and looks them both over, putting his face too close.

"Ever do any mining?"

"Some." Hod answers him. "I can handle a Burleigh and I can work the timber, and hell, anybody can lift a shovel."

"How bout you, Chief?"

Big Ten takes a long time to answer, considering his options, and when he speaks he looks at Hod instead of the man in front of him. "They'll stick me underground when I'm dead," he says. "No need to push my luck."

The deputy and the other man with a badge and the railroad bull all laugh at this, then the deputy puts the irons on Big Ten and takes him off to jail. The Indian doesn't look back. They aren't friends, exactly, but when you travel with someone for a distance—

The man whose badge is for the Ibex Mines leads Hod outside and off in the other direction.

"What's your name, son?"

They are stepping over the shunt tracks and in between cars being shifted back and forth, the business of the yard continuing despite the threat of two hungry, jobless men stealing a ride on a boxcar. For an instant Hod considers giving his real name but then thinks better of it.

"Metoxen," he says. "Henry Metoxen."

"What kind of name is that?"

"Polish." The headache is back now, worse than before, and he is having a hard time catching his breath. "We're pretty high up, aren't we?"

"This is Leadville, son. The Cloud City."

There are lots of lights up on the hill they have started to climb, and from the flats off to the right Hod can hear music. They pass a little cemetery, crooked stones and crosses leaning into the slope, and he thinks of the Indian girl behind the school. He thinks of his mother's lonesome grave back on the old man's folly of a quarter section, the Mennonites shaving a little closer to it with their plows every year.

"You'll make two-fifty a day—three dollars if you really can run a drill. First week goes to the deputy down there—that's your fine."

"Thought the silver kings all went bust."

"We're still pulling gold out of the Little Johnny, lots of it." He indicates ahead of them. "This is Carbonate Hill—we'll put you up in the company barracks here, charge a dollar a day."

"Meals?"

"That's your lookout."

Hod wishes there was more air to breathe, and he made three-fifty back in Butte, but he's done enough jail for a lifetime. The mine dick gives him a look as they climb.

"You a drinking man?"

Kansas was dry and his old man a temperance fiend and somehow that has stuck with him. "No sir."

"You stay in Leadville," smiles the man with the badge, "you'll want to take it up."

OUR "BOYS" AT CAMP

The game is friendly till the ladies arrive. The 12th are regulars, at least, though Sergeant Jacks is convinced their moundsman is a ringer, snuck in from the Atlanta pro team after the officers made their wagers. He has a smoking fastball and a wicked, late-hooking curve that has the right-handed batters back on their heels and popping up. It has stayed tight only because the boys he's picked for the outfield, especially Scott in center, cover their ground at a gallop and rifle the ball to the proper base when the white team makes a hit. Private Coleman, who they call Too Tall, has been adequate in the box, but is starting to tire from whipping fastball after fastball over the batters' slab.

"Don't you have a change-of-pace pitch, son?" Sergeant Jacks asks him when he trots forward from second after calling time-out.

"Course I do," the veteran answers. "I rolls the ball to the catcher."

"What I thought. How's the arm?"

Too Tall spits tobacco and works his shoulder a few times, cocking his head as if listening to something inside the muscle. "Won't be able to lift her tomorrow," he says. "But now she's fine."

Jacks nods and moves back to his position. They are down four runs to two, a runner on third and a single out. A couple hundred of the 12th are gathered along the first-base line cheering their batter, a big, sunburned boy with a dent in his nose, while an equal contingent of the 25th urge Coleman on from the third-base side. Colonel Burt and his rival sit together with some other officers and the sheriff from Lytle and other dignitaries on a little set of bleachers that has been set up, sipping whiskey from tin mess cups and enjoying the contest like plantation lords, while the rest of the cracker civilians over from town are either clumped behind home pulling for the whites or scattered in the outfield, moving out of the way or becoming obstacles depending on which team's ball is in play. It is dusty as ever but enough breeze to keep the flies from settling on you. Jacks tries to spit but can't make enough water.

The batter, overswinging, fouls the first two pitches off, and as they are playing the old rule there is no count against him. Coleman has been throwing for seven innings now, putting the mustard on every pitch, and it's clear the white boys aren't afraid of him anymore.

"Come on, Pitch," Jacks calls, adding his voice to the infield chatter. "Throw that pellet past him!"

Coleman delivers high and wide for a ball.

The 25th was the first unit to arrive at the Chickamauga camp, helping to clear new roads in the park, to dig the near-useless wells. Then the other regulars started coming and finally the state volunteers with their swagger and their suspicion and their amateur officers. There are too many men here and not enough for them to do and if something doesn't change soon the flies are going to win the campaign. Combat will be no problem, combat keeps them occupied, but this—a hodgepodge of units waiting for orders, regulars and volunteers all mixed together under the pines, their sentries challenging each other for the pure spite of it, Lytle a hellhole for the colored troops and Chattanooga, if you've got the time to get there, not much better. Missoula was pie, the town used to them, friendly even, cheering them onto the trains and telling them to be sure and come back. But the reception has cooled with every mile farther south traveled and they are still only to the very top of Georgia. Short of combat, of course, a ball game is always the best way to let off some steam.

Even better if you win.

Too Tall bounces one off the plate for another ball.

"Bear down, big man, bear down!" calls Jacks, taking a step back into the shallow outfield. Let the run score, just get the out.

It is then that the ladies appear, a good dozen of them with pastel dresses and parasols, a lane parting among the white spectators, chatting with each other as they walk without a glance to the field, confident that play will be suspended till they are settled. Too Tall just looks at the ball in his hand, rolling it around as if counting the stitches in the cover, and most of the others break out of their crouches and kick at the uneven pasture, waiting. But Dade at first base, who is from Rhode Island of all places, puts his hands on his hips and stands gawking at them like an idiot.

The tin cups disappear and the officers jump up to be gallant, smoothing their moustaches and brushing off the boards so the ladies may be seated. From the corner of his eye Jacks can tell that these aren't camp followers or sporting gals, but the cream of whatever Chattanooga claims for society. He checks the sky for rain.

The umpire, a second lieutenant from Headquarters staff with a whimsical sense of what qualifies as a strike, waits until the last parasol is positioned before starting again.

"Let's play ball!" he calls out. "And mind your language."

Coleman puts a strike past the batter then, grunting as he releases the ball, and Jacks can tell he's hurt. It's the first time the whole regiment has been together in years, and each company has voted two men to make up the squad, forgetting that pitching is half the game. His only left-hander, Gamble, is in the sick tent with dysentery and Ham Robinson mustered out a week before the *Maine* blew up. The next delivery is slow and wide but the 12th man swings anyway, dribbling it foul off the top of the bat. The ball rolls dead at the feet of one of the young ladies in the bleachers, the others twittering as she picks it up and holds it as if it may bite her. Before any of the officers can relieve her of it that fool of a yankee first baseman Dade steps right up and plucks it out of her hand. It gets too quiet then. He is a pretty boy, Dade, buff colored with reddish hair, and he smiles to show the blond girl his gold tooth, tips his cap, and trots back to the field.

Nothing happens right away, but Jacks can feel a change in the air, like it gets on the Gulf in Texas before a big blow, backs stiffening among the local crackers behind home, an edge to the cheering from the men of the 12th standing on the sideline. Too Tall throws again, wincing, and Jacks doesn't like the sound when the batter lays into the ball. He turns, expecting the worst, but there is Scott backed up deep in center, the boy waiting, waiting, then charging a few steps forward to catch the ball and winging it in on the fly, Jacks letting it sizzle past him to skip off the front of the mound and continue to the catcher so quick the runner is four feet from home when he's tagged. Double out, inning over.

The whole regiment lets out a Comanche whoop then, slapping the Carolina boy on the back when he comes in from the field, sharing out a sack of oranges somebody has foraged. Water at the camp is not much for drinking, boiled and allowed to settle it still tastes like mud, so even hot from the sun the orange soothes his throat.

"I took something off it," says Too Tall. "I knowed he's gonna pop up."

The pop-up would have been out of reach in any fenced ballpark Jacks has played in, but he leads off the inning and can't deal with the pitching now. He digs in at the plate, splits his grip on the bat for control, and watches the white boy's legs. His fastball still has too much pop to do much with, but his curve is a lot slower and starting to break earlier. In his windup for the curve he twists his hip and swings his lead leg across his body, almost stiff at the knee, while he bends the knee and lifts it high for the straight pitch.

Jacks waits for a curve.

"Come on, Sarge!" calls Cooper, not playing but plenty active on the sideline. "I got some serious paper on the line!"

Laughter from the men then. There is no cash left in the camp, soldiers writing "checks" to each other in their card games and charging what little there is to buy at the colored canteen against next month's pay. Jacks waits out two fast ones, a strike and a ball.

On the next throw the hurler keeps his lead leg stiff and Jacks steps back while he's still in motion, waiting on the ball then slapping it hard between the shortstop and the third baseman.

"Atta go, Sarge! Runner on board!"

The pitcher has a good quick-throw to first and has almost caught them napping a couple times. Jacks hasn't stolen a base in ten years and stays close to the bag while Curtis strikes out on a pitch in the dirt. Dell Spicer who married the Blackfoot gal back in Montana comes up then and swings late on the first pitch, slicing it just fair of the first-base boundary that has been laid down with lime. It gets lost in the spectators, who complicate things by trying to help, and Jacks ends up on third with Spicer standing up at second. The umpire makes them both move back a base, claiming interference. Jacks knows it will do no good but needs to make a show for the boys, calling time and stomping over to complain.

"If they hadn't grabbed it, it would've rolled for a triple!"

The umpire is in military uniform. He taps his second lieutenant's bar. "All decisions final."

Jacks returns to second with the white side of the field catcalling after him. Horace Bell from B Company is up now, the swiftest of their runners but not much with the bat. Jacks sees the 12th infield playing back, and signals for a bunt.

"Good look now!" he calls, catching Bell's eye and tugging twice on his cap. "Wait for your pitch."

But the curve snaps in on his hands and hits the neck of the bat before he can pull it back, popping up easily to the catcher.

Jacks calls time again and has them wake up Sergeant Lumbley, who has been snoozing in the shade under the bench. Lum can't run any more on account of the bullet he took in the knee during a scrap in Bozeman, but he can grit his teeth and march the boots off most of the boys. And with a hickory club in his hands, well—

The big sergeant steps up to the plate, a pattern of field grass dented into one side of his face, squinting sleepily and looking around the bases. He hasn't been awake enough to know what stuff the pitcher has got, but with Lum it's never mattered much.

"Strike this darky out!" hollers one of the locals and Lum turns to stare at him as the first pitch sails over for a strike. The crackers laugh.

Lum turns his sleepy gaze back to the pitcher then and knocks the next one over the left fielder's head and it just rolls and rolls, rolls so far that two runs score and he is able to quick march all the way to third before they get the ball back in. Jacks sends a runner to take his place and Lum returns to the bench, rubbing his eyes.

"We ahead or behind?" he asks.

"Tied."

"What inning?"

"Top of the eighth."

"Damn." He looks up at the sun. "This day done slip by me."

Shavers bounces out and they take the field, Jacks walking out next to his pitcher.

"Can you do this?"

Too Tall spits tobacco. "I'll keep it low."

The first batter up for the 12th is a pinch-hitter too, a long-limbed drink of water who has been corked black wherever his skin shows out from the uniform. The crackers behind the catcher think this is a riot, and the boy coons it up, dragging the bat to the plate, dangling his loose limbs like rubber, turning to doff his cap, revealing a shock of yellow hair, and bow to the ladies who cover their mouths as they giggle.

"Send one to the moon, Rastus!" calls the sheriff through cupped hands.

"I sho'ly do mah best, sah!" he answers, bugging his eyes wide. He walks with his buttocks stuck out and arched high, and waggles them to great amusement as he settles in at the plate.

"Send me the sauce, Boss!" he calls to Coleman.

It is bad enough down here in this shithole Georgia not knowing if there's going to be a war or not or if there *is* will they be allowed to go and wearing the damn woolen tunics in this heat while you drill and then what's supposed to be your own people who you are fighting for treating you like dirt every time you wander off the reservation.

Jacks sees it coming.

Jacks sees it coming in the way Coleman holds his body. In the way he grips the ball, but he just stands at his position and says nothing.

Too Tall sends one upstairs and the blackface boy hits the dirt.

It is dead quiet for a long moment.

"Ball one!" calls the second lieutenant, and gives Jacks a look.

The crackers and a good number of the boys from the 12th are screaming as he walks to the mound this time, faces red, a few stepping across the lime onto the infield to make their threats. He hears nigger this and nigger that, something about when the sun goes down. The 12th are regulars, a good outfit, but the pastel ladies are here now and it changes everything. Both the colonels are standing up in the bleachers, looking concerned.

Jacks takes the ball from Too Tall. "You don't really have nothin left, do you?"

"Spose not," the pitcher says, turning to spit tobacco, face a mask as the crackers shout. "If I still had it, I'd of tore that boy's head off."

"You walk straight for the middle of our fellas over there, keep your eyes to yourself."

"I can get these bastards out."

"You done enough today, Trooper. Nice job."

The private walks extra slow to the waiting wall of blue shirts, tucking his glove under his arm and seeming not to notice his life is being threatened by the mob on the other side. Jacks waves for Hooks to go in at center, and brings Scott in to take the mound. The word is that the Carolina boy can throw it some, and at this point he wishes Colonel Burt would step down and run the damn team like he did when they played the railroaders in Missoula.

"Get us through this inning alive," Sergeant Jacks says to Scott as he hands the ball over, looking him hard in the eye. "You know what I mean."

The boy, Royal is his name, gives him a big grin. "Sure thing, Sergeant."

He takes his time getting ready, strolling over to say something to Corporal Ponder at third base and giving him his glove. Ponder trots to the bench, whispers something to the one they call Mudfish, and returns with a different one. The crowd, impatient, are shouting for action as Scott puts this one on. He winks to the second lieutenant.

"My pitching glove," he says.

He asks for a couple warm-up throws then, which brings a new howl of protest from the white side, and proceeds to out-coon the batter, wind-milling his arm in an elaborate windup, catching the return throws behind his back like the boys do when they're just fooling among themselves. The white folks aren't sure what to make of it, and neither is his own side, but the burned-cork boy looks a little embarrassed now, waiting to take his turn.

"Batter up!" calls the second lieutenant. Jacks crouches and pounds his glove.

Scott rears back and throws hard overhand—only he doesn't let go of the ball, instead wheeling off the mound and striding over to the bench, the 12th men and the locals catcalling again as he gets his original glove back from Mudfish.

"Sorry, sir," he calls to the umpire as he takes the mound again. "Just didn't feel right."

The minstrel boy digs in, looking pissed off to have the attention of the crowd pulled away from his antics.

"You aint gonna need a glove if you'll throw me that thing," he calls. "You gonna need binoculars to follow where it's goin!"

"Comin right up," smiles Scott, and goes into his windmilling wind-up.

The pitch he lobs in is so fat Jacks could run to the sidelines, grab a bat, and still get to the plate in time to hit it. The white boy in the blackface takes a mighty swing, connecting with it square over the plate—but instead of a crack of wood there is a heavy, soggy THOOMP!, the ball flying apart into a hundred little bits that spray outward like a fireworks explosion. Jacks is hit on the shoulder with a piece of it, a wet scrap of orange, the peel made white with lime from the basepaths.

People are stunned at first, minds taking a moment to grasp the phenom-enon. Then the whole 25th falls out laughing, whacking each other on the back and miming the batter's dumbfounded reaction. Even a few of the white folks join in, the white ladies clapping their little gloved hands with delight. The second lieutenant, though, is not smiling as he steps to the mound.

"Let's cut out the nigger show and play ball."

"Nigger show is at the plate, sir," Scott tells him, nodding toward the batter, who is looking sheepish and still picking flecks of orange off his front.

"You gonna get serious," says the officer, "or do I call a forfeit?"

"Yes, sir." Corporal Ponder tosses Scott the real ball. "I will seriously strike this coon out."

And proceeds to put the side down with only nine pitches—in-shoots and drop-offs, fast balls that seem to hop at the last moment and a big round-house curve that starts out heading halfway between home and third before hooking back over the heart of the plate, the regiment whooping louder after every strike. The last man to whiff slams his bat down in frustration and Jacks hurries to join Scott as they leave the field.

"Don't smile, don't wave your hat," he says. "Just walk off."

Of course Scott is the first batter up to begin the ninth. The pitcher gives him a long look and then throws a steaming fastball into his ribs. There is a sound like the orange exploding and Scott drops to his knees and then it is very quiet again.

If this was two white teams or two colored teams it would just be base ball, part of the game, and if there was a fight with nobody sent to the hospital they'd all meet after at the canteen to compare bruises over beer and pretzels. But instead Jacks and Mingo Sanders have to grab Cooper to keep him from running across the field and the officers are out of the bleachers waving their arms to keep the regiments apart and the crackers are asking Scott if he thinks he's so damn smart now and when the whistles start blowing Jacks thinks it's the provost guard come to make some arrests. But there is Colonel Daggett with a quartet of majors around him, marching up onto the mound, and in a flash the junior officers and noncoms have their people in formation, base-ball uniforms scattered among the blue, the 25th formed on the third-base side of the field and the 12th on the first, and Daggett waits till even the civilians are on their feet and silent before he speaks.

"I've just received a wire from Washington," he says, "and it applies to both regiments present. We have orders to break camp, pending transport to Tampa. The Congress has voted and it is *on*, gentlemen."

A cheer erupts on both sides of the field. Hats fill the air. The ladies in the bleachers spin their parasols in excitement.

The game has begun.

THE YELLOW KID

WAR! is the one word the Yellow Kid can read. The rags have been hustling the **WAR!** for months, and now here is Specs passing it out in the day's first special edition behind the *Journal* building. Specs has got an ink smudge on one of the lenses of his cheaters, ink all over his hands.

"By the time you little bastids unload this batch," he says, "we'll be ready with another extra."

The Yellow Kid elbows in, slaps down a quarter's worth of pennies and Specs slams a bundle of fifty against his chest, nearly knocking him over.

"Watch it, four-eyes!"

"Yer lucky I let you have em, you little Chiney piece a shit."

Just because there is **WAR!** doesn't mean their daily battle with the circulation gink is off.

"He aint Chiney yella," explains Ikey for the hundredth time as he grabs his bundle, "he's *sick* yella."

"Yer both a friggin disease. Get outta here and sell those papers."

They run around the building, shouting "**WAR!** Congress declares **WAR!**" and selling a few on their way.

"The Chief gotta be shittin himself," says Ikey, pausing on the corner of William Street to adjust his load. They've seen him arriving late at night a couple times, Boy Willie himself pulling up in his hack with the white horse and his two sweet babies who look like the Riccadonna Sisters in the *Hogan's Alley* comic he stole from the *World*, one on either side, fresh from some uptown theater or lobster palace. Big smooth-faced character in his glad rags. As far as they can figure he runs the dogwatch shift at his *Journal* dressed just like that, still in his silk top hat and swallow-tail coat. He always calls hello but never throws any mazuma their way.

"Willie been peddlin this yarn hard all year," says Ikey. "Gonna be bigger than Corbett and Jeffries!"

They step out into Newspaper Row and the Yellow Kid takes the north side. They are at the center of the whole friggin works here. There is the tallest building, the *World* with its gold dome towering above, the glass boxes of the Electro Monogram out front swiveling to tell the folks that it is **WAR!** with the Tryon Building behind where the *Staats Zeitung* used to roll and the *Sentinel* and the mick *Freeman's Journal* still do and then the *Tribune* Building with its clock tower showing that it's nearly noon, the Yellow Kid better with the numbers and the hands of time than with letters, then the *Times* and the *Sun* behind it on Nassau, all of them flying their own flags along with the Stars and Stripes or even hoisting some kind of Cuban banner like Boy Willie's paper, and then there's the construction on the Park Row Building, already got the four giant Amazons with their giant stone melons up front and just across Ann Street the St. Paul Building is racing it story by story, both of them sposed to top the *World* by a good eighty feet when they're done say the birds who bring the tours past and "**WAR!**" cries the Yellow Kid, waving a rag to display the scarehead, "Congress Declares **WAR!**" stepping over into the park in front of City Hall, geezers snatching papers and flipping him their pennies on the way in and out of the building. The Kid tries the can't-find-change-for-a-nickel dodge on one old whitehair with a pair of muttonchops halfway out to his shoulders but the geezer is wise to it and waits with his palm out, the cheap bastid.

The Yellow Kid's corner, by common understanding, is at Broadway and Warren where the omnibuses stop at the park and you can sell to the top-hat crowd heading for the Astor Hotel, with Graub's restaurant, where the builders go if they haven't brought their lunch, on one side of Warren and Donnegan's, which is the reporters' favorite gin mill, on the other. A hell of a location. But because today there is **WAR!** he can make a quick run through City Hall Plaza with the horse trolleys turning around and the noise and the dust and the drays pulling up with stone for the new buildings or the new bridge over to Brooklyn to the east and the Tammany hacks and city clerks coming and going and boys hawking the *Journal* and the *Sun* and the *World* and the *Times* and the *Herald* and the *Trib* and the *Telegram* and the *Telegraph* and the *Daily News* and the *Mail and Express* and the *Star* and even one poor clueless little street rat trying to pawn off day-old copies of the *Weekly Post*, just don't stop moving and there's no trespass, before he takes up position on his own spot.

"**WAR!**" he hollers. "Special edition, Congress Declares **WAR!** Only in the *Journal*!"

It isn't only in the *Journal*, of course, at least he doesn't think so, but the geezers don't know that yet, do they?

Nobody muscles you off your spot, the place that is understood to be yours by the Unwritten Law. The one time somebody tried with him, big stupid spaghetti-bender wearing a different color shoe on each foot, thought just cause the Kid is sick-looking and little and skinny he'll roll over easy, he sold maybe three papers before the Kid come back with a brick in each hand and half the newsies below Canal Street to teach him how it works. The wop tried to run but they caught him and knocked the stuffing out of him till he just rolled into a ball on the cobblestones and then they all pissed on him.

The Yellow Kid took the spot over from Dink Healy when Dink got too big and switched over to the Western Union, working as his striker for halvsies the first year, buying the corner a nickel a day. Dink has the glimmer that don't focus right and was maybe a little scary toward the end when he got tall, so the Yellow Kid would sell most of his bundle.

"You look like death on a friggin soda cracker," Dink would always say, tugging the Kid's cap down over his eyes. "I couldn't have a better striker if you was crippled."

"Read about the **WAR!**" hollers the Yellow Kid. Some of the builders coming out of Graub's buy on their way back to work, then he tries Donnegan's but the joint is empty.

"Haven't seen em all day," calls Sweeny from behind the counter. "They're all at work, poor miserable bastids, slapping together them extras."

The Yellow Kid sells out to a mick priest heading for St. Paul's and hotfoots it as fast as he can go back to the *Journal* building.

"You get the last dozen," says Specs, jerking his nose at the pallet.

"When's the next run?"

"Sposed to be out at three o'clock. All new headers."

The Kid buys the dozen and heads up Centre Street. "**WAR!**" he cries. "Spanish Invasion Plans, this issue!"

He does a circuit around the Tombs and the Criminal Courts Building, always good for a few sales to the turnkeys, got nothing to do but sit on their keisters, pick their noses, and read. He unloads two under the Bridge of Sighs on the Franklin Street side, then stops in front of the Bummer's Hall and looks up from where Maminka brought him to wave up at the windows the first time Janek got pinched. The food was lousy in the Tombs, said Janek, but Alderman Burke from Tammany treated him to steak and spuds the day they sprung him.

There is a horse trolley running up Broadway that the Kid manages to catch up to, hauling himself aboard as it rolls and hollering his way up the aisle to the front.

"**WAR!**" he cries. "Spanish Fleet Sighted in East River!"

He sells all but one, hands it to the conductor before the old grouch can lay a collar on him. "Read all about it," he says, then ducks under the man's arm and leaps off the moving trolley in front of Blatnik's.

The working stiffs have fed their faces and gone back to their stalls so now it is only newsies who have peddled their morning bundle at the counter—Nub Riley and Beans and Ikey and Chezz DiMucci and Yid Slivovitz. The Kid grabs a stool and shouts for his burger and pie and a chocolate fizzer which Yid likes to call an egg cream though they don't put neither egg nor cream in the thing.

"About friggin time with this **WAR!**" says Nub, who is a fiend for red-hots and always has two, one with onions and one with pickle relish, laid on thick. "I mean shit or get off the friggin pot."

"This is gonna be big," says Ikey, pushing the scoop of vanilla under the surface of his root beer with the spoon. "You remember how we sold when they sprang the Señorita?"

"That was only the *Journal*."

"So? This'll be good for everybody."

The *Journal* made a big deal out of this beautiful Cuban Señorita the Spanish bastids had violated and tortured and locked up in a dungeon in Havana, got the Women of America to write letters to their king or queen or whatever they got over there, then finally lost patience and sent their own guy, just a scribbler, down to spring her out of the joint with a ladder and some men's clothes for disguise. Boy Willie hogged the headlines for a week.

"Well it's a damn sight better than that Cross of Silver malarkey they were floggin. Jesus, Mary, an Joseph, how's a guy spose to sell papers, they can't make up better news than that?"

"You at least need a society dame floatin in the river. Or a riot where the Army gets to blast away—"

"Like that Pullman strike."

"Okay for a week," says Chezz DiMucci. "But them labor things burn out quick."

"What about that Coxey's Army circus?" says Beans.

"Or Dr. Holmes who croaked all the people in Chicago?" says Yid Slivovitz.

"Most of youse weren't born yet," says Slow Moe Hershel who is flipping burgers behind the counter, Moe who used to be a newsie himself when the *Sun* was the hottest rag in town, "but when they brung Geronimo in off the warpath, that was a *story*. Couldn't print em fast enough."

"And leave us not forget—" says Nub Riley, spreading his hands to signal he's got the topper, "Remember the Friggin *Maine*."

They all have to pull their faces out of their feedbags for that one. What a day that was, what a week.

"I had a guy bought my whole bundle, gimme a buck. Couldn't of been more than fourteen, fifteen left."

"Jeez, the way they played it out—Day One, the ship blows up. Day Two, who blew the ship up? Day Three, we think we know. Day Four, we sent down our experts, here's the facts—and on and on and on—"

"The extra where they printed the names of the diseased—"

"You mean de*ceased*."

"You sure?"

"Diseased is your mama's bunny hole. Deceased is them unfortunate sailors on the *Maine*."

"But **WAR!**—"

"**WAR!**—"

"Fellas, I been in the newspaper business a long time," says Yid, who is thirteen, "but nothing we been through in our lives has prepared us for this."

Slow Moe lays a burger down and the Yellow Kid flips the lid and dumps ketchup on it. It comes with potatoes cooked in the same grease and half a kosher dill.

"Over in Europe, China, Italy, places like that," Yid continues, "they got a massacre every day of the week. But here in America, what—" he looks to Moe. "When was our last big **WAR!**?"

"Week ago Saturday," says Moe, not looking up from the grill. "The Eastmans took apart a social function the Five Pointers was hosting."

"Friggin numbskull. Don't you read the papers?"

"Even when I sold em," says Moe, "I never looked past the headlines."

"It must have been the Civil **WAR!**, that they put up all the statues about," offers Ikey.

"Yeah," says Chezz. "When we took over Mexico."

"I bet Boy Willie goes down there to Cuba himself, bags a couple Dagoes for the front page."

"Yeah, then what's Jewseph Pulitzer gonna do? He's too old to ride a horse."

"Any stunt Hearst pulls, Poppa Joe's gonna try to top him. If we're sellin this good already and nobody's fired a shot yet, just wait'll the lead starts flying. We just gotta pray they can keep it going awhile."

The pie is hot and full of apples and cinnamon and his stomach is full, tight even, like the chocolate fizzer is still bubbling inside him when they cross the street to Newsome's Palace of Pleasures. Music blasts them as they enter, the Coinola Orchestrion that Gruesome Newsome who owns the arcade feeds to attract business pumping out a version of *Down Went McGinty*, piano tambourine bells xylophone woodblock triangle snare bass and cymbal all-in-one mechanically slamming out the song punched on the paper scroll. Ikey and the Yellow Kid march straight down the center aisle, past the bagatelle games and the Big Six slots that never friggin pay off and the Electro Shock Machine and the Fortune Teller and the Automatic Billiards and the Lung Tester and the Skill-Shooter Pistol Range and the box-ball setups and the Scientific Punching Machine and all the Black Diamond Gum vendors to the last Mutoscope viewer on the left.

"This is the one," says Ikey, pointing at the photo card above it that advertises the view. "I seen it the other day, twice."

The Kid feeds it a Lincoln and gets on his toes to get his eyes to the slot. They put the ones that are spose to be for adults up on a board to make them taller, but not really so tall you can't look if you want to. The light comes on and he starts to crank, nice and steady, so the Lady Undressing for Bath moves a little slower than normal.

"Careful you don't run it out," says Ikey. "She don't ever make it into the tub."

The Kid cranks it backward then, which Gruesome Newsome says you can't do cause it hurts the machine but really cause he doesn't want anybody getting more than a minute view for their penny, but what fun is it to see the lady put her clothes back on?

He cranks it forward again, real slow, till what must be nearly the last card flips into view and holds it there.

"Nice melons."

"What I tell you?"

The woman is down to her unders, a white corset cinched tight in the middle and black stockings you can follow all the way up to her—

Whap! His cap flies off as Gruesome smacks the back of his head.

"What I tell you little shits?"

"Hey, I paid!"

"That don't mean you can park yourself there with your tongue down the slot."

The Kid bends to retrieve his cap. "Don't cost you nothin extra."

"You monopolize the machine, nobody else can see it." There is ten or eleven of the guys in the joint at the moment, and plenty of machines to go around.

"Besides, you got the same crappy pitchers every week," says Ikey. "Even Fine changes his once in a while."

Fine runs the Garden of Delights two blocks down, but it's smaller and dirtier and there's a character they all call Creepy Drawers who seems to hang there all day long.

"You don't like it," says Newsome, "you can hit the bricks."

They stroll around a few more minutes just to show him he can't boss a paying customer, and then the Kid has to blow.

"I told my sister I'd come by," he says.

The Yellow Kid, running, always running in the daytime cause there is money to make if you are quick on your feet and loud and fearless, cuts across Worth Street, the morning's pennies rattling in the grouch bag tied around his waist and stuffed into his crotch, four more in his pocket in case the guinea kids catch him when he hurries past Mulberry and Mott and he needs something to surrender, running all the way to Chatham Square where he stops in front of Altgeld's to look at the crates.

All the downtown Social Clubs buy from Altgeld when one of their brothers kicks the bucket, the crate from Altgeld and flowers from Kilmurray's. There are three in the window now, two full-size and one cut short for kids. One of the full-size is the basic model, a wood rectangle with no metal fittings like the old-country hebes have to use, but the other is a real beauty, a polished box that juts out wider at the shoulders, with the shiny brass handles for your pals to hang on to and all kinds of fancy carving on the lid. If he'd had the dough he'd have popped for something like that for Maminka, instead of her riding the damn barge that might as well be a garbage scow up to Hart Island where One-Nugget Feeny says they just dump you in the common trench, shoulder to shoulder packed three deep with the other dead. Or worse, give you to the junior croakers to cut apart and learn their trade. But there was no dough and the Old Man fell apart, stupid Bohunk bastid, so there she was.

The child's coffin looks more like a cake you want to eat than something to get planted in, all white and smooth on the outside with red plush trimmings and a little satin pillow. You see that crate roll by on the back of the wagon and you know it was *somebody* inside, not some pile of horseshit scraped off the street. A steam train curves overhead on the Third Avenue El, making the window glass vibrate and blurring his view of the coffin. He's told most all of the guys that's what he's saving up for, figures it's half the size it should be half the price of the ones they use for big people, but he has not quite got around to going in and asking old Altgeld what the ticket is.

The Kid turns up Bowery then, trotting, and at the corner of Pell runs into Janek shuffling out into the sun. Or Hunky Joe, which is what the other pugs in the Eastmans call him these days. He's got the goo-goo eyes already, not even two o'clock, which means he's just come from the Chinks.

"Frantisek," he says, grinning stupidly, using the Yellow Kid's Bohunk name.

"Janek."

"It's Hunky Joe—"

"Yeah, yeah, I got it." The Kid looks him over—nose crooked where it's been bust a couple times, jacket too short on his long arms, bowler too small for his fat Bohunk head. "You been on the hip?"

Hunky Joe shrugs, grins wider. "I like to do a pipe or two in the mornin. Takes the edge off things. What you doin up here?"

"Going to see Vera. The Old Man been around?"

His brother spits on the bricks. "I aint been over there for weeks," he says. "If she's lucky the old bastid'll finally drink hisself to deat'."

"Yeah, well—"

"You doin all right?"

"Can't complain." The last time the Kid saw Hunky Joe his brother touched him for a buck. The Eastmans are spose to be such a hot outfit and there he is stumblin up Chrystie Street with his mitts out, practically begging.

"Money's a little tight," adds the Kid, looking away.

"Good news, though—"

"You mean the **WAR!** Yeah, as long as the papers don't rise the price up on us."

Hunky Joe gives him a once-over, the wheels in his head clunking the way they do when he's trying to pretend he's not doped up. "Listen, I got a proposition," he says. "You still on your corner, right?"

"Yeah—"

"I and some of my associates have branched out into the policy racket. We are currently scouting for operatives—"

"Nigger pennies."

Hunky Joe shrugs. "You got the location, a steady flow of clientele—"

"Brannigan just barely leaves me alone as it is—"

"Brannigan owes his uniform to the Hall. We, I and my associates, are the mighty right arm of Tammany. Brannigan, therefore, works for—"

"The thing is, Joe," says the Yellow Kid, searching quick for a believable lie, "I just can't handle the numbers. Anything past two plus two, I'm lost. I didn't get up to the fit' grade like you."

"Just tink about it, all right?"

"I'll do that. And stay away from the friggin Chinks. You look skinnier than I do."

"Numbers, bullshit," grins Hunky Joe. "You was always the smart one."

The Yellow Kid runs away from his brother then, runs up Bowery till he hits Hester and cuts right to where the pavement ends and there are so many people you can't run anymore. The sheenies are all out selling their second-hand everything, horsecarts and pushcarts and funny-smelling geezers wandering around wearing wooden trays full of buttons or ties or hot Jew food. Little girls empty ashcans or finger through yesterday's bread to find a roll softer than a rock or watch from the stoops, latched ahold of the ones who can just walk or carrying the ones that can't yet, the ragpicker yelling out but outyelled by the pots-and-pans hondler who knocks his metal together and both of them whispers compared to the big raw-throated ladies hollering down from their windows, lowering baskets and hauling up whatever they bought from the street vendors. Chickens hang by their feet, pickles float in barrels, and if Mott Street was garlic Hester is salt herring.

The Kid squeezes through till he finds the Hat Man. He needs a new cap. The one he's got One-Nugget Feeny says looks like he took a dump on it, which is fine for the paying customers, the rattier you look the better you sell if you're little, but it's nothing you want topping your knob when it's just you and the guys.

He tries on a few lids, checking his reflection in the butcher's window behind as the Hat Man watches him warily, sure that he's going to bolt with the merchandise. The Kid has his eye on a pair of shoes one stall over, light brown and shiny, with real laces that were made to go with them instead of string, a buck for the pair. His own old high-tops that Janek—that Hunky Joe passed down are split at the sole up front and his toes stick out if he doesn't curl them under.

"*Nu?*" says the Hat Man, impatient, but the Kid knows the Customer is King and just keeps trying on lids. There's a yellow-checked number that he pulls down over one eye.

"How much?"

The Hat Man holds up way too many fingers, so the Kid counters with a few fingers of his own. They keep it going for a while, the Kid knowing the bastid has a bottom price and when the old zid hawks something gray into the dirt at his feet and starts to shake his head and mutter in sheeny it's clear they've reached it. The Yellow Kid has to go to his grouch bag, not so easy here on Hester where there's a dozen eyes every way you turn, so he just digs into his pants, what Ikey calls cradling the cubes, and comes up with the mazuma.

"I'd say it's been a pleasure doin business with you," he says, "but it hasn't."

The Hat Man looks at the pennies in his palm like they might be slugs, exactly the kind of old tightwad who deserves a wooden crate with no brass, and the Kid takes a last look at those sweet brown shoes and shoves his way back out to Bowery.

There is a horse down on the corner of Broome. Little kids are circled staring like they never seen a dead nag before and a wop is trying to sell them shaved ice with lemon syrup from his bicycle box and a cop stands with his hands on his hips, thinking up what fine he's gonna strongarm out of the dinge whose wagon it was pulling. The dinge is down on his knees wrestling the harness off in a big puddle of horse piss that's still steaming hot though it smells like the nag's been dead for weeks. Friggin cops always got their mitts out for a donation and get one or not he'll just walk away and leave the carcass for somebody else to deal with it.

While the big mick has his back turned the Kid hops the back of a milk wagon headed uptown at a pretty good clip, the cans rattling empty over the cobblestones. Angelo Pino who shined shoes in front of Donnegan's got rolled over a couple weeks back hopping a dray full of crushed stone leaving the Park Row Building, the wheel popping his head open the guys said, but he was lugging his box and only had one hand free and that's when accidents is bound to happen. Angie's little brother Pasquale has the spot now, but the newshounds that drink in Donnegan's can't tell the difference and call him Guido, which was the name of the kid who worked there before Angelo.

The Yellow Kid lucks out and the milk wagon keeps rolling across Canal, keeps rolling uptown, the driver never looking back, carrying him up to Houston where he hops off and runs five blocks up to see Vera.

The old place don't look any worse. They moved a whole lot of times before he was old enough to know about it, is what Hunky Joe says, but this dump is the one the Kid remembers. Three stories, front and back entrance, toilet for the whole building out back, bring your own paper, jammed up next to three more shitboxes just like it. The Nemecs' kid Dusan who's never been right sits slobbering on the stoop and the Yellow Kid takes a minute to catch his breath before going in. His heart is racing. If the Old Man is there the odds are he's not conscious, and even if he is the Kid knows he can outrun the bastid, even in these damn flap-sole high tops. It got worse after Maminka died but he was a guzzler from Day One, old Kazimir. The Kid used to rush the can for him on the one outside job the Old Man had, making bricks. Wrestle a big pail of beer over to him twice a day, never a tip like some of the other kids got. Get plastered and moan out those old Chesky songs, go on one of his cursing, spitting stomps, pacing all five steps from one side of the apartment to the other. Bohunks come in Catholics and Free-Thinkers and the two brands just friggin hate each other. The Old Man is an *ateista*, a Free-Thinker, always going on about the idiot Pope and the idiot Bohunks who kiss his holy ass, like any of that matters here on East 5th Street. Make you glad to be an American. He was a miner back where they come from says Hunky Joe, but left to get away from Germans and Catholics and the coal dust. After he drunk himself out of the brickyard he holed up and started rolling cigars like every other stupid greenie on the block, Vera and Maminka stripping the leaves and Janek out getting into scrapes with the neighborhood gangs and him, Frantisek back then, running up and down the friggin stairs with buckets and bottles to keep the old bastid lubricated.

It's dark in the downstairs hallway and somebody is sleeping right by the stairs, got to step over to climb up. It smells like cabbage. At the door he hollers—you knock and they figure it's the landlord's collector come to jerk a few shekels out of you—and Vera answers. From the look on her face he can tell the Old Man is not at home.

"Frantisek!"

She looks like a ghost, Vera, pale and big-eyed and already a little bit stooped though she's only a year older than Hunky Joe, a couple of her teeth gone missing since the Kid saw her last.

"I come to say hi."

She pulls him in though he's happy to stay in the hallway. The room smells like the inside of a cigar box, tobacco winning out over the kerosene, with piles of leaves and stacks of wrappers and the day's work spread out thick on the table. Enough to make you gag. The window was always closed before to keep a breeze, should such a thing ever wander onto East 5th Street, from getting in and drying the leaves out. Then after Maminka jumped the Old Man nailed it shut forever.

"You are hungry?"

Vera never went to any school and speaks Bohunk English when nobody in the room, like the Kid, is willing to talk Chesky with her.

"Got a bellyful right now. He been around?"

Vera smiles, shrugs. He has tried to get her to give up on the Old Man, to walk outside in the sun and never come back, but it's like she's been sentenced to live in these little rooms forever, doing a jolt for some crime she can't even imagine.

"He is very sick."

Sick was how Maminka used to call it too, especially once he'd passed out and couldn't hit or kick anymore.

"You o.k. here? You need anything?"

It is a stupid question. She needs everything.

"I am no problem," says Vera. "Where do you sleep?"

This is always the big question with her, worrying about where he lays down at night ever since he told the Old Man to shove it and run off for good.

"Here and there," says the Yellow Kid. "Depends on where I am when it gets dark."

It was looking at the same damn walls every day that done it, finally, more than the Old Man going off with his hootch and his temper. "It's worse than the friggin Tombs in here," said Hunky Joe just before the last big fight, the one where he ended up on top of the Old Man with both of them bleeding and it was time for him to move on. The walls that Maminka tried to wash once and gave up on cause you had to haul the water up so many stairs, the walls with lighter-colored squares everywhere the Old Man took down pictures of saints the last poor bastids, some kind of Catholic Germans who snuck out a month behind in the rent, had left hanging. You put a nail in the window in this apartment, it might as well be in your coffin lid.

"Listen," he says, "you gotta forget that old soak and take care of yourself."

It's a waste to try to get Vera to take money, so he says he's got the afternoon extra to deal with and lets her hug him once. When he steps over the body propped against the bottom of the stairs he bends to see that it is the Old Man, in the tank again, wheezing a little as he breathes.

Any other day he might head over to the bathhouse on Rivington, give you a towel and chunk of soap for two cents and let the shower run a good five minutes before they shut it off on you. But there is **WAR!** and special editions waiting to be peddled.

The fellas got a crap game running behind the *Journal* when the Kid gets back, breathing hard from running the last six blocks. Ikey is holding the stones.

"Look who's got a new lid!"

"Yellow hat for the Yellow Kid!"

"You're so flush, you oughta get in on this," Ikey calls, shaking the dice softly by his ear the way he does, as if they are whispering to him. "I'm rollin hot here."

"I'll pass."

"Cheap bastid. You don't never play."

"He's savin up for his goin-away party," says Beans. "Gonna invite the whole city, get planted in a solid-ivory crate."

"That's all a racket," says Specs, rolling out a dolly loaded with a pile of specials. "Them coffins got a false bottom. Everybody goes home and they yank out their goods, leave the stiff in the dirt with the worms. Everybody knows that."

The newsies scoop their pennies off the ground and scramble to line up by seniority, boys who been selling the longest first, and the Kid takes a chance on another fifty. The schoolboys are out and ready to sell now, waiting at the back of the line.

"Bunch of friggin amateurs," says Ikey, who left classes after the sixth grade, "cloggin up the sidewalks."

Most of the stores and offices have dicks in the lobby to keep newsies and peddlers out, but the saloons are always open for business. The Kid stuffs his new cap inside his shirt, slaps the old one on his head, and makes a show of staggering under the weight of the bundle as he comes into Donnegan's.

"Lookit this kid," says Boylan from the *Sun*, who likes to sit by the door and listen for sirens to chase. "Little bastid's on death's door, he's still hustlin papers. Lay em down here, kid."

He offers his stool and the Kid parks his bundle, pulling a dozen off the top to work the room. It is elbow to elbow with reporters now, trading rumors about the **WAR!**, guzzling whiskey, ribbing each other. They are the best customers for print, some getting their own rag to crow over a byline, or buying three or four of the competition to see what the poop on the Row is.

"What's Boy Willie got to say now he's finally done it?" says Pope from the *World*, grabbing one from the Kid. "Probly wants to be made Admiral."

"Over Roosevelt's dead body."

"If that could be arranged," says Callan from the *Journal*, "the Chief would be only too happy."

"I'm takin names for the Regiment," Sweeny calls from behind the counter, waving a paper that dozens have signed. "Shall I put you on it, Kid?"

"Sure," says the Kid. "Sign me up."

That gets a laugh and somebody says he's already got the Yellow Fever so why not and he sells more papers and there is lots of kidding about who is too old or too young or too much of a hopeless souse to go to **WAR!** Then Lester Schoendienst gets up on his hind legs and calls for order.

"I've got me colyum fer tomorra ready," he says in the voice he puts on like a Ninth Ward mick, "and I'd aprayciate yer opinions."

From what the Kid can tell this bird writes a column where he pretends to be these two bog-trotters, Gilhooley and O'Malley, the former who is spose to be a beat cop and the other a sanitation worker who specializes in horse pucky.

"My opinion is it stinks," calls Pope, "and I haven't heard a word of it yet. Finley Peter Dunne, on his worst day—"

"Can outwrite you on yer best, we're all aware iv that, we are," Schoendienst comes back as he steps up on a chair to be seen over the crowd. "Now kape yer pie-hole buttoned while the true gentlemen iv the press give a listen."

"You break that chair, Lester," calls Sweeny, "you bought it."

"*So Martin O'Malley is plyin his trade,*" starts the scribbler, reading from his ink-smeared notebook, "*with a shovelful of road apples in mid-air, whin Officer Gilhooley strolls by on his rounds.*"

The reading is always good for the Kid. He keeps moving through the room as the newshounds listen, jamming papers under their elbows and into their hands, the men paying without looking at him.

"'*It's quite a swagger yer walkin with today, Tom,' says the man with the spade. 'Have they lowered the price on whiskey?*'

"'*Sure and hasn't the Congress itself signed the Articles iv* **WAR!**' *says the copper.*

"'*Ohhh—have they finally done the dade? Tis a hysteric occasion—*'

"'*It's got me martial spirit inflamed,' says Gilhooley. 'If there was a Spaniard at hand I'd pop him in the beezer meself!*'

"*O'Malley throws a glimmer around the street. 'And where is the swarthy little fandango-dancers whin you nade im? I don't suppose an Eyetalian would do?'*

"*'Diffrint race altogether, Martin. Yer Dons has been a haughty and crool outfit since the days of the conquistadoros, whereas your Eyetalian is more iv a Jovanny-come-lately to the Table iv Nations. Columbus himself was wurrkin for the Spaniards whin he bumped into the United States.'*

"*'They're a seafarin paypul, yer wops,' agrees O'Malley. 'Sure and haven't ye ivver seen em on the Staten Island Ferry, with the rag and polish in their hands? All the grrreat ocean voyages—Magellan, Cook, Henry Hudson sailin up our own West Side—there was always a little Jewseppy aboard to kape a sparkle on their boots.'*

"*'There's a call out fer fightin men,' says Gilhooley, twirling his stick. 'I've half a mind to throw me name into the hat.'*

"*'Half a mind indade,' says O'Malley, filling the back of his wagon.*

"*'Tis a grrreat day fer the Republic,' continues the officer, a far-off look in his eye. 'And the Cubings will be throwin a party as well.'*

"*'The divvil with the Cubings,' says O'Malley, tamping down his haul with the back of his spade. 'This is* our *donneybrook now. They want a fight, they can attack Porto Rico or one iv them ither islands in the Carrybium. Forst come, forst served is what I say!'*

"*'That's the spirit—'*

"*'And whin the Pearl iv the Aunt Tillies is free,' he adds, 'can the Emerald Isle be far behind?'*"

There is cheering and banging on tables then and Schoendienst buys a round for anyone who can shove their way up to the bar. At the door the Yellow Kid runs into Maxie Schimmel, lugging in a stack of *Herald*s.

"Two more rounds in these jokers," he shouts to Maxie over the sound of the scribblers stomping their feet in time and singing *Glory, Glory Hallelujah*, "and they'll buy *yes*terday's paper."

He heads over to the Park Row turnaround then and attacks the commuters getting into their trolleys to go home.

"**WAR!**" he hollers. "Spanish Threat to Burn Washington!"

He is bumping shoulders with One-Nugget Feeny, who's got an armful of the *World*.

"**WAR!**" cries Feeny. "*World* Exclusive, Cuba Declared Newest State!"

"**WAR!**" yells the Kid. "Houdini Disappears in Havana!"

"**WAR!**" shouts Feeny. "The *World* Remembers the *Maine*!"

"**WAR!**" screams the Yellow Kid. "The *Journal* Declares **WAR!** on Spain!"

* * *

The Kid is down to a handful by the time it is dark, hanging outside the New Citadel, the Delmonico's downtown joint on South William Street. He has all but one paper stashed under a trash barrel across the way, and every time a couple sports wander out with their bellies full of oysters and alligator pears he goes into his crybaby routine.

"Wah-hah-hah-hah!" he goes, tears running down his cheeks, standing smack between them and the hack stand, bawling and snuffling and holding the lonely paper out with trembling hands.

"What's the matter, sonny?" says one out of three.

"I wanna go to home!"

"Go home then."

"I can't! I gotta sell all my papers or my fadder'll knock the tar outta me! Whah-hah-hah-hah! Dis is my last one ony won't nobody buy it. I wanna go home!"

"Here, then. What's this, the Hearst paper? There ought to be a Commission to look into this—forcing young children out on the streets to peddle this trash! Here, go home now."

And before he's halfway down the block they're gone in their hack and he runs to grab the next one.

There is a woman, a young one, all dressed in satin and foxtails with a big hat with feathers and a bucket of perfume on her who bends down to take his face in her hands.

"Isn't he adorable?" she says. He has the ratty old cap on still, and he's been blubbering so much there's snot hanging out his nose and his toes are sticking out the front of Hunky Joe's old clodhoppers and he's yellow as the flophouse sheets, but what the hell, she thinks he's adorable that's her business. "What's the matter, little boy?"

There's nothing much the matter, he's never made so much mazuma in one day, ever, but her hands feel nice on his cheeks and the perfume is o.k. too, so he just keeps sniffling.

"I gotta sell—my last paper—before I can go home," he manages to whine out between sniffs, lips trembling. "An if I don't—"

"Hush now. Rupert?" And with this the skinny geezer scowling down at him sighs and digs into his jacket. "Rupert, buy this poor child's newspaper. How much is it, darling?"

"Only a nickel," says the Kid in a very small voice. "Onnaconna it's my last one."

Rupert slaps the coin into his palm and snatches the paper away.

"And where do you live?" asks the pretty woman, straightening up.

"Baxter Street," he answers without pause, "with my fadder and six baby sisters."

By the time he is making the long walk back up Broadway, legs weary, he has only four papers unsold. The *Journal* doesn't give you nothing back for returns, none of them do, so he is out the four cents.

He is passing Fulton Street, yawning already, when Sluggo Pilchek calls from under a streetlight.

"Yo Kid," he calls, "lookit what I got here."

At first when Sluggo peels the paper back he thinks it is dead, but then he can see its face is red and that it's only too weak to cry, little eyes blurry and almost clear blue, naked inside the front page of the morning *Telegraph*.

"Some lousy break, huh?" says Sluggo, who works for the *Sun*. "Ditched on the street wrapped in a stinker rag like that."

"What you gonna do with it?"

"What am I spose to do with it? The old lady's already got a squaller at home."

"We can't leave it here."

"Its mother did."

The Yellow Kid rewraps the baby, lifts it awkwardly. "Grab my papers."

"You aint gonna sell these now—"

"Grab em."

"What are we doing?"

"Look for a cop."

Sluggo picks the Kid's papers up, shakes his head. "This hour? They're all up on Bowery, suckin at the tit."

"So we'll bring it to the nuns."

They walk, the Yellow Kid wondering if it's still alive but not daring to check.

"How'd you do today?" asks Sluggo.

"Knocked em dead. They can't get enough of this Spain business."

"It'll only get better."

"That's what they say."

Sluggo cocks a doubtful eye at the Kid's new bundle. "So how you figure the nuns feed these things?"

"They keep milk."

"Just sittin around?"

"Maybe."

"Cause they got no tits, nuns."

"Really?"

"Brides of Christ," says Sluggo. "They're not spose to have em."

"They must keep milk then."

"It goes bad awful easy."

The Kid shrugs. "They do what they can," he says, "then send em to Randall's Island."

"What's that?"

Maminka had gone out there for a while, after she was big with the last one who was going to be Anezka if it was a girl or Miklos if it was a boy, the last one that came out blue, not yellow, and didn't breathe. She went out there for the money a couple weeks, before she got so low she just sat and stared out the window that wasn't nailed shut yet, frozen for hours like the Lady Undressing for Bath. You took a ferry to Randall's and nursed the orphan babies and the nuns at the Infants' Hospital paid you.

"They bring women out there to feed the squallers," says the Kid. "It's like a dairy."

"Well whoever ditched this kid should of ditched it out there. Stead of the friggin sidewalk."

"Women get moody," says the Kid, "you never know what they'll do."

"You can say that again," says Sluggo.

Most of the shops are closed up. A lone horse trolley rolls by in the opposite direction, nearly empty.

"Where you sleepin?"

"They got a room by the presses at the *Sun*," says Sluggo. "We can stretch out on the benches. Don't cost a penny."

"Yeah, but you sleep at the *Sun*, you gotta sell the *Sun*."

Sluggo shrugs, his feelings hurt. "It's a good paper. Everybody says so."

There are no cops on lower Broadway, so they cut across City Hall Park, nearly empty now, the fountain shut off, and angle up to the Five Points Mission on Pearl. They used to have a stroller outside, one of those nice wicker jobs with the wheels pulled off so nobody would nick it, but people would just ditch their babies in it and blow, no matter what the weather, so now you got to rattle the knocker.

"Lord save us, not another one," says the Sister of Charity who answers. "And at this hour."

"We could put it back if you want," says Sluggo.

"You'll do nothing of the sort." She takes the little thing from the Kid, holds it up to the light. "Only a few hours in this world, the poor thing. Not much hope for him."

"You gonna put it on one of those trains?" The Kid has heard about Sister Irene and her trains, sending orphans out to lonely people in the far West, out past Jersey.

"He'll be lucky to see the sun rise," she says, hugging it close and turning to go. "We'll have to get the sacraments taken care of, save his little soul."

"What I tell you?" says Sluggo when she has closed the door on them without a tip or even a thank-you. "No tits."

Sluggo gives the Kid his papers back and heads off for the *Sun* building. The Newsboys' Lodging House is close on Duane, where everything is a nickel-and-a-penny—six cents for a bunk, six cents for coffee and roll in the morning, six cents for pork and beans at night. You can wash up, bank your money, even get a stake to buy the next day's papers if they know you well enough. But it is a warm night and doesn't feel like rain. There is a headstone, a big tall hunk of polished pink rock that shields you from sight of the street in the old St. Paul cemetery yard. Big letters on the front of the stone, somebody important planted under it.

The Yellow Kid spreads his newspapers carefully on the ground, lies down on them and looks up at the stars. The Sunday edition is best for this, at least a hundred pages, three color supplements, a regular mattress of a newspaper, but two afternoon extras will do. If the baby lives, he thinks, probly it will get sent out somewhere with nothing but dirt and trees on the ground, where the horses got no trolleys hitched to them, where you look up in the sky and there's nothing but clouds. Poor bastid. The Kid can hear the thrum of the presses rolling in the giant buildings a block away, can feel the rumble of them through the ground here at the center of America. They will run all night and tomorrow there will be fresh news to sell. The baby is safe with the nuns and the Spanish fleet is creeping who knows where and the Yellow Kid has a full belly and a new hat and the moon is rising nearly full, smack behind the chapel spire. There is **WAR!**, and fat times lie just around the corner.

EXILE

Wu sits back among the crates as his assistant pores over a page of sums, clacking an abacus. The warehouse smells of sandalwood and machine oil. Wu speaks English with Diosdado and never ceases smiling.

"You are an emissary."

"I assure you that the money is secure," Diosdado explains. "Here in a bank in the city."

"We have all heard of your General's settlement with the Spanish crown." Wu slumps with his hands folded on his stomach, a round man dressed in the Western style, with a white fedora tilted back on his head. His assistant wears a blue cotton work tunic and makes small noises as he calculates.

"We can make a purchase, then?"

Wu shows Diosdado the palms of his hands. "The merchandise you seek is unavailable."

"I was told that if anyone in Hongkong could accommodate us—"

"It would be I, yes. But our new administrators, in their wisdom, have forbidden trade in weapons."

It is always hard to tell with them, the Chinese, what is bargaining and what is fact.

"Many things are forbidden in the Crown Colony," says Diosdado blandly, "and yet you are known to deal in them." Wu is alleged to be head of the Three Harmonies Society and an exporter of illegal coolies from Macao. He continues to smile.

"This city is alive with rumor. Weapons, however, are of a great concern to the British government. May I inquire what purpose you might have in acquiring so many of them?"

"For our people," says Diosdado. "To fight the Spanish."

"But the terms of your Treaty—"

"Have been violated repeatedly."

Wu sighs and shakes his head. "Politics. Irresolvable conflicts. I am so very content to remain outside of their sphere."

"If you were to quote me a price—"

"The Germans in Shandong are growing wary of our—our more *exci*table citizens," says Wu, leaning forward to make his point. "And the British do not wish to upset the Germans—"

"We are not going to give weapons to the Boxers."

"Be that as it may, there are none here to be purchased."

Wu turns and tells the assistant, in Cantonese, that Diosdado wants to buy guns for the naked savages back home, as if they could be taught to use them. The assistant has a coughing laugh that rattles his abacus. Diosdado remains expressionless.

"Do you know of anybody who might have something we could buy?"

"If you are going to fight the Spanish," says Wu, "surely there will be wounded. I can offer you an excellent deal on medicinal herbs—"

"I'm not authorized to buy opium." Diosdado stands to leave. "Thank you for your time." At least this one did not promise like the Japanese, promise and never deliver. Only Dr. Sun, the Chinese revolutionist, actually sent them weapons, but the boat foundered in a typhoon and all was lost.

"So very sorry to disappoint you," smiles Wu from his throne of crates.

"We carry one foreign power on our back," Diosdado says in Cantonese as he bows goodbye, "while China opens her legs for a dozen."

The streets west of Central Market are packed with the usual swarm of humanity, the only relief from the noisy mass of them an occasional unobstructed glimpse up to the slope of Victoria Peak, where the humanity thins out and the British and the wealthiest of the Chinese merchant kings have built their palaces. It is green up there, with unfouled air to breathe, quiet. Diosdado's rickshaw boy grunts as he trots up a slight incline, weaving them through vegetable stalls and charm-sellers, past an oversized British official sitting pinkly on a pallet borne by four sweating lackeys hustling in the opposite direction. A pair of carriages rattle by, full of wealthy Chinese heading to the Happy Valley racecourse, shouting out joyously as they go.

A city built on trade, thinks Diosdado, with the soul of a whore.

Junta activities in Hongkong emanate from the two houses on Morrison Hill Road in Wanchai. Don Felipe Agoncillo lives in the smaller one with his family and whoever spills over from the other. Diosdado calls to the boy when they reach the house, steps down, and reluctantly parts with a few coins. There is, of course, no more money from Don Nicasio, and the Junta can only spare a tiny stipend for its exiled patriots. But it wouldn't do to arrive soaked in perspiration from the climb, not with the General back from Singapore.

It is Señora Agoncillo herself who answers the door, beautiful and gracious.

"Our young linguist," she says, smiling and stepping back to allow him passage. "You must come out of the heat."

He is ushered to the study, where members of the Junta and a few of the exiled government stand around a table, frowning over a drawing.

"I understand why the sun has a face," says one, "but shouldn't it be smiling?"

"In a Masonic triangle—"

"Just a triangle—"

"All triangles are Masonic. You can't avoid the association."

"The three points of the triangle represent Liberty, Equality, and Fraternity."

"The French—"

"The French have nothing to do with us."

"I thought the three stars—"

"They represent Luzon, Visayas, and Mindanao—"

"Wonderful. Mindanao. Why not a half-moon and a scimitar?"

"The *moros* are Filipinos, whatever their beliefs."

"And the rays emanating—"

"Eight rays, eight provinces that rose in '96—"

"You make eight?"

"Batangas, Bulacan, Cavite, Laguna, Manila, Nueva Ecija, Pampanga, and Tarlac."

"You allow a more generous definition of *revolt* than I."

"Blue and red, like the flag of independent Cuba."

"You're forgetting the white triangle."

"Red, white, and blue—"

"Symbolic," says the slender, large-eyed man who has been sitting quietly at the head of the table, "of our hopeful friendship with the United States."

He smiles shyly. "Or at least that's what I told their Consul in Singapore."

The men laugh. Diosdado has never seen the General in person before. He seems too slender, too gentle a man to be the strongman of Cavite, who outfought and then outfoxed the Spanish *cazadores*, who had the grit to order the execution of the Bonifacios and risk tearing the movement apart.

"He suggested that we have a new banner, to rally the people."

The voice is soft, seemingly without irony. He didn't order the executions, Diosdado corrects himself, he merely allowed them to happen.

"Do you trust them?" asks Mascardo.

"The hulls of their Great White Fleet have been painted gray for battle and they have been asked by the British, in the interests of neutrality, to leave the harbor. We can only hope that they are trustworthy." The General turns and looks directly at Diosdado. "And what do you think, Argus?" He indicates the drawing. "About my design?"

The men of the Junta all turn toward Diosdado. He is speechless at first, that the General would recognize him, would know his code name, would ask his opinion.

"We are a complex nation," he answers in Tagalog. "We deserve a complex flag."

The General laughs. "You went to see the Hong man?"

Diosdado nods. "Not a single rifle."

Malvar, who sent him on the mission, scowls, but the General's expression does not alter.

"No matter," he says. "The Americans have promised to sell us as many as we need."

"When?" asks Riego de Dios.

"We are to wait here for their summons," says the General.

"Our people are already fighting in the Ilocos."

"There is little else to entertain oneself with in the Ilocos," says Alejandrino, and the men laugh again.

The General turns back to Diosdado. "We will be waiting here for the summons," he says, "but you, young man, are to go immediately to Manila."

Diosdado takes a deep breath, trying to appear unfazed by the order. Manila. He has been condemned there as a traitor, drawings of him, poorly rendered, circulated by the *guardia*. He thought he might never see the city again.

"And what is my mission?"

The General smiles. "To wait for our American brothers," he says, "and embrace them when they step ashore."

THE CLOUD CITY

Leadville is a wound festering between the Mosquito Range and the Wasatch Mountains, a high-plains sprawl of new-built structures surrounded by treeless hills pocked with diggings, hills that at closer look are only piles of tailings excreted from the holes men have torn into the earth. Blasted rock spews from tipple chutes into ore cars that rattle and slam down tramways behind coal-devouring engines, wooden headhouse towers marking the mine portals where hoist cables screech lowering men crammed in steel cages down tomb-dark vertical shafts, tongues of candles flickering on their hats, oil lanterns in hand, dropping with stomach-shifting speed past the played-out silver, the abandoned tunnels, past Level Three, Level Four, Level Five, down four hundred feet more sucking air hammered into the ground by a compressor, Level Eight, Level Nine, then *thunk* to bedrock and the door clanging open and the men spilling out into the main chamber to face a half-dozen galleries. The newest of these, the rawest, leads back a thousand feet, only half that distance with track on the floor. At the end of it, in the nervous light of three candles, Hod braces himself in a narrow fissure and rams a seventy-five-pound stoper drill straight up into the stony roof above him, rock dust filling the crevice, filling his nose his mouth his lungs, ear-shattering trip-hammer roar as he drives the cutting bit into hardrock a thousand strokes per minute, vibration coursing through his chest down his backbone and out through his legs into the rock he is wedged in, muscles of his arms taut cables pushing the drill steel up, up, every part of him straining and concentrated on the shoot-hole above till Cap Stover reaches up to swat his leg. Time to change bits.

Sudden quiet.

Hanging rock dust.

Hod hands the drill down to the chuck tender, who twists the bar stock and pulls out the old steel, still hot to the touch. The edges of the star-shaped cutting bit have been hammered smooth. Cap jiggers in a new rod of drill steel, twists it to lock.

Grimes, the foreman, calls up through the winze from the level below. "You all right up there?"

"Changing steel, boss," Cap calls down into the little opening.

"How's it coming?"

Cap looks up to Hod, who shows him fingers. If he tries to talk it will start the coughing again.

"Three more to go, then you can shoot," calls Cap.

"Keep on it," calls the foreman, and then nothing.

Hod starts the tip of the steel into the shoot-hole, then guides the rod as Cap hoists the body of the hammer drill back up to him, unkinking the wire-belted cable that leads back to the compressor at the head of the gallery.

"Need a minute?"

Hod shakes his head, then braces himself again and muscles the heavy drill upward till the bit jams against the unyielding top of the hole. The air is almost clear now and he takes a big gulp of it and squeezes the trigger—shriek of metal cutting rock, vibration filling his body once again.

Maybe he'll find her tonight.

One of the girls on the Row who recognized him from Skaguay said Addie Lee is in town, staying at the Crysopolis, but the desk jockey said there were no redheads upstairs and nobody going by any of the names Hod recalled her using. Hod drills and thinks how it would be to be with her, to hold her. He searched the town last night and the night before, she'd been there and gone, sure, happy to pass it on, what was his name again? Hod drills and concentrates on a single image, her cheek resting in sleep against his bare breast, the smell of her hair, her breath warm and steady against his skin. He'll find her tonight, or she will find him.

The shooters are on their way into the drift by the time Hod and Cap come out on the tracks.

"Got some holes need packin," says Cap to Greek Steve as he passes with a box of blasting powder and a spool of fuse cord. "And you might ought to shore the roof up some before you set anything off."

"Fockeen guys," says Greek Steve, his usual greeting and the only English he's ever been heard to utter. They step out into the gallery to join the others coming off shift, Hod's arms floating slightly without the bulky widowmaker in them. Flem Hurley is honking into his crumpled bandanna, trying to muffle the echo in the stone chamber. The other men look away. Miners' con is carried as a dirty secret, something shameful. A weakness in a tough business.

Me in six months, thinks Hod. He only smiles and nods as the others swap reports from their different drives, each ore face a more grievous affront to the human body, darker, narrower, dustier, the timbers bent with stress, the sides unstable and the top threatening to come down.

"Damn roof make more noise than a Chinaman in a fish market," says old Arlie Bogle through cheeks bulging with tobacco. "The more you wedge it the more it complains."

"The sides where I'm at is all crumbling," mutters Dog Dietrich. "Got so many hay bales piled up you got to walk sideways to get through, but it aint but sand holdin the whole deal up."

"Leastways it's dry, down this level."

"Hell, you don't ever know," says Cap. "She be dry as a bone and one day some mucker pokes his shovel into the wrong crack—"

"Seen a couple fellas blowed straight out of a hole down Idaho Springs once, long with a half-ton ore car and a quarter-mile of track. Busted through to a whole underground lake—"

"All that pressure built up, waitin there centuries for some dumb hunkie—"

Fell down shaft

Hod was on the Grievance Committee in Butte, had memorized the litany of Cause of Fatality they had stolen from the coroner's office—

Fall of ore
Crushed in machinery

It was all in the same handwriting, and he imagined the functionary, poker-faced as he listened to the shift boss's explanation, trying to compress each man's grisly end into a one-line epitaph—

Rock fall
Suffocated by carbonic-acid gas
Shot of dynamite
Struck by cage
Explosion of powder
Bucket fell down shaft

Hod has been on rescue crews, has helped dig the flattened remains of a half-dozen miners out from a collapse, bodies spread and pressed to the thickness of a floor plank—

Car tipped on man
Returned to blast area too soon
Caught between loaded ore cars
Rope broke on cage
Pinned against post
Cave of dirt while timbering
Fell into ore bin
Caught between trippers, bled to death
Refiring missed hole
Killed by gas in bag house

There were quick deaths and slow deaths, deaths that blew out the lights in the drive and deaths not discovered till the next shift stumbled on the scene—

Picking out missed shot
Caught between timbers and cage
Pinned under a motor

There were deaths caused by stupidity—

Thawing powder in open fire

—greenhorns fed to the mines, men from desperate countries who nodded with incomprehension when instructions were given and marched into the drives armed with every tool they needed to murder themselves and the man next to them. There were deaths caused by the inescapable nature of the job—

Bad air

There were mines that rumbled and growled and warned you not to challenge them, and sneaking mines, mines that invited you deeper and killed you with gases invisible and odorless. The truth was that the air was always bad and the roof always unstable and the laws of gravity without pity. Hod has them all in his head, the jacks and the shooters, the muckers and timbermen, the chute-loaders and motormen and cagers and jigger bosses and whistlepunks, the seasoned miners and the hapless immigrants, and knows they are a scant fraction of those dead or dying from what he already carries in his lungs.

"A mine has got more ways to kill a man than Carter got liver pills," says Cap as they step into the elevator. "You can't take it personal."

Grimes comes then to count heads and the men grow silent. He fired a boy the other day, a little nervous Dago kid, accusing him of high-grading. The boy had turned his pockets inside out, dropped his pants and opened the flap of his long johns and not so much as a lead pebble fell out, but Grimes chased him anyway.

Hod and the shift boss face each other, nose to nose in the press of miners as the man-skip hoists them up through the levels, Grimes chewing tobacco and avoiding Hod's eyes. Hod is one of the few who passed on shitting in Grimes's lunchpail this morning when the muckers got hold of it. They had not been short on volunteers.

The cables shriek, cage shuddering as they jolt to a stop. The bar is drawn and the miners crowd out through the split-log shafthouse and into the late sun filtering through the refinery smoke.

The mine dick who pinched Hod and Big Ten stands at the side of the tramway with another company gun, a pimple-faced kid with a worried look on his face. The dick points at Hod.

"You."

Hod can feel Grimes shifting behind him as he steps away from the others who cross to pull their tags off the shift board, brassing out, and don't look back.

"Say your name was?"

"Metoxen. Henry." Hod has recognized two or three other jacks on the job from his Butte days, men also digging under bogus handles. They usually don't much care who you are if the ore keeps rolling out.

The mine dick steps up to look him in the eye. He can feel Grimes's breath on his neck.

"There's somebody got you pegged as a fella name Brackenridge. Officer in the Federation."

There'd been a riot in Leadville in '96, and the Federation led a strike just last year, shut most of the works down and had the owners worried some till the Colorado Guard was brought in to keep the workers starving and away from the driftmouths. One hothead had snuck through the sentries and sabotaged the pumps up on Carbonate Hill, flooding some of the mines beyond repair.

"That aint me," says Hod.

"Somebody says it is."

"Who would that be?"

They keep a blacklist, he knows, but he's never been kodaked by the bulls or sat for a police artist. Not yet.

"Don't matter who it is."

"Well it's not true."

"That don't matter neither," says the mine dick. "You're done."

The nervous kid puts his hand on the butt of his gun. "That means out of company lodgings. Tonight."

"He knows what it means."

This is where you always have to be careful, Hod thinks, not admit to anything but not give them an excuse to unload on you.

"I worked three days already this week," he says.

Grimes speaks up behind him. "That's your lookout." Grimes who a year ago was just another rock donkey like Hod, Grimes who for another fifty cents a day drives them and curses them, hollers cause they're going through drill bits like green corn through a goose then hollers louder cause the jacking is going too slow, Grimes who missed his lunch because the day shift left their opinion of him steaming in it.

"We don't pay off no Reds," he says.

Hod smells apricots, acid and thick in the air, the separation plant upwind running their cyanide process, and the ball mill rumbling louder than thunder even a half mile away, and everywhere around them smoke, black smoke hanging over the tailing dumps and the smelters and the ore trains and over the hodgepodge shitpile of a town itself, hanging like a bad mood from Ball Mountain to Pawnee Gulch.

"Sure will miss it," says Hod and steps quickly past the mine thugs.

He wanted to greet her with a job and a bankroll. He has twenty-five dollars hid in his street shoes but that won't last long here, nothing but a man's labor cheap in Leadville.

The boys in the washhouse are careful to avoid him, not sure who might be a spy scrubbing under the steaming water, sympathetic but living from payday to payday themselves. Hod sniffs shower spray into his nose and blows out gray clots, swishes the grit out of his mouth and works the carbolic soap deep into his hide, feeling it burn a little before he lets the cold water blast it off. The smelters pay only two dollars a day, two and a half tops, but they haven't been struck so often and are less vigilant. In town there are only pimps, faro dealers, and respectable folks, the doctors and lawyers and assayers for the big outfits, and then a lot of former rock donkeys missing arms or legs who are living, more like slowly dying, on the bum. The clothes shed is empty but for Hod by the time he laces his shoes up and is ready to leave, hair wetly combed, shoe tops polished on the backs of his legs. He wishes he'd shaved this morning.

They take one look and say they aren't hiring at the Thespian, or the Irene Number Two or the Julia Fiske or the Eclipse or the Forsaken or any of the other diggings and by the time he gets to Harrison Reduction it is dark.

It takes a while for the floor boss upstairs to understand what Hod is yelling in his ear, bulk ore thundering down the chute onto crushers and the crushers spinning, cannonballs inside tumbling to smash the biggest chunks into smaller ones that rattle walnut-sized to the shaker screens then tip into the grinders, iron ore-cart wheels screeching over the thrum of the conveyor belts and the roaring furnaces below, but finally he points down through the floor and hollers back "See van Pelt!"

The smelting works is not allowed to cool, men feeding the furnaces day and night, and Hod has to pause halfway down, air searing his lungs, till the heat of the metal steps prods his feet into movement. A bare-chested worker jams his lance into the mouth of the nearest furnace, which erupts with blue-green flame before the glowing red tongue oozes out, bubbling and smoking as it fills the sluice and rolls forward, the heavier matte beneath channeled off to the side as the molten surface waste spills over the front edge to splash, hissing viciously, into the conical slag pot below. Another sweat-drenched worker rushes forward pushing a cart frame, jacking the pot up off its stubby legs and rolling it, still sizzling, out through the low opening to the tip. Cones of just-dumped waste glow on the spoil bank, their light fading as they cool to ash, piles flickering here and there, dying, smoke wisping up toward the moon. Van Pelt is a balding man scribbling on a production log steadied against his assistant's back. Both men wear flannel jackets and appear not to perspire.

"Worked in a smelter before?" Van Pelt gives Hod the briefest of glances and continues to write in the log.

Hod nods at a worker rolling a slag cart past, head turned away from the trailing fumes. "I can do that."

"But you just come from a mine, didn't you?"

Hod's hair feels like it's on fire, each breath scorching, and his high-mountain headache sits right behind his eyeballs, sharp as a fresh drill bit. He is in no shape to invent a plausible lie.

"Yes sir, I have."

"Fired."

"They didn't have no complaint with my work."

When the supervisor turns to look at him again there is the reflection from the angry furnace in his eyes. "Agitator."

"No sir," says Hod, cap held twisted in his hands. "Just a working man needs a job."

Van Pelt lifts the production log and the assistant straightens his back. "Won't find one in Leadville, not in the mines, not in the mills. Word's gone out on you, son."

The man was a colonel in Horace Tabor's light cavalry, Hod remembers, the vigilante outfit that tried to boot the union out of town before the militia came in. The man is on the list Cap showed him once in the company dormitory before lights out, high up among the ones to be dealt with if the class war ever really boils over into something serious, something final. Hod is wasting his time here.

When he gets back to the dormitory he finds his lower bunk stripped bare, his few belongings piled on the mattress. Mrs. Mapes sits scowling and rocking and smoking her pipe in the entryway, snorting once when he passes with his roll to go out the back stairs.

There is a burro standing in the path down the hill, a slat-ribbed jenny with scabs on her rump, staring at nothing and still as a painting. Most of the wild pack wandering around the gulches are too old or too ornery to work anymore, no longer worth a prospector's handful of feed, but this is a loner with a mad gleam.

"Look like you had your fill of it," says Hod softly, making a careful arc around the animal. "Don't spose I blame you."

There is not the slightest movement in the creature's eye as he passes, only the stare, angry and infinite.

There are men in tailored suits and ladies not for hire outside of the

Delaware and at Tabor's Grand Hotel on Seventh. Hod fights the notion that he should go inside and search out someone higher up the pyramid than Burt Grimes, maybe surprise old J. J. Brown or John Campion or any of the top-hatted, champagne-swilling bonanza kings who own the town and suggest where they might stick the Little Johnny and the rest of the Ibex works, but they are probably forted up in their Denver mansions and unavailable to entertain his opinions. Instead he drifts down slag-paved Harrison to Chestnut Street, already bustling with miners determined to throw their hard-earned money away, and begins to search the thirst parlors and love shops for Addie Lee.

He begins asking in the saloons. He has taken up whiskey, to scour the deep dust out from his craw, and it seems only polite to order at least a small one in each place before asking questions.

"Couple days ago, sure," says McCormack in the first of the gin mills. "It isn't like ye could miss her in a crowd. Had a bad cough, though." The bartender pours Hod two fingers' worth. "Word has it ye've been chased."

Company spies are rampant in Leadville, and more than one miner has been dumped, bleeding and unconscious, on the railroad platform late at night, a paper with *Out of State* scrawled on it pinned to his back.

"They got me confused with a Federation man."

"False witness is a terrible thing," says McCormack. "Not that I've any-thing against the union."

There are Federation men in town as well, and the mine dicks, the smart ones, never walk abroad at night unless they're heeled or in a group.

"I suppose we all look alike to them." Hod pours the whiskey straight to the back of his throat, still not reconciled to the taste of it.

"I've heard they're hiring again in Blackhawk," says the bartender. Behind him hangs a painting of naked women being chased by bearded men with goat's legs. There was an identical one in Skaguay, Hod can't remember which saloon.

"The thing to keep in mind," Jeff Smith used to say, *"is they'll never catch up with those females."*

There are a dozen flockie miners taking up the rest of the counter and talk-ing whatever it is they talk, a couple assayers losing at hi-lo and Riggins, who used to be a foreman at the Morning Star before his leg was shattered under an ore car, passed out face-down at his table. No women yet. Hod feels the wel-come numbness start at the roof of his mouth. Addie Lee tries to dress in green, to compliment her hair, and wears a scent like nothing else smelled in Leadville.

"Of course, if yer on their list, ye might consider a change of careers," says McCormack, who the men say worked the hard coal back in Pennsylvania, lowering his voice as he leans in. "Speakin from me own experience."

Hod drains his glass and wanders back out onto the street, packed with miners now, men speaking in a half-dozen tongues and searching, searching for a fight, a card game, a woman, searching for some proof they are alive and of some consequence on the earth's shaft-pitted surface. Music spills out from the saloons, from house ensembles and melodeons and groups of soon-to-be-drunken men harmonizing—

Oh show me a camp
Where the gold miners tramp
And the buncos and prostitutes thrive
Where dance halls come first
And the faro banks burst
And every saloon is a dive!

Hod steps into the street to avoid a strutting mucker with blood in his eye. If she is here and he can find her he doesn't know what he'll do, no money, no job. There are men, he knows, who live off their women, who set them up in cribs or turn them onto the streets, but he has never considered it. And she never offered.

He looks for Addie Lee in the Saddle Rock and the Cloud City Saloon and in Hyman's and in Curley Small's pool hall and behind West Second in Stillborn Alley and even passes by the Crysopolis again to get the same answer, payday girls sitting in the lobby offering to take her place it's all the same in the dark honey but he continues, throat not so raw now, a swallow or two in each of the saloons and nobody has seen her, not the faro dealers or the sporting women or the men dishing poison behind the bar, and by the time he finds Spanish Mary in the Trail's End he can't feel his nose and even the American miners are speaking words he doesn't understand.

Spanish Mary has one crooked eye and seems always to be looking over your shoulder.

"Sure, I know her. Skinny as a broomstick."

"She been around tonight?"

If the woman recognizes him she doesn't let on, neither of her eyes making contact with his as she watches the action in the saloon. "She gone off to Cripple Creek with the others."

"Others?"

"Fellas get tired of the same old slop buckets, they shift em around. There's a bunch just come in from the Creek if you're looking for something new."

"She just left?"

"The Poontang Special rolled out yesterday."

"But you said she just got here—"

Spanish Mary shrugs. *Down Went McGinty* is on the pianola and she absently taps her fingers on the tabletop, a little behind the beat. "Maybe she'll end up at the Old Homestead, spreadin it for the carriage trade. The cough she got, she sure can't stay up this high."

Hod grabs the back of a chair to steady himself. He's only passed out once, climbing the hill back to his bunk, and woke with his pockets empty and his shoes gone. He feels like if he doesn't find his girl, his skinny, tubercular whore of a girl, there will be nothing left to tie him to the earth, that the whiskey will float him somewhere else, somewhere darker and less solid than the deepest mine he's ever crawled into.

Spanish Mary snorts. "Think they getting something new," she smiles, "when it's only been relocated."

He doesn't quite remember how he gets to the next place, but there he is, standing in the middle of the narrow, unsteady room. There are paintings, mostly of gaudily dressed women, balanced on a strip of wood trim high on one wall and a herd of animal heads—deer, antelope, elk, mountain goat—hung on the opposite. There is a sallow little professor sleep-walking his fingers over the piano keys in one corner and a heat-blasting woodstove, a bar with a dozen Polish muckers swilling beer and, at one of the three faro tables, little Billy Irwin and Niles Manigault losing to the house.

"Behold," says Niles, "a fellow pugilist has graced our presence."

Hod knows Irwin as a tough little mick who works at the Maid of Erin mine when he's not fighting.

"This scruffy mine rat, is it?"

"Hands of stone," winks Niles. "In the land of Gold and Hardships he was legend."

Hod stares at him and tries to keep his balance.

"He's the one was bounced at the Ibex today," says the Irishman. "The story's all over Leadville."

"I note that you have finally succumbed to the nectar of the grain," says Niles, raising his own glass. "May I offer you a libation?"

Hod sits heavily in the empty chair next to the gambler. "I've had enough."

"Yes—extemely discouraging to lose one's employment. Or are we still pining after that underfed daughter of joy?"

"Ye won't find any work in this town," says Billy Irwin. "Unless it's a potwalloper in some hash house."

"You left Skaguay." It is hard for Hod to form the words.

"Shortly after your own retreat. A rather large sporting debt to a person of lethal temperament—"

"Soapy couldn't fix it?"

"We run that skulkin little rat out of town years ago," says the fighter.

Manigault's expression does not change. "Soapy has met his Maker."

"Bastard still owes me money," says the little mick.

"Billy here is on a card in Denver this Friday—"

"I'm not fighting," says Hod.

"Dago Mike Mongone, and I'll lay the bye flat in less than five rounds—"

"I'm not fighting."

He has managed not to think too often about Ox Knudsen. Real fighters, if the bout is straight, know what they're getting into. Like soldiers on a battle-field. But a fella like Ox, all swagger and no sense, sooner or later in Skaguay somebody was bound to—

"Of course not," says Niles, "Only a desperate man would deign to step into the prize ring."

The professor is playing *Break the News to Mother* and Hod wants to cry. He's not sure exactly where Cripple Creek is, only that it is downhill from here. Everything is downhill from Leadville. Niles jiggles his stack of blues in one hand, studying Hod as if his face is the faro layout and he is figuring his next play.

"Only a man with nothing left to his name."

Hod feels himself falling, falling into the center of the earth, lights begin-ning to flicker, the man-skip plummeting too fast, and reaches for something to hold on to.

ERRATUM

Here we scribe truth in hot lead.

The phrase makes Milsap smile as he sits at the machine, compositing the front page for the morning edition. It's what Mr. Clawson always shouts out when he's giving someone a tour of the paper and stops by the Linotype. The visitors, whether they're schoolchildren or adults, will have their hands over their ears against the din, but they nod, understanding, and it makes Milsap swell.

"*Drew, here,*" Mr. Clawson will say, putting a hand lightly on his shoulder, "*is an extension of this wonderful machine.*"

The left header has been set, in 24-point Clarendon—

NEW OUTRAGE IN EAGLE ROCK
RURAL WOMEN LIVING IN FEAR

—another violation in what seems to be an epidemic throughout the state. Milsap's fingers fly over the keys, brass and steel rattling into the assembler box and molten metal flowing down to make the slugs. He did it by hand in what they're already calling the old days, building sentences a letter at a time with a dozen other setters in the room. Mr. Clawson got the Model 1 five years ago and Milsap is the only one left who can look into the machine and savor its intricate beauty, the interplay of belts and blocks, gears and wheels, the way it cycles the matrices back into the distributor, every letter into its distinct channel, drink in the thick, hot-metal smell of it. And he is the only one who can glance at a piece of copy, even something scrawled with hasty hand, and see it in solid block columns before his fingers touch the keyboard, edit the wording on the fly without resorting to awkward hyphens or loose lines for his justification. There are no orphans or widows dangling from Milsap's paragraphs. He understands better than anybody that words are not sounds made of air but solid objects, with weight and consequence.

Milsap hesitates for a scant second—Mr. Clawson prefers not to separate *black* and *brute* on a line break—he adds *burly* and it squares off nicely. Milsap is hammering out slugs faster than little Davey, his printer's devil, can supply him, but as he moves down the column the feeling begins to creep on him. It is upsetting, naturally, what has been going on throughout the state this fall, every day another story or two he types in, not to mention what he reads in the Raleigh papers Mr. Clawson lays out in the lunchroom. It is enough to make a white man pick up a gun. But this is different, it's not anger—it's that other strange sensation, that feeling where you're sure you've seen it before, read it before, even if it is plain you could not have—

What tips it is that *nameless crime* is naked, unsheathed of its inverted commas, which Mr. Clawson believes add impact to the phrase without offending delicate sensibilities. The upstate papers, the *Caucasian* and the *News and Observer*, leave them off, though, just like they prefer to throw exclamation points on their scareheads, which Mr. Clawson considers vulgar and unnecessary.

None of the other compositors actually read the copy, allowing some very sloppy errors into print. But Milsap has the gift, has had it since he was a boy and could read the *McGuffey's* across the room and upside-down, the gift of seeing and understanding a whole block of story at the same time instead of plodding through it word by word. Mr. Clawson says he ought to be an attraction for P. T. Barnum, only Barnum couldn't pay him enough to give up Milsap. There were other boys growing up who called him freak, and his mother once had Reverend Calhoun from the Pentecostal cast devils out of him, but here, tucked into the metal racket of production, he is indispensible. "Drew practically resides here," Mr. Clawson is fond of saying. "I'm only a daily visitor."

Milsap finishes the page and stands slowly. Sometimes he is at the machine for so many hours without a break that the blood rushes from his head when he gets up. Once he even fell over.

Davey looks puzzled to see him step away before the paper is all set.

"I'll be right back," he says, and heads for Mr. Clawson's office.

He passes Stokely Burns, preparing the line block for a cartoon for the editorial page, the negative photograph of the drawing clipped up on his lamp shade. Milsap likes to decipher the images from the negative—

"I see a lot of clear," he says, pausing to cock his head and examine it.

The clear will become pure black when printed, and anything opaque will be white.

"If we keep running these nigger pictures," Stokely says without taking the cigarette out of his mouth, "we gonna run out of ink." Stokely's greatest skill is burning a long ash on his cigarette but never dropping any onto the gel plate.

"He's a big one." Milsap can see it now, the negative reversing in his mind to show a huge black negro complete with plaid pants, vest and coat, bow tie, top hat, walking cane, sparkling diamond stickpin, lit cigar, spats and enormous black shoes, one of which is pressing on the splayed body of a tiny, underfed white man.

NEGRO DOMINATION reads the caption beneath. HOW LONG WILL IT LAST?

"Is this ours?"

"The *Journal* sent it over. We run it tomorrow." Without looking Stokely flicks an inch of cigarette ash into his wastebasket.

Mr. Clawson's door is open and a poker game is in progress. There is Mr. Stedman and Mr. Parmelee who used to be the chief of police and Mr. Walker Taylor whose father was mayor once and is a colonel in the State Guard, sitting around the editor's desk with cards in their hands, chewing over the important questions of the day. Milsap waits in the doorway, crossing his arms to hide his hands under his armpits. There are dozens of little burns from the hot lead on each, pocked up as bad as his face from the smallpox when he was eight, and away from the machine they draw attention. Mr. Clawson is studying his cards and doesn't see him right off.

"Most of em, whether they admit it or not, would be pretty damn happy if we just stepped in and took over the whole shebang."

"The people are crying out for Christian guidance, for responsible hands at the tiller—gimme two—"

This is the quietest part of the floor, but living in the machinery has taken away Milsap's hearing and he has to strain to make out what they're saying.

"A few of the you-know-whos might put up a fight. The ones that got big ideas in their heads. But push come to shove, I don't think they'll find a whole lot of support, not even from their own people—drawing one—"

"There's a financial side to all of this, of course. A nickel."

"Of course—"

"See you. No way we can hold our heads up out in the world if we just let nature take its course. We've got to be *firm*."

The sudden wave of rape and terror in the state has pushed the Cuban situation off the front pages, but Milsap has been following that story, too, reading everything he can find in Wilmington. Victory, if the enemy is engaged, is less of a question than the fate of the natives once they are liberated.

"I'll fold. The thing is, some people can deal with free will and some can't. Poor witless bastards don't know if they're coming or going. I think it's nothing short of our Christian duty to take over the reins."

"The timing will be tricky, of course. Some people will need to be brought along."

"The first thing I think we need to do," says Milsap, forgetting that he has not been invited into the conversation, "is to get this Teller Amendment repealed."

The men look up at him through the smoke in the room, a bit surprised. Mr. Clawson squints as if trying to make out who he is.

"Something wrong with the machine?"

"No sir. I just—"

"Then to what do we owe the honor of this visit?"

"I was setting the front page and—"

"What's the Teller Amendment?" asks Mr. Stedman.

"It's the one that says if we boot the Spaniards out we can't keep the island," Milsap explains. "You were talking about Cuba, and—"

The men all laugh, even Mr. Clawson who had seemed annoyed before.

"I'm afraid the conflict we were discussing is much closer to home," he says. He indicates Milsap and addresses the others. "Drew here is the reigning mechanical genius of the *Messenger*. The *con*tent of our publication, however," he adds, smiling, but his eyes going cold as he looks back to Milsap, "is not within his purview."

"Our lead story, Mr. Clawson, the nameless crime—"

"Yes?"

"I've read it before. In the *News and Observer*, over a month ago."

The smile remains fixed. The eyes remain cold.

"And what of it? We frequently reprint items of public interest—"

"The headline says *New Outrage*. If the story is that old, how can we say—"

"Do you believe our average reader is as diligent as you in perusing the upstate dailies?"

"No, but—"

"If they have not read the story before," Mr. Clawson says with an edge in his voice, "the story, and the outrage caused by it, is new to *them*—is it not?"

The card players are chuckling.

"Yes, but—"

"But what?"

"In the original story the crime was in Zebulon. This version says it was Eagle Rock."

Mr. Clawson sighs and then exchanges a strange kind of smile with the seated men. "Were you at the scene of the violation, Drew?"

"Mr. Clawson, I only know what I read in the papers—"

"And that, gentlemen," interrupts the editor, "may well be the salvation of our fair city."

The men laugh again and Milsap wishes he had just let it slide.

"I thank you for your concern for our—our ve*ra*city, Drew, but we have a public duty to fulfill. We mustn't let mere facts stand in the way of larger truths."

"Yes sir."

"And I've decided to move the article describing Mrs. Felton's little *soirée* tonight to the first page, bottom right."

"I'd just ignore the old crow," says Walker Taylor.

"You may do just that," smiles the editor. "But she has the more soft-headed of our local ladies in a dither, and that makes her appearance in our city *news*. And I have heard tell that her advocacy has been drifting in a more—a more *per*tinent direction of late."

"I'll make it fit, sir," offers Milsap.

Mr. Clawson looks away from him then, finished, and glances at his hand. "I am going to raise you gentlemen ten cents."

Milsap turns and immediately passes Mr. J. Allen Taylor, the colonel's younger brother, looking impatient as he always does when he visits. Half the big wheels in town in the office, something big cooking no doubt, and he has to go pester Mr. Clawson with trifles.

"Fresh meat!" the editor calls from inside his office. "Sit down, young man, and we'll deal you in."

* * *

There are more men in the hall this evening than Miss Loretta has ever seen at a Suffrage lecture. One will note a half-dozen scattered, sympathetic clergymen, a few scoffers who come to sit with folded arms and tight smiles or stand at the side of the aisle for the entire program making the ushers uneasy, now and then a reporter for one of the newspapers scribbling unkind observations and chuckling to themselves. But tonight they are nearly a third of the audience, including some hard-looking types who might not be expected to be able to afford the "donation" at the door. The fellow beside her, a solid little man in a brown checked suit, needs to be reminded to remove his bowler by the woman behind.

As for the women, Miss Loretta is surprised at some of the faces she recognizes, representatives from many of Wilmington's finest families among them. The controversial nature of Mrs. Felton's views has no doubt kept the meek, the uncommitted, from attending so public a gathering, and she is heartened by the turnout. If the cause is to succeed it will need the support, the strength of Southern women.

"It has been said that we are *whiners*."

The Suffragist is in excellent form. Miss Loretta has always admired her aptitude for speaking forcefully and intelligently without surrendering any of her feminine grace. She is credited, not always unkindly, with being the mastermind of her husband's political campaigns, and somehow his popularity with an all-male electorate has not been damaged by his wife's outspoken advocacy of a widely derided position.

"It has been said that we are the most privileged class the world has ever known."

The Suffragist's voice is strong, almost musical. She stands on the stage behind a lectern draped with the American flag, wearing a slate-gray ensemble and a hat enlivened by a corona of violets.

"It has been said that we are so elevated in the regard of our menfolk, so cosseted, that to desire more is a display of not only folly, but greed."

Miss Loretta has seen Mrs. Felton unravel the plans of an inebriated disrupter with nothing more than her Southern woman's irony, drawing him sweetly into a logical argument, seeming to agree with him, leading him deeper and deeper before delivering her fatal thrust. She has perfected the tactic of presenting men's intransigence about Suffrage not as brutal and hard-hearted, but as weak and unworthy of their manhood.

"I will admit it for myself," she says with a coy smile. "Yes, I am greedy."

Polite laughter from the ladies, some of whom have heard this gambit before and know where it is leading. Miss Loretta realizes that the man beside her is making a noise, a perhaps unconscious growling sound, barely perceptible during the speaker's dramatic pauses.

"And yes, I would venture, many of you fine women sitting before me share that greed. *Yes*, women desire to be educated. *Yes*, women desire to escape the drudgery and debasement of rural servitude. And *yes*," here she looks to every corner of the hall, seeking out the eyes of the men, "women desire Suffrage. Without the vote we are mere spectators, fated to serve as handmaidens to the powerful but never to share in the administration of that power. Slaves, if you will, to the whims and stubbornness of the so-called 'stronger sex.'"

The man in the brown suit sits coiled and tight beside Miss Loretta, growling, if that is how one would describe the noise, even more loudly now. She leans out into the aisle and casts a glance backward to see where there might be someone to intercede if he proves dangerous.

"But with power," the Suffragist continues, "comes responsi*bil*ity. A responsibility that is sadly lacking in our present administration in regards to their unholy alliance with a—" and here she looks around the hall again, as if searching for the parties she is about to malign, and though finding none, lowers her voice with the delicacy appropriate to public criticism, "—a less morally de*vel*oped segment of our citizenry."

It can't be.

Miss Loretta feels her cheeks begin to burn. This is wrong, this is not where it is supposed to lead. She had not believed Daddy when he told her, had refused to read the article in the newspaper, replying that as she had never heard him refer to its editors as anything but liars and scoundrels, why would she believe a slander they printed about Mrs. Felton, whose views they so airily disparage whenever given the opportunity?

"See for yourself," he grumbled, "but don't blame me for being the messenger."

Daddy is a man with no idols. Even Mr. Lincoln, whose words and deeds he admired on the whole, was "still a politician" and therefore the object of some contempt. Even Socrates, endlessly quoted during her childhood and ever since, is not beyond reproach. "A Greek," Daddy will say cryptically, leaving the nature of that particular shortcoming to her imagination.

"For the want of political gain," the great lady goes on, indignation creeping into her voice, "these white men have initiated the *ne*gro into the mysteries of the ballot box, confounding him with tall stories and outright bribery in exchange for his vote!"

The Suffragist says *vote* with disgust, a dirty thing in her mouth. The man in the brown suit has begun to rock slightly to and fro in his seat, the movement somewhat indecent, his burning eyes fixed on the speaker. There have been reports, a new one practically every day, that indicate a rash, no, an epidemic of black men inflicting the "nameless crime" upon innocent white women. Six of them—or is it nine, or fourteen? Some of the stories end with the tree and the rope, others with only the howl of outraged Southern Manhood. Daddy, of course, with his contempt for the Fourth Estate, especially as it is manifested in North Carolina, remains unconvinced.

"Can it then surprise us that once allowed to break our election laws with impunity, these creatures assume they may engage in theft, rapine, and murder without fear of retribution?"

Grumbles among the audience members, male voices for the most part. The Suffragist begins to increase her volume, laying a foundation for her *crescendo*, lowering her register, now that she knows she has the men with her, from a soft *coloratura* to a hearty *tenore spinto*.

"As long as your politicians take the colored man into their embrace on election day and make him think that he is a man and a brother, so long will lynching prevail—for familiarity breeds con*tempt*."

She is brilliant, as usual, in her use of the language. "Your" politicians, leaving the unenfranchised women innocent of the outrage, the twist in logic that makes misplaced benevolence the handmaiden of murder. Daddy was president of the Forensic Society in his Princeton days and has drilled Miss Loretta in the uses and abuses of rhetoric. She feels tears beginning to form. The man beside her presses his hands, curled into fists, against his thighs as he rocks and growls, his knuckles white.

"And if it needs lynching to protect women's dearest possession from these ravening human brutes—" a tiny caesura, the intake of breath before the final chord, "—then I say *lynch*, a thousand times a week if necessary!"

The little man springs to his feet, smashing his hands together in approval, joined by half the audience, the women applauding as fervently if not as athletically as the men. It is what they have come for, the air in the room with a different charge than she's ever felt before, a raw and terrible energy. Miss Loretta rises and walks quickly up the aisle toward the rear of the hall, a tight smile on her face, the tears coming now.

She recognizes the man standing at the very back. He is not applauding but writing on a pad, a frown fixed on his handsome face. Their eyes meet for an instant and he nods, though they have never been formally introduced.

It is Alex Manly, the editor of the *Wilmington Daily Record*, who is engaged to her dear little Carrie.

Miss Loretta may be the only person in the hall who knows he is not white.

"The manhood of the South," she hears the Suffragist continue as the applause dies down, the words echoing, distant and hollow now as she hurries across the lobby, "must put a sheltering arm around innocence and virtue. The black fiend who lays his unholy and lustful hands on white women must surely die!"

An ancient negro waits, leaning against his hackney carriage at the bottom of the steps.

"M'am," he says, tipping his battered cap, and offers his hand to help her up.

Miss Loretta experiences a twinge of—what? Discomfort? Fear?—as she takes it, and is immediately furious with herself.

"Thank you," she says when she is settled. "Eighth and Market, please."

The old man tips his cap again and climbs up into the driver's seat.

"Listenin to Mrs. Felton," he says as he urges the horse into motion.

"Yes. She's—she's quite an orator."

"Womens at the ballot box," he says, shaking his head at the wonder of the idea. "That be a new day."

VOLUNTEERS

In Denver they don't make him undress.

The meeting is in the bigger bar downstairs at the Windsor, the one with the silver dollars inlaid every few feet in the floor and walls. Masterson perched on a stool pulled away from the bar counter as the pencil artist sits and stands and squats to draw his face from different vantage points, Niles Manigault obligingly skittering out of the eyeline whenever it changes, the fat man blocking most all the daylight from the open doorway.

"He knows the deal?" asks Masterson, flicking his eyes briefly at Hod.

"He fought Choynski," says Niles. "Held his own."

"The three great virtues of a prizefighter," says Masterson, lifting his chin a bit to catch the light angling in from Larimer Street, "are Talent, Heart, and Obedience. In my book the last of these is the greatest."

"He's a sharp lad," says Niles. "Once the deal, whatever it is, has been agreed upon—"

"Twelve rounds," says the fat man, slowly circling Hod, poking his bicep once with his cane. "Reddy needs time to sell beer, and if the Kid and Mongone are fighting straight—"

"For eight rounds they're fighting so that both stay on their feet," interrupts Masterson, "and then they can knock each other's brains out."

"You've placed some wagers."

"Move, Otto," says Masterson, holding his pose and wiggling a finger sideways. "You're throwing a shadow."

The fat man snorts in annoyance but moves to the side a few feet. He wears a bright checked suit and a red vest. "If you'd just have a photograph taken like a normal man—"

"It lacks the human dimension," says Masterson. His face is fleshier than Hod has imagined, his eyes sharper. In their boyhood games he always insisted on being Masterson, his brother Zeb left with a choice of badmen to represent. "It lacks the *soul*. These likenesses, which will appear in—what's this one to be called?"

"*Bat Masterson, Plague of the Kansas Outlaw*," answers the crouching artist, eyes fixed on his sketchpad.

"These likenesses convey the *spirit* of the man, his sense of vitality. A photograph freezes time, character becomes a mask, motion a blur—"

"What about the moving pictures?"

"Overrated."

Hod catches the eye of Niles Manigault, who discreetly motions for him to sit back at the bar. He wonders what they do to keep men like himself, desperate men, from prying the silver dollars out of the woodwork.

"They could have used one of those cameras in San Francisco when your friend Earp handed the fight to Sharkey—"

"The man fouled—"

"Fitz had him all but knocked out."

"On a punch delivered when the Tom's knees were on the canvas."

"A film wouldn't have lied—"

"Were you *there*?"

The fat man pushes the skimmer back on his head. "No. But if there had been a camera—"

"*I* was there. It was the correct decision."

The artist clears his throat. "Do you think," he asks softly, "you could assume a gunfighting stance?"

"About to draw or piece in hand?"

"Either one would suit me."

The Hero of Adobe Walls stands and pulls a short-barreled Colt from inside his jacket. The fat man takes a step backward.

"That isn't loaded, is it?"

"What fucking use under God's blue firmament would it do me to carry an unloaded firearm?"

Hod looks down to the end of the bar. A large man has folded his arms on the counter and is dozing upon them. Tabor had the hotel built during the first gush of silver from his holes, had supervised the details in both of the bars. This is a drinking man's dream of heaven—inlaid panels of ebony and oak, cherrywood on the bartop, enamel spittoons with Chinese designs, gleaming brass and silver metalwork and a dozen cut-glass chandeliers hanging overhead. A bartender in sleeve garters is polishing glasses, feigning indifference to the negotiations.

"They wanted to make a moving picture of the border fight," says Masterson, crouching slightly and pointing the iron held at his hip toward an imaginary foe. "I'm down in El Paso with Tom O'Rourke, sitting on the ten thousand cash prize, when the Rangers run the lot of us—fighters, managers, promoters, fans—out on a rail. So Roy Bean down in Langtry says he can handle it and he builds a little bridge out to a sandbar in the middle of the Pecos. 'It's not Texas and it's not Mexico,' he says, 'and is subject only to the laws of Nature.' The fellow with the camera had paid a bundle to Stuart for the right to photograph, and when Fitzsimmons's people demand a percentage of his profits, he turns them down cold. As it was, Ruby Robert put Maher away with one of his corkscrew punches in less than a minute of the first round."

"A disappointing afternoon," ventures Niles.

"Not for Judge Bean, who had the liquor concession. He sold out his stock to the sporting crowd, then issued an ordinance that not a drop could be consumed in Langtry. It was a memorable train ride." Masterson turns and points the gun barrel at the fat man. "What's this I hear of the 'Otto Floto Circus'?"

The fat man shrugs, embarrassed. "One of Harry's ideas. The newspaper would promote it."

"And you could donate one of your old opera capes," says Masterson, turning away, "to use as a tent."

The fat man grips his cane with both hands. "If you weren't armed, Masterson—"

"Gentlemen," interrupts Niles. "We agreed that this would be civil. Have we settled on a referee?"

"It's Reddy's hall," says Otto Floto. "He wants to run the bout."

"No objection," says Masterson. He sits back on the stool, looking at the pistol held in his lap. "There was a different filmist in Carson City," he says. "This one had a special tower built by the ring, with a slot cut out for all three of his cameras, and he made sure to throw some money at both Fitz and Corbett before the battle."

"Ensuring a prolonged contest," ventures Niles.

"I was there," says the fat man.

"As was I." Masterson's glare is like a bullet. "Earp and I providing security in case a riot ensued—"

"Like the one Earp started in San Francisco."

Masterson idly twirls the pistol on his finger. Niles takes a few cautious steps to the side. "Photographed every bloody minute of it. Jim knocking the starch out of Fitz, but the bald-headed little bastard hanging in, and his wife there by the corner—I wouldn't like to meet her in a prize ring, either—'Hit him in the slats, Bob!' she hollers. 'Hit him in the slats!' and out he staggers in the fourteenth and does just that, square on the mark, and Jim is done for the day."

"The film is a sensation," says Niles. "They set up a special projecting machine called a Veriscope, and—"

"I've seen it," says the gunfighter flatly.

"And your impression?"

"Greatly inferior to my own remembered impressions of the bout," says Masterson. "Smaller than life."

"The man has made a fortune."

"That I do not deny. At the presentation I attended more than half of the spectators were females, and I do not mean those of the lowest stripe. Something is afoot here that I mislike." He stands and looks at Hod again, then at the sleeping man beyond him. "Do you know what they showed before they put the fight up on the wall? Professor Welton's Boxing Cats! The noble art, turned into a raree show." He turns to Floto.

"Your man," he says, pointing to the sleeper at the bar, "Chief Rain-in-the-Face—"

"He'll be fine for twelve if I tell him."

Niles interrupts. "The Blonger brothers specified ten."

"The Blongers can lick my kiester," says Masterson. "Do you think he'd put the warpaint on?"

Otto Floto makes a face. "We tried that once. It got on the gloves, in the fighters' eyes—"

"A headdress perhaps? When he comes in the ring—"

"I think Harry has one at the paper."

"Little prick probably puts it on when nobody's looking. And your boy here—"

"Brackenridge," Hod calls out.

"A name that is neither here nor there," says Masterson. "Something Irish—"

"I'm not Irish."

"And Fireman Jim Flynn is a Dago, what of it?"

"He fought before under Young McGinty," Niles blurts.

Niles promised Hod before that it wouldn't be McGinty, just in case the warrant has traveled from Alaska, but now only puts a finger to his lips to warn him off.

"Young McGinty versus Chief—?"

"Strong Bear," says the fat man.

"It's a match. We advertise a prize of five hundred dollars, and out of that the fighters share—"

"Excuse me," says Niles, holding up a hand. "If we're talking business—"

He holds a fiver out to Hod. Masterson and Otto Floto and Niles and even the artist all stare at him as if he shouldn't be there. Hod takes the five and steps to the back of the room.

"That's to feed yourself," calls Niles jovially. "Not for an excursion to Holliday Street."

He gives the sleeping man a nudge as he passes on the way out the back door. "Lunchtime, buddy."

They are out on 18th before Hod realizes that the man is Big Ten.

"If you don't mind," says the Indian, eyeing the five, "I haven't eaten in days."

They find a place two blocks up serving steak and eggs and settle in.

"The fat gink," says Big Ten, "is some kind of newspaper writer who also promotes shows. I pulled his coat for a handout over by the Opera House and he pitched this boxing idea."

"Jail in Leadville?"

"One week, they got tired of feeding me. Took me to the freight yard, told me to catch the first thing smoking."

The Indian doesn't look any thinner. Fighting him will be like punching a tree stump.

"You know what you're doing in the ring?"

"Hell no."

"What they paying you?"

Big Ten shrugs. "The fat man got me a flop for the night," he says. "Then it's twenty for showing up and then the sky's the limit, he says, depending on how I handle myself. What about yours?"

"I think he owes Masterson a lot of money, so this is mostly on the cuff," says Hod. "But if I catch him before he can reach a faro table I might see a few dollars."

Big Ten sighs as the food arrives and they dig in.

"There was a sign over that bar," says Big Ten. "Said it was against the law to serve an Indian—less he's been cooked first."

"The whole deal sounds like lots of lumps for short money." Hod stares out the window at the characters circulating on 18th. "I'd recommend taking a powder, only these people always got an in with the law. If they catch us—"

"If you promise not to hit too hard," says the Indian, "I promise not to fall down too quick."

They linger over their coffee, just thinking, and are on their way back to the Windsor in a light drizzle when a tramp steps up on the sidewalk to block their way.

"You fellas spare some change?"

The man is swaying a little as he stands, skin and bones, hair wet and wild, looking slightly through rather than at them like fellas will do when they put the touch on you. Big Ten gives him a nickel and a penny.

"That's it, buddy," says the Indian. "Now we're as busted as you."

"That's white of you," says the tramp, who Hod recognizes from Butte, a mucker on the day gang with a Polish name longer than an ore train. The man staggers around them, almost falling off the curb.

"Always does the heart good," says Big Ten, "to see somebody worse off than you are."

On the next block they see the recruits.

There are three of them, two normal sized and one half-pint kid, standing at stiff attention in the middle of the sidewalk in front of the Elite Saloon.

"Our sergeant said he needs to kill his thirst," says the kid, who the others call the Runt. "Or maybe he just gone in to *wound* it. One way or the other, we got to stand here at attention till he comes out."

"We're volunteers," says one of the normal-sized ones.

"Sure you are," says Big Ten. "I can't see how anybody'd *pay* you to stand out in the rain."

"In the *Army*," says the Runt. "Off to battle the Spaniards."

"You don't say."

The Runt closes his eyes, then opens them and begins to spout.

Oh it's Tommy this, and it's Tommy that
and it's "Chuck him out, the brute!"
But it's "Savior of his Country"
when the guns begin to shoot!

The biggest one looks embarrassed. "He does that. Right out of the blue."

"We come up from Pueblo and he latched on to us," says the middle one. "But they took us anyway."

The sergeant comes out from the saloon then, a long man with a long moustache drooping off his face. He glares at his volunteers. "Have you been talking to these civilians?"

"They were asking about enlistment, sir," says the Runt, eyes forward, chin tucked in, his scrawny body held rigid. "And I was explaining the opportunity."

The sergeant turns to look Hod and Big Ten over. "I've got one deserted already and one lost to the clap shack," he says. "You boys ready to take the trip?"

The Polish miner wasn't a drinker, Hod remembers, just a steady, hard-working fella trying to keep grits on his table. He looked like hell, a ghost of a man out there alone in the rain. This is not Hod's war, the plight of the oppressed Cuban a subject he has barely considered. But it had felt right, that one moment, marching with the Skaguay Guards, and there will be three squares a day and a chance to see the palm trees and it won't be Soapy Smith or anyone like him running the deal. Hod, light in the pocket and blackballed from the mines, exchanges a look with the big Indian, who he can tell is also considering the offer.

"Where to?" asks Big Ten.

"Five blocks over to the Armory," says the sergeant, "and then on to Glory."

ARMADA

The Americans are there before the sun comes up. Just *there*, out in the bay, somehow passing the Corregidor batteries without a shell being fired.

"*Como Pedro por su casa*," says the Spaniard next to Diosdado at the sea wall, a long-nosed *ayuntamiento* clerk wearing the yellow armband of his volunteer unit. It is first light and already there are hundreds lined up along the Malecón to watch, men only, though there are a few women among those fleeing behind them on the Paseo, the poorest with their rolled *tampipis* over their shoulders, the wealthiest trailed by barefoot coolies staggering under bulky pieces of furniture. This day has been known, has been inevitable, for weeks—what can they have been waiting for?

"Do you think they'll bombard the city?" asks Diosdado. His orders are to gauge the mood of the people, both Spaniard and Filipino, and it has required a sociability he never thought himself capable of.

"That is the present subject of discussion," the clerk tells him. "Do you see their light?"

At the bow of one of the still distant American warships a beam flicks rhythmically on and off. The clerk points across the road behind them, where a corporal and his capitán stand on top of the Baluarte de Santa Isabel, the capitán watching the signaling ship through binoculars and the corporal wig-wagging a pair of flags, one red, one white, in a complicated sequence.

"If General Augustín promises not to fire from the shore batteries," the Spaniard explains, "their Admiral Dewey may agree not to level the Intramuros."

"So you think no shells will fall on our heads?"

The clerk gives Diosdado a weary smile. "Leaving more available to murder our boys in the fleet."

The fleet, if the less-than-a-dozen Spanish ships fanned out uncertainly in front of Las Piñas, escape route blocked by Sangley Point, may be conceded that name, has nowhere to go.

"What are they doing?"

The clerk watches the closer ships for a moment.

"One would hope," he says finally, "they are making their peace with the Creator."

This same bitter humor, this mix of exasperation and stoicism, has infused every conversation Diosdado has engaged in or overheard since the news arrived that the Americans were steaming away from Hongkong. Haunting the Escolta in his moustache and country planter's outfit, in for a quick drink at the Tabaquería Nacional or La Alhambra or the San Miguel beerhouse, rubbing shoulders with the *peninsulares*, infantry, cavalry, volunteers—for every Spaniard between sixteen and sixty has been called to service—it has been the same shameful story.

"We have been abandoned," said the *teniente*, said the merchant, said the cargo inspector. "The people in Madrid make speeches and wave their fists, but they send us no ships, no arms, no men."

"They have the insurrection in Cuba to deal with."

"An insurrection fueled by *yanqui* gold."

"Nonetheless—"

"They have abandoned us. They have hooked a monster this time, have roused the interest of these overgrown Americans, and have decided to cut bait rather than endure the fight."

"But *we* will fight," they all add. "If only for our sense of honor. If only to stand as men, under our flag and God's eyes, till the very end."

And then, enraptured with their own tragic Iberian nobility, intoxicated with sentiment for their beloved archipelago, their Pearl of the Orient, each Spaniard will turn to lay a hand on Diosdado's shoulder and speak as if to a brother.

"*Y tu, amigo*—what will you do?"

They do not mean what will Diosdado Concepción do, or Idelfonso Ledesma, the name on the newest *cédula* the Committee has given him. They worry, they obsess, about what the Filipino people will do.

"So many of our prominent figures," Diosdado reassures them whenever asked, "have sworn to stand with our mother Spain against these invaders. Look at those already leading volunteer battalions—Pio del Pilar, Buencamino in Pampanga, Paterno, Ricarte, Licerio Gerónimo, the Trias brothers—"

Diosdado has spoken to almost all those that Alejandrino, too well-known by the Spaniards to operate secretly, has not been able to reach. Hurrying about the provinces in his flimsy disguise, General Aguinaldo's faceless envoy to those he hopes will follow him in a revived insurgency. They are all, perhaps with the exception of Ricarte, practical men, and have deduced that the safest position in the coming upheaval is at the head of a large body of armed men, preferably from one's home province.

"But will they stand to the end?"

And because he is an imposter, with a radically different notion of what that end should be, Diosdado can look the Spaniards in the eye and say, honestly, "I hope so. With all my heart."

He raises his binoculars as the American ships form a line, one behind the other, speeding past the Malecón now, the shore batteries silent. The lead vessel is within two hundred yards when the Spaniards begin to fire. One by one the American ships turn hard right and run parallel to the Spanish line, rapid-fire cannons delivering a continuous broadside, balls of smoke and then the booming report over the water. The *Regina Cristina* and the *Don Juan de Austria* charge forward and immediately begin to come apart. They are old, badly fitted, wooden-hulled relics facing gray-painted fortresses of steel. It is target practice. The *Mindanao* is on fire off Las Piñas beach, the *Castilla* is sinking, only its chimney stack still above water, and the *Regina Cristina* explodes with a concussion that jolts the solemn watchers all along the sea wall.

The clerk has the side of his hand in his mouth, biting down on it. There are men in the water now, some of them on fire, swimming away from the wrecks or rowing lifeboats, desperate to be out of killing range. The American ships each take a second, then a third and a fourth turn, as evenly spaced as a line of mechanical ducks at a shooting gallery, only they are the sportsmen and the thrashing Spanish *marineros* the prey.

Most of the Filipino leaders were evasive, or at the best noncommittal, when he spoke to them, noses to the wind.

"Give Miyong my regards," said Buencamino, who fought for the Spaniards in the '96 uprising. "Tell him I will do what is best for our people."

Any of them watching this carnage will have chosen sides by now.

Diosdado has planned for this day, he and his fellow *universitarios* have longed for it, but at this moment, with the mighty Spanish Navy revealed as a floating scandal, his heart is with the men struggling to keep their heads above the waves. Morning sun flashes off the steel hull of the last American warship in the procession as it turns, then the rolling smoke and the roar of cannons and one of the long lifeboats is blasted into flying splinters, the rowing men simply gone, gone from the world. Somebody beside him is sobbing.

READER

Quiroga sits on his platform, surveying the bowed heads below. They never look up, not even if he pauses for a very long time, not even at the most emotional moments, as when poor little Nell died in Mr. Dickens's wonderful tale—only a wagging of the bowed heads, maybe a cry of *"Ay, Dios!"* from one of the women at the back benches, stripping the fibers from the leaves, and the one instance where Fermín Pacheco was so upset that it seemed one of the Musketeers had been killed he slammed his fist down and ruined a Corona. No matter what Quiroga reads or how powerfully he presents it, the work, the chopping and pressing, the rolling and wrapping, the tap-tapping of wooden boxes being assembled, continues unabated, the fingers keep on moving.

"MUCH CONJECTURE IN LIBERATORS' CAMP," he reads in the tone he reserves for newspaper headlines and chapter headings. *La Verdad* and most of the other Ybor City papers invariably refer to the American force as *"los liberadores"* unless they choose to use the more fraternal *"nuestros hermanos de la Causa."* Don Vicente allows him to read the Cuban papers if he sticks to the reporting, the editorials invariably too inflammatory and likely to injure the sensibilities of the Spaniards at the *fábrica*, who are, after all, his key employees.

"General Shafter Cites Progress in Organization."

Still declamatory, but at reduced volume. Quiroga prides himself on delivering the sensation of reading, even for those few illiterates in the factory, prides himself on finding an equivalent for the effects of font and justification. He has a vocal technique to match everything in the arsenal of author and printer.

The fingers keep moving.

"*United States Major General William R. Shafter, in an interview granted today from his headquarters at the Tampa Bay Hotel, displayed a cautious but optimistic viewpoint when asked about the readiness of his force for the impending confrontation on Cuban soil. 'The logistics of transport and supply for an army that has not been employed on foreign shores in one hundred years are daunting,' he stated. 'But I am confident we shall overcome them in time to engage the enemy to our best advantage.' When pressed to verify that Havana will be the primary focus of the assault, he reiterated that all sensible military options remain open. Major General Shafter reassured this newspaper that contacts with Cuban patriots already in arms on the island are being maintained, and that these groups are considered an invaluable part of the liberation process.*"

Though the author of the article, a Cuban zealot of his acquaintance named Flores, employs a very high and impassioned style, Quiroga tries to deliver the story in the matter-of-fact tone befitting a news dispatch. He is paid by the workers themselves like any other *lector*, but he understands he is here at the sufferance of Don Vicente.

Quiroga notes that Señor Aragon is not at his bench. It has been entrusted to him, Quiroga, to "keep an eye" on Aragon, a Spaniard of openly Royalist sympathies. But Aragon is a crafter of *perfectos*, an artisan paid by the bundle and not by the hour and thus able to stroll out onto La Séptima whenever he wishes. When a special order was presented to the wonderful writer, humorist, and cigar *aficionado* Mr. Samuel Clemens, it was Aragon who was honored to fashion the *puros*. Any man who makes nearly three cents per cigar is an aristocrat among workers.

The elite here and at the Sanchez and Haya *fábrica* down the street are Spaniards. Cubans, thus far, are only the masters of a few storefront operations, full of moody Sicilians churning out inexpensive cheroots for those who can tolerate them.

"LOCAL MERCHANTS OFFENDED," Quiroga announces, switching to the other front-page story. "*Colored Troops Behind Disruptions.*"

Aragon has never so much as acknowledged his existence, even when he is reading from the more exhortatory of the Cuban papers. In fact, the only Spaniard he can be sure is listening is wizened old Infante, the blade-sharpener, who puts something especially dull and noisy on his wheel if the writer's opinions upset him.

"Several Tampa merchants have complained of distasteful and sometimes violent incidents involving bands of negro soldiers set loose on the city streets each night. They complain that military officials have not considered the effect on local sensibilities of encamping such troops in the area without adequate supervision. 'We are left at the mercy of these insolent brutes,' a prominent merchant accuses, 'and ask at least that the authorities disarm them before allowing them to leave their bivouacs.' The murder of a white man by members of the colored 10th Cavalry, prompted by his refusal to serve them in his establishment, has terrorized the inland community of Lakeland recently, and residents there warn of impending retribution. 'We have plenty of white boys down here ready to fight, and more coming from our Western states,' continued the downtown merchant. 'The colored should either be sent home or immediately dispatched to Cuba, where their loss on the battlefield will be no great misfortune.'" Quiroga folds the newspaper carefully. "Reprinted from the *Tampa Post and Defender.*"

A few of the *negros americanos* stand in the rear talking softly to each other, the ones who tend the wagons and carry crates to and fro. He wonders if they have any Spanish. Most of the Cuban rollers know only a scant handful of English words, and with the Sicilians it is impossible to tell. English is not necessary here in Ybor City.

His facility with the two tongues, his *lector*'s erudition, has led the Junta to employ Quiroga as an interpreter for their overtures to the American command. But the latest meetings on the vast porch of the Tampa Bay have been polite in protocol alone, the Junta being told in no uncertain terms to tend to their flag-waving and leave military intrigue to the professionals. Undaunted, they have convinced themselves of dire Spanish plots to reveal details of local troop maneuvers, when in fact the schedule of Don Vicente's trolley service into Tampa City is harder to divine than the open and predictable drilling of Shafter's regiments. No doubt the Crown has spies in Tampa, feverishly translating the reports of the flock of war correspondents that hovers about the palatial hotel waiting for something, anything, to happen, but Aragon the *puro* artist is not likely to be one of them.

It shamed him, the American officers smug in their rocking chairs, cocktails in hand. Arturo Quiroga knows when he is being condescended to. He wanted to tell the *yanquis* to keep their ten thousand men and send instead fifty thousand rifles with twenty rounds of ammunition each, to tell them that with these Cuban patriots would control the country in a week. It made him wish he was a true orator, not just a medium, a channel for other men's words. Martí—he met the man at the Pedrosos' boarding house just after the Spanish tried to poison him—Martí should have been on the porch of the

Tampa Bay Hotel. *"The belly of the Beast"* Martí called America in his speech at the Liceo, the speech praised or blamed for starting the Ten Years' War, *"he vivido en la barriga del Monstruo del norte,"* and offered no apologies when the quote was picked up by the *yanqui* papers. He was a little man, slight of build and stature, but the voice, the eyes—he spoke and every Cuban in Ybor became a believer. Quiroga was there listening on the stage with his own brother, Pablito, not much more than a boy, who was moved to buy a pistol and join Martí's fated expedition of '95, and gunned down in Dos Ríos at the side of the Apostle.

He is no orator though, Quiroga, only a channel for other men's words, other men's ideas. The *torneadores* have their favorites, books they love to hear again and again, Mr. Dickens and Monsieur Dumas *fils* prominent among these, but occasionally he is able to widen their scope, to introduce them to authors and ideas of his own choosing. It is a tiny act of persuasion, an act not of revolt but of subversion. *"Each serves as he may,"* said Martí, standing not an arm's length away from him in the boarding-house parlor, *"and ideas may triumph while weapons fail."* Are they listening, these bowed heads, stacking, pressing, rolling, binding, cutting, fingers ever moving, these human machines spread at the benches below his platform? And if listening, do they intuit a connection, decipher a metaphor, find instruction or reassurance in the lives of those fictive characters? Or is it all just a story, buzzing over their heads?

Quiroga is beginning a novel today, and has some question as to how its content will be received. Don Vicente Martínez-Ybor, though a Spaniard by birth, is said to be sympathetic to La Causa, allowing on the premises the collection of monies to arm and organize the revolt, Quiroga faithfully tithing his ten percent like most of the others. But Don Vicente's opinions on organized labor are less tolerant, the move from Key West blatantly an anti-unionist stratagem, and though the old man rarely enters the factory these days, his ears, as they say, are long. Freedom, true freedom, is not only a matter of what flag flies above your head. After the star and the triangle are raised over Havana, the struggle will truly begin—

The fingers keep moving.

Quiroga opens the new volume gently, attempting not to crack the spine. *"Germinal,"* he announces. *"Escrito por Don Émilio Zola. Capítulo Uno."*

A GENTLEMEN'S
AGREEMENT

The White Admiral sits in a wicker chair in his quarters on the flagship of the victorious Fleet. He is dressed in white, with a white head of hair and a thick white moustache, resplendent against the stateroom's dark, polished wood. This could be a room in a grand hotel, the *Olympia* so huge that they are barely rocked by the waters of the Bay. The White Admiral crosses his hands and rests them against his middle, while the smaller brown men sit facing him with their hats in their laps, afternoon rays slanting into their eyes from the skylight above. One of them, the exiled General, ventures to speak in careful Spanish.

He congratulates the White Admiral on his great naval victory.

The White Admiral smiles and nods when this is translated for him.

"We have come," the Admiral says in English, looking the exiled General directly in the eye, "to lift the yoke of Spanish rule from the backs of the Philippine people."

Diosdado sits behind and to the side of the White Admiral, hired by the Americans to help if the exiled General cannot say what he wishes in Spanish and needs to revert to Tagalog. But Aguinaldo's Spanish is adequate if not elegant, and Diosdado only listens.

The exiled General expresses his admiration for the grandeur and beneficence of the American nation. It is a courtly dance, between partners who have been only recently introduced.

The White Admiral asks if the exiled General will not soon return to his country and lead his people against the Spanish forces still occupying it.

"My people are willing," replies the General, "but lack arms with which to demonstrate their patriotism."

The White Admiral and the exiled General discuss details of bringing arms into the country. A quantity of Mausers and ammunition are already here, carried up from Corregidor Island, and many more can certainly be purchased and shipped from Hongkong with the help of the U.S. Consul. An aide to the White Admiral, standing discreetly to one side and speaking as if it is a somewhat insignificant consideration, mentions the sum of seven American dollars per rifle, of thirty-three dollars and fifty cents for a thousand rounds.

The exiled General is soft-spoken and polite as always, his expression guileless. Did his face look like this, wonders Diosdado, when the Bonifacios were led away to be slaughtered?

"I must tell you," says the General to the White Admiral, "that there is some uneasiness among my fellow patriots, men who worry that once the Spaniard is vanquished and we are weakened by the struggle, your country may decide to replace them as our masters."

The White Admiral nods pleasantly. The floor of his stateroom is littered with wicker baskets overflowing with congratulatory cables and letters and gifts. There is a rumor that his cook travels into the blockaded city by launch every day, to buy fresh fruit. He answers slowly in English, as if reassuring a child frightened by a storm.

"America is wealthy in both land and resources," he says. "It has no need of colonies."

Pepito Leyba, younger even than Diosdado, translates for the General, managing to transmit both the White Admiral's condescending yet friendly demeanor and his lack of specificity.

"This is reassuring for me to hear," responds the exiled General. "My colleagues, however, will be more reassured, more likely to rally to our cause, if they could read of your intentions in an official statement."

"An official statement like the one you signed with Spain," counters the Admiral, sitting back on his wicker throne, "that stipulated your permanent exile?"

There are men, friends of Diosdado's, who will never forgive the General for the Treaty of Biak-na-Bato. To accept money from the Spaniards, to accept amnesty and exile, even if—

The General appears unperturbed. "The Spaniards did not honor the Treaty," he says flatly.

"And so you will see," smiles the White Admiral, "that the word of honor of an American is more positive, more irrevocable, than any piece of paper."

The exiled General flicks his eyes to Diosdado when Leyba says the word *irrevocable.*

"*Manatili,*" Diosdado translates. Leyba speaks Spanish, French, English, Tagalog, and who knows what else, but perhaps the General is asking for more than a word here. *Do not trust these people*, Diosdado thinks, and hopes the thought is transmitted through his eyes.

The General's expression does not change. The White Admiral either will not or has not the power to promise their independence if Filipinos lead the fight to expel the Spaniards. If they do not fight, however, do not show their willingness to kill and be killed, how much more likely, with German warships hovering in the bay, with the Japanese so rapidly building up their own navy, that the *yanquis* will choose to stay?

"We must proceed with the liberation of the islands," says the White Admiral, "and must act toward each other as friends and allies."

On being introduced, Diosdado feigned that he had never before met the General or Pepito Leyba, had shaken hands formally and stepped back into his place. After the General is gone the Americans will ask him for his impressions, and he will say "I think he believes everything he said." And then later he will report to the General and be questioned and say he thinks the Americans have not yet made up their minds. And though both statements are obvious and true he will be a spy, and neither side will give him their complete trust. The Americans have destroyed the Spanish fleet, the dreaded gunboats that precluded any chance of Filipinos attacking Manila, their blackened hulks still visible in the shallows off of Sangley Point. The Americans have taken the Cavite Arsenal and have their big guns trained on the Spanish garrison within the Walled City of Manila. There is no saying how they will fare in Cuba, the liberation force as yet to leave American shores, but here, here they have been godlike in the speed of their devastation. If the White Admiral lacks guile, it is because up to this moment he has not required it. Whereas Aguinaldo—

"I am willing to sacrifice my own life in this great undertaking," says the exiled General, "as is every true patriot in our nation."

In the pilot boat on the way out the American ensign who came for him was much amused by the crowd of *lanchas* being poled back and forth with their loads of *zacate* fodder and piled stems of bananas.

"Look," he winked to Diosdado, "it's the Filipino Navy."

The White Admiral rises above them, an avuncular smile on his face, and offers his hand.

"Go and start your army," he says.

THE LOST WORLD

Tampa is a fever dream.

They wake to a fusillade of noise, every regiment on the Heights with its own drummer up and driving the sticks, men cursing on their ponchos before the bugle's first assaulting note. The chigger bites along Royal's ribs remind him where he is. The scramble for socks, the insult of the woolen pants and he's out with the others, the canvas of the tents whiter than the sand, ghostly rows like headstones in the failing wisp of moonlight. There is no warning of the heat to come. Royal pulls the flannel shirt on, sits to wrestle with his boots. Junior crawls out from the tent, then Little Earl, looking surprised, as he always does, to find himself awake at this hour. No one speaks. The air is bitter with the coffee Stewpot Sims has begun to boil on his cookfire, one of a half-dozen glowing throughout the camp. The 25th stumble forward to be counted.

Sergeant Jacks knows his book and expects the same from you. His eyes remain calm, even when chewing on some rookie who does not know his left from his right or his bunghole from a bayonet. He allows them to drill without their blouses due to the heat, except for the one day the company dogged it so bad during the morning close-order routine the lieutenant let him lead them on a five-mile jaunt around the camp weighed down with full kit, Merriam packs, and three days' provisions.

"You think this is bad," he said during one of their pauses to see if a fallen man was dead or just resting with his face in the sand, "wait till we get to Cuba. They got your *steam* heat."

There is a rumor that their winter-issue uniforms will be replaced soon, but that seems the unlikeliest of all the many stories contaminating the Heights. Yes, the Army might load them into their transports tomorrow or send them to China to pacify the yellow hordes or make peace with the Dons and call off the whole Cuba invasion, but the idea of Supply, in this fly-ridden dump of men and munitions, coming up with anything to make a common soldier's burden lighter is unimaginable.

Sergeant Jacks wears his blouse though, all day long, service stripes half-way down to his wrists. No one has ever seen him take a drink of water, or step away to relieve himself, through Coop won a two-dollar bet the day the sergeant allowed himself to squash a mosquito crawling up his neck.

"Man eat bricks and shit gravel," Coop will say when the sergeant is out of earshot. "Probly kilt more nigger privates than he ever did Indians."

Jacks calls their names and the men bark out in response and then he announces Sick Call, which nobody who can stand dares report for since the Doc has taken to dosing all internal complaints with a ginger-root concoction that cleans you out, and not gently, at both ends.

"We have the healthiest regiment in the camp," muses Sergeant Jacks with the tone in his voice that substitutes for a smile. "Fall out."

They make their way to the chow-line then, and as Junior is first it falls on him to do the honors.

"What have we today?" he says, raising his voice to be heard by all. "Sowbelly with no bread or sowbelly with no eggs?"

"No breakfast," says Stewpot Sims. Thick, stumplike Sims, who if he even hears the kicking anymore does not respond to it. "Coffee if you want it."

Royal dips in, coffee scalding in his pint can, dark coffee this morning, with an acid taste that lingers for an hour after but is better than nothing. He tried to drill one day with nothing in his stomach, hung over from a night in Ybor, and by noon his legs were jelly.

"No breakfast. Maybe they packed it all up on the transports, we be leaving today." Little Earl is the source of many camp rumors. Royal likes to hear how they have grown, have sprouted arms and legs by the time they've circled back to the company at the end of the day.

"Maybe it just smelt so bad they had to bury it," says Corporal Puckett, one of the veterans from Fort Missoula.

"Not yet, they haven't," says Coop. "Don't no hole get dug in this camp but what I digs it. Something to eat got buried, I'd know."

The men laugh. Coop is the sergeants' favorite goat, though there is nothing visibly wrong with his soldiering. He jumps when jump is called for and flops on command. Something in his eye, though, the way he stands, an attitude. I am here, it says. Royal and the other greenhorns all with their shoulders pinned back, chins down, guts pulled in, trying to be invisible to the officer of the moment while Coop stands there taking up his space as if it belonged to him. As if he still belonged to himself and not the 25th Regular Infantry, Colored.

"You ever been hanged, Cooper?" Sergeant Jacks asked him just the other day at muster, body almost pressed up against the taller private.

"Not yet, Sergeant." Voice innocent of tone, but steady.

"Must be an oversight."

The men who smoke keep one eye on the bugler, Kid Mabley, trying to burn one down before he brings the metal to his lips. The sand crabs are up now, skittering from hole to hole as if their business, whatever it might be, needs finishing before sunrise. Royal forces the coffee down and takes a few steps in place. The blisters are still there, no chance to heal, but not too angry yet. The worst is taking the boots off at the end of the day, something Junior and he help each other with, comparing the size and state of their raw spots.

Dellum from Company C moves close to him. "Any tobacco on you, rookie?"

"Don't use it."

"That's no reason not to *have* it."

"I get hold of any," says Royal, "I'll let you know."

The veterans ragged them pretty hard at first, pushing at the new recruits to see how far they'd give, but there was nothing mean in it. Except with Coop sometimes, coming back weary from whatever punitive duty he's caught that day, Coop will go right back after them. Even Scout, the little spaniel they keep for a mascot, spoiled on mess-hall scraps and stolen biscuits, knows enough to slink away when he sees Coop with that look on his body. Once he held Little Earl by the throat so hard, over a remark that had nothing to do with him, that there were bruises the next day, bruises that showed on a black man's neck.

At a nod from the lieutenant, Kid Mabley blasts into *Drill*, humping his chest down hard to let the whole camp hear. Mabley is the best on the Heights and knows it, all the other buglers, even the white boys, coming by in the evenings to trade licks with him, holding their campaign hats over the horns to mute their playing in case someone wants to get a head start on their shuteye. No shots have been fired in camp so far, that's what town is for, but a few men have been left bloody in the sand.

"Spaniards don't get him," says Dellum, a nervous sleeper, eyeing Mabley as he starts away, "Imonna kill that boy."

Tampa is a fever dream, fever rising with the sun.

The Krag, even unloaded, makes it seem real. The weight of it in his hands, the heat of the barrel once the sun comes up, the way every action must be altered to accommodate the ever-present fact of it makes Royal feel like a soldier. Sergeant Jacks makes sure the Krag never leaves their grasp from the instant drill begins till Kid blows *Recall.* They are drilling by companies today, Junior and Royal and Little Earl in Company L marched with most of the other recruits, four abreast, two miles south of camp skirting the City of Tampa to end up in the dunes facing Davis Island across the bay.

"Company halt!"

To the east, in a jumble of masts and stacks and flagpoles, is the mongrel fleet of coastal packets and converted yachts that word has it will take them to fight the Spanish. Some of them. The men are winded from keeping up with Sergeant Jacks, but stand as steady as they can at right-shoulder arms, waiting. Royal casts a glance at the surrounding dunes, deep pockets of shadow forming among them as the sun begins to creep over the horizon, and wishes there had been something to eat.

"Form by platoon—march!"

They separate into their two platoons. The lieutenant hasn't come along. Drill is shorter when he comes—he gets hot or bored and pulls out his pocket watch which Sergeant Jacks somehow senses without looking and wraps things up. Without the lieutenant it could be a long morning.

"First platoon, deploy as skirmishers, on the flank—march!"

Royal pivots around Corporal Pickney and the rest follow, stepping off their two paces from the next man, each squad spread out fifteen paces from the other. It seems a waste, now that they've gotten the hang of it, of the manual of arms, of close and extended-order marching and maneuver, now that they've learned to stack and take arms, to clean, repair, and fire their weapons, to adjust sights and judge distances, to respond correctly and with dispatch to vocal, whistle, or bugle commands, to make and break camp and dig entrenchments and all of the thousand daily duties of the Regular Army soldier, a waste for their Company L to be the one left behind in Tampa to look after equipment and maintain a base of operations. But that is the order, straight from the Colonel.

"Second platoon, in support, as skirmishers—march."

The rest of the company spreads out behind them. They have their backs to the bay, facing a series of dunes.

"Observe Sergeant Cade."

Cade appears at the top of a dune over a hundred yards away, waves his hat.

"That is the enemy position. You will advance by rushes, maintaining your lines, on my command. Company, port arms!"

The shadows of a phalanx of pelicans ripple over the sand in front of them. Royal feels the first little bit of heat on his cheek.

"First platoon, double time, forward—march!" shouts Sergeant Jacks and they are off, Royal aware only of the other seven men in his squad strung out beside him, boots sinking into the soft sand as the dune slides away beneath their feet, stubbornly surrendering as they lift their knees and pound it under, climbing till Cade is just visible over the crest and—

"Down!"

Royal flops forward, easier on the uphill slope than on flat ground, raising the Krag to aim—

"Three rounds—fire!"

A metallic clicking all down the line as the men sight their weapons and pull the trigger. Sergeant Jacks always has them check the magazine and set the cutoff before they leave camp, and Royal has only had two brief sessions with live rounds back at Chickamauga. Jacks calls behind them.

"Second platoon, double time—march!"

Royal has put three imaginary shots through Sergeant Cade's forehead by the time the second platoon comes huffing past—

"First platoon cease fire!"

The second line kicks sand back, Royal catching a noseful, as they double-time over and past the men lying on their bellies. They are down the far side and halfway up the next dune before Jacks calls out.

"Down! Hold fire! First platoon up, double time, march!"

His heart is hammering against his ribs by the time he reaches the upslope of the second dune, his grime-stiffened wool starting to loosen with his sweat, sand down his collar and in his pants and in his eyes and gritty in his teeth and *Down!* and firing, at will this time, Royal not aiming so much as pointing the barrel in the general direction of Cade and the second line slogging past and down and up to the crest of the next one and then *Up!* they are charging forward again, shirt soaked and stuck to his body, sand stuck to the wet on his face, the day suddenly very bright, legs leaden on the last slope and then *Down!* flopping at Sergeant Cade's feet and heaving for breath, a flock of gulls mocking noisily overhead now, till the second platoon thumps down next to them.

"On your feet, gennemen!" calls Sergeant Cade. Cade has dull black skin that is creased with age and exposure, is missing several teeth and rumored to have fought the Confederates at Fort Wagner. "Form your skirmish lines! You all bunched up, dammit!"

Shuffling and side-stepping to get their intervals back. Little Earl is throwing up beside him, a thin yellow liquid that smells like coffee.

"About face! Rifles, port arms! First platoon—"

Sergeant Jacks stands back at the shore, waving his hat over his head.

"—observe the enemy position. Advancing by rushes, first platoon, double time—"

If you drop they let you lie there a bit but then there is kicking and shouting and even the ones who are carried from the field have to make it up later, in spades, and the veterans spit their tobacco and look at you like you're nothing. "You can rest when you're dead," Sergeant Jacks will say, the toe of his boot digging into your ribs. "And there will be no dying without my permission." There have been times, since the regiment has been here in Tampa, when Royal has been amazed to survive the day, amazed at what his body can endure, and thought this must be the last test, the worst they will ever put us through—

"—forward *march!*"

They charge back and forth between the sergeants in rushes, first by platoons and then by squads, till the sun is straight up in the sky. The only break is for the few men detailed, one at the shoulders and one at the feet, to lug the five troopers who collapse and lie motionless to the edge of the water and leave them there in the rising tide. All but one is able to stand by the time Sergeant Jacks has the company clean the sand out of their rifles and start the march back to camp.

The insects are out in force for the return, sand fleas and biting flies, and Royal's rifle weighs twice what it did in the morning, digging into his shoulder. His eyes sting with sweat and they take a longer route, swinging well clear of the sunburned Georgia Volunteers learning the rudiments of their old trapdoor Springfields at the base of the Heights. When they trudge into camp the other companies are already sitting around confronting the midday meal.

"Yo, Junior," calls Coop, fish-eying an open tin of stringy beef trimmings packed for the Japs four years ago, "hold your rifle on me so's I got a reason to eat this shit."

* * *

Tampa is a fever dream of commerce.

Tampa is a fever dream of war.

Jacks leads the detail of recruits along the trolley tracks that lead down Seventh to the railhead, old Patch following with the supply wagon. He likes Ybor, likes the noise and the pace and the mix of people. The white folks lord it over you in Tampa City, even now that they are outnumbered by soldiers, and the colored who live in the Scrub are a sorry-looking bunch, just scrabbling along, but here there is color and music and industry, more fun than anything he's seen outside of Mexico.

The signs are in Spanish, of course, though there are hasty translations painted below them on the establishments catering to soldiers. Two little brown boys, barefoot, fall into step with the detail, thrusting forward an old shoebox filled with live baby alligators.

"*Caimanes aquí, muy chicos, muy baratos!*" they sing. "*Caimanes vivas!*"

"*Para comer?*" says Jacks, poker-faced, and the boys peal with laughter, both at the phenomenon of this *yanqui* speaking Spanish and at the idea of eating the lizards.

"*Como quieres, hombre.*"

The lingo here has a different music than border Mex, the Cubanos dropping their esses and never sounding like burros. Jacks puts his hand over his stomach to indicate he is full. "*Acabo de almorzar,*" he tells them. "*Gracias, no.*"

"You understand everything they're saying?" asks Lunceford. Lunceford is a schoolboy, full of big words and big ideas.

"Picked some up in Arizona Territory, some in Texas. Know a little Apache too, not that it do any good here."

A good half of the buildings are spanking new, unpainted board shacks tacked together to sell something to the soldiers while they last here, saloons and gambling dens and whore cribs and stands selling fresh fruit and candy and everything not provided for in Army rations, which is just about everything. The new structures are wedged in between the larger brick buildings—the cigar factories, the huge Centro Español, the Dago bakery where he likes to get bread and eavesdrop on the little gamecock Cubano patriots bragging on how they'll fix the country up once it is liberated. Not the ones drilling, or their pitiful approximation of drilling, in the streets with their white linen uniforms and drawn machetes, but the vest-and-watch brigade who wave their arms and pound their fists, faces reddening, voices rising into what in any other language would be poetry about the plight of their *isla desconsolada*. Oaths are sworn, tears are shed, hours of entertainment for a three-cent loaf of bread. More little boys, even darker skinned, cluster at the corner of 14th selling deviled crab.

"*Cangrejo, cangrejo, muy rico, muy fresco!*" they shout, holding the platters over their heads. Jacks has tried it once, nice and spicy with a mug of beer, but a lot of work for the harvest. He waves the boys off and presses forward. The shavetails are dragging, the morning's drill in the dunes knocking the go out of them. If there was time he'd have them all with their feet in pickling salts, he'd have started with shorter marches and built them up, he'd have really taught them how to shoot and not just fumble with their sights and blast away. But the regiment is under strength and there isn't time. They've been split up all over the West for decades now, usually no more than three companies at any one post, and it is no great surprise the unit isn't in step with itself.

"So Sergeant, give it to us straight—" Lunceford again, who they call Junior, a real barracks lawyer, with the same damn question they all been pestering him about. "How can they leave behind a company of highly trained regular soldiers to make way for some volunteer outfit with inferior weapons?"

"You greenhorns got a long road to tramp before I'd call you *soldiers*," says Jacks without turning. "But even if you *were*, somebody got to be left behind. There aint enough war to go around, and every damn body, regular or not, wants a piece of it."

The Rough Riders pulled in just a few days back, college sports and ranch hands and little Roosevelt who belongs at the Ferlita bakery singing his own praises with the Cubano peacocks, four-eyes Roosevelt strutting all over the camps and the Port trailing a remuda of so-called war correspondents and Kodak fiends. Jacks is a professional soldier and his pride, the one thing he has to show for his years of service, is wounded.

"Volunteers nothing but a bunch of ward heelers and merchant princes leading a bigger bunch of saloon trash who couldn't find their way out of a half-acre woodlot. But they got *pull*, see, and there's only fifty-some buckets out in that harbor ready to steam away, and even packed like sardines that won't do for the whole force we got mustered here. So the regulars leave without their full compliment and the cavalry leave without their mounts and the volunteer outfits with friends up high leave without a clue among the lot of em as to what they be facing when they get there." They are passing out of town now, and the sergeant can hear a hurdy-gurdy playing, a Dago selling shaved ice and colored syrup by the stables where the American teamsters congregate. Once he starts the boys jacking crates from the boxcar he'll come back and get one. He likes the green syrup, the mint, best in the heat of the day.

"And then at some point they expect there will be slaughter," he says with no bitterness, "or there'd only be white boys going over."

"And somebody's got to clear the roads and bury the dead." Scott is a smart one, not book-educated but quick to pick up on what's needed.

"Oh, we'll do our share of that, too. If there's a shit end to the stick we get to hold it. But there's times in battle," he says, a little uncomfortable to be sharing this with rookies, "when your job is to go soak up bullets."

"Cannon fodder."

"Mexicans call it *carne de cañón*. Cannon meat. You stuff that first wave of troopers down their mouth so's they can't bite no more, and then send in the boys that are gonna survive and pose for the statue."

"There's companies greener than ours set to go on them boats," says the one they call Little Earl. "How come ours got to stay?"

"Your company has to stay because your company has been *or*dered to stay, Private," says Jacks, putting a little steel into his voice. "You're in the Army—don't be trying to figure out a *rea*son for what you're told, don't be trying to guess what comes next or why. Aint a thing you can do about it one way or the other, and the sooner you give yourself up to that, the sooner you'll make a soldier."

Still, he thinks, it would be wondrous duty to be deployed in China.

They reach the little single-track rail depot and Jacks finds the boxcar and shows the dozey white sentry his orders. Patch gets his fly-addled mules in order and pulls the wagon alongside. There are crates inside the boxcar, unmarked, and the orders don't specify what is in them either, only that they are to be loaded and delivered to the Wisconsin Volunteers, wherever they might be found. It's just enough work to keep the four rookies busy and afford him a stroll around Ybor.

He pulls his dollar watch out and pretends to study it. "When I get back here," he says to the private soldiers, already wrestling crates onto the wagon bed while Patch hunkers down in the shade of the boxcar, "this wagon best be ready to *roll*."

"No problem, Sergeant." Poor Lunceford, thinks if he hustles and pleases and keeps his buttons shining he can somehow earn the privilege of accompanying the rest of the outfit to go have their heads blown off. So far this deal is more like the game the Mex kids play at their birthdays, blindfolded and batting wildly at who knows what swinging creature, than it is a war.

"If it isn't ready, we might have to revisit those dunes," says Jacks, turning back toward town, always careful to leave with a threat.

Maybe the purple one, he thinks, that they say is blackberry flavor. No telling if they'll have that in Cuba.

Tampa is a fever dream, a snake swallowing its own tail.

Coop digs and the sand slides in from the sides. He's spent more time with a shovel in his hands than a Krag, something about him that makes sergeants' eyes get big when the shit details are handed out. "*You! Cooper!*" they say, and he knows it's something down and dirty they've got in mind. The white officers, lieutenant and up, don't even see him, which is happy news. Coop keeps on digging and the sand keeps filling back in.

Sooner or later somebody with chevrons will come and see it is impossible, that the company will either have to be let to shit where the white boys do or walk through their territory to firmer ground. Coop has his shirt off, suspender straps cutting hot into his bare shoulders, red bandanna soaked on his forehead. I'm just a latrine-diggin fool here, staying in rhythm, throwing sand and watching it slide back in. And this after they try to kill us on them dunes. That's one thing with the Army—half of what gets ordered is just doing to be doing. There's no goods that come out of it, no cotton, no tobacco, no tree gum. Back home they happy to let you lie easy till the harvest, and then a black man better jump quick and get him a job before the sheriff put him on the work gang, same work but you got nothing to show at the end of it but marks where they put the irons on. But nobody let to lie in the Army—

Dewey comes by and watches for a moment.

"You wants to help," says Coop, not breaking his rhythm, "kill up some a these damn flies be pesterin me."

"I don't want to help," says Dewey. "I just come to see where we going tonight. That's if they let you out."

"Tampa City," says Coop, making Dewey hop back from a shovelful of sand heaved at his feet.

"Been having an awful row with the white folks in there."

"Yeah, and I aint been in on it yet." Coop likes Ybor well enough, but the idea that there is something he's not supposed to do, somewhere he's not supposed to go, even in the uniform their own damn Army give him—well. "Hear they got some ladies there make your toes curl."

"Not for us they don't." Dewey has been in for ten years and likes a good time without too much trouble.

"Well if them others wants to know," says Coop, "that's where I be."

Dewey watches him shovel for a moment. "That hole gonna just keep filling up."

"You see Sergeant Cade, you tell him about it."

"Oh, he knows, Coop. He just don't want you cooking up mischief. Idle hands is the devil's instruments."

Dewey steps away. Though Coop has made some kind of shallow bowl the back-sliding sand is halfway up to his knees now. Keep this up long enough, he thinks, and I bury my own self.

They don't whip you in the Army, or chain you up at night. They give you real folding money, thirteen dollars a month, instead of cardboard scrip you got to use in their own store and they give you a rifle and teach you how to use it. Just show up telling them you're Henry Cooper, jump over a stick, cough while the Doc puts his fingers on you, and you can wear the blue. He was skinny, bleary-eyed, a week hiding in the piney woods and two more tramping north and west, with nothing in his pockets and clothes that didn't fit he had to steal on the way. The recruiter in Kansas City barely looked at him. "Cavalry is full up," he said, "but if you don't mind walking we got a place for you."

Even in war there's got to be nigger jobs, he figured. Not just the digging and hauling and minding prisoners, but bloody work, something they don't want to put their white boys in front of. The Indians had been settled in for some time and there wasn't much talk of this Cuba war yet, they hadn't blown that ship up, so killing wasn't even on his mind.

Beats slaving in a damn turp camp with iron on your legs.

One of the white outfits, volunteers, double-times past him in formation, a blue rectangle moving against the bleached sand. Coop recognizes the look on their faces, trying hard not to think beyond the moment, not to wonder when is this particular hell going to end. There been nothing regular about their life since they pulled out of Fort Missoula, the brass just guessing their way along, and you got to grab your chances when they come. Get a chance to get drunk, or for a woman, or for a decent bite to eat and you damn well better jump on it. "*We not paying you boys to think*," Sergeant Cade likes to tell them, "*just pick em up and lay em down.*" The sun is lower now and Coop tosses his sweat-heavy campaign hat to the side of the pit. He hasn't been to stockade once since he joined, they can't break him and they can't shake him and he knows it bothers old Cade, on his tail from first bugle to *Taps*, but Cade don't rile him none. Just keep smiling and shoveling and tonight they owe him a pass, strap on the pistol and step out with the boys. Coop can't read, as such, but he knows his letters, knows when there is a big *W* on a brand-new sign it likely means "Whites Only" and was stuck up there just for him. There was more of that back home when he visited too, making a point of what a man already know on his own, rubbing you raw in a public way. We will see. The Cubans in Ybor just want your money—hell, they all shades themselves, ebony to ivory, and got all manner of Italians and Chinamen running around in the bargain. But Tampa City it's your standard-issue crackers, sun-baked and nasty, and a nigger won't get too many chances in this life to run it down their throats, to carry a sidearm and dare them, just dare the sorry sons of bitches to make something out of it.

Coop pulls his feet free of the sand. Without the uniform, of course, he be a dead man. Dead swinging on a rope or tied to a tree and burned or just shot and left lying for the dogs. Or dead soon enough from the way they work you. It come clear to him in the turp camp before he run off. So whatever the Army or old Geronimo or the Spanish or the Chinamen, if that's where they end up, got to throw at him is nothing. Better a bullet on a battlefield than be scraped by the week and bled by the season.

And when Sergeant Cade step by to see how the latrine is coming, here is Coop pouring sweat, ankle deep in a long, shallow ditch in the sand, smiling. Shoveling and smiling.

As the sun falls Tampa is a dream. The yearning of a war-hungry nation.

Father—

Junior in the shade of the tent, sides pulled up hoping to catch an afternoon Gulf breeze, Merriam pack across his knees to support the paper, voices shouting cadence drifting from every direction. Junior writes with dashing penmanship—

We have encamped at Tampa pending orders for embarkation. It is a hodgepodge of a town, given over to cigar-making and tourism, the former mostly in foreign hands and the latter in the minds of certain as yet unrewarded entrepreneurs. The arrival of our force, some eighteen thousand men in uniform, has no doubt been a huge economic boon, though one finds nothing but complaint in the local (white-owned) newspapers. Nearly one out of four of the fighting men gathered here is colored, and your pride would certainly swell to observe the account we are making for ourselves. My own 25th is in the thick of the training, and our surrounding volunteer units can only gape in wonder at the precision and brio we bring to field maneuvers and review.

Junior has his boots off, risking a sudden call back into action, his feet throbbing—

There are flying columns of "Cuban freedom fighters" clamoring about town in white linen uniforms, brandishing their long machete *knives and waving the one-starred flag. A notably underfed and overheated group, I'm afraid, and if their compatriots on the island are no more impressive it explains a great deal about the lack of success they've met over their decades of struggle. These aggregations are notable, however, for their inclusive nature, the white* insurrectos *marching shoulder to shoulder with the sable sons of Maceo. Emancipation came to the island a mere twelve years ago, and it stirs the blood to see these dark warriors accepted as brothers in arms by their erstwhile masters. We hope the performance of our own colored regiments in the coming battle will weigh heavily against the efforts of segregationists to discredit us, and that the call for Negro officers will be met. Whatever honors we win here will be an advantage for our entire race.*

The volunteers are a mixed lot, their comportment and training varying, as one would suppose, with their state of origin. The 71st New York share the Heights with us and seem a steady bunch, while the contingent from Georgia have proved less congenial neighbors. They are all "spoiling for a fight" while my fellow regular soldiers seem content to await orders. The "Rough Riders" have arrived with much fanfare, though we have little contact with mounted units. There are of course more horses and mules in their area than troopers, with the attendant sounds and odors, and I see no hope of transporting them all to Cuba in the "mosquito fleet" so far assembled.

Junior hoping no one will see him writing again, already the butt of jokes, the bearer of nicknames. If Royal hadn't been there, Chickamauga would have been the end of him—the heat, the veterans' insults, the grueling days of mindless drilling. It was a mistake to have come in as a private. A man with his background and education, with his standards of conduct—but there are no colored lieutenants and the war would not wait. Junior writing, holding pen hand aside to keep his sweat from dripping on the letter, as Little Earl naps sprawled beside him and the others steel themselves to face another meal—

The food has been an adventure. Hardtack is universally reviled and taken, if necessary, broken in pieces mixed with stew or canned tomatoes. It resembles nothing I have seen before, certainly nothing edible. A good deal of humor is spent imagining its proper employment (our Navy is said to be caulking the more ancient wooden vessels with their version of it, known as sea biscuit). "Bacon" is seen at nearly every meal and is another source of bitterness and objurgation, large blocks of sowbelly meant to serve as fresh meat for our diet. Of the tinned variety the less said the better, and though foraging is officially condemned the practice here is rampant. Yesterday I saw a man pay 5 cents for a single egg.

Junior paid the nickel and was later shamed to learn Private Cooper sold the rest of his clutch for two cents each. The poundcake Jessie mentioned in her letter was purloined somewhere in transit, not a crumb of it left, and the prices in Ybor shoot up between every visit. Junior, who was nauseated the first time he managed to finish a plate of sowbelly and half-cooked beans, who suffers the same dysentery his tentmates do but in silence and disgust, who has never been so filthy in his life and imagines all manner of crawly things breeding beneath the sour-smelling wool of his uniform—

I have had little time to reflect on what Fate may hold in store for me. My comrades do not speak of it, and from all appearances give little heed to the gravity of our situation. I am confident, though, that when the time for action arises, the men of the 25th will comport themselves as champions of liberty and fulfill without hesitation whatever duties shall fall upon their shoulders.

Junior thinks of little else. They are not slated to leave with the first wave, no, but he is confident the call will come, Company L into the breach, and then—

A wound, grave enough to be carried from the field but that will slowly heal, leaving a scar visible but not disfiguring—acceptable. A bullet to the head, neither seen nor heard—if the highest price is to be paid, that would be the best. The veterans have their stories, skirmishes in Indian territory or on the border, men with parts of themselves shot away, maimed, suffering agonies before they die, the veterans tell it with little emotion and some of it must be true. Or worse, to go home untried, untested, never to face an angry shot, left on the beach as others sail to glory. The privations, the insult, are only bearable if they lead to a moment in arms, under the flag, caught in a desperate fight. If we risk that for them, Junior thinks, Junior believes with all his soul, how can they deny us the rest?

Our bugler is warning of the evening mess and I must close. Please send my love to Mother and Jessie. I shall write them separately as time permits. I ask that you share the general observations enclosed with Manly at the Record, *whom I have promised a correspondence. There are other Wilmington men here besides myself and Royal Scott, but none of a literary bent. I will make you proud.*

> *Your son,*
> *Aaron*

Junior considers his boots for a long moment, then grimaces and struggles to pull the first one on. Little Earl sits up, sand stuck on his face, looking bewildered.

"Chow?"

"That's right."

The private frowns, trying to dredge something from his memory. "When was it they give us biscuits and butter?"

"Chickamauga," says Junior, starting on the other boot, "the first week."

Little Earl shakes his head. "Shouldn't ought to play with a man like that."

Tampa is a fever dream. Tampa is for sale.

Coop and the boys wait at the trolley stop, resisting temptation. Gasoline torches light the area and vendors at the various wood-and-cardboard stands shout out their attractions. Oranges are sold at one, imported from California since this year's killing frost, while others have soap and cocoanuts and local souvenirs and lemons and writing paper and sandwiches and there is a forty-foot-long ice-cream-and-soda-fountain counter at which prohibited items may also be purchased if the Provost Guard is either absent or willing to settle for a share. A crap game proceeds at one end of the counter.

"We leave that one alone," says Coop, "unless we way behind by the time we get back here."

"That be sometime tomorrow," grins Willie Mills.

"Don't you worry none. Ice cream might be run out, but them craps still be rollin day or night."

There is a new building, a two-story barnlike structure slapped together with raw pine, that sits just across from the trolley tracks.

"Pompton Stiles from B Company won hisself a pile in there playing chuck-aluck," says Willie.

"Yeah, and then he lost the whole thing on the roulette." Coop lets his hand rest on his pistol grip, a dozen white volunteers arriving and standing in a group to wait. "I stick with them bones. Bones always treat me right."

A barefoot little black boy comes by, selling polished conch shells.

Nobody wants to buy but he lingers, staring at the men. Coop pulls the Colt out of its holster, offers it.

"You want to hold this here?"

The little boy stares, awestruck, at the heavy weapon. "Naw suh." He shoots a glance toward the white soldiers, who are studiously looking in another direction. "They lets you ca'y that?"

"They insist on it," says Too Tall, who claims to have been a preacher once in Alabama. "Soldier aint a soldier less he's armed and ready for action. What if a boatload of them limejuicers land here in Tampa tonight, commence to attack the population? We might not have time to run back and get our rifles."

The boy nods, wide-eyed.

"Someday, if these crackers don't run you down first, maybe you be a soldier too," says Coop.

"Yeah?"

"Hell," says Willie Mills, "they take Coop here, they take about any old body."

They are laughing when the electric trolley arrives. Only a few passengers get off, mostly more vendors arriving for the nightly festivities, but there is a crowd of soldiers squeezing onto the two cars. The conductor scowls and stares hard out at the carnival booths, and Coop finds himself pressed tight against a short, nervous corporal from the Ohio Vols.

"Anybody seen that Jim Crow on board?" Coop calls out, grinning, just before the bell and the first lurch of motion.

"Naw," answers Too Tall from the other end of the car. "He aint been invited."

Tampa is a fever dream. Tampa is a dream of Hell.

The song ends and Little Earl feels the Spirit move within him. Earlier it was the stew and one of the sweats he's been having, the ones that come even when they're not running you over the sand, but this is different, tingling out through his whole body and urging him to stand and shout no matter what the white folks think.

Moody, the famous Moody of Chicago, steps to the podium on the plank stage at the front. He is a stocky man, with a patriarch's beard and a deep, booming voice that fills the great tent without strain—it impresses Little Earl that the evangelist is only *talk*ing with them, man to man, though there are women scattered in the rows. There are at least five hundred souls gathered under the canvas, with many uniformed soldiers among them, whites taking up some three-quarters of the space and the blacks crowded behind a rope to the left.

The subject is the Lost World.

"The Spirit of God tells us that we shall carry our memory with us into the Hereafter," says Moody, lifting his iron gaze to the volunteers standing by the rear of the tent, still whispering among themselves. "Memory is God's officer, and when He shall touch these secret springs and say, '*Son, daughter, remember*'—then tramp, tramp, tramp will come before us, in a long procession, all the sins we have ever committed."

The whisperers fall silent, not sure whether to retreat or hold their ground. "Do you think Cain has forgotten the face of his murdered brother, whom he killed six thousand years ago? Do you think Judas has forgotten that kiss with which he betrayed his Master? Do you think when the judgment came upon Sodom that those wicked men were taken into the presence of God, or did they find themselves in the other, darker realm, in the Lost World of Hell itself?"

Mam made him swear upon the Bible—Earl can feel the dry leather in his hand—to walk the path of Righteousness no matter where the Army might take him. That she is back in Arkansas, breathing still, is a comfort, for if the dead can indeed look down upon the living, oh, Lord, the sins she be witness to!

"Many in that Lost World would give millions, if they had them," Moody continues, "would beseech their sainted mothers to pray them out of that place—but all too late. They have been neglecting salvation until the time has come when God says, '*Cut them down, the day of mercy has ended!*'"

A note of laughter from the men standing by the entrance. Moody does not deign to look their way.

"You may make sport of ministers, but bear in mind there will be no preaching of the Gospel in that Lost World. There are some people who ridicule these revival meetings, but remember, there will be no revivals in Hell."

Little Earl wonders is there a rope, a line of barbed wire perhaps, that separates black and white sinners in Satan's realm? Or will their bodies be hurled unsorted, stewed together like offal in a cauldron, and that wicked proximity yet another torture they must bear? And in the place above, should he somehow rise to see it, will his people there be asked to sit to the left, crowded on unpainted benches?

"A deacon was one day passing a saloon as a young man was coming out, and thinking to make sport of him, the young man called out, 'Deacon, how far is it to Hell?'" A chuckle from the audience as they sense what is coming.

"The deacon gave no answer, but after riding a few rods he turned to look after the scoffer, and found the man's horse had thrown him and broken his neck. I tell you, my friends, I would sooner give my right hand than to trifle with Eternal things."

At least, if what the lieutenant said is true, they won't be going right away. There is time to repent. It strikes Little Earl that timing figures larger in the stories the preachers tell than the amount of wickedness engaged in—a monster of lechery pardoned at death's door while a Godly man might transgress only once, but if struck down leaving the address of sin, be cursed forever.

In Missoula he sported with most all of the women who made themselves available outside the Fort every payday, before settling on the Mankiller sisters, Jewel and Ortha, Flathead girls who weren't really red. Copper maybe, with long, coarse black hair that took his breath away sliding against his bare stomach and strong legs that didn't let you loose till it was finished. Ortha was moody while Jewel was gay, but both knew your company and rank and called you soldier—"*Get those trousers off, soldier*"—and Jewel even gave Elijah Barnes a free one to celebrate when he made corporal. Then the one in the Chattanooga house he visited a couple times, dark little thing with the beautiful eyes who called him Daddy and could bend herself like a pretzel and now the whole shooting gallery available over in Ybor, Francine with huge breasts that have a life of their own, pillowing his ears as she works on top of him or Zeidy who snarls words in Spanish he doesn't understand but thrill him all the same and Caridad his exact same shade like they were formed from the same patch of clay and Esther who could pass for white or the skinny Chinese girl the guys call Poon Tang with her nipples like the tips of his little fingers or any of the other ones, all shades and all sizes, all the other ones he's looked at but never tried in Ybor or here in Tampa City.

Little Earl shifts on the bench to cover the evidence of this line of thought. Moody seems to be looking directly at him.

"We are trying to win you to Christ," says the man with the patriarch's beard, sincere, forceful, singling Little Earl out from the others. Can the man read minds?

"If you go forth from this tent straight to Hell, you will remember this meeting, and the golden opportunity we have offered you here. For in that

Lost World you won't hear the beautiful hymn *Jesus of Nazareth Passeth By*, no, He will already have *passed* by. There will be no sweet songs of Zion there, only the mournful lamentations of the eternally condemned. If you neglect this salvation, oh sinner, how will you escape? Remember that Christ stands right here—" Moody holds his arm out to indicate the Redeemer is standing only feet away from him, "—here in this assembly tonight, offering redemption to every soul. For the reaping time is upon us, brothers and sisters—if you sow the flesh you must reap corruption! If you sow the wind you must reap the whirlwind!"

The evangelist pauses dramatically, and Little Earl can hear the life on the street beyond the tent, hear horses passing and carriage wheels rolling, the drunken shouts of men, can hear, as if they are calling to him, the brazen voices of the women of the night. They are out there, a hundred Jezebels, no, a thousand, waiting with eager lips and soft skin, with enticing words, with—

Moody changes tone.

"I was called once to the bedside of a dying man, a man who had tried to follow the word of God but let the opinion of his worldly acquaintances obstruct his progress, a man who had turned away from the Light to bask in the false warmth of his comrades' admiration. 'You need not pray for me,' he said, 'for my damnation is sealed.'

"Nevertheless I fell upon my knees and tried to speak with the Almighty, hoping in His charity He might comfort a sinner come to the final day—but my prayers did not go higher than my head, as if Heaven above me was like brass. 'The harvest is gone,' said the poor unfortunate from his bed, 'the summer is ended, and I am not saved.'"

Moody turns his lion-like head slowly, seeming to look deeply into the soul of every person in the tent, black and white. He speaks softly, sadly, yet such is the silence in the tent that even Little Earl, crammed in the rear of the colored wedge, can hear his every word. "He lived a Christless life, he died a Christless death, we wrapped him in a Christless shroud and bore him away to a Christless grave."

The Golden Orator of Chicago slams his hand down on the top of the podium. "*Fly* to the arms of Jesus this hour! There is yet time! You can be *saved* if you will!"

And then the choir, bursting into song with Sankey's beautiful voice rising above the others, the man nearly blind now but God-possessed, calling them, calling them forward to Glory—

What means this eager, anxious throng
Which moves with busy haste along,
These wondrous gath'rings day by day,
What means this strange commotion, pray?
In accents hushed the throng reply,
"Jesus of Nazereth passeth by!"

Tampa is a fever dream.

Tampa is a fever dream lying by the fetid Gulf, writhing hot with fear and desire. Camp followers have swarmed the miasmic city to feed upon the soldiers and each night, drawn to light and noise, those soldiers dare each other to be the drunkest, the loudest, the lowest. The pianos are all warped out of tune, the liquor smells of kerosene and the Army is a guest who has stayed overlong. Tampa wishes he would leave but can't help selling one more cocoanut, one more drink. And there are guns everywhere, guns are the point of it, guns and flags and men marching or staggering in groups and the hard slap of a black man in uniform a reminder that there is a price for this boon, this bonanza of war, an insult that must be swallowed to keep the riches flowing. Tampa is a cackling reverie, flushing hot in fevered temples, teetering on a point of chance—

Finally, Coop is the shooter. It's the first time he's held the dice all night and up to now he's just nibbled around the edges of the table, for it is a table and not a poncho behind a tent or chalk marks on a floor, throwing the nickel minimum in on hopping bets with long odds and the house has taken his nickels. The house used to be a butcher shop from the hooks on the ceiling and the smell of it, with a half-dozen games working and Army-issue tin cups, a boxcar-load of them seems to have been stolen and spread around Tampa, that you rap on the pine three times when it's time for a refill. Coop puts his half-full cup down to press the dice between his palms.

"These bones been waitin for a man knows how to treat em," he says, closing his eyes and rubbing the cubes. "They feelin awful cold."

"What you play?" The boxman is a Chink in a vest and bowler hat. A light brown boy with a harelip is ragging a tinny little piano at the rear where the heavy breakdown used to happen, blood stains mottling the wall beside him.

"No pass, what you think? Lay a dollar down, Willie." Willie always handles his money when he is rolling. Making change interrupts the flow.

"Train leaving the station," says Coop, rattling the dice next to his ear now. "You boys better jump on board."

Some of the boys he knows and some he doesn't get on it while he heats them up and then Too Tall shouts "Come out, brother!" and he whips them down on the felt. It really is felt, too, recently razored off a billiards table from the marks on it, and an easy eight bounces off the rail.

"No pass," says the Chink with the bowler hat. "Point is eight."

Coop will play whatever is running but he likes craps the best. Straight poker is slow, feels like you're slaving at the mercy of all that royalty on the cards, and roulette you can't ever hold nothing in your hand, but craps is ever-shifting, like trying to catch fish in a river while bouncing through its rapids. And he's always been good with numbers.

"What you paying for hard-ways?" he asks as he scoops the dice up.

"Nine to one." Jerome, who is black as a wood stove and twice as wide, is dealing and wielding a bamboo cane for a stick at the same time. "But for a sportin man like yourself we make it ten."

Coop smiles. "Put me down five, Willie." Cheers and whistles from the boys. "Gone roll me a hard eight."

The floor man is a tough-looking cracker who sits on a high stool with a shotgun across his knees. Coop has never seen a white man shoot craps, one of the things he likes about it, but has no doubt that's who owns the bank here. Willie puts the cash on the layout.

Coop rolls a five, and then a ten. Fagen, a big old local boy from the Scrub who soldiers with the 24th, leads a few men over from the other games. Coop feels their heat around him, feels snug and happy in the smoke and noise and music, gulps whiskey and bangs for more. He knows the secret and they don't. He rolls a four.

"The man is *hot*!" Willie calls out. "Keep back or you catch fire off him."

Yes, there is luck, he knows, but it smiles on nobody. The rain is going to fall or not fall whether you put a crop under it or not, enough people scratch for gold someone is likely to find it, and you can be the slickest thief in the Carolinas but a day will come when you're in the wrong place with the wrong mule.

"Show me a five, keep it alive," he chants and snaps them down on the table and yes, it is a five but it could have been anything. He starts to laugh.

"He got the *pow*er," calls out Rufus Briscoe from A Company, who is sweating the way he does when thoroughly drunk. "He got the touch." And doubles his bet on the point.

Most of them are making deals with God, but Coop knows better. He knows the secret. *"Oh Jesus, if You love me slip me a queen on the draw."* Jesus don't play that game—Jesus is the house and the house always wins. The black come up five times in a row it's just as likely to come up a sixth as to go back to red. Company of men go running at a lot of people shooting a lot of bullets and some number of them, good soldier or bad, is going to get killed. That's the odds Jesus will give you. You have to forget about winning and just be happy to hold the dice for a while.

Coop hurls them down and the twin fours come up. There is a cheer and men slapping him on the back, half the room following his game now, and even fat Jerome pretends to smile.

"The Lady didn't just smile at this boy," says Fagen when the shouting settles down. "She done sat on his face."

Coop nods and Willie pockets his winnings. He rolls an eagle to the Chink. There are shots then, just outside the door.

"Bout *time* the show got started," says Coop before he rolls boxcars and craps out.

Tampa is a fever dream.

When they step out of the arcade there are men with guns and a woman screaming and a child held upside down. It is hard for Royal to focus at first, he's been looking at the views in the little machine, a train coming straight at him but contained on the rectangle and if he looked away it wasn't there. But this is all around him on the street and won't go away, a black woman screaming and cursing as the white boys, Ohio Vols, laugh and hold her back and another down the street holds the child, who is screaming too but with an animal terror, swinging by his ankles gripped in another soldier's hand, the man holding him out like a rabbit just killed, a shell on a leather thong dangling down from the boy's neck, and then Junior grabbing Royal's arm, Watch out he's saying and then the shot, coming from behind him. Yet another Vol, feet spread apart but body swaying with liquor, one eye closed as he aims his Colt at the swinging shell.

"You don't hold that pickaninny still," he calls, "Imonna plonk him for sure."

The man fires again and then the street seems to brighten under the gas lamps, colors flaring as Royal steps toward the one with the Colt, Junior dragging on him and the woman screaming "God damn you! God damn you to hell!"

But before Royal can reach him the Vol with the Colt grunts and collapses on one knee, a dark stain blooming on the man's light blue trousers
just below the hip. He looks around, stupid with drink, sees Royal and raises
his pistol but his balance is all gone and he pitches sideways to the street.
More shooting then and there are others, Coop is one of them, running out
from a raw-pine building across from the arcade, many of them firing and it's
then Royal realizes he left his pistol in camp. Junior said it would be best,
but Junior is now shouting and waving to get off the street, dammit, and a
blue shock cracking behind his ear and the pavement comes up fast to thump
him hard. There are night-pass boots in his face, stomping, he can smell the
wet polish, and then he's rolled under falling bodies.

Junior pulls him up out of the writhing pile and he sees the weeping
woman holding her child, the child still shrieking and the street filling up
with white men.

"This is no good," says Junior, seeming to have a clearer idea of what is
happening. "We got to run!"

How do they know what it's about so quickly? These white men, a few
of them soldiers but mostly shopkeepers and corner sports and family men in
white skimmers with their shotguns and pistols already, their bats and pool
cues—how do they know the moment they step into the heat of the gas-lit
street that it's get the niggers and not some other disaster, some other entertainment, here on a block full of drunken men and a dozen clashing musics
and gunfire commonplace since the encampment began? Some instant signal, some electric connection has hurled them out here and every white man
is searching for a black one to shoot, to beat, but now suddenly there is a
counterrush of black and blue out from Miss Sadie's on the north end of the
street, Miss Sadie's Lovely Ladies where Little Earl has been spending his pay,
a wave of black men wearing bits and pieces of their uniforms and several of
them firing pistols and the ground is sparkling, sparkling with broken glass
as Junior pulls him back into the arcade.

Royal is coming and going now, dizzy, hurting sharp behind his right
eye and missing some pictures in between like the Mutoscope he was viewing before when you crank it too fast and each time he comes back the
Orchestrion is still playing *Goodbye, Nellie Gray*, pumping the piano and
drums and cymbal and tambourine but the shots outside not in time with
it and then he's gone for a moment, the pictures blurring together till they
slow and he reels, caroming off the bagatelle table they were playing at then
stopped hard at the hips and doubled over, vomiting on the surface of the

beanbag toss, looking up woozily into the goggle eyes of the target, a monstrous laughing jigaboo head, its open mouth the hole you have to aim for.

"You get outd of heer!"

The proprietor, a big German with pop-eyes, comes at him from a tilted angle, raising an ax handle in his boiled-ham fists.

"I break you in the hedt!" he cries, voice surprisingly high. "You get oudt *now*!"

And where, in a penny arcade, did he find a brand-new ax handle?

"We're just going," calls Junior, ever the gentleman, as he lifts Royal by the shoulders and steers him away. "We don't want any trouble."

Royal sees they are the only customers left and the Orchestrion switches to *Bill Bailey* as he is hustled out the back entrance, stumbling over a drunken soldier sleeping curled on his side.

"I've been hit," says Royal, the fact dawning on him with another wave of nausea. "Somebody hit my head and I'm sick."

There is too much water in the air to breathe right and there is more shooting, shooting and shouted curses from the other side of the building. A small soldier hurries down the alley toward them, looking back over his shoulder and he is almost on them before they see it is Little Earl, his eyes shining with more excitement than fear.

"I been saved," he says. "I'm prepared to meet my Maker." And then, as if an afterthought, "Why everybody shooting?"

Tampa is a fever dream bubbling acid to the brain. Old hatreds are resolved in a flash, strangers try to murder one another, property is destroyed, storefronts violated.

A fire wagon races down the street, horses wide-eyed and prick-eared, thick-armed men ready to shoulder through doorways, but nothing is burning yet. Tampa is unhinged, thoughtless, thrashing in its own worst nightmare.

Coop has one round left in the chamber and they're running. Not running away but running wild, running to spread it as fast and as far as possible, to do what is needed till it can't be done anymore.

Too Tall trots with a sack of cans, beans and tomatoes and succotash they pulled from the grocery where the clerk spat at his shoes, and whenever one of the boys says There, they wouldn't serve me there, they all reach in and grab a can and let fly at the glass. Coop wonders what the Army name for the formation they are running in is, a wide V with a few pedaling backward behind to cover the rear. Willie Mills has a new Winchester and a pocketful of shells he took from the hardware and hasn't got to use yet. Now and again some white head will look out from a doorway or window, take one look and disappear before he can get a shot off.

"They sposed to pop up again," Willie complains. "Give a man a chance."

Coop is feeling good, feeling free and bold and keeping that one ace back in the chamber in case he needs it. The first one he knows he hit cause the man fell out, aimed at the balls and cut him under the hip, and two more must have hit somebody cause it was such a crowd of them coming all together he fired into. The Krag, what he would give to have the Krag in his hands right now and a belt packed with ammunition. Put these rednecks to school.

"It's there on the left," says Rufus Briscoe and they see the girls, most all of them white, looking down from the second-floor balcony. The V swings right and again Coop is sure the Army has a name for it, Too Tall shattering the door with the heel of his boot and the rest squeezing shoulder to shoulder to push it through.

A thick-necked black man sits on the parlor stairs, shotgun leveled and his face glistening with nervous sweat.

"You go upstairs," he says, "they gone kill me for sho."

"You put that shotgun up." Too Tall spreads his arms out wide, drops the sack with the last few cans in it. Men still outside are shouting, wanting to know what the hold-up is.

"Don't you make me do this."

Coop drifts off to the side, toward the parlor. He has the pistol loose in his hand.

Too Tall takes a small step forward, arms still spread.

"We gonna get what we come for. These gals anything to you?"

"This my job."

"It worth dyin for?"

"Ax you the same thing. White-woman pussy worth dying for?"

Too Tall laughs. "You all right. What's your name?"

"Jawge."

"There's at least seven, eight of us here, Jawge. Aint no white man gonna blame you, overwhelm eight-to-one."

Coop watches the man's trigger finger. He's seen a man taken apart by a shotgun this close once, in Raleigh. Saw backbone come out white behind and the man lifted clear off his feet.

"And this aint just no common layabouts, Jawge," says Too Tall, easing his hands down. "You got professional soldiers here, out on a rampage. If you think your white man blame you for that, give us his name and we go get him."

The man on the stairs ponders this for a moment, not happy, then looks over to Coop.

"Lay your shotgun back," says Coop, smiling, "and step out the way."

Coop eases back closer to Too Tall, not taking his eyes off the weapon. George stands, then swings the gun around and unloads both barrels into the parlor, shattering a mirror and blowing stuffing from a pink divan. Screams from upstairs.

"You done lost me this job," he says accusingly. "But you tell them gals I peppered some hides down here, maybe Mist' Carlyle won't come after me."

He steps aside and the men charge up the stairs, cheering.

"Aint a thing up there that's worth it," he says to Willie, left behind with his rifle to watch the street.

Coop is the first in the room. A blond woman with a face round as a pie plate, dressed in red silk, stands in front of the others with her hands on her hips.

"We don't fuck no niggers here," she announces.

"Aint nothing to it, darling," says Coop. "And how things is, tonight you got no choice."

The blond woman eyes the roll of money as he pulls it from his shirt pocket.

"You gone pay?"

"Yeah, darling, we gone pay," says Coop, laying his winnings on the bureau and smiling. "One way or the other."

Tampa is a fever dream, lingering through the night, a nightmare that won't end.

"Who goes there?"

There are five of them, sharp-eyed boys from the 2nd Georgia. The boldest has the barrel of his rifle jammed against the center of Junior's chest. There is enough light to see color now.

"What we got?" calls another as he steps around the side of a scrapwood shanty.

"Got a bunch of plantation monkeys all dressed up like sojers." A scrawny dog is sniffing loudly at Royal's leg and growling, its tail rigid. There is a distant popcorn-rattling of gunfire from back in Tampa City but here the black folks have barred their doors, or what they have that will pass for a door, praying the fight won't blow their way.

"What you doing out here, Rastus?"

"Private Aaron Lunceford," says Junior as calmly as he can. "25th Infantry, Company L."

"Not what I asked you, is it?"

They cut through the Scrub hoping somebody might hide them till day-break. Little Earl knows a house with two women who host card parties but nobody was in there and then they got turned around because the streets are just sand paths with no signs anywhere.

"We were just visiting here," says Royal, feeling sick again, "and then heading back to the Heights."

The leader looks down to the fyce, growling louder now and staring tense at Royal's leg, ready to snap if he makes a twitch. "Dog botherin you, boy?"

"No." Royal realizes it should have been "No sir" but the Army training has taken hold and this boy has only got one thin stripe on his arm.

"Bothers me," says the leader.

Royal feels the force of the bullet passing close by his leg. Just a single startled yelp, the kind they do when they're sleeping and you step on their tail, and it flops to the sand. He can smell the blood, and something else, urine. He shifts his leg slowly and is relieved to find it's not his own.

"Oh Lord," says Little Earl.

Another one comes close to peer hard in their faces, a boy with light green eyes, cat eyes, and a lump in his cheek. He spits tobacco next to the body of the dog. "Our regiment been delegated to get you darkies in line," he says. He nods at the leader. "Lester here was fast asleep and yall put him outta bed. He fit to kill, he is."

"If you'll deliver us to the provost tent, I'm sure they'll—"

The leader, Lester, jerks the barrel of his Springfield up to crack Junior under the chin. "You open your mouth again, nig, I'll knock them pearly whites out." He points. "Yall prisoners now, you march where you're told and shut the hell up. Now hop to it."

Lester winks to the others and waves his rifle. They start to walk, one of the Georgia boys on each side and two behind, with the cat-eyed soldier leading the way.

"Just follow Jimbo," says the leader, "and keep your hands where we can see em."

They aren't walking toward the camp. Lost as he is Royal can tell that much but can't bring himself to raise the question. You raise the question you have to live with the answer. The pain behind his eye has dulled somewhat, the dizziness gone. He could bolt away before they're clear of the houses, maybe outrun them. The ones behind have their rifles shouldered, strolling casually. He could bolt away but that would leave Junior and Little Earl to the volunteers with their blood up. They step out onto a foot trail through a tangle of palmettos and Jimbo begins to sing—

Oh Ireland has her harp and shamrock
England floats her lion bold—

He has a beautiful voice, a sweet tenor—

Even China has a dragon
Germany an eagle gold
Bonny Scotland loves a thistle
Turkey has her crescent moon—

He turns and walks backward, green eyes smirking, dropping to an exaggerated bass like a minstrel darky—

An what won't de yankees do
Fo they red, white, an blue?
Every race got a flag but de coon!

Jimbo finishes, the Georgia boys sniggering, then turns and leads them deeper into the palmetto thicket. Royal sees tiny spots of orange dotting the horizon to the left, campfires on the Heights maybe a mile away.

"Where they taking us?" whispers Little Earl.

"Don't know," Royal whispers back, his knees going to water for an instant. "Don't say nothing."

"You know any?" Jimbo turns again and backpedals slowly. "Any of the old-time songs?"

"Christ, Jimbo," moans Lester. "Let's just get this done."

"They all of em can sing. Aint that right? Let's hear something."

Royal's mind is only pain and sickness. He looks to Junior, who is walking stiffly, eyes fixed forward, as if being judged on his carriage.

"I know you," says Little Earl.

Jimbo stops, brings his rifle up. They all have to stop not to walk over him. "What's that?"

"I seen you," says Little Earl. "Tonight at the Moody revival. You was singing and I looked over and there you was, giving note for note with Mr. Sankey."

Lester looks from Little Earl to his comrade. "That's what you do with a pass?"

"It's a hell of a show, Les," says the cat-eyed soldier, shaking his head in wonder. "Ought to try it sometime."

"I thought you was part of the choir, put out among the sinners, till I seen the uniform." Little Earl has a terrible smile on his face. The other 2nd Georgias have surrounded him now, crowding close, watching Jimbo to see what they should do.

"Let's hear it, then," says Jimbo softly. "Hear how the niggers sing it."

Little Earl, breathing hard, closes his eyes to remember the words. His voice is shaky at first—

> *There is a fountain filled with blood*
> *Drawn from Emmanuel's veins*
> *And sinners plunged beneath that flood*
> *Lose all their guilty stains—*

He gets his breathing in line with the melody and gains a little strength. Royal feels like he is watching it all from some high place, him and Junior waiting to be murdered and Little Earl singing and the white boys with their rifles gathered round and the palmettos taking detail as the sun teases the edge of the earth—

> *The dying thief rejoiced to see*
> *That fountain in his day*
> *And there may I, though vile as he*
> *Wash all my sins away—*

Jimbo joins in then, singing counter to Little Earl's steady declamation, bending the words here and there—

> *Then in a nobler, sweeter song*
> *I'll stay Thy pow'r to save*
> *When this poor lisping, stammering tongue*
> *Lies silent in the grave*
> *Lies silent in the grave*
> *Lies silent in the grave*
> *When this poor lisping, stammering tongue*
> *Lies silent in the grave*

It is very quiet when they finish. No nightbugs anymore. A rooster announcing itself over in Ybor. Little Earl's breath coming hard.

"Jesus," says Lester to his friend, his look more confused than admiring. "You sound more like a nigger than he does."

Jimbo grins as if it's a compliment, cocks his head at the prisoners. "You boys carryin any money?"

Tampa wakes from a fever dream, damp and confused, hoping that none of it is true.

The Georgia boys look wounded when it is Sergeant Jacks they turn their prisoners over to. They peek past him into the provost tent and there are white men there, officers, and Lester steps in to speak with one of them. The lieutenant glances out and nods that it is okay.

Lester walks back past them, muttering, and joins the other Georgians at the coffee boiler.

"They took all our money," says Junior when he is out of earshot.

Jacks yawns, leads them back toward the bivouac. "Won't be needing it where you going."

"But we're stuck here."

The sergeant shakes his head.

"Had a bunch of our fellows shot up in town last night," he says without turning. "Sent em to Atlanta. We short in H Company so you three and Cooper are moving over. With me."

Junior brightens. "That's terrific! When do we go?"

"They'll move us to the Port tomorrow, then I spect we'll sit some more." He falls back into step alongside them, looks at Royal's boots.

"Who that blood is?"

"They kilt a dog."

Jacks nods his head slowly, as if this explains it all. "Yeah," he says, "you lucky niggers going to Cuba."

CAMP ALVA

Hod looks up from the chow line at Camp Alva Adams and can see the flophouse he stayed in the night before he enlisted. The camp is laid out just across from the brickyards above Denver City Park, and it is raining, as it has been for weeks now, the volunteers drilling in the mud and eating under a patchwork canvas awning that sags with collected water and promises to collapse under the weight. Runt has been taking bets as to which unit will be soaked when the inevitable occurs. He and Hod and Big Ten and the other late recruits have been reassigned almost daily, landing just this morning with Company G, whose men are mostly from Cripple Creek.

"Reinforcements," says a private with a ratlike face as they join the group waiting with mess kits in the drizzle. "And we aint even been shot at yet."

"We've been sent over to shape your outfit up," says Runt, who is from Pueblo and claims to be a newspaper reporter, "and provide a model soldier for you to study."

"You'd think they'd have sent a full-size model, then."

Runt only comes up to Hod's shoulder, fair game for the wags in every company they've been stuck in.

"You figure the bigger the soldier," says Hod, "the bigger the target he's gonna make."

The rain comes harder then and they are soaked by the time their tin plates are weighted with stew and they can duck under the sagging canvas to sit on wet benches.

Big Ten slaps water off his hat, looks to Hod. "To think we could be in a nice dry variety hall, pounding each other's brains out."

"It rains every day in Cuba," the rat-faced soldier tells them.

"You been there?"

"I read all about it in the papers."

"That's your tropical climate," says the Runt. "Hot and wet."

The soldier looks at him suspiciously. "How old are you, kid?"

"Old enough."

"The Regular Army got standards," says the soldier, considering Runt and shaking his head. "But us vols—you ought to see some of the officers."

"Any more poop on when they ship us out of here?" asks Hod. Today he is feeling especially stupid to have signed on. Marching and saluting and yes sir and no sir and sleeping in tents on the muck and slop for food—at least in a mine you've got hours working alone up at the face where the bosses can't ride you.

"Depends on how much weight Colonel Hale carries with the high muck-etymucks. Every outfit in the country is trying to be the first to Havana."

"What's the hurry?" says Big Ten, shoveling stew into his mouth.

"No hurry," grins the long-faced private. "Long as they save a couple Dagoes for me."

After chow there is Battalion Drill, sloshing with rifle on shoulder through the mud and the cactus, trying to stride and turn as one man, laborers from the brickworks pausing to watch on their way home. Once the whole battalion is moving Hod feels better, losing himself in the mass of it, one little part of four hundred rifle-toting, cadence-shouting men shifting into rectangles of various sizes or swinging in great flanking maneuvers, over and over, the mind numbing with repetition as their boots grow heavy with mud. Since the news of the embarkation at Tampa hit camp there is the real possibility that they will actually get to use the old trapdoor Springfields they've been given, to kill and be killed. So far they've barely fired a round, the officers more worried about a stray shot hitting the neighbors than the fighting prowess of their troop. If it does come to a real fight, thinks Hod, then hell—the Dons are nothing but bosses, bosses of the cruelest sort, and freeing the poor Cubans from them is a good thing, a noble thing, an American thing to do. There will be breakfast tomorrow, possibly hot, and the next day and the next, his decisions worried out by other men and his hours regulated by trumpet calls. Men like him, homeless, desperate men, are blown about the world like cinders from a locomotive stack, and the Army is as good a place for them to end up as any.

The overcast day loses the last of its light and there is the six o'clock whistle from the Denver and Rio Grande tracks and finally they can march no more. The men stand in ranks and a major struts in front of them and barks loud noises about discipline and teamwork and then they are dismissed till evening meal. Big round Sibley tents have been put up in rows, and the men, sixteen to each, sit on their bedrolls in the gloomy interiors, pulling their sodden boots off, feet facing the center pole, smoking and talking by candlelight.

"Makes you feel right at home, don't it Chief?" winks a corporal named Grissom to Big Ten. "Back in the old teepee."

"I never been in a tent," says Big Ten looking at the simple rigging above. "Except once at the circus. My people live in cabins."

"We get to Cuba," says their squad sergeant, LaDuke, "you'll get a chance to lift some tonsures. Bet that greaser hair comes off easy."

"Wasn't nobody in my family ever a barber, neither," says Big Ten, in a way that announces he's done with the topic.

"I figure we either go for broke blasting our way straight into Havana," says Runt, who is full of strategy he reads in the editorial pages of the *Post*, "or we slip around to the other end of the island and take them from behind. Santiago de Cuba."

Grissom snorts a laugh. "Oh, they see you, Half-Pint, they'll be shaking in their boots."

"Long as you save a couple Dagoes for me," says the rat-faced soldier.

There is dinner, canned bacon and undercooked beans, and then a little time for card games and another installment in the running debate over which is the finest passion parlor, accessible on a soldier's pay, on Denver's Holliday Street. The trumpet signals lights-out at ten. Hod lies back and listens to the rain on the canvas and, only blocks away, the music and shouting from the saloons on Larimer. Once he and Zeb made a pup tent from a tarpaulin and some fenceposts and slept out behind the barn, pretending they were Army scouts out on the range, pretending to listen for hostile Indians and thrilled to feel the ground tremble when the night train from Salina rushed past. He feels like he is pretending now, their little cluster of tents surrounded by the great city, feels like it might as well be the Salvation Army he has joined and not the 1st Colorado Volunteers.

Big Ten begins to snore and it seems as if the ground is trembling.

*   *   *

In the morning the sun is out, and after breakfast the men in Company G decide to kangaroo the Runt in celebration.

"Think of it as an honor," suggests Corporal Grissom as they toss the boy up from the blanket again and again, one soldier at each corner and dozens gathered around to cheer. "An initiation into the brotherhood of fighting men."

"I'll tear your fucking heads off!" the Runt replies, red-faced, trying to keep from turning face-down as he is flung skyward. Hod stands at the edge of the crowd, not bothering to smile. Runt is new and wears glasses and is small enough to throw really high, but it could as well have been him and he doesn't like the look on Grissom's face or the way Sergeant LaDuke chants "*Up* she goes, *up* she goes—" with each toss. Hod has his usual morning regrets, uncomfortable in the uniform, Army breakfast sitting heavy in his stomach.

They heave Runt higher each time, bringing the blanket almost to the ground on the catch, till a familiar voice calls out that that will be enough.

Hod feels dizzy. It is Lieutenant Niles Manigault.

"Put that soldier down."

The men are confused at first, not recognizing the new officer, but field the Runt in the blanket one last time and lay him on the ground. Manigault, wearing a spanking-new tailored uniform, stares at Runt as the little soldier crawls to find his glasses on the ground and stands unsteadily, still red-faced.

"Name?"

"Runyon, sir. Company G."

"That is *my* company now. And I won't have anyone in it more fit to be shot out of a cannon than to charge one on a battlefield. Collect your gear and see the pay clerk."

"But sir—"

"You are mustered *out*, soldier. Remove yourself from the training field."

LaDuke laughs out loud. Manigault turns to the gaping men.

"Let's get those haversacks squared away," says the Lieutenant. "We'll be laying siege to Cherry Creek this afternoon. *Move!*" He holds a hand up to Hod and Big Ten as the others hurry away, Runt moving dazedly in the opposite direction. "A word with you two."

This is some confidence trick, thinks Hod, that they planned all along. The bait and switch. Niles steps close to speak quietly, drilling them with his eyes.

"You gentlemen left me in a rather untenable position."

"Our nation pleaded," says Big Ten, "and we answered the call."

"I owe the Blonger brothers a considerable sum. Your participation," he pokes Hod in the chest with a finger, "in the fistic enterprise would have squared me. Instead I have been forced to seek, like yourselves, refuge in this aggregation of halfwits and slackers."

"You made lieutenant awful quick," says Big Ten.

"I was a major in the Skaguay Guards," Niles corrects him, "but have accepted a lesser commission for the good of the cause."

Hod snorts. "But that was just Soapy doing the whole town."

Niles pokes him with the finger again. "You are the last person who should be telling tales from the Yukon, Private McGinty."

"Atkins," sighs Hod, and nods toward the Indian. "He's McGinty now. It's what we told them when we enlisted."

"Whatever. I hope you understand that any assumptions based on our familiarity have been precluded by rank. You stand warned."

"What about me?" asks Big Ten. "I'm not familiar."

"You, Private," explains Lieutenant Manigault, arching his eyebrows, "are not even *white*."

BOOK II

A MOMENT
IN THE SUN

BEACHHEAD

Nobody is shooting at them. Royal has been imagining it, dreading it, the green mat of jungle facing them crowded with armed Spanish, every one of them sighting his rifle at a spot dead between his eyes. But nobody is shooting, nobody here but a passel of sick-looking locals, nary a one of them got shoes on their feet. At least that, with all the orders shouted and screamed, with the waves washing over the rowboats and the mess with the livestock. The muscles in Royal's stomach ache from all he's thrown up on the big ship, his legs feel weak and it is hotter than it ever got in Tampa, but as he lunges out of the boat, waves breaking around his knees, and hurries after the others onto the little strip of sandy beach he is flooded with relief to be here, on solid ground, on Cuba.

"Company H stack rifles here!" shouts Sergeant Jacks, standing on a small rise in a swarm of mosquitoes he chooses to ignore. "Then get on those crates. *Move!*"

"I don't see any of the white soldiers unloading cargo," says Junior. He and Royal butt their rifles into the sand, bringing the muzzles together, and Little Earl adds his to make the pyramid stand.

"Somebody got to do it."

Junior follows back to the boats. "But it's always us."

Royal shrugs as he wades out, then staggers backward into the surf as a crate of ammunition is pushed into his arms. "Didn't send us down here to sit on the beach and eat cocoanuts."

*   *   *

In the drawing a barefoot *insurrecto* stands behind Uncle's massive calf, sticking his tongue out. Just in front of Uncle's knee is Teddy in his campaign outfit, gloved hands on hips, glaring. The object of scorn is a Spanish don, greasy moustache ends dragging the ground, peeking up timorously at the towering American Icon whose top-hatted shadow covers him.

A NEW "BULLY" ON THE BLOCK

But he'll have to start again. It's impossible not to sweat on the paper here, to smear, and the Cuban isn't right yet. He's drawn a Mexican before, but the *sombrero* is different here and what cactus there is grows only a few inches from the ground. And the Chief is not fond of Mexicans. There are Cubans in Tampa of course, cigar kings and soapbox politicians, but they look nothing like this motley rabble grinning at the edges of the American throng, looking for something loose and preferably not terribly heavy to steal.

And then every few moments one of the damned illustrators drifts by from the operations at the shoreline to peer over his shoulder, maybe chuckle, and say how wonderful it would be to just be a lampoon man and not have to render the realities of life.

It is not meant kindly.

Remington is here, glued to the Rough Riders, the younger illustrators all kowtowing each time he passes, and Glackens from *McClure's*, and Howard Christy from *Collier's* and Macpherson drawing for the London papers, and a claque of photographers hung with leather-covered boxes and even a fellow from the Vitagraph company who thinks he'll make a motion picture of the fighting.

The quandary is which type of *insurrecto* to draw. All the ones here to greet them are barefoot and starving and wear tattered white linen pajamas and slouch hats, the wide brims rolled back in the front so as not to hamper their aim. They carry their *machetes*, but for the few who sport captured Spanish Mauser rifles or ancient Winchesters, and have a beaten, hangdog look to them. Something less than your ideal plucky freedom fighter. A handful look like his Mexican or have the long El Greco faces of dignified European gentlemen, *sans* monocle and trapped in beggar's rags. But more vexing, two out of three are clearly negro, and many of the others some mongrel mix. The Chief has not been promoting a slave rebellion, or an endorsement of miscegenation. He is sailing down on his yacht, due any day now, and Crane and a few of the other wags insist no real fighting will be allowed till he comes ashore. Perhaps when presented with the facts, when he sees the actual ebony-skinned, barefooted article—but no. Higher ideals are at stake here.

This place, Bacquiri, Daiquiri, something like that, is pleasant enough but for the heat and the mosquitoes. They were expecting a hot reception, and the Navy guns plied the coastal hills for a good while, a fireworks exhibition that perhaps induced the Dons to scurry inland. The only real excitement was the unloading of the beasts, which, in the absence of a landing dock, had to be improvised. A mule or horse would be led to the cargo port and given a glance at the beach, some four hundred yards distant, then shocked on the hindquarters with a blacksnake whip, the animal bolting forward into an awkward plunge. Quite a bit of braying and screaming when they first went in, but then each got down to the grim business of survival, many considering the floating transports to be their only safe haven and circling back to try to climb on board. There had been a particularly persistent mule just below him, somehow managing to lift its forelegs clear of the swells and thump the hull for a solid hour before going under. Teamsters and sailors were out among them in rowboats, talking softly, trying to herd them, occasionally managing to rope and guide a few to shore. Fitzpatrick was beside him at the rail, sketching furiously, doing an especially nice job on their eyes, huge with terror, and with the already drowned rolling about on the surface. And glancing over at the Cartoonist's own empty hands as if to say, You're not getting this?

Oh, he can draw a mule, all right. His Democratic donkey is second only to old Nast's, and the Chief loved his Bryan riding backward on a Populist nag. But he likes to think he is more an interpreter of events, an editorialist, colleague to Davis in his pith helmet and Crane and Creelman, to Stephen Bonsal and Poultney Bigelow and the other correspondents who stand querulous in the seething mass of blue uniforms, pumping the regulars for information and priming the volunteers for quotables, colleague to men of ideas, rather than a mere draftsman.

"Look there," he said at one point, and Fitz was obliged to reckon with the despatch boat chugging past with a half-dozen Kodak fiends and the Vitagraph man cranking his bulky apparatus, all capturing the bedlam on celluloid. "There's your future, old man," he added, in what was meant to be a kidding tone. "You'll go the way of the buffalo."

So no bloated equines, but he has done a sketch of one of the scurrying land crabs, terrible little brutes with their eyes, in perpetual astonishment, suspended above their bodies on little stalks. Very promising—perhaps a Spanish diplomat, or one of their key generals, or even Spain itself as a crab, side-stepping in terror beneath Uncle's giant impending footstep. It is a shame they've recalled General Weyler, the "Butcher" sobriquet license for wonderfully gory analogies, cleaver in hand, dripping innocent Cuban blood, clasping horrified black-eyed maidens to his offal-smeared apron.

Keep Your Claws Off! Uncle will say, or some play on *scuttling*.

It needs work.

Wooden crates of ammunition are being hauled ashore, negro soldiers staggering wet to their armpits, while sergeants everywhere bark regiment numbers and company letters and order their milling warriors to fall in. The men are casual, light-hearted even, no doubt relieved to be making the landing without Spanish interference and exuberant to be free of the stifling, overcrowded transports. Like a football rally, American boys all in blue, or an especially crowded 4th of July picnic, and if not for the steaming heat you could imagine it was the Jersey shore.

He ran into Rudy Dirks in Tampa, Dirks who draws the Katzenjammers, wearing the uniform of one of the volunteer regiments, and Post who'd sketched at the *Journal* is here with the 71st New York, a private in arms. Taking things a bit far, he feels, though maybe for the German it is a dec-laration of his patriotism. Personally, he needs to take the Olympian view, to distill the essence of a situation, to perch on a general's shoulder, if need be, and view the larger canvas. He has done several drawings of Shafter, his favorite the one where the commander's bulk is sinking the flagship of the invasion fleet. But the Old Man has so nurtured this war, is so thoroughly in the jingo camp, that in everything he's submitted Shafter is merely "sub-stantial" rather than the gout-ridden colossus he's made to appear in the Havana papers.

In the drawing, now, the *insurrecto* is scrawnier, clinging onto Uncle's massive thigh, not even a *machete* to protect himself. And his face—

The Chief's favorite, Davenport, is not here, nor is Fred Opper or any of the other big-money cartoonists. He is the only one who has made the voyage, not in uniform but here nonetheless, with beasts of burden still washing ashore, some of the colored Ninth detailed to drag them out of the surf. The native militia are offering doughboys huge green bananas from their flour-sack carryalls, offering short stalks of sugarcane and exotic fruit, hoping to trade for tinned beef, and the strip of beach is just as crowded and disorganized as the dock at Tampa the day they left. This, this whole thing, could be a disaster, a folly. A great mulatto approaches him, smiling, holding out one of the oblong yellow-green fruits.

"*Mango?*" says the giant *insurrecto*.

He waves his pen in the air to decline. "No, thank you very much." He tilts his head back and closes his eyes then, feels the relief of a slight breeze off the ocean, and tries to imagine the Cuban face.

FORAY

It is unseasonably cool, chilly even, a stiff breeze coming in off the Cape Fear as the cab rolls along Water Street to the train station. It will be colder up there, Harry knows, snow eventually, and his coat will be inadequate. Perhaps his first purchase in the great city. He has only the new-bought wall trunk and his old leather satchel, amazed at how few possessions seemed vital enough to warrant inclusion. The wheel shop is only padlocked, no sign indicating his absence or likely return.

The familiar sights roll by—Harry knows the owners of most of the commercial properties, the residents of at least half of the private dwellings—and he muses that away from the noise and smell of riverside industry Wilmington is a lovely town. But compared to the northern metropolis he has read and imagined so much about, only that. A town.

He wonders if there will be trees.

The cabman is one of the sullen rather than cheerful types, a tubercular old negro who sighed and staggered dramatically as he lifted the snugly packed trunk into his vehicle. His horse needs washing. The Judge will be at his Front Street club now, trading stories with his contemporaries, and then on to his nap in the leather chair by the south window. Harry's note, rewritten several times and left at home in the Judge's box by the door, presents an orderly rationale for his departure. Harry is not, in fact, getting any younger. Opportunities do exist, up there, which may never be available in Wilmington. And it is his own money, after all, that is being ventured, his own life to lead.

And yet he feels furtive as they pass the busy Sprunt works, cotton press slamming bales together, and roll into the yard before the Atlantic Coast Line depot.

"Wait here a moment, please," he says to the moping cabman as he carefully lowers himself to the ground. Train schedules have been known to change.

He does not recognize the station agent, which is a blessing. Tuck Simmons, who mans the booth until noon, is a familiar of the Judge, having procured the position through the old man's kind agency after his cigar emporium was destroyed, uninsured, in a suspicious blaze. Wilmington is full of such gentlemen, beholden to his father for this or that act of generosity, and as a boy it seemed a wonderful thing. Only lately has it become oppressive, Harry unable to miss, behind the effusive greetings and inquiries as to the Judge's health, the silent evaluation.

He must be such a disappointment to the old gentleman.

The agent sits behind his window, contemplating the front page of the *Messenger* and shaking his head.

"Hell in a hand basket," he mutters before looking up. "Somebody got to make a *stand*."

It is suddenly very close, though it is only Harry and the station agent and the empty benches inside. He removes his hat.

"May I inquire," he begins, though he has three printed schedules folded in his pocket, though he has all but memorized the timetable, "how one would proceed from here to New York City?"

The agent cocks his head to one side, looking Harry over. "My, my, my," he says, then glances up at something that must be posted on the wall above the window.

"Monday, Wednesday, and Friday there's a Florida Special coming through, northbound—it leave here at one-ten, stops in Wilson and Rocky Mount before you reach Richmond. At Richmond you change from the ACL to the Richmond, Fredericksburg, and Potomac, take you to Washington. From there you switch to the Pennsylvania Railroad, trains to New York nearly every hour."

Harry nods at each point of the itinerary. "And the fare?" He has it counted out, folded in an envelope, in another pocket.

"To Richmond, or all the way through?"

"The entire journey."

"Private compartment?"

"I can share."

The agent smiles at him. He knows the Judge, knows who Harry is. He must. Harry feels the perspiration on his lip, feels his color coming up. Nobody of his immediate acquaintance, other than Niles, has ever ventured beyond Charlottesville, Virginia, and certainly none has entertained the idea of actually living in what the Judge still refers to as "enemy territory." The few yankees Harry has met—mostly snowbirds on their way to one of Mr. Flagler's sunshine resorts—have been less intimidating than he expected, though of course not in their native element. All have commented on the charm of an accent he was not aware he possessed, and assured him that he would be regarded in the North as a creature of refreshing novelty. *Rara avis.*

"If you were to travel on a single ticket," says the station agent, "it would cost you sixteen dollars and seventy-five cents. Meals not included."

It will cost me a great deal more than that, thinks Harry. His legs, both the healthy and the malformed one, do not feel as if they can support his weight. Perhaps he is coming down with something.

"I thank you very much," he says to the agent as if his idle curiosity has been satisfied, then turns to go. His footsteps, uneven as always, sound very loud on the depot floorboards as he makes his retreat. The Judge will be at cigars and brandy by now, and there is ample time to return home and cover his tracks.

The balers at the Sprunt works seem to be operating inside his head as he steps into the yard, pounding, throbbing. He is short of breath. It is the farthest he has gotten, the last attempt only a long sight-seeing ride past the depot and then up to visit his mother's grave at Pine Forest. He is ashamed of himself, but not enough to turn and march back inside to make the purchase.

"Not today," Harry smiles sheepishly to the cabman, who does not seem to care.

EL CANEY

They are up and moving before sunrise. No breakfast, not even coffee. The order is silence, though Royal and the others are too tired to have much to say. It has been days of marching since the landing, marching in the heat and the bone-soaking rain and at night only rolling the wet poncho and blanket and tent-half canvas out on the ground to try to stay dry on at least one side and feeding the mosquitoes or out on sentry. At night there are shots, shouting, crabs rustling in the underbrush. And then that whole day spent hurrying in circles in the jungle, trying to relieve the ambushed Rough Riders at Las Guasimas but never finding them, lost, a dozen men falling from the heat and Royal nearly one of them. It is a wet heat that sits heavy on you, like being a steamed oyster says Junior, only oysters don't carry forty pounds of supplies and a horse-collar blanket roll over their necks.

Parrots and *tocororos* begin their squawking in the canopy above as the men form twos and start down the pathway that is being called a road. Light filters in through the branches, giving shape to the trees, and by the time they come out into the first canefield the morning mists are rising, then thinning to reveal the distant Sierra Maestras. Royal had never seen mountains, never left the Carolina coast before the Army and Fort Missoula, and these don't look real to him, their slope too sudden, too steep. He is already sweating under his sodden uniform, haversack strap digging in, already feeling tired when a squad of Cuban fighters lopes past their line. The men and boys are dressed in thin, light cloth, a few with sandals, most not, and every shade under the sun. A few look like white men, a few like the Chinese he's seen in picture books, and a few are blacker than any man in North Carolina. Achille Dieudonné from G Company who speaks Creole French and border Mex says these dark black ones are Haitians, floated over on rafts from that island where the going is even rougher.

These Cubans are smaller, mostly, than the Americans, and very thin, though that is exaggerated by how little they carry—a sugar sack and a machete, maybe a rifle, their cartridge belts rigged from stiff cloth or no belt at all, just a leather pouch worn round the neck holding the few bullets they have. Thin, but nothing like the ones back at Firmeza, the *reconcentrados* they found behind barbed wire who looked even more miserable than the drawings in the newspapers. Royal has never seen people so poor, so starving, white, black, and brown thrown in together, hollow-eyed with their bones poking up under their skin.

"I wouldn't treat a dog that way," said Too Tall Coleman as they passed. The people only watched them, mute, too wasted to muster an expression.

There is a sound ahead, a deep, coughing, compressing of air like truncated thunder. Four of them, one just after the other. Sergeant Jacks turns to call softly over his shoulder.

"The dance has begun, gentlemen," he says. "Let's keep moving here."

They continue marching, in and out of the thick trees, and Royal can tell by the mood of the sergeants that today it will be real. Last night they were given extra rounds to carry, two hundred more he has twisted into the spare socks in his pack, and the chaplain was busy and the officers were huddling together with maps. The mosquitoes are up now and at their business but Royal knows to crush them not swat them and to strap his load tight so it doesn't rattle and to not ask questions. He and Junior and Little Earl are rookies but not so green as they once were, real soldiers now except for the one thing and after today that will be done.

They have been marching almost three hours when volunteers begin to appear, coming in the opposite direction in twos and threes, men from the 2nd Massachusetts who have been pulled off the firing line. Many are wounded, pale and a little stunned, a few shot through the body and walking as if it is a conscious effort to hold themselves together, their gaze gone inward.

"Don't bother, fellas," says one man with a bloody crease across his stubbled cheek. "They're sittin up there where you can't even see em, pourin it down on us. You won't have no more show than we did."

"Volunteers can't see through their own smoke, is what," says Sergeant

Jacks flatly after the man has passed. "Got them old shit Winchesters. Black powder will draw enemy lead like bees to honey. Smart to get them off the field."

Jacks sees another man moving toward them against the flow, a top sergeant like himself, with a sunburned face, holding one arm close to his body.

"What they dealing out?"

The sunburned sergeant stops ahead of them. "Maybe a couple Hotchkiss guns up there, Mausers." He grabs his wounded arm by the wrist and raises it to display a small black stain on the bicep of his uniform shirt. "Put one right through me."

Jacks cocks his head at the wound. "Mauser ball make a nice clean hole, don't it?"

"We lost a boy in an ambuscade on the way, some of these guerillas up in the trees. Went in over the lung and come out his back the size of a fist."

"That'd be a Winchester round. She'll tear the hell out of you."

Royal wonders if he is saying this for effect, trying to scare the greenhorns like the other veterans do. The two sergeants could be talking about fishing.

"You like a bullet to stay in one piece when it hits you," adds Jacks.

The white soldier shakes his head. "Don't know what they think a man can do," he says. "Aint nobody going to take that hill."

They continue to move forward, the men watching the treetops now. On the third day ashore they saw a few of the *guerillas*, hacked dead with machete blows and laid out on the side of the road, already stripped of equipment and some of their clothes. Cubans who fought on the Spanish side of this mess, but not looking any different from the *insurrectos*.

"Why would a man want to fight against his own people?" Junior wanted to know.

"We used the Crows to track the Sioux," said Achille, who did a stretch in the 9th Cavalry when he was a young man. "Used the Tonkawa to fight the Comanches. But to a man outside they all just Indians."

They march past a dead American, sitting propped at the base of a huge ceiba tree bordering another canefield. His whole middle is wet with blood, and there are a half dozen vultures circling in the sky. If the man's head was at a normal angle it would look like he was resting.

"There's the music," says Bevill ahead of Royal and yes, he can hear it now, very light and distant but lots of it, no break between gunshots, just louder ones and softer ones.

They cross the field and fall out under the shade of the mango trees by a big plantation house. Men hurry their fixings out, rolling smokes, Too Tall cutting open a green cigar he has bought from some roadside *muchacho* and wadding the tobacco into his pipe. Royal drinks, realizes his canteen is already half empty. It is a beautiful spot. It is all beautiful country but for the heat and if you had the right clothes and nothing much to do and nobody was shooting at you it would be a paradise. Royal's stomach is still not right from the green mangoes they boiled down for dinner last night, smelled like turpentine but tasted sweet. His stomach hasn't been right, in fact, since the trip over on the *Concho*, the drinking water warm and brownish, the food no better than usual and all that rolling in the hold, sick even at night and having to take turns for time up on deck.

"Somebody's catching hell," says Gamble. "That firing aint let up once."

The men listen. Birds are still singing, the high-pitched frogs are awake and throbbing, and through it they can hear the rattle and roll of rifle fire punctuated with an infrequent bass note of artillery.

Junior points. "Over there."

They look and can see a cloud of white smoke rising above the jungle canopy to the right, maybe a half-mile away.

"That'll be our battery," says Sergeant Jacks. "Four pieces. Working kind of slow."

They listen awhile, then lose interest, some men unhitching their loads and lying back on the ground, some talking quietly, most sitting alone with their own thoughts.

"*Insurrectos* say they cut the Spaniards' heads off if they catch em," muses Achille. "Say the Spanish do the same, put em out on a stake."

"What that mean to us?" asks Coop, who lays back with his eyes closed and his hands folded on his chest.

"Means maybe some of them Spanish boys been wanting to surrender, get sent back home. Now they got us to give up to."

"Don't sound like nobody surrenderin to nobody up there."

"They got their officers behind em, stick em with a sword they don't keep fighting."

"So alls we got to do is kill all their officers."

"That would do it."

"Good," says Coop. "I keep that in mind."

Sergeant Jacks comes by to inspect rifles, just the rookies, and Royal pulls out the oiled rag he keeps stuffed down the muzzle.

"There's a village called Caney," says the sergeant as he handles the Krag, "behind a fort on a hill. We sposed to take that, then swing over and help the main force at San Juan." He has never volunteered this kind of information before, never explained, and Royal wonders why he wants them to know this now. "We get into the shit, you just do what you see everybody else doing."

The sun is directly overhead when they are formed up again and marched toward the gunfire. Royal is out off the path as a flanker with Junior, struggling through the brush, when they come to a man hanging upside-down from a tree, a rope tied to his ankle. Another Cuban, a *guerilla*, with palm fronds fastened around his body. Blood has run from the hole where his eye used to be to collect in his hair and spatter down onto the broad-leaved plants below.

"Sniper," says Junior, pausing to look up into the nearby treetops. "No telling how many of ours he killed."

The battle is louder now, flankers called in as they approach the end of the cover. Now and again there is the whine of a closer bullet, leaves and palm branches fluttering down from above, snipped by the spillover from the fighting in front of them. A sharp crack here and there and wood chips flying. The men strip off the load of bedrolls and haversacks, jettison everything but rifle, rounds, and canteen. Royal imagines he is dead.

If he is dead they can't kill him.

He crouches with the others at the end of the woods and looks through the trees at what is waiting. A rugged stretch of mostly open ground, green-brown chaparral with a few spindly trees leading to a steep hill crowned by a stone fort. There are wooden blockhouses stretching off to the left of it, and then, on another hill slightly behind, a village with a tall stone church. Royal imagines his mother at her table, quiet and all cried out. He imagines Jessie with a black armband over her white shirtwaist sleeve, wearing it for him, solemn for a year, maybe more. Being dead is nothing, exactly that, nothing, so much better than being afraid, being injured, in pain, maimed.

He is dead and whatever happens next cannot hurt him.

Lieutenant Caldwell strolls in front of them, still inside the first line of trees, shouting to be heard over the gunfire that seems to be mostly off to the right of the hill.

"We will need to step into the open to form ranks," says the lieutenant. "And we will advance in extended order at once. We are part of a larger maneuver—people are counting on us and we cannot fail them. Sergeants!"

They step out and form a firing line then, sergeants trotting parallel and shouting, getting the intervals right while the volleys from the fort swing their way. There is nothing to hide behind, and though most of the rounds sing over their heads a few men fall and soldiers sidestep to fill in the gaps. G and H Companies are out front in the firing line, Royal near the far left, with C and D to follow a hundred yards back in support, the rest crouching back in reserve. Royal sees the 4th Infantry, who had been with them on the *Concho*, whites to port and blacks to starboard, step out to form on their left flank. There had been lots of jokes across the bowline stretched between them about who was being protected from who.

"Firing line, forward—march!"

Kid Mabley blows the order and they quickstep ahead.

The idea seems to be to keep moving forward and hope all of them are not dead by the time they reach the top. Royal checks to each side to be sure he is not getting out front too far and sees that more men are falling. He feels the bullets singing past as much as he hears them and keeps walking through the chaparral, everything very bright, very clear and thinking he should be firing like some of the others but there is nothing, nobody up there visible to shoot at. The line reaches some small trees and there is barbed wire stretched between them, a half dozen strands of it and posts every three feet to kick and club through, something to concentrate on furiously as chunks of wood crack into splinters and more men fall. Somebody is screaming behind him. The line is scattered when he comes into the clear again, Royal trotting with the few left on either side of Sergeant Jacks.

"In rushes!" shouts the sergeant. "Keep moving!"

There are whistles and bugle calls behind but now it is just rush and flop, rush and flop, desperate lunging forward then extending the Krag and diving to the ground. It's a wildly uneven field with spiky pineapples in rows upon the churned earth and hard to navigate without tripping. Royal flops in a furrow and fires his first shot, not really using his sight but just pointing at the fort and pulling the trigger. Others are firing and the sergeant said to do whatever they did. The thick spat of a bullet near him and there is hot sticky fruit on his cheek and he is up and rushing forward again.

He can see something at the top of the hill, movement, behind the line of barbed wire staked in front of the rifle pits before the fort, and he fires again, trying to aim this time, if not at a person then at a spot a person might be in. The hill is steep, steeper than the sand dunes back in Tampa, Royal holding his rifle in one hand and using the other to grab roots, plants, anything to help haul himself up and something sprays his face again, not a pineapple this time but somebody, a wet part of somebody, men dropping, men stopping movement around him but he climbs upward, upward till he is exhausted and needs to lie with his face on the hot ground a moment, then roll on his back and let his lungs work. The dead can be exhausted, they can be thirsty, but they are never afraid. Royal drinks from his canteen and sees down the hill to the second line coming up past the bodies of the first, sees D Company double-timing forward on the right as flankers, then rolls and struggles upward again.

He reaches a little dip, a depression running across the hill for several yards in which Jacks and half a platoon are lying, and falls down beside them. The artillery has been firing from behind them all this time and finally it seems to have found the range, one shell blowing a breach in the barbed-wire fencing and the next blasting the front of the fort itself, snapping the flagpole off and sending the Spanish colors tumbling to the ground. The men around him cheer. Royal is heaving for breath and drenched in his own liquid and he burns his hand on the barrel of the Krag, hot only from the sun and not his few random shots and he drinks again as more men reach the dip and flop down. They are only a hundred yards from the first of the trenches now and the Mausers are cracking, bullets spanging off rocks and flicking up dirt in front of their faces and it is unthinkable that he will have to stand and go forward.

"Sharpshooters!" yells Jacks, who seems to be the ranking officer on this part of the hill. "Articulate fire! Get those loopholes in the fort, get those bastards in the pits!"

Sharpshooters have been designated back in Tampa and Royal is not one of them. He looks down the ragged line of soldiers, sees men pushing up on their elbows to sight and fire, some rising on a knee, pulling the trigger, working the bolt, rolling on their sides to reload. It is methodical, hot work, and he is suddenly filled with awe for these men and hopes some of them will survive.

Coop aims at the spot where the white hat had just been. Fuck em. Kill em. The hat reappears and he fires and it drops out of sight. He cranks the empty out and pans down the trench line searching for another. Take your time. Sons of bitches have been trying to shoot him all the way up the fucking hill, had hours to get the job done and here he still is so fuck them, kill them, blow their damn brains out. He empties his magazine once, twice, three times—yes they're shooting back still but they better not pause to aim or he'll put one in their Dago skull. He stops once to refill his cartridge belt, slow and steady, not dropping a round, and when the corporal beside him gets it he slithers over to use the body for cover, propping the Krag barrel on the dead man's hip. They are taking fire from the left, from the blockhouses and the village and whatever passes high over the 4th is hitting them but that will have to come later. Now it is the fort, bullets pocking the stone front like hard rain on dusty ground, the fort that has to be taken before the men inside it can kill him.

The little ditch isn't much cover, not with the crossfire from the block-houses, and it's Sergeant Cade who jumps up to scream Let's go and all of them rise at once, up, screaming their Comanche yell, scrabbling up the last steep pitch of the hill through corn stubble, the 4th still pinned down but Company C filling in to the left, Coop firing and running and firing and running till he flops again just short of the first of the trenches and jams his barrel through the barbed wire to fire down into it. A man steps out into the doorway of the fort with a white flag and Coop drops him, then another picks it up and is torn apart by several shots down the line then the sergeants are screaming to cease fire. No fire from the fort now, though still from the blockhouses and the village to the left. Another rush comes up behind him, men yelling Let's take it and Coop stands to join but is banged from behind into the barbed wire, wrapped by it, kicking and chopping with his Krag till he tears his skin away and rolls untangled into the firing pit on top of a carpet of dead men. All of them lying in their blue-striped, mattress-ticking uniforms with holes in their foreheads, jumbled on top of each other. Coop gets hold of his rifle and squirms to his knees and sees one still alive, weep-ing, sitting on top of the others with no weapon in hand. Coop jumps out of the pit and dashes to the fort.

There are dead men lying in the way and he runs over their bodies and slams hard against the front wall, then joins the others who have made it, firing a few rounds into the loopholes cut in the wooden window plugs then rushing for the doorway. He loses his feet just inside, hip cracking hard on the blood-slick floor, then stands and steadies himself. Bodies everywhere and a few on their knees begging not to be shot. Fuck them, Coop thinks, kill them, but he is out of ammunition.

Men from the 12th have come up behind the fort on the right and Sergeant Jacks waves at them to keep down, heavy fire sweeping across from the blockhouses now. The firing pits are filled with dead and more lie dead and dying amid chunks of stone blown off from the fort. A black-bearded civilian in a long coat, maybe a newspaper man, sits on the ground beside him with a hole in his shoulder and the dust-covered Spanish flag in a pile in his lap.

"I did it," says the bearded man, looking dazed at the red and yellow cloth. "I did it for the *Journal*."

Jacks scurries, bent low, a quick lap around the hilltop to see what's left. He saw Lieutenant McCorkle get it at the beginning, saw Bevill go down in the pineapples and Gilbert knocked backward on the hill, but there are a lot of blue shirts up here and some of his people who have stripped to the waist in the heat. They're taking heavy fire from the blockhouses and the town but the bulk of the firing line has made it and the 12th is here and the 4th and their own reserve companies hustling up and they hold the high ground now, can swing even higher and shoot down through the roof of the nearest blockhouse. No officer up yet, no telling what is happening with the main force at the San Juan Heights, no orders. He sees one of the rookies, Scott, crouching behind the fort wall next to another who is holding the side of his neck with a bloody hand and having a hard time breathing. The rookie's cartridge belt is full.

"Take him back," he yells to Scott, who is shaking hard but seems to understand. "If he can stand take him back down where they can do something."

The rookie gives him a searching look. "Where do I take him?"

"Back the way we came. Somebody will know where the field hospital is." The other one is shaking too, his eyes starting to glaze over.

"Get him as far as he'll go," says Jacks, "then get your ass back up here. Move!"

They just be in the way, both of them, and there is work left to do.

A captain from the 12th strides past trying to separate his white boys from the 25th. "Form up!" he is calling. "Form companies!" He is walking upright and stiff-legged, feigning disregard for the bullets still chipping away at the stone walls, but the men on the hilltop are too busy to be inspired. The rookie helps his friend up and they stagger away together.

The artillery has been hopeless all day long, the little battery still a half-mile back in the jungle, and if the Spanish send reinforcements over from Santiago the hilltop will be impossible to hold. Jacks curses, then rises and runs, tapping men splayed out on the ground as he goes, calling them to follow. He makes it into the trench on the west side of the fort, facing the village, and a dozen men pile in after.

"We take the blockhouses one at a time," he tells them, "then go get that fucking church."

They lift the bodies of the dead Spaniards up then, and add them to the breastworks behind the barbed-wire fence.

The shaking seemed to catch up with Royal, chasing him all the way up the slope and over the wire and the bloody pit and overtaking him only when he was safe and solid against the stone wall of the fort, catching him like a chill hand at the back of his neck and then down through the rest of his body and now only movement will mask it. Royal leads Little Earl back down the hill, passing much of C and D Company still struggling up, sidestepping down and reaching back to support his friend when it gets too steep.

"They got surgeons," he says. "Surgeons that know all about bullet wounds. They got drugs for the pain and on one of the ships they got the X-ray machine, look right into your bones."

If Little Earl is reassured he doesn't say so, keeping his hand pressed hard to his neck. There is blood but it isn't throbbing out, just keeping his fingers wet, and he stares at a spot level with his eyes as if he can't look down or at Royal for fear of losing his balance. They move in silence, past more troopers climbing and broken bodies left on the slope and bodies left in the pineapple rows, bodies left in the scrub and suspended awkwardly on the *trocha* of barbed wire. Royal leads Little Earl back as quickly as he can without dragging him, certain that now that he's been to the top the ones still shooting from the village will discover he's no longer dead and will murder him.

Hardaway is back guarding their bedrolls and haversacks behind the treeline.

"We done it!" he says with a gap-toothed smile. "Can't deny the 25th."

"Where's the field hospital?"

"Sposed to be at El Pozo."

"Where's that?"

Hardaway just points back into the trees. "Think we was near there two, three days ago. You keep walkin, somebody bound to know."

Royal finds his gear and pulls the first-aid roll out from it. He folds the arm sling a few times, making a compress.

"Look pretty hot up there," says Hardaway, watching Royal's hands. Hardaway is another rookie and feeling sheepish he wasn't on the hill.

"Hot enough."

Royal gives the folded cloth to Little Earl to hold against his neck.

The sun is slanting low and the firing from behind more sporadic by the time they find the dressing station. It is only one young doctor's assistant and a pair of litter bearers with a small supply of bandages. The doctor's assistant looks at the hole in Little Earl's neck, blood starting to ooze out again, then scribbles on a red-white-and-blue tag and loops it with copper wire through a buttonhole on his shirt.

"There many more behind you?" he asks.

"Hard to tell. Half of who was on the hill run over to the village. Don't think we be much help for San Juan."

"Oh, we took that near two hours ago," says the taller of the litter bearers. "They shot the hell out of us getting there, but the boys run up and took her."

The shorter of the litter bearers walks a ways with them to be sure they are headed right. He reads Little Earl's tag, gives Royal a dark look.

"Don't give him no water till they say so," he says. Little Earl seems not to be listening, seems barely to be there at all anymore but keeps following, putting one foot in front of the other. "And don't be stopping to rest."

Coop stands in the plaza in front of the church in Caney, looking down on a dead Spanish general. There are only scattered shots popping now, back in the village. The general is a goat-bearded, white-haired man spread out on a stretcher on the ground, shot through the legs and in the head. Some of his hair is stained with blood and stuck to the canvas of the stretcher. Coop nudges the body with his foot.

The village is mostly just palm huts but in the stone and stucco houses there were holdouts, most of them civilians, who had to be burned out and shot. Achille and Too Tall have a group of maybe forty prisoners, fever-looking Spanish soldiers, standing by the church doorway with their hands up on their heads.

"Get over here," calls Too Tall. "We gone need you."

"Need me for what?"

"We spose to march these boys back and hand em to the Cubans."

"If they know where they headed," Achille adds, cocking an eye, "they try to bolt for sure."

"You mean if they know where they *be*headed," says Too Tall and they both laugh.

In their light blue pinstripes the captured men and boys look like hospital patients in pajamas.

"Why I want to hook up with your detail?" Coop asks.

"Cause come nightfall everbody else gone be digging trenches for the white boys over on San Juan."

Coop laughs and crosses to join them. "At your service, gennemen."

It is nearly dark when Royal finds the Santiago–Siboney road. They follow it to the field-hospital tents, sitting in high wild grass between the road and a little brook, three big ones for operations and dispensary, one slightly smaller for wounded officers, then six bivouac tents for enlisted men. These are all full, a hundred men crowded inside each where only sixty should be, and a dozen long rows of wounded lie on the ground outside.

Royal has to grab the shoulders of the orderly trotting by to get his attention.

"I got a wounded man here."

"You aint the only one."

"It's real bad, I think."

The orderly glances at Little Earl's tag without looking at his wound, then points to a line of men lying at the base of a cluster of piñon bushes. "Set him down at the end there," says the orderly. "He'll get his turn."

"They any blankets?"

"Not less you brought one."

Royal pulls Little Earl to the end of the line of waiting wounded. Some of them are moaning and rocking, or weeping quietly, and more sit or lie staring blankly. A few are dead. Little Earl tries to rest on his side but starts to choke and Royal helps him sit up.

"Won't be long now," he says to his friend. There are nearly thirty men ahead of them. Some of them have had their shirts or trousers stripped off to uncover their wounds, and as the light goes the temperature is dropping. There seems to be no system to bring water to the waiting wounded or to the hundreds more who have already been through the tents. Royal squats on the guinea grass and realizes he is dizzy himself.

"I'm going for water," he says, squeezing Little Earl's arm. "I be right back."

He passes the open flap of one of the big tents on his way to the brook. A white soldier makes choking noises, writhing on a table as a pair of orderlies work a rubber hose down his throat, blood frothing out the sides of his mouth while a blood-spattered surgeon stands waiting, his eyes closed as if sleeping on his feet.

"Easy does it," coos the orderly who is pinning the wounded man down on the table. "Easy does it."

The brook water is cool and Royal drinks from his cupped hands till his stomach starts to hurt. Litter squads are still arriving, adding their damaged men to the line of the waiting, then staggering back toward the front. The night frogs begin to chirp. He fills his canteen and a pair of orderlies come carrying something heavy rolled in a blood-soaked sheet between them, leaving the whole load just up the bank from him and stepping away quickly.

Royal has an idea what it is but looks anyway.

When he lifts the sheet up he is not sure at first why it seems so wrong. Then he realizes it is because they are all together, white arms and black, white legs and black, stripped naked, obscenely intertwined. One of the legs, cut off below the knee, still has a boot on it and that seems wrong too. Royal covers the limbs and hurries back to find Little Earl.

"Take some water in your mouth," he says, offering the canteen, "but don't swallow."

Little Earl tries but begins to choke again. He spits bloody hunks of phlegm and tissue onto the ground, looks to Royal with fear in his eyes.

"Won't be long now," Royal tells him. "They moving along."

A table has been set up in front of the nearest tent, a doctor just back from the front working on a soldier's chest, an attendant holding a lit candle close to the wound to help him see. The moon is almost full, peeking over the treetops across the road. Sergeant Jacks said to hurry back, but they'll be plenty more chances to kill him tomorrow and he's not going to leave his friend lying alone here.

Little Earl takes his wrist, pulls him near, then whispers a request into his ear.

"I'm not much of a singer," says Royal.

His friend only looks at him, waiting, blood soaked through the folded cloth he presses to his neck. Royal sees that Little Earl's arm is shaking now, that even in the moonlight you can tell he isn't the right color.

"I can't think of anything from church."

Little Earl gives a slight shrug. The only song that comes, the one they sing marching sometimes, doesn't seem right and the lyrics he knows are mostly dirty. Little Earl squeezes his wrist, hard, and Royal is as scared as he's been all day.

The old gray mare
She come from Jerusalem
Come from Jerusalem
Come from Jerusalem—

—he sings, softly—

The stud had balls but
He lost the use of em
Many long years ago

RALLY

The Judge sits in the last car with seven maidens in white. The soot and cinders from the engine can't reach them here, and there is no excuse for the rough element on board to come passing through. Sally has set her heart on riding the Float of Purity since she heard of it and the Judge has had to explain more than once that Cumberland County is hosting the event and has its own supply of maidens. She has insisted on wearing white from head to foot, though, stating that every other woman attending in Fayetteville will be similarly attired.

"I have heard no such thing."

"Neither have I, Father, but trust me, they *will*."

So she jabbers with her school friends and fellow debutantes while the Judge chaperones the whole clutch of them, unable to so much as light a cigar. Clawson from the *Messenger* and one of the Meares brothers and George Rountree and Sol Fishblate who used to be mayor and some of his cronies from the ousted board are in the dining car, passing the Scotch, no doubt, and the Judge would join them but for the way those White Government Union layabouts were running their eyes over Sally on the platform this morning.

He looks out at the overcast landscape. It is still drizzling a bit, puddles lying gray in the fields from last night's downpour, and he wonders if the weather will keep people away. There is a burst of raucous laughter, men's laughter, from the car ahead. It is the age-old dilemma of revolution—for that, after all, is what they have embarked upon. The rabble, the *sans culottes*, are needed to storm the barricades, but then must be held in check before they run rampant, mistaking the power to destroy with the sense to rule. Most of the contingent, already four railroad cars full when they pulled out of Wilmington, seems responsible enough, many in the uniform of the Cape Fear Militia. But the White Government clubs, ranks swelled by brother organizations at each whistle-stop, have changed the tone of the excursion. The call themselves a Union, but the only thing uniting them is their mutual unemployment and a hatred of negroes, seeming more like the dregs of Coxey's Army than the solid base of a political-reform movement. White Emancipation, the purpose of this rally, is too important, too vital a cause to allow it to be sullied by vulgarians.

The train slows to a stop and up in the second car the Fifth Ward Cornet Band blasts into *Onward, Christian Soldiers* to greet the new passengers, giving it a bit more Sousa than you'd likely hear at a revival meeting. It is the station in Tar Heel, a buggy ride away from the rally site, and only a handful of pilgrims step aboard. A red-cap porter backs away from the train as it begins to roll again, looking a little stunned as the men in the car ahead begin to shout at him from their open windows. The Judge closes his own, hoping to spare the young ladies, but they are too involved in their own excited chatter to have heard anything.

The epithets linger in the air like train smoke.

He was asked to join the hooded riders when they were at their peak back in '68, when, many would still insist, they were most needed. They performed important services, vital to the day, but the society included too many men of the wrong caliber. The Judge sensed how easily they might sink from moral vigilantism to mere revenge and thievery, and regretfully declined. Roaring Jack Butler was in his heyday then, enrolling blacks in the Union League, ringleader of the Republican militia formed to stamp out the Klan, promoting his version of the "new South." He made certain allegations against the Judge, merely a lawyer then, in the carpetbagger press, which in his father's day would have resulted in a duel. But his father's day had ended with the Capitulation.

"The only thing a man can truly carry to his grave," the old man would say, "is his honor."

The Judge realizes now that this was his only lesson, repeated in many forms over the years. Even the nightly treat of Sir Walter Scott, read or recited from memory, was an affirmation of that basic principle. His father said they were descendent from Jacobite Scots who had fled to France after the '45 uprising, that the blood of kings flowed through their veins. The blood of kings flowed, quite literally, through most of his stories, often to the point of death defending an untenable cause. It was his father who taught him the original meaning of the burning cross, the beacon calling the clan, men of the same blood, together to defend their families, their land, their honor. It was such a potent image—fire, religion, family, the premonition of torture and death—blazing its message through the dark night of oppression.

"Symbols matter," his father had told him. "They stir men to action. They must never be degraded."

"Father?"

It is Sally, turned to look over the back of her seat to him.

"When we get there, I'll need a moment to arrange myself. We all will."

"I'm sure there will be time."

The rallying of the clan.

If they had done their work in the daylight he might have joined. But in the uncertainty of darkness, men with masks and firearms—there was too much opportunity for blunder and mismanagement. The only act he ever regretted committing had been at night, in the company of other men. It was at Chancellorsville, though the battle had no name then, just another endless day of slaughter, mostly in a tangle of woods that allowed little opportunity to know if you were in the van or outflanked, no chance to reform ranks on the flag. His only brother, Robert, had been killed that day, as had many other good friends in the 18th. There was murder in his heart and when they assumed the picket they were told that yankee cavalry was operating in the area.

You only had time for one shot if horsemen overran you, the object being to fire quickly and hope to dodge the saber. They heard hoofbeats, a small party approaching at a canter and he joined in the volley toward the loom-ing silhouettes, muzzle flashes on both sides of him, then the cries and the terrible discovery that it was their own officers they had fired upon, with General Jackson unhorsed and sure to lose his arm. He looked into the great man's eyes when they carried him to a tent—they were glossy with shock and he was moving his lips very slightly, whispering a prayer. There was no knowing if his own bullet had found its mark on any of the wounded, but no comfort in that ignorance. Jackson was stricken with the pneumonia just after his surgery, and died a week after. A few days before Gettysburg the Judge saw a photograph of the coffin, covered by the new Stainless Banner that he thought, with its massive white field, too much resembled the flag of surrender.

They arrive in Fayetteville shortly before noon, a fine mist of rain still in the air, and hurry without organization the few blocks to the Lafayette.

"Oh my," says Sally, thrilled, "just look at all of us!"

Thousands choke the street. Every sunburned farmer in the county, with wife and tow-headed brood, has come for the festivities, a logjam of buggies and haywagons that needs breaking up before the procession can get under way. Sally and her friends duck into the hotel to freshen themselves, and the Judge finds himself waiting, watching the frantic last-moment pushing and prodding of the rally organizers who shout and wave over the throng, trying to shape the energy and good will present into concerted action.

A half-dozen bands tune their instruments at once, grunting and blatting, snare drums rattling, while wearers of uniforms struggle through the crush of bodies to find each other. The rain stops, which is a blessing, and the Judge manages to get his back up against the hotel and avoid being jostled by the crowd.

The battle flag has reappeared.

During the Occupation it was outlawed by statute, and even after the yankee troops marched out it was rare to see one. But today, from his own limited viewpoint, the Judge can count nearly a dozen. It is the old square cloth of the Southern Cross with thirteen white stars upon it, the flag that came from the St. Andrew's Cross of Scotland that came from the *crux saltire*, the X-shaped cross the Romans had used to crucify the apostle. His father, years before the War, told him how St. Andrew had appeared in a dream to King Angus MacFergus the night before battle, how his Picts and Scots had looked above the battlefield to see a great white cross in the sky and were inspired to drive back the Northumbrians. There was no mistaking that banner, held high above the artillery smoke, no mistaking it for the enemy's flag as with the Stars and Bars. It thrills him to see it again, rippling in the little breeze that has come up, and makes him anxious as well.

They must never be degraded.

He tried to call Jack Butler out. They were boyhood friends, fished and hunted together, their fathers partners in law and business. But the war of ink, each letter to the editor surpassing the last in vitriol, degenerated from *my esteemed colleague* to *notorious scalawag* and *Secessionist assassin*. Action was called for. His father was wounded in a duel as a young man, precipitated by a point of honor so complex he was never able to fully explain it to his sons. He described the confrontation, the deadly honor and solemnity of it, as the event that finally made him a man.

The Judge met his adversary by chance on the courthouse steps, Butler descending with a gang of the officeholders from that benighted time, himself with only poor tubercular Granville Pratt as a witness.

"Sir," he said, blocking the other man's way, regretting that the terrain put him at a disadvantage in stature, "I demand satisfaction."

Butler smiled with condescension. "You won't receive it from me."

The carpetbaggers laughed then, as they had been laughing since Appomattox.

"You are no gentleman," the Judge observed.

"That may be true," Butler replied, and here held a finger in his face, "but neither am I a cutthroat and a terrorist."

The Judge did not carry a cane then, or he'd have done more damage before they were separated.

It was so clear, in his father's time, so personal. Insults were redressed face to face, with seconds and pistols, both parties often able to walk away with honor restored or maintained, unharmed.

"I was young and hot-headed and in the wrong," his father said of his own ceremony. "But the time had passed for apologies. The gentleman grazed my ribs, then I fired into the air. He did not demand a second exchange."

The Judge looks about at this as yet unfocused mass, this storm-sea of discontent, and thinks of the worst of the fighting. The days when, blackened with powder, he fired into smoke and hoped to hit flesh, days when he felt the indifferent calm of the butcher.

Or felt like the man who killed Stonewall Jackson.

The march begins the moment Sally reappears on the front step of the hotel, as if they have all been waiting only for her. The Cornet Band heads out playing *The Carpetbaggers' Lament* and Sally beams and God Himself smiles on their activity, opening the clouds for the first time in days to bathe them all in gold. And then, cutting in from the side street where they must have been assembled and waiting all along, come the Red Shirts. There is a collective intake of breath as they appear, then applause and wild cheering from those lining the streets and leaning out their windows. There must be at least three hundred riders, four abreast as they flow past, smiling and waving their hats. The shirts are not uniform, ranging from silk to the roughest flannel, but together they make a river of color down Hay Street and once again the Judge's heart is lifted.

"It's so beautiful," Sally exclaims, taking his arm. "Niles should be here."

A passing horse lifts its tail and deposits a steaming load at their feet, but Sally, imbued with her departed mother's gentility, will not recognize it.

"Our own cavaliers," she says.

That many or most are mill hands up for the day from South Carolina is not worth mentioning. They were the mailed fist of the Redeemers in that state back in '76, and their presence here, the Judge can only hope, will inspire a similar rising in the Old North State. It takes ten solid minutes for them to pass, and then, drawn by four mottled Percherons, comes the Purity Float. Twenty-two lovely Christian girls in white dresses, one from each district in the county, smile and wave as they pass on a decorated logging trailer. Sally presses her gloved hands together in delight.

"Oh, they've done such a wonderful job of it!" she cries. "Considering what they have to work with."

The carriages come next, with the Mayor of Fayetteville, the editor of their *Observer*, the Democratic chairman, and Pitchfork Ben Tillman himself riding in the first. The Senator waves energetically, a solid man of fifty dressed like a middling farmer come to church, his one eye bright with the excitement of the occasion.

"If we had a firebrand like him," the Judge shouts to his daughter over the tumult, "crisis would not be upon us."

Mr. Bridgewater, father of Sally's dearest friend Emilia, beckons them then, and they walk to the elegant landau he has rented for the day. The driver, an Irishman in a jacket a size too small, eases it into the procession once they are settled, the girls facing forward, waving delicately as if they are the true dignitaries and the Judge and Bridgewater facing the rear, with an excellent view of the Fayetteville White Government Union lads footing along on either side in homburgs and plugs and slouch hats, strutting to beat the band.

She has a sense of purpose that neither of his boys possess, Sally, able to chart a course and stay true to it. Harry leaps from one fascination to the next, while Niles—the less he thinks about Niles the better. Sally has her mother's soft-spoken perseverance, plus an intellect that if not restrained within the limited purview of her sex would be formidable. She is no suffragist, though, feigning no interest in what she condescendingly refers to as "men's business." He was surprised that she asked to come with him, until the display of maidens was revealed, and she has asked no questions about the gathering that might not pertain to a country fair. The girls have their parasols up, as it has begun to sprinkle again, and look a picture. One of the White Government boys, transfixed by them as he walks alongside, steps into a lamppost and is heartily mocked by his companions.

Cannons boom across the fairgrounds as they enter, the Cornet Band greeting them with *Dixie*. The judges' stand on the racetrack infield is serving for the speakers' platform, and dozens of benches have been set up on the turf to accommodate those who cannot fit in the grandstand. Tom Mason, a fine academic speaker from up by the Virginia border, is already holding forth when they find seats, Bridgewater having brought a blanket to cover the damp pine. The crowd is only half paying attention, the fairgrounds no venue for fine points and historical flourishes, but all rise to applaud when he introduces the Senator from South Carolina.

The approbation continues for some time. Here is the stalwart of the backcountry farmer in his struggle with robber barons and tidewater Bourbons, the Free Silver man who offered to stick a pitchfork in Grover Cleveland, his own party's candidate, if he continued to acquiesce to combinations and goldbugs, who lost an eye in the War and proudly claimed to have instigated the Hamburg Massacre. That he lost the eye to disease and saw no battle does not dampen the enthusiasm of the gathering, nor does the fact that his role in the historic first blow of Redemption is greatly exaggerated. He is the people's man, though never an avowed Populist, blunt-spoken and unapologetic. The Judge's Charleston acquaintances, of notably bluer blood, complain that Tillman's accomplishments as governor have been limited to outlawing Greek letter fraternities and denying citizens the right to buy liquor by the glass, but that was ignoring the larger picture. The man has stemmed the tide of defeat.

"They call me Pitchfork Ben," he opens and there is another cheer, punctuated by rebel yells throughout the gathering.

"Out on the farm we employ a pitchfork to handle manure. And I can tell that you want a long-handled one to deal with the recent political shenanigans in your state."

The Wilmington contingent, mostly around them on the grandstand, are particularly amused by this.

"As a United States senator, I am asked to consider matters which at first might seem to have little to do with one another. But during my tenure there I have discovered that a great number of the things which affect us here in the South adversely—are all of a piece. Our former candidate, Mr. Cleveland—" booing here, though rather good-natured, "—has been revealed as not only a mono-metalist and a tool of Wall Street, but an accomplice to the international thieves who doom the poor farmer and the honest white working man to patches in his clothes and slim pickings on his table!

He so damaged our economy he was forced to bring in Rothschild and his American agents—" more boos now, with an edge of anger, "—to maintain the gold standard. The richest and most powerful nation brought so low as to allow a London Jew receiver to its treasury!"

The Judge looks over to his daughter, the smile never leaving her face, as if she might be at a garden party back home.

"With such men in power, we here in the South are doomed to economic servitude. New York shall ever be the center of manufacture and usury, and we here in the heartland of America shall never be more than drawers of water and hewers of wood, toilers on another man's plantation."

The Judge understands that this is the root of Tillman's popularity, that it brings the bulk of the populace to the fold, but class hatred is a dangerous brew to stir. Easy resentment, simplified solutions—

"Let me talk about numbers for a minute here. There are three negroes in our state to every two white men. Let that sink in for a minute. With a free vote and a fair count, how you gonna beat those numbers? The Federals come down and handcuffed us and threw away the key, propped up their carpetbagging negro government with bayonets—" he looks around at them, indignant, "—and ever since they left we've had the damn Republicans trying to put white necks under black heels!"

Applause now, murmurs of outrage and agreement.

"But we took the government away from them in '76. We *took* it. We have had no organized Republican party in our state since 1884, and we have fewer negro voters than a hen's got teeth!"

Handclapping, some stomping on the footboards of the grandstand.

"My people," he says with humility, "were but simple farmers. They never owned negroes. And I wish to God the last one of them was in Africa and that none had ever been brought to our shores. But that is not the case. So when we began our great movement we scratched our heads to figure out how we could eliminate the last one of them from the election process in our state. How? We stuffed ballot boxes. We threatened them. We *shot* them. We are not ashamed of it."

Many are standing to cheer now. The Judge looks around uneasily at his confraternity. It is one thing to gain power and change laws—another to openly break those that exist. It should be possible, he believes, to challenge unjust institutions without fostering contempt for the law itself. He is beginning to understand more fully his Charleston friends' aversion to the Senator.

Tillman turns to address the Red Shirts, dismounted now and standing in rough formation at the base of the judges' stand. "It stirs my heart to see the demonstration of patriotism, the show of backbone, that these men have offered us today. When the Redemption got going in South Carolina I recall seeing more than five thousand Red Shirts in one gathering, and when they mounted up and rode together through the precincts of our adversary, believe me, those people ran back into their holes like rabbits."

Laughter again, and a cheer for the Red Shirts, who raise their right fists into the air as one.

"We did not disenfranchise our negroes till 1895," Tillman continues, easing back a little. "Then we had a constitutional convention which took the matter up, calmly, deliberately, with the avowed purpose of disenfranchising as many of them as possible under the 14th and 15th Amendments."

Serious booing of the Amendments in question ensue. The Judge has taken them apart in front of a law class, revealed their basic incompatibility with the Founders' intentions. A federal law must be truly iniquitous, he thinks, for the common man to know of its existence.

"We adopted the educational qualification as the only means left to us," Tillman explains. "Now, I hear you got a few overeducated niggers up here in North Carolina—" laughter, applause, "—but if they so smart, they'll learn to stay clear of the polling places soon enough! Our negro is as contented and well protected as in any state of the Union south of the Potomac. He is not meddling with politics, for he has found the more he meddles in them the worse off he gets. And as to his 'right'—" Tillman pauses masterfully, seeming to look into the eyes of each man present, letting the last charged word hang in the air, "—we of the South have never recognized the right of the negro to govern white men and we never *will*!" He pounds the podium with a fist as he shouts. "And we will not submit to his gratifying his lust on our wives and daughters without lynching him!"

This is what they've come for, and the reaction is enormous. Sally is swept up by the excitement of it, standing and applauding with the others. But Tillman is in no hurry, and draws back.

"Now I've been told," he says, "that your numbers up here come out to two *white* men for every black." He makes a puzzled face, holds his arms out at his sides. "Now if that is true, what, short of idiocy, has kept you people from prevailing over negro domination?"

An uneasy laughter follows this. The Judge notices that Colonel Waddell, who he had not seen on the train, is but two rows below them, chuckling and shaking his head.

"This is not meant as an insult, for I am your guest. But I have been invited here as a man of some experience in these matters, a surgeon, if you will, and as such I must not spare the knife when it needs be employed. Your politicians have betrayed you, they have delivered you into the tender mercies of the negro party for their own profit and glorification, and you are seeing the fruits of that irresponsibility, of that treason, in the increasing boldness of those who would put big ideas in small minds."

Tillman looks to the Float of Purity below him to the right, extending a hand to indicate the ladies, then swinging it toward the audience before him, seeming to look directly at Sally. "I can't help noticing," he says, "how many very beautiful girls we have among us today. They are our pride, they are our greatest treasure."

Yes, thinks the Judge, this is it. This is it exactly.

"And every one of these fine young Christian ladies," Tillman continues, voice rising in power, "lives in constant peril of losing her most precious possession!" He slams both fists down on the podium. "Why don't you people get your damn niggers under *control*?"

And if any had been present they certainly would have been torn apart, with bare hands if need be, such is the vehemence of the reaction. Sally seems bemused, looking around her, taking the curses and protestations as a compliment. Which in a way it is. What do we fight for, thinks the Judge, if not the virtue of our women?

"I have three daughters," says Tillman when it is quiet enough to be heard, sadness and reflection creeping into his voice, "but so help me God I had rather find any one of them killed by a tiger or a bear and gather up her bones and bury them, conscious that she had died in her purity, than to have her crawl to me and tell me the horrid story that she had been robbed of the jewel of her maidenhood by some black fiend!"

Again the Judge marvels at his daughter's powers of concentration as men all about forget themselves and curse at the top of their lungs. It is the Southern woman's great ability to shape reality by recognizing the existence of only those things they wish to, to smooth a rough or awkward moment with a pleasant phrase, to remain pure in the most compromised of situations. His wife, may she rest in peace, was a nonpareil of the breed, in command of any social situation, able to float above the unpleasant, able to disengage herself from—from everything. Sally has inherited much of this, but there is a warmth in her, a womanliness—

Judge Manigault looks at his daughter and Tillman's image, a sooty paw on her pellucid, ivory skin covered with the finest golden down, overwhelms him to the point of nausea, his hands curling into fists. He knows that much of it is buncombe, an orator's trick, but the diamond-hard kernel of it is undeniable. Their women will not be dishonored.

"From this day forth," cries the Senator, "let the enemy live in terror of the slumbering giant he has awakened! The Anglo-Saxon will not be ruled! I don't care if you been a Populist, Democrat, Fusionist—there must be only one political party in the great state of North Carolina, and that is the White Man's Party!"

The Red Shirts wave their fists, the maidens on the float wave their hats, the White Government Unionists screech and stomp, flasks of whiskey passing from hand to hand. The Judge holds on to Sally's arm and to the rail as the grandstand shakes, men pounding the boards with their booted feet. The old Confederate battle flag is waved atop a dozen poles. The rabble have been roused, the fuse lit for an explosion that will rock the state. The Judge decides that they will return on the train after the picnic, though they had planned to stay over at the hotel.

Tonight, he is certain, Fayetteville will not be a safe place for a young lady.

CONQUERORS

The moon is bright and high in the night sky by the time Royal stumbles back to the 25th.

They regroup, those not dead or wounded, in the mango grove to reclaim their blanket rolls and haversacks. The order comes to take the road back to El Pozo. Trudging through the dark jungle, too tired to talk, unsure if the day has been victory or defeat, Royal surrenders himself to the sight of Junior's back in front of him and the mindless rhythm of one step after another. In the middle of the night they are allowed to stop and sleep next to the La Cruz plantation house, lying on their gear with their hands on their rifles.

Royal dreams of bullets.

A horizontal hail of bullets, singing down from the top of the endless slope in deadly sheets, no hiding from them, no cease in their nightmare wasp-whine swarming till Kid Mabley blows him awake an hour before sunrise.

They are ordered to move to a ridge overlooking Santiago under light fire, intermittent pops and the occasional cry, a man from Company C catching one that smashes the bone of his elbow, his forearm hanging useless. Some of the red-tile roofs below them show damage from artillery. Black smoke rolls up from a fire. Only Cooper seems serious about hitting the few uniformed Spaniards moving behind the breastworks.

"Them I didn't get yesterday, Imonna get em today," he says, up on the firing step in the trench some other outfit has left them, peering over his Krag. "Counted a dozen I'm sure is dead and a couple I knows I winged em."

"Watch out for them truce flags," says Willie Mills. "You pop one whilst they under that, Sergeant Jacks nail your ass to the shithouse door."

"White flag only last till I hear a shot comin our way," Cooper tells him, squinting to aim at a spot where he's seen movement. "Then all bets is *off*."

There is thunder from the bay in the afternoon, the men wondering if the counterattack has begun, if the Spanish reinforcements have come with artillery. It lasts less than an hour, then stops as suddenly as it began.

By dusk Cooper's count is up to seventeen despite the white flags hustled back and forth and Royal has identified three different kinds of lice living on his body. The regiment is marched back down to the base of the ridge and told to hack a new trench from the hard ground. They were given three days' rations before the attack and there is nothing left to eat. They dig through the night.

"What they got us down here doin nigger work for," grumbles Cooper, "when they Spanish left to kill?"

Royal's hands are bleeding, his bowels starting to twist. The Captain has them pile the breastworks on the rear side, as if they might be attacked from behind.

"You don't eat nothin," says Willie as they finally lay out their gear to sleep in the open again, "you starts to shit your *body* out. Keep this up and we won't be nothin left but eyes and assholes."

In the morning, refugees from Santiago appear on the road that cuts through their trench line. Hundreds of them, hungry-looking and scared, old men, women and children, even a few dogs skulking along nervously at the edges of the sorry stream, casting a suspicious eye on the watching soldiers.

"Dog look like stewmeat to me," says Willie.

"If you kill it, I'll eat it," adds Cooper, but nobody shoots the dogs, pre-ferring not to scare the wretched Cubans any worse. Some of them are dressed well enough, one lady wearing cotton gloves and walking stiffly under a parasol, but most are barefoot in rags with a numb, unfocused look on their faces. Where they can all be going is unclear.

"Counterattack comin today," says Corporal Barnes. "Rats always climb off the ship when it's set to go down." Barnes, whose experience of ships is like their own, puking over the rail when he could get to it and in the hold when he couldn't.

A mule train comes, teamsters haggard and mud-spattered, with sacks of raw beans and cans of embalmed beef and the news that the Spanish fleet attempted to run the blockade the day before and was smashed by the American gunships. There is a cheer, echoed along the lines as the word spreads.

"It's the 4th," says Junior, stabbing a can of the slimy meat open with his knife. "We ought to celebrate."

"Celebrate what?" asks Cooper, who has sworn off the beef since it made him sick in Tampa.

"Celebrate our naval victory," says Junior. "Freedom from tyranny."

Cooper and some of the others laugh. "Why'nt you step up on that ridge and make us a speech?" he says, pointing to their former perch, occupied now by a white regiment. "I guarantee we see some fireworks."

They stay just beneath the ridge the next day, and the next, when the rain starts in the evening and the men push rags into the barrels of their Krags and the water runs down the slope and into the backside of the trenches and Royal just barely makes it to the tiny ditch of a latrine before the beef runs through him. He has been thinking about Jessie but decides to give it up, something dirty about even the memory of her while he's in this obscene place, this place where dead men and dead animals lie still unburied. There are a dozen other men squatting in the rain beside him, pants at their ankles, including one being held in position by his bunkie.

"He got the shakes," says the standing bunkie apologetically, holding his moaning friend by the wrists, head turned sideways to provide the illusion of privacy. "We aint gonna fight no more why don't they pull us the fuck out of here?"

It rains through the night, wet coming up through their groundcloths and soaking the little half-shelter tents, water over their ankles when they climb back in the trenches, rubber peeling off the flimsy ponchos of the men who bother to wear them. Royal is shivering too, now, though the rain feels warm on his face.

"Guess I'm not one of them Immunes," he says to Junior, who looks away without comment, mouth tight. Royal's hands shake as he tries to shovel muck on one of the pointless details the officers are inventing to keep them busy during the endless back and forth of negotiations with the Spanish.

"I can imagine they're eager to surrender," Junior says. "Even if they do have us outnumbered. They've spent a fever season here before."

"Don't let your guard down," warns Sergeant Jacks, glaring at the make-work he's been ordered to supervise. "It aint over till the Fat Man says so."

The Fat Man is Shafter, who they have seen only once, being loaded into a carriage after a visit to the front, the huge, gouty pile of general in charge of the whole circus.

"Spanish just got to wait," says Pres Stiles, who has been coughing up black, tobacco-looking hunks of phlegm. "Nother week in this shithole gone do us in."

Heads have been counted. In their company Cousins and Strother are dead and Little Earl is lying under a tent back at Siboney waiting to be shipped home. When Royal left him he couldn't talk but was still breathing. Lieutenant McCorkle from G was killed right at the beginning with Leftwich, and three men from D were lost on the barbed wire. A few more of the wounded might not make it, but considering the volleys that were poured into their firing line, the impossible open slope they had to cross, it is a wonder to have so few casualties.

"Aint been the bullet made can bring me down," brags Cooper, who was a good ten yards ahead of the rest of them during the charge to overrun the trenches.

"Yeah, but they makin new ones every day," says Sergeant Jacks. Royal remembers Jacks walking backward up the hill, heedless of the Spanish volleys, checking to be sure the men didn't bunch up and blowing his whistle when it was time to flop or rush ahead.

"There's a lot of stupid things you can do to get yourself killed," Jacks likes to say, "but there aint much *smart* you can do to stay alive, except quit the damn Army."

On the 11th they are marched back to the front lines in the pouring rain. Royal has a fire in his throat and something pressing behind his left eye, has to step out from the column twice to drop his pants and let go. By now it is one man out of four with the aches and chills and they are down to hardtack only, which they break apart to fry in the little bit of rancid sowbelly left to them. Royal threw away his last bit of that days ago but the smell clings to the cloth of his haversack, grease spots attracting swarms of tiny ants if he lays it on the ground during the few hours it isn't raining. Pete Robey sings at dinnertime when they are making their desperate little fires, smashing charred coffee beans with the butts of their bayonets—

There's a poor starving soldier
Who wears his life away
Clothes are torn and his better days are oer
He is sighing now for whiskey
With throat as dry as hay
Singing "Hardtack, come again no more!"

Pete has a deeper voice than Littler Earl's, a voice that rumbles out of his barrel chest, and the others are too beaten to join him for the chorus—

It's the song, the sigh of the weary
"Hardtack, hardtack
Come again no more
Many days you have lingered
While worms crawl at your core
O-oh hardtack, come again no more!"

When they reach the trenches overlooking Santiago again the white unit who has been holding them staggers away, scrawny and unshaven, filthy uniforms hanging from their bodies.

"You boys are welcome to it," says a sunburned, runny-eyed sergeant. "Skeeters'll get you if you don't drownd first."

It rains all through the night and for most of the rest of the week. The officers, some of them just as sick as the men, give up on everything but keeping the pickets out and every day another dozen can't hold themselves upright in the morning.

The day the Spanish leave Santiago, Royal is shitting blood.

Not mixed with anything, just a hot slick stream of blood out where it shouldn't be coming from and he is on his way to tell Sergeant Jacks something might be wrong when he sees the Spanish marching out, hears the bitter grandeur of their drums and horns as the side of the hill tilts up and smacks him hard in the cheek. He lies in the mud a while, dry-heaving, before Junior comes to find him.

"You o.k.?"

Royal manages to roll himself on his back.

The sick tent is just back down the hill, too many men down in all the regiments to transport the private soldiers all the way back to the coast. There is no medicine but for a spoonful of bismuth once a day and the treatment amounts to checking for dead every few hours and hauling them out.

"You got it easy now," says Junior, trying to seem cheerful. "Just lay back and wait to ship out."

After Junior leaves, a delirious man, a corporal from D Company, starts to thrash in his cot and rave about missing buckwheat cakes.

"I catches the one who took em," he repeats, over and over, "I cut him to the *bone*."

There is a different kind of time inside the sick tent, fever-time, each man in his separate sticky hell. It keeps raining, rivulets, then streams running under the tent edges and cutting away the ground beneath their cots. Royal finds himself tilting, feet higher than his head, and no one comes to set him level again. The delirious man is shouted at, told to shut up, threatened, but none of them lying there has the strength to get up and strangle him.

When he is conscious enough to sustain a thought, Royal realizes that all of it—the drumthumping of recruitment, the long training, the weapons and uniforms, the soul-wearying marches, the waiting in vomit-sloshing ship holds for the bilious, ocean-tossed transport of their blue horde to this steaming island, the flags and the stirring horns and the frank judgment in his comrades' eyes pushing him forward, willingly if not eagerly, one foot in front of the other, obeying the order of the moment—are just parts of an intricate, implacable process meant to bring a sharp-nosed, shrieking bit of metal and his own forehead to the same spot at the same instant.

But the machine has failed somehow, too many moving parts, too much room for error, and so he lies here with rotting bowels waiting to feed the sweet-smelling, poisonous green jungle that grows and decays around him.

Royal is swept by waves of fever. The heat generates inside him then flashes through his body, a shimmering liquid heat beneath his skin cooking out in fever-sweat, his clothes sodden with it, heat concentrating as it rises to a place behind his eyes, brain boiling, images flashing, images first of battle, of the angry whine of bullets sizzling by, of metal ripping through flesh, but then as the days pass (if they are days and not only waves of clarity and unconsciousness) the images soften and swoon and there are times that Jessie comes to him, Jessie in a way he's never dared to imagine her, loose and naked and steaming amid the hot green jungle plants, Jessie smiling, her tongue impossibly red, her breasts oozing sticky white pulp that drops, *spat*, on the broad green blades of the foliage below, her skin slick and oozing like the fleshy succulent plants and hot and wet and her sex a purple orchid red at the pistils yielding hot and wet and fleshy to embrace him, tightening in a sweet hot grip around him, squeezing, constricting, pulsing hot until he bursts and she is gone, his uniform cold and wet and heavy as a shroud on his trembling body.

The chills start then, shimmering through bone-aching limbs, pulsating

Northern Lights of sensation that flutter, icy and electric, clear through him and he understands that he is dying despite Junior talking somewhere close You're o.k. you'll be fine don't worry and piling on blankets—where did he find blankets?—that press on Royal but bring no relief from the icy wind that blows in his blood. And sometimes, suddenly, a patch of smooth water after the chilling rapids, Royal vaguely conscious and aware of sounds, a snatch of voices from the living outside the tent, the ones who can still prop themselves up at their posts and shiver under the searing noon sky, aware of where he is and who he is, aware of bright light strained through dirty white canvas overhead and mosquitoes whining by his ears and dying men groaning and Junior there again, giving him a drink from his cool metal cup and Royal hasn't the strength left to lift his own head, then, slipping back down, flushing hot with fever as he is swept under another wave, lost to another steaming nightmare.

Days pass in waves of heat and chill.

Rain drills the tent canvas at night, stormwater cutting a deeper furrow below the cot, somebody weeping, weeping.

And Royal is a sidelong bulge of panic in a horse's eye.

The horse is churning without direction in a hot, acid sea, snorting saltwater after each new wave slaps its upstretched head, nostrils barely above the surface, legs pedaling desperately, hooves seeking solid ground and finding none, not lathered despite the effort but huffing and pedaling in a lather of ocean, slapping waves incessant and blocking sight on every side, the powerful forelegs beginning to tire, saltwater rushing into the nose and down the long gorge and still it struggles, frantic, without the sense to surrender to liquid, a machine of slamming heart and burning muscle torn from its mooring but powering forward nonetheless, no thought, no plan in the beast's mind only a shrill unwavering note of fear—

!

!

!

Royal is a sidelong bulge of panic in a horse's eye.

If it was me, thinks something just a little removed from what used to be his conscious mind (not a thought, really, or a voice, just a knowledge that is separate from his body), if it was me and not this thrashing animal I would give up, give in, let the water fold over but they can't see ahead, horses, eyes set off on each side of the great head, they can't see what's straight in front of them, can't understand that there is no safe harbor to swim to, that the kicking and huffing and bulging out of eyes is a waste. When the dying man, Royal, saw something like this there were dozens of them, horses and mules churning the sea into a lather with their fear and their pedaling legs and a few of the last ones saved, that's right, saved when a bugler already on shore played *Boots and Saddles* and they obeyed the order of the moment, unthinking like good soldiers and swam to the shore that led to the pathway that led through the poisonous jungle to the steep murderous slope where the angry waspwhine bullets waited to burn through them and carry their parts away. But that's over now, and he's not needed anymore, different fevered men crouch atop the hill, and he is free to give in, to accept the warm caressing water if he was Royal still and not the sidelong bulge in a horse's eye, was not thoughtless panic and thrashing and here it comes, a big one, more than a wave a mighty lathering swell rising up and over, blotting out the sky, and the nostrils swept under and the powerful forelegs spasm, barrel chest pressed in a vice, lungs flushed with acid saltwater, no air, no air, no air, till the machine jolts, wrenching his throat open with a crying gasp and wheezing, dragging the hothouse sick-tent air into his lungs, sopping wet and cold now lying on solid ground with the taste of brine in his mouth.

"What happened?"

Junior is standing over him. "Fever broke." Junior is hollow-eyed, unshaven. He holds himself upright leaning on his rifle.

"You look like hell, Junior."

"You want to see hell," says Junior, smiling a gaunt, death's-head smile, "I'll get you a mirror."

"No calls," says Royal. Something that has been gnawing at the edge of his consciousness, a lack, something missing in the air. "No reveille."

"Kid Mabley's in the other tent, almost as bad as you. And none of the others got the wind left to blow."

Royal shifts his weight slightly and feels the pool of sweat beneath his back and buttocks. He is lying on a cot, beneath a tent, and knows now that he's not going to drown. But the rest of it is distant, unformed.

If there's no bugle, he wonders, how do we know which way is the shore?

*   *   *

Father—

Junior off on water detail, writing hidden behind a tree so the others won't know he has paper. His hand trembling, paper propped on an empty canteen on his thigh. Something dead is nearby, buzzards wheeling overhead.

You have no doubt read reports by now of the gallant show made by our force at El Caney and the San Juan Heights. It was, from a military point of view, an inelegant and possibly ill-advised assault, though the results appear to be much more auspicious than expected. The Spaniards put up a desperate fight, and any doubts about their valor on the battlefield have been put to rest. Santiago, and possibly the war, have been won at the cost of much precious American blood, and certain notables with political aspirations are already elbowing their way into position to take full credit. We have not received any papers since our arrival, and thus I have no way to know if the role played by our colored troops has received adequate attention. The 24th Infantry and the 9th and 10th Cavalry were instrumental in the capture of the San Juan Heights, while my own 25th led the last desperate dash to take the fortifications at El Caney. The sons of Ham have made quite a military record for themselves here, and I can only hope that this will be justly recognized and celebrated throughout our homeland.

He hears the shouts and splashing of the others on the detail, naked in the river scouring themselves with the little yellow cubes of soap they've been issued, black men with ribs showing through their skin, a few just sitting at the edge of the flowing water, too weak to risk the current. Junior, with everything he's just experienced, still can't fathom bathing in front of others.

What the citizens at home should also know is that our great victory is in danger of betrayal by the incompetence and self-serving of powerful men far from the clamor and deadly consequence of the battleground. If we are not brought home from this place immediately we shall all be lost to fever and starvation. The rains are upon us—dysentery, malaria, and the dreaded yellow jack have leveled over a third of the regiment, with more taking ill each day. My own company lost Private Charles Taliaferro this morning—a good soldier and a good friend—and the brass have forbidden the firing of a last salute and playing of Taps *for fear the constant burials will undermine morale. But there is no morale, only the desperate realization that we have been abandoned here to die by an unprepared and uncaring government. There is insufficient food, medicine, shelter, no provision for dealing with the fever season and seemingly no plan for what follows the "liberation" of this island and these people. On the 12th we took high ground and encamped with our backs to the enemy city, told to defend the Spaniards from any incursions by our* insurrecto *allies wishing to wreak vengeance. These Cuban patriots now mutter among themselves, wondering, no doubt, if we have designs on their sovereignty.*

Rumors of beheadings, a good deal of theft. The Cuban fighters have kept themselves apart since the rains and sickness began, cutting the strange local fruits open with their machetes and offering them in trade for whatever they don't have, which is everything. The refugees are beyond pitiful. Apparently the custom here is to be buried by your peers—how many times has a cortège of little boys or little girls passed shouldering the tiny box that bears their stricken playmate? And those are only the ones with enough spark left to care about their sacraments.

Royal Scott, who you will remember from Wilmington, has been through a terrible bout, touch and go for a while but if we receive transport soon he may stand a chance of pulling through. He asks me to send his regards. Desperation is a great leveler, and the observation of "Jim Crow" rules has all but disappeared among the men here, trapped in the same dire circumstances. Sad that it requires such an extreme of suffering to break down the habits of color prejudice. I am eager to see, once privation and the threat of annihilation are lifted, whether our white comrades will return to their former ways.

Junior can smell whatever it is that has died. When the jungle is wet there are many odors of decay, but none so sweet as rotting flesh. The evening of the charge he was on burial detail, pulling Spanish boys out from the trenches where they had been shot and clubbed and bayoneted and smashed apart by artillery. The bodies were surprisingly light, though they had swelled in the heat, and after the first few he was careful to turn them face-down so he wouldn't have to see dirt thrown into their mouths and eyes. That had bothered him more than the smell. And then yesterday, when they found the mule mired with a broken leg and Coop shot it and the cooks tried to dress it and make a meal it had not been the smell but the color of the meat, deep purple, that made his gorge rise and sent him stumbling toward the blood-splattered latrine.

The dignity of brave men who have faced death in battle is now dragged through the filth, the best men of our generation to be lost in this pestilent wasteland. We are soldiers, and deserve the support of a grateful nation. Please spread the word to any with the ear of those in power.

Junior has a wound, infected now, a long trough cut in his arm going through barbed wire during the ascent, a wound he didn't notice till they were marching away from the hill that first night. He flexes his hand, feels the ache. The doctors have nothing left to treat it and he worries it will swell and have to come off, like what happened to Briscoe of A Company.

"Bad enough a man go home, take his uniform off and the white fokes don't want to know about him," Cooper said when they got the news of the amputation. "But you take a whole arm off, you might's well throw way the rest of the nigger."

As for my own performance in the tumult of mortal conflict, you have nothing to be ashamed of. I acquitted myself as an American patriot, no more or less, and though I know now I will never love the military life, I am confident I can at least uphold the honor of my family and my race. My love to Mother and Jessie—

Your son,
Aaron

SURRENDER

They put the white flag out an hour after the *merienda*.

The *chino* camp followers came up from Manila, and the men paid them to prepare some *pancit canton* and *baboy*, and Bayani, the new sargento who reported to him this morning, had the idea of throwing a few of the pork ears on the fire once the breeze shifted to send the odor over the thornbush breastworks to the Spanish garrison crouching without food in Guagua. He is insolent, this Bayani, addressing Diosdado with the *tú* when he speaks Spanish, which he does ironically and with an atrocious accent, moving among them with a kind of assurance, as if already the platoon belongs to him. It was a good idea, though, a very good idea, and Diosdado shrugged in what he hoped was a manner becoming an officer and said he supposed they could give it a try. The siege has been on for over a week, the Spaniards never even stirring to snipe at their positions until nightfall, Diosdado's men dug in all around the town and kept busy shuttling from one trench to the next to try to appear like a much larger force and gambling away their meager three-and-a-half-peso monthly pay. Almost all the people from Guagua managed to sneak out with their livestock the night his platoon arrived, and are camped in the fields behind them complaining constantly about how long it is taking to drive the Spanish away.

"If you would like to lead the charge," said Kalaw, the private with the big nose, to one delegation, "we will be two steps behind you."

But an hour after they are finished with all the *pancit* and the *baboy* and the fried bananas the *chinos* have brought up, the white flag appears from the belltower of the tiny church in the plaza of Guagua, the high spot from which a Spanish sniper hit Anacleto Darang in the knee, their only casualty so far.

"Come and talk to them with me," Disodado says to Sargento Bayani, who claims he was a *cuadrillero* for the Spanish in the Moro islands and understands the thinking of their officers.

"*Con placer, hermano,*" says Bayani with his strange, insolent smile. "Let me get a flag together."

It takes nearly a half an hour for one of the privates to run back to the *hacienda* they liberated a week ago and borrow a sheet. Sargento Bayani holds this banner of truce, tied to a long bamboo pole, high over his head as they step out and approach the Spanish breastworks.

"Our boys need practice," says the sargento as they walk. "They'll never get it this way."

"The point is to regain our country, not to test ourselves in battle."

"And when we have to fight the *yanquis?*" He has that smile on his face.

"The *yanquis* are our allies," says Diosdado. It is ridiculous, this cynicism. If not for the Americans the Spanish would still control the harbor in Manila, would still be able to resupply themselves, be able to send fresh troops to relieve any besieged garrison. Education will be the key, as Scipio always says. Of all the ills that plague the people, this overriding cynicism, this ignorance, is the worst.

"We're sending you into the field," Scipio told him in Cavite. "Very soon, when we are in power, the people will want their leaders to be men who bore arms against the Spaniards, men of action." Scipio, never a weapon in his hand, has moved up in the hierarchy, though he will never tell Diosdado his official title.

Diosdado had expected to rejoin the Supremo's staff, Pepito Leyba at one side of their diminutive leader and himself at the other, translating, rewriting proclamations in a more confident Spanish, offering his opinion when asked. He had a detailed scenario worked out in which Ninfa Benavides, looking up at him contritely in the rags of one of her fabulous gowns, begged for his intercession to save her collaborationist father from the wrath of the Philippine Republic. She was so very grateful—

"This is because of my accent," he said to Scipio at the time, hurt. "Because I'm not a Tagalo, much less a Caviteño."

His friend did not deny it. "This will be good for you," he shrugged. "Believe me. Just avoid being shot."

Diosdado has no training, of course, but there doesn't seem to be much to it. Setting a good example, being a model of character for the men, explaining the importance of doing one's duty and not leaving in the middle of an engagement to deal with problems at home. The uniform—he had the foresight to have a pair made in Hongkong before he left—does half the job. When he caught the men looting the *hacienda*, Diosdado made them replace everything that was not of immediate use in the military campaign, and put Sargento Ramos in charge of making certain the goods taken were shared equally.

"We are soldiers of the Filipino Republic," he reminds them constantly, "not a gang of *tulisanes*."

There is only an *alferez* under a smaller, improvised white flag on the other side of the breastworks.

"My *comandante* wishes to hear your terms," he tells them.

"You will leave your arms and ammunition stacked, neatly, in the church," says Diosdado. "You will form ranks and march out fifty yards on the road to San Fernando and halt. There I will accept your surrender."

"Stacked neatly," echoes Bayani, mocking, and Diosdado shoots him a look.

"And there will be no reprisals?"

"You will be treated with the consideration due to fellow soldiers."

The *alferez* looks uneasily to Bayani, then back to Diosdado.

"We are starving."

Diosdado nods. He wanted to ask the men to save some of the *merienda*, but realized it would never be enough to feed the garrison.

"There is food in Malolos," he says. "You will be taken there to join your defeated comrades."

He has no idea if there is sufficient food for them in Malolos, only that that is where prisoners are to be sent. The *alferez* nods and offers him a salute. "I will inform my *comandante*."

"There is no reason to make them feel ashamed," he says to the sargento on their way back to the men.

"Of course not. We may shoot them, cut their throats, hack them to bits, but we wouldn't want to hurt their feelings."

The ideal is to keep the best of the Spanish—learning, culture, a certain code of honorable behavior—and jettison all that is base and hypocritical. The friars will have to go, of course, though the Jesuits might be allowed to remain if their political inclinations can be discouraged. The native clergy will do well in the villages, but for the *ilustrado* class a more elevated approach to

Heaven will be required. Sadly, there are aspects of the Filipino temperament, shortcomings, brought into sharp relief by a character like this Bayani—

The Spanish begin to come out of the plaza. They are trying to stay in ranks, but the men sent ahead to make a gap in the breastworks are weak and struggle with the spiky mass of aroma bush and a few men collapse while they are waiting. It is thirst, really, Diosdado knows, no well dug within the garrison's fortifications and his own people tearing down the bamboo *acueducto* that fed the town from the hillside stream, and finally the *alferez* appears beside a tall, emaciated *comandante*, leading the men who can walk, maybe sixty of them, out onto the San Fernando road. Before they left for this outpost, no doubt, these soldiers knelt in their ranks before the *Arzobispo* in Manila, receiving his blessing and swearing before God that they would never surrender the sacred banner of their nation. Bayani sends two squads of the men who have rifles to quickly flank them, worried about their reaction when they discover how few of their tormentors are present. Diosdado steps up to the tall officer, who salutes him.

"I am Comandante Ramón Asturias y Famy," he says. "We are at your mercy."

"We will take you first to the stream," Diosdado tells him. "And then on to Malolos. Are there wounded left behind?"

"Perhaps a dozen. Sick, not wounded." The officer looks Diosdado over. He is glad that the uniform fits him well, that he has managed to keep it nearly spotless during the siege. "May I inquire about your training?" asks the *comandante*.

It seems a strange, if not presumptuous question for a prisoner of war to put forth. Diosdado wonders if he should reveal his inexperience, even to a man unlikely to resume arms against the Cause. Filipino forces will be at the outskirts of Manila soon, circling the final gem of the crown, and the troops inside the Walled City must be made to believe they are outmanned, outgunned, outgeneraled—

"I believe he is very well trained in philosophy," Bayani interjects, an innocent look on his face, "with an interest in the Classics."

It is cruel, yes, and Diosdado wonders how he knows. He has not spoken to anyone in the platoon of his education. Asturias y Famy is weeping.

"A university boy," he says, tears making channels in the grime on his cheeks. The Spaniards have not bathed for a week. "I am surrendering to a fucking university boy."

REPRIEVE

After the swim they stop at the Iolani Palace for a picnic. President Dole came aboard looking like Father Christmas with his long white beard and invited the whole sorry bunch of them from the *China*—Colorado Volunteers and the 8th Infantry and the Utah Battery and the engineers and the hospital people, everybody but the damn mascot goat—and now they're breathing air heavy with the smell of flowers and spread out at long, long tables set on the grass under the trees with plates and utensils and cloth napkins for what they call a loo-wow. Hod still has water trapped in his ears from the surf, the bottoms of his feet scraped by coral. There were Kanakas riding the waves in on their wooden boards, men and women wearing almost nothing at all, but they disappeared quick once the beach was mobbed by the sickly-skinned, boat-dopey soldiers, peeling their uniforms off to give themselves up to the sea water. Only Big Ten chose not to go in, sitting on the shore with all his uniform still on, even his boots.

"My people will row on top of the water all day and all night," he says, "but swimming is for fishes."

Hod thinks it's so the others won't see how dark he is all over.

The food is hard to believe and just keeps coming. The local Americans, celebrating the Annexation Bill just passed in Congress, have roasted a whole herd of pigs down in holes in the ground, serving up steaming chunks from them wrapped in palm leaves, and then there are crabs and fish and chickens and yams and huge sweet potatoes and pineapples that never been in a can and bread and cocoanut milk and the best coffee Hod has ever tasted and dates and cocoanut pudding and something called alligator pears that Big Ten at first tries to eat without peeling the hide off. Inside they are light green and creamy and nutty tasting and you eat them with Worcestershire sauce. Everybody eats twice as much as they can hold, the food on the trip so far just pitiful, salthorse and sea biscuit, and no reason to think it will improve for the rest of the way. Three days into the voyage they let some carrier pigeons loose up top, supposed to fly with their messages back to San Francisco.

"I was gonna eat them birds," said Big Ten, watching them fly. "Now we stuck with fishee ricee."

The Chinamen and Japs who serve as the crew of the transport always have something you can buy to eat, a nickel here, a nickel there, even dough-nuts if you catch them at the right time, but they won't take Army grub in trade. The yellow men were left on board, helping the stevedores load coal into the ship, when the regiment marched away.

"Yo, Chief!" calls Corporal Grissom down the table. "Introduce me to your sister."

There have been a lot of them telling Big Ten he looks just like the Kanakas and he takes it like a sport. He turns to the long-haired girl who is serving and speaks some of his lingo at her, but she just covers her face and giggles. There are dozens of the Kanaka girls serving in their bright shifts with flowers in their hair, and white women too, white women in clean white dresses with high collars and little straw hats moving around the long tables under the banyan trees with platters of food and urns of coffee.

"I think she's a Princess," says Big Ten. "They aint spose to talk with commoners."

Corporal Grissom points to the Palace, just visible through the trees. "They say they got the Queen shut up in there. Once the Americans bumped her off the throne she hooked up with some bunch that wanted to put her back on it, so they stuck her under house arrest."

"Tough duty. Lookit that place."

"She should of behaved herself."

"If this was my island," says Big Ten, looking around, "I'd sure as hell want to get it back. In fact, I think I better volunteer to be on her guard detail, make sure she don't bust out and cause any more ruckus."

They all agree that duty here would be paradise, even without women serving you a feast every day. There is a kind of orchestra playing for them while they eat, natives wearing bright-colored shirts and ropes of flowers around their necks and some of the instruments Hod has never heard before. Suddenly it is their table's turn to give back the compliment and they stand to sing *On the Banks of the Wabash Far Away* only with the words changed for their section of the country—

Oer my Colorado Rockies flies the eagle
Down the slopes flow rushing rivers clear and cool
Oftentimes my thoughts revert to scenes of childhood
Where I single-jacked for silver, Nature's school
But one thing there is missing in the picture
Without her face it seems so incomplete

On the ship it is a whore they sing of, each verse nastier than the next, but this is polite company, with officers hovering and white ladies present—

I long to see my mother in the doorway
Of our cabin years ago, her boy to greet

Big Ten has a strong bass voice and can harmonize with anybody. Hod sings along, letting the other voices carry his, wishing he could feel a part of this like he did on the run with the Butte contingent of the Commonweal Army. But all he feels is that he's hiding from something, that his life is not real, and being here in this dreamland, pleasant as it is, doesn't help any. When the *China* was towed up to the wharf there were little Kanaka boys and girls swimming all around the hull who smiled and shouted and dove down under to grab for pennies the soldiers threw overboard. *That's me*, Hod thought as he and Big Ten, throwing nothing, watched them splash and shout. *That's my whole damn life.* Scrambling for pennies to entertain the folks up high—

Oh, the moonlight's fair tonight in Colorado
From saloons there comes the sound of men at play
Oer the glory holes the caution lights are gleaming
In my sweet Colorado, far away!

"So the Philippines is just like this, right?" says Private Neely when they have received their applause and are allowed to sit down and gorge themselves again.

There has been a lot of talk during the long, stomach-heaving days at sea as to where exactly the islands are and what the nature of the people on them is.

"They're just like Cuba and Porto Rico," insists Corporal Grissom, who has never been to either of those places, "only farther away."

"It's part of China," says Private Falconer, "only the Papists got there before the other religions."

"You sit under a tree," says Sergeant LaDuke, "and take a nap, and when you wake up your lunch has dropped down into your lap."

Runt, before they booted him out for being too small and too young, showed them the islands on a map he got hold of somewheres.

"Jesus, lookit em all," said Neely, impressed. "We got to liberate every one of those?"

"We just wrap up the big one here," said Runt, poking his finger onto an island called Luzon, "and the rest of em tip over like dominoes."

Manigault strolls by them, wearing a white duck uniform and white canvas shoes like the navy officers.

"Dig in, fellows," he says jauntily. "This will have to last you quite a while."

"We been hearing plenty talk here, Lieutenant," says Corporal Grissom. "There was some sailors at the wharf who see everything that comes on the wire, and their scut is that after what Dewey done to the Spanish fleet it'll be over before we even get there."

Manigault gives him a pitying smile, then nods toward an enormous roast pig being carried past on a litter by two barefoot Kanaka men.

"There is no feast," he says, "without a slaughter."

FURLOUGH

Halfway home on the *Comanche*, Royal is strong enough to climb up to the steamer's aft deck and see the dolphins. The creatures, sometimes three, sometimes four, power along in their wake then leap again and again, sleek and glistening, to the cheers of the men. It is the best he has felt since Chickamauga.

There is a full band on one of the battleships plowing alongside the returning fleet, and several times a day the thump of bass drums is heard across the water, military airs and the new Sousa marches pounding out to cheer their passage. Royal is not stirred. He grips the aft rail tightly, still weak at the knees, and thinks of what a small thing his death would have been. His mother would have mourned him, and his brother Jubal, and his uncle Wicklow and Junior, for a while. They turned to waste so quickly, the bodies of the dead. A white man with a clipboard came through the sick tent, stopping by the cots of the ones who were thought to be dying.

"Next of kin?" he asked Royal.

"Jessie Lunceford."

Her name came without thought, and when it was out it seemed right. To be mourned by Jessie Lunceford would mean you were someone in the world. You were not easily replaced. The Luncefords kept a horse and carriage, they lived in a house with white folks on either side of them. They were people the world looked at, wondered about, tried to be like.

"Relation?" asked the man with the clipboard.

"We're going to be married," Royal answered.

He is no longer delirious, or dying. But he will make it happen.

The Judge confronts him halfway into the street, brandishing a newspaper.

"Have you seen this?"

It's hard for MacRae to make out anything on the paper with the Judge still waving it. "What is it?"

"It's today's *Record*, is what it is, and it is the most vicious slander."

"I'm not in the habit of reading the colored sheet, Judge." MacRae pulls his watch from his vest, glances at it. There's a meeting with the fellows across the street in Bellamy's building and he's late already.

"Nor am I. But when it was brought to my attention——" the Judge slaps the rolled newspaper hard against his open palm. "Measures must be taken!"

"Are you mentioned by name?"

"I am not, damn it, but if he ever dare print it in this vile rag, I will——"

"Mr. Manly is not reticent with his opinions."

"His opinions are criminal! This is part and parcel of what has become of the entire state. Our homes are no longer safe, the streets are overrun with insolent darkies who have been told they are our equals, no, that they are superior to us, men of proven value and social standing are ignored while the governor doles out state commissions to every shitheel Republican with two nickels to rub together——"

"The governor," says MacRae, laying a calming hand on the Judge's shoulder, "will not plague us for long."

"His term is——"

"His term has meaning only so long as he controls the legislature. We have an election coming up."

"And every one of these grinning monkeys will be lined up at the polls, lording it over us——"

"That will not be allowed. Not this time."

The Judge is brought short by the bluntness of MacRae's reply.

"And who will prevent it?"

The difficult part will be the timing. Building the pressure without letting it explode too soon, keeping secrets from your friends as well as your adversaries.

"Men of substance," he says. "Men of honor. Men, as you put it, of proven value."

"But the legalities——"

"The legalities will be dealt with as they arise. Desperate times call for desperate measures."

They are distracted then by the loud rattling of an empty dray, a high-stepping horse heading directly at them and the teamster, a young, hatless negro, pointedly neglecting to rein it in.

"Pardon me, gennemen!"

The Judge and MacRae both have to scramble back onto the curb to avoid being trampled. Both men stare after the wagon as it speeds away toward the river, incredulous.

"When the time comes, Judge," says MacRae, his voice shaking with anger, "trust me—you will be called upon."

Jubal pulls the dray in front of the loading dock at the lumberyard. Dap Mosely, the foreman, is sitting with the others eating their lunches, legs hanging over the edge of the platform.

"Got Mister Rankin load ready?" asks Jubal.

"Lunch don't end till I say it do," Dap smiles. "An I aint said so yet. What's your hurry, young man?"

"This one always in a rush." His Uncle Wicklow sits on a pile of railroad ties back in the shade of the awning, shoes off, wiggling his toes. "In a big rush to get nowhere."

"What you doin here, Wick?"

"Oh, just resting my feet. Listening to Broadnax here read the news."

Percy Broadnax, who is missing two fingers from a sawmill accident, waves a copy of the *Record*. "Gonna be trouble over this one. Get all the white folks in a fuss."

"I just put a few of em up on their toes," says Jubal, stretching out on the seat of the wagon. "My Nubia pert near run Mr. Hugh MacRae and that old Judge Nannygoat over."

"What you want to do that for?" says Wick, leaning forward with a frown.

"They was standing right out in the middle of Market Street like they own it. You got to leave people room to do their bidness."

"Hugh MacRae probly does own Market Street," says Dap. "Spect he thinks he does, anyway."

"What you care about them, anyhow?" says Jubal. His uncle has done livery work for plenty of white families over the years, but none of them lived in a castle. "They aint your people."

"Got to treat white folks and snakes just the same," says Wick. "Don't rile em less you got to."

"Well this gonna get em hissin and spittin, all right—" Broadnax holds the paper at arm's length to read it, *"If these alleged crimes of rape were so frequent as has been reported in our state's newspapers, Mrs. Felton's plea might be worthy of consideration."*

Teeter Williams, brushing cornbread crumbs off his pants, whistles. "Damn. That boy Manly can ar*ti*culate."

"Say his grandaddy was governor back before the war, had him a fondness for the gals back in the cabins."

"Well, he act like he's king of somethin." Jubal shakes his head. "I haul his paper around every morning to them that sell it. I see him up there in his office—he hardly look at a man. Just cause you look white don't mean you got to act it."

"It's his mama the one got the brains in that family," says Dap Mosely, who is nearly as old as Uncle Wick and seems to know everybody in the city. "Woman is *sharp*. She aint so light-complected as her boys, cause she don't come from the Manly line, but she don't miss nothin."

"However," Broadnax reads, raising his voice to regain their attention, *"some white women who cry 'Rape!' in this regard may be exaggerating the truth."*

"How you do that?" says Jubal. "Exaggerate—"

"He means lying."

"Right. Some lowlife dog either rape a woman or don't. Aint no exaggerate about it."

"Only the truth and a lie. But either one get your neck stretched."

"Many black men," Broadnax continues, *"are sufficiently attractive for white girls of culture and refinement to fall in love with them."*

Jubal straightens and shows them his profile. "Yeah, an I'm one of em."

The men laugh, all but Wicklow.

"You be careful how you talk," he says.

"Relax, Wick—"

"Here it's a joke. Somebody else be listening, you find yourself tied up to a tree."

"Uncle Wick still got them old plantation ways in his head." Jubal winks to the others. "Fraid the Massa gone come back and get him. Them days over."

Dap stands and stretches. "You go back and ask your Mr. MacRae about that, young man. See what he got to say about it." He turns to the others. "Stir your bones, gennemen. We got some wood to load."

*   *   *

Judge Manigault is in the editor's office when Milsap arrives. The Judge comes at least once a month, fulminating about one outrage or another that must be redressed in print, but Milsap has never seen his face quite this crimson before.

"*Furthermore*," reads the Judge, shouting though Mr. Clawson sits only feet away from him, "*in the light of the continued rape and seduction of black women by white men, we must ask these carping hypocrites how they can cry aloud for the virtue of their women while they seek to destroy the morality of ours*. Sir, I ask you—"

"It came across my desk this morning," says the editor, calmly.

"This must not be tolerated!" The Judge hurls the folded newspaper on Mr. Clawson's desk. "Scurrilous, vile—"

"Yes, Judge, they gone way past cheeky in this town."

"And what do you intend to do about it?"

Clawson swivels in his chair, scooping up the paper. Milsap can tell from the doorway it is the *Record*. Eight pages, cheap paper.

"I have only just begun to formulate my editorial comments—you may read them in tomorrow's issue. Mr. Manly's absence from our community is strongly advised. As for this fortuitous bit of calumny," the editor slashes a blue pencil across the first and last paragraphs of the piece in front of him, then holds it out toward Milsap, "we must first be sure that our readers are aware they have been so maligned." He finally looks over. "This goes in today, Drew."

Milsap steps in to take the paper, glances at the article. "Just the middle part of it?"

"Cut to the heart of the insult. Header—" the editor tilts back in his chair, musing for a moment—"'A Negro Defamer of the White Women—of the *Chris*tian White Women of North Carolina.' Lead column left, change the typeface from our own."

"They use Baskerville—"

"That will be fine. And the other front-page piece—"

"'Attempted Assault by Black Brutes.'" Some colored boys had thrown stones at a trolley on Fourth and Red Cross. "I've already set the column."

"Redo it with a subhead so it looks like a continuation. Then beginning tomorrow we'll run Manly's statement in a box, center bottom, front page."

"Yes, sir." Milsap turns to go.

"And Drew—"

"Yes sir?"

"Be sure to have them hold onto the slugs. We'll be reprinting this in every issue till Election Day. Center bottom, first page." The editor swivels back to smile pleasantly at the Judge. "In a box."

The justification of the article is terrible, as it always is with the *Record*, but the text makes it hard for Milsap to concentrate on the borders of the column. His fingers dig into the keys, matrices rattling down the chutes of the Linotype—

We suggest that the whites guard their women more closely, as Mrs. Felton says, thus giving no opportunity for the human fiend, be he white or black. You leave your goods out of doors and then complain because they are taken away.

Milsap is not married, never even engaged, but can imagine the anxiety of leaving a wife or daughter at home unprotected with marauding beasts at large, intent upon rapine and murder. Is that all the provocation necessary, to let them step out into the light of day? Seeing old Manigault has made him think of the Judge's daughter Sally, strolling past his room with her friends on their way to Bible class, made him think of his own furtive thoughts, the few regrettable instances of self-pollution that have followed them. But to violate another, to touch them against their will—

Poor white men are careless of protecting their women, especially on farms. They are careless of their conduct toward them, and our experience among poor white people in the country teaches us that women of that race are not any more particular in the matter of clandestine meetings with colored men than are the white men with colored women.

Milsap feels dirty just to read this, and setting it into the machine makes him sweat, the seat of his pants sticking damp to his chair. It always makes his stomach go funny if one of them is pressed against him in a crowded trolley car, man or woman, especially on a hot day. They have a smell that is peculiar to their race and are unpredictable in their moods. In Charleston when he visited his Aunt Hepatha they had the Jim Crow rule in effect and everybody seemed comfortable with it. But here—

Meetings of this kind go on for some time until the woman's infatuation, or the man's boldness, bring attention to them, and the man is lynched for rape

Milsap stops halfway through the line. His pulse is racing. He tries to imagine what sort of white women would willingly, no, willfully submit to—has he ever met such a creature? Haskins the inker and some of the others who work the cylinder press like to go on about the women in Patty's Hollow, teasing him about what they could show him if he'd only come along with them some night, but those places are only for white men and as far as he knows the negroes must have prostitutes of their own color. It is not something written about in the newspapers, except for a rare mention of a *disorderly house*. How debased a woman would have to be to—but that is the point, it is a lie, a projection of this Manly's own twisted fantasies. A window into the criminal mind—

Every negro lynched is called a Big Burly Black Brute, when, in fact, many of those who have thus been dealt with had white men for fathers, and were not only not "black" and "burly," but were sufficiently attractive for white girls of culture and refinement to fall in love with them, as is very well known to all.

The light-colored ones were always like that, impressed with themselves, making assumptions. There is a condescension, a challenge in that *as is very well known to all* that makes Milsap burn. He knows no such thing. That he knows no women of culture and refinement, not personally, is beside the point. Such ladies would naturally be even closer to the feminine ideal than those he is familiar with. When tomorrow's *Messenger* reaches the public, with Mr. Clawson's editorial—

And then he understands it. Understands it all. The daily headlines of outrage, the editor's meetings with important men, the cartoons reprinted from Raleigh, even the arsenal he stumbled upon the other day in the storage room—cases of shining new Winchesters and Colt pistols. It is a campaign. Not a campaign like the trash collection or the county voting or the smallpox warnings earlier in the year. Intricate plans have been made, strategies devised, and the press, the shining jewel of American democracy, is to be the sharp point of the sword. He should have known. The way Mr. Clawson was with the Judge, so relaxed, a player with all the aces in his hand. He looks at the last line again, seeing now that it is somebody's death notice, and is thrilled to be here, humble as his part in it will be, the man who feeds the machine.

Milsap yanks the lever and the hot metal flows.

It is Frank, with his usual long face.

"He wants us out."

Manly sits by the electric lamp, writing. They are so much superior, steadier. Stay with gas light and he'll be blind by fifty.

"We have a lease," he answers. Frank can be an alarmist. Frank has assured him, many times, that the newspaper will ruin them all.

"He says there'll be a county sheriff here at ten o'clock."

"What gives him license to do that?"

Frank sighs, points at the article he has pinned upon the wall. "Your reply to Mrs. Felton. What do you think?"

"It's been out for days. Old news—"

"The *Messenger* just reprinted it. And the *Raleigh News and Observer*."

"Ah."

Manly rises, looks around at the press crowding the tiny room. "I suppose we'll have to cease operations tomorrow, make arrangements—"

"Anything left in this room," says Frank, "they destroy or confiscate."

"They can't do that."

Frank keeps staring at him. Of course they can do that, and much worse.

"It's already dark out."

"Good," says Frank, beginning to stack piles of paper on other piles of paper. "Maybe nobody will see us."

"I have nothing to hide."

Frank shrugs. "Course not. You're the one that pass for white, not me."

* * *

His sharpest memory of her is on a train. He was at the station to help his brother Jubal load crates onto the wagon and she called to him from the window of an excursion train, dressed in white like always, the only girl he knew who wore gloves that weren't for scalding chickens. It was the AME Zion youth group off on a day trip to Lake Waccamaw, laughing and shouting, and he was down on the platform with bare feet and stains on his shirt.

"Royal," she said, excited, "there's going to be a boat race!"

Junior is sleeping in the seat by the window as the passenger car clicks over the rail joints and the dark countryside rolls by. They are in uniform, but there have been no parades. The station in Washington was full of soldiers, the hearty, sunburned ones just mustered out from volunteer units that were never shipped to Cuba, and a few of the hollow-eyed men, too, regulars discharged or chasing their regiments, who had made it back. Men, black and white, like Royal, who'd had to punch another hole in their belts and cinch tight to keep their pants up, men who looked dazed as they passed through the crowded waiting room, shades among the living throng.

The porter who works the dining car, still awake, comes back to sit across from him, grinning.

"Allus likes to see another man in uniform."

It is a joke, the porter running his finger down his long row of buttons.

"Yours fits better."

"You boys was down there?"

Royal nods.

"You in the Nigger Ninth?"

Royal shakes his head. "25th Infantry."

The porter smiles and lifts his cap. "Yall was in the middle of it then. Regulars."

"That's right."

"You done us *proud*. Ever time you or the Cavalry boys or the 24th make a move down there it's all up and down the line." The porter waves a finger back and forth to indicate the rail they are riding. "This here the colored man's telephone."

Royal forces himself to smile. Since he's been back in the world the white people just look through them like always, even with uniforms on, but everywhere the colored folks stop and gladhand and want to know where they served.

"How far you headed, son?"

"Just to Wilmington," Royal tells him. "Then we'll get on something headed west, catch up with our regiment in Arizona."

"Out to the Territories."

"Fort Huachuca. Near where Chief Geronimo gave up the warpath."

"Wa-chew-ka," the porter sounds it out. "But you too young to be in on them Indian wars."

Royal nods. "I suppose now we'll just sit back and watch the jackrabbits run by. Unless the Chinamen get up in arms."

The porter chuckles. "Young man your age, you seen nearly as much of the world as me. And I *been* some places. You got people in Wilmington?"

"Yes sir. Born and raised."

"Got a gal there, I suppose."

Royal is surprised to feel his heart race at the question. He still gets dizzy if he stands up too quickly, still feels like his insides have been bruised. "I suppose I do," he answers, glancing over to Junior, snoring softly now by the window.

"She aint around, young war hero won't have no trouble findin another. If we could change uniforms for one night," the porter winks, "I be a happy man."

Alma opens the cellar door to a racket and a swirl of black dust. She shuts it quickly, grabs the house bucket and steps out back to find Wicklow shoveling the morning delivery into the chute.

"Got some of that for me?" she calls, loud enough to be heard over the rattling coal.

Wicklow turns, leans on the wide-bladed shovel and cricks his neck to the side, wincing. The Crosbys' rooster over on Queen Street is announcing himself, and the backyard is still in shadow.

"Miss Alma," he says, smiling. "My first ray of sunshine." He has a sweet tongue, Wicklow, but is never free with his hands like Calvin Hines who brings the ice. Alma always keeps her broom in hand when Calvin comes by.

"How you be this morning, Wick?"

"Sore all over, truth be known."

"You getting old."

Wick laughs. "That's true enough, young lady, but also I been helpin my boy Jubal, got the dray bidness, move Mr. Manly's press."

"He leavin town?"

"No, M'am, he only been ast to vacate his office by the white man owns the *build*ing."

"What I heard," she says as Wicklow scoops smallish chunks with his hands to fill the house bucket, "he lucky he still got his head on his shoulders. Though Lord knows what he use it for, talking like that."

"He didn't say nothin, Miss Alma, he *wrote* it. Wrote it out in his newspaper."

"That's even worst. You speak out wrong and they come after you for it, you can always tell em folks just misheard what you really said, or even that you was *drunk* when you said it, act the fool and save your neck. But to print it out in black and white—" Alma shakes her head, lifting an armful of kindling from the pile against the back wall and crossing to add it to the fire already crackling beneath the huge galvanized kettle.

"Wash day again," Wicklow remarks, watching her hips as she moves.

"Blue Monday." Boiling the clothes and linens, wringing them out and hanging them up, the endless ironing—on top of all of what she usually does for the Luncefords. "Ever damn time I turn around it come up on me."

"You got to admit," the old man continues, "wasn't nothin he wrote in his article that's un*true*."

Alma doesn't read the newspaper. She barely has time for a chapter of her love stories at the end of the day, measuring them out so a book will last a month, all through work wondering at what will befall the poor girl next and then finding out by candlelight and falling hard into sleep. But she's heard about what was written, heard that it had to do with colored men and white women, and if Manly is so smart and educated he ought to know better.

"*True* don't have one little thing to do with it," she says. She licks her finger and touches it to the kettle—getting there. She tosses a handful of the powdered bluing in. If she's lucky Miss Jessie won't lay up in bed too long and she can strip the sheets off. "You know Mrs. Beauchamp, got that big red whatever-it-is growing on the side of her neck?"

"Sits two pews ahead of me in church."

"Well then, you meet up with her on the steps, no place to look her but right in the face, and *she* know it's there and *you* know it's there—but do you say 'Lord, Mrs. B, if that aint growed twice its size since I see you last!'? You do not."

"That's just po*lite*," says Wicklow, turning back to the pile of coal. "This here with Mr. Manly not about manners, it's about *prin*ciples."

Alma snorts. "Who tole you that?"

"Mr. Manly. Last night whilst we were hauling all his machinery upstairs over the Love and Charity Hall."

"Where Doctor have his Lodge meetins."

Wicklow nods. "That's the new headquarters of the *Wilmington Daily Record*. Would you believe ever damn one of them letters they use to print the paper is made of *lead*? I'd knowed all that mess was going to the top floor I'd of told Jubal to go chase hisself."

"Manly help you carry?"

"Him and his brothers. Course Mr. Alexander that's the editor is the one that look most like a white man. Talk like one too. He wanted to, he could move off somewhere and *pass*, easy as pie."

Alma has seen the Manlys out in their carriages, has heard the story of how their grandfather was governor of the state, how the great man set their father, his son, free, even before the War.

"Don't matter how white he *look*," she says. "People read that paper they see a colored man speakin through it, and a colored man got to have more sense than just shout out whatever little idea fall into his head."

Wicklow draws himself up to his full height. "A man can't live thout principles."

"Well *I* can live without em," says Alma, picking up the coal bucket and heading inside. "Specially ones that's bound to get me lynched."

Wicklow shovels in silence for a moment after the screen door bangs, frowning and flinging the coal hard into the chute.

"Man laid out the *truth*," he mutters finally. "In black and white."

Alma feeds coal into the maw of the cooking range, flicks water on the stovetop to see if it's ready. She has the bacon sliced and the eggs ready to fry for Doctor, who will be out early on his rounds. Jessie and Mrs. Lunceford only take toast and tea before climbing back upstairs to face their corsets, but Doctor is an old farm boy no matter how he works to cover it over, and wants some fuel for the day.

The bacon is sizzling, starting to curl in its fat when someone, probably Wicklow asking about the carriage, knocks at the back door. Alma flips the slices and hurries out. It is Clerow, Hattie Pettigrew's boy, with a telegram.

"This here just come."

The telegraph office won't send their white boys to the colored houses, but their colored messengers are allowed to deliver to whites and get in the habit of coming to the back. He looks cute in his little hat, wears uniform pants too long and shoes too big. Hattie can't shut her mouth bragging about the boy, maybe because her older one is the worst hophead in the whole Brooklyn section.

"It need a reply?"

"No M'am."

She gives Clerow a penny from the dish she keeps by the door and steps back in, worried. Before the Spanish War she would have just put it by Doctor's plate at breakfast, but now, with Junior still in uniform and so many sick up north on Long Island, she hurries through the kitchen to pull the skillet off the heat. A telegram is not a letter. A letter, with Junior's handwriting on the front, means he is well enough to write it, no matter how long ago it was sent. The news inside might be bad but not the worst. A telegram is short, maybe just one hard fact in it, and Alma keeps it in her apron pocket, unread, till she is upstairs.

Doctor is doing his men's business behind a locked door so she brings it to Mrs. Lunceford, sitting in her bedroom in her dressing gown, looking pretty by the window that takes the morning light.

"This just came."

Mrs. Lunceford looks at the paper like it might be a snake in her hand.

"Leave it on the dressing table, Alma."

Except for Jessie, the Luncefords don't want her witness to their private life. The Hightowers, the white folks she kept house for just before, would scream and holler and curse and then make up with tears and little private names as if Alma wasn't standing there an arm's-length away from them. And then that mess working for the Judge and his boys—well. But she has never been seated in a room with either Doctor or Mrs. Lunceford, has never been taken into their confidence.

And still knows everything she needs to about them.

Alma waits halfway down the stairs to listen, hand gripping the banister to keep from shaking, until she hears Mrs. Lunceford cry out "Oh, wonderful!" and then she is called and rushes back up to find Mrs. L and Jessie and then Doctor, all excited and smiling cause Junior is visiting them on leave this very day.

"It's sent from Washington," says Doctor, scrutinizing the little note. "He must have just wired it from Union Station on his way."

"You're certain it's today? There's only the one sentence."

"With telegrams you pay by the word," Doctor explains. "It's a virtue to be con*cise*."

"We need to have something special—"

Jessie takes the telegram and reads it. "*Coming today on leave arrive 4:20 Love Jr.* It doesn't say how long he'll be here." She shoots a look to Alma.

"Alma," Mrs. L says again, "we'll have to have something special."

"No trouble, M'am," she smiles, and hurries back down the stairs. It *will* be trouble, with the wash and breakfast not even started and the extra cleaning that will be expected, but she feels lightheaded as she steps back into the kitchen. Junior can't be the only soldier on the train.

Jessie nibbles toast. Mother is going on about what needs to be done, what needs to be cleaned, and Father has already gotten his Lodge brothers busy setting up a reception for Junior tonight.

Their eyes meet first—his are wounded, smoldering with unexpressed longing, hers misting with the sudden release from her lonely vigil. He crosses the room with long strides, ignoring all the others, no object in his mind but her, the image he had carried through the hell of battle now real, made flesh before him, and taking her, who he has barely touched before, taking her full in his arms—

It does not seem possible, after all her thinking, all the scenarios, each different in at least one detail, that she really will see him, Royal, again, that he is a person who walks the earth and not a character from books.

"I'm just so relieved he's out of that horrible quarantine," says Mother. "The conditions he described—"

"Scandalous neglect," says Father, getting up to go on his rounds. "If the stories you read about how badly they've served the white soldiers are true, you can imagine what our colored boys have been through."

The last she'd heard of Royal was in one of Junior's letters. *Failing* had been mentioned, and *We can only pray*. Nothing from Royal himself, though Alma said she asked the carrier each day when he came by if there was anything for her. Alma never got mail at home, she said—her street, just an alley really, was not on the official route. But surely if something terrible had happened since Junior's letter he would have found a way to let her know.

There were stories told about the young woman, about her silent, almost mute demeanor, the sadness that always seemed to fall upon a room she had entered, the black gowns, always black, that she wore. The stories were only conjecture, of course,

*attempts to fathom why one so young, one so seemingly full of life should have come to
be this mysterious, selfless Sister of Help in such a remote corner of the world—*

No. It couldn't be. She would have felt something, would have sensed it
somehow. Her mother is right—there is so much to be done. If Royal is in
Wilmington and Junior does not bring him home, how will they see each
other? The one time Jessie mentioned him, in passing, at the dinner table
there was a long, strained silence until Father began complaining again
about the black layabouts in Brooklyn who made his vaccination work so
difficult. What if Royal is already sent away, off to another post in another
forsaken country? Or still in the death-camp in Hempstead?

"I suppose he'll be different," says Mother. "A man on his own."

Jessie lays her toast down and hurries upstairs to study her wardrobe.

Alma throws the last of the linens into the boiling water, poking them under
with the paddle, adds a double handful of soap flakes, then stirs the mass of it
around till soap foam comes to the surface. She has the shirtwaists, petticoats,
and collars in a pile by the starch tub, has Doctor's clothes all separated the
way he asked her to after the smallpox hit in January. She has to lean over the
kettle for leverage, working the paddle with both hands, and the rising steam
wets her face and forces her eyes shut. It's a relief when she hears Honniker's
man down the street and can leave it for a moment.

Alma pulls her wet shirt away from her body, smooths it down, and
walks around the house. Honniker's man, Simon, tall, gap-toothed, cinnamon colored, has a bell on his wagon so he doesn't need to call out. There are
always a half-dozen dogs, strays mostly, following him around town, though
he swears he never throws them a scrap.

"Alma Moultrie, needs some poultry," he smiles when she steps out to
the curb and he pulls the reins in.

"Today you right," she says to his usual greeting. "Two big fryers."

"Company coming." Simon leans back to uncover the birds and Alma
picks out a pair. Honniker mostly sells to white folks, but you can buy what
he calls the "colored cuts," the head and trotters and innards, out the back
door or off Simon's wagon. Doctor draws the line at anything below bacon
or cured ham, though. "If these low-class negroes attended to their diet," he
says, "they wouldn't fall ill all the time."

"We got Mr. Lunceford Junior coming back from the war. Usually I'd
make him a stew, but that's more time than I got today."

Simon wraps the birds in butcher paper, hands them down. "So after you got your family all squared away here, nine, ten o'clock, think you like to step out with me?"

He's a nice-looking man, Simon, and Wilma Reaves says that Lula Mae who used to live with him is gone and not coming back. But there's the chance that Clarence—Henry—whatever name he's carrying now, will show up and as tired as she is—

"Spect I'll be later than that."

"Party at Brunjes' still be goin no matter when you free."

The dogs are up around the wagon now, sniffing.

"Imonna walk into Brunjes' all by myself."

"Plenty of ladies do."

"They some that might, but they aint no ladies."

Simon laughs and twitches the reins to wake his horse up. The dogs shy away, heads low, as the wheels begin to turn.

"I'll have Mr. Honniker put this on their slip."

Wilma Reaves said he was just too good to Lula Mae, that some women need a rough man and she left to look for one.

"Simon," she calls, and he looks back to her from his seat, the motion of the wagon ringing his bell. "Ast me again sometime, you think of a nicer place to visit."

Coop is the last one off the train, checking the platform on both sides through the windows before he makes his move. There are people he doesn't want to see, not all of them lawmen. Snapper Jones is at his little stand like always, unseeing eyes a milky blue, fingers stained a half-dozen shades of polish. Coop hasn't spoken to the man in years.

"Shine?"

"Wouldn't mind one." Coop sits and props his feet up. The old man is surprisingly limber, squatting down to probe at his shoes with an oxblood finger.

"Black."

"That's right. Make em sparkle."

Snapper wipes the leather down. "New in town?"

"May as well be," says Coop. The old man's scalp is yellow brown where the hair is gone on the top. "How things workin for us these days?"

"Oh, lively, lively." Snapper taps a dab of polish onto one shoe, begins to work it in. "Repubikins got the mayor's seat again, ony there's three different gangs of em claims it. Mist' Wright seem to won out, an he aint a bad man. Then there's that old fox crowd, they's Democracks, been rilin up the peckerwoods somethin awful. Got these Red Shirts and Rough Riders—not the Teddy Rooseville kind, these is local boys—marching around, makin speeches, shootin off their pistols, say they gone make this a white man's city again."

Coop snorts a laugh. "What they think it is now?"

"I spose they won't be happy till they push us all the way back down to slavery days." Snapper starts to buff the shoetops, popping his rag. "We got three of us that's aldermen, we got police, mail carriers, Mr. Dancy who runs the Customs at the port, got Mr. Miller that own so much property he got white folks owes him money—and that don't sit right with these plantation colonels. What they want is our *vote*, see, and we aint givin that back."

"They took it in Georgia," says Coop, standing to hold the shine in the light, one foot at a time. "South Carolina too."

"Well, then, they got some sorry niggers down there."

Coop has never voted. It starts with giving your address to register, and why make it easy for them to find you? "So where's a black man ought to go after dark?" he asks, changing his tone. "I only got tonight."

Snapper glances up at him. "What you lookin for?"

"Hot dice and cold beer," says Coop. "That'll get me started."

"Oh, there's Darden's, there's Pompey Galloway's place on Castle, there's Brunjes' saloon in George Heyer's store, he allus got a crap game goin."

"Probly usin the same old bones, too. Lopsided little pocket-robbers."

Snapper grins. "I know you! You Clarence Rice, took off four, five years back!"

"That boy dead and forgotten," says Coop, tossing an extra coin into the blind man's cigar box and stepping down to go. "Let's keep him that way."

Jessie is thrilled to see her brother, of course, to feel the new strength in him when they embrace, but then there he is, Royal, standing back out of the light like a word that nobody will utter. Father is smiling, it's so wonderful to see him really smile, but when he turns to Royal it hardens somehow and her heart sinks, the impossibility of it all, the silliness of her fantasies coming home to her and she stands immobile in the spot she has chosen where the best of the afternoon light slants in, smiling prettily but no more than that, not even able to take his hand.

"I'm pleased to see you've passed the test as well, young man."

"Yes, sir."

"Scott, isn't it?"

He knows it's Scott, of course, Royal's own mother cleaned his office for years before he discovered she was selling home cures to her neighbors and had to dismiss her. Jessie's cheeks burn with embarrassment.

"Yes, sir."

Royal says it evenly, without deference, and she sees he is different too. He is thin, sickly thin, but it's like he knows something about them he didn't know when he left. Mother feels it as well, made uncomfortable, and does not call to Alma for cool drinks.

"Your mother must be so relieved to have you back," she says. "You have seen her, haven't you?"

"I'm on my way," says Royal. "Just wanted to pay my respects, M'am."

"That's very kind of you." Mother, who tells her that an awkward situation can always be defused with the proper grace and charm, Mother just smiles at him and lets the moment hang and Junior is about to step in when Royal saves him the trouble.

"Thank you M'am," he says, and turns to her and nods—only that, or is it a bit of a bow?—and says "Miss Jessie," and turns to leave.

"In the morning, old man," calls Junior.

"I'll be there."

Then he is gone and all the strength rushes out of her while Mother reacts to the hard news that Junior has only the one night to spend here before he's off to the West and Royal too, thinks Jessie, I've lost him, lost him before I ever had him! Unless, and this is all that gives her the strength to stir herself from the suddenly oppressive patch of sun and take part in the family conversation, unless she read the haunted look in his eyes correctly, the look he gave when he nodded or half-bowed to her upon leaving, a look that made her hear his voice, his true voice, inside her head.

Save me, he said. *Save me*.

Alma is in the kitchen peeling yams, one of Junior's favorites, wondering why they haven't called her out to greet him yet, she wiped that boy's nose enough times, when there is a rap at the back door. It is Royal Scott, looking tragic in a uniform too big for him.

"Little Roy," she says, wiping her hands on her apron. "Aw honey, you come back all right."

Royal nods, hands her a folded note. "Would you give this to her?"

Jessie has pestered her with a thousand questions about him, about what he's really like, about what he might think of her, but Royal has never asked Alma to go between them before. She stuffs the note in her apron pocket. It will be trouble, whatever she does with it.

"If I get a chance," she says. She thought she heard him out front before, so this is secret business, not just a hello. "You back for good?"

"Just tonight. We're chasing after the regiment."

"You know the one calls hisself Cooper?"

"He got off the train with us."

Alma smiles. "Well, sometime later, I get alone with her, I'll pass this on."

"I preciate it." He steps away.

"And tell your mama Imonna be by for more poke root."

"I'll do that."

She can hear Junior telling stories in the music room when she goes back to the yams. He'll come in, by and by, and make a fuss over her. A thoughtful boy, Junior, and she wonders if he had him one of those Cuban gals in the drawings, if he's more than his daddy's little echo after being to war. Maybe Clarence—Coop—will be by later. Man like Coop is a cool breeze in August. It don't last long, feels good when it turns your way, then leaves you sticky and wanting more. Never know when a breeze like that coming up, but you won't get through the heavy days without one.

"Alma!" cries Junior when he stomps into the kitchen. "How's my best girl?"

Early is at the crate and Coop knows it's his lucky night. A quick peek from the swinging door that leads from the store in the front—nobody here yet he's got bad blood with—and he steps up to the bar.

"Look what crawled back from the grave!" calls Brunjes, laying him down a cold one in a mug. "Must be the Judgment Day."

There is a table of young sports in the corner who look over wondering who he is, Early playing it fast and ragged, nodding to him over the keys, three or four women he doesn't recognize and the usual Harnett Street crowd. Simon Green is there, like always mimicking the sausage-eater he works for.

"*Gott im Himmel!*" he cries when he sees Coop. "*Ist der schwartzer goniff!*"

There is some back-slapping and old jokes then, a few happy to see him and the others with one nervous eye on the door. He almost killed Pharaoh

Ballard here one night, or Pharaoh almost killed him, and the police must have come sniffing round more than once after he left town.

"Somebody told me you was on a work gang down South Cahlina," says Brunjes.

"Still there," Coop gives him a look. "If you know what's what."

Little Bit appears at his elbow.

"Clarence. Gone, but not forgotten."

"Little Bit. Forgotten, but not *gone*."

The old boys laugh at this. A couple of the sports drift over.

"Way I recollect, you owes me fi' dollars."

"Damn, must of left it in my other pants."

More laughter.

"How bout that uniform, brother?" asks one of the young ones, who Coop can't place. "You was down there fightin?"

"Smack in the middle of it."

Some of the women are pressing close now. There is a short one in a green dress, little bit of a thing, got her hair in a Indian braid.

"What them Spanish look like?"

"Oh," says Coop, turning to rest his back against the bar, "mostly they look just like white folks. Dark hair, but white-complected."

"And they let you shoot em?"

"As many as I could hit."

The crowd laughs and Brunjes tops his beer off. "On the house tonight, brother."

Little Bit has stopped looking at him. "Fi' dollars aint a *pit*tance."

You don't want to take Little Bit too light. Smallish man like that, known to handle a wager, he's got to back it up with steel.

"I'd of paid you back already, brother, if *cir*cumstances hadn't come between us." A few chuckles. Coop can feel the others, especially the young ones, hoping for a fight. But he's not in the mood for one yet. "What you say," and he puts a hand on Little Bit's shoulder, "we get up a card game later, and the first fi' dollars you bet comes out of my pocket?"

It isn't a surrender and it isn't a holdout, either, and in front of all these eyes Little Bit knows it's the best he'll do without killing the man. He tips his little bowler. "I looks forward to it."

Early switches to a waltz now, but cutting it up with his right hand. After the thudding *oompah* of the regiment band it brings a smile to Coop's face.

"Almost forgot what *mu*sic sound like."

"But you got a band come with you to the battles." It's the young sport that asked about his uniform.

"Yeah, and a mule got a dick." The Indian-looking gal laughs with the others. "But aint much gonna result from it. Way the military is, everything by the *numbers*, see, which means right square on the beat."

"You carry a pistol?" Another of the young ones, more familiar.

"Officers got the sidearm—that's for shootin snakes and deserters. Fightin men, that's the sergeants on down, we carry a Krag rifle. Drill a hole in your skull a hundred yards away."

The boy, cause he is not out from his teens yet, looks once to the door before asking. "Any way a man get one of them without he's in the Army?"

Coop recognizes him. "You Twyman Wilson's brother."

"That's right."

"How he is?"

The boy shrugs. "There was a accident at Sprunt's." Sprunt owns the cotton press and half of the waterfront. "He passed."

Coop nods. "Sorry to hear that. What you want a rifle for?"

"Things getting bad."

"Things always bad."

"Fire and pitchfork bad," says Twyman's brother, and nobody contradicts him. "Man gonna need to protect himself."

Both Simon and Brunjes look away. Coop thought the blind man was only passing gas, entertaining a customer for the length of a shine.

"You try somebody in one of them volunteer outfits," he tells the boy, moving away from the counter. "Regular Army aint handin out no rifles." He takes the hand of the girl in the green dress, Early pushing the waltz tempo a bit, and calls across the room.

"Loosen them cards up, Little Bit! Imonna carry this pretty thing round the floor a couple times and then we play. What's your name, darlin?"

"Hazel," she says, not even pretending to be shy.

"Let's see what you got, young lady."

Jubal is riding. Just riding. Aint so many colored men in this town got a horse just to ride on its back, not hitched to a damn thing, and sure as hell not a horse like Nubia. He got some Arabian in him along with whatever else, got the blood and the high-stepping pride and when Jubal make him shine there aint a gal in Brooklyn won't turn her head and stare. There is men put their pay into clothes, and they do fine with the ladies, but a *ride*—

A skinny man in a blue uniform is leaning up front of his stalls and it is Royal.

Jubal jumps down and ties Nubia off and feels how much of his brother is gone, a rack of bones when he hugs him.

"I told em all," he beams. "They can't kill no Royal Scott!"

"They did their best," says Royal, quiet like always but sounding moodier with his face so thin.

"You home now?"

"One-day leave," says his brother. "Let us see our people on the way."

"You been to Mama?"

"That's next."

"She gone bust out, man, see you back and in one piece."

"You moved out."

"Couldn't take the *smell*, man. Them medicines old Minnie brew up—"

Royal laughs. "And this all is yours?"

There is a room over the two stalls, stairs to it on the outside of the building.

"I rents it from Mr. Longbaugh."

"Mind if a take a look?"

"Be my guest. I just put my ride here in with old Dan."

"That's a fine-looking horse, Jubal."

Jubal can't stop grinning. "Aint he though?"

Jubal's room smells fine. He has hung a half-dozen of Mama's lavender sachets from the low ceiling, cutting the horse odor from below. The bed is narrow but almost level, and there is a pile of clean linen on a chair, which makes Royal smile. Mama still doing his wash. There is a little window, with a view out to Swann Street and Love Alley. He sits on the bed. There are pictures of famous racehorses tacked up on the walls. It could be worse.

Jubal steps in, steps to the little basin to wash his hands.

"I been savin," he says. "Got my eye on a nice hinny mare, team her up with Dan. Once I can haul the big loads, I make some real money in this town."

Royal looks at his brother and is suddenly enormously relieved that Jubal has asked him not one thing about Army life. One colored boy they won't get to kill.

"I need to ask you a favor," he says. "Bout using this place tonight."

Jubal's grin does not change. "This aint who I think."

"The less you think," says Royal, knowing she probably won't come, that he will spend his night of leave staring at pictures of long-dead racehorses, "the better it be for all of us."

Minnie Scott always brings a rake and her collecting basket. The rake is for the acorns, which can pile up inches deep on the graves in the late fall, rotting underneath, getting musky and black if you don't keep on top of them. There aren't so many headstones here in Oak Grove, sometimes just a rock with a name scratched on it or a rusted child's toy or something about the departed. One man who was a plumber before he gambled it all away is under a cross made of pipe, and another beneath a dented, discolored trumpet. Leaper, gone to Glory these many years, has a proper stone now, that she was able to buy and have scribed. But that's only for the sake of the living. The Lord don't care what you lay on top, He's only after souls.

Minnie rakes his site clear, acorns making a neat little rectangle around it when she is done. He was a good man, Leaper, never raised a hand to her or the children, did his best to find work. But the weakness for spirits was there from the beginning, it dogged him his whole poor life and left them nothing to send him off with when he turned yellow and died. Most of her family was in Pine Forest behind the white folks, but they were all so cross at Leaper, even her brother Wick and Reverend Christmas at the Central Baptist, that they let the town bury him here.

"No sense pourin money into a hole," Wicklow said when she came to him. "Just like when he was with us, you give him money, you knowed what it was going for."

Leaper had said it himself, coming home sweet and unsteady, sitting hard at the table and looking around like he could barely recognize his own house. Then smiling that beautiful smile when he'd see her, smile that could break your heart. "There's my girl," he would say. "There's my Minnie." And then later, after she'd helped him out of his clothes and maybe bathed him, he'd say in that far-off voice he got when he was tired, "When I go, just lay me out in the Oaks."

She blames it on the yankees. The first story he told anyone about himself was him and Jimmy Shines tippin off one night from the indigo plantation, ten years old, stealing a boat and rowing out to the blockade ships. How they shouted and banged their oars on the hull of one till the yankees hauled them up, how Jimmy fell out of the ropes and drowned a few days after but Leaper, they give him a little sailor suit and made him mascot and filled him up with rum most every day, setting him up on a box to sing dirty songs and curse the Rebels. And him thinking it was all right since he was already bound for Hell, having robbed Mr. Ralston of himself and Jimmy.

"I caught a taste for rum," he like to say, "that I never lost."

Minnie bends carefully to wipe the headstone clean. She's got the water on the knee now, too many years cleaning floors and pulling up roots, not so easy to get back off the ground. Taking liquor isn't a sin, not the way some would have it, it's how you act once the liquor is in you. Leaper called it "his medicine" and without it he would brood, he would lay up in the house without moving for a whole day, or if he thought she couldn't hear he'd weep like a child. The only people he had were sold away before he came to know them, and when the boys was born he would look but never touch, smile at her admiringly like a baby was something she'd done on her own. The *Royal Scot* was the name of the blockade ship, and he had taken Scott for his name when a yankee census man came through to count heads and explain the voting. Leaper had been one of Mr. Ralston's favorite hounds that he said was the same shade of brown as the little nigger boy and as many times as Minnie begged him to be born again as someone with a Christian name, Luther maybe, he wouldn't have it.

"If a man's name not even the truth," he'd say, "than what about him *is?*"

Minnie stops to pick some goldenseal that grows just beyond the oak trees, pulling the plants up, shaking the root clean and stuffing them in her basket. Wilma Reaves's daughter has the pinkeye again.

She takes the long way home, stopping in a stand of pines on the way to gather some deertongue.

She believes that the Lord listens to prayer, but is mighty picky about which ones He answers. "Please, Lord," she would beg every night, sacrificing her knees one last time before sleep, "deliver my man from that devil's brew." And maybe He tried, as He is a merciful Lord, but Leaper had as tight a hold on rum as it had on him. Neither Jubal nor Royal never took up with it, praise Jesus, and she lies in bed worrying about her younger son been off to this Cuba, which Reverend Christmas says is one of the islands where they make it.

It is a long and halting two-horse trolley ride back toward the river and then having to pay again to transfer onto the new electric line. No wonder the acorns build up, she thinks, moving to the front since there's no old horse's behind to smell on this one—poor folks can't afford to get out there. The car is crowded enough by the time they pass Queen Street that the white man who has avoided sitting beside her for three blocks finally surrenders and stiffly takes the seat, body angled so his feet are in the aisle. The Jim Crow has come as far up as Charleston, she knows, but here it is still just a rumor. The man hurries off at City Hall and Minnie can relax till the depot and then take up walking again. By the time she turns down Terry's Alley the sun is low and she is exhausted, bone-weary from cleaning Judge Manigault's house all day, man can't keep no permanent help even with his boys gone, weary from raking at the cemetery and picking the herbs and knowing it will start again before sunrise tomorrow. Halfway to her door she smells the yarrow, overpowering the rest of what she's got hanging and drying inside. It takes her eyes a moment to adjust, someone standing inside, a flicker of fear and then her knees gone to water as she realizes who it is, how skinny he's gotten. She drops the rake and the basket.

"Royal! My poor baby! What them people done to you now?"

The Love and Charity Hall is full to bursting when they step in, almost all the Lodge membership present plus a smattering of Masons and a few of the city's unaffiliated colored men of importance. Mr. Lowery the carriage maker is holding forth in one corner and Reverend Moore from St. Luke's next door and Valentine Howe with a crowd of firemen past and present and at least two of the Manly brothers, who have apparently moved their newspaper operation to the floor above. John Dancy from Customs is already seated, looking up patiently as old Mr. Eagles, elegant as always, jabs his silver-headed cane to make a point.

"I want to know the purpose," he is saying, "of raising hopes, of assembling a fighting force, of the training, of the marches and the grandiose speeches, when all along they knew we'd be mustered out before the first angry shot was fired!"

Mr. Eagles accepted a commission with the North Carolina Volunteers and feels used. There was much public contention over whether officers would be white or colored for the colored companies, and the regiment's sudden dismissal in February, with the halfhearted explanation that there were already sufficient forces to defeat the Spaniards, was at least an embarrassment to him, if not an insult.

"The marching and the speeches *were* the purpose," says Dr. Lunceford in passing and is treated to a glare. They are on opposite sides of the Russell question, the "Black Eagle" a regular, arguing that the governor should be supported no matter what his printed disparagement of the race, while the Doctor has joined Lowery and Fred Sadgwar and some of the others to form the Independents around the issue of "character." And him walking in with Junior, a soldier fresh from battle, can only be salt in the old man's wounds.

Junior is smiling and shaking hands, modest but firm, grown up in so many ways so rapidly, and the Doctor has a sudden rush of hope that it might be here, Wilmington, that the tide is turned, here that a final, desperate battle against ignorance and disenfranchisement is fought and won. Such hopes had been pinned on young men before, Lowery and Eagles carried the burden in their own day, but look at him, Aaron Jr., handsome, educated, confident—and a war hero. Dr. Lunceford's own father bore arms for the cause, and was wounded at New Market Heights, and now Junior—

"Got to be a proud day for you, Dr. Lunceford." Dorsey Love, moving up behind him.

Dr. Lunceford nods. "A very proud day."

"A credit to his race," says the barber, smiling admiringly at Junior as he fends off compliments a few yards away. Dorsey cuts white people's hair at the Orton Hotel, owns a shop on Brunswick where his employees serve negroes.

"I can only hope that the credit will be rendered."

"Oh, they got to take note, Doctor, *got* to take note. That San Juan Hill—"

"Junior was at El Caney."

"That too, that too. And how is your lovely wife?"

"Mrs. Lunceford is well. Extremely happy for a visit from her son, of course."

"And little Miss Jessie?"

The barber always calls her "little Miss" to disguise his interest, but the Doctor is not fooled. Love is a decent sort, industrious, a man of property, but uneducated. He has no more chance of success than that Royal boy who always attaches himself to Junior in order to skulk around her.

"She has a recital coming up in November, after the election. And of course, she'll be off to Fisk soon."

If the mention of the University fazes Dorsey Love in any way he does not reveal it. He has a constant, bemused smile, perhaps a manner he's adapted for his profession, as if life is a perpetual wonder.

"That's a clever girl you got, Dr. Lunceford," says the barber, shaking his head at the unique quality of the phenomenon. "Gonna make a prize for some lucky gentleman."

Dr. Lunceford reminds himself to have a word with Junior about the Scott boy before he leaves tomorrow. The way he looks at Jessie—those people, well-meaning some of them but bone ignorant, living over in the Brooklyn section with their liquor and their crime and their disease. When the small-pox hit in January he was asked, with Dr. Mask, to administer the vaccination program. One would expect open arms, gratitude, at the least a grudging submission to the public good. But instead they were met with suspicion, with lies, with violence. After Dr. Mask's carriage was despoiled and him-self threatened by a drunkard wielding an ax, they petitioned to be relieved of the duty unless law officers were dispatched to accompany them. It was superstition, of course, distrust and fear of the unknown stirred up by those jealous folk practitioners, like Scott's own mother Minerva, who persist in bilking their neighbors with roots and potions and Indian cures despite the legal prohibitions. Had she not accepted vaccination herself, and made no observable effort to dissuade others, he would have had her arrested.

Isham Joyner has the gavel by now, rapping the gathering to order.

"Gentlemen, if you'd please arrange yourselves!" Isham loves his voice like a preacher, and is always the one chosen to recite epic poems or quote Patrick Henry's exhortations on Emancipation Day. The men still standing begin to find seats.

"Brothers of the canton, honored guests, this is not an official meeting of our Lodge, and we will dispense with the customary observances and invo-cations." He is the Noble Grand Sire and a stickler for protocol, Isham, a stern master of rites when Degrees are awarded. Dr. Lunceford is a Patriarch himself, Treasurer of the Lodge, but is uncomfortable with the swordplay and passwords, the mysteries and symbols, the play-acting around Abram's Tent and the Oak of Mamre. He would be content to *visit the sick, relieve the distressed, bury the dead, and educate the orphan*" without any of the baroque ceremony, but perhaps his Brothers' secret, allegorical selves are preferable to their everyday ones.

"We have gathered instead to honor and to listen to remarks from a young man who not long ago was my pupil—" Isham tutors Latin in the foyer of his undertaking business, "—but, as we will see, he has survived that ignoble apprenticeship to become a guiding star among our youth."

Isham spotted Junior first when the young boy's oration on Remembrance Day overshadowed his own. What to do with the competition but take some part in, and therefore some credit for, its development? Latin was a must for a medical career, of course, but Junior has always exhibited more interest in the Doctor's political efforts than in his profession.

"To introduce this paragon, I cede the floor to one who took part in his development at a much earlier stage than I—" laughter here, "—Dr. Lunceford?"

Polite applause as he steps to the podium they've pulled out from behind the bar.

An excellent turnout, really, Fusionists, many of the more wary Republican die-hards, men who voted but chose to leave their allegiances unspoken, even a few who owe fealty to the Old Fox Crowd, employees or functionaries of powerful white men or those, like Dorsey Love, who are under their constant scrutiny. In light of the racial enmity that has been so publicly encouraged in the state, all will need to pull together to survive this next election, and he hopes this common celebration, this moment of shared pride, will help drive that idea home.

"When Mr. DuBois," he begins, knowing that the mention of that controversial gentleman's name will assure their attention, "speaks, as he often does, of the 'Talented Tenth'—and I would argue that we can boast of a much higher percentage than that—he is being both practical and political."

He sees that Alex Manly is already scribbling. A word to him later about editorial restraint.

"It does not ordinarily, in this section of the country, behoove us to celebrate our gains too openly. However, the showing made by our colored regiments in the recent conflict—" and here there is more hearty applause, "—brings credit to all of us. I confess my particular pride in sheltering one of these fine young men under my roof. Gentlemen, I present to you—Aaron Lunceford Jr."

Men stand on their feet when his son takes the podium. Dr. Lunceford has made many speeches, has won election to a post vital to the community's welfare, has saved lives even, in his professional capacity, but men have never stood to applaud him. He could be the one, Junior, to build it on. An orator, a tactician, a man with the sound of cannons on his record. A black Bryan, perhaps, a stirrer of men's souls.

Junior looks the gathering over slowly before speaking.

"We are honored tonight to have in our midst men who defended the Union, and I need not add, freed our people, bringing us honor as they fought beneath the flag in the desperate days of '64," says Junior, bowing to old John Eagles sitting ramrod straight in the first row. "I have had the honor of carrying that banner to a foreign shore to liberate its oppressed citizens, many of them of our own hue, and can only hope that our performance there is a worthy reflection on the glory of those illustrious patriots."

A black Lincoln, thinks Dr. Lunceford, but a handsome one.

Later, Alma will decide that she was just too weary to oppose it. Her own clothes are hanging between lines of the Luncefords' sheets, Mrs. L never objecting as long as she keeps them hidden from the neighbors, and dry by the time Jessie reveals her plan. Or is it pure treachery? They pay her a bit more and treat her at least as well as any of the white folks she has worked for, but there is something about Doctor's tone with her, about the way Mrs. L always says "a young lady of her standing" when she's talking about Jessie. White folks don't know any better, plus they're white and don't need to do anything to be sure nobody mistakes them for the help.

And Jessie has treated her as a sister.

Nothing will come of it, of course, no matter what kind of goodbye they say to each other tonight. Soon enough they'll ship her off out of sight to the school in Tennessee like they did with Junior, where she'll play her piano and make friends with other "young ladies of her standing" and meet someone Doctor will approve of. Doesn't hurt a girl to have a little heartbreak at her age, get used to what's in store for her.

If Coop was coming he'd of been here by now.

"It fits me perfectly," says Jessie, excited, turning in front of the mirror to see herself in Alma's gray shift. It is, in fact, a little high at the ankle for her, but uncorseted and wearing a pair of old shoes Mrs. L has ceded to Alma, she even moves like a different person. "Are you sure about your coat?"

"I got all my clothes in a basket by the cookstove," says Alma. "I'll just bundle up."

Mrs. Lunceford is at the Household of Ruth meeting, bragging about her son, and gave up looking in on her sleeping Jessie years ago. They have worked out which light will signal what in the house—Jessie has promised to be home at least by ten but there is some little risk of her running into Doctor or Junior when she's sneaking back.

"Tell me which way you gonna walk, child. Don't matter what you passin for, they places won't no woman go by if she got sense."

Jessie sighs dramatically, impatient, and crosses to her dressing table to read the crumpled note from Royal again. "This isn't the worst part of the city," she says.

"You don't know the first thing bout what's bad in this city. Let me hear the street names."

"Why should I feel like a criminal?" It is one of her favorite sayings lately, along with "They're determined to ruin my life." Jessie stands next to Alma, looks at the two of them in the mirror. Jessie is lighter of course, younger, with the good hair and the way of holding herself that says Quality to folks who never seen her before. "Sometimes, Alma, I am so envious of you."

Alma smiles. She will pay for this, maybe, if it ever becomes known, but now she is too tired or too weak or too low and contrary to deny her sweet baby Jessie this wish.

"You want to change places with me, darlin," she says, "there's a mess of dirty dishes waitin downstairs."

Miss Loretta always says to Jessie that it is the things she never did that haunt her.

Ruth Hall, where her mother is meeting, is just on the corner. Jessie hurries by, hoping she looks like someone else. She plays at the Hall when there are musical programs, the ladies always very kind, but tonight she doesn't want them to see her face. She hurries north on Seventh, passing the Williston School that somebody, and Father has his suspects, keeps trying to burn down, and wishes she had a shawl to cover her face with like in the books. Anyone who knows her family who sees her will report back—What was your daughter Jessie doing out alone at night, dressed in serving girl's clothing? She hasn't been allowed to walk alone like this since she was twelve and even if she were only to circle the block and return home right now it would feel like a wicked transgression. She crosses Ann Street, crosses Orange, then Dock, then stops at the edge of Market to look up and down. Across the way looms the MacRae castle where once as a little girl she stood outside with Father and was frightened by the screeling of bagpipes, Father telling her it was only a kind of music the white folks had played across the seas before they invaded America. Right next door is Mr. MacRae's sister who married Mr. Parsley. It was on the street just in front that their little Walter Jr. had run out and been hit by a bicyclist last year, the shades pulled down in their windows ever since, a house in mourning. Jessie waits for a carriage to pass, then hurries across the broad avenue to the north side, tilting her face away as she sees the city lamplighter, Primus Bowen, with his ladder against a pole up on Eighth. Miss Loretta lives on that corner, and just beyond her Carrie Sadgwar who was famous with the Jubilee Singers and teaches at the Williston now, whose grandfather was a white man raised as a slave and whose father is building a house down on Fourteenth for her to live in with Alex Manly, the newspaper man, when they are married.

She continues up Seventh, using the sidewalk on the east side, and realizes she knows who lives in almost every house, black or white or Jew—the Solomons and the Davids and the Bears all off to her left within a few blocks of each other—knows who is related and what their businesses are, knows, from hearing Father and Junior talk, where each of the men stands in the complicated tangle of city and state politics, and she feels a wave of hopelessness course through her. How can she imagine being anyone but Miss Jessie, daughter of Dr. and Mrs. Lunceford, who plays piano and sings passably well, soon to be presented in colored society for the consideration of young men whose fathers know and have the deepest respect for her own? "We must set a standard," he is always saying, mostly to Junior, but she is included within her more circumscribed sphere of activity, "that others will strive to raise themselves to."

But here she is walking unaccompanied and "unbraced" as the Shakespeare play put it, in an increasingly strange part of the city, to meet a man she loves—

The gas lamps end at Red Cross Street. Jessie finds herself caught in a flow of people, mostly older women, making their way into the Central Baptist for an evening service. They are dressed for church, of course, and she is not, but they might expect her to be one of them—floor-scrubbers and pot-washers, laundresses, seamstresses, cooks and caretakers. Aunt Sassy— she never learned the woman's proper name—who was her great friend Fannie Daltrey's nanny when Fannie lived on Front Street, passes within a foot of her, walking with difficulty on swollen legs, a hat with glistening raven feathers fastened on her head. The woman barely glances as she goes by. Mrs. Sharpless, who Father treated for palpitations and who sold pecan clusters at the train station for years, looks her full in the eyes with no recognition, no "How we doin, Miss Jessie?" and maybe it is working, maybe the clothes and Alma's simple, fraying straw hat tilted low over the eye have transformed her. She rushes to cross the street away from the church entrance, and has only taken a few steps into the darkness beyond the spill from its open doors when the crazy man blocks her way.

"Tender chicken," he says, smiling with all his face, "pitter-pat away from her roost."

His clothes are filthy, his face streaked with grime, his hair hangs in gnarly ropes past his narrow shoulders. He is the skeleton of a man who calls himself Percy of Domenica, King of the Creole, and appears throughout the city with his message of Repentance.

"You frighten of Percy, child?"

She could run, turn and run back toward the Baptists shouting for help, but that would be the end of it, would mean explanations and recriminations and the end of trust and liberty. "No sir," she tells him.

"Little chicken tell me proper." He waves a Coca-Cola bottle in his hand, the liquid inside it not the right color. "Only ting we got to fear now is the Wicked One come out when sun is down, work himself into our heart." People say he is from the islands, which ones they don't know, and his speech is like song. "You let the sun shine on your body, child?"

"I do."

"*All* your body?"

He is blocking the sidewalk but not crowding her. She saw him almost on this very spot, last year when she talked Alma into taking her to the tent that had been set up to exhibit the Nightingale. It was ten cents admission, collected by a man who claimed to be a Doctor of Deformity and sold the sisters' pamphlet, "Written by One of Them," which contained the details of their unfortunate birth and subsequent adventures. But once inside Mille-Christine McCoy herself recounted those events. Mille, who was on the left as you faced the Nightingale, concentrating on the harrowing incidents of kidnapping and privation, while Christine countered with tales of rescue and impressions of European nobles they had met in their travels. As they demonstrated their facility with six languages, sang prettily in close harmony, employing all four legs and all four arms as they moved about the platform, Jessie was so enthralled she did not notice who it was who took the seat beside her. It was his odor that distracted her first, sweet and thick, like over-ripe pears, and then his constant chuckling drew her to look.

"God make a joke," he said as the sisters were reciting *The Rhyme of the Ancient Mariner*, Mille in English and Christine in German. "Bond two woman together, give them only one hole for pizzle, one for poop."

Tonight he smells of persimmons.

"Do you let the sun shine on *all* your body?"

"Whenever possible," she answers.

The King of the Creole smiles again with all his face. "The High Spirit loves you, child. How many year you got?"

"I'm sixteen." She thinks of telling him she's older, to seem less vulnerable perhaps, but his gaze, guileless and unblinking, has her transfixed.

"Then you must fast for sixteen day, purify the soul. You promise Percy this?"

"I will do my best." She has fasted once for two days, after reading *Robinson Crusoe*, pushing her plate away at every meal until Father gave her a dose of ipecac, thinking she had been poisoned by tinned fruit.

"Percy sense a young woman at her crossroad, cyannot decide which trail to accept."

"I don't—"

"*For*ward. Always forward to the Light. The Wicked One dog our passage—turn back and we are lost forever." He holds the Coca-Cola bottle out to her. "But first you must partake from the Source."

"I really couldn't—"

"Cyannot refuse the Blood of Christ, child! Drink, and it make holy everting you do this night."

Jessie holds the neck so it doesn't touch her lips, tilts the bottle. It is warm, just water, and she manages to swallow a tiny bit. Percy smiles and takes the bottle from her and steps aside with a gallant half-bow.

"Go forth, then," he says, "and mul-ti-ply."

He moves aside and she walks toward the river, resolute, the lunatic's blessing filling her with courage, till she turns right to cross over the railroad bridge into Brooklyn. The gaslights are far behind her and the grand houses too and the paint is peeling on many of these houses, or was never applied, someone is making frightening noises on a piano a few blocks ahead but this is the only way, the way to save Royal, to save the two of them, to come to him in servant's clothes and do something she can barely imagine.

Something irreversible.

Coop is leaving Hazel, smelling her on his clothes, when Toomer steps out with his hand on his pistol. They stand a few yards apart, facing each other, Coop feeling himself reel slightly with the gin that followed the beer, and stare at each other's uniforms. Toomer laughs first.

"Who you steal that from, Clarence?"

They are on Brunswick Street, just the two of them. Toomer keeps his hand on top of the holster.

"Second squad, Company H, 25th Infantry," says Coop. "And what you sposed to be doin?"

"Keeping the peace. Protecting folks from the likes of you."

"I'm just passing through, man—"

"Far as I know," says the police officer, "you still a fugitive round here."

"White people's bidness."

"I work for the law. Law cuts both ways."

"Yeah? They let you 'rest a white man?"

"If it come up, that's my *job*. Only don't many of em show their faces this part of town."

"So you out keepin us wild niggers in line."

"Let's say old Pharaoh Ballard come around, find out some soldier boy passin through has been next to his gal Hazel," says Toomer, easing his hand off the holster and hooking his thumb in his belt, "and Pharaoh commenced to waving his blade around and bragging how he's gonna cut a certain lowlife son of a bitch up for fishbait." Hazel didn't say nothing about Pharaoh, but it make sense she got somebody. "It be my responsibility to advise him to reconsider, and if he go ahead and do it, to bring him to justice."

"That happens, you best shoot before he sees you."

Toomer nods. He was the best pitcher on the Cape Fear Mutuals when Coop left, a long-armed house-painter whose brother Granville owned a furniture store Coop and Tillis had hit once. "You understand my position."

"I didn't come here to mess with him."

"Then you best stay clear of the waterfront. He get off his shift at Worth and Worth in a half hour."

If he was staying they'd need to have it out, him and Pharaoh, no way he was skulking around Brooklyn avoiding a fight. But passing through like this—

"Don't spect we'll meet up."

"How long you plannin to be in town, Clarence?"

"When the westbound pull out this morning at seven," he says evenly, holding Toomer's eyes so the man knows it's his own choice and not the threat, "I be on it."

Toomer smiles. "25th Infantry. The heroes of Santiago."

"That's us."

"*With feet to field and face to foe,*" he intones, "*In lines of battle lying low— The sable soldiers fell!*"

"That's the Ninth. We were on a different hill."

"Lots of folks walking tall in this city when that news hit town." Toomer steps aside to let Coop pass. "You done more than free them Cubans, brother."

It smells like lavender. She is shaking so hard, even just hurrying up the stairs outside, that he thinks she is freezing and takes Alma's coat off her and holds her tight. The shaking calms down some but he kisses her on the mouth and it starts up again and she says she's sorry.

"Got nothin to be sorry about," he says.

They both know what they are up to, though. That going all the way through with it means there is no going back, not for Mother and Father either. It is the only way. Jessie can hear the animals stirring below, hooves on hollow wood, snortings and shiftings. *Once the horse is out of the barn*—she has heard her father say it more than once, treating ruined girls over in this section of town or closer to home.

Royal is looking her straight in the eye, his face so close it makes her shake even more. "I just got to know," he says, "that this is what you want."

Jessie takes his hand then and places it over her breast, something she read once in one of Alma's love books. She doesn't have much there, she knows, and she is still in the shift, but in the books it is always how the chapter ends and you've got to imagine what happens next.

She nods.

On the bed he puts his hand on her thigh, Alma's shift riding up, and then he moves his fingers under. She never thought of that, even when touching herself. The shaking stops and she has to breathe deep and he is still looking at her, that is the most incredible thing of all, looking deep into her eyes right as it is happening. She reaches down and curves his fingers just the right way, leans herself against him and closes her eyes when it happens. Amazing that he would know. Even this much, she thinks, if I went home now having done even this much maybe they would be forced to reconsider, but she sees how his pants are, just like Alma told her they get, and knows there is going to be more.

His bare skin is reddish in the lantern light, darker than hers, and she is glad there are no mirrors on the walls, only pictures of beautiful horses. How did he know how much she loves them?

She is shaking again and really cold now, she is never naked except in a warm bath, and he has her squat on the edge of the bed facing him and then lower herself down. Junior showed her a picture in one of Father's medical books once, but it was pink and wrinkly and not hard like this. This is not in Father's book, this is not in any book she has ever read or imagined.

"Easy," he says in her ear, "easy."

And it is like when Alma draws the bathwater too hot, you have to let yourself down a little at a time and maybe come back up a little bit and then ease down and the second time down it isn't so bad, a little farther, a little deeper, and then suddenly you are all the way in and it only stings for a tiny instant.

"I can't believe this," Royal says, looking at her, their faces even closer now, his eyes digging into her and she kisses him so maybe he will close them. He has his tongue up past hers, even that, they even put that up into you.

When she opens her eyes he is still looking.

"We won't get stuck, will we?"

He smiles. He has a kind smile, never teasing. "You mean like dogs? That doesn't happen to people."

"You're sure?"

He takes hold of her under and lifts all of her up a little and then eases her down, once, twice, three times. She must be wet or he must be wet because it slides. "If it could happen, there's nobody I rather be stuck with than you."

Who is doing this? she thinks as he somehow lifts her around so she is on her back and he is standing on the floor with it still in her, pointing down. She is not wearing Alma's clothes anymore, not any of them, and when he pushes it deeper, if that is possible, it is her name he whispers hot into her ear.

"Jessie. Jessie Lunceford."

He is as beautiful, in the lantern light, as she imagined, thinner even, muscles and bones standing out under his beautiful dark skin as he pushes in again and again and now each time she can't help but squeeze it a little, like you do when you hold your water, like she won't let him pull it back.

"Jessie," he says, "I can't hold back anymore," and then he sighs deep and lays heavy on top of her, holding her tight.

He is the one shaking when he steps away and cleans himself off at the basin and then brings the lantern over to look at her closer.

"Sorry," he says. "I been sick."

"Something you can catch?"

She means it as a joke, but he doesn't smile.

They don't talk much after, Jessie telling him no, he shouldn't write to Father, not yet. She has no idea what time it is. They lie under a rough blanket for a while, her cheek on his chest, listening to his heart beat, and she wishes she could sleep here, sleep and then wake to discover it is fine, everyone has agreed and they will be allowed to be this way forever. Jessie reaches up and touches his face, moved by the incredible fact that this is now something allowed between them, that for the moment she owns this right, at least while they are alone together. The books are no use now. *Debased* has no meaning for her, nor *virtue* or *ruined*, the familiar litany of traps for the young and foolish do not seem to apply. She cannot imagine, now, being Alma—how can she have been intimate with more than one man, how can the heart bear it?

"I should start home," she says.

"You're not walking," says Royal. "Not alone."

How can he know?

It was her very first dream of him—night, black night with a full moon and her arms around him and the horse's body hot between her legs, no saddle, just the power of the muscles flowing. And waking out of breath.

"What does he call it?" she asks as Royal guides the beautiful horse over the railroad bridge.

"Nubia," he says, eyes wary for whoever might be out this late. "I think he calls him Nubia."

Alma has left the back door unlatched. Jessie finds her asleep in a hard chair in the kitchen. She frowns when she wakes, taking Jessie's hand and looking her in the eye.

"Child, I'm sorry. Don't know what I was thinking."

"I promise you won't get into any trouble."

"Not me I'm worryin about."

Jessie turns away from Alma's eyes. "Did yours come?" Alma has let it slip about her soldier being in town.

"Not a sign of him." Alma crosses to the range, rubbing her eyes, lays a pot on the heat. "You gonna drink some tea."

Jessie sniffs the few inches of brown liquid in the pot. "What's in it?"

Alma shrugs. "Squawroot, pennyroyal, little bit of rum." She doesn't add that she bought the herbs from Royal Scott's mother, for her own use, a few months ago. "If you been up to what I think, you need to drink some."

Jessie wrinkles her nose. "I don't think so."

"You got five, six weeks I can maybe help you, girl," says Alma, pulling down Jessie's favorite cup. "After that you in the hands of the Lord."

*   *   *

Royal puts the horse back in its stall, rubs it down. Steam comes off the sides of the animal as he works, and he can feel his own muscles, feel the blood moving in him again, back with the living. Just maybe on his way to being somebody in the world instead of a little barefoot nigger whose daddy had a dog's name. The horse is asleep and the sun just rising by the time he locks up and starts for the train station. He falls in with the early shift heading for the docks, many of them, the colored workers, asking about his uniform and reciting the highlights of the campaign. Ben Chesnutt is among them, and Moses Toney and Nat Washington who he knew from his days working at the creosote yard, and Vernel Underwood who played left field to his center on the Mutuals.

"Always knew you was gonna turn out o.k.," says Vernel, winking. "No matter what anybody say."

Henry Cooper is there, dozing on a bench, Junior a few feet away looking unshaven and exhausted.

"I feel like I'm running for governor," says Junior as Royal sits.

"Your daddy has his way, you be doing that soon enough."

"How's your mother?"

"Fine. Living along."

"Jubal?"

"Jubal got his horses, keeps him happy I guess."

Coop wakes then, making a face. "Mouth feel like cotton," he says. "And that water fountain is bust." He looks at them, disoriented. "Yall made it."

"With time to spare."

Coop stretches, yawns. "Met a gal last night, like to wore me out. How bout you, Roy? You plant the flag somewheres?"

Royal knows he's just ribbing, but with Junior looking at him, a little smile on his face, the question prompts a guilty sweat.

"Naw," says Royal. "Just took care of some family bidness."

THE MARCH
OF THE FLAG (II)

Hod and the others walk toward Fort San Antonio Abad in double file, wading knee-deep in the river where it spreads and spills into the sea. To the left he can see Dewey's ships steaming parallel to them, moving into position for the attack. It is cold still, having rained all night, and the men clutch their rifles with grim resolve. There has been shooting and shelling almost every night since they replaced the Filipinos in the positions facing the fort, but nothing much to shoot back at. Rumors of surrender without a fight have been running through the regiment, but here they are, marching straight into it. There is no cover as they climb up onto the sand and move forward toward the stone walls, only the Bay to the left and the flat beach ahead. A perfect killing ground.

"Fear not, gentlemen," says Niles, or Lieutenant Manigault as he must now be called. "This is mere formality. Our worthy adversaries have their backs to the ocean and a hundred thousand overexcited niggers seething at the gates. They know we've come to preserve their posteriors."

Niles hints that he is privy to the inside dope, that the men with stars on their shoulders confide in him, that today's action will be a stroll in the park. But even he flinches at the first percussive boom of the cannon.

"It's the Admiral, gentlemen," he calls out, recovering. "He'll soften them up for us."

Smoke coughs out from the five-inch guns of the ships, broadside to the Spaniards, in a piston-like sequence. The return fire from the shore battery is sporadic and ineffectual. They are close enough now to see chunks of masonry flying from the seaward walls whenever Dewey's guns find their mark.

"If the Dagoes haven't shot me by now," says Big Ten, walking big as a house just behind Manigault, "they aint even trying."

The barrage is a brief one, followed by much wig-wagging of signal flags on board the *Olympia* and atop the wall of the Spanish fort, and then there is only the sound of the waves spilling out over the sand. The fort looks something like a beached stone vessel, triangular in shape, with cannon on the parapet walks and poking out from holes in its walls, several of them, it seems to Hod, pointing directly at him. Major Moses organizes them, Hod's 2nd Battalion spreading out on the sand in support of the firing line before them, and then it begins. Rifle fire from the Spanish trenches in the sand in front of the fort now, a thin whining of Mauser balls overhead, and now and then a Dago running frantically to get the fort between him and the advancing volunteers. Hod holds his rifle ready but does not fire as they walk forward. He feels very calm. Not me, he thinks. Not today. If they're really shooting at us, why aren't rounds kicking up the sand?

There is a hatless correspondent scampering ahead of the firing line, pausing here and there to snap with his Kodak—now toward the fort, now turning back to photograph the approaching Coloradans.

"Get the hell out of there, you stupid son of a bitch!"

It is Colonel Hale himself, shouting over a megaphone, advancing along with the reserve line.

"I'll have you thrown in the brig!"

The correspondent, looking sheepish, stops to allow the firing line to pass him.

Three dead Spaniards have been left like rags, tangled in the sand, when they enter the first of the trenches. Some officer, thinks Hod, some boss told them to sit there and put up a fight or go to jail or maybe be shot if they didn't. Big Ten turns to look at the reserve line behind them, still advancing.

"I could hit those stiffs from here with my eyes closed."

"What did I say?" Niles waves his walking stick toward the fort. "More of a foregone conclusion than a test of arms."

"You don't think it's a trap? Drawing us in?"

"I think," says Lieutenant Manigault, strolling ahead, "they're all back in the city by now, packing their valises."

The fort is unmanned by the time they enter. A few dead left from the naval barrage, a boy soldier who has shot himself in the foot so he won't have to flee and be killed somewhere farther up the beach.

"Check inside," says Niles as men scatter in groups to search the structure. Hod and Big Ten flank the doorway to one of the low stone buildings, one corner of it collapsed from the bombardment.

"I'll throw it open," says Big Ten, "and you shoot anybody who makes a fuss."

Hod positions himself on one knee, sighting down his rifle, and Big Ten yanks the door. Inside the room is packed with soldiers sitting or lying down, covered in blood. A man with a Red Cross band on his arm turns to look at Hod and says something in Spanish. He does not seem grateful to have been saved from the Filipinos.

Diosdado now regrets the uniform. The old Chinaman wrapped strips torn from the margin of a newspaper around his arms and legs, penciling measurements and mumbling to himself. It fits perfectly, white cotton drill for the jacket and pants, sturdy canton for his shirt, and looks not unlike the other officers' dress, but the *taos* they have assigned to him regard it with a mixture of awe and resentment. Sargento Bayani, who they turn to for confirmation every time Diosdado issues an order, seems only amused.

"If I were a *fusilero*," says Bayani, "I would forget all the others and aim at the one in the pretty suit."

Diosdado has them spread out along the puddle-filled trenches left by the retreating Spaniards a week before, a defense line of earthworks now and then reinforced with logs and topped with sandbags that stretches the full mile from here out to Fort San Antonio on the coast. When the *yanqui* ships began their shelling he sent runners to bring the remainder of his platoon from their homes, but none have come back yet. General Luna throws a daily tirade against this practice of treating the army like any other job and walking back to your family at the end of a shift, but the Tagalog officers only make faces behind his back and tell their men to be prompt in returning.

"*Bahala na*," shrugs Bayani with seeming indifference. "As long as they leave their rifles at the front, it's probably better to have them out of the way."

And now the sun has broken through the clouds and the *yanquis* seem to be marching north to Manila.

A thick column of them stumble out of the inland swamps behind the line and spread out along the muddy entrenchments, big men like all

Americans, each one with his own new-looking rifle, glancing with curiosity and mistrust at Diosdado's cheering platoon. Caught up in the moment, several of his men stand and begin to shoot into the trees in the general direction of the Spanish. A sweat-soaked officer, seeing the uniform, walks directly toward Diosdado.

"You people are not supposed to be here."

Diosdado salutes the American. "We await orders, Captain."

The captain does not seem surprised that Diosdado speaks his language. "Your orders are to clear the hell out of here. And stop those men from firing!"

Gunfire is coming back from the Spanish position now, twigs and leaves falling from above, clipped by bullets. The captain stands a full head taller than Diosdado.

"I am sorry if there is confusion, but our orders must come from our own commanders—"

It is not so much a directive as a wave of the hand and suddenly the entire company of *yanquis* has taken a knee, pointing their weapons at his handful of men.

"Sargento," Diosdado calls in Zambal, which apparently this Bayani speaks, voice as calm as he can muster, "tell the platoon to hold their fire." He turns back to the captain. "May I ask you to identify yourself?"

"This is the 13th Minnesota," answers the American. "You people are slowing us down."

"There is more difficult terrain ahead of you. Wire fences, forests of bamboo, flooded fields of rice—and your naval guns cannot reach this far inland. If you were to move to the west—"

"We've already got another column coming up the beach parallel to us. How many more of your outfit along this line?"

"There is a blockhouse lying ahead," says Diosdado, "that commands the Pasai Road. If we were to guide you—"

"All you need to do," interrupts the American captain, poking Diosdado in the chest with a finger, "is have your men put their weapons down and stand aside."

The men are looking to Sargento Bayani and Bayani is looking at Diosdado. The Americans seem carved in stone, the barrels of their rifles unwavering, at least three of them to every one of his own. He turns and gives the order. The men, grumbling and looking sideways at each other, lower their rifles, stick the tips of their bolos angrily into the mud.

"We'll be back in no time, fellas," winks one mud-splattered Minnesota private as he clambers over the sandbags. "After we've whipped them Dons for you."

"What are they doing?" asks Sargento Ramos, who is a Kawit from Bacoor.

"They're doing what we should be doing," Bayani answers him in Tagalog. "They're going to the Walled City to kill the Spanish."

"We can't let that happen!"

There has been no warning of this attack, only the long siege and the knowledge that without proper artillery the walls of the Intramuros cannot be breached. The Americans have promised that *insurrectos* who try to enter Manila will be shot, though up to now it has seemed an idle threat.

"We will not advance until ordered," Diosdado tells the sergeants. "Pass the word."

The *yanquis* form into lines just ahead of the earthworks, each man stretching one arm out to touch another to establish their spacing, then move forward in a great wave through the woods. The gunfire from the Spanish positions thickens, crackling uninterruptedly now, and the *yanquis* return it in a seemingly haphazard, random way, barely pausing to aim.

Diosdado's men begin to pour out of the trench around him.

"Halt! Come back here! There is no order to advance!" he shouts, but each word sounds weaker and more ridiculous than the last. Bayani is by his side again, with his customary hint of a grin, speaking in Spanish as he does to emphasize his contempt.

"Our nation is about to be liberated, *mi teniente*," he says, "and our loyal soldiers wish to have a part in it."

Diosdado raises the field glasses he bought second-hand in Hongkong and can see smoke through the trees, smoke coming from the loopholes in the blockhouse, the hornets' nest awakened now and responding as the *yanqui* line approaches it, a hail of rifle fire and the sound of at least one Hotchkiss gun and his own men firing their sorry mix of Enfields and Metfords and old Mausers captured from the enemy and the *yanquis* seem confused, caught in between, looking behind and then throwing themselves on their bellies to join in the fight. Diosdado, almost alone in the ditch behind the earthworks, climbs over and strides forward to join his men. He has been given the leftovers to command, Tagalos and Ilocanos and Pampangans and even a few Zambals who volunteered late in the struggle, men who, except for Bayani and Ramos, have never been in combat before. There has been very little shooting in their engagements with the Spanish so far, one starved garrison of fuzz-faced conscripts after another surrendering with only token resistance, the best of their officers and soldiers sent to Cuba. But now there are more bullets flying through the air than he has ever experienced, buzzing and whining and thwacking against the trees and Diosdado breathes deeply and wills himself to appear calm, unconcerned even, as he steps into the lethal, buzzing air in front of the earthworks. His uniform is a target, of course, an officer honor-bound to be the most visible and least intimidated man in any troop, willing to take a greater risk than the private soldiers. He reaches the spot where his men have paused, kneeling behind trees for cover, firing over the *yanquis* at the blockhouse, intently struggling to reload their antiquated weapons, and stands with his hands clasped behind his back as if judging a competition, gazing this way and that as the forest splinters apart around him.

"I'll remember that pose," laughs Bayani, sitting on the ground just to his left, leaning his back casually against the thick trunk of a *narra*. "For when they carve your statue."

Teniente Diosdado Concepción calls out to his troops, trying to keep the anger from shaking in his voice.

"Do not waste your ammunition," he shouts to them over the rattle and whine of the fight, "and attempt to avoid shooting the *yanquis* in the back!"

There are Spanish firing at them from a thicket of bamboo across from the dirt road that runs parallel to the shore, probably the same men who just abandoned the fort, and Hod is thankful for the trenches they've left along the west side of it. He squats with the others, bullets thapping against the low earthworks, and turns when he hears a band playing *Dixie*. Big Ten raises himself up slightly to look.

"It's our outfit, all right," he says, ducking back down. "Couple hundred yards back, out in front of the fort."

"Somebody ought to tell them this isn't over yet."

"I'd aim at the tuba, I was them," says Big Ten, nodding toward the bamboo thicket. "Knock out the heavy artillery first."

By the time the order comes to eat, the band has retreated back behind the shelter of the fort walls, playing *Hot Time in the Old Town Tonight*. There is only hardtack and canned goldfish that has to be hacked with bayonets out of the tin and whatever is left in their canteens. The salmon stinks like something left on the beach for a week.

"It's said that the Dagoes holed up in the city all these weeks have been dining on rats," says Donovan, who is from Lake City by way of Sligo. "And there's come to be a shortage of those."

"Maybe we could trade them some of this," says Thorogood, who was a timberman in the Thespian Mine back in Leadville.

"The divil that ye know," says Donovan, mashing some of the oily fish onto a slab of sea biscuit and trying to chew it down, "is to be preferred over the divil ye don't."

The artillery boys bring up their one-pounders then, wheeled behind a trio of the enormous water buffalo they've borrowed from the natives, and begin to blast the thicket. Niles, scanning the bamboo through his binoculars, orders the platoon to fix bayonets and prepare to advance.

"I thought this was in the bag," says Hod.

The lieutenant puts the field glasses down and turns to address them. "Your Spanish Don is, above all things, a man of honor," he explains. "Despite the odds, one must keep up appearances."

"We've got to slaughter each other just so's the Spanish brass don't get their medals tarnished?"

Manigault smiles. "'Ours is not to reason why.'"

The Captain calls down the line, "Skirmish formation, in rushes—move out!" and they are back into it.

Hod scrambles over the wall of dirt and joins the others, nearly trotting now, bayonet catching a glint from the mid-morning sun. The one-pounders are still firing, bamboo shaking and splintering ahead as the shells rip through it and only a few scattered shots coming back at them. Shit, shit, shit, thinks Hod as he hurries toward the thicket, my feet are going to stay wet all day.

There are only a handful of dead men left in the bamboo when they get there, one man missing his head, and the band catches up, playing behind them as they move over the open ground and into the wood-and-thatch buildings at the outskirts of Malate, spreading out five abreast on the Calle Real, turning every few steps to look up at windows and roofs. A few dogs trot away from them, looking back over their shoulders and yipping nervously, and a startled young native girl, pregnant, stands frozen on the steps of a large stone church. They pass a building that from the wall of sandbags out front appears to be the Spanish headquarters in the neighborhood and Major Moses orders the color bearers to decorate it, halting their advance for everybody to watch and cheer. The boys hang the regimental flag out the second-story window and then the Stars and Stripes and the whole 1st

Colorado hurrahs together, nearly covering the sound of the sniper fire, bullets whanging in from at least three directions. Phenix, a sharpshooter in Company I who is still wrestling with the banner in the window, takes one in the neck and is carried, writhing and blood-soaked on a stretcher, to the rear.

Hod and Big Ten hug the buildings on the west side as they advance again, watching the rooftops across the street.

"Somebody runs up a flag," says Big Ten, "you best hustle your hindquarters clear of it."

It is late afternoon before they loop around and face the bridge over the flat, lazily curving Pasig River that leads to the north walls of the city. The band, following only a few hundred yards behind their lines all day, strikes up *Marching Through Georgia*. Some of the boys begin to sing along as they form up in flying columns to cross—

How the darkies shouted when they heard the joyful sound
How the turkeys gobbled that our commissary found
Even sweet potatoes leapt out willing from the ground
While we were marching through Georgia!

—singing still as they double-time across the bridge by squads, bullets from hidden assailants flying at them from every direction, from the rooftops of the tall church steeples visible over the moss-covered walls ahead of them, from the covered barges tethered in the water below, from the bamboo shacks they just left behind—

Hurrah! Hurrah! We bring the Jubilee!
Hurrah! Hurrah! The flag that makes you free!
So we sang the chorus from Atlanta to the sea
While we were marching through Georgia!

—Hod bending over his rifle as he runs, as if there is anything but pure dumb luck keeping him, keeping any of them, from being hit—

And so we made a thoroughfare for freedom and her train
Sixty miles of latitude, three hundred to the main
Treason fled before us, for resistance was in vain
While we were marching through Georgia!

But there are no cheering darkies at the far side of the bridge, only Lieutenant Niles Manigault waiting for them, pistol in hand and a look of displeasure darkening his countenance.

"The next man who utters a line from that blasphemous ditty," he announces, "will have his brains blown out."

Blockhouse 14, though manned by the *cazadores* of the 73rd, who have never retreated before, is finally abandoned and Diosdado and his men follow the *yanquis*, marching just far enough behind that it is not worth the Americans' effort to turn and try to disarm them, following as they circle wide around another blockhouse that is already burning, ragged shards of wood blown out from the walls as the munitions inside explode, then squatting in a rice paddy to shoot past them again as the Spaniards try to make a stand in the little *baryo* of Cingalon, the *yanquis* leaving their wounded in the church to be cared for later and moving on as the enemy retreats northward. Diosdado's men linger in Cingalon after the Minnesotas march out, searching the dozen Spanish dead but finding no weapons.

Then the firing from the north stops. The navy guns to the left are silent. Diosdado has the sergeants form the platoon into a ragged skirmish line and they hurry to catch up.

The Americans have dug in behind the trenches on the far side of the Paco road.

Their rifles are facing south.

Bayani and Ramos walk forward with him to meet the Minnesota captain in the middle of the road.

"Show's over, fellas," says the *yanqui*. "This is as far as you go."

Diosdado points. "The enemy is that way."

"Enemy no more. We just got word, there's a white flag been up for hours."

Bayani asks what the captain is saying and Diosdado tells him. He asks to borrow the binoculars.

"Orders now are to make sure you *insurrectos* don't slip in and queer the whole deal. Take revenge on the Dons, loot the city—"

"It is our city," says Diosdado.

"Not at the moment," says the American, his ocean-blue eyes unblinking. "I suggest you take your outfit and back off a ways. Don't want any trouble if we can avoid it."

"The flag isn't white," says Bayani in Zambal. There are tears of anger in his eyes as he takes the binoculars away from them. "It is red and white stripes, with a blue square in the corner. It's the fucking *yanqui* flag!"

Diosdado takes the glasses and adjusts them until the field becomes clear, turning to the northwest, searching till it comes into view. There are American soldiers sitting on the ground in the Luneta, American soldiers marching on the drawbridge that crosses the overgrown moat that faces the thick walls of the Intramuros, American soldiers already posing for photographs on top of the Revellín de Real like a group of tourists, and above them, rippling in the late afternooon breeze that comes off the Bay, their gaudy banner.

There is no breeze on the Paco Road. It must be low tide, the little *esteros* that run inland from the bay beginning to smell.

"I am still waiting for orders," he tells the captain.

"Well, you just move back on out of sight and wait for them there. It wasn't for you little monkeys riling up the Spanish we could have marched in there hours ago without a single casualty." The captain turns as his men cheer. Very faintly, from the direction of the Walled City, come the wobbling strains of the *yanquis'* strange anthem.

"We should have been first into the city," Diosdado says bitterly, and turns to stride back to his own lines.

More *yanquis*, the reserve units of the day's campaign, step around Diosdado's men as if they are fence posts, crossing the road to join their countrymen. Bayani and Ramos follow Diosdado back.

"You fucking people," says Bayani, in Tagalog for the sake of Ramos, "you fucking people have given them our country."

He means all of the *ilustrados*, of course, the educated, the wealthy, the ones who make treaties and wear tailored uniforms and get to float safely to Hongkong in between massacres, but under Bayani's unwavering glare Diosdado feels personally responsible.

This wasn't a battle, he realizes—it was a show staged by white men. Not a liberation but a changing of the guard. And still not a word from Aguinaldo.

Ramos is red-faced, chest heaving as if it is hard for him to breathe. "What do we do now, *mi teniente?*"

"Now?" The platoon has gathered around them, confused, suspicious, angry. They stare into his eyes. He is the only one of them who has ever been out of the country, the only one, excepting maybe Bayani, who can read. He feels exhausted, though they have not traveled so very far today.

"If the Americans have the city," he tells them, feeling his own fury rush to his head, "we will have to take it back."

ANGLER

The fishhook pokes up through the northern tip of Luzon, snagging it securely.

The Cartoonist has arranged the other islands, eliminating many of the smaller ones, to suggest the body of something long and twisted, a fighting pickerel perhaps, with Luzon the head and Mindanao representing the tail flukes. Sitting forlornly upon the northern isle, under a drooping, sickly-looking palm, is a Filipino man, hatless, elbows on knees and head in hands, his tattered shirt open to reveal the slat-ribbed torso of the undernourished. A poor brown little bugger despondently facing away from the hook and its line, which extends tautly across the Pacific to the tip of the slightly bent cane pole held in Uncle's firm, knobby-knuckled hands. Uncle has rolled his striped trousers up and cools his bared legs to the shins in the rolling sea.

SHALL I REEL HER IN?

—asks the caption, Uncle turning his head to query the reader with bushy eyebrows raised. An extremely unseaworthy-looking dinghy is being rowed away to the northeast of the hooked fish by a white-moustachioed Spanish admiral, with a greasy merchant balancing a bag of loot at the prow, and a fat, tonsured friar in the rear, turning his head back for a last sad glimpse of his Paradise Lost.

The Cartoonist has modeled the friar after Hastings in editorial, and hopes no one will notice till after the paper hits the street.

SOLDIERS
OF MISFORTUNE

Hod watches the cards pile up in front of him, still a little dizzy from the wine Neely smuggled in. Company G is back from the defensive line that's been set up north of the Pasig, scattered now in the nipa huts serving as their cantonment by the reservoir at the edge of a neighborhood called Sampalac or Salampoc or something just as hard to get your mouth around. They've named it Camp Alva after the governor, just like back in Denver.

"The women won't show in public without their chaperones," explains Corporal Grissom, who has declared himself the squad's expert on local customs and has a nasty-faced little monkey named Aggy perched on his shoulder. "Daylight catches a señorita on the street, you can bet she's got one or two old bulldog aunts clearing a path for her."

"You mean the Spanish girls," says Big Ten.

The Spanish haven't all gone, merchants and friars and even a few soldiers awaiting transport still hanging on in the Walled City, depending on their new *amigos yanquis* to protect them from the locals. There are days Hod feels like a militia guarding a mine boss.

"I mean the Spanish girls." Grissom finishes the deal, takes a gander at his hand. He has managed to teach the monkey to throw cocoanuts and other fruit down from the trees and to shit anywhere but on his own shoulder. "And the half-breed ones with money. The dark ones, the whatever—Indian ones, that sell stuff on the street and slick their hair with cocoanut oil, they'll stare you straight in the eye."

"Which leaves the field open for you, Chief."

Big Ten shrugs. "Don't talk the lingo."

The locals, the ones who aren't in Aguinaldo's so-called army, just stare at you. There are rich folks' houses here with Filipinos living in them, even the bigger bamboo huts in this neighborhood look comfortable enough, but it is hard to get a peep into their lives with them scowling at you. Worse than being a Gentile in Utah.

"Ye just rattle some of them Mexican cartwheels in front of their noses," says Donovan, who has already been busted down to private for wandering into a posted district. "They'll get the idea, all right."

"I wouldn't fuck a googoo on a bet," says Grissom.

"Ye'd fuck a rockpile if ye thought there was a squirrel in it. A dead squirrel."

Hod has had the trots for a week now and the Dhobie itch real bad and it feels raw where he sits. Some of the guys wear red flannel bands around their middles, even to sleep, but they've been getting sick just like anybody else. The wine was a bad idea. Hod is tired of their talk, always the same, tired and bored and worried about his insides turning to mush. He hasn't been right since a day out of Honolulu, stuffed in the three-tier bunks, only two hours on deck a day, trying to eat the slump they shoved in front of you with puke sloshing around your feet. Here inside the hut there are mosquitoes that come out at dusk and dawn, lurking at the edges of the light from the single kerosene lamp they've hung over the ammo box they play on, a half-dozen men sitting around it on a woven-mat floor. They don't buzz, these mosquitoes, and the only strategy seems to be to let them land and fill up with some of your blood before you crush them.

"The young ones don't look so bad."

"Monkey faces," scoffs Grissom.

"Just close your eyes," says Winston Wall, a private from the Kansas Vols who it seems is a third cousin of Hod's, demonstrating with his hips. "And then imagine the woman of your dreams—"

Neely reddens, slaps his cards down on the crate. "She wouldn't do nothin like that."

The men laugh.

"You in this game or not, Atkins?"

It takes Hod a moment to react to his Army name.

"Let's go, buddy, shit or get off the pot."

Hod doesn't want to think about shitting. He spreads his cards out. Garbage. "Sure. Gimme two."

A boy in a white provost uniform ducks into the hut, squints at them through his glasses.

"Hey fellas," he says cheerfully, "long time no see. What we playing for?"

The men take a moment, in the weak light, to recognize the boy.

"It's Runt!" grins Big Ten.

"How the hell you get over here, son? Thought they threw you back for being too puny."

Runyon squeezes onto the floor next to Hod. "Stupid bastards. I snuck on the train to Frisco, hung around the camps—" He shrugs. "There was a Minnesota company that come up a few men short one morning, I talked to the sergeant—"

"They must be desperate."

"It's a good outfit—"

"That uniform appears a might roomy on you—" says Winston Wall.

"It fits just fine. They got us policing the city now."

"Well," says Sergeant LaDuke, scowling at his hand, "least there's one of you short enough to look the googoos in the eye."

The boy scrutinizes the backs of the men's cards as if he could see through them, cards decorated with a lanky Gibson Girl holding a bicycle. "They're not a happy group of people, our comrades in arms," he says. "Had their hearts set on chopping up the Spanish, and then along we come—"

"What I want to know is where they keep the sportin gals."

Runyon grins. "Just down the street here in Sampaloc. What're you, blind?"

Grissom deals Runt in, the boy throwing a ten-centavo piece into the ante.

"So you Minnesotas are pullin the provost."

"For the moment, yeah," he says, studying his hand. "But we were in the thick of it the day the city fell."

"*We* were in the thick, what there was of it," corrects Sergeant LaDuke. "I don't remember seeing you."

"Me neither," says Wall. "Less it was way back in our dust."

"We hooked up with the Astor Battery, hauling their pieces with those water buffalo," says Runt, standing pat, "and all day long whatever we run into, Spanish in a blockhouse, Spanish holed up in a church, whatever, we get the Astor boys set up and they blast the hell out of it."

"Imagine having so much money you can field your own artillery," muses Big Ten.

"I wish old John Jacob would come over here, build us one of his swanky hotels," says Donovan. "I can't sleep in these feckin rat-holes no more."

"And the rats aint too happy about you snoring like a freight train—"

"I don't snore."

"And shit don't smell. Tell him, Neely."

"I was a googoo sneaking up and heard that racket coming out of your tent," says Neely, "I'd turn and run for my life."

"General Otis has ordered all the saloons closed down on Sundays," says Runt. "But the boys have discovered this *beeno* home-brew stuff—"

"General Otis," complains the Kansas private, "has parked his fat ass on a supply of Krag rifles and won't give em out to us vols."

"What we need with new rifles if we're going home?"

"Hate to break it to you, pal, but we aint going anywhere."

"I signed up to slaughter Dagoes," says Donovan. "And at that I've been sorely disappointed."

"You'll get home when they squeezed the last drop of blood outta you."

"So they got you playing nursemaid to the drunks and goldbricks," Sergeant LaDuke says to Runt, "while we keep the googoos in line."

LaDuke was a militia back in Colorado, and when Private Thorogood called him out as a scab and a strikebreaker the sergeant put him on report for a week.

"For a while they had me guarding this herd of buffalo calves," says Runt. "When they're little they're kind of pink-colored—"

"And when they grow up they wallow in the mud and taste like shoe leather."

"These aint for eatin. They grow the pox on em, for vaccine."

"Evry time ye turn around this place there's a feckin doctor with a needle in his hand—"

"Now we're inside the walls, keeping order. Most nights it's about what you'd see in Pueblo on a Saturday after dark. One of our fellas got cut by a pimp and his patrol partner shot the little bastard, almost had a riot on our hands." Runt and Grissom's monkey trade a look. "What's the stakes here?"

They gamble, dice and cards and side-bets about what time it is going to rain or how many insects will they find in a plate of beans or anything that comes to mind, many of the men owing next month's pay and the one after that, gamble, Hod included, because so far they have only time to kill and nothing to save for.

"Fifty-centavo minimum," says Grissom, "and if one of our Mariquina googoos picks you off before you settle your debts we don't pony up to bring the body back."

Manigault steps in then, and Sergeant LaDuke nudges the wine bottle behind his body.

"As I assumed," says the officer, looking over the spread of cards and pesos on the ammo crate. "Uncle Sam's finest issue, ever vigilant, girding their loins for battle."

"We're rarin to go, Lieutenant," says LaDuke. "Only the coons have decided to take the night off."

He was not popular in training or on the ship, Manigault, the men going through "that cracker peacock" and "Niles Manlygoat" before settling on "Lieutenant Tarheel" when he was out of earshot. Opinion improved on the day of the so-called invasion, Niles striding out in front of the company with a malacca cane in hand, seeming to grow more cheerful with every flurry of sniper fire.

"I wouldn't be so sure of that," he says, tapping the cane twice on the edge of the crate. "I had the opportunity to visit headquarters today, and from what I was able to glean—" he winks to the men, a hint of conspiracy in his voice, "—I wouldn't wander too far from your weapons."

They've been sleeping in their boots for a week, but other than insults tossed across the two hundred yards the forces are ordered to maintain between each other, there has been no action. Hod feels it coming again, stomach churning, but holds to his seat.

"Merely a suggestion to the more prudent among you," says the lieutenant, raising his eyebrows, then sees Runt.

"Runyon, if I recall."

"Yes sir."

"I thought I cashiered you in Denver."

Runt grins. "But I caught on with the Minnesotas. Some real fighting men."

"With real officers," adds Hod, "from what I hear."

Manigault moves to stand behind Hod. "Insubordination is not looked upon kindly, McGinty. Even in the volunteers."

"He's Atkins," corrects Big Ten. "I'm McGinty."

Manigault narrows his eyes at the Indian. "I am acutely aware of *what* you are, Private." He turns to the others. "None of that wine had better end up in your canteens, gentlemen. I miss nothing." He gives Hod a smart tap on the shoulder with his cane and steps out into the darkness.

"What's with the shavetail?" asks Runt when he is gone. "Is that the real goods?"

"They like to start rumors. So's we don't become lax and undisciplined."

"As if the little monkeys would dare start anything."

"Who says they'll be the ones to start it?" says Big Ten.

"Give me something to shoot," declares former corporal Danny Donovan, "or send me the feck home."

If respect is not forthcoming from the lower ranks, one must settle for *fear*. Niles strolls toward the entrenchments, the night beginning to cool, startling a private so overcome with the sprue that he has dropped his trousers to do his business at the side of the path.

"Name and company," Niles barks as he steps around.

"Bollinger," says the sweating youth. "Company I."

Niles only nods curtly and continues. He may or may not pursue the matter. Unpredictability is a valuable tool, even the worst dullards forced to attend, to remain vigilant. Jeff Smith was the master of unpredictability, his moods, genuine or feigned, keeping his pack of thugs and grifters on a very short leash, his pistol always prominently displayed and judiciously brandished. Niles reflects that his own sidearm, an Army Colt ransomed from a pawnshop on lower Larimer, is rather plebeian for an officer of his caliber. It is not a gentleman's weapon.

"Who goes there?" calls a sentry at the Cossack post, whirling around.

"Lieutenant Manigault," he answers. "Had I been a skulking googoo, you'd have been dead three times over."

Command suits him, thinks Niles—he seems to have been born to be a leader of men. The Colorado Volunteers are a ragtag outfit, true, with a criminal element personified by Hod Brackenridge and his redskin cohort, but such a group demands a finer, firmer class of officer to be effective. When this Philippine fracas has petered out he will look in on the political situation in Wilmington, and, if it is still impossible, offer his services to the Regular Army. *Colonel* Manigault, at least.

Niles strides past the discomfited sentry and climbs up on the earthwork wall that faces the enemy—no, they are not yet that, officially—the Fili*p*ino lines. Conversation, in their atrocious ning-nong dialect, drifts across the no-man's-land with the sound of a guitar being strummed. If, when, the reckoning comes, they shall not prove an estimable foe.

There is a man standing on the opposite earthworks.

He is wearing boots and a short-peaked cap, sporting a pistol on his hip. He sees Niles and mimes pulling the sidearm, pointing it at him and pulling the trigger. It is too dark, the distance between them too great, to see if he is smiling or not.

Niles lifts his hat and gives the nigger a stiff bow.

Soon enough for you, my friend.

IMPROMPTU

The keys have changed their pattern. Jessie stares at them, trying to remember, trying to let the music in. She feels like her body is sinking, heavy, into the floor as her head floats dizzily above it. The Conservatory is in Virginia, not far from Hampton where Junior went to school, and if she can be the first colored girl accepted there, living away from her parents—

"Jessie?" calls Miss Loretta, the voice, echoing in the near-empty hall, a shock.

"Yes, M'am," she says. The white man's eyes challenged her when he said hello, his steady gaze asking *Just what do you think you're doing here?*, and at the moment she has no answer for him. Usually she has only to lay her fingers on the keys, all in their proper pattern, and the music is there.

Royal can come to her in Virginia, they can have the ceremony, and if this is what she dreads the most, everything will be made right. She will be forgiven. She only has to survive this test, to prove herself worthy.

The white man clears his throat, impatient, out there somewhere in the staring rows of seats with Miss Loretta. Jessie looks at the sheet music, notes drawn on lines, swimming.

G-Minor, she thinks, and wills her fingers into motion.

It isn't wrong, really, just not what is accepted. Miss Loretta sits on the aisle, a few rows behind the Maestro, and can't help but try to read his reaction from the set of his shoulders, the tilt of his head. It has been such a trial to convince him to come up, and she worries she may have overstated Jessie's abilities. What is outstanding in Wilmington may not impress Atlanta or Charlottesville, though her ear and her intuition have not deceived her before.

"Another Hottentot prodigy," the Maestro smiled tightly when she met him at the station. "You've become something of a missionary."

He is listening, though, eyes closed as always, fingertips of his right hand gently pressed against his temple as if the music is being played inside his head. Jessie has chosen her favorite ballade, and though it is meant to begin in a pensive mode there is something—not tentative, exactly, for the girl's fingers know where they're meant to be—something other*world*ly about her playing as she begins. The caesuras are much too long, Jessie listening to each phrase, pondering it, before proceeding with the next. The massive hall is cool, as always in the early afternoon, and Miss Loretta realizes she is shivering.

There will be only this one opportunity with the Maestro. She has made an effort not to frighten the girl, tried not to overstress the importance of the audition. But the fact remains that it is one of those rare moments in which the course of one's future is determined, the road dividing, only one path leading forward. She is so young, Jessie, innocent yet of the terrible knowledge that certain actions, certain decisions, cannot be undone. Miss Loretta dabs at her neck with her handkerchief, then fans herself, suddenly flushing with one of the vaporous attacks she is prone to lately, worse always when she is tense or upset, and then Jessie stops playing.

Just stops.

The ballade is meant to change character here, gaining power and certitude, but Jessie only sits staring at the keys as if this more resolute music is a forest she dare not enter.

The Maestro turns his head to Miss Loretta, arches an eyebrow.

"I'm sorry," says Jessie, her near whisper carrying out to them.

The girl stands and steps off into the wings, footsteps hammering. Miss Loretta is up and leaning in to placate the Maestro.

"Perhaps if I speak with her—"

"She understands," he says, shaking his head slightly and reaching for his coat as he rises. "Left to their own devices, they prefer to dwell at their own level." He pats Miss Loretta's hand as he steps into the aisle, as a father pats the hand of a child who has lost her balloon. "Your efforts for the girl are commendable, and I'm sure you saw the spark of something there," he says, slipping his coat on, "but the Academy is not a settlement house."

"I apologize for—"

"No need. I'll be able to catch the three o'clock if I hurry."

Miss Loretta sits then, suddenly exhausted, till she hears the door to the lobby thump shut behind him. The chill that so often follows her hot spells shudders down her spine from the sides of her neck. It is very quiet in the great hall. She stares at the piano, mute and reproachful at the center of the stage. She remembers hearing Anton Rubinstein from this very seat on the aisle, enthralled at thirteen years of age, the music filling her soul. Miss Loretta sighs and stands to find the girl.

Jessie sits on a stool by the bank of pulleys that control the scenery and curtains. Her cheeks are wet with tears as she looks up to see her teacher.

"I am so very sorry."

"Not as sorry as I." Jessie flushes as if she has been slapped. Miss Loretta regrets the phrase the moment it is uttered, but she has suffered the Maestro's condescension, has confused her own thwarted hopes with those of this colored girl.

Softer now, "You're not feeling well?"

The girl's forehead is damp, the neck of her shirtwaist darkened with perspiration.

"I was afraid I was going to be ill."

There was a girl at Conservatory, Antonia, a lovely girl who played like the wind and had great dark eyes that were rumored to be the result of gypsy blood in her family. Miss Loretta and the others would gather outside the rehearsal room and marvel at her facility, her passion. But if more than one of them stepped in to listen Antonia would break off and return to playing scales or pretend to study the score. The morning of her first *recitif* she began to tremble and by noon was burning with a fever so intense an ambulance was called for. It was said that her symptoms had disappeared by the time she reached the hospital, though none of them ever saw her again. The porters were there to remove her belongings from her room the next morning.

"The nature of your sex," said Professor Einhorn without mentioning Antonia by name in his next lecture, "disposes you to a heightened sensitivity. It is both your glory and your undoing."

Miss Loretta chooses her words carefully. "You have performed in front of people, important people, before this," she says. There was the concert in February, the *haute monde* of Wilmington present, and but for the girl's parents not a dark face in the audience. She was brilliant.

"I feel ill all the time," says Jessie. "Not just today."

It is unthinkable.

The girl has been rounding out lately, her body ripening. Nothing more. These are growing pains, perhaps, the unruly sway of female humors. We women are slaves to our bodies, thinks Miss Loretta, and our emotions rule our health.

"Have you had—"

She is not the girl's mother, after all, not responsible. But at the end of all her pleading to lure the Maestro here for a trial, after all her steady instruction and guidance through the years, her investment in this child, there must be an accounting.

"Have you started having your flow?"

The girl seems to understand. "It began last August," she says. "But since I've been ill—"

Unthinkable.

Miss Loretta feels her own tiny swoon of nausea. She is a music instructor, nothing more. "How long has it been interrupted?"

The girl looks at her with fearful eyes. "It can't be that."

"Of course not." It is very stuffy, here in the wings, the air stale and motionless. "Because you've never engaged—" they are familiar, Miss Loretta and this colored girl, more familiar than teacher and student, more familiar than society will normally allow, given what separates them, "—because you've never engaged in improprieties with your young man."

It is not a question.

It is a statement begging confirmation and the girl lets it hang too long, another caesura, the sound of Miss Loretta's words decaying in the narrow space that is heavy with the mildew of the side curtains bunched around them, and then the realization that they are not alone.

"Pologize for disturbin you ladies," he says, pulling his cap off and holding it over his chest, "but you finish with that pianner?"

It is the day man, old Samuel, a fixture at Thalian Hall since Miss Loretta was a girl, known as Songbird because of his constant humming while at his tasks. He has appeared without a note, however, and stands frozen in a slight bow awaiting her instruction.

"We are quite finished with it, Samuel. Thank you."

He turns to the girl. "I seen your Daddy out the hallway, here on city bidness," he says. "He ax if I know how it's goin for you in here."

"I'll have to tell him when I get home," she says quietly.

Samuel bows again and puts his cap back on. "Yes M'am, Miss Jessie." He leaves them to attend to the piano.

"It was only the one time," she says when he is gone, as if this may provide absolution.

Slaves to our bodies.

"Yes," nods Miss Loretta, wishing there was a place for her to sit. "You will need to tell your father when you are home."

"I've let you down," cries the girl, Jessie, her Jessie. "I've betrayed you."

Jessie is weeping now and Miss Loretta finds herself holding her, cradling her head against her chest as she stands and the girl sits on the stool, feeling the tight-coiled black tresses she has always wanted to touch, if only from curiosity, stroking her hair now and this is too much, too much to bear. She has lost her, lost her dear Jessie forever.

"What can I do?"

"Oh my dear," says Miss Loretta, weeping herself now, "there is so very little you can do."

"They'll find out."

"You will tell them. Today."

She is amazed to discover that she does not think any less of the girl, that there is, in fact, no betrayal. Only sadness. There are worse fates, of course, but she wanted more for this one. Colored society—what, society in general being what it is—the young man may suffer no consequences. Off in the Army somewhere, at liberty, in the eyes of the world, to shoulder his responsibility or not. What must it be to move with that freedom, to love without care. What reckless joy to saunter through life with only your conscience as restraint, ever the raptor and never the ruined.

"You will tell them today, and you will be married, and you will have your child," Miss Loretta says to Jessie, as gently as she can muster.

"Is that all?"

It is more than she herself has achieved, it is what women are raised to do. Jessie looks up to her from the stool, holding tightly to both of her hands now, waiting for her response.

"You can pray that it is a boy," says Miss Loretta.

"First you loosen the set screw—that's right, now lift that lever pin."

Milsap wills himself to patience, standing over Davey's shoulder while the boy tries to pull out the distributor clutch. He can follow instruction, Davey, but every time he puts his hands into the Linotype it's like the first time they been there. No sense of the machine, of what sets what into motion.

"Now you can take the lever and the spring away—get a good holt on it—you drop these little pieces in there we got to tear the whole thing apart."

"All right—"

"Now—you're gonna take the screw from the bracket *there* and loosen the other screw over on the right front so the whole clutch bracket comes off its dowel pins without springing the clutch *shaft*—"

"There's so many parts."

It could have been done with an hour ago but part of the job is seeing if he can train anybody else to fix the apparatus. Maybe come a day when he's not there and there's important news and the machines go down, both of them, could be one of a thousand things. What happens then if it's only Davey or Clifton Lee or that half-wit German they just brung in? The people must be informed, that's how a democracy functions.

"You do as many things as this machine does, you need a lot of parts. And they got to be in *har*mony, which is why we're changing out this clutch."

Milsap sees that there is God in the machine, in the active interplay of slides and matrices, of wheels and pulleys and discs and shafts and springs and ejectors, of hot lead and cold steel, just as there is God in the holy, complex cycles of rain and seed and growth and harvest, in the cleverness of the human mind that can, like Mr. Merganthaler's, discover a system so intricate yet so obvious once invented that it surely must be divine.

The copy boy comes up and stands by them but Milsap isn't ready to see him.

"Anything in this life," he says, "got to be in harmony to operate how it's sposed to. Your church organ—how many moving parts you think that has? One of them, just one, gets out of kilter and you gonna hear *noise* in the house of God, not music. Our society," he says, picking up a theme that Mr. Clawson has been developing in his editorials this week, "has got some intricate workings of its own. Something, somebody, steps out of their *place*—well, that's when you get chaos. That's when you get *an*archy. What you want?"

The copy boy, staring into the guts of the machine, is startled to be addressed.

"Oh. Mr. Clawson need you."

The boy runs off. Milsap considers leaving instructions with Davey, then decides against it.

"Don't touch anything till I get back," he says. "*Any*thing."

When you put the clutch back on the beam you have to be sure that the timing pin in the distributor screw meshes into the clutch-shaft gear, where the tooth is cut away, so that the screws will be in accurate time with each other. It seems plain enough, like holding a bottle of milk the right way up before you pull the cap off, but some people got no feel for machines and Davey is one of them.

Clawson is in his office in the tilt-back chair, reading, when Milsap ducks his head in.

"I got a telephone call from over at the Armory," he says without looking up from the copy in his lap. There's only a handful of telephones in town and the *Messenger* got the first. Milsap can read the subhead, upside-down, of the copy that lies in the editor's lap—

FEDERAL BAYONETS TO BE USED IN
CARRYING ELECTION IN NORTH CAROLINA

The yankees are threatening to come back and escort their friends to the polling places and the *Messenger* is making the proper stink about it.

"They need you to go over and help them with something. Right now."

"What is it?"

Mr. Clawson looks up and gives him one of those Do I pay you to ask questions? looks.

"Bring your tools."

Davey is still staring into the machine when he comes back.

"You touch anything?"

"No sir."

"You might's well clean out the magazines while this is down."

"Yes sir."

If there is God in the machine, his printer's devil will be the last man on earth to recognize Him.

You got to take note when old Dan start rubbing his ass on everything in sight. Rubbing his ass and jerking his tail around and pulling his lip up to show his teeth like he got something to say. Jubal leaves him tied out front on Terry's Alley and goes around behind the shack. Mama is off cleaning for somebody, hardly ever find her home this time of day, but she say come by and get herbs whenever.

The wormwood plant is in an old wood tub half-buried away from the rest of the garden. Jubal pulls the leaves off, few from this side, few from that, and stuffs them in a leather sack. Brew up some tea with them, lace it with plenty of honey. Dan won't take nothing that bitter less you sugar it up some. Maybe mash some garlic in with his oats, lace some honey in that too. He had the roundworm once before, Dan, had to shit every three blocks and fought when you cinched the traces on him.

Jubal has the four-wheel dray with the headboard and seat hitched to him out front. Got to get four, five more years out of Dan, the way prices are. The horse leaves a pile, sick-smelling, in the sand as they turn south to head out of Brooklyn.

If there was some way to know ahead, like these white folks do who got the telephone, you would never roll empty. Drop one load off and pick up another on the same block, and just keep doing that, making triangles all over town. But how it is, they send some little barefoot boy they give a penny to that finds you or he doesn't and some other man he sees with a wagon get your job. Jubal pulls back on the reins to slow and ease alongside Mance Crofut, walking along Fourth.

"How they treatin you, Mance?" he calls.

"They's mischief afoot."

"How you say?"

Mance is a hunting friend of his uncle Wicklow, do up a stew with squirrel or possum make you slap your brains out. Mance have to roll around in this one spot where the deadfall trees are going back to dirt before he goes stalking, cause he always smell of creosote from his years on the dock. Jubal went out with them once when he was maybe twelve—Mance hit a doe neither him nor Royal nor Uncle Wick could even see it was so far back in the trees, little hole just under the ear.

"You know my ole Trapdoor Springfield I got," says Mance, leaning on the edge of the front wheel as the dray comes to rest. "I allus gets my bullets at Mr. Yaeger store, maybe some chaw that he hang out back. Only this mornin he won't sell me no bullets, says he fresh out of em. I can see the boxes right there behind him on the shelf, but you don't want to call no white man out as a liar, specially if he one of the better ones, sell me on credit now and then when there aint no work. So I goes down to Dothan's and to Bailey Catlin's and even all the way up to the Phoenix Genral Store, they say they got none either. You know that's a .45-70, aint like half the town don't shoot with them old Army rifles, so's I *know* somebody tellin stories. I come back to Mr. Yaeger's, buy a hank of that chaw, an I look right at them boxes behind him an I says 'You haven't got noner them .45s in since I come by this mornin, have you?' Now he look round that storeroom to be sure aint nobody listenin and he lean crost the counter and he lower his voice down, say 'I be honest with you, Mance, they is an inner*dic*tion on us sellin no weapons nor bullets to the colored folks till we told it's o.k. again.' Seems it's this White Man's Union, going bout making rules and you break em they gone shut you down or burn you *out*."

They are quiet for a moment, pondering this.

"Election coming up," says Jubal.

"Well I wish it was already past," says the old man, shaking his head. "White people start actin skittish, you got to step lightly."

Jubal offers him a ride but the old man is almost home and cuts off into Campbell Street, still shaking his head. Dan whickers and farts as they cross over the railroad tracks on the Hilton Bridge. Mostly it's the foals you got to worry about with roundworm, eat their whole insides up. A mule Dan's age has had em more than once, and they don't usually suffer too much with it. That's just life, is what Uncle Wicklow says, whatever bad happens to you, you don't ever lose it. Just learn how to carry it inside.

He turns at Princess, and then again on Seventh, crunching on the shell road now, passing little Jessie Lunceford who his brother is so sweet on, walking alone, dressed pretty and wearing a face like she lost her last friend. He calls out to her but she doesn't seem to hear him. Jubal pulls Dan's head to get them off the main street, then stops the dray crosswise to the rear of Turpin's Pharmacy like they asked. Mr. Kenan is there waiting.

"We not going far," says Mr. Kenan, winking, "but this here's a load."

Jubal has never liked a man, specially a white man, to wink at him, and it makes him uneasy when Mr. Turpin and Mr. Kenan commence to joshing while he helps them lift the big crate out.

"Boys at the Armory gone preciate this," says Mr. Kenan, winking again. "After this party done, they be some young men wish they *had*n't."

But the crate is way too big and way too heavy for liquor, dead weight that staggers the three of them getting it out from the back and onto the dray. The springs complain when they thump it down.

"Yes sir," says Mr. Turpin, "there be some heads hurtin fore this wing-ding over."

Jubal just smiles the way they like and shoves the crate farther onto the platform. No need to tie it down with the Armory just about around the corner.

"Whatever you gennemen got in there," he says, "they's a good deal *of* it."

Mr. Turpin throws a tarp over the crate and goes back inside. Mr. Kenan rides beside Jubal on the seat, looking glad there isn't nearly anybody around, and hops down quick when they pull up behind the Armory. Mr. Kenan was the Customs House man, where they say you make more salary than the governor. When they give it to John Dancy, who is colored, a lot of people thought there would be trouble but so far it's just noise.

"Get us some more hands," says Mr. Kenan, and hurries inside.

Jubal pulls the tarp off and tries to peek between the slats of the crate but it's covered in there too. Sure as hell aint no whiskey bottles. Mr. Kenan comes out with Colonel Moore and another man Jubal doesn't know, young man with blisters on his nose. Colonel Moore won't hardly look at him but then he is one of them die-hard Confederates, marches with the Klan and still hasn't give up the emancipation war for lost.

Jubal climbs up and kneels and puts his shoulder to the crate to get it sliding, while Mr. Kenan and the white boy take the weight of the back end. He hops down to take a corner but Colonel Moore shoulders him away.

"We got it from here," he says.

So Jubal holds the back door open for them and when they're through Colonel Moore calls, "You shut that, boy."

He's got to wait to be paid then. It's always better if you help them carry it in cause then you just stand there in the way till somebody notices and pays and usually give you a tip on top of it. When they leave you outside there's no telling, you just wait and even if they have forgotten about you they act like you done something wrong if you knock to remind them.

But Mr. Kenan hurries out and gives him an extra twenty-five cents even though he didn't help them bring it in, and winks.

"Don't be careless how you spend that, now," he says. "Don't let the devil get it all."

Dan is pulling his lip up and farting more as they roll empty back to the stable, but keeps on pulling strong and steady, and every time they pass a white man Jubal sneaks a look at their face to see if he can guess what they up to. Mance is right, he thinks. Acting strange and skittish.

Not knowing what their problem is, Milsap has to lug both boxes of tools, but it's just a short walk to the Armory. It used to belong to the Taylor brothers' family and is more a clubhouse for the Light Infantry and their friends than a real fortress like in Raleigh or Charleston. There's a long wait after he knocks and then it's Mr. Kenan who answers the door and pulls him in.

"He didn't tell you to come to the back?"

"No sir."

"Least you're here. Come on."

Kenan leads Milsap to a room in the rear and there it is, laid out in pieces on a tarp on the floor, beautiful. Colonel Moore is there and a young fellow, maybe one of the Shiner clan from over in Dry Pond, who they don't introduce to him.

"It's got an instruction sheet for assembly," says Colonel Moore. "But we didn't want any slip-ups."

The cylinder is already put together, ten blued-steel barrels, smelling of oil and metal shavings.

"Look like it come straight from Hartford."

"We thought it was heavy," says the boy, "but they just thrown all the ammo in the same crate with it."

Colonel Moore holds out the assembly sheet for Milsap but he steps past without glancing at it.

"They done most of it for you," he says. "Just kept a few things apart to pack easier."

He sits and opens one of his toolboxes as the men look on, excited. He saw one pulled behind a wagon once when he was a boy, but it was a yankee parade and his father wouldn't let him go closer. It is one of those inventions that once you see it makes perfect sense, that plenty of people had thought of only the machining wasn't up to it then or the cartridges weren't uniform or any of the dozens of little things that have to fall in place at the right time.

"The beauty of this," he says, cradling the cylinder and beginning to attach it to the frame, "is each barrel got its own breech and firing-pin system. And by the time you crank her around again, your spent cartridge has fell out of the ejection port and a fresh one has slid in from the hopper. What's this take?"

"Krag rounds," says Mr. Kenan. "You work it right she'll put out six hundred a minute."

"That's some monkey-buster," grins the boy, who surely resembles a Shiner.

Milsap sets the brass crank in the socket, gives it a turn to check the action, then begins to secure it.

"It's a Peace-keeper," says Mr. Kenan. "Best way to keep the peace, you let the other side know what you capable of, militarily speaking. Deters any ideas they might get about disruption."

"Or voting," says the Shiner boy.

"You gone roll it into place?" asks Milsap.

"Haven't decided yet," says Colonel Moore.

"Well, it's best you mount this plate on first—shipboard, wagon bed, wherever you want, get it rock solid, and then bolt the apparatus on top of that. It'll tolerate some cant, but the more level the better. And if you expect to be firing a good deal," and here Milsap looks up to Mr. Kenan, "you best put some plugs in your ears. Don't want to end up deaf like me. Imonna put these on now so you can move it easier."

Colonel Moore and the Shiner boy lift the assembly up while Milsap wrestles the carriage wheels onto the axle, tightens the nuts on the hubs. When he is done they all step back to behold what he's put together, silent for a long moment. There is nothing in the magazine yet, the boxes of cartridges stacked against the wall, but there is no mistaking the purpose of this machine. There is God in this design as well, thinks Milsap, the God of swift and terrible retribution. He realizes he is in a sweat, though it's the others who done all the lifting.

"You think it's likely to come to this?" he asks.

"It might and it might not," says Mr. Kenan. "But we'll sleep better just knowing it's here."

"You have ruined us."

Yolanda has seen him angrier than this, furious over some defiance on Junior's part, some pointed slight at a Council meeting, but never so cold.

"You understand that, don't you? You understand what you've done?"

Her daughter stands before him, chest heaving with sobs, near hysteria since he began his relentless questioning of her symptoms. He has not touched her, and Yolanda can tell that she is not yet allowed to.

"I was going to tell you earlier," Jessie manages to say between sobs for breath, "but I wasn't sure."

"Sure of what? There is no question about your relations with that boy—"

"But that doesn't mean—"

"So you think your behavior would be acceptable if there hadn't been this consequence?"

Yolanda wishes he would stop. Her daughter's girlhood is shattered, that is all that matters now.

"I see this sort of behavior every day across the tracks," he says. "I expect it from those people. But in my own family—" He is shaking his head now, eyes fixed with censure on Jessie. He is not a man to hurl objects, not a man to kick and curse. She knows he is gentle with the other ones, the fallen girls he treats north of Red Cross Street, she knows from the way they smile and proudly show off their fatherless infants when encountered on the street. But this is their daughter, their jewel, their gift to the world.

"How could you do such a thing?"

It isn't shame she hears in her husband's voice, though public shame is certainly on his mind. It isn't shock or disappointment or even the fear of how this will be used against him, against them all, that she senses in his tone.

He is jealous.

"I'll write to him," Jessie sobs. "Or if you let me, I'll go to him—"

His smile, his pride, walking arm in arm with her, showing her off to the world—

"The next time I see that boy," he says, "will be his last day on earth."

He walked that way with her once, Yolanda, when she was his young wife, but time passes and daughters love their fathers and fathers return that love—

Jessie runs and throws herself on the divan, covering her head with her arms, wailing. Yolanda takes a step but he stops her with his eyes.

"It's that white woman," he fumes. "Filling her head with scandal."

"She's a piano teacher."

"And a Suffragist."

"You've never had a problem with—"

"It isn't the voting, it's everything else that goes along with it!" He is pacing now, pointedly looking away from Jessie, pacing the way he does when he returns from the city meetings and condemns the latest outrages. "The father is practically an anarchist."

"You know that isn't true."

"And that boy—"

"His name is Royal."

"His name," says her husband, raising his voice so Jessie can hear over her sobs, "will never be spoken in this house again!"

It is easier, it must be, for the rest of them, the people north of the tracks. Nobody is watching them, nobody hoping for them to fall. And there are women there, midwives and roots women, who can erase an indiscretion if engaged in time. More than once he has spoken of having them arrested, but never made a formal complaint. And some just have the child, acknowledging the father whether he reciprocates or not. Easier, yes, but no option for a decent Christian girl.

"I'll write to his commanding officer," he says, "and have him discharged."

"And what purpose will that serve?" says Yolanda. She is amazed to feel so calm. It is the same calm that came over her when Junior went under at Lake Waccamaw and she was the one to pull him out, the one to flip him on his stomach and work his arms and squeeze his little ribs till the water was forced out and he took his first gasping breath. Jessie is making those sounds now on the divan, drowning in her misery, but Yolanda is calm and already thinking ahead to what can be done. What must be done. The worry will come later, as it did with Junior, trembling every time he came near the water after that, her first thought when he announced his enlistment the anxious relief that, thank the Lord, he had not signed on to be a sailor.

"We need to be strong now," she says. "We need to think very clearly."

Jessie is weeping more quietly, having made her last effort and eager to hear what fate will be decided for her. Dr. Lunceford stops pacing, turns to face his wife. We have been so fortunate, she thinks. I will not allow this to destroy us. Jessie has been foolish and weak but not wicked, never that, and what they've planned for her is gone. But there will be no tragedy. We have endured worse than this in our lives, she thinks. And then, with the tiniest guilty twinge of excitement—there will be a new baby.

Her husband begins to pace again, but now his eyes are inward, calculating, his step the measured stride that always follows his diatribes.

"We find a husband," he says. "Immediately." He shoots a look to Yolanda before she can raise the possibility. "Someone respectable."

Alma sits on the stairs, waiting for the storm to pass. Her own father had taken his belt to her the first time and for a while she blamed him. The next she lost before she was showing much and by the third he was out of their lives. That was the story with railroad men, her mama said, they went off down the tracks and one day didn't come back.

Dr. Lunceford uses suspenders to keep his pants up and she's never known him to raise a hand to any of his family. Not like the Judge, thrash his arm stiff whipping his younger boy's behind, and him, Niles, only waiting for it to end and taking no lesson from the punishment. The last fight was the worst, with blows exchanged and blood on the rug and her in the middle of it.

And now little Jessie down there sobbing like she's got it hard.

Alma hurries back up to their bedroom when the girl's begging loses steam, when Doctor's plans are fixed and Mrs. Lunceford stays quiet. Alma finishes making their bed, sheets smelling the tiniest bit of smoke from the fire over on Castle Street the day she hung them out, and she hears Jessie running up and slamming the door to her room.

She waits till it is clear Mrs. Lunceford won't be following, still reasoning with Doctor down the stairs. She steps in without knocking. The girl is sprawled on her belly, exhausted from crying. Alma sits on the edge of the bed. It is a long moment before Jessie pulls her face out of the pillow and stares, red-eyed, toward the window.

"Did you hear?"

"I heard."

"They won't let me have him."

"You didn't tell him before this? Write to him?"

"I wasn't sure."

"I *told* you, girl—"

"You're not a doctor."

"I aint a farm girl, neither," says Alma, "but I know when a melon is set to bust." She puts a hand on Jessie's shoulder, tries to remember being this young. By the time she got shoes, ten, maybe eleven, she knew enough not to hope for things. You try to get what you can out of life, but only white folks and the few there is like the Luncefords, the educated colored, bother to make big plans and expect them to work out.

"Can't spen' what you ain' got," her mama always said, *"and can't lose what you ain' never had."*

"What you gone do now?"

"What can I do?"

"That boy want you. That's all you been tellin me—"

"He's in the Army."

"So? Texas somewhere—"

"Arizona."

"It aint the moon. If it's on the map, there's a train will get you there."

Jessie throws her arm across her forehead. "I'm just a girl," she says in a very small voice.

If there was one like Royal Scott wanting her, she'd *walk* to the damn Territories if that's what it took. But she is not this girl and never was.

"You gone marry who they say?"

Jessie covers her face with her other arm.

If I'd been able to keep one alive, keep maybe a couple of them, Alma thinks, I'd of schooled them better than this. Not the way her mama did, no time to do more than warn and worry and pray every night to the Lord for His divine protection, but really telling what was what and keeping the men off them long enough to have some little-girl time, making mudpies without a worry in the world. But after the fourth one came out looking like a tadpole the white doctor told her it was never going to happen for her, and the only mothering she'll ever do is letting this fool girl know she isn't licked less she lets herself be. She just got to deal with it, one way or the other.

"You aint so far gone," says Alma, softly, stroking the girl's arm. "There's things that can be done."

Jessie uncovers her face, looks scared at her.

"I thought them teas and baths was gonna fix you, but it's caught hold now and there's—"

"I can't do that."

Alma shrugs. "Then you can't."

The girl keeps staring at her. "Did you? Ever?"

"Never had to, never wanted to," says Alma. "Nature done it for me."

"Oh."

First time out and this girl end up with a baby, everything goes regular, and she don't even want it. Alma offers the other possibility.

"You need a train ticket, whatever, I got some money put by. You welcome to it, darlin."

It will be the end of her job here, for sure, though it probably won't be long before some of the blame for this spills her way and she'll be fired anyhow. "Junior will take your side on it if you get there," she adds. "I just bet he will."

Jessie takes too long to answer. Alma remembers sitting with her just two years back, maybe three, playing dolls and talking nonsense, the girl laying her head against her when she laughed, little braids back then—how she worked every morning doing up those little braids for Jessie. Girl could melt your heart. Jessie takes too long to answer, but when she does she tells the truth.

"I'm just a girl," she says.

* * *

It never happens in the books. Ruined girls are mentioned, pitied, but there is never one you get to know as a character, as a friend.

Jessie studies herself in the mirror above her vanity. Maybe they're all wrong. Her father never took her temperature, never listened to her heart or even put his hand on her forehead the way he did when she was little and had a fever. And if they're wrong about it there is still time to win them over, to make them see who Royal is. If he knew he would come, Army or no Army, he would come and make everything right.

It was his tongue that surprised her more than the rest. Alma told her about the rest, told her not to expect so much the first few times, but that part was nice, was sweet and thrilling, building up after the first strange invasion of his tongue into her mouth, touching her own, breathing into one another for a moment. Intimate. They were intimate. And that is all they will ever have.

Jessie studies herself, studies the swollen wreck this day has made of her face, feeling like a powerful hand is squeezing her throat shut, like each breath is a hill she has to climb. She turns the corners of her mouth down and wonders what it will be like to never smile again.

MAIL CALL

Tombstone is closer but the boys say there's more cooking every night in the Gulch so that's where they are. It is most of a day's ride and none of them are cavalry.

They ditch the mounts at a stable and come into the Calumet Saloon all together, nine of them, uniforms but no sidearms, and the miners are too drunk to care. Royal's sitter is sore as hell so he stands at the bar drinking from the stone jug they fill from a barrel, what they say is Old Crow but tastes like creosote and it doesn't matter.

My dearest Royal—

Mail call was early, with Corporal Puckett handing out the letters.

"Royal Scott got him three," he shouted out, holding the envelopes under his nose. "Smell good, too."

Oohing and aahing and catcalling from the boys then, like they would with anybody.

"What you want to do is read the last one first," said Hardaway. "Get to the grit."

But Royal started with the first one and wasn't one line in before he couldn't swallow.

My dearest Royal—

It hurts me so much to have to write this to you.

The thing with a jug is you can't see how much whiskey is left. He hopes there is enough. The miners are singing one song and the boys from Companies A and H something else, but happy, it is early Saturday night and the holes around Bisbee are puking out copper like there is no tomorrow and the Papagos and the Apaches are quiet and the boys will have half of Sunday to sober up in the saddle and Royal is slugging his way through a gallon jug.

My dearest Royal—

Her handwriting is beautiful, like you'd expect, and at first it was hard to understand that something so wrong could be hiding in such gracefully crafted shapes. If she is as upset as she says she is, he thinks, why can't you see it in the writing? If the handwriting in the letters was a voice it would be soft, reasonable, calm—

My dearest Royal—

It hurts me so much to have to write this to you. Nature itself has betrayed us, and I am with child.

Something he heard from the Bible once. *With child.* Too Tall is down the bar telling a story about Coop, who is back digging slit trenches at Huachuca cause they caught him smoking hemp on guard duty. Whatever is in the jug feels better when it gets down now, though swallowing is still a chore. His throat started closing right while he was reading, his insides trying to push up out of him, and by the end of the first section he could hardly breathe.

My dearest Royal—

It hurts me so much to have to write this to you. Nature itself has betrayed us, and I am with child. But our love cannot be.

Fort Huachuca is nothing but heat and dust. They drill, they march into the mountains with full packs on, they listen to the officers tell them they may be needed in the Philippines or in China, but finally it is only Army makework and not nearly enough of it.

"Stick the niggers where they can't make too much trouble," Coop grumbles whenever they are out on maneuvers. "Any further an we be in Mexico."

"All I know," says Too Tall, who got the trench foot so bad in Cuba they almost had to amputate, "is it aint rainin."

It is crowded in the saloon, crowded in all of the dozens of saloons in Brewery Gulch, and the boys will tie one on and then climb uphill to buy women but Royal is looking straight ahead, past the two busy bartenders who run back and forth, looking to the even busier picture behind them of the 7th being slaughtered by Indians on the hills he has ridden over on a bicycle. At the lower right there are men already stripped of their clothes, others having their scalps lifted or being trampled by horses or shot or stabbed or tomahawked, and only a few able to fight back. More Indians on horseback are on their way, galloping from the mountains at the top of the picture. The General himself is just up and over from the middle, dressed in buckskins, hatless, empty pistol held as a club in his left hand and saber raised high in his right. Above the frame it says that the beer company presented the original of the painting to the regiment, though why you'd want a picture of your friends being murdered and mutilated is not explained. On the bottom it identifies RAIN-IN-THE-FACE and HALF BREED and GENERAL CUSTER and some others and at the far right SQUAW KILLING WOUNDED. Sure enough above it there is a woman in a red dress grabbing a downed soldier at his collar and raising a club overhead to brain him. No prisoners.

We have no engagement to break off, of course, no, we have nothing but our one night of love to remember—

He has seen *Custer's Last Fight* in bars before but never studied the details. The old troopers say you kept the last bullet for yourself because if you weren't finished they would scalp you alive and then do other things. Coop said that in Caney they found a Spanish officer who'd stabbed his woman, a Cuban girl, and then shot himself in the head. But that is just meanness and honor, Dago stuff, and no model for his present situation.

Father will not be moved and I am not of an age to defy him. If it was not for my condition we could wait—

Junior is sitting over with the boys but quiet. And feeling bad, Royal hopes. He drinks more whiskey from the jug. He read all three letters, the second two just more of how bad she feels but she is not the mistress of her own fate, her hands are tied, she suffers with each breath, each word seeming more of a fake than the next, and only the first one has anything for him, scrawled as an afterthought below her name—

I will always love you.

He will not always love her, not if he can help it. He thinks, in fact, that he has already stopped, but that doesn't make it any easier to breathe. He wants to paint his face like the Cheyenne and the Sioux in the picture and ride straight over somebody, wants to pound somebody to jelly with a club. Dorsey Love is an old man, almost thirty, and he will be the one lying with Jessie, he will be the one raising up Royal's baby boy or girl, he will be the one that sits at the Luncefords' big table and the Doctor will have to smile at him and pass the chicken and pretend he is happy about it. The liquor has no bite now, just a smell, and Hardaway is up on a chair reciting *The Charge of the Nigger Ninth* for everybody in the saloon, though Hardaway is in the 25th and didn't come up the hill till the second day.

"What you got there?" he called out, passing by as Royal pondered the letters, sitting on the barracks steps. "Some gal that won't leave you be?"

"Just news from home," Royal said and looked across at Junior, who was reading his own letter from his mother and knowing by then. "Junior's sister is getting married."

"That right?" Mudfish Brown joined in. "Fore you know it he be a uncle. Uncle Junior."

They were still calling him that on the ride across the scrublands, Junior shooting Royal a sorry look now and then but not saying anything. There is not much he can say that won't end with Royal hitting him.

I have never understood why Father is so ill-disposed toward you—

Royal understands. Royal has always understood. Junior is the one who doesn't fit in here, Junior with his little half smile watching the men thumping Hardaway on the back, not a spot on him from a day of riding, Junior the one who grinds through every stupid detail without complaint, who acts like someone even higher than the white brass is watching his every move, judging his deportment, keeping score, while Royal accepts that he is just another sorry-ass nigger no matter how you dress him up.

The second letter didn't say she would always love him at the end of it, it said how in the light of the terrible circumstances they should probably not correspond any more. And the third one was to apologize for the second one, but it was only a few lines, like she was in a dungeon somewhere and had to write it quick and smuggle it out.

I shall soon reap the consequences of my own weakness. Do not mourn for me, do not even think of me—

She doesn't say if she means she was weak to come to him at Jubal's place or weak not to fight more against the Doctor. It doesn't matter. She is as gone from his life as if she was dead, worse even. Squaw killing wounded. The boys are having too much fun now and he is afraid they will try to pull him into it and the jug is feeling awfully light. He takes it with him, reeling out through the back to the alley behind where you piss and there are two men already sick there, heaving what is probably not really Old Crow and he decides to get the horse and ride somewhere.

But on Commerce Street there are too many men, the town overstuffed with miners come in desperate to spend their pay and get at least as drunk as Royal is. There are three different fistfights in progress and men peeing right out on the curb and a man who has taken his shirt off standing out in the middle and screaming, just screaming. The Gulch rises up steep to the next block, drunken men stumbling down past as he climbs and thrusts the jug into the arms of an already weaving white miner and then passes through an alley between two buildings and just keeps climbing, up the slope and away from the racket of Bisbee and the glowing lights of the copper smelter just below it. It is steep enough that sometimes he has to put his hands down and climb on all fours but finally he is on the ridge, standing unsteadily, looking back down at the lights and the shouting and the raucous music and now and then a gunshot and he can think of nothing more than Sodom and Gomorrah in the Bible story. They had it coming and so did he, it looks like, and he wheels around and walks farther away from the light and the noise.

A different story—forty days and forty nights in the desert, Jesus maybe, or maybe Moses. Mama tried to take them regular to church but for a long time was caring for some white people's children on Sundays and he and Jubal would go but sit in the back and sneak out sometime before the sermon, so sometimes the stories get mixed up in his head. Forty days and forty nights in the desert and turning away from Temptation and then coming back clean and holy but mostly being away from everybody, away from their ribbing and their eyes able to see the shame of it on your face and them talking about you when they think you can't hear. Might as well give the damn letters to Hardaway and have him read them out loud. He keeps walking up a dry gulley away from the town, don't look back, don't look back, that is another story, and it is getting colder fast now and the wind picking up and he starts to howl back at it. There are coyotes at night, of course, a couple big tribes of them around the Fort that set each other off with their noise that can go on for hours, but you don't see much of them unless you're out on maneuvers and cook up a mess of bacon and then they'll come sniffing, head low and ears back. The stars are gone now, no moon, the sky feeling suddenly low and heavy above him and then there is thunder, rolling at first, and sheet lightning flickering up in the clouds, one section of the sky lighting up for a moment, then another, like the clouds are packs of coyotes calling to each other then *CRACK!* a bolt sizzling down not so far from him and *CRACK!* another behind and then it is hail, hard and scouring and there is nowhere to shelter, the land here even more wasted, even less friendly than Montana and the hailstones sting like hell where they slap against his skin, Royal ducking his head in under his arms, left his hat on the bar in the Calumet, and thinking I looked back, dammit, I forgot the story and I looked back and now I will turn into a pillar of shit. And *CRACK!* it answers, close enough to smell fried air this time, answering him, reminding him how small he is, how it don't care a thing about his troubles.

Royal sits heavily onto the spiky ground, covering his head and waiting for it to end.

Sergeant Jacks is skirting around Bisbee with Guadalupe and the new mule when a mine foreman riding in the opposite direction tells him there is a soldier sitting in the desert. The mule is the end result of a transaction among Lupe's hundreds of cousins that started at least two years ago, and he hopes to hell it isn't stolen. El Chato, who sold it to him at his shack down near Naco a hundred yards from the border, is from the Apache side of her relatives, a son of old Hernán whose sister was one of Geronimo's wives, and likes to brag about what great stock thieves his people are.

"Some of my fellas hauling timber in seen him," says the mine foreman, trying not to stare at Guadalupe on the grulla mare beside him. "They stopped and walked all the way over from the wagon road but he said he'd just stay where he was."

Lupe is half Mex and half Indian, which Jacks didn't know till they were hitched and nobody come to congratulate her. Relatives on both sides will nod hello if they pass by but that is about all. And then up in Missoula with her it was a whole nother kind of people, white ladies who couldn't be bothered and the Flathead gals who don't speak Spanish or Apache. So it is mostly just the two of them, which has been just fine so far. Marriage is a tricky enough deal without the in-laws thrown into the pot.

"*Es un loco?*" she asks about the soldier when they are riding away.

"*No sé cual soldado es,*" he shrugs. "*Quizás es solamente un borrachón.*"

There are men in the company, good men in a pinch, who can't handle peacetime duty and fall into the bottle. And it is worse out here in the Great Nowhere, easy for a soldier to think the Army has just forgotten about you, that you'll shrivel up in the sun like a dead rattler. Which is some of why he chased after Lupe so hard on his first tour here, knowing only that she wasn't white and she wasn't for sale and that she was one tough trader. They still had a sutler at the Fort then and whenever he would try to swap canned provisions for her wild game or Navaho blankets or other souvenir goods she would pick a can out at random and make him eat the contents, all of it, before she'd close the deal. Wouldn't talk any English, either, though even back then Jacks could tell she understood it fine.

She points to the sky.

There are nearly a dozen buzzards wheeling lazily in the air, enough to know that what's below them is bigger than a *javelina* and high enough to guess that it isn't dead yet. Lupe leads the mule on a rope. It is maybe a three-year-old, bred in the Mex style on a mustang mare, and is way too curious to have been used in the traces. Its big ears start twitching every which way when they cut off the road and into the chaparral.

From a distance he does look dead, though he is sitting up, cross-legged in the middle of a big patch of *ocotillo* and *cholla* cactus. There were maybe twenty each from A and H got the two-day pass, let them blow off some steam and keep the barracks scraps to a minimum. Men are not mules, which would be happy to eat mash and switch flies all day, they get mean and skittish if there's too little to do, if there's nobody else to fight but each other. Huachuca isn't bad duty, laid out just like Fort Missoula only the mountains are scrub instead of evergreen, but riding herd on the cursing, whining, sweat-stinking lot of troopers will wear a man down, so whenever there is a chance to spend a night at the cabin he grabs it. If there was ever a person don't need taking care of it is Guadalupe. She won't come on the Fort any more, not even to sell, and he figures it is on his account. The old hands know better than to call him Squaw Man or tamale-eater but still it is nice to keep the two things separate. Army owns enough of you.

It is Royal Scott.

It is Royal Scott and he's lost his hat and the skin on his face has started to blister. He sits cross-legged, hands resting on his knees with his palms up, eyes closed. Lupe hands Jacks her reins and gets down, stepping carefully over the horse-crippler and around the *cholla* till she can bend down and look at him close. He opens his eyes to see her.

"Here she is," he smiles. "Come to kill the wounded."

"You got lost in the desert," calls Sergeant Jacks, giving the boy an out. Scott looks over and doesn't seem too surprised that he is there.

"No, Sergeant, this is just where I come to a stop."

"You were due back in camp sometime yesterday, I expect."

The boy shakes his head. "I need to go home."

"You *are* home, son. Till they tell us different."

He keeps smiling, one of those don't-give-a-damn-no-more smiles Jacks has learned to be wary of. Guadalupe is still bent over the boy, studying his face.

"Just leave me here, Sarge. I aint worth shit for a soldier."

He is mostly right. "Army will be the judge of that, son. Get up and we ride in together."

Private Scott holds his hands out. At some point, probably in the dark, he fell and tried to catch himself and got both hands full of *cholla* spines.

"I can't hold no reins."

"You just get up. Lupe can pull you along."

Lupe helps him stand. He teeters some when he walks, but there is no bottle left on the ground so it is just thirst and hunger and being out in that crazy hail that made such a racket on the cabin roof.

"Thank you, M'am, I think I got it now." He looks up to Jacks. He isn't the worst in the company, but he is no warrior, not like some of the old boys or that wild-ass Cooper. "This is her, isn't it? Mrs. Sergeant."

"That's her."

"I thought it was just a rumor."

Jacks gets down from his buckskin quarter horse to help her hoist him up onto the mare.

The boy's hands are useless so it is not easy. The circle of buzzards loosens, disappointed, and one by one they peel off to search for a less active prospect.

The private is still watching Lupe. "She write you letters when you're away?"

"She don't write."

"Good. Don't teach her."

When the boy is settled in the saddle Guadalupe rides bareback on the new mule, who is surprised but doesn't kick, pulling the mare along by the reins.

"*Es que se le parte el corazón*," she says to Jacks when they are on their way to Huachuca. "*Nada más.*"

The Army will occasionally grant leave on the death of a soldier's mother, but makes no provision for broken hearts. Every time the damn mail comes there is somebody left in a funk, and he wishes the people at home would have the decency to lie if they don't have good news to report.

"We'll stop on the way, deal with them hands of yours. Lupe got something to put on it."

"She a medicine woman?"

"Horse doctor. If she can fix saddle galls and glanders and poll-evil, I figure she can't do too much damage to a colored infantryman."

It is only a glue that she makes that you paint on after the big spines are pulled out and wait for it to dry. When you peel it off all the little cactus hooks and hairs in the wounds come out too. They ride for some time, Scott still smiling his smile though he is facing at least a week in the brig and won't see another leave for months, though it must be some effort to keep seated being weak and dizzy and riding with his hands crossed in front of his chest.

"You were out there a good five miles from Bisbee," Jacks says finally. "Mind telling me where you were headed?"

"Not headed anywhere. Just waitin."

"Waiting for what?"

The private stops smiling and looks off to the right to the Dragoons, where old Cochise holed up with his people. "You sit there long enough," he says, "and the Dark One is spose to come and offer you the world."

A CALL TO ARMS

It will take a day or two for the word to drift back from Magnolia, and with the election tomorrow it won't likely compete as big news. The Reverend and Mrs. Cox seem like they've hosted plenty of these—wedding party of four, no announcement in the papers. The *Record* has shut down, of course, Manly supposed to be halfway to Philadelphia, and the *Messenger* doesn't bother with colored society. Dorsey doesn't mind a bit, not any of it. Only too bad Mama passed before she could see him married to Miss Jessie Lunceford.

"From the beginning of creation God made them male and female," says Reverend Cox with his big deep voice, "that they might be one flesh." Dorsey has seen him preach once or twice, coming back from Raleigh on a Sunday and stopping halfway for church. A joyful messenger for the Lord. Dorsey is joyful now, surely more joyful than Mrs. Lunceford with her handkerchief to her eyes and Dr. Lunceford grim-faced and wishing it was over and Jessie, so beautiful in her yellow dress holding the yellow roses it was so hard to find, a brave little smile on her face like a girl waiting for her smallpox needle. Dorsey doesn't mind any of it. There is joy in his heart, and in time hers will follow.

"Therefore a man leaves his father and his mother and cleaves unto his wife," booms Reverend Cox, voice filling the tiny nave they've requested to avoid the empty, accusing pews in the main hall. Reverend Cox knows this is not a judge's sentence but a joyful sight under Heaven, and thunders out the Scripture while Mrs. Cox keeps an eye on the clock. Dorsey noticed the party waiting in the main hall when they passed through, the girl showing six months if it's a day. With Jessie you'd hardly guess, maybe just a little butterfat here and there, make her look more womanish.

"Love bears all things, believes all things, hopes all things, endures all things—"

Dr. Lunceford endures the Reverend's words with shoulders set and chin thrust upward. Dorsey has cut him once or twice, in the days before he moved to the Orton Hotel for the white trade. A serious man, Dr. Lunceford, a race man. People have nothing but good to say for him as a doctor, but the rest scares them some, showing so proud in the world, making the white folks jumpy. They are Episcopalians, the Luncefords, but have chosen Reverend Cox because it's Magnolia where nobody of any account knows them and because the Reverend is understanding of what he called the *ex post facto* of the situation. Dorsey expects some heavy ribbing from the boys who cut for him over that, maybe even from some of the white gentlemen at the Orton when they finally hear. But no matter the circumstances, from this day forward Dorsey Love and Miss Jessie Lunceford will be bound in holy matrimony.

"I do," says Jessie, quiet and sweet and dry-eyed as she speaks.

"I do," says Dorsey, feeling shivery as the words come out. His life will never be the same.

There is no way to cross the river of white men. Jubal pulls back on old Dan and sits as still as he can, watching them pass, white men in red shirts riding through the colored section of Wilmington, whooping their rebel yells, some already taken with liquor and all of them shiny-eyed with the power of their numbers. Jubal watches and is careful to avoid meeting the gaze of any of them, knowing how easy they can spook. There are the horsemen in the red shirts under the old slavery flag and then a bunch on foot, the first two holding up a banner that says WHITE CITIZENS' UNION which is the ones he has been losing hauling jobs to, the bossman saying Sorry, Jubal, I got to hire white till this election business blow over, three dozen Paddy-looking characters ambling along in sloppy rows singing—

Onward Christian sojers
Marching as to war—

Making it sound more like a drinking song than a hymn—

With the cross of Je-sus
Going on before

Then there is another mounted group, ten or twelve riders in buff uniforms and campaign hats. ROUGH RIDERS is written on the banner the first two support, the third man carrying the American flag on a long pole. This bunch gets the biggest noise from the white folks lining the street, as if they are all veterans of the recent triumph.

Two of them detach from the rank and ride up on either side of Jubal, a big one with a beard and a mean-looking little one.

"Come to gawk at the parade, Rastus?" says the little one.

"Nawsuh. Just waitin to cross."

"We aint holdin you up, are we?"

"Naw. Yall go ahead first."

"That's white of you, Rastus," says the little one and the big one laughs. The little one tugs at the front of his shirt. "You know what this uniform mean?"

"Mean you been to the Spanish war," says Jubal. "Like my brother Roy."

The white men trade a look.

"We was *meant* to go," says the little one. "North Cahlina Volunteers. Only they pushed them nigger outfits in front of us."

The big one indicates the parade passing behind him. "Know what this all about?"

"Aint sure I do."

"This here's the White Man's Rally. It's about how we gonna take this city back."

Jubal says nothing.

"What you think about that?"

There is always the point where you got to guess which way it's best to move. *"You don't never show a mad dog your back,"* his uncle Wick always says, *"and you never look a papa bear in the eye."*

"Don't spect I think nothin about it, one way or the other."

The little one nudges his horse closer. "You playing with me, boy?"

Jubal is a little above him on the wagon seat. Dan won't bolt no matter what you hit him with, been trained for that, so even if the path ahead was clear there is no way out of this. He just hopes they won't look into what he's hauling under the tarp behind—Dorsey Love would surely skin him alive if that got messed with.

"Nawsuh, I aint playin."

"You gonna vote tomorrow?" asks the big one.

"And there aint many white folks," Uncle Wick always finishes, *"who merits the truth."*

"I aint never voted," says Jubal, looking the little one in the eye with as empty a face as he can muster. "And I don't spect I start up tomorrow."

The big one grunts. "Sounds like a wise plan of inaction."

"We gonna be out here tomorrow, supervisin," says the little one. "We see you anywhere near a polling spot, you be one dead nigger."

They yank the reins and are gone then, trotting to catch the other Rough Riders. There are gaps in the flow of the white people coming down Bladen now, just the stragglers, black folks starting to pop their heads back out from their houses, but Jubal is in no hurry to push through.

Her father insists on running up the colors when they pass. He has lost several flags to vandals in the past, even after he fenced the yard with pickets, in the annual battle of the dead. When Miss Loretta was a girl and the bluecoats still a presence in town her father would march with them up to the National Cemetery on Decoration Day, though he had never been a soldier, would drag her along by her skinny arm, mortified, to hear the yankees speechify and the negroes sing. Honoring the Nation's Sacrifice is what they said, but really it was only the graves of the Union men and some of the colored who had served with them they were praying over, and there were many in town who wanted to reroute the New Bern Road so they wouldn't have to pass by the entrance gate. She was twenty-four when the bluecoats marched to the train station, gone forever, and since then every tenth of May when the rest of white Wilmington flocks to the Oakdale flying the old Dixie flag to mourn the Confederate Dead her father raises his defiant Stars and Stripes to shame them all. And here he is today, Roaring Jack, ramrod straight beside the pole, banner rippling above him, glaring his contempt over the white pickets to the horsemen passing by.

"Daddy," she says gently, stepping out on the lawn to touch his arm, "just come in and pull the shades down. This will only spur them on."

"White Citizens' Union," he snarls, then raises his voice in a shout to the men on foot who follow the Red Shirts. "Passel of damned layabouts, got nothing better to do with their time! Shiftless trash—"

The men, singing, turn and wave their hats—

Christ the royal Master
Leads against the foe
Forward into battle
See His banners go!

"It's just noise, Daddy. You know how elections are."

"It is rebellion," he says. "Armed insurrection."

"Nobody has fired a shot yet."

"The voting doesn't start till tomorrow. There will be bloodshed." The old man's face suddenly drains of color. "And what is this?"

A group of men dressed as in the photographs of Roosevelt's famous cavalry appear, riding two abreast. One of them carries the Stars and Stripes, what Daddy calls the Flag of Freedom, on a pole jammed into a scabbard on his saddle.

"How dare they?" says her father.

Miss Loretta feels her stomach clenching. If those men can use that flag for this purpose—

"Sacrilege!" cries Roaring Jack, striding forward to the fence, cheeks flaming now. "You have no damned right to drag those colors through the mud!"

A rider who seems too much the runt for his enormous campaign hat pulls his mount up on the other side of the fence, spurts a gout of black tobacco juice back over his shoulder.

"What's your trouble, Granpaw?"

"That flag—"

"We fought the Dagoes for that flag, old man. It's *ours* now."

"Never."

The runty man looks past Roaring Jack to Miss Loretta.

"You want to keep him tied in the yard the next couple days, M'am. Might could get dangerous for people who can't control what they say."

"If that was a uniform," her father says, looking the rider up and down, "you would be a disgrace to it."

A larger man with a beard walks his horse over. He touches his hat. "Afternoon, M'am."

"There are laws in this country," her father continues. "Men have rights by the Constitution. Anybody put themselves in the way of those rights commits treason."

"You tell em," says the big man.

"What's your name?" asks the other.

"Daddy, come away from there." Miss Loretta stays rooted where she stands, her father as likely to turn his wrath on her if she interferes. "You don't need to tell them anything."

"My name is Jack Butler. And you skulking sons of bitches know where to find me."

Miss Loretta holds her breath. Rolling past the two Rough Riders, past the last of the white men parading on foot, is a carriage with two men in gray tailored suits and derbies sitting impassively in the front. The one with the reins is Frank Manly, beside him his brother Alexander, and though the latter is at least as light-skinned as she with her mother's touch of Cherokee blood, the word has circulated that he is to be lynched on sight. The carriage is headed north.

Alex meets her gaze for a moment in passing, holds her eyes.

"You gentlemen will have to excuse my father," she says, moving sideways to draw their attention. "Whenever an election comes up he can become somewhat in*flam*matory."

Her mother said a lady can diffuse the most awkward of situations with a compliment and a soothing word. "You all make such a stirring sight, up there on your mighty steeds—" and here she sugars her words with the tiniest lilt of flirtation, "it's no wonder you've got him all riled up."

"I forbid you to speak with these scoundrels!" snaps her father, turning to her, furious. He slapped her once, only that one time.

The carriage is past, out of sight. In the one cartoon of Alex Manly she has seen, waved in front of her by her father during one of his jeremiads, he is depicted as a coal-black fiend in the loud clothing of a Dock Street procurer, leering at a young white woman with her leg uncomfortably exposed as she steps down from a carriage very much like the one he just drove past in.

Miss Loretta spreads her arms apologetically. "He can be so *dif*ficult," she says, nodding at her father. "If you gentlemen don't mind—"

The big one attempts a bow on horseback and leads away, while the runt turns to glare back at them as he follows.

"Names are being collected," she says quietly to her father when the riders are gone. "Mischief is being planned. They have lists."

"Well sign me *up*," says Roaring Jack Butler, standing fast beneath his flag.

It is the piano that makes her cry.

All the way back to Wilmington in the carriage he's rented she is strong, she is polite and respectful the way her father says she has to be. Dorsey is a good man, like her mother says, and mostly tends to the reins as if he isn't used to driving, tipping his hat now and then to the loud collections of white men, carrying banners on horseback, who seem to have invaded the city. Dorsey makes no mention of them, as if not acknowledging nasty looks and leering comments means they didn't happen, and instead compliments her dress, remarks on the Reverend's beautiful voice. She understands how he can cut their hair all day. His house is on Eleventh just north of Red Cross, smallish, but his own house, he remarks with pride, bought and paid for.

I will bear this, she thinks, this is my life now and I will be strong. Then he opens the door and the first thing there, too big for the room, is the gleaming piano and Dorsey turns to her proud and hopeful, gleaming himself, and it is too much.

"I don't need you to play for me," he says when he has her sitting in the one soft chair, Dorsey perched on the arm of it holding her hand in his, patting the back of it as if comforting a child. "Just whenever you want—if you get the notion."

"I am so sorry," she says, wiping her eyes and trying to catch her breath. "I didn't mean to do like this." My room, she thinks, her heart racing. I won't ever sleep in my own room again.

"We got lots of time, Miss Jessie." She hasn't called him anything yet, not Dorsey or Mr. Love or Dear or anything, just making sure he is looking at her before she speaks. He is always looking at her, sneaking sideways glances, and she wishes he wouldn't. "Lots of time for everything," he says. "Aint no hurry about it when you married. You just let me know when you ready for—you know. When you ready."

She was hoping to get that over tonight, but now, with the piano filling up this room, pushing her back against the wall, maybe not.

"Thank you," says Jessie. He's looking at her again, looking at her like she could break and she's feeling like she might just, might shatter into a million pieces. White men are singing on the street outside, drunken, and she wants him to pull the shades down.

"That's the deal, being married," he says again, squeezing her hand. "Aint no hurry about a thing."

Later, when he is gone to return the carriage wherever he hired it from, she plays a chord on the piano. It wants tuning.

The gunfire begins when the sun goes down. There has been commotion all day, horns and drumming and the devil yells of the horsemen, and now the gunshots, singly and in volleys, accompanied by animal whoops and laughter. Dr. Lunceford can see the reddish glow over their bonfire on Chestnut, can hear the men shouting and carrying on from several directions, the rally having spread throughout the city. Yolanda, still mourning for their daughter, calls him in off the porch.

"No reason to give them the satisfaction," she says quietly when he steps back into the parlor. "Those kind of people get into the drink, there's no telling what they might do if they come by and see you out there."

"This is my house," says Dr. Lunceford, sitting heavily beside her on the settee.

They have only the one gaslight lit on the wall and the piano throws a long shadow. It is so quiet with Jessie gone.

"They see you on the porch of this house," says Yolanda, "owning it, not doing the yard work, and it makes their blood boil. You know that."

During his visits to Brooklyn the previous morning the people were tight-lipped and grim, near whispering when they spoke of the election. The positions at risk on the state level are not so vital in themselves, and this is not South Carolina, or Mississippi, God forbid—but every new day there has been another warning. In the evening yesterday he and a handful of the others prominent in the colored community were escorted with an undertone of menace out onto the water, that huge gun bolted on the foredeck, the white men smirking as they neared Eagle Island and the deadly machine demonstrated. A simple cranking motion, like operating a meat grinder, then the hammering of bullets, all of them covering their ears as they watched thick wood reduced to flying chips on shore in an angry hailstorm of destruction. All this followed by a quiet but pointed lecture on civics and security. His companions were duly impressed.

There is a crackle of gunfire, not too distant, and Yolanda puts her hand on his arm.

"They say they'll be watching the polls tomorrow. Carrying weapons."

"We've petitioned the governor," says Dr. Lunceford. "He doesn't want to know about it."

More gunfire, and a distant, drunken cheer. "Do you suppose Jessie is safe?"

"They're mostly down by the river."

"But tomorrow—"

"She'll have her husband with her."

He knows this comforts his wife no more than it does him. They ran into the procession on the way back from Magnolia, a lot of white trash from Dry Pond strutting about, displaying their banners and their ignorance. But they are only the hounds, set loose to yowl and slather. The ones behind the hunt are the cigar-puffers in the Cape Fear Club, the planters and pressers of cotton, the lawyers and land-speculators and ambitious sons of the men who lost their city to the Union and now want it back. The ones who are listening to that old Confederate wind-bag in the gilded embrace of Thalian Hall, not those scorching pig and swilling whiskey behind the post office.

"Will you go out tomorrow?"

Yolanda asks in as neutral a tone as she can produce, neither a challenge nor an admonition.

"I am an Assemblyman, elected by the people," says Dr. Lunceford. "I am responsible for more than my own personal safety. I am going to vote."

It is very quiet in the parlor. This is the time of day Jessie would play. Not practice, just play a whole piece, Brahms perhaps, something slow and sweet while they all waited for Alma to call dinner.

"They say they're out to hang the Manly boys," says Yolanda. It is her attempt to caution him, to remind him of the atmosphere on the streets.

"They're safe out of town," says Dr. Lunceford. "Rode out this afternoon."

Yolanda looks to him. "You had something to do with it?"

"Several people came together," he says. "White and black. They're long gone now."

"There's one thing we can be thankful for."

Someone is walking up their street, singing loudly. As he moves closer the words become distinct—

The Paddy has his attributes
His love of drink and song
He'll serenade the stars the whole night long
The Dutchman is a stolid chap
Beneath his heavy brow
But I don't like a nigger—nohow!

Yolanda puts her other hand on her husband's arm and leans into him.

"If I could go," she says, "if I was allowed to vote, I would not allow anyone, *any*one, to steal the ballot from my hand."

The Judge moves through the men standing at the back as the old Colonel begins his aria.

"We have seen our institutions destroyed," says Waddell, standing wraithlike on the Thalian stage, "our ideals trampled upon, our women dishonored."

Most of them are up there behind him, basking in the reflected glory of the moment, MacRae and Parsley and Rountree and the Taylor brothers. The hall is packed with men and not a few women, emotion running high.

"But the time for smooth words has gone by, the extremest limit of forbearance has been reached," Colonel Waddell's voice trembles with righteousness as he exclaims, pounding the podium before him for emphasis, "and the blood of warriors rises in our veins!"

The Judge reaches Turpin, smiling as he leans against the center-aisle doorway, gazing out over the cheering throng.

"You know what's going on outside?" calls the Judge over the shouts of the audience.

"Some of our brother Redeemers having themselves a barbecue," says Turpin, not taking his eyes off the stage.

"We are Anglo-Saxons," Waddell sings out, spreading his arms to include every person in the gathering, raising his eyes to the balcony—

"They're a bunch of hooligans staggering around in the streets. I almost ran over two of them coming here, weaving straight up the middle of Princess passing a bottle between them." The Judge is listed on the Businessmen's Committee that has sponsored the evening's oration, and he is a part of what is brewing, for better or worse.

"We are the sons and daughters of those who won the first victory of the revolution at Moore's Creek Bridge, who stained with bleeding feet the snows of Valley Forge," cries the old man on the stage, "and only left the service of our country when its independent sovereignty was secured."

"It's like the old coot been born again," Turpin chuckles. "Just what you worried about, Judge?"

"If this whole deal is going to work we must operate within the law, we must be beyond reproach. We can't have the rough element taking over and blackening the name of our city."

"Our city got a pretty black name in the world as it is," says Turpin. "That's the whole problem right there."

"We are the brothers of the men who wrote with their swords from Bull Run to Bentonville the most heroic chapter in American annals, and we ourselves are men who intend to preserve, at the cost of our lives if necessary, the heritage that is ours!"

Ben Tillman might hold an audience with his plainspoken grit, concedes the Judge, surveying the eager faces in the Hall, but this old Confederate has the gift, the voice—

"We maintained that heritage against overwhelming armies of men of our own race—shall we surrender it to a ragged rabble of negroes led by a handful of white cowards who at the first sound of conflict will seek to hide themselves from the righteous vengeance which they will not escape? No!" he thunders, the audience joining his shout. "A thousand times no! You are armed and prepared," he says, and looks among the aisles with piercing gaze, "and you will do your duty. Go to the polls tomorrow," Colonel Waddell commands, "and if you find the negro out voting, tell him to leave. If he refuses, *kill* him."

A massive cheer erupts in the Hall, men and women standing, shaking their fists and applauding, many with tears in their eyes.

"Negro domination shall henceforth be only a shameful memory to us and an everlasting warning to those who shall seek to revive it!"

The Judge takes a step down the aisle toward the Colonel. The old man looks forty again, reanimated, a spirit back from the grave. And yes, sometimes the only course is to let the dogs loose and have at it. Order can be restored later. They are only dogs, after all, and tire even of blood.

Turpin claps him on the shoulder. "Don't worry, Judge," he winks. "Every move been planned out. Gonna be like clockwork."

"We shall prevail in this election," cries the old rebel, "even if we have to choke the Cape Fear River with carcasses!"

Somebody has to shovel the coal. To feed the engine. Mr. Clawson said as much when he left for the Thalian with the others. "Drew," he said, "you got to mind the fire while we gone."

Milsap perches on his stool setting type as Colonel Waddell speaks in the great Hall and the others rally outside. He can hear the Red Shirts through the window as his fingers fly over the keyboard, shouting and singing and shooting off their pistols, celebrating tomorrow's great victory. When he ducked his head out before, he could see flaming barrels of tar on the street corner, could smell sweet pork cooking. But somebody has to set the front page of the *Messenger*, Special Morning Election Edition, somebody has to ensure that the lightning bolt of truth, hurled before a yearning public, will be properly spelled and spaced.

Milsap has filled the hoppers with italics, and the words quicken his heart as they fall into line—

Rise ye sons of Carolina!

The clandestine pamphleteers of the Revolution must have felt this way, peeling Tom Paine's seditious manifesto off the blocks—

Proud Caucasians one and all;
Be not deaf to love's appealing—
Hear your wives and daughters call;

That Milsap has neither wife nor daughter does not lessen the chill that rises up his back as he commits the phrases to metal—

See their blanched and anxious faces
Note their frail but lovely forms;

Slender, pale girls with arms thin as broomsticks, eyes pleading as they submit, horrified as they stare the Nameless Crime in its brutal visage, breasts heaving, thrilled—

No. No. Horrified. Milsap strikes the keys and the matrices rattle down the slides, lining up like soldiers for a volley—

Rise, defend their spotless virtue
With your strong and manly arms!

CONGRESS

Diosdado is here because of the uniform. The one that has not been torn or stained in his few desultory engagements with the disheartened Spanish, nor in the weeks of guiding his mongrel company from post to post facing the American defenses north of the Pasig.

"If you've still got a decent uniform," said Scipio, passing close to the front in white linen and straw boater, "I can get you on for the Congress."

So he stands here at attention beneath a bamboo arch, borrowed sword raised in salute to the delegates as they file past from the train station nearly a mile away. It is all nipa in Malolos, roof panels woven here sold throughout the island, nipa huts strung along either side of the narrow main road, lined now with excited citizens eager to greet and evaluate their representatives.

These great men, perspiring in full evening dress, pause now and then to lift their silk top hats and acknowledge the throng, wiping their brows with dazzling handkerchiefs. There are not nearly enough carriages. The Banda Pasig, up ahead at the massive stone church, are pumping out *Alerta Katipunan!*, though that old secret society of workers and peasants, wellspring of the people's revolution, has recently been dissolved by General Aguinaldo.

The entire Philippines is now the only Katipunan, read his decree, published in both Spanish and Tagalog, *the real Katipunan, where all are united in saving the Mother Country from the depths of slavery.*

A cunning piece of diplomacy, thinks Diosdado, standing at attention, eyes forward, sweat rolling down his face. Certainly none of these gentlemen parading before him were in the original organization, their *cédulas* torn with Bonifacio's at Pugad Lawin, nor did they rise up valiantly in '96 to battle the oppressors. Most have not been elected by the regions they represent, regions they may never have set foot in, but have been appointed by the Supremo to impress the *yanquis* and the ruling powers of Europe, reassuring them that the new republic will be administered by educated men, men of means and culture.

Here, riding in an open *calesa*, is the lawyer Pedro Paterno, who after his role in brokering the truce of Biak na Bato petitioned his well-connected Spanish supporters to have himself made "at least a Duke" of Castile, with the position "valued in dollars so that the common Filipino will not hold it in contempt." Paterno who made his best efforts to rally those Filipinos to the cause of Spain, certainly *his* Mother Country, when the Americans declared war on her.

And here is Don Felipe Calderón y Roca, grandson of a Spanish friar, who balked at recognizing the Revolutionary Government and decries those who "cater to the ignorant masses" who have shed their blood to make this day possible, with Buencamino just behind him, only a month ago jailed for intriguing with the Spaniards, now strolling at the head of a gaggle of his minions.

One of whom is Scipio Castillero.

Scipio, in a swallowtail coat he never wore to the theater, favors Diosdado with his customary smirk and a discreet nod as he passes, and now the sun is almost unbearable, the dust stirred up by this herd of strolling dignitaries thick in his nose, the Banda Pasig, playing an overwrought version of *Jocelynang Baliwag*, perceptibly out of tune.

Two local *kasamas* have camped behind him, men in their forties who look sixty, missing teeth and, in the case of the taller, several fingers.

"So who are they," asks the shorter, whose name is Eulalio, "these men in the tall hats?"

"*Ilustrados*," replies Zacharias of the severed digits. "Men who know things."

"And what do they know?"

"For one thing," Zacharias states confidently, "they can speak *kastila*."

"But if we have defeated the *kastila* themselves, if they are banished to their home across the seas, why would we speak their language?"

"Because it is the language of learning," explains the taller man. "When Padre Fulgencio stole the last five *hectares* of field from you, in what language did he read the legal decree?"

"*Kastila*," Eulalio concedes.

"And when he gives his sermon to admonish us on Sunday, what does he speak?"

"*Kastila*, again. After speaking that other one for Mass."

"That is called Latin. The language God uses to speak to His angels."

"I've never understood why the padre does this before us, we who are no angels," says Eulalio, "when he can speak our language passably well."

"To remind you of your ignorance," Zacharias explains. "And to take advantage of you. What is the point of knowledge if you can't use it to prevail over others? Look at this one—"

It is the fiery Ilocano newspaperman Antonio Luna, tricked out in a general's regalia, strutting down the center of the road at the side of Dr. Trinidad Pardo de Tavera. A strange and symbolic pair, thinks Diosdado, though comrades from their wild *indios bravos* days in Paris and Madrid—Luna's brother Juan, the celebrated painter, very pointedly shot his wife and mother-in-law, Pardo de Tavera's sister and mother, to death in a jealous rage.

"There are only ten, maybe a dozen families who matter in this country," Scipio likes to say, "eternally bound by blood and commerce."

The last of the pedestrian delegates pass. The *kasamas* and many of the other spectators drift toward the Barasoain Church. Diosdado holds his pose till his arms begin to tremble, then eases the sun-heated blade back into its scabbard and allows himself to look around.

The honor guard is mostly infantrymen, privates favored with footwear and intact *rayadillo* uniforms, troops who no doubt fought for the Spanish at some point, with junior officers like himself spaced at the bamboo arches for decoration. Capitán Janolino, charged with the detail, hurries down the line with an aide.

"He's getting in his carriage," announces the capitán breathlessly. "We'll greet him at the church."

They form in double file and march, the rest of the spectators tagging along on either side, till they come to the huge churchyard and create a passageway with their ranks, two hundred yards long, leading to the neoclassical grandeur of the basilica. The shadow of the three-story belltower gives relief to a good half of the waiting soldiers, but Diosdado is not among them. He waits, at attention, in the sun.

Malolos is renowned for its churches, "infested with them" as Scipio would say, and within them many of the Spanish friars captured in the central provinces are being held prisoner. Humiliated, yes, but fortunate to have been spared the wrath of the poor villagers they have bullied and defrauded for so many years. If it had not been for the Church some sort of reform acceptable to Filipinos might have been possible, some link with Spain preserved. But the religious corporations had the ear of the Queen Regent, that girl of sixteen years who famously stated that she would "rather lose all of the Philippines than a single soul for Christ."

There will be a Philippine Republic now, with Philippine laws and a Philippine Constitution, each new proclamation, Diosdado hopes, no matter how compromised by the *principalía* in their top hats, further refutation to American designs on the archipelago.

Cheers erupt from the crowd as they see the carriage, drawn by four enormous white horses, passing over the small bridge and under the towering, hastily constructed triumphal arch, a trotting phalanx of infantrymen to keep the well-wishers from mobbing it, now swinging into the passageway of soldiers and stopping in a waft of dust at the foot of the great church.

Diosdado can see the delegates crowding at the entrance to the basilica, the Banda playing the newly written national anthem, cries of *"Viva Aguinaldo! Viva la República Filipina!"* filling the air.

He is a small man, even smaller than Diosdado remembers from Hongkong, carrying a large ivory cane with a golden head, flanked by his taller subordinates as he mounts the steps. The mass of cheering delegates part to allow him entrance.

A small detail of Janolino's men is left to guard the doorway, and Diosdado is able to squeeze his way back through the spectators who press forward hoping to catch a phrase or more of the Supremo's opening address, till he reaches the shade of a huge mango tree. It is an honor to be here, he knows, but he can't escape a twinge of disappointment at being left outside like this, after his close and valuable service—

Eulalio and Zacharias are there beside him, squatting on their heels and fanning themselves with their hats.

"First Don Emiliano will give a speech," says Zacharias, "and then the rest will make up the new rules."

"And what will these be?"

"Better ones, God willing."

Eulalio indicates a dozen Augustinians, no doubt receiving their daily allotment of exercise, being shepherded across the rear of the yard by a pair of armed soldiers. Robes wrinkled and dusty, the *frailes* hide their unshaven faces from the happy *indio* throng with their parasols.

"Will they be sending these ones away?"

"Without a doubt. As soon as it is allowed by the Americans."

Eulalio ponders this. "Why do we need their permission?"

Zacharias sighs at the ignorance of his friend. "Because the Americans control the harbor of Manila and every ship that sits upon it. We can't make the *prayles* swim home."

"I would like to see them try," says Eulalio, his face brightening. "I bet the fat ones can float for a long time." He looks around the churchyard. "Are the Americans here?"

Zacharias stands to look over the heads of the crowd, then approaches Diosdado, holding his hat over his heart.

"Excuse me, *po*," he says, bowing slightly to the younger man. "Do you know if any Americans have attended? Their great Admiral Dewey, perhaps?"

Every *anuncio* has been full of praise for "the Mighty and Humanitarian North American Nation, cradle of Liberty," who has "offered its disinterested protection" to the fledgling republic, but the *yanquis* remain distant, cloistered within the Walled City and on their menacing gunships, like dark clouds of a typhoon hanging over the sea whose very mention may draw their fury screaming about one's ears. We have mounted an impressive spectacle today, thinks Diosdado, but our most important audience is absent.

"Perhaps," he tells the barefoot *kasama*, "the Americans have other plans."

ELECTION DAY

They're supposed to burn the city down. Sally Manigault strolls up Princess, giddy with fear as she carries the basket, but at every corner there is only another pair of men she knows, tipping their hats and warning her not to be long on the street. The only smoke in the sky is behind her, a long black tail from a steamer heading upriver. They're still working at Sprunt's and the other big places on the water, but most of the downtown businesses are closed for the voting. It is the quietest Election Day she can recall.

Myrtle Talmadge said he was up on Tenth, so she passes the corner sentries feeling like Little Red Cap from the Grimm brothers' story, swinging the basket and smiling and greeting the men. Niles would be out here if he hadn't had his tiff with the Judge and been forced to go out West. Sally is wearing the lavender dress with the leg-o'-mutton sleeves and gloves of a darker purple, embroidered in rose, and the pink and black chiffon touring hat she bought in Charleston last year. Her boots, of course, pinch like the devil, but there is no remedy for that short of surgery. If she had only gotten Niles's slender, modest feet instead of flat monstrosities like Harry's, but one is not consulted when physical attributes are being handed out.

The men carry shotguns and rifles and all have a white handkerchief tied on their left arm. They are ever so brave, volunteers all, and she gives them her brightest smile as she walks by. The Judge wanted to send her out of town like many of the other women in their acquaintance, but she told him if the men of Wilmington had suddenly discovered their backbone the least their women could do is be there to encourage them.

He is on the northeast corner of Tenth, as dazzling as Myrtle said, standing a few yards away from a crowd of rough-looking men outside an old carriage barn being used as a polling place.

"Excuse me, Miss," he calls out shyly. "May I ask where you're heading?"

"You may not," she answers, sweetening her response with a smile.

The boy flushes. "It's just that we have orders—public safety—"

"There are armed citizens on nearly every corner. I can't imagine any harm coming to me."

"We don't know their plans. There's been all kinds of rumors."

The burning will be the most difficult to control. One deluded soul with a tin of kerosene, a waterfront piled with cotton bales and wooden shacks—

"Besides," says the blue-eyed volunteer, "this is where the First Ward begins. You don't want to be up here."

Sally casts a glance at the men hanging about, joking and jostling, many of them wearing the red shirts the Dry Pond ruffians have adopted, crudely sewn garments with sailor-type collars bordered in white stitching. She can picture their wives, hair a mess, big feet working the treadle, hunched over the machine by a sooty oil lamp. If anybody is to burn the city down, these are the prime candidates.

"You believe there's going to be trouble?"

"Pretty sure of it, M'am." He shoots a look to be sure nobody is listening, bends close and lowers his voice. "In fact, it's been planned. Gonna be a bit of a rush come time to count the ballots."

"Indeed." The Judge has been grumbling around the house about secret plots and cabals all week, more upset by his exclusion from them than by the fact that they seem to exist.

"I got to keep em under control till then."

"All alone?"

"My—my fellow volunteer was—he had to attend to something."

"How long do you think you'll be out here?"

"Oh, as long as it takes, Miss. I haven't laid eyes on a nigger all morning, which has got to make you suspicious."

"Perhaps they've been discouraged from showing themselves—"

"That's the general idea, Miss."

Sally cocks her head and allows herself to look him over. He is a good foot taller than she, a few years older, clean-shaven. He looks a bit like the young man in the Arrow Shirt advertisements.

"I don't believe we've met before—"

He straightens, touches the brim of his hat. "Robert Forrest," he says. "I come down from Raleigh yesterday."

"All the way from the capital just to help us out?"

"Least I could do, Miss. The stories in the paper—"

"We are so very grateful." Sally offers her hand. "Sally Manigault."

He takes her hand, once more looking to the crowd outside the old barn. Being forthright, she always needs to remind the Judge, is not the same as being forward.

"My father, Judge Manigault, is a great friend of Mr. Daniels of the *News and Observer*. We visit him there quite often."

"Well, if you're ever up there again," says dazzling Robert Forrest, then leaves the rest to her. He is polite, this young man, and brave, but certainly not *gallant*.

"Have you and your companion had anything to eat or drink since you've commenced your duties here?"

"No, actually—"

"In that case you are in good fortune," she smiles, and lays the basket on the ground. "I have a tureen of coffee here, sandwiches, some pie—"

"Oh—"

"In response to your initial question, Mr. Forrest, where I was headed was here—to lend my support to the cause, so to speak." She flips the lid of the basket open and the boy looks into it, somewhat stunned.

"That is very kind of you."

"Nonsense. It's the least I can do. Let me pour you some coffee—"

Flirt with them, Myrtle Talmadge always says, and you win their hearts. Feed them, and you own their souls.

There are two dozen outside the icehouse, staring at him. One of them, a red-haired man with a face ruined by smallpox, steps out to block his way but is whistled back by Turpin the druggist.

"This is Dr. Lunceford," he says with a hard smile.

Turpin is a Fourth Ward man, yet seems to be in charge of this bunch blocking a polling place in the Fifth. Dr. Lunceford himself would not be here were his house on the west side of Eighth rather than the east, though geography and race are not so closely wed in Wilmington. Colored and white are poor, uneasy neighbors in much of the Fifth Ward, and not an inconsiderable show of white workmen live north of the Creek in Brooklyn, outnumbered five to one in the First.

"How we know he supposed to vote here?"

"Dr. Lunceford represents this ward." Turpin touches his hat and gives a tiny bow. "One of our distinguished aldermen."

"If he was extinguished," says the pox victim, "we'd all be better off," and the white men laugh.

"Now, now," says Turpin. "Make way for the gentleman. We don't want any complaints once the numbers come in."

They stand aside ever so slightly, eyes mocking.

Dr. Lunceford can't help but think of the revolving gun. The cylinder that housed the barrels was on a swivel, and one could direct the torrent of projectiles easily, back and forth, like a fire hose. He imagines the crank in one of his hands, trigger finger of the other squeezing hard as he faces this clot of leering white men, imagines their flesh and bone tearing apart, the terrible swift justice of it, the job done in five quick heartbeats. His father must have killed men, white men, when he wore the blue uniform. It was, however, like his youth in bondage, a matter he would not elaborate upon.

"Expect we'll have quite a turnout today," says Turpin as Dr. Lunceford passes through their gantlet, eyes fixed straight ahead. "Hell, we got folks been buried five, six years coming out to vote."

The white men laugh.

Dr. Lunceford feels his perspiration chill against his body as he steps into the icehouse. There are only a handful of men there by the table, a pair of kerosene lanterns hung from the rafters to light their task. Laughlin is behind the Republican box, and Dr. Lunceford wonders how many of the other white Fusionists have dared come out today. He fills his ballot out quickly, stuffs it into the slot. Laughlin meets his eyes.

"How is it out there?"

"About what you'd expect," says Dr. Lunceford, "given the saber-rattling that has preceded. Will you be safe here?"

Laughlin looks to the other men in the room, two of them colored, all of them worried. "It's the end of the day that worries me. When it's time to count."

"We petitioned the governor—"

"Yes, well, none of those famous yankee bayonets seem to be at our disposal. You be careful out there."

The poll-watchers are less interested as he steps out, and he can't help then but to think of the rest of it. The shredded flesh, the blood. He treated a man once who'd been shotgunned at very close range, a pox of buckshot on the parts of his body that had not been torn away by the blast, tissue crushed, bones snapped. He amputated what was left of the right arm, cut out a ruined eye, extracted a palmful of lead pellets. He is no surgeon, but none was available at the moment, and the man died a week later from blood poisoning. He can't help but wonder, should the rapid-fire gun be turned today on its owners, on its inventors, if he would lift a hand to treat them.

"We know who you are," calls the red-headed man as Dr. Lunceford turns to walk home, "and we know where you live."

Jessie is rewriting her last letter to Royal in her head, for the hundredth time, when Dorsey steps through the front door. She can't help but cry out, feeling guilty—

"Dorsey!"

He crosses to her, takes her hand. "You're shaking—"

"I was so worried," she says. "Worried about you, out there—"

She will no longer allow herself to lie, she tells herself, unless it is to spare the feelings of another.

"I'm fine."

"How is it?"

He sits at the table, right where she was just thinking about her lover who she will never see again, and slumps like he has been carrying a great weight for a long time.

"I went around to see some of the boys." He calls the men who work in the tonsorial parlors his boys. "Hoke Crawford say he was by the polling spot, there was a mess of white folks with guns outside, taking names."

"So you didn't go."

Dorsey turns his face away from her. "No point to it. Won't be an honest count."

Jessie fills the coffee pot with water, places it on the stovetop. He says he drinks coffee when he comes home from work, that it helps him think.

"I expect my father voted," she says and immediately regrets it. Now he looks at her.

"Dr. Lunceford treat colored," says Dorsey, "so he got nothing much to lose. Half my business is white heads."

"I'm glad you're back safely," she says, and it is no lie. "There's been so much talk about violence—"

"Something else afoot, I can smell it." He was on one of the Fusionist ward committees for a while, then quit it when the infighting boiled up. "Word is they got a couple reporters from up North in town, come to watch the ruckus, and it's gonna wait till the yankees leave town. Something tricky afoot."

He waits till she drifts to the piano stool, sits, and meets his eye again.

"You think bad of me? Cause the polls don't close till—"

"You did the right thing," says Jessie. What she means is that if men insist on keeping politics to themselves, they may do with it as they wish. With Royal the unsaid was always something you couldn't risk yet because you weren't certain, the unsaid was tantalizing and delicious—

"I can march right down there and look them in the eye, tell them here is Dorsey Love, make what you want out of it—" Dorsey has straightened up now. He sounds like Father— "—throw my ballot on the fire—cause that's where it's going—and let the Devil have his due. If it make you think better of me, Jessie, I am willing to suffer the consequences."

Dorsey has no trouble with words. Maybe because he has never read the books, not the love stories anyway, and has not learned to lie from them. Dorsey hides nothing from her and at the moment it brings tears to her eyes and she crosses to put her arms around him. She has never been the first to touch before.

"You stay right here," says Jessie to her husband. "I don't want you to suffer a thing."

There was some talk of using the Dance Hall for a polling place, but the Exalted Africans didn't think it looked good. "Think of who we'll be associated with," said one of the reverends. "Put a ballot box among the low crowd that congregates there and we'll look like a cartoon from the *Messenger*."

Jubal doesn't read the *Messenger* or any of the other white papers but has been forced to look at some of the comic pictures, inky coons smoking cigars and bug-eying at white women, and stood for the usual *"Aint that you, nigger, how long you have to pose for that picture?"* and sometimes wishes he could draw to point out how funny white people look. He doesn't mess with the Exalted Africans either, the whole crowd with their clubs and their college degrees that his brother Royal been sniffing around, as if Dr. Lunceford was ever going to let that boy lie on his daughter and act happy about it. So it's not any polling place, but when Jubal steps into the Dance Hall there are a pair of ballot boxes set up on the bar counter and you got to put your money in a slot if you want a drink, one with an old post-office WANTED FOR ASSAULT drawing of Pharaoh Ballard pasted on its front and the other with the same for Clarence Rice who disappeared some time ago. His drawing says WANTED FOR LARCENY and Jubal is about to drop a dime in the slot when Pharaoh Ballard himself calls out from the corner. "Don't you be feedin that box, boy, or you answer to me."

Gus Mayweather behind the bar takes his dime and puts it in Pharaoh's box. "Right good turnout we had today," he says. "Half the First Ward been in to vote."

"Can't get a drink nowhere else. You got beer?"

"Wet and cold." Gus bends to pull a bottle from an ice chest at his feet, pulls the cap off. "Yeah, when we heard the mayor was thinking of closing down the saloons we laid in some supplies. Imagine that—no liquor on Election Day."

Simon Green, the butcher's man, steps up next to Jubal. "That mayor up for office this time around?"

"Not for another two years."

"Well he aint getting my vote." Simon drops money in Pharaoh's box. "You register?"

"No."

"Then you can't vote or *not* vote for the man. You aint even counted as a person."

"They put somebody up that's worth the trouble, that's the day I register for their little game."

"Like who?" asks Jubal.

Simon thinks a long while. "Mr. Miller."

"Thomas Miller?"

"That's the man. I owed Mr. Miller ten dollars, he let it ride for two weeks and didn't charge me no extra."

"That aint no reason to vote for a man."

"Yeah, well he got white-people kind of money, owns lands, owns buildings, only he don't try and act like them. These other high-tone sonsabitches—"

"Exalted Africans," says Jubal—

"That's the ones. I deliver to their houses all the time, mostly got to bring it to the *back* door."

"You sellin em pig guts, Simon," says Gus. "You think they want that mess coming through their parlor?"

"These ones won't eat no innards, they rose *above* that. They eatin high off the hog."

"Still, any kind of quality folks, you expected to deliver to the back."

Simon isn't having any. "Just cause a man is a nigger," he says, "aint no reason to treat him like one."

"How's this vote going?" asks Jubal, sipping his cold beer and nodding at the ballot boxes.

Gus leans in and lowers his voice, glancing over to Pharaoh and Little Bit and some of the others sitting at a corner table. "The calculations won't happen till late, but I'd say our friend there has opened up a fair lead since he come in to supervise the proceedings."

"And old Clarence aint here—"

"Changed his name," says Jubal. "Went off in the Army with my brother."

"You heard of a absentee ballot?" says Gus. "Clarence a absentee candidate."

"It's pretty much that way outside, too."

"You tried to get in?"

Jubal shrugs. In here it seems silly but their Mama took both him and Royal down to register the minute they came of age. "*Your Daddy risk his life for that vote,*" she always says, "*and you boys damn well gonna use it.*"

"You never know," he says, feeling like it's an apology, "maybe somebody you help to get in do something for you later. Get you a job or something."

"Post office," says Simon Green, nodding. "Wear that uniform. Or on the police like old Toomer."

"That's right," says Jubal, feeling better about it. "Give and take. That's politics, right? Or maybe the white folks got something planned, take one of our schools away, and we got a black man up there he can stop them."

"So you get there?" asks Gus.

"Got close. But there was a line of peckerwoods outside, showin off their hardware."

"Guns—"

"Pistols, rifles, shotguns—"

The bunch from the corner has drifted over, listening in.

"You got to pick your ground," says Jubal. "Like they taught my brother in the 25th. The ground aint right, you back off and fight another day."

"So you didn't get in?"

Jubal feels them watching him. "It made me think. If the vote don't mean nothin—how come they so set on taking it away from us?"

"How many was there?"

It is Pharaoh Ballard, leaning his back against the counter so his coat falls open to show everybody the pistol in his belt.

"Oh—nine, ten of em."

There had been six, but two had shotguns and they looked desperate to shoot somebody.

"Don't no white man deny me entrance, I wants to go in," says Ballard.

Gus laughs. "You can't vote, Pharaoh. You a convicted assaulter."

"Maybe I just want to walk in the door, see how things is comin along—"

"You gonna mess with a posse of rednecks, you only got that old—what is it—"

".45."

"Man got a Colt was old when they buried Custer and he wants to start a war."

"The point is how they get to strut about our section of town, wavin their iron? What happen if we march down Market Street all loaded up and ready to shoot?"

"That *would* be a war."

"This is *ours*," says Pharaoh, indicating the empty dance floor, but Jubal knows he means the whole of Brooklyn. "They want to block off the Fourth Street Bridge like they done today, keep us from crossin in, fine. But stay the fuck out of where we *live*, man. That aint nothin to ask. You may own the world," says Pharaoh, pointing his finger toward the door, "but you don't come in my *house*."

Gus and Simon applaud, and there is no mockery on their faces.

"Can't have a proper Election Day," says Gus, "without a speech."

The numbers make no sense. Even the big number—two years ago the Republicans outpolled the Democrats by five thousand, and now he's supposed to set into the morning edition that the Democrats took this one by six thousand. Of course there should be a sizeable swing, everything they've printed in the last year has been pushing folks that way, to come back to responsible, white government, but if the colored were discouraged from the ballot how can they be showing up in the Democrat boxes? Milsap climbs down from his stool and goes looking for Mr. Clawson. The editor had just handed him the slip of paper with the election returns though the polls aren't due to close for another hour. The big number is confusing enough, but these ward returns—

Mr. Clawson is in his office entertaining Mr. MacRae and the younger Taylor brother, pouring out liquor into the glasses he keeps in his bottom drawer. He raises his eyebrows at the interruption.

"Do we have a problem, Drew?"

"It's these figures, Mr. Clawson," says Milsap, holding up the slip of paper. "I think maybe somebody pulling your leg."

Clawson smiles and winks to his guests. "And what makes you think that?"

"Every one of these precinct tallies is just way over—look here, the Third Ward, there's not more than six hundred forty or fifty men registered to vote, but here just for the Democrats we got over eight hundred and—"

"I trust my source."

"Yes, but—"

"Lots of new people been moving into the city," says Mr. MacRae. "And this business with the colored editor got people motivated to come out and vote."

"But I know the registration numbers," says Milsap, frustrated. "It just doesn't add up."

"Got all those figures in your head?" asks Allen Taylor.

"Yes, sir, I make sure and bone up before Election Day, keep an eye on our reporters. We are the paper of record here in Wilmington."

"Well I am impressed. City government could use a man with a head for figures and that kind of diligence."

"Thank you, sir," says Milsap, and now he realizes what this is, that the numbers are—what—sym*bol*ic of the will of the people, not actual counts. He feels like an idiot. "But I'm a newspaper man."

"And an outstanding one," adds Mr. Clawson. "Drew serves as my watch-dog here—misspelling, grammatical infractions both grievous and minor, errors of punctuation. But *facts*," and here the editor's eyes lose their twinkle and his voice takes on an edge, "facts he leaves to the men in the field. Isn't that right, Drew?"

"Yes sir."

"The numbers may be a tad ex*treme*, but these are extreme circumstances we are faced with, aren't they Drew?"

"Yes sir."

He indicates the paper in Milsap's hand. "My source for these figures is unimpeachable."

"I understand, sir."

"I'm confident that you do. So you go ahead and set that front page. And this here—" he holds up another slip of paper, "goes in a box, bottom center. Bold."

Milsap steps in to take the paper from him. "I get right on it."

Milsap is not so far down the hallway to avoid hearing Mr. Clawson's summation of the incident to his guests. "That is the most infuriatingly *lit*eral sumbitch," says his employer, "that ever trod the earth."

The other men laugh and Milsap feels his ears grow hot. He glances at the paper. It is an announcement not written in the editor's hand, perhaps the work of one of his visitors. At the top, in thick capitals, it says

ATTENTION WHITE MEN!

* * *

The Judge understands why they've chosen to do it in the courtroom, but it makes him uneasy. There was no legality in the summons, an admonition on the front page of the *Messenger* for "every good white citizen" to meet here this evening, and though every man in the throng is white, he knows for a fact that several are not good. Merchants, lawyers, doctors, ministers, men of property— a large proportion of those who make the city function. No trial he ever judged here at a decent hour attracted as many spectators, the jury box filled, and the gallery, and men standing shoulder to shoulder in the aisles and on the floor watching MacRae and Sol Fishblate and the few others who, thankfully, have chosen to stand in front of the bench rather than rule behind it.

MacRae is holding some sort of document and Fishblate, who's been mayor and clearly wants to be again, shouts for order.

"We're going to make history here today," he says, and calls up Colonel Waddell to read a statement.

There are cheers as the old man steps out of the crowd, looking pleased but puzzled. MacRae hands him the few typewritten pages and whispers something in his ear.

"I am as uninformed as the rest of you as to the purpose of this meeting, or the content of this document," he says, holding the pages at arm's length and cocking his head as if trying to make sense of a foreign script, "but I shall endeavor to do it justice."

The Judge looks around the room. A handful of the men, all up by the bench, are clearly the impresarios here, standing with folded arms, confi- dently studying the faces of their public, while others seem either eager to be led or, like the Judge himself, annoyed to have been excluded from the decision-making.

"*The White Declaration of Independence,*" the Colonel intones, and there is wild cheering.

The election is not in question, the advantage gained will tip the scales and the city charter can be amended to negate the sway of pure numbers in local government. What they hope to gain with this display—

"*Believing,*" the Colonel sings out, "*that the Constitution of the United States contemplated a government to be carried on by an enlightened people; Believing that its framers did not anticipate the enfranchisement of an ignorant population of African origin, and believing that those men of the State of North Carolina, who joining in forming the Union, did not contemplate for their descendants' subjection to an inferior race—*"

This is all true, no doubt, but legally insignificant given the Fifteenth Amendment, ratified in their own state legislature. The Judge recognizes the argument, has written statements not dissimilar, but that was when he was young and they were justifying the Secession. If this is indeed a declaration of independence they had better be damned clear about who they plan to be independent of—

"*We the undersigned citizens of the City of Wilmington and County of New Hanover,*" the Colonel continues, one hand holding the proclamation and the other held over his heart now like some touring Shakespearian, "*do hereby declare that we will no longer be ruled, and will never again be ruled, by men of African origin.*"

Cheers and stomping. The Judge is stirred, what white man would not be, but the arbitrator in him hovers above the clamor, awaiting the specifics—

"*While we recognize the authority of the United States, and will yield to it if exerted—*"

The Judge smiles. The lawyer's hand reveals itself. Iradelle Meares is standing up there between the Taylor brothers, and this bears evidence of his precision. They will *recognize* and *yield* to preclude any whiff of sedition, but only if *exerted*, to maintain the boldness of the assertion—

"*—we would not for a moment believe that it is the purpose of more than sixty million of our own race to subject us permanently to a fate to which no Anglo-Saxon has ever been forced to submit.*"

Playing to the jury here, and not the judge, appealing to what even the most hard-hearted white yankee must admit—

"*We hereby proclaim—*"

It is the same appeal the great Calhoun made to the Senate when he was at Death's door, his last plea to settle the differences of North and South or part amicably. That the original intent had been perverted, the original balance irrevocably lost, and that it was only the North with its numbers and control who could save the day, unless "her love of power and aggrandizement is far greater than her love of the Union." The *sine qua non* here is not Union but the deeper, more holy sense of what it means to be a white man and a Christian—

"First—That the time has passed for the intelligent citizens of the community, owning ninety percent of the property and paying taxes in like proportion, to be ruled by negroes."

It is common sense, but common sense and statutory law are distant cousins. The Colonel continues down the list of resolutions to much noisy approbation, that whites who manipulate the black vote to dominate the public sphere will no longer be tolerated; that the negro is incapable of understanding where his best interests lie; that the practice of hiring blacks to fill the predominance of positions in the workplace has encouraged their present impertinence and must be curtailed; that the responsible white citizens of the city are prepared and determined to protect themselves and their loved ones—

"We are prepared," Waddell continues, with none of the vacillation of the unrehearsed, *"to treat the negroes with justice and consideration in all matters that do not involve sacrifices of the interest of the intelligent and progressive portion of the community—"*

The flattery is brilliant, for who will not desire to be included among the intelligent and progressive? Who will argue that the interests of such exalted citizens should not be paramount? And then, without ever mentioning his name, the Colonel comes to the fate of Alexander Manly.

"This vile publication, the Record, *shall cease to be published and its editor banished from our environs within twenty-four hours."*

Men are standing on chairs to applaud now, pounding the walls in a frenzy. Were this a trial he would clear the courtroom, but it is no legal proceeding but an exercise in *posse comitatus* that he hopes will preclude a lynching, or, if that act be done, indemnify the citizens in this room from responsibility.

Sol Fishblate thanks the Colonel profusely and thanks the press, looking pointedly at Tom Clawson, for serving as secretaries for this historic gathering and for their vital efforts to inform and inflame the public preceding the election. Then the wily Jew recommends a few amendments to the

Declaration, requiring the resignation of the mayor and the chief of police and the Board of Aldermen, and there is more celebration and the Judge feels the gear click into place, the machinery of it all too clear to him now. A coup has been planned, no waiting for the slow evolution of political reform, for the months of proposal and legislation to effect the needed changes—it is a *coup d'etat*, despite all the eloquent verbiage, and when his name is called to be on a Committee of twenty-five to enforce the provisions of the document he steps forward and agrees to join it.

MacRae is on the Committee, no surprise there, and Allen Taylor, and Meares and Frank Steadman and a pair of ministers and Dr. Galloway and a quorum of the intelligent and the progressive, of good white men, and he is proud to be included but relieved that there is no swearing in, no palms pressed to Scripture to legitimize the moment. His emotions are just as divided as he lines up with over four hundred others to put their names on the Declaration.

"This is how the Founders must have felt," says John Bellamy, who will be their new congressman, "waiting to sign the parchment."

Perhaps. But to the Judge it feels more like the uneasy night in the Masonic Hall, when, surrounded by his fellows in the Craft, he knelt bare-kneed beneath the blue ceiling, cable tow wrapped three times around his body and swore, upon no less a penalty than having his body severed in twain and his bowels taken hence, never to violate the Obligation—an emotion both solemn and false.

It takes the citizen behind him in the line, Junius Hargeaves, who butchers swine on Front Street, to cut to the bone of the matter.

"If it stick the niggers back where they belong," he twangs, "I'll sign any damn thing."

Dr. Lunceford has never been in the Cape Fear Club before. The two white men in red shirts who came to get him with their pistols showing bring him in through the front door and lead him to a large meeting room. Inside are Hugh MacRae and two dozen white men neatly arranged on one side of a long table and a greater number of black citizens who have been summoned like himself crowded haphazardly on the other. His fellow alderman Elijah Green is here, and Dr. Alston and Henderson and Moore and Scott the attorneys and Tom Miller and his own son-in-law Dorsey and some other barbers and even Mr. Sadgwar, the old gentleman looking confused and upset to be awake at this hour.

"That should be enough," says Mr. MacRae on the other side of the table. "Let's get this thing started."

The next surprise is that it is old Colonel Waddell who seems to be presiding over whatever this gathering is supposed to be.

"I'm going to read you a statement," he says, "and you're going to listen."

Dr. Lunceford studies the faces of the white men as Waddell reads. A few meet his gaze with glares or stoic indifference, but none shows the slightest hint of the shame they should feel to be associated with the racialist tripe the old man is flatly reading. White Man's Declaration of Independence indeed. It is a clever strategy, he admits, to adopt the language of patriotism and liberation to cloak their designs on absolute power, but it is also as vile and cowardly a course of action as he can imagine. He looks to his fellow "leaders," whom MacRae has taken it upon himself to dub the Colored Citizens' Committee. They have no doubt been escorted here at gunpoint as he was, and sit with a kind of stunned resignation as one preposterous resolution follows another. The election results have been tampered with beyond the credulity of even the most prejudiced observer, the Democrats apparently not content to merely threaten their competitors away from the ballot box, and this farce of a proclamation seems a pointless reiteration of their contempt—

"*It is further resolved,*" reads the old Secessionist, "*to demand the immediate resignation of Mayor Silas Wright, Chief of Police John R. Melton, and the entire standing Board of Aldermen—*"

Elijah Green makes a small groan beside him. This isn't a declaration of independence, it is a demand for submission.

The Colonel finishes, lays the typewritten sheets of paper back on the table. "This is not a proposal," he says. "There will be no discussion."

Nobody on his side of the table speaks, so the Doctor clears his throat. "In regards to Editor Manly," he says softly, "he has acted entirely on his own. His newspaper has ceased publication, and, I have it on good authority, he has already absented himself from the city."

"We will require a written response as to your acceptance of these demands," says Waddell without acknowledging him. "It shall be delivered to me personally at my residence by half past seven tomorrow morning. This meeting is adjourned."

With that the white men remain seated, staring at the colored committee they have invented, insulted, and now dismissed. Tom Miller is the first to comprehend, standing without a word and walking quickly for the door. Dr.

Lunceford takes a final glance at the faces across the table and finds no hint of bluff or reservation, only the florid glow of righteousness.

"I'd had my .44," says Tom Miller when Dr. Lunceford catches up to him on Dock Street, "I'd have blown his cotton head off."

Dorsey has never actually sat in David Jacobs's shop before. He's looked through the window in passing, David or one of his boys snipping over the white men who come in, a three-chair tunnel of a room. It is packed to the walls now as most of the men from what they're calling the Committee and some others who have caught wind of this new threat have all crowded in. Dr. Lunceford stands in front of the middle chair and tries to pull them together.

"The mayor is useless," he says. "Once the hope of Federal troops was gone he crawled under a rock to hide. Which means it's up to us."

"They got the guns, they got the power."

"They've asked for a reply." The Doctor seems almost calm. "We should give them one. We reject their declaration and all of its provisions. If they can achieve the same ends through legal means, let them try. There's no reason we should take a part in our own disen—"

"There's a couple hundred reasons still wandering around town," says David Jacobs. "They're just aching for an excuse to let fly at us."

"I'm not talking about a physical confrontation. I believe it is important, for the record, to—"

"Who's gonna write that record?" Tom Miller holds the lease on Dorsey's Dock Street shop, owns the pool room he used to hang in before he married Jessie. "Anything don't look good for them they just change it."

"If there's nothing to be gained by defiant language," says Mr. Henderson, "I suggest we just distance ourselves from Alex Manly and appeal to the cooler heads among them. If those Red Shirts had their way—"

"Those Red Shirts don't do a damn thing the big folks don't put em to." Miller is by the door, angry, holding up a fist studded with rings. "And no matter what we say in any letter it's already been decided whether they be let loose or not. But lemme tell you, they come huntin niggers where *I'm* at, they gonna find one who bites *back*."

Dorsey finds himself stepping up on one of the chairs by the back wall to be seen. "They think we got some say about how other colored folks act," he says. "But the ones they worried about, all that wild Brooklyn crowd, them shack people live down south of town, they don't go to no church service. And they sure as hell don't care what *we* got to tell em—"

"Just like how we had nothing to do with what Alex Manly wrote in his paper."

"That boy was here," says Tom Miller, "I'd put my boot to his near-white behind."

"So what will our response be?" asks Dr. Lunceford.

"You seen that gun they got," says John Goines, who was Manly's printer at the *Record* before it shut down. "Seen what it can do. You want to be responsible for that machine being turned loose on our people?"

"The responsibility rests on the head of the man who pulls the trigger," says the Doctor.

"Yeah, and the man who gets caught in *front* of it," adds David Jacobs, who is also the city coroner, "won't have no head left."

Jubal spends the long night down with his animals. Old Dan is still poorly, shedding the worms, and Nubia is flighty from the white people all day. They've been quieter and more sober than for the marching, but so many *of* them about, crowded around the polling places, laughing and waggling their rifles and looking their looks at you. Jubal take her out for her little trot, Nubia a horse you can't leave in a stable all day, no matter what, and she got a sense for it, contention in the air make her shy just like a shotgun blast, and now her skin is still quivering on her back in sudden ripples, her ears switching this way and that listening for it to start for real. Jubal listening just as hard.

"Best thing for it," he says softly as he moves around her stall, "is they drink some more and fall out from it, wake up happy they won this round. Things go back to normal."

Dan is farting as he dozes, not a mule to worry about people business. There is hauling to do tomorrow and Jubal wants people back in their homes and forgotten about the election. He uses his time now, too jangled up to fall asleep, to put the tiny stable in order, hanging tack and polishing leather, talking soft to his nervous riding horse.

"Maybe this Sunday we head out to the beach," he tells her. "Let you go on them mudflats. You like that, I know."

It is a quiet night, a long night, and dawn is peeking in through the cracks between the planks before Nubia's head finally drops low and her ears relax. Jubal eases the bar up silently and steps out onto Love Alley.

Across the way, sitting in the sand with his back against a slat-and-wire chicken coop, is old Caleb who used to drink with his father, who was a slave on the indigo plantations and then rolled turp barrels on the loading dock till the liquor made him useless, which he's been as long as Jubal can remember, Caleb who never in his life give a damn about anything you couldn't pour down your throat. There is no telling what shade the old man is under the crust on him, with yellow eyes and yellow nails thick as horse teeth on his toes.

"They done stole it back," he says, looking in Jubal's direction, the way he does, but not really *at* him. "Everthing we won in the War, everthing we built up, they done took it back." He shakes his head, lets his turtle eyelids drop shut, tears making channels in the grime on his cheeks. "Aint that some shit?"

And then there are roosters crowing.

POSSE COMITATUS

When Milsap turns onto Market Street a thousand armed white men are marching toward him. At least a thousand—they fill the wide thoroughfare from side to side all the way from Sixth to the Armory two blocks down. The flood must have come like this through the streets of Johnstown, he thinks as he waits for it to sweep him along, no chanting or haranguing in the ranks, only an inexorable force of nature unleashed to run its course. He knows where they are headed.

Colonel Waddell is in the van, the old gentleman riding ahead with a Winchester held up like a standard, grim as fate. Many of the town's leading men hurry to keep beside him on foot, armed or not, determined to be noted by the swelling throng behind them. Mr. Clawson is up on the sidewalk staying parallel, with Walter Parsley and Hardy Fennell trailing after, Clawson scribbling in his notebook as he walks. Milsap falls into step—where else in the wide world should he be?—and feels the power of a thousand bodies with one deadly purpose in their consciousness as the mass surges hard right down Seventh Street, picking up speed, more men and boys pushing into the torrent from the side streets as they cross Dock and Orange and Ann and Nun, small brown faces goggle-eyed at the windows of the Williston School till they are pulled away by their teachers and then Waddell raises his rifle over his head and the righteous horde washes out around him facing a two-story clapboard house just south of the colored Methodist church, modest in façade and seemingly empty. The Love and Charity Hall.

Milsap has only seen it once, when he was a boy in South Carolina. By the time he and his friends got there the beating and burning was well over and somebody had strung a cord through the calves like it was a slaughtered deer and three of the Knights were hoisting it by rope over the branch of a sycamore tree. The top part was more charred than the legs, but as it swung, poked by gleeful older boys with long sticks, it was evident that it had been a man. Mr. Hudson, the town's only photographer, had been summoned to set up his apparatus and there was repeated posing with the trophy, Milsap and his friends sneaking in just before the cord was pulled to be included among the huntsmen. He had not, at that point in his life, seen himself in a photograph. He remembers them all being queasy with excitement, remembers the bitter smell and the strange rush of saliva in his mouth, this confluence of blood and gathered neighbors always in the past leading to fresh cracklins and pickled souse.

"You know who it is?" Milsap asked one of the older boys wielding a stick and the boy laughed and poked the hanging carcass again to make it spin and said "Say hello to Albert Lee."

But Albert Lee was a man he knew, a man who sat on the dock at the feed store and had once given him a gator he had carved from a chunk of tupelo, and this thing with half a head left strung up by the sinews could not be him.

One of the Red Shirts steps forward to pound on the door and there is shouting from the men who have flowed around and behind the structure and then Milsap is borne in a rush, feet barely touching the ground, in through the door just smashed open with axes and wrenched hard, fighting to keep from falling under the stampede of men squeezing into the downstairs hall, chairs and benches hurled shattering before them, Milsap grabbing a belt and lifted at the head of the crush up the steep incline to the crowded press at the top of the stairs. It is all he can do to avoid being brained by wood or glass or metal as the furies attack Manly's den and wreak upon his tools of outrage what they had hoped to inflict on his person.

They have been, as Milsap often surmised, still setting by hand here at the *Record*, and he cannot help but make a hasty inventory as the smaller pieces of equipment whiz past his head to smash against the walls, as stacks of papers are flung about to carpet the floor and sloshed with kerosene from the lamps snatched up from below and a man next to Milsap is beating on a folding table with a compositor's stick, smashing down again and again screaming "Nigger! Nigger! Nigger! Nigger!" while four burly men struggle to tear the bulky rotary press from its moorings and, failing that, allow others to rush in and have at it with ax and sledgehammer. Then fire, the flames whooshing across the floor and the angry wave that has scoured this room becomes a desperate scramble of men fighting to escape, men leaping down the stairwell rolling over those still struggling upward to claim a shard of glory. Milsap is shoved and then rides another man's back to the ground floor, someone stepping on his neck, then lifted and pulled to safety, hundreds of voices roaring in exaltation as white men pour out the bottom of the house and black smoke pours from the top.

Milsap doesn't remember having grabbed the chunk of metal till he feels it cutting into the palm of his tightened fist. It is a rectangle of brass with a raised shape on one face, only a shape to most but to Milsap unmistakably a capital N when reversed in a newspaper headline. He jams it in his pocket and hurries back from the sudden wave of heat roaring out from the building, flames licking out from the smashed front window above now, nearly stumbling over the guts of the defenestrated printing machine.

They could have stripped the office of the equipment, he thinks, and given it to someone who would have used it responsibly. He learned his trade on an old four-cylinder press just like the one now busted at his feet, which Mr. Clawson himself had bought cheap then sold on credit to the Manly brothers. A pity to butcher the horses, he thinks, when the coachman is to blame.

The heat has driven them all to the west side of Seventh and the fire bells are sounding their alarm when Davey finds him in the throng. Tiny points of orange are reflected in the printer's devil's eyes.

"Manly wunt in there," shouts the boy over the clanging of the bells and the cheers of their companions. "That bird done flew the coop."

Milsap nods. His neck hurts where it was tromped on. "Then we've all got something to thank him for," he says.

The alarm bells are clanging and then it's their new hose wagon come rattling down Fourth behind those two big iron grays. Jubal ties Dan off to a light pole and runs alongside till Elijah Gause can pull him up to the siderail.

"What we got?"

"Seventh and Church," shouts Elijah, pointing ahead to the left where the smoke is billowing up.

It is a mixed neighborhood and it might be three other companies there first. Jubal used to drive for these boys, the Phoenix Hose, before they went on the city payroll at the beginning of the year. Back then it was every company for itself and a race to be first at the scene for a crack at the insurance money. Uncle Wick told him once how he and Mance Crofut killed a bear years ago, how it reared up big as a hillside and threw their dogs through the air and took a couple pounds of lead shot and a smack on the head with a railroad spike before the light finally went out in its eyes. There are no bears left around here, though, and maybe a fire is the biggest thing left worth fighting, where at the end you feel like you done something important and come out alive.

They whip around the corner, wheels sliding in the dirt, and Jubal calls forward to Elijah. "You know what's burning?"

"Not yet," Elijah shouts back. "But I got a feeling it's more than a fire." And then Johnson has to pull back the reins as they come into the white people.

There is a shifting sea of them all around the fire at the Love and Charity Hall, men and boys, lots of them waving guns around. White men catch up the horses and surround the wagon, looking ugly, though Bud Savage is grinning as he struts up to hand them the word.

"False alarm, boys," he says. "Chief says we gone let this one go to the ground."

None of the other city companies have come. Heavy wood is shifting and cracking inside the building now, glowing embers floating down all around them, but not one of the Phoenix boys budges from the rig. Jubal can feel crackling heat from the blaze ahead and the acid glare of the white men closing in.

"You mean to let this church burn too?" asks Johnson, nodding to the St. Luke's Zion. "Cause that's what's gonna happen next."

An old gray-haired white man walks his horse over.

"What's the problem here?" he says.

"Boy claims the church gonna burn," says Bud.

The old man looks at the church and then back at the Hall, frowning. "Our work here is done," he says. "Let them through."

It takes a minute for the others to catch wind that they've been vouched for, every few yards another knot of white men throwing up their guns to challenge, but finally Elijah's brother Frank jumps off and hooks them up to the hydrant as Jubal runs the hose out to within twenty yards of the fire with the other pipemen, his face feeling like it is blistering, and then Frank yanks the valve. The hose jolts stiff on his shoulder and then, despite themselves, the crowd of white men cheer as the first gout of water spurts skyward and smacks down on the St. Luke's roof. Hot sweat boils off Jubal's face, stinging his eyes as he wrestles the line with the others, water pressure pretty feeble here and thinking they could use one of the steam engines to pump while he hears the old white man's voice, singing above the noise of the fire bells and the now roaring flames and suddenly the greater part of the white men start to move back north up Seventh, many of them ducking under the hose as they go. Something cracks under his feet and when he glances down he sees it's a sign that's been torn off the front of the house and hacked with axes, a sign you can still tell said THE RECORD PUBLISHING COMPANY.

He helped carry the printing gear up into that house just a little while back and now it is burning away, and he has to wonder was anybody trapped inside or shot when they run out from it, such a low, spiteful thing to do when they already took their damn election, the faces on the couple hundred whites who stay to watch not twisted with meanness, but just looking happy and curious like it's the 4th of July and next there's going to be rockets. Johnson directs them to wet the outside of St. Luke's and then do a quick knockdown of the fire on what's left of the Love and Charity top floor.

"What's the use setting it on fire," says a disappointed white boy, stepping up close with two of his friends, "if you gonna let em come and put it out?"

Dorsey was born on the day of the Capitulation, when the rebels give up to the Union at Appomattox, and his mama says that's why he's bound to keep the peace. But nobody seems to be in the mood for that right now. There is a big crowd of them come out from the cotton press, maybe a hundred men, worried about their families or their homes or just so mad they want to fight back, all facing the double row of white men lined up across Nutt Street with rifles raised and ready to shoot, some with uniforms and some without, and a Gatling gun mounted on a wagon with a white man sweating at the trigger.

Dorsey stands in the middle with Mr. Rountree and Mr. Sprunt and old James Telfair.

"What we heard is they strung up Alex Manly and burned down the Love and Charity Hall and St. Luke's Zion," says James, who manages the floor for Mr. Sprunt and sometimes preaches at St. Stephen's. "And now we hear they coming over to Brooklyn to shoot us up."

"No truth to that at all," says Mr. Rountree, whose hair looks like he hasn't put a comb to it this morning. "You got to get these people back inside."

"—*that if any persons, to the number of ten or more, unlawfully, tumultuously and riotously assemble together to the disturbance of the public peace*—" Mr. Roger Moore shouts out, reading from a paper and marching back and forth in front of the line of riflemen, "—*and being openly required or commanded by invested authority to disperse themselves*—"

"Dammit, will you stop that?" snaps Mr. Sprunt.

Mr. Roger Moore is in some kind of made-up uniform, wearing a sword. "We got to make this legal," he explains.

"There hasn't been any disturbance here and there's not going to be any," says the press owner. Dorsey was cutting Mr. Sprunt in his shop in the Orton when a couple men run in and yelled "Your niggers are coming out!" and then run off again. He should have just stayed and let the white man deal with it, but they put his name on that Colored Committee, which maybe was an honor but felt more like a responsibility, and so here he is in the middle of it. He knows they at least won't start shooting while the man who owns the cotton press and the Orton Hotel and a good deal of the rest of the city is right beside him, but the big mounted rapid-fire gun keeps swiveling to follow every time his nerves force him to move a little bit.

"If there's nothing to it about a mob coming," says Dorsey quietly, trying to be still, "I don't see why the men can't go and see for themselves."

"The situation has got beyond that," says Mr. Roger Moore. There are stripes and other shapes on the shoulder of his uniform but Dorsey doesn't know what rank they add up to. "We can't let a whole gang of these people out into the streets when they supposed to be working."

"It's the rumors, suh," says James Telfair, who belonged to the de Rosset family when he was a young man and knows how to talk to white folks. "Rumors beset a man's mind. But if you let a few out, two or three at a time, they can go look and come back with the real story."

"That would be fine with me," says Mr. Sprunt. "They won't get any work done till this is settled, one way or the other."

Mr. Rountree turns. "How bout that, Roger? Two or three can't do us much mischief."

"I'll let these two go," he says, pointing to Dorsey and Reverend Telfair. "And then I want the rest of them inside." He flips the Riot Act paper over, holds it out.

"Write your names here, if you can write."

Dorsey writes, and thinks how this is the second time in two days the white people got his name on a paper.

"You hurry your asses back here," says the man behind the Gatling gun as they pass. "This deal won't hold water long."

Men and boys are posing for photos when Jubal leaves the fire. It's only just smoldering now and he's got Dan tied across the Creek on Fourth with a wagon full of coal left to deliver. He tries to stay on the far side of the street from the white men who are drifting back toward Brooklyn in small groups, rifles slung carelessly over their shoulders, talking excitedly. The ones that got jobs must be taking the day off, as they are none of them in any hurry. When he crosses Chestnut he sees Toomer hurrying up in his uniform.

The police gives him a look. "Where you been, get all sooty like that?"

"With the Phoenix boys at the Love and Charity fire. Where were you, man?"

"Bad business popping up all over town. Somebody got a plan," says Toomer, "but they aint let me in on it."

Jubal nudges Toomer's stick as they walk. "You gone 'rest somebody?"

"Not if I can help it. I be happy I get out of this day alive."

There are a couple dozen black men outside when they get to Fourth and Bladen, glaring diagonal across the trolley track at as many whites carrying rifles who have bunched up between Brunjes' store and the St. Matthew's church. Dan is tied up by the white men.

"Help me with this," says Toomer, heading for the black men.

"I aint no police."

"Yeah, but you was over at the Love and Charity. You can put them straight."

The one they call Little Bit who you don't want to mess with at craps is out front of the men with his chest puffed out.

"Look who comin," he says. "Pet nigger in a blue suit."

Toomer steps very close to Little Bit. Jubal doesn't understand stepping that close to a man known to favor a knife. "What you think you gonna settle out here?" says Toomer. "All this shit blow over fast if you let it."

"They lynched a man."

Toomer turns to Jubal.

"You see anybody swinging?"

Jubal shakes his head. "Burned down Manly's paper but he wasn't there. Not that I seen anyway."

"Then what they all doin over here now?"

"Most of em lives here," says Toomer. "Now why don't alla you just—"

Little Bit pushes Toomer back a little and there is a pop and then another and a couple of the men around him have pistols out and there is a volley from the rifles across the street and a half dozen men fall. Jubal squats down as more shots are fired and glass shatters and one white man is down in the dirt with Dan rearing and bucking to tear himself loose while other white men take cover behind the wagon, shooting, shooting at him, and then Dan is down and screaming, kicking and writhing and Toomer stands tall and disgusted in the middle yelling "Damn you! Damn the bunch of you!" and then more white men with rifles arrive and Jubal is running, running with the rest, first down Fourth and then right up Harnett but there are men in houses shooting at them there and they retreat, a few men turning to fire back at the houses and then toward the river but more shooting now, whites chasing and black men coming out of their houses shooting and on Third another man goes down, Sam Gregory, he thinks, but Jubal just jumps over the body as it sprawls and keeps running, cutting back with three other men toward the railroad tracks and maybe a bridge to hide under, the fire bells ringing again all over town and marching up from Nutt Street to their right comes what looks like the Wilmington Light Infantry and a hundred of the Vigilance Committee with a rapid-fire gun mounted on a wagon.

"In volley, front line," calls a white man on a horse, "fire!"

The front line fires and two of the runners fall, the other two just sprinting on through and they continue to march, the Light Infantry in the van, not a one out of step as Milsap follows the loose squadron of irregulars behind them.

"On your left," calls Captain Kenan as they take fire from another house on Brunswick, "top-floor window. Fire!" Another volley and the front of the unpainted house is blistered with rounds. A pair of the infantrymen stop when they reach one of the men who was just mowed down. The top of his head is gone, and there are brains spread in the sand.

"Nigger got himself a haircut," says one Red Shirt to the other.

Milsap feels dizzy, and then sees Mr. Clawson up by the wagon that carries the Gatling. He has heard there was a demonstration, a display for the colored that he was not invited to, and he would love to see the mechanism in action but not today. The detachment moves over to Bladen Street where the original trouble was reported and continues to move west, firing at whatever moves unless it is white and sensible enough to throw its arms up and declare loyalty.

"Keep your eyes open, Drew," Mr. Clawson tells him cheerily, dropping back a few yards as they head for Manhattan Park. "Won't see many a day like this one."

Milsap nods, but when the editor strides away he lingers and then crosses to sit on the porch. There is gunfire from every direction now, screams and cursing, black powder smoke hanging in the air. A straggling Red Shirt with a shotgun steps over to him.

"Can't stay here without us, buddy," the man says. "They see a white man on his lonesome, they kill him for sure."

This is probably true and his hands are shaking but he feels more weary than scared. "I live here," says Milsap, nodding at the little shotgun shack behind him. "This is my home."

Dorsey had this nightmare just last night. Trying to find his way back to Jessie but every path blocked, knowing she's in the house and something might be wrong. Reverend Telfair went back to the cotton press hours ago, left before the worst of the shooting began to tell them it was not so bad. But now the alarm bells strike a constant warning, a clamor of metal in the air on every side, and all of Brooklyn is a running gun battle. Whatever street Dorsey turns down there are men who want to shoot him and what began as a search for a safe passage home has become nothing but flight, turning to walk, not run, away from the spots where they are killing.

If you run you're just a target.

Without Jessie it would be easy, just get down to the river and make his way to the Orton. The whole colored staff will be there, safe, behind their wall of quality white folks. But without Jessie nothing matters and the least thing a man can do and hold his head up in the world is to protect his woman from harm.

"That's him!" he hears, and his heart falls.

There are too many of them, and too many with rifles to run. They back Dorsey up against a building, dozens of them, wild-eyed and cursing, so close he can smell whiskey, and he thinks he sees Mr. Turpin at the back looking on. He holds his palms up in front of himself.

"I'm just trying to get home, people," he says. "I don't want no trouble."

"That's the one!" A different voice this time. "That's the one shot Bill Mayo!"

"I don't know any Mr. Mayo," Dorsey says, trying not to sound as scared as he is. If you're too bold or too scared they lose control—

"I saw him up on a roof! Shot right down at Bill!"

"I aint been on any roof," Dorsey says, feeling the bricks hard at his back. He wants to put his hands down over his privates where one of the men keeps poking him with the barrel of his rifle but you have to keep them up where they can see. "I don't own any gun."

"Crafty nigger, huh? Think we believe that?"

"I'm Dorsey Love," he says. "I own property. Mr. Turpin, he can tell you—"

But Mr. Turpin, if he had been there, has disappeared. A man grabs Dorsey by the collar and yanks him stumbling out into the middle of the street with the others jeering and the rifle barrel poking him hard, again and again, in the ribs now and then a hard blue shock of light and he is down with his face in the sand and he smells blood and it is his own making mud next to his cheek and they kick him, kick him over onto his back and there is a big one with a chunk of lead pipe in his hand peering down.

"Did you kill him? Is he dead?"

"I hit him in the head," says the big one. "You know they got skulls like cast iron." And there is laughing and hands pulling him up till his jaw is grabbed and forced open and someone, he can't see who with the blood stinging his eyes, jams a pistol into his mouth cracking his teeth and he can taste blood now, his own, and you can't talk peace with a gun in your mouth.

"We gonna give you a chance to do what niggers do best," says the man pushing the pistol into him. "Either you run or you stay here and eat this."

He always knew it couldn't last, that they'd find out sooner or later and put a stop to it. Raggedy-ass little orphan boy, what he do to deserve all he got, own himself a business, got the most beautiful young wife. Dorsey blinks till his eyes clear. He can see the way to Jessie. The man pulls the pistol out and gives him a shove, the others screaming for it now, veins standing out in their necks, spit flying. He runs to her.

Jessie listens to the gunshots and wishes he was here. She knows he will be trying to get to her, that's Dorsey, sweet and courtly, though he should just stay in his shop and let it blow over. She will be fine, she knows, if you don't step outside it's only noise, the havoc of the alarm bells and the angry popping of guns. There's nothing you want to see happening out on those streets.

Jessie sits at the table watching the door and misses the trees. At home— at her parents' house—there are trees lining all the streets, white ash and chestnuts and live oaks and a kind of shade and shadow they make that smoothes the sharp edge off life. Over here north of the Creek the trees have mostly been cut down and the few left are twisted and scraggly. Sand blows into the house from the street and though there's colored and white living side by side the feeling is different than where she grew up—harsh words and meanness all the time. She wishes he was home. If he gets here she will hold him and be glad and he'll know it, he'll feel it even if she can't find the words for how good he's been to her and what he's done for her and what she thinks of him as a man. She's been holding herself inside and that isn't fair to him and she feels him out there, worrying, that's Dorsey, a worrying man, and her heart lifts at the first hollow footfall on the wood of the front step.

The door is kicked in so hard it smashes against the wall behind it and sends a hung picture crashing to the floor. There are six of them, two in the red shirts, and one has a list he reads from.

"Dorsey Love," he says.

"He isn't home." Jessie stands, thinking strangely of her mother all of a sudden, the lady of the house. What she would do.

"He's on the list."

"You may not come in here," she hears herself tell them. This is Dorsey's home. He works so hard to keep it—

"Look under everthing," says the man with the list. "He's probly crawled under somewhere."

The men spread out, kicking and throwing and tearing and smashing, not looking at all, and Jessie can only stand where she is and hope they won't turn on her and that Dorsey won't arrive till they are long gone. One of the men stands scowling at the piano, as if its presence is a grave insult.

"Look at this," he says. "Can you believe this?"

When the inside of the house is in ruins they come back to the man with the list.

"He shows his face," the man says to Jessie, "tell him he got to report to City Hall, give himself up."

"But he hasn't done anything."

"He got his name on this list," says the man. "That's enough."

As they leave the man who is angry at the piano gets two others to help him. She has barely touched it. The keys give up a moan as the men bang through the doorway.

"That's mine," she says and feels the first tears rolling down her face. "He gave it to me."

* * *

Harry has somehow located the only cabman left working on the streets of Wilmington, a poor little hare-lip negro with a spotted dobbin who has seen better days.

"Oh my *Lor'*," says the cabbie as they are blocked and redirected and once even chased by the marauding white men, jerking his reins this way and that till they are thoroughly lost. Harry was at the wheel shop when the shooting began, cataloguing the inventory, and was struck with the sudden knowledge that it was his duty to join his father at home. He has seen the Judge's signature on some sort of proclamation this morning, pasted crookedly on the display window of his shop, and it has troubled him deeply.

"A sense of impending shame," Niles used to say, but always with his mischievous grin, his touch of irony. There were names far more prominent than their father's on the ridiculous document, but he had an impulse to mount one of his speedier models and pedal to the old man's side. As if he could.

A cripple running a bicycle shop, he thinks. An apt metaphor for the situation in this city. This city, he promises himself, that I am leaving.

"Oh my *Lor'*," says the cabbie beside him, pulling up on the reins.

Men are butchering a piano in the middle of the street. Polished wood cracks sharply under the backside of an ax head, pieces of the beautiful machine yanked free and hurled about. The men, white men, look up from their furious work but say nothing, make no threatening move.

"Don't worry," says Harry to the rigid cabman. "You're with *me*."

He has his cane in hand, but is not suggesting he will use it in defense. It is their contract, the one race serving the other, that protects them, that has even elicited a smile or two from the rampant Caucasians they have encountered. The man in the red shirt, the one with the ax, is smiling at them now.

"You can pass by here, Mister," he says to Harry, then winks. "I see you got yourself a tame one."

Harry elbows the poor hare-lip, who chucks his ancient nag forward. It is a tense, jittery passage, the cab wheels bumping over the scattered ivory keys, black and white.

It is one thing to bear witness as the disgraced ones sign themselves out, but another to compromise his office by swearing this new crowd in.

"You haven't been elected," says the Judge. "Not a one of you."

Mayor Silas and the white aldermen and Melton the police chief have just been sent off with their tails between their legs, having signed the paper and said the words to relinquish their positions, and here is Waddell shoving this new slate under his nose for confirmation.

"But you agree, Judge," says Hugh MacRae, who is listed as one of the new aldermen, "that we need somebody in charge to deal with this riot we got outside."

"It appears to be running pretty much how you planned it," says the Judge. They can jockey for position all they want, but nobody is going to ride on his back.

"We need this board in place," says Waddell, who has windbagged himself into the mayor's spot on the list. "We need our new chief of police to get active weeding the troublemakers out of town and we need at least a couple hundred special constables sworn in to restore the peace."

"Now that you've burned down everything you wanted."

The old man stiffens. "Mob violence is the most terrible occurrence. I dispersed those men myself, with words of conciliation."

"I can hear them out there spreading fellowship." The alarm bells have been ringing since before noon, the gunfire constant and not so far to the north of City Hall.

Allen Taylor is pacing behind him. "You going to do this for us or not?"

There was no subterfuge in the Secession. He remembers the euphoria of those first days, how free they all felt, free of compromise and secret agendas, their defiance proud and open. But this, despite the legal filigree and the old Colonel's stirring peroration about saving the city from an African uprising, is nothing but clubhouse politics under the cover of wholesale slaughter.

"No, I will not," he says.

"Dammit." Taylor looks to the other men, the self-declared saviors of Wilmington, already occupying the old board's seats. "Somebody go dig up a Justice of the Peace," he snaps, "that got more sense than scruples."

The men seem almost awed, standing on the carpet in the Doctor's house. Alma shows them in and then Mrs. Lunceford comes down to tell them no, he is not home, and yes, if they must they may search the house. Alma wants to take a fire poker to the one that sits in the Doctor's favorite chair without being invited and sticks his dirty boots up on the hassock, but Mrs. L is as gracious as if they were guests.

"My husband is a physician," she says, using the fancy word. "I suggest you go look for him where the victims of this outrage," and here she drills the one sprawled in the Doctor's chair with a look that would melt lard at forty paces, "are being treated."

Mrs. L doesn't blink as they get up and shuffle out, a few grumbling, the others looking like boys just been whipped by the deacon. She turns to Alma.

"Would you'd help me pack a few things?" she says. "I suppose we need to be prepared for the worst."

It feels like the alarm bells are in his head. They should shut them down—everybody knows to watch out by now and it's only adding to the panic. Jubal ducks behind a light pole as a riderless, crazy-spotted Appaloosa comes barreling down the street, big eye swimming around in terror, lathered beyond what is healthy. Horse like that will run till those bells stop or it falls down dead.

He finds Uncle Wicklow at the stable, calming Tobey and Socks and Strider with wet blankets over their heads to dull the sound.

"They killed Dan," Jubal says as he steps in, glad to be out of sight of the street. "And they done their best to kill me too."

Wick is running the curry-comb down Strider's shivering flanks with long, easy movements. "They done step past the line," he says with a look in his eye his nephew has never seen before.

"Aint nothin we can do about it."

Wick snorts in disagreement and comes out of the stall, carrying his hunting rifle with him. "They after you?"

Jubal shrugs. "Some that know who I am got a look at me when it come to gunfire. Right now they just huntin black hides, don't care who it is, but I expect they been takin names."

Wick pulls the bridle and steps in with Tobey. "Best thing for you is ride out of here tonight and don't look back."

"Leave Wilmington?"

"This city dead for us now. Won't never be the same."

Jubal is not so sure it won't settle down, that tomorrow or the next day he can't be back hauling coal and ice and whatever else they want, but he gets the saddle and throws it over Tobey's back.

"I got near one hundred dollars in a tin box under them grain sacks," Wick says, nodding to the corner. "Take all the paper money—it won't weigh you down."

There is shooting only a block away and Strider whinnies and shifts about, then lets loose with his pizzle and the barn starts to reek. Smells like fear, sharp and nasty.

"That horse don't never foul his own nest like that," says Wick, shaking his head. "Done step past the line."

Jubal has never been farther north than Raleigh. "What I'm gonna do?"

"You a strong young man, nearly smart as your little brother. You find something."

Jubal cinches the saddle tight. Tobey don't hold a candle to Nubia, but won some races when he was younger, his dam covered by a thoroughbred, and can still cross some ground if you keep him at a canter. And he is jet black, hard to pick out after dark.

"You'll tell Mama?"

"I get through this day I will."

Wick has the Remington up in his hands again, watching the door. Jubal remembers the day the postman brung it from the Montgomery Ward catalog, wrapped tight in brown paper, and how proud his uncle was, bragging about the pop it had, how it took the smokeless powder and shot the pointed bullets. It looks puny after what he's seen on the street today.

"They got soldiers marching in lines," says Jubal. "They got a whole army out there killing people."

"They want to start a war with me," says his Uncle Wicklow, who takes his hat off when he talks to ladies, who he's never heard mouth an angry word against any man, black or white, "I'll shoot their damn eyes out."

The Judge walks with his hands over his ears. The bells and the gunfire and the drunken scoundrels hollering from every trolley that careens up Market and his own heartbeat hammering in his ears—all such a racket he can barely think. At least Sally is safe in the church basement with the other ladies and children, at least for once in her life she's obeyed his instruction, and the new girl will be cowering in the pantry, no doubt, rolling her crooked eyes with consternation and useless to fix him anything to eat. Not that he's hungry. A queasiness, a mild nausea has settled in his gorge since he came down the steps of City Hall and had to push through the insolent crowd of rednecks loafing there waiting to be set on whatever victims this Secret Seven or Clandestine Nine who are behind the whole sorry business have chosen next. A dizziness.

The Judge turns onto Eighth to get away at least from the raucous trolleys and suddenly his left arm cramps and he feels like he's been rammed in the chest with a lodge pole. He grabs on to the picket fence beside him, unusually high, then his legs go to water and he sits hard on the ground. The sky has gotten very bright, too bright, and the alarm bells are like his life-pulse made sound, screaming through his body, and then there is a woman, young but not so young, someone he knows he should recognize, kneeling beside him.

"You just be still, Judge," she says, laying a hand on his arm. Kindness, he thinks. There has not been a moment of kindness in days. "My daddy's coming out to help you."

If there are white men wounded and dying at the main building, he doesn't know and doesn't care. Dr. Lunceford supposes he would be even busier if the ambulances were willing to bother with black men and if they could get through the fighting. So far there has been a steady stream of injured, most of whom have walked in on their own two feet, nervous about the neighborhood around City Hospital and still shy of medicine from the whole smallpox disaster at the beginning of the year. There was a riot then, too, a couple of the pest houses on Nixon burned to the ground and both black and white invading the Board Chamber to declare the vaccination law a violation, people pointing at him as if he were a poisoner of children. But gunshot wounds are not the province of root doctors and so they come in, half in shock, to ask will it cost them to get the bleeding stopped. They've only needed to use the ether once, as most of the bullets have passed through clean, but all the beds are full and there are wounded sitting on the floor in the hallway, waiting.

Dr. Mask comes in with the next one, laid out on the stretcher and looking like he's been used for target practice. Tom resigned from the Health Board along with him, surrendering science to superstition and leaving the smallpox rampant, but his practice has not suffered.

"They left this one lying where they shot him," he says, looking angry. "It's been some hours and he can't have much blood left, but there's still a pulse."

Dr. Lunceford has the man nearly naked on the table before he realizes it is his son-in-law.

Dorsey has been shot many, many times, his back torn apart, a few of his fingers missing, the side of his head swollen. He is breathing shallowly, not conscious, which is, as the shack people never fail to say, a blessing.

"Where do we start?" Mask says, spreading his hands to indicate the extent of the damage. "That's bile leaking out there."

He thinks immediately of Jessie. "Where was he found?"

"Down on Hanover," says the orderly, Barnes, examining the blood-soaked canvas of his stretcher.

"On the street? And no one with him?"

Barnes only shrugs. "White boys from the ambulance said they keep coming back but them with the guns say leave him out here for an example. Like there aint enough examples still layin out in the dirt." Barnes pulls out a buck knife and starts to cut the ruined canvas off. "Finally Judge Manigault's boy, the cripple one, stop and make sure he get picked up."

There is hollering then, Millicent who runs the nurses booming from out in the hall and then white men with rifles push her in and look around.

"You're not allowed in here!" shouts Millicent. "This area got to be *clean*."

The men try to ignore her, though she is bigger than any of them. "Which one of you is Lunceford?"

Dr. Lunceford steps away from Dorsey's body. "I'm Dr. Lunceford," he says.

"You got to come downtown with us."

They are in the uniform of the Light Infantry and the barrels of their rifles are pointed at the floor. Not one of them glances at Dorsey lying raw under their noses. Dr. Lunceford suddenly finds it difficult to breathe and knows to take this slowly so the contempt will not show. It was his first and most important lesson in politics.

"If the board has determined to take action," he says evenly, "they will have to proceed without my vote. We have patients to tend to."

"There's a new board been put in," says the one who seems to be the leader, "and you aint on it. Just come with us and there won't be any ruckus."

Barnes has the buck knife held low in his hand and Tom Mask is seething, and he has seen Millicent lift an intoxicated watchman up and slam him against the wall, but these men have weapons and there is murder in the air. Dr. Lunceford takes hold of Dorsey's bicep on the arm that is not shot away and gives it a squeeze. There is no way to know how much a dying man is aware of.

"If he wakes up," he says to Dr. Mask, "just be sure he's not in pain." And then he lets the white men lead him away.

*   *   *

The Judge lies propped on the sofa, looking up at Roaring Jack Butler.

"You had yourself a heart attack," says his old enemy, his old law partner. "Smack in front of my house."

"I'm sorry," says the Judge, still working to catch his breath.

"It's catching up to us all," says Jack. "The best and the worst."

They are quiet for a moment, and as if to honor that the last of the alarm bells stops ringing. There is still gunfire, distant and sporadic, and the Judge has a sudden crushing feeling of shame to be lying here.

"I am sorry," he says again, "for the inconvenience."

"If you'd been Alfred Waddell I'd have had the girl leave you out there."

"You know what he's been up to, then."

"A great deal of wind," Jack says, "of the overheated variety, has been rushing past my ears of late."

"He's our new mayor."

Jack laughs then, and if he could the Judge would join him and then both men are in tears.

"Look what we've come to, Cornelius," says Jack, shaking his head. "Look what we've come to."

When the newly minted Special Constables knock and the daughter, Loretta, who never married, lets them in, the Judge is beginning to get some feeling back in his fingers and toes.

"I am Judge Cornelius Manigault," he tells them, the fist behind his lung tightening again. "You leave this man be."

"Manigault not on our list," says the cretin in charge of the arrest, and they haul Jack away before he can find his hat.

He didn't think there would be so many people on the tracks. It is raining now, and cold, raining since the sun went down. Jubal keeps Tobey at a trot, leaning forward in the saddle to try to make out where the flat ground along the track bed is. You got to know what's ahead or there can be trouble. There are folks walking up on the rails or resting along the way, some empty-handed and some carrying canvas tarps or mattresses rolled up, set to spend the night outside. They startle when they hear Tobey's hooves coming up behind and Jubal keeps calling out, softly, "It's all right, it's all right."

It is not all right, and the people, mostly women and children, are fleeing out of Wilmington in the rain and the cold and none of them sure when it will be safe to come back. Even Tobey knows something is wrong, skittish and sharp-eared, a horse that's never been rode at night without a carriage hung with a lantern hitched behind him.

There are lanterns on the bridge up ahead, sentries. The Hilton draw-bridge has been raised up all day to keep people on the poor side of the Creek, and this way, the tracks over the railroad bridge, is the only stretch they haven't been patrolling. Jubal has his friend Denson up in Mount Olive and if he can follow the rail far enough out of town and then cut north— unless the whole state gone crazy. Used to be a black man got worried, white folks in his town mad at him or just looking at him funny or there's no work, he pull up and come to Wilmington. This *our* town, people used to say, don't nothing move unless it's us that moves it. It's the only place he's ever lived.

"Who's that?" calls a voice from up on the bridge and he feels Tobey twitch with fright under him and he kicks hard with his heels and they are galloping, rain hard in his face and shots coming after and cursing and dark shapes of people leaping out of the way and it is dark, dark, so dark that for all he knows there might be nothing up ahead—

The cemetery is filled with living souls, wandering in the rain. Jessie lights her kerosene when she comes upon the first miserable group of them, but is shouted at to kill the flame.

"Them men still about," says a woman with a half-dozen sniffling children clinging at her. "They see a light in here they shoot at it."

Jessie lays the lantern on top of a stubby tombstone and keeps searching, pushing her face close to whoever she meets to see if it might be him. There are dozens, maybe hundreds among the headstones, all with a different story.

"They decided to kill us all. It come down from the governor."

"Naw, it's the North and South War that's started up again. There's Federal soldiers with bayonets coming on a train to take our side."

"It just got out of hand, is all. Fed them redboys too much liquor."

A very old woman tells her there are even more people run all the way to the swamp back of the Smith Creek Bridge.

"Nobody can survive out there," Jessie protests. "Not on a night like this."

"You be surprise what folks can get through," says the very old woman, who sits on the wet ground with her back up against a stone angel. "Even your own little self."

Jessie is wet to the bone and cold, her hair plastered down on her head and streaming with rain and there is no shelter, no shelter, only the wet, cold stones and the frightened people haunting this ground waiting for the sun to come up or to be chased farther into the woods and it feels like this rain, this dark, will last forever, a sodden limbo of fear and not knowing.

She hadn't started out to be here. When the shooting had settled down to a distant pop she'd taken the lantern and set out to find him. She'd headed first for his colored shop and there was a dead man spread out in the middle of Brunswick Street in the rain, but too tall, not his clothes, and another man curled in a ball at Hanover and Third and she'd had to put the lantern down by his face to be sure. The man's lips had curled back so he looked like a dog about to snap and she hurried on, sand turning to mud in the streets and at Campbell the sentries began, white men and sometimes just boys challenging and a few just letting her pass when they saw she was a woman, while others had to step close and throw their lights over her and tell her to go home, there was nothing she could do now for her man. Dorsey's colored shop was closed up but none of the glass broken, no fight there, and she thought of going back to Dorsey's house, going home, but with the inside torn up and the piano smashed apart out front it didn't seem safe anymore, didn't seem like where she should be.

She was trying to get to the Orton Hotel, maybe they'd kept the bunch of them there from leaving, there were so many guns around town, when the boys stopped her. Boys almost men. They had rifles and mocking eyes and had draped their jackets over their heads against the rain so they looked like neckless creatures, surrounding her.

"Look at this one," said the boldest of them. "She got a pickaninny on the way." Then he touched her belly and she swung the lantern hard but only hit him in the side and they told her turn back, nigger bitch, before we get any ideas.

She felt numb walking back then, soaked and shivering already, and met the people carrying their crippled boy up to the cemetery.

"I seen em outside the Central Baptist," the mother told her. "Whole mess of them in their uniforms, come up with that big swivel-gun in a wagon and set outside whilst a dozen of em go in and tear the place apart. Churches aint safe, house aint safe, we got to get out where they can't find us."

They cut through backyards and under fences, Jessie swept along, numb and cold, taking her turn with the boy on her back. His arms were tight around her neck and his legs no more than little sticks and he weighed nothing, nothing at all.

"They tell me they coming back to kill my Charles," said the mother, "but I aint seen him all day."

Jessie wanders through the gravestones, looking for life. She can't really imagine that Dorsey will be here, he'll be all about finding her, the last man to think only of himself. But she approaches everyone she finds, seeing in their eyes the same searching, the same hope to recognize somebody who's been missing. There is a figure alone by a tall pillar.

"Little Dove," he says. "Caught out in the wet."

It is Percy of Domenica, smiling. How can his eyes shine so bright when it is so dark?

"Little Dove," he says, "got to fly from the nest."

The wet has bushed out his matted locks of hair, making him wider, more substantial. He places his palm on her belly.

"I see we been fruitful, Little Dove."

Jessie steps back. Nobody should be touching her there but Dorsey.

"You know bout Armageddon, child? We seeing the End of Days now. Satan have gathered him Host, arm them to challenge the High Spirit. Today begin the Final Battle."

"I need to find him," says Jessie.

"Oh, Him soon come, don't you worry. Pronounce upon the wicked and the righteous." Percy points to her belly and she takes another step backward. "Even them what never see the light."

"What have we done?" she asks. "What have we done to deserve this?"

Percy laughs. "He make the black man to sin," says the King of the Creole, eyes gleaming, spreading his spindly fingers over his chest, "and the white man as our punishment."

"It wasn't a sin." He is crazy, she knows, but there has been murder all day and she is standing soaked and freezing in a cemetery on a moonless night. "Nothing done in love can be a sin."

He laughs louder now and gives his cape of hair a shake. "Only one question for you, Little Dove—are you prepare to accept His judgment?"

"No," says Jessie, backing into a row of tombstones. "I have to find my husband."

Rain blows in over the Cape Fear River, rain dousing the small fires that have been left unattended, rain puddling around the bodies left uncollected, cold, steady rain that drives the last of the vigilantes, hoping for one last triumph for their cause, finally to shelter. Rain falls steady and cold on the people huddled in the cemetery and in the dark swamp, rain collects and rolls in sheets from the sides of the bridge others have sheltered beneath, sudden creeks of rainwater appearing on the downtown streets, rushing downhill for the swollen river, the storm drains backed up with debris, the city unable to swallow any more.

It is still raining early in the morning when they pull them out of the jail. Dr. Lunceford is tied with rope to the others, to Ike Lofton and Toomer the patrolman and William Moore who represented the anti-vaccination crowd in court, to Arie Bryant the butcher and Bell and Pickens the fishmongers and Tom Miller at the rear complaining that his watch has been stolen. There is little slack so when the major raises his hand for them to halt each man bumps into the back of the one in front. At least their hands and legs are free, the deputies all on their first day of service and ignorant of how to attach the shackles.

White people, men and women, line the street jeering at them as they are herded to the station, nigger this and nigger that, some walking parallel with the soldiers to unload their contempt, a group of boys trying to time their spit to fly in between the gaps in the escort. It is very early in the morning for such outrage, and he assumes these are people unable for whatever reason to participate in yesterday's action and feeling left out.

And then he sees them, standing on the other side of Third, his wife holding the broad umbrella and his daughter, looking exhausted, huddled beneath it. They are safe. Now he can bear anything. He catches Yolanda's eye and she covers her mouth for a moment, then waves, regally, the way she does when she sees him off on any other train journey.

"When you think they'll let us get off?" asks Salem Bell.

"Told me there's a lynch mob waiting at every train stop from here to Washington," says Frank Toomer. "I aint getting off till I seen the last of Dixie."

"Close your yaps," the major calls back to them. "Else I'll put a muzzle on you."

Dr. Lunceford wishes he could have been present to see their faces when they came looking for him and found his wife instead, in her parlor, when they got a dose of Yolanda Lafrontiere. They'll steal the house, of course, they own the law now and there will be taxes due or ordinances passed and within months some white man rewarded for his participation in the coup will be sitting in his favorite chair. A house is wood and brick. His Yolanda has come through it safely and will be with him for whatever comes next. She will save what she can, will help Jessie bury her husband, and then, as is their long agreement, the plan almost a joke between them, she will reunite with him whenever she is able in the city of Philadelphia, on the steps of Independence Hall.

Jessie wants to follow him to the depot but her mother says no, he knows we're safe now and there is so much to do. She means putting Dorsey into the ground. Jessie spent the night in the cemetery and then walked home, to her old home, to find the windows shot out and Alma weeping and her mother saying He's gone, you poor child, he's gone. She thought it was her father and then could tell from the tone it was Dorsey.

"Your father has been banished from Wilmington," her mother told her, holding her shoulders and looking straight into her eyes, "and your husband has been murdered."

Jessie is still shivering even after the bath and changing her clothes and her throat is raw, frantic and without sleep all night in the rain in the cemetery. There is a woman walking straight at them from the jailhouse, somebody she should know.

"Jessie," says Miss Loretta. "Mrs. Lunceford."

Jessie looks at her like she doesn't recognize her. She hasn't seen the girl in months and here she is on this terrible morning with her little belly sticking out.

"They have my father in there," Miss Loretta says, indicating the jail. She wishes she could hold Jessie for a moment, for her own comfort if not for the girl's, but even if it was allowed she is not sure it would be welcome. "He's being sent away. I shall follow, I suppose."

Mrs. Lunceford nods.

"He'll be on a later train than your husband," she says to Jessie's mother, then smiles bitterly. "So there won't be any race-mixing."

Dr. Peabody says it is only a twinge, brought on by the Judge's extreme choler and the unnecessary exertion. The old man lies in his bed upstairs, frowning out at the drizzle, Harry standing awkwardly to the side, hat in hand. He has not slept, and there is blood on his shoes, acquired while he was attempting to help the ambulance men with their gruesome duty.

"I have made my decision, Father," he says. "Or, rather, it has been made for me. I will be leaving."

The words do not seem to register.

"Today."

The Judge turns his head to look at him then, eyes not unfriendly, nods. "Don't let them make a yankee of you," he says.

Alma is trying to get all the glass up from the carpet when Wicklow looks in.

Once the sun went down the shooting began, first the windows on the ground floor, then the second, and finally even some around the back. If it had been all at once it would not have been so bad, but they just come every half hour or so all night, shooting another pane out and yelling their filth and strolling away to brag about it. She sat on the upstairs bed in their big bedroom while Mrs. L wrapped the silver and sewed her jewelry into the lining of a jacket and fussed about what clothes she should bring for him if they had to leave.

"You folks made it all right?" asks Wicklow when he peeps through the open window.

"They kilt Dorsey Love," she says, trying not to cry again. "Who my little Jessie married."

Wick shakes his head. "Sorry to hear it. That was always a nice polite boy, Dorsey. They killed a good score more than him. Talk is about bodies in the river, people thrown in ditches and covered over—"

"Don't make any sense."

"Got what they wanted, I spose. Had to send my nephew off. Jubal. There's hundreds pulled out last night, hundreds more gone follow as soon as they can. They made it plain enough that this aint a town for us no more."

Alma leans on her broom for a moment and sighs. She has never felt this tired.

"Don't make any sense at all," she says. "Who gonna do all the work?"

Milsap knows he is already late for work but he doesn't care. He has been drawn back to the blackened, dripping ruins of the Love and Charity Hall, no screaming mob now, no Kodak bugs snapping photographs. He steps into what's left of the ground floor, rain collecting in the burned-away remnants above and funneled into little waterspouts that drizzle down onto the debris. There is a large hole in the ceiling where the bulk of the press fell through, machinery lying tilted on its side draped with a layer of charred newspaper.

Milsap picks his way across the floor, poking with his toe till he finds a melted hunk of lead. It is still warm in the palm of his hand. He turns it over a few times, deciding that there is no telling what letter it was, then sticks it in his pocket with the brass N he found yesterday. He comes out from the ruined building, then absently switches it to the other pocket. Force of habit—you always want to keep your brass and your lead separate.

BOOK III
THE ELEPHANT

CURRENT EVENTS

"Tis gggreat news from the islands," says Gilhooley. "Victhry has bin wan at a pittance—the haughty Dago vanquished with barely a show."

"Manila is ours, then?" queries Officer O'Malley, jiggling his keys.

"Fer the time bein it is, it is. The Stars and Stripes gallantly flappin oer the pallum trays, the downbaten Spaniard shipped home with his tail betwixt his legs. Whither we *kape* the place or not, that's another tale altogither."

"The Fillypeens—"

"Thousands of islands it is, from the size of the Auld Country down to some not bigger than Battry Park, each with its complymint of grateful salvages."

"We've enough salvages already," frowns the roundsman. "Or have ye nivver strolled through the Tinderloin on a Saturdy night?"

"It's *mar*kets we want, Pat, or so says the powr behind the trone."

"Mark Hanna himself, is it?"

"An appytite with legs and a mighty repository of balloon juice, but a jaynyus win it comes to the spondoolacs. Whin the President does a jig, it's Hanna that's pullin the sthrings."

"Markets in Manila," muses the officer. "If it's exotic goods I'm afther I could easily stroll over to Chineytown—"

"We're not to buy from *thim*," explains the horse-follower. "They're to buy from *us*. As well as the Chinamen and the Japanese and the whole gang of yella monkeys as they've got over there. Providin a positive outflow of resarces and a ginerous influx of the auld roly-poly."

"And can they afford it at all?"

"We're only discussing the chayper sart of goods, O'Malley, nothin you or I might purchase. Have ye seen the suit that's hangin in Hymie Ziff's store winda?"

"What would a nekkid salvage be wantin with a chape Jew suit?"

"Ye'd be surprised. I've bin readin up on it—did ye know that on sortin iv the islands the majoority is Cathlicts?"

"They're all Cathlicts on Skelly Michael back home," says O'Malley, "and a more salvage, poorly dressed lot ye've nivver seen."

"The idee is," Gilhooley continues, "to bring thim the fruits iv dimocracy and cappytilism first, which projuices a desire for the finer things in life, like shoes or newspapers or whiskey."

The policeman appears distraught. "Is there no whiskey there at all?"

"None that I've heard of."

"Me admiration for our byes in uniform incrases."

"Think iv all thim barefoot Fillypeeny byes who could be out rushin the cans fer the workingmen or shinin the shoes of thim what has shoes—"

"Unimplymint is a turrible thing—"

"—but instead have naught to do but hang about and kick the cocoanut."

"A turrible thing."

"Don't I know it meself? Think if these new automobiles was within the means iv any but the Asthors and the Vanderbilks—no more horses. And without horses what's there left staming on the streets fer yers truly to shivvel off into a wagon?"

"So it's democracy, is it? Will they be sindin Croker over?"

"Not the Tammany brand, that'll come later. No, I belave it's Jiffersonian dimocracy will be the first dose."

"The lucky divvils."

"It's all part iv a natural progrission—first you had the concept of immynint domain, then it was mannyfist destiny, and now we've got binivilint assimilation, which leads, inivitably, to cappytalism. Plant the desire to improve yer lot and thin install the twelve-hour day."

"How long is their days at the present?"

"Sunrise to sunset, and not a moment of it spent in gainful implymint. Mostly they run errands for the friars."

The policeman winces in sympathy. "Franciscans, is it? Ah, the poor, sufferin brown bastards."

"Aye, Franciscans, and iv the acquisitive variety."

"Now, Franciscans aren't the worst of the orders. They'll go easy with the rod, is my experience. But yer Christian Brothers——"

"Sakes, set them byes on 'im and there wouldn't be a Fillypeeny left standin."

The copper ponders for a moment. "So——we kape the flag flutterin above, injuice thim to buy our chape suits, and in the course of time innerjuice the finer concepts iv patronage and quid pro quo."

"Tis the very thing Senator Hanna advises."

"A sound course of action."

"Ah, but there's a sorpint in the Garden."

"Wherivver ye've got pallum trays there's sure to be sorpints crawlin about."

"This wan's name is Aggynaldo."

"An Eyetalian in the Fillypeens! And is he an arnychist as well?"

"He's only a Fillypeeny insurrictionalist, is all. Wan iv their ginrals that was on our side agin the Spaniard, and now perhaps he isn't innymore."

"That quick, is it?"

"Imagine, if ye will, what the poor monkeys are thinkin——here they've bin fightin agin the Spaniard since shortly after the Flood, and in stames Admiral Dooley to knock the tar out iv the Dago's flotilla——"

"Our byes to the rescue, jist like at the San Wan Hill——"

"Ah, but there the Cubing insurrictos had their own flag at the ready——"

"Many's the time I've seen it, hung outside the hoonta office on New Street."

"And the Fillypeenys might've had some sort of a banner waiting, fer all I know, but the race goes to the swift, or in this case to thim what's got the Great White Flate floatin in the harbor set to bombard Manila with dinnymite. So there's a bit iv a dustup around the fort——Murphy, the policy banker from Twelfth Street, says it was in the bag before a shot was fired, and he ought to know——and poor Aggynaldo and his stalwarth companions look up to see the Star-Spangled Banner itself wavin high over the walls."

"Ye say the battle was not on the up-and-up?"

"D'ye know Finnegan that works on the gas lines?"

"He's felt the hard ind iv me stick more than wonst."

"And d'ye remimber last August when his missus set out afther him with a lead sash-weight in her hand——"

"And Finnegan run into the station hollerin bloody murther——"

"And him no great friend of the byes in blue——"

"He'd curse us to Hell as soon as look at us."

"Aye, but at the moment he was in mortal peril from a far more turrible inimy. Can ye imagine fallin into the hands iv Big Annie Finnegan in all her fury?"

"A fate worst thin Death itself."

"Well, thim Spanish Dons trapped in the fort in Manila was thinkin the same thoughts as Finnegan. Better their kaysters thrown on a quick boat back to auld Madrid than their noggins on a pike in Manila."

"Which manes this Aggynaldo is in Big Annie's boots."

"He takes a smaller size," corrects Gilhooley, "but the principle is the same. He goes to Admiral Dooley, does Aggy, and he says—in Spanish now, fer that's what the eddycated wans spake, none of yer googoo lingo fer thim—he says, 'Thanks fer yer help in the matter,' he says, 'and whin exactly will ye be pullin anchor?' And the Admiral strokes those great white chop-warmers he wears and he says, 'Ye'll be informed whin inny consinsus has bin arrived at.' Bein a polite way iv tellin the little monkey to bugger off. So it's our byes with their kit and rifle versus the salvages with their bolo knives, waitin fer the other brogan to fall."

"And will they lift a man's tonsure, the Fillypeenys?"

"Worst than that—they've got torters and depprydations to make a red Injin blush fer shame."

"There's bows and arras involved?"

"Spears even, like your African headhunters use. Oh, it's a primitive type of conflict they'll be wagerin on thim islands, what the Royal British who's fightin the Boors in Praetoria are callin gorilla war."

"Gorillas, too! A turrible thing." O'Malley ponders. "What exactly is a Boor, then? I've hoord iv the thing, but I don't have me finger on it—"

"It's a type of Dutchman," says Gilhooley, "that's gone wild on the African felt."

"That's a soberin thought, that is—a salvage Dutchman. The worst iv two wurrulds."

"Spakin iv red Injins," says Gilhooley, "me own opinion is that what's needed over there is Ginral Miles, late iv the gggreat victhry of Sandago Cuba, him that injuiced Geronnymo and his haythen band to come back on the riservation. He's the bye fer the job."

"Aye," the policeman nods, "he'd make short work iv this Aggy fella." He taps his stick absently against the wheel of Gilhooley's wagon, thinking. "So—whin the Fillypeenys have bin subjude, d'ye think we'll have another star on the flag?"

"Not on yer life. The Fillypeeny himself is somethin between a Hottentot and a Chinaman—with none of the positive attrybutes iv ayther race, what-soivver as those might be. Them islands is more likely to become a Turritory, like this Porta Reeky or Oklahoma. As such they injoy some of the bennyfits iv citizenship, but kape their noses out of trouble come Illiction Day."

"It seems like a great deal iv bother to go to," opines the lawman, "to sell a few chape suits."

"Tis the white man's burthen," replies Gilhooley, bending once again to his task. "And we'll all need to buck up and carry our portion iv it."

COCKFIGHT

There are roosters at the front. It has been quiet along the line all day, even with the Americans setting up their artillery on the heights across the river, quiet enough for General Ricarte and Colonel San Miguel to join Aguinaldo and the rest of the general staff in Malolos for a ball to celebrate the new Constitution.

"Keep a third at the outposts," the colonel called down to Diosdado from his rented barouche. "But there's no reason the rest of the boys can't have some fun." And then was gone.

So there are roosters in the long pit dug just behind the sentry posts, at least three sets of birds preparing to tear each other apart, and torches stuck below ground level to light their battles. Diosdado's men crowd around, betting coins and cigarettes, using old lottery tickets as promissory notes, bantering about the relative merits of Cubans versus Jolos, feathery birds versus sinewy, orange versus black. Gambling has been outlawed by General Aguinaldo, of course, but like many of his orders this one seems to be understood in principle and ignored in practice. The boys at the outposts turn to call back their observations to those in the pit, feeling persecuted to have drawn sentry duty on this night of celebration, the war over and Manila beckoning from behind the American lines on the other side of the San Juan River.

"I'm holding the Death of all Chickens in my hands," sings out the one they call Kalaw because of his big nose. "You bet against him, you bet against fate." Kalaw holds his champion, a squirming bundle of rage, within inches of the beak of the other combatant still pegged to the trench floor while his friend, Joselito, yanks the bird's tailfeathers to anger it even more.

Nicanor from Cavite squats behind the pegged gamecock. "My Butcher will cut him up," he states calmly. "Anybody who doesn't think so can show me their money, *ba?*"

Locsin, the *chino* from Botolan, is serving as the *sentensyador*, mentally recording bets shouted out by the soldiers crammed down in the pit or kneeling just above it. Kalaw's bird, hackles up, whips its snakelike neck forward, beak snapping just short of Nicanor's stocky half-breed. Nicanor pulls the cock back into his lap and his second, Corporal Pelaez, straps the razor-edged gaffs, still in their leather sheaths, onto its feet. Joselito is waving a cookpot from the mess at them.

"This is where your *kawawa* Butcher is going," he taunts, "after we tenderize him a little!"

Diosdado pulls himself away from the fight and walks along the outposts, fully exposed to the other side. Providing an easy target and pretending not to care is part of being an officer. They had started a full hundred yards back from the river, like the Americans on the other side, but after San Miguel took over Third Zone both parties began to creep up, and now each is dug in at the foot of the bridge itself, more convenient for shouting drunken insults at each other. Diosdado has been pulled in to translate, standing with San Miguel at the center of the bridge to parley with the American officers, a volunteer general from the mountains of Colorado and a Colonel Stotsenberg.

"Encroachments," the volunteer general stated in the direct, seemingly affectless American way, "will not be tolerated."

Diosdado pauses to kick one of the boys who has fallen asleep face-down on his rifle.

"Wa—?"

"This isn't a dream, soldier. What if the Americans decide to attack right now?"

The soldier looks over the lazy San Juan, the bridge paralleled by the water pipeline from El Depósito, as if the possibility has never occurred to him. Diosdado can smell that the soldier has already celebrated the Constitution.

"Then they will be very stupid."

It is probably good, this confidence, this cockiness. Spirited. When Luna suggested digging trenches, one of the Caviteño generals retorted, in Spanish, that "true men fight with open breast." Only Sargento Bayani seems to doubt that the Americans, most of them volunteers and soft from inactivity, will be no match if it comes to open hostilities.

"And what if General Luna were to appear and find you sleeping at your post?"

The private sobers visibly. "You speak the truth, Teniente. I will try to stay awake."

Luna is the boogeyman, the *aswang* who all the officers use to frighten the troops when they don't want to risk their own popularity. Luna has already sentenced two poor Manila boys to be executed for sneaking home while on sentry duty, has screamed at and slapped men of every rank below colonel. He is regarded as an Ilocano phantom, likely to materialize in three different places at once, implacable in his mania for discipline, fingers eagerly caressing his pearl-handled pistol. He is known as El Furioso, El Martillo de Dios, El Loco—

"Did you know," the men whisper to each other as Luna struts past them, eyes searching for the next junior officer to be humiliated, "that his brother, the painter, murdered his own wife and mother-in-law? And got away with it?" The whole family are *locos*, go the stories, *locos Ilocanos*, and all you can do is hope that when he explodes you are somewhere else.

But Luna is the one who knew they should have taken Manila before the *yanquis* strolled in, no matter what the cost in lives.

Sargento Bayani sits on the slope of the riverbank at the end of the outposts, smoking, smiling his private smile. Diosdado stops by him to gaze across the water.

"You're not interested in the *sabong?*"

Bayani shrugs. "I'll have some stew tomorrow." He jerks his head toward the American lines. "They had a busy day."

Diosdado watched it all through his binoculars, reporting constantly on their progress till Capitán Grey y Formentos told him to leave him alone and put it in writing. Artillery positions dug and leveled and sandbagged, the pieces rolled into place, painstakingly sighted on the San Juan del Monte hill. If it starts in earnest it will be there—the Americans will try to capture the old Spanish blockhouses and push on to take El Depósito where Bonifacio's uprising floundered not so many years ago. The powder magazine and the waterworks will be their objectives, and to take them they must pass straight over Diosdado's celebrating patriots. It has been a week of incidents, escalating each day, insults called back and forth, rumors of American sentries taking liberties with Filipino women passing through their lines, stories of the Spanish garrison back in the Walled City acting more like conquerors on leave than prisoners, stray bullets winging in one direction or the other with greater frequency each night. But orders, from Aguinaldo himself, are to avoid engagement, to accommodate their "allies" wherever possible. To wait.

"The Americans are going to vote," Diosdado tells the sargento. "Back in their own congress. About what to do with us."

"What to do with us," Bayani repeats. He addresses Diosdado in Zambal, as always now, as if it is their private language. Diosdado has not garnered the nerve to order the sargento to speak Tagalog like the others.

"The bird that loses, the *talunan*," says Bayani, "goes to the owner of the one that wins."

"We're not the losers—the Spanish are."

"Is that right?" Bayani stares across the bridge, shakes his head. It is too dark to see any movement but there is a harmonica playing, laughter every now and then, shouted challenges and passwords from the river's edge.

"The generals know more than we do."

Diosdado hopes it is true as he says it. There has already been too much dissent above him, the Caviteños resenting Luna, the veterans of '96 discounting the newcomers, each general a warlord threatening to pick up with his regional clan and march home if he isn't deferred to, flattered, given his proper share of glory. And this only in Luzon. Hard to imagine controlling what develops in Negros, Cebu, Samar, controlling the crazy *moros* on the southern islands.

"Of course," says Bayani. "The *ilustrados* always know what is best for us."

He says the word in Spanish, with the slightest touch of contempt.

"It's what I heard up in Malolos," shrugs Diosdado, angry to be made to feel guilty about his education. "The American congress is meeting. Important men are said to support our cause."

Bayani cocks his head and studies Diosdado's face, making him feel as if he is being judged for something long past repair. "If you were a *yanqui*," asks the sargento finally, "and you wanted your government to vote to take our country away from us—what would you want to happen here?"

Diosdado looks down along the outposts, looks to the men lit by the glow from the torches in the cockpit behind them. Most of the sentries have their backs to the river, talking softly with each other or calling to see how the cockfights are progressing.

"The Americans are not the Spanish," he answers, hedging. "They don't have the priests whispering in their ears—"

"I'd want a fight. I'd want some dead American boys to throw at the feet of these voters, these ones who will decide what to do with us."

He is a simple *tao*, a peasant, Bayani, in manner of speech and appearance, but there is an understanding, a cunning—

"Yesterday the Americans fired every Filipino working behind the lines for them," says the sargento, spitting into the darkness. "Today they point their cannons at us."

There is a burst of laughter from the cockpit, then shouting and the squawking of birds. "If they attack tonight," says Diosdado, indicating the sargento's lit cigarette, "the first one they'll shoot is the *tanga* sitting in front of his breastworks smoking."

Bayani leans back on his elbows, relaxed. "Unless they hit the *teniente* standing up next to him in a white uniform."

The uniform is impossible, a chore to keep clean at the front. Once a week he gives it to a girl who smuggles it past the *yanquis* into the Intramuros and brings it back the next morning, clean, starched, and smelling of woodsmoke.

"Maybe the vote will go our way." Diosdado starts back down the line. The men should at least be facing in the right direction.

"You know, in the *sabong*, if you hold the birds back from each other too long," Sargento Bayani calls after him, "they will burst and die."

In the daytime it seems very little like there will be a war. The land on this side belongs to the Tuason family, the rice mostly harvested, a handful of their *kasamas* wandering over from Santol to compete with the flocks of maya birds, gleaning what has been dropped in the fields. The Englishman McLeod has a house on the hill above them, as do a couple of the Tuasons, and the carabao, untethered, pass their days dozing in the shade of the cane thickets and lumbering down to wallow at the edge of the San Juan.

"An orderly transition," Diosdado says in his lectures to the men about not drinking on duty and taking more care with their firearms. "We can only hope these people will be as civil as the Spaniard when they decide to leave."

In the pit, Kalaw and Nicanor hold their cocks head to head, the birds pecking furiously at each other, neck plumage bristling—

"*A ra sartada!*" cries the *chino* and the men let the cocks go and step back quickly, the birds smacking together in a flurry and shooting upward, squawking and clawing, feathers flying, the razor spurs unsheathed.

"*Vaya*, Destino!" call the men who have bet on Kalaw's bird. "Cut him to pieces!"

"Get on him, Butcher!" call the others. "Don't let him go!"

They are both well-bred, Diosdado notes, standing with his back to the pit but looking over his shoulder. Small heads, long thighs, necks like steel cable, one rusty and barrel-chested, the other sleek, gray with black stippling and now flecks of his own and the other bird's blood.

"Take his eyes out!" cries Kalaw, crouching with his hands balled into fists, doing a little dance as he shadows the movements of the fight. "What's wrong with you?"

The fowl leap and flap and peck and claw, chests heaving, blood spattering, their tiny eyes red and implacable in the torchlight, till both stagger back, exhausted.

"Break!" calls Locsin, and the men gather up their champions, Kalaw spitting water into his wounded bird's face and cooing endearments, Nicanor taking Butcher's comb into his mouth and sucking the fighting blood back into it as Private Ontoy hovers over both with his needle and thread in hand, ready to sew off a torn artery if needed.

"*Ristos!*" calls Locsin, who receives a good deal of teasing because he can't pronounce his *l*'s, and the men again push their gamecocks' faces together.

"*Rucha!*"

The renewed struggle is easier to follow than the opening brawl, both birds clamping on with their beaks and trying to pull the other down, Destino dragging a broken wing, Butcher blinded on one side, yanking at each other desperately and then resting as if by agreement, their tiny hearts visibly hammering in their bodies, feathers slick with blood and gaffed claws digging for purchase in the trench dirt. Diosdado hears fireworks coming from the east, his first thought that at least his men are not the ones out of control with their celebrating, and then a private whose name he has never learned falls into the pit, shot through the eye.

"They're coming!" shouts Bayani from the river. "The *americanos* are coming!"

The fireworks are on top of them now, the air filled with angry wasps and the men scatter, most leaping down into the pit, some going for their weapons and the rest just going.

"To the front!" calls Diosdado, standing tall and feeling sick about it. "Everybody to the front! Cover the bridge!"

The birds, excited by the noise and the movement, break apart and begin to swipe at each other again and two more that were pegged waiting for the next fight are kicked loose in the scramble and go for each other and

Diosdado finds himself stepping forward to the nearest outpost and pointing at the foot of the bridge as if his men don't know by the muzzle flashes where the attack is coming from.

"There!" he shouts, over the whine of bullets and the hysterical squawking of gamecocks. "Concentrate your fire over there!"

There is no cover, he thinks, a tiny redoubt next to the bridge on the American side but then the exposed, low-railed bridge itself and the open water—they must be insane. They will be slaughtered, even at night. He turns to shout an order to Sargento Ramos, but for some reason Ramos is down on his hands and knees, crawling—

Most of the officers have gone to what is advertised as "Warren's Combined Shows," but Niles has never cared for the circus. He sits in his white drill playing bid whist, no jokers, with two Nebraska lieutenants and a major from the Signal Corps. There is money on the table, gold and silver coins and paper bills, and he and his partner, the wire-stringer, are only a trick away from taking the pot. He's pulled all the trumps from the Nebraskas, and his partner, eyebrows wig-wagging a code they set beforehand, has made clear what he's still holding.

"I had my doubts about this game," says Niles, pretending to consider his cards only to prolong the losers' agony a few delicious moments more, "but I'm beginning to see its merits."

Niles can recite the order of every card played in last week's poker game, has memorized the nicks and flyspecks on the backside of the worn deck they are using, has caught two reneges already this evening, Lieutenant Coombs too distracted by the lizards on the rectory walls to follow suit.

"They still haven't moved," he keeps saying. "But if they were dead they'd fall off the wall, wouldn't they?"

Niles has suggested that the friars glued them in place for some manner of reptilian penance, but the Nebraskan remains fascinated, much to his partner's dismay.

"Coombs here is as much help in a card game as our little brown brethren were in taking the city," says Lieutenant Spottiswood. "With friends like these—"

Niles slips the jack from his hand, raises it high—

It is something like the effect of rain on a metal roof. A few hard drops, scattered and tentative, then thickening, the thin pop of Mausers and louder bang of Springfields and then a hammering onslaught of gunfire, really pouring now, all coming from the defensive positions to the north.

"That sounds like us," says Coombs, laying his hand down with a frown and rising from his chair. The lizards skitter out of sight.

Spottiswood, much relieved, begins to sweep money into separate piles, as if he can recall who wagered what. "Afraid we'll have to call it a night. That is most definitely us. Trouble with our *amigos* across the river."

Jeff Smith once held a pistol on a steamship captain, forcing him to play out his hand despite the news that his vessel was sinking off the Juneau Pier. Niles can only scowl at the Nebraskans' abandoned cards. "If you don't have the queen of spades in there," he says, "those niggers are going to *pay*."

It is coming out of Hod, hot and liquid and seemingly with no end as he squats alongside the convent and listens to the bullets chip the stone away. All hell has broken loose and there are signal rockets streaking across the sky and I got the trots again, fuck these fucking islands and please let me die with my pants pulled up. The googoos must be shooting high, well over the heads of the boys on the front, for their bullets to be landing this far back and now here's Lieutenant Tarheel, chuckling, stepping around and over the men who have grabbed their rifles and laid down on their bellies to wait for orders.

"Word is we've got them coming in all through our lines, gentlemen," he says, pointing to the north with his cane. "It looks like the dance has begun."

Hod gets himself buttoned up and joins the others, shaky legged, as they are mustered on Calle Alix, Companies F, G, and E marched quickstep in Indian file out past the dark cemetery to dig in just south of the Balic-Balic road, looking across at the googoos that must be holed up in Blockhouse 6. It is all bamboo thickets and just-harvested rice fields around the road, Hod peering into the dark every few yards of the march for a good spot to flop if they run into an ambush. By the time they are in position the firing has thinned out, the blockhouse a black shape against a blacker sky ahead. Hod manages to crawl over an irrigation dike and pull his pants down around his ankles again. He is only just started when Sergeant LaDuke slides down next to him.

"You too," he says, unbuckling his belt.

"It aint nerves, Sergeant," says Hod, wishing he could be left alone by the Army for one solid minute, if only to relieve himself in peace. "This country's got my bowels in a twist."

"Artillery will start in on that at sunup," says the sergeant, eyes bright with excitement, jerking his head back toward the enemy blockhouse as he squats to deliver. "And then the shit is gonna *fly*."

The moon is just peeking over the horizon when the Chinese come with coffee, a huge tureen of it suspended on poles they carry across their shoulders, running and squatting, rising and running again with their quick bow-legged shuffle that always makes Corporal Grissom laugh so hard he almost chokes. It is quiet over by the big bridge and only a random potshot from the blockhouse now, but the Chinamen are trembling like gun-shy puppies by the time they arrive.

"No toast and jam?" says Neely. "That tears it—Sergeant, I want to go home."

"Sugar and cream?"

"Hey, it's still hot. Attago, Chop Suey."

All the Chinamen are Chop Suey or Chow Mein or Foo Young or You Yellow Pigtail Bastard and they give Hod the willies. Windy Bill Bosworth who he double-jacked with in Montana worked with them in California and said they were demons in a hole, do-anything rockbusters who the white miners eventually ran out so they wouldn't have to compete. These two just stay close to the ground and watch the tureen, wishing for it to be empty so they can hurry it away from the front.

"Just think if they'd sent us to China," says Grissom, poking one of the coolies with his boot. "This is what we'd be facing."

"I doubt these two are Boxers."

The coffee is hot and acid, better than nothing but only just. Hod doesn't expect it to stay in him for too long.

"Same breed," says Grissom.

Donovan is shivering as hard as the Chinese. "If we're not to fight," he says, "lave us go back under our blankets and wait till it's serious."

"Do they even have rifles, the Chinamen?" Grissom is still staring at the coolies as if he's never seen one before.

"Chopsticks. They fight with chopsticks."

"I seen one swing one a them laundry skillets at another once—"

"And the tong gangsters use hatchets and meat cleavers—"

"Wouldn't stand much show in this mess."

Hod can see the front of the blockhouse, washed by moonlight now, a solid square built of wood beams with one eye-level firing slit on the side and a little roofed lookout platform on the top. He hopes if they have to make a charge the artillery will have had time to work on it some.

Grissom tosses the dregs of his coffee into the ditch at Hod's feet. "Then they oughta get them a couple breech-loaders and a Long Tom rifle," he mutters. "Join the human race."

It is cold, bone-cold, when Capitán Grey y Formentos announces the counterattack, a heavy dew gathering, Bayani's breath visible as he complains to Diosdado.

"Why did he wait?" hisses the sargento, crouching with his back to the wall of the cockpit as they wait for the order to charge. "He can't look into the fucking sky?"

Diosdado looks, the moon rising over the hill behind them, and then Grey y Formentos fires his pistol and cries for them to charge across the bridge and he is up out of the pit and running, men beside him shouting and he fills with pride to be leading them as their feet strike the planks of the bridge and the whine of American bullets concentrates to a roar, a solid typhoon wind of destruction sweeping across the river at them and the pride is replaced by something else as they begin to stagger and fall. "*Con pecho desnudo*" he thinks as he stumbles on the body in front of him. *With open breast—*

"*Retíranos!*" the capitán calls then and it is worse going back, Diosdado forcing himself to retreat slowly, facing the fire as the men rush past him, helping Bayani drag a boy hit in both his legs to the base of the bridge and then the artillery begins to blow the hill behind them apart, the shells falling just short of the waterworks, each one louder, closer, walking down the slope to the edge of the river where the remnants of his ragged company are huddled. The ones who have rifles fire, none really aiming, reloading frantically and firing again while the enfilade from the American line continues steadily, Diosdado's men dug in only as deep as bayonets and tin cans can scratch in desperation, dew-moistened dirt spattering up to slap against his white uniform pants as he wills himself to stroll, hands clasped behind his back the way Luna does when he drills the men, some of his boys wounded, crying, Reynaldo Puyat dead, yes, that is what dead looks like up close and the bodies they left on the bridge still lying there and the *whump!* of the shells behind them, the shock of each blast like a thick board smacked against his body and the fighting cocks crowing and flapping and he is tired, tired as the sun seeps over the land to the west, understanding now how men can charge into certain death, so exhausted they can think of nothing better to do and he can see the others now, moving across the bridge and along the pipeline, huge men, Americans, hurrying a few steps then taking a knee to fire again and then a sharper bang tearing the air and it is shrapnel, his men beginning to run, run back up the hill where the big shells are plowing the ground or sideways along the river with canister-bursting jagged shrapnel screaming slicing and *whump!* the section of the bank he is standing on lifts suddenly into the air and the ground slams him on the side, punching the breath from his lungs and more earth, heavy, falling on top of him and he starts to leave, body floating out into the fragrant earth, dirt in his mouth in his nose in his hair and something wet and hot mashed against his cheek.

Something with feathers—

BETRAYAL

The soldier is young, not much more than a boy. Fit-looking in his uniform shirt and trousers, leggings wound tight over the calves, square-chinned under a battered campaign hat, but no Adonis. The rifle slipping from his stiffened fingers was at parade rest, butt on the dusty ground, no bayonet fixed to its barrel. There is a look of confusion on the young American's face, of innocence betrayed, his lips parted in surprise, his lower back arched in where the *kris* has been thrust from behind. The Cartoonist has actually seen a *kris*, hung behind glass on a wall in a Boston museum, but has added a few extra serpentine curves for effect.

The wily Filipino is a bit of a problem. The feet are bare, the clothes the same peon's rags he has used for the Mexicans the Chief hates so much and more recently for the noble Cuban *insurrectos*. The straw hat is equally ragged but less round, coming to a point suggestive of a cutting edge at the peak. Even the shade of the skin he has left relatively unaltered, a delicate cross-hatching to give shape to the exposed areas and suggest something between white and negroid. He hopes that if it pleases the Chief enough to be reprinted on Sunday the color-ink boys will render it a yellowish-tan, like a bilious weak tea. He's done the features over several times before hitting on something that looks right, the cheekbones high and sharp, the eyes narrow, up-slanting razor slits, the mouth twisted in a cruel, treacherous grin as he drives the crooked blade through his victim's spine. Only a slight exaggeration from the one photo published of their *jefe* Aguinaldo, who—though reputed to be of a Chinese-Malay mix—bears the angular, cunning stamp of the Jap.

Beneath the assassin's feet, trodden into blood-soaked foreign soil, lies Old Glory.

The Cartoonist roughs in the caption, noting below it that he wants the heavy Gothic font they use for *In Memoriam* buys on the obit page, sober and declamatory at once—

THE THANKS OF A GRATEFUL NATION

HOMECOMING

They are waiting for him on the dock, notepads gaping like the mouths of baby magpies, insatiable. They are waiting for him everywhere these days, in the hallways, in the lobbies, in front of the hotels, on street corners and under lampposts, in gentlemen's clubs and workingmen's resorts, starved for quips, for observations, his every vocalization sandwiched between quotation marks and rehashed for the delectation of the reading public. Having sent his wife and daughter ahead, the Humorist nurses a cigar that has burned down to a stub, waiting, as the steward has requested, for the other passengers to absent themselves. No sense obstructing the disembarkation.

He has seen some of the caricatures occasioned by his political musings, forwarded to London by friends and accompanied by suitable proclamations of outrage. His favorite is the senile literary lion, toothless perhaps but still full-maned and regal compared to the bonneted schoolmarms they've made of Hoar, Carnegie, and poor, hapless William Jennings Bryan, his once voluminous bag these days nearly bereft of wind. The fellow at *Punch* had some sport with him after an interview sympathetic to the Boers, drawing him as a grimy, wild-haired *Voortrekker* shooting himself in the foot with a blunderbuss. There is a sort of glee in it, the illustrators attempting to outdo each other, attaching his physiognomy to a menagerie of outlandish creatures, both extant and mythical.

"All in good fun," chortled the editor from *Lloyd's Weekly* at the Travelers' Club, though his countrymen slaughtered at Mafeking and Ladysmith might be excused for undervaluing the hilarity involved.

"Thank you very much, sir," says the steward, appearing beside his deck chair. "I believe it will be all right now."

The Humorist rises, lifts the tattered carpetbag he carries more as a prop than as a necessity, and descends the gangplank of the *Minnehaha*, flash powder fulminating with each step, to feed the Beast.

The *New York Herald* is there, and the *Sun* and the *World* and the *Times* and the *Mail and Express* and the *Chicago Tribune* and the *Philadelphia Inquirer* and, for all he knows, a representative from the *New Yorker Staats Zeitung*.

"How does it feel to be on American soil?" The *Sun*.

"A good deal superior to being under it," answers the Humorist, setting fire to a long black article and taking the first puff. "But then I've only just arrived."

Chucklings of appreciation.

"What are your plans?"

"If I am drafted to serve as President, I will not shun the honor. Short of that I will settle for schnitzel and ale at Luchow's."

Knowing laughter. Winks. The *World* steps forward, features devoid of mirth.

"In regard to the statements attributed to you during your stay in London—"

"I found the Prince of Wales an admirable drinking companion and all-around good egg," the Humorist interrupts, "and I shall defend that position with my life."

More jollity, but the pack is on the scent now and won't be shaken.

"I meant your reaction to the situation in China," clarifies the newshound from the *World*.

"The Boxer is a patriot," replies the Humorist, pausing for effect as pencils are jabbed into notebooks. "No less a patriot than you or I—and I am giving *you* the benefit of the doubt."

The *World* man stiffens, not certain as to whether he has been insulted.

"He defends his land and his culture," continues the Humorist, "barbaric though it may appear to our eye."

The gauntlet hurled. The scribe from the *Times* picks it up.

"But the murder of Christians—"

"Should a handful of Celestials descend on the nether regions of your gashouse district and begin to proselytize for Confucius, they would be made equally short work of. The fate of the missionaries is lamentable, but they were well aware of, if not secretly titillated by, the risks involved."

It is not that there is nothing left to lose. Yes, he can choose exile again, circling the globe with his stories and being well rewarded for it, can find an innovation equal to the damned compositor to squander his earnings on, can decorate the dining halls of Europe till they grow nauseous at the sight of him, but he longs to be home, in familiar surroundings with Olivia near her most trusted physician. These people can turn on him, decide there is no Humor left in the old man and hound him from their fervently patriotic shore. But he has seen too much, lived too long, to temper his opinions for the mollification of jingoes. He lays the carpetbag on the dock.

"And the Boers?" The representative from Mr. Hearst's publication, goading him on.

"The British are in the wrong in South Africa," states the Humorist, holding the cigar away from his face so the smoke cannot obscure his seriousness, "just as our own nation is wrong in the Philippines."

The jasper from the *Herald* grins wolfishly. Pencils dance merrily on notebook paper.

The *Tribune* scoops up the banner. "Don't you think that while our boys are in peril—"

The Humorist knows where this is heading and will not allow it to arrive. "I am an anti-Imperialist," he states, raising his voice slightly. "Opposed, on principle, to the eagle sinking its talons into any other land."

"We have had nothing but victories there."

He is not yet clear of the dock and is already exhausted. These men have the bright, excited look of those whose experience of battle is the thunder of scareheads on the front pages of their journals, who look at carnage as a starving dog regards a beef shank dripping in a butcher's window. It was the look on the faces of his young friends when reports of those early victories came down from the North, friends boasting, as they strutted off to enlist, of how fast and how far they would set the yankees running. It has been the young, covetous of their grandfathers' fading glory, who have campaigned for the present war. His stomach slides up toward his gorge. He was content, happy even, on the leisurely voyage home, safe from the long reach of the telegraph, but now this queasiness, this sudden weight on *terra firma*. Land-sickness. Jingophobia.

"Our situation in those islands," he says slowly, giving them time to write, "is an utter mess, a quagmire, from which each fresh step renders the difficulty of extraction immensely greater—"

"Our flag has been raised," declares the pedant from the *World*. "To lower it now would signal defeat."

"Our flag, my young friend, must be wrenched from those shores before it is further sullied."

Silence then, scratching of heads and pencils. This is not risible, this is not what they have gathered for, the return of the nation's favorite wag with tales of European fatuity and American common sense. Then the stutterer from the *Mail and Express*, prudently mute up to this juncture, steps into the breach.

"So Mr. T-t-t-twain, w-w-what you are saying is that you are op-p-p-posed to w-w-*war*."

The Humorist smiles, takes a lung-tickling pull on the cigar. "I could not have said it better myself. You have no doubt read in your own papers that Czar Nicholas of Russia declares he wants the entire world to disarm." The Humorist gestures across the harbor with his stogie. "The Czar is ready to disarm." He touches his chest with both hands. "*I* am ready to disarm." His friend has arrived behind them with the hack, the Humorist recognizing the driver, a foul-breathed Fenian who excoriates his slat-ribbed nag in the Mother Tongue. "Collect the others and it shouldn't be much of a task."

The Humorist winks at them, lifts his carpetbag and hurries through another poofing barrage of flash powder to the open door of the cab. Only the opening salvo, he thinks, what the frogeaters would term an *hors d'oeuvre*. They will be back tomorrow, pencils sharpened, hungry for more.

BARREN ISLAND

The City eats horses. Dozens and dozens are floated over from New York in a day, more than a hundred when it is hot, they say. Some shot in the head by a horse doctor or one of the Cruelty people but mostly they just fell over in their traces and are unharnessed and left in the street till one of the wagons picks them up. If the shoes have been left on they get pulled off and tossed into the pile and sold back to the ferriers. Jubal yanks the hooks into the tendons just below the hocks on a big roan's back legs so it can be winched down the slide, then pops the shoes off as fast as he can. It goes a lot faster when they're dead.

The scrapers are next, running their quick blades over the body, razoring off manes and tails, separating the hair by color if it's for brushes or not if it's for plaster, and then the skinners step in slicing and tugging, tossing the heavy wet hides into a heap for the tanner's boy to haul off in his wheelbarrow, a cloud of flies bursting apart with each new toss and then settling back on top. A man comes in to fog the whole floor three times a day but the flies always come back. The blood-smeared butchers come last, one on each side of the chute, hacking out the cuts they want and dropping them into steel carts, stripping one side of the skinned animal then digging in their meat-hooks to flip it over and do the other. What is left gets hauled up the ramp, unhooked, and slid into the enormous rendering vat. His first week on the Island Jubal was up there on the catwalk in the heat and the fumes and the smell, but he come on time every day and didn't complain and didn't fall in so they moved him to horseshoes and now they got a new colored man at the vat. It is mostly Polacks and Irish here, lots of them with the whole family working. Some of the Polacks speak American, and other ones, like old Woytak who skins the dogs and the raccoons and the fox that come in sometimes, talk old country or don't talk at all. Mr. Tom says if Jubal does a good job and stays out of trouble on the Island a few more weeks maybe he will put him on a wagon.

His first day up from Wilmington he went to all the stables in the City, telling what he could do and asking for work. There were stables for four horses and stables for twenty and stables for more than a hundred that had three stories with wagons on the ground floor and the horses brought up a ramp to the second and their feed on the top. One place that was for trolley horses had five hundred stalls but the trolley gone electric now and near half of them were empty. Jubal asked and walked and asked and walked, teamsters on the street happy to tell him where to try, but there was no work till he come to the West Side stable for P. White's Sons and they said they would start him out on Barren Island.

The horses on the streets of the City are all blinkered, as close to blind as you can do and still get them to work. The people don't look to the sides much either, staring a tunnel down the street and hurrying through it. Wherever he went that first day he was in the way of something, and both times he tried to sit down a police appeared to eyeball him to his feet again. There is places in Wilmington where you got to state your business if you're colored, but there is also a dozen white men Jubal could say he hauled for, who would stand for him as a honest worker with a feel for the animals.

The room he stays in now is not so big and belongs to P. White's Sons, like all the other rooms and houses on Barren Island. They built the school and the firehouse and the little grocery and probly own the two saloons that he's never seen any colored in. Rent comes out of his pay, double for the first week. A small steamer boat, the *Fannie McKane*, travels over to a place called Canarsie and back two times a day and once for church on Sunday. He hasn't gone back over yet, his credit good on the Island but nowhere else. They cook garbage here too, at a plant on the other side of the pier, but it pays just the same and there's no chance to get on a wagon. There is a neighborhood or two in the City where colored live, even some from Carolina, but this is the job for now and if you work here you got to live here.

Halecki steps past pushing a train of carts full of tankage that will be dried and sold for fertilizer. They don't waste a thing, P. White's Sons, and the next passel of horses bound for the City will come up grazing on grass grown on their grandaddy's bones. Some of the horses come in you can tell they broke a leg or got hit by another carriage, but mostly they are old and gray-muzzled and just been worked out. Jubal hooks carcasses and pops horseshoes till one of the Irish who do errands, little Darby, runs up to say there is a load coming in.

Jubal is the only one suppose to come off the line. It is chilly, his breath showing white and the winter wind blowing strong when he steps out of the building, blowing black smoke from the huge brick chimney over to Rockaway and lifting some of the smell away with it. It is not so bad as he worried, kind of a old-coffee thickness in the air that never goes away, and he is used to it by now. A steam tug pushes a scow piled with carcasses across Dead Horse Bay to the pier, the dark hides nearly hidden by a blanket of feeding gulls. Most every carcass Jubal handles is missing at least one eye and he's come to hate the birds.

No telling how they bring the horses out when the river finally ices over.

Smitty and Pops are waiting with their wagons by the wharf crane, both with a blinkered four-in-hand team. Uncle Wicklow taught him to handle a big team like that when he was in livery for Mr. Sprunt, and once Jubal got to work six mules rolling a house from Queen Street to Market. A mule won't let you kill him with work, but horses—these ones coming in on the scow probly just got pushed past what they could do, too heavy, too steep, too fast. Driver got to make up for the sense that a horse don't have, and Jubal has always had a feel for them. Once when they were little and times was hard Mama bought some horsemeat from Honniker and cooked it in a stew. Mama could make a sump-digger's boot taste good, but Jubal couldn't touch a bite and Royal laughed at him and ate the whole mess.

"Jubal think he know who this stew is," he said. "Know the name of every horse in town."

The gulls stir some when the scow bangs against the pilings and Jubal hops down to tie her up. He kicks at one of the birds that stays too close when he climbs onto the pile of carcasses.

"Got room for you in that renderin tank."

Hruba who operates the crane sends the tackle down and Jubal gets busy, muscling the first cold body around with his gaff while old Inkspot fixes lines in place and sets the hardware. Inkspot is drunk whenever he's not working but still moves quick, hopping around the jumble of bodies and legs like a flea, tapping where he wants Jubal to lift, trussing the animal to be lifted. He sits back on the rump of a Cleveland bay and jerks his thumb up at Hruba.

"You got im!"

Half the gulls are still on the pile and half are flapping in the air, looking for an opening. The winch chain rattles till it goes taut and the hooked horse is hoisted straight up, eyeless head flopping to one side, then swung over Smitty's wagon bed and cranked down. Smitty got his whole team in feedbags for the loading—it could be sacks of concrete coming down for all they know. Some horses will shy at a corpse, but they can be trained around it. Jubal drove Mr. Rivers the undertaker's matched black Tennessee Walkers for a spell, wearing a top hat that was a mite too big for him, and never had to use an overchuck on them, the horses raising their heads up proud the minute they saw the hearse rolled out. Except for the Phenix fire pumper, that was the finest team in Wilmington, stepping high, pulling even, standing tall. Dignified.

Jubal knows how old a horse is from twenty paces, can feel its legs and tell you is it a lead or a swing or a wheelhorse, can tell you how it's been hitched and how much it can pull, can riff his fingers in the coat and let you know what kind of feed it's lacking. But these ones don't tell much of a story, just dead weight to gaff till old Inky has got the lines fixed and then you move on to the next. Uncle Wick owns a little patch out on the way to Winnabow and sometimes he move an old horse off a team and onto a single-pull and then one day when it isn't good for even that he put it out on that patch, lets it feed and sleep all day and go rheumy-eyed and ski-footed. Might be four or five of them old horses out there at any time that Uncle say weren't to be rode.

"That hoss done carry his share of the world," he would say if Jubal or Royal would ask could they climb up. "Leave him rest now."

Smitty's wagon fills and he pulls the feed bags off and puts the bits back in and clucks the team back toward the rendering plant, steam showing out their noses, a few gulls resettling on top. Smitty is good, can dock that rig backward into the loading slot first try every time. Used to run them eight-up for a moving company, he says, till it was bought by a bigger company that wanted all white horses and all white drivers.

Jubal gaffs a broke-legged pony and rolls it back for Inkspot. The pony has been shot in the head and has a pinto hide, which the skinners always put away special. Be on somebody's easy chair in no time. Jubal looks over to Brooklyn while the old man kneels by the pony with lines in hand. It is part of Greater New York now, part of the City. Word is that the colored man's future is up here, even if won't nobody look you straight in the eye.

"You just don't stop movin, is what," old Inkspot told him the first night in the room they share, his breath sharp with whiskey. "You stop movin, black or white, you gets throwed in the *pot*."

How many horses there must be over there, for this many to come in dead every day? Every one of them horses need caring for, feeding, somebody who know how to work them. It only makes sense. This the place for me, Jubal thinks as the pony is hoisted and swings upside down next to him for a moment. I just got in on the wrong end of it.

With a piano she could give lessons. Or even just to play for Mother and Father at night. Jessie has read the bulletins posted at the Academy of Music and the Metropolitan Opera and at the Carnegie Hall. It is possible that these instructors don't have a piano in their homes, but they have positions that give them access to one, or money to rent a music room. In this city nothing happens until money passes hands.

Even if they could afford it, of course, a piano is an impossibility in their two crowded rooms. Walls would need to be moved and a crane employed to bring one in, the lopsided stairs too narrow, too weak to bear the weight. The only music she hears now is from the pianola at the corner saloon, drifting up from the street till halfway through the night. Some of the songs are lively but the machine lacks at least a quarter of the notes and depends on the stamina and interest of whoever is pumping the pedals, and the saloon keeper insists on having his rolls played in the same order every night. If the neighborhood is being graced with *Hello, Mah Baby* it is a quarter past seven.

Jessie has passed the women before, standing in the cold under the elevated tracks on Ninth just north of Paddy's Market, arms folded, chatting in small groups, waiting to be picked up. At first, unsure of their business on the street, she walked by pretending they weren't there, but eventually began to nod politely and respond to their questions and listen to their suggestions. She has solicited as far south as Park Row and as far north as 80th Street, venturing all the way to the East River once to see about a position in a laundry. She has learned that the shops on the Ladies' Mile do not hire colored girls to meet the public, and that most of the small manufacturing concerns employ workers who speak the same language as the floor managers. She has learned to hide rather than reveal her education when seeking a position as a domestic, and she has learned, in her two torturous half-days of employment, that she can neither cook nor sew. She has been left more than once outside an employment-agency door while dozens of white women were ushered past her and discovered how long a lady can sit alone resting her legs at a park bench before attracting unwelcome attention. It is not more than a few minutes.

"Is there a line for me to put myself at the end of?" she asks Alberta, the friendliest of the colored girls, who says she is from Charleston.

"Naw, honey, you just stan out here like the rest of us. If they like what they see they ask you over, then you make a deal and get in."

"Sometimes they remember if they had you before," says her friend Clarice. "Sometimes they want to look at your hands or hear you say your name or there's a uniform you got to fit into."

There is Alberta and Clarice and Queen, who is big and looks angrily at everyone, then an Irish woman called Wee Kate who doesn't stop talking and four other Irish girls who listen to her and then two dark-haired girls who speak something Jessie doesn't recognize, all of them standing in the dirty slush beneath the rattling trolleys waiting for someone to pick them up.

"They've been hiring to cover baseballs across the river," says Wee Kate. "Hand stitching. It pays by the piece, but an able girl can do well for herself."

"Ye've done it?" asks Sorcha, one of her listeners.

Wee Kate looks insulted. "Let them transport me to New Jersey? Of course not."

"Then what does it have to do with us?"

"Only that there's opportunities available, is all. Ye only have to put yerself forward."

A white man with a stubble of beard rattles up in an old omnibus that has seen better days. There are five women already inside, staring out the windows at them.

"I need three more," he says, and Jessie is left standing, the others all rushing forward. Two of the Irish girls climb on first and Wee Kate has a foot on the rung before Queen shoulders her out of the way and falls heavily into the final seat.

"That's three," she calls and the unshaven man, who has not turned to watch them, flicks his reins and the omnibus jerks away.

"Fecking black whoor," grumbles Wee Kate, watching the vehicle rattle south toward the Market. "I'll deal with her tomorrow."

Jessie feels short of breath though she hasn't moved from the spot.

"They didn't ask what the pay was," she says.

Alberta shrugs. "The sooner in the day you get started the more you can make."

"Is it safe?"

"There were three of them, and more in the bus."

"But if you're alone—"

"Some girls do," says Alberta. "Not me."

Jessie is surprised that no one passing turns to stare at them. They have the snow banks to navigate, of course, and the wind cutting between the tall buildings, but still—if there is a place in Wilmington where women congregate and offer their services she does not know where it is. The two foreign girls are taken after a long conversation with a man who speaks their language and then the remaining six of them wait for what seems like hours. Wagons full of ice and meat and fish and fodder for horses pass by them and the trolleys rumble overhead and an Italian man pushing a cart goes by singing praises to his melons and uniformed servants of various races hurry to and from the Market and once a policeman looks them over but does not say hello.

"It's the Jews ye have to look out for," says Wee Kate when she has gotten over her tussle with Queen. "They'll try to cheat ye out of it every time. And very free with their hands, if ye know what I'm sayin. They can't help themselves in the presence of a Christian girl, it's a well-known fact. And it's them that runs the whole city."

"And I thought it was the lads at Tammany," says Sorcha, raising her eyes in an exaggerated way. "Croker and that lot."

"They're merely the custodians," corrects Wee Kate. "It's your Jews, the bankers and financiers and such, that own the whole shebang."

The Jews that Jessie has seen so far in the city don't seem to have much. Mrs. Kastner, who lives below them with her half-crippled son who sits mooning on the stoop, twists colored cloth and wire into flowers from early morning until she blows the candles out at night. A boy who wears the black hat and curls next to his ears comes every morning to take what is finished and bring her more material.

There must be different Jews.

"I was a waiter girl for a time," says Wee Kate. "At Auchenpaugh's Beer Garden. Now your Dutchman is tight with the gratuities until he's poured a couple down his gullet, and then he's as generous as the next fella. I could carry six steins of lager in each of me hands," she says, holding her skinny arms out wide and making fists. "More than once I've navigated the floor with every Fritz on the East Side crowdin the place, and never spilt a drop. 'Katie,' they'd say to me when they was feelin no pain and waxin sentymental, 'yer a drinkin man's angel.'"

"How come you quit?"

Wee Kate raises her chin at Clarice, looking offended. "I didn't *quit* at all. Auchenpaugh comes in one day, cocky as a magpie on a pump handle, and declares that from now on we're to wear this get-up as a unyform—" she indicates with the side of her hand, "—down to here and up to there. A decent woman wouldn't be caught dead in it. 'Tis only the traditional costume in the village that I hail from,' says Auchenpaugh. So I says, 'Then, traditionally, yer women is whoors.'"

Sorcha keeps her eyes wide. "And he took offense, did he?"

"Thick heads and thin skins, if ye ask me. I don't have a word of the German, and it's a lucky thing too from the tone of what he was sputterin. Lost his best waiter girl that very night."

"So the skirt was small, ye say?" Sorcha winks at the other women.

"Not enough to keep a field mouse warm. It's all showgirls there now, the ones as can't get on to wiggle their fannies at the Casino Roof. Arms like pipe cleaners that can barely lift an honest mug of ale, much less six in each hand. Strumpets, is all, and if that's what the Dutchmen want I'm well rid of em."

Wee Kate goes on to tell of her trials in a hotel kitchen and sewing undergarments and assembling cardboard boxes and pretending she was an experienced typewriter girl.

"They had me believe I was just to copy what was already there on the page, not to read it and make corrections," she complains. "It's been me own Stations of the Cross. An honest girl has nowhere to turn."

It is nearly noon and Jessie feeling lightheaded from hunger when a drayman with a carbuncle that looks like a raspberry on his nose stops and calls them over to his wagon.

"Easy work," he says. "Making toys. It pays two dollars a day—only half the day is gone already."

The women look at each other, then begin to climb in. There are some crates to sit on but by the time Alberta pulls Jessie up these are gone. She sits, awkwardly, on the floor of the wagon bed, holding on to the side. A mismatched pair of horses pull them forward, one bleeding from under its harness.

The women bump shoulders and knees as they roll east on 44th Street.

"Will he take us back to the same place at the end of the day?" Jessie asks, and the others laugh. Alberta looks her over.

"You aint brought nothin to eat."

Jessie shakes her head. Her too-thin coat cannot hide from their eyes that she is several months pregnant. She feels alternately famished and bloated these days and is suddenly prone to headaches. Nobody on the street is even looking at them, a wagon full of women, colored and white, loaded like sacks of grain. Alberta pulls something wrapped in a handkerchief from her waist and unrolls it, breaking off half a corn cake and handing it down to Jessie.

"Eat this here," she says. "You gone need it."

"You're very kind."

"Yeah," the dark girl smiles. "I feeds the crumbs to the birdies."

It is a little stale and there is no butter but it is the best corn cake Jessie has ever eaten.

The building is on 25th between Sixth and Seventh Avenues, six stories high, floor-length windows separated into tiny panes by iron mullions. The drayman ties his horses to a light pole and then lets the back gate of the wagon down, stepping back to stare at their legs as they climb onto the street.

"Follow me."

There is an elevator and a board beside it with the names of different manufactories and the floors they reside on, but the six from Paddy's Market and two more they gathered on the way are led down creaking wooden stairs to the basement. It takes Jessie's eyes a moment to adjust. The ceiling is low, with only a few oil lamps hung from the pipes running overhead. A huge boiler dominates the middle of the room, faced by two long benches with stools placed next to them. It is sweltering and smells like food has been stored here recently, cabbage maybe, and the only exit is by the narrow, unsteady stairs. There is no place to hang their coats, so they hurry to pull them off and lay them in a pile on the floor in the corner. Jessie is perspiring already and has to fight back a panic that there is not enough air for every-body to breathe. Eight or nine women are already seated along one of the benches, painting metal figurines.

"All of you take a stool over here," says the wagon driver. "It don't mat-ter which one." He ducks under a lantern to reach the end of the first bench, frowning at several fully painted figurines lined up on a thin metal tray at the end of it.

"You gals been sleeping here, or what?"

None of the working women, who are all white, look up to answer him, faces set in the dim light.

Jessie sits at the empty bench, Alberta on one side of her and Clarice on the other. There is a glass pot of orangey-pink paint in front of her, a small paintbrush lying on a scrap of cardboard beside it. The wooden bench top is gouged and scarred but not spattered with paint like the other that has been in use.

The drayman steps to the head of their bench and picks up one of the metal figurines to wave at them. "I'm only going through this once, so keep your ears open. Anybody here don't speak English?"

None of the women at the table respond. It occurs to Jessie that if she didn't speak English she wouldn't have understood the question.

"All right, this is your basic piece, and each one of youse is going to paint a different part of it. The paint dries fast but not so fast you can't smudge it up with your hands, so you never pick it up by where the gal before you just painted."

The figurines are American soldiers, marching men with a rifle over their shoulders. They are bigger than the lead infantrymen Junior played with when he was a boy, nearly a half-foot high. The top of each figure has been dipped in blue, the bottom in a buff color, meeting unevenly at the belt line.

"The base, all around here, is green. Number One, that's you."

The drayman walks down the line to point to the section each woman is to paint.

"Number Two, you do the hands and the face with this—don't get none on the bottom of the hat—and Number Three, you got black for the belt and the boots. Be careful with that damn black, it's murder to cover up. Four, you got the little brush, that's brass color for the buttons. Just one little dot on each of em, don't go crazy with it. Five, the whites of the eyes. Six, dark brown for the hair and eyebrows and the rifle, Seven, a dab of blue in the center of each eye—don't fill the whole thing up—and Eight," he has reached the end of the bench, "you do the hat light brown and line the pieces up on the tray here. I want them facing the same way and none of them touching. Now do we all know our colors?"

Jessie thinks that to make a figurine of the drayman they'd need a pot of red for the berry on his nose. He slaps the top of the bench with his hand.

"You mess it up, stick the wrong color in the wrong place, just put it aside on the table and keep the line going. You'll have to fix those later. Let's get cracking."

He hands Alberta the figurine and goes to the stairs, turning back to glare at them just before he starts up.

"Oh yeah—I come back and catch any one of you flapping your gums—you're *out*. No pay, no nothin." He taps his temple with a finger. "A word to the wise."

They begin to paint. Alberta has a wider brush and slaps the green onto the base sloppily, so it is dripping when she hands it to Jessie. None of the oil lamps is directly overhead and it is hard to see, but she does her best with her brush. The figurines are hollow cast iron, molded with great detail. Her paint is light but doesn't look like any skin color she's ever seen when it goes on. She used to love painting eggs with Mother at Easter and has done watercolors for years, but something about this makes her anxious.

"I've got the hardest task by far," mutters Wee Kate, squinting as she lines a soldier's eyebrows with brown. "The bastard done it on purpose."

"Shut up with ye," says Sorcha. "Ye'll earn us all the sack."

Jessie has passed five pieces on to Clarice when a skinny white boy steps out from around the boiler carrying a tray with a dozen of the finished soldiers on it, all the colors, especially the skin, looking better now. He is wearing gloves and a sweat-soaked undershirt, quickly unloading the figurines into a crate painted on the side with a similar-looking soldier standing in front of a giant American flag. He takes a tray of painted men from the end of the first bench and hurries back behind the boiler.

"He'll have an oven back there," announces Wee Kate. "To bake the color on."

The women continue to paint, silently. Jessie already has green stains on her sleeves and wishes she had worn a different waist today. She does the neck and face first, not worrying if it overlaps with the hairline, then takes more time with the hands, careful of the blue uniform cuffs. If it wasn't for the low ceiling and the smell and the heat from the boiler and the unforgivingly hard seat of the stool it wouldn't be the worst of occupations.

Another man comes down, this one tall enough to have to bend over to fit under the pipes, and stands behind them, watching.

"Jesus Horatio Christ," he says finally, kicking the back of Wee Kate's chair. "You're sposed to paint the damn things, not play with them!"

He stomps, stooped over, to stand in front of them. He has bloodshot eyes and long, crooked teeth, and his breath smells like his lunch when he starts to shout into their faces.

"You people got half a day to give me a hundred fifty pieces. Didn't he tell you that? You don't make one-fifty, nobody gets paid!"

"Ye've given me three things to paint," says Wee Kate, holding up the soldier she is working on, and then nodding toward Sorcha beside her, "and this one has only got to spot the feckin eyes on it."

"You don't like your job," says the tall man, raising his eyebrows, "you know where the stairs are."

Wee Kate thunks the soldier down on the bench top and angrily jabs her brush at it.

"And the same goes for you!" he shouts at the women at the other bench before clumping away up the stairs.

"There's a Jew for ye," mutters Wee Kate when he's gone.

Jessie has no idea if the man is a Jew or not, but the threat of not being paid puts a frantic energy into their work, Jessie perspiring, her brush hand beginning to cramp, and a dull pain is forming behind her eyes. A few of the women still have food with them and hurry a few bites in between soldiers. How they can stomach anything with the cabbage smell and the heat—

Jessie is aware that she needs to relieve herself. Nothing has been spoken of this, and she looks around desperately. No sign of a convenience. She paints a few more pieces, resolving to put it out of her mind. But the problem is not in her mind. She is barely keeping up with Alberta, but it can't wait.

"M'am," she says, turning to a woman behind her at the other bench, a woman with a touch of gray in her hair, "excuse me, but—"

"Past the boiler, on the left," says the woman without looking up from her work.

"Now ye've sunk us," snarls Wee Kate, who has three soldiers lined up waiting for her attentions as Jessie hurries past.

It is only a closet, with a toilet of sorts and a single candle for light, the ceiling open around a thick pipe that runs upstairs. She hurries through her business, holding her breath against the smell for as long as she can. There are footsteps above, and then the voices of the wagon driver and the tall man.

"It's all that was left," says the drayman.

"I told you before—"

"You want all white, you got to send me out earlier."

"How am I supposed to know half of em don't come back?"

"And what's the difference?"

"Campbell rents the room," says the tall man, "and he don't want niggers in the building. That's the difference."

Jessie is suffocating in the closet. She arranges her clothing and steps out to see the skinny young man carefully stoop to slide a tray of soldiers into the mouth of an oven standing on stout legs near the back wall, a brazier filled with glowing coals beneath it. He turns and holds her eye for a long moment.

"You don't want to be here," he says sadly, and then turns back to his work.

"Here's our ladyship, come back for a visit," says Wee Kate, but none of the others even look up. Alberta is finishing the face on a piece for Jessie, and hands back her brush.

"Thank you," says Jessie, sitting into her spot. There is no clock in the basement, and without a window there is no way to know how much time has passed.

"You do it for me when I gots to go," says Alberta.

Jessie begins to paint again, head and hands, head and hands. If this were a novel, she thinks, the Dark and Brooding Man would appear at the bottom of those stairs to sweep her into his arms and carry her away. He would have vanquished those who ruined Father, restored their fortune and their home. The women left behind in the basement would be stirred by the scene, and Wee Kate, a tear in her eye, would have an appropriate and sentimental comment to put a cap on the story.

But then she is not the Wronged Heroine, honest and stalwart. She is the Fallen Woman, the lass alluded to as a caution to flighty girls, the one who through her own fecklessness and perfidy has earned her fate.

Jessie has to struggle to keep the soldier she is holding in focus. Her head is swimming. If this is the influenza, how will it affect the life growing within her? How will she not pass it on to her parents living in the cramped quarters of their apartment? She feels flushed, light-headed, she feels—ashamed. That is what she feels most acutely. What would Junior say, or Father, if they saw her here, doing this work for these men? Or Royal, if he ever overcame his rightful anger to look at her again?

Junior's infantrymen were Union soldiers, and he fought the battle of New Bern over and over with them, using clothespins to represent the Confederates. They were all white men in blue, set in various poses, and he would erect battlements of dirt in the backyard or in the coach house when it was raining, making the noises of rifle and artillery fire and the occasional cry of a wounded man. Jessie remembers how heavy they were for the size of them, barely able to lift the box that Junior kept under his bed for years.

She wonders who is living in their house in Wilmington now. They will be white people, of course, and she wonders if they have a daughter who sits dreamily at her piano, if they have a small boy who plays in the carriage barn with lead soldiers whose blue uniforms he has painted gray—

Jessie stands shakily, takes a few steps and dips her brush into Wee Kate's paint pot.

"Christ Almighty, what're ye up to now?"

Jessie steps back to her place and quickly paints a soldier with brown face and hands, then sets it in front of Clarice. Clarice looks at her, giggles and starts to paint the hair and eyebrows black. The figurine moves down the line. Jessie dips her brush back into her own pot, but there is still some brown on it and this one comes out closer to Junior's shade.

The first was more like Royal Scott.

The next one she paints might be an Italian.

"Jesus, Mary, and Joseph!" exclaims Wee Kate when the figurines reach her. "Have ye gone mad?"

"I done the rest for you," says Clarice. "You just paint that rifle and pass em on."

When the skinny boy takes them away on the tray he says nothing, nor when he returns and crates them with the color baked on.

Head and hands, head and hands, head and hands. Figurines pass down the line of women who have become one long, many-armed creature that occasionally sighs but does not speak. At some point each of the women excuses herself, even Wee Kate, the slack taken up by the others and the flow of pieces uninterrupted. Once, when she was little, Father let her come with him to treat a man injured at the cotton press, found her a safe place to stand and watch the gang at work. At first it was the sound that terrified her, steam exploding to drive the heavy metal press down onto the loose bales, the big, sweating men shouting at each other over the clank and grind of machine parts. But as she watched, the noise and confusion began to fall into a pattern—men hoisting bales up from the wagons with a pulley, dankeymen pushing them along a slide to the mouth of the press where the snatchers cut the ropes away and shoved them in onto the huge metal teeth and the leverman pulling the arm to trigger the press down and back up and then the tyers pushing metal bands through the teeth and then pulling them over to fasten them snug around the tight-pressed bale and jumping away when the press kicked the bale out with its tongue to slide down the chute onto the back of another wagon. And all through it the caller—singing out instructions, sometimes even riding on top of the press itself to see the entirety of the operation, nearly disappearing into the hole as the press hammered down.

Ready when you hear me call—

—he sang—

Pull that stick and let her fall!

Limbs, bodies, heads moving out of the way just in time not to be destroyed by the monstrous works—

Haul the next one when you able
Put the bacon on you table!

And the men singing back now and then, never taking their eyes off the machinery—

Won't be liquor, won't be sin
Cotton gone to do me in!

It was thrilling and terrifying and she felt a mixture of awe and pity for the men working there, a sadness to their labor that she thought at the time was due to their fellow worker having his leg crushed that morning, due to the danger and the deafening bursts of steam and the heat and having to breathe the cotton lint kicked up and filling the air till you were coughing, coughing without a hand free to cover your mouth, coughing blood sometimes and spitting it out onto the hot metal beast. But now she understands that it is not the work itself, so much harder and more dangerous than her own, of course, but the repetition, the repetition of the work that is nightmarish. The same process, the same motions over and over, day after day, year after year, knowing the job will not change, that it is waiting for you, impatient, demanding, insatiable, and that this is all that life will ever have to offer you. Jessie tries to become an automaton, to drive complaint from her head and to make her motions as efficient and mechanical as possible. She tries to count the pieces as they pass through her hands, hoping to mark time with the sum, but twice loses track just past thirty.

At the end her eyes are dry and smarting, the headache settled just behind them, and the brush is trembling slightly in her hand. The tall man has been down twice to check on their progress, shaking his head and muttering, and finally there are no more figurines left to paint. The skinny boy climbs the stairs, carrying a crate full of finished pieces, and promises to tell the men that they're done.

"Are ye here all the time?" Wee Kate asks the women at the next table, who are all standing and trying to straighten their backs.

"A few of us were in yesterday," answers the woman with the gray in her hair. "I think they set up in different places whenever they get a contract."

"I made dolls once," says another. "Stuck the hair in their heads. Pay was the same but at least we had a window."

"Oh, I done worse," says the older woman. "I done plenty worse."

The tall man comes down with a cloth sack and begins to pay the women at the first table their two dollars, most of it in coins. When it is Jessie's turn he gives her a pair of Columbian half dollars, the ones with the explorer's ship on top of two globes on one side and his face on the other. Junior has a collection of them. Had.

"Don't bother coming tomorrow," the tall man says to her.

Jessie holds the two coins tightly in her hand, rubbing them together, as she pulls her coat back on and follows the other women up the stairs and out through the lobby into the street. It is almost dark now, big flakes of snow falling lazily between the high buildings, and cold.

"Where you live?" Alberta asks her.

"On 47th, just west of Eighth," she says. It is the third apartment they have lived in, and if she can find steady work they won't be there long.

Alberta nods at Clarice. "We walk you far as 39th."

As they are leaving she sees the skinny boy and the drayman loading crates onto the wagon. Her soldiers are in there somewhere, she thinks, no telling where they're headed.

.

New York is a machine with too many parts. Harry braces himself on the ice-slick sidewalk, a flood of bodies rushing past on either side of him, attempting to decipher the intermeshing rhythm of its gears, the design, if any, of its incessant motion and counter-motion. He has cranked his way through every clamshell Mutoscope in lower Manhattan, harem girls and saucy parlor maids up to their customary antics, has thrilled to the *Roosevelt Rough Riders* thundering off the screen at Proctor's Pleasure Palace, mourned *The Burial of the* Maine *Victims* and marveled over *Mules Swimming Ashore at Daiquiri* at Koster and Bials, suffered through an interminable and decidedly unfunny comic opera at Keith's Union Square to witness the *Cuban Ambush* on their celebrated "warscope" and eaten a hamburger sandwich at a counter with fellow lunchers' elbows digging into him from both sides.

A tiny newsboy with yellowish skin starts across from the other side of 23rd, disappearing behind careening carriages and screeching trolley cars but sauntering yet, unconcerned, when they have passed, till he stands at Harry's side tugging at the sleeve of his new heavy coat and raising plaintive eyes.

"REBELS ATTACK MANILA, Mister. Read all about it."

"No thank you." The boy is peddling Hearst's sensational *Journal*.

"Two cents, fer cryin out loud. How can you go wrong?"

The boy looks unwell, malnourished at the least, possibly contagious. Harry tightens his grip on his cane, takes a sidestep away. "You aren't allowed to read this scandal sheet, are you?"

The boy makes a disagreeable face. "I look at the pitchers. You got a problem widdat?"

Harry gives him a weak smile, steps off the curb.

"On Sunday they got em in colors."

He makes his cautious dash then, using the cane to push off on his short-leg side, narrowly evading the wheels of a rattling landau, and finally gaining the broad, recently shoveled front steps of the Eden Musee.

The building is steep-roofed and ornate in the French Renaissance style, statuary perched on decorative stone ledges, stairs leading to three high-arched entryways. Harry pays his dime to the young lady in the kiosk and waits for his heart to stop thumping before venturing on to the exhibits.

"The *Passion* has already started," she informs him. "They're probly up to Palm Sunday."

The clientele in the Musee are more genteel than in Proctor's or Keith's or the Huber Museum, well-dressed ladies perusing the tableaux with their young ones, gentlemen in bowlers and ties, no crush of workmen and street urchins popping in here for a quick and prurient thrill.

"There will be a display of sleight-of-hand in the Egyptian Room at four o'clock," adds the kiosk girl.

The first grouping of figures depicts President Lincoln at his famous Gettysburg Address. The tall wax figure, bearded and hatless with the suggestion of a stiff wind in his hair, gestures nobly with one hand, the handwritten speech clutched in the other, flanked by a pair of Union soldiers with rifles at port-arms while a half-dozen onlookers stand at the foot of the platform in attitudes of reverent attention. The eyes are dark and deep-set as in the Brady photographs, but there is no light of life in them.

"—*that from these honored dead*—" drones a hound-eyed older man dressed in a '60s mourning cloak who stands beside the tableau with hand over heart, "—*we take increased devotion to that cause which they here have thus far so nobly carried on*—"

Harry moves on, the unalloyed yankeeness of it giving him a guilty twinge. "*A freak of Nature*," the Judge was wont to say of the North's martyred saint. "*Malformed and malignant.*"

He wonders how many times a day the man must repeat the speech. Perhaps a phonograph recording of it would be more effective, not placed so it seems to be coming from the motionless figure, but amplified from above, like a voice from the Great Beyond. Harry has already worked out a mechanism whereby a spectator's foot triggers the phonograph and is pondering the nature of sound waves when he wanders into the execution of Marie Antoinette.

"—*this moment, when my troubles are about to end, is not when I need courage, Father,*" recites an acne-scarred youth in peasant garb. "And with that the lethal drumroll began—"

A tumbrel filled with filthy straw and doomed nobles, a long-faced *curée* intoning from his open Bible, the buxom Marie with her hair shorn, hands tied behind her back, kneeling with neck stretched out over the block, the *sans culottes*, faces distorted as they jeer from every side—there is a sudden skreek of metal and the heavy blade falls in its slot—*CHOK!* neatly separating the Queen from her head! There are screams and cries from the flesh-and-blood spectators and one young lady in lavender quite close to Harry swoons and is caught in the arms of a man who might be either her husband or her father.

"French degenerates," mutters the man, legs bowing under the weight of his charge as he fans her with an orchestra program.

Harry hurries past the other gatherings—the signing of the Declaration of Independence, Moses parting the Red Sea, a rather grisly evocation of one of Jack the Ripper's attacks—waxen, three-dimensional versions of a Kodak snap and in that way inferior, no matter what their subject, to the moving actualities he's just seen in the variety halls. Harry is about to climb the stairs to the Concert Hall when he hears a familiar voice boom out through the open door of a workroom.

"If you don't hurry with this I'm going to suffocate!"

Looking in, Harry sees a man seated on a workbench, his face completely obscured by plaster bandages, while another man painstakingly pries the cast away from the skin with a metal instrument coated with petroleum jelly.

"Mr. Teethadore?"

"Who's that?" The voice, even somewhat muffled behind the appendage, is deep and resonant.

"We met in Wilmington. After a performance."

"You find me at a disadvantage."

Harry takes a step into the room. There are white wax heads, nearly featureless, lined up on a shelf, historical costumes hanging on a pipe and torsos made of wire. "Are you all right?"

"Having my mug reproduced. It seems that General Custer shall soon be *hors de combat* from his Last Stand exhibit and donating the better portion of himself—body, hands, flashing saber—to our noted Rough Rider."

"It seems to be stuck somewhere," says the other man, gently pulling on the mold.

"If I lose so much as a hair from an eyebrow," says Teethadore, raising a finger, "there shall be dire consequences."

"You said I should come see you," ventures Harry with what he hopes is an ironic lilt in his drawl. "If I ever came to New York."

"And you've followed me here?"

The recent disturbance in Wilmington seems too complicated, too tawdry to mention. "Actually I came for the views. This is something of a Mecca—"

"Foreign subjects. Very uplifting. Celluloid novelties for the carriage trade."

"It's really the camera that I—"

"Of course. I remember you now—waxing poetic over the mysteries of the projection device. Drat!"

"I'm sorry," says the wax sculptor. "I told you to shave your moustache."

In Wilmington the actor's moustache had been applied with spirit gum. "No use dragging the character onto the street with me," he'd said then. "It's enough to portray the little runt on the boards." But that had been before the San Juan Hill.

Harry watches uncomfortably as the sculptor wiggles the plaster this way and that, trying to loosen it.

"It was very nice to see you," he says finally.

"You shall *see* me, my friend, when this *moulage* is removed from my face and not before. I suggest you go up and watch the other fellow suffer a bit. It's quite a presentation."

When Harry steps away the sculptor has taken up a hammer and chisel and seems about to do something drastic.

He slips quickly into the rear of the hall, a few patrons looking back with annoyance at the intrusion of light. The seats are all full. On the screen, Christ carries a huge wooden cross past idlers and loose women, a pair of spear-carrying Roman soldiers trailing behind Him. There is bright sunlight above and a backdrop painted with the stone buildings of Jerusalem, but this cannot be what they've advertised out front. The Oberammergau Passion, Harry knows, is staged once every ten years, and the equipment to photograph motion did not exist at the time of the last performance. Christ falters, catching himself with one hand. The soldiers snatch Simon of Cyrene from the crowd and force him to shoulder the cross for a moment. Finally, after much prodding with spear tips and flogging, Christ exits the right side of the screen, the rough wooden post dragging behind, the mob turning to jeer his passing. The moving image fades in brightness, immediately replaced by a lantern view, a hand-tinted diapositive of El Greco's *Christ Carrying the Cross*. It is one of Harry's favorites, angled as if the painter were on his knees when the Nazarene passed, his eyes fixed on the hill above, dark sky brooding behind him.

"Imagine the weight of it," intones a white-haired gentleman wearing a pince-nez, his head barely peeking over the lectern set up beside the screen. "Imagine the rough stones underfoot, the scourge of the Roman whips, the raucous contempt of those who, only days before, had waved the palms of peace and cheered your entry into the city."

Harry is aware of a man standing next to him in the darkness at the rear, a man nodding vigorously as the lecturer continues.

"Are these the souls He has come to save, these torturers, these blood-thirsty, mocking Jews and Philistines?"

The El Greco fades into a new still image, this the circular Bosch painting with the turbaned Pilate at the left, the soldier reaching to wrench Him away, the potato-faced onlookers. These men do look like German peasants, rough and primitive.

"'*Ecce homo*,' the Roman judge pronounces," continues the lecturer. "See the man. Not the Messiah, not their Lord and Savior, but simply a man. This, we now understand, was the greatest degradation of all. Humble as He was, this was the only Son of God brought to His knees before the dregs of humanity, beaten and reviled, driven, at last, to Calvary."

Harry can hear several women in the audience begin to weep as the Bosch is replaced by a moving view. Three crosses, three crucified men, low hills in the background, a tall palm to the right, the centurions crouched below, throwing dice upon the ground and laughing. The shadows of the crosses are visible on the backdrop sky, of course, and no breeze stirs the painted palm fronds, but there are gasps and outcries in the hall when one of the Romans thrusts his spear into Christ's ribs, and then a sigh of wonder as He lifts His eyes one last time to Heaven before letting His head drop in death. A golden nimbus, some sort of dye-process, no doubt, spreads from His body and suddenly a choir, previously unseen, is lit on the other side of the screen, a dozen angelic voices singing *When I Survey the Wondrous Cross* and it is then that Harry has his revelation. What drives the picture forward, the vital armature, could at the same time drive some phonographic device *in synchrony* with the celluloid. Not only could this holy music be joined to the film strip, but His dying words, "Lord, hath Thou forsaken me?," audibly delivered by the actor portraying Christ *as if he were in the room.*

Or is this sacrilege?

The man who stands beside him has joined in the singing, a rich, full basso—

> *His dying crimson, like a robe*
> *Spreads o'er His body on the tree*
> *Then I am dead to all the globe*
> *And all the globe is dead to me!*

The moving view gives way to a lantern-slide of Rembrandt's moody *Descent from the Cross*, Joseph of Arimathea hugging the Body as he descends the ladder, Mary swooning into sympathetic arms in her own golden patch of light. The choir finishes the song, softening their voices into mournful oohs and aahs as the professor intones once more.

"There is, of course, a simple human side to our story," he says. "That of a mother's love for her Son."

The Rembrandt gives way to the final moving view, the *Pietà* staged before the same backdrop. The thieves still hang on either side, the Roman soldiers gone now, replaced by nascent Christians who watch in sorrow as Mary clutches His thorn-crowned head to her breast. Harry can't help wishing they had moved the camera closer so that the Virgin's face could be seen, wishes he could walk into the view to comfort her.

"A mother's grief knows no bounds," says the lecturer. "But we can take comfort, we can find solace, in this story. For the Lord God on high loved us so much," and here the projectionist, for it must be his hand, causes the image on the screen to begin to glow and then brighten further to a blinding whiteness as the voices of the choir climb to an almost unbearable crescendo, "that He gave His only begotten Son that we might be saved!"

The electric house lights flash on then and there is stunned, then uproarious applause.

"What did you think?"

It is the man beside him, dark-haired, with an intense, hawklike face.

"Very powerful," says Harry. "But it can't be Oberammergau."

The man smiles. "A ruse to deflect the protestations of clergymen," he says, offering his hand. "Such as myself. Reverend Thomas Dixon."

"Harold Manigault." Harry shakes the preacher's hand. "You had no objection?"

"On the contrary. I've hosted a similar production at my church down the street, though I must admit our moving views were not as—as *sump*tuous as these."

"I wonder, though, if the spectacle does not overwhelm—"

"We are poised to enter a century of *light*, my friend." He grips Harry's arm and looks deep into his eyes. "This—" nodding toward the screen, "—this in the proper hands will move men's souls. I detect that you are of my home section."

"Wilmington."

"Goldsboro, in the Piedmont," smiles the reverend. "And I pastored in Raleigh for a year." He leans close, lowering his voice conspiratorially as his eyes move over the departing audience. "Some rather propitious events have taken place in your lovely city."

Harry looks around—the room is nearly empty of spectators but it feels close. "Unfortunate events—"

"I am something of a novelist, in addition to my efforts from the pulpit, and your Wilmington situation strikes me as one of those instances in which history does not need to be greatly modified to instruct us. There is a great lesson to be learned."

"And what might that be?" Harry asks.

Dixon regards him with a hot gleam in his eye. "That corruption unaddressed will fester," he says. "And that the leopard, no matter how one paints him, does not change his spots."

Harry tries to approximate the carefree grin that Niles would use. "What a pity—I've been hoping to change my own."

Dixon pats Harry's arm as he would to comfort a child, and starts away with an indulgent smile on his lips. "Breeding will out, I'm afraid." He pauses in the doorway and spreads his arms as if to indicate all of New York. "Where better to bring our struggle than to the belly of the beast?"

Harry is sitting alone when Teethadore, face raw from scrubbing, comes to join him.

"Did you get here for Salome's dance?"

"I'm afraid I missed it."

"Charming girl. Travels with a sister act, the Singing Simpsons, but she's the only one who hasn't had her knees glued together. Did you see me?"

"In this?" Harry finds it unsettling to think of the diminutive variety artist rubbing elbows with the Savior.

"Herod's minion, Elder of Zion, St. Matthew, Pilate's clerk, bad Samaritan—I'm all over the thing. The days we spent on that rooftop—"

"And Christ—?"

"Splendid fellow. Long-suffering. He and those thieves were strung up there for hours, waiting for the clouds to open. I suppose you'll want to examine the device?"

"Do you think that would be possible?"

Teethadore gives him the smile and a wink. "The operator is an old friend."

A youngish man named Porter is blowing air from a bellows into the workings of the cinematograph as they enter.

"The hero of Santiago," he observes.

"Merely his theatrical counterpart," grins Teethadore. "I bring you a worshipper at the altar of celluloid."

Harry nods but can barely take his eyes off the machine. It is even smaller than he imagined.

"This is the French model?"

"Greatly modified," says Porter. "This can't double as a camera."

"The image was so smooth."

"Thank you." Porter gives the crank a whirl. "Two revolutions per second."

Harry looks out through the small window toward the screen. "You watch the view as it's projected—"

"Only the edge of the screen, I'm afraid. We've improved the pull-down claws quite a bit but she'll still jump around on you. Nothing like that mess Biograph uses."

"I witnessed some this morning." Harry puts his hand on his stomach. "Still queasy."

"Did you notice the odor?"

"There's an odor?"

Porter pokes at Teethadore. "From this fellow's acting. For whom, I believe, the term *rank amateur* was coined."

"*Touché.* Mr. Porter is a photographer as well. We have toiled together in the wilds of New Jersey."

"*Gramps Gets Hosed.* You can catch it on the Bowery."

The apparatus is dark metal and glossy wood, mounted on a sturdy tripod. Harry fights the urge to put his hands on it. This is closer to the thing, to the intricate, holy apparatus, than he has hoped to come—

"Mr. Porter," he ventures, "if you were ever to hear of a place, of an opening within the—"

"Edison's always looking for new lackeys," says the projectionist, rewinding a strip of celluloid onto a spool. "I can give you a name."

Harry holds the folded slip of paper with the name written on it in his hand, thrust safely into his jacket pocket, as he crosses back through the maze of waxen statuary. He pulls up short at the French Revolution, a young cleaning woman on her knees scrubbing what looks like vomitus from the floor.

"Oh my," says Harry, stepping back from the spreading puddle of wash water. "Someone's been ill."

"We get one or two every day when the Missus loses her head," says the girl. She is Irish, and when she glances up she has the brightest, clearest green eyes Harry has ever seen.

"I'm sorry."

"It's none of yer fault, is it?"

"I meant—that you have to deal with it."

She looks up at him again, cocking her head, then she indicates the bloodstain painted on the guillotine block and the floor around it.

"And wasn't it a poor girl like meself had to mop up that mess after the killin was done?"

"You work here?"

"At the moment, yes." She goes back to scrubbing.

"Have you seen the attraction in the Hall?"

"The death of Christ? No, I haven't, as a fact. But I know the story well."

Of course she would. Harry resists the impulse to hand her a dime, not knowing how the gesture would be received. "Have you ever seen a moving view?"

The young woman sits up on her knees. She has a breathtaking smile. "Ah, I love the fillums, I do, but I rarely have the money nor the time. They take my breath away."

He feels a little dizzy and wonders if the hamburger was a miscalculation. "Do you think," he asks, once she has turned her head back to her task, "you might like to attend a show with me some time?"

The eyes grow sharp. "Yer foolin with me."

"I assure you I'm not." He lifts his skimmer off. "My name is Harry Manigault. I'm very new in this city—"

"Brigid," she says, still suspicious. "It's another name in Irish but here they call me Brigid."

"May I call for you?"

"Fer that ye'd need to know where I'm situated. Number and street."

Harry flushes, in deep now and not sure how to get out of it. "I suppose I would."

"And what would ye think of a girl who told that to a man who'd just stumbled upon her workin?"

He hadn't thought of that, with her on her knees in bucket water, an immigrant. A scrubwoman. He wonders if he could ever capture those eyes, not the color of course, but the brightness, the life of them, in a photograph.

"Quite right."

What would Niles say? Even if he didn't mean it, he would have something.

"Perhaps I could return at closing time and escort you—"

"My work is just beginnin then. It's only me and the wax heroes, havin a grand time together."

"Ah."

She watches him for a moment with her green eyes. "Sunday afternoons," she says finally, "I've been known to pop into the Hippodrome on Houston Street. A persistent gentleman might find me there. By accident, ye might say."

"A most happy accident." He puts his lid back on, then tips it to her. "A pleasure making your acquaintance, Miss Brigid."

"And where do ye come from, Mr. Mannygalt?"

"North Carolina."

"Right," she nods sagely. "I had ye spotted fer a foreigner. Twas a pleasure makin yer acquaintance as well," she says, raising her scrub brush, "considerin the circumstances."

Harry tries to walk as steadily as he can around the wet spot, not using the cane till he reaches the stairs outside. The cold hits him like a fist, still a surprise. It is night now, the streetlights glowing. He stands on the walk in front of the Eden Musee, the folded paper forgotten in his pocket, slightly dizzy. His heart is racing again, and he hasn't even started across 23rd Street.

REGULARS

The armbands are supposed to make it all right, but you never know in El Paso. Royal is holding the reins, Junior never much with a wagon team, as they roll along Second, white folks' brick houses to the left and Mexican baked adobe to the right. They are both wearing the armbands and strapped with pistols, usually forbidden, but this is a provost detail. Royal keeps his eyes straight ahead, glad it's noon and most everybody is inside.

"We'll be back in the thick of it in no time," says Junior beside him, rubbernecking around like a tourist. "The Philippines, China—"

"You don't know that."

Junior has been on him all week to reenlist, their hitch officially over tomorrow and lots of the boys who come in with them at Missoula saying they're going to hang it up.

"It stands to reason." Junior holds tight to the seat as Royal turns the team left on Campbell. "We're experienced, disciplined—"

"Don't want to shoot them people any more than I wanted to shoot a Spanish."

"We don't get to choose our enemies, Royal."

"If you're not in the damn Army you do."

"It will be more like police work by the time we get there. Maintaining order—"

"Don't care for that neither."

Junior scowls. "Suppose you were to accept discharge. What would you do?"

Royal has been trying not to think of this. He shrugs. "Go back to Wilmington."

It is a sore point between them, Junior bragging after every letter he gets about how good his people are making it up in New York, like they never lost a step, while Royal, who gets no mail at all, doesn't call out the lie. If he even says the *name* Wilmington, Junior gets all tight and says that's over, that the colored man's future all up North now.

Or in the regulars.

"What I've heard," says Junior, turning his head away, "is they even told Mr. Sprunt he can't hire colored anymore."

All Royal knows, from the other Wilmington men in the unit, is that his mother wasn't hurt and Jubal took off and hasn't been back. It was Junior who told him Dorsey Love is dead and Jessie gone up to a better life in New York.

"Set me there with one dozen of these wildass colored regulars," said Coop when he heard, Coop who used to be Clarence Rice at home and didn't come back from leave last night, "and they be a mess of redneck crackers floating in that Cape Fear River."

Royal pulls the wagon off the street, hitching the pair in the shade of the alleyway next to the jail. He and Junior straighten their uniforms out, set their hats, and step inside.

The deputy leans back in a swivel chair behind a scarred-up desk, chewing tobacco and spitting the juice into a coffee cup in his hand while an electric fan blows air on his face. Another man, an Easterner by his dress, sits across from him writing in a notebook.

"We don't use it so much as the old days," the deputy is saying, "but we keep the hinges oiled. I'll show it to you in a minute, up on the third tier of the tank."

"And is it usual to have multiple executions?" asks the dude, who must be a reporter.

"Hell, there probly been a double-header before this," chuckles the deputy. "But not since I been here in El Paso."

"Excuse me, Deputy—" Junior starts, and the white man just holds his hand out and keeps talking.

"The thing is, we had Flores set to go, and we been trying to get old Geronimo Parra back here to stretch ever since he kilt Charlie Fusselman in a shootout up in the Franklins near ten years ago."

Junior steps forward and places the folded order in the deputy's hand.

The white man does not look up, and Junior takes two military steps back to stand by Royal again, not quite at attention.

"But Parra slipped under the border, then got caught rustling over in the Territory and ended up coolin his heels in the Santa Fe lockup."

The deputy glances at the paper.

"Cristy!" he shouts, then spits a big gob of black liquid into the coffee mug.

The newsman never stops scribbling. "You tried to extradite?"

"They wouldn't stand for it. Only our Captain Hughes, who's from the same Marfa outfit of Rangers that Charlie Fusselman come from, has been on Parra's trail all these years and that old boy don't *quit*. He runs into Pat Garrett in a saloon—"

"Garrett who killed William Bonney?"

"The very same, still a Territory lawman. Garrett says how they'd do anything to get holt of this bad character name of Agnew, spose to be hiding out in Texas, and proposes a swap."

"An exchange of prisoners."

"Agnew wasn't a prisoner *yet*," grins the deputy, teeth flecked black with tobacco. "But with a chance to bring Geronimo Parra home to justice, Captain Hughes jumped on his pony and went looking. Caught Agnew working as a ranch hand on the Big Bend, and we had our deal with the Territory."

A jailer in a blue uniform appears, the deputy waving the colonel's paper at him.

"Bring that nigger trooper out."

Sergeant Jacks, who grew up in this town, has warned them all about dealing with Texans, the white ones, told them scare stories about John Wesley Hardin and lynch law and the Rangers, especially the Rangers, who are death on Mexicans and not much fonder of colored. The colored and Chinese here live in the Mex section, Chihuahua, and there's even supposed to be a couple of the old black Seminole scouts left over in Juarez. Royal has come in on leave with the others a dozen times, tequila making quick work of him.

"Cristy there," says the deputy, nodding after the jailer as he leaves, "was one of them got stabbed by our desperadoes."

"They had knives in jail?" the reporter's bowler sits on the desktop beside him. He writes with a pen that doesn't need to be dipped in ink over and over.

"Made them some daggers. When boys are gonna make the drop, you got to let them say farewell to their families, which with a Mex is half the damn county. And they go in for all that hugging, even the men. *Abrazos*. Don't know how you spell that—"

Royal is used to white men not looking at him, pretending not to see him, but with the uniform on it is more of an insult. He is just a private, "lower than muleshit" as Too Tall would say, but still—

"Some one of these folks slipped some fence wire to them that they twisted into shape and sharpened on the wall blocks that night. Next day, there's thousands outside, mostly Mex, fillin the streets, up on the rooftops, like they gonna see us do our business inside here. The hour arrives and we open the cells, and they both jump out—Parra and this Antonio Flores who's already stabbed to death some little señorita over in Smelterville who'd turned him down one too many times. Flores commences to jabbin my buddy Ed Bryant in the gut with this wire contraption while Parra goes after Cristy there and Officer Ten Eyck who was the first ones in. Took a half dozen of us to pull them frog-stickers away and get the cuffs on. The Mexicans call handcuffs *esposas*," winks the deputy. "The same word as *wife*."

But the uniform, thinks Royal, is something. Enough, maybe, if you break no laws and stay south of Second, east of Santa Fe Street, to keep a cracker deputy off of you. He wasn't much back in Wilmington, just another nigger millhand, and from what they tell of the white folks' takeover he be even less now. At least in the regulars it's always clear where you stand—look on a man's arm and you know how tight your asshole got to squeeze.

"None of the wounds were fatal?" asks the writer.

The deputy grins, spits into his mug. "You can't hurt a Texan with no fence-wire dagger," he says. "Nothin but chicken scratches. We sent Flores up first, and he wasn't too pleased about it, from what I could tell with the hood over his head. Made a good loud snap when he run out of rope, didn't need no doctor to know the job was done right. With Parra, well—Geronimo put on some weight in the Santa Fe hoosegow, and with his drop it popped that vein in your neck, blood pourin out from under the hood and all over the floor, and when Captain Hughes pulled it off the man's head was just barely holding up his body by one little strap of tendon."

"Oh my," says the Easterner, laying his pen down.

The deputy spits. "He needed killin."

Royal sees someone coming down the corridor toward them, a colored man in a regular's uniform, with the jailer Cristy behind him.

"We let the gory details out to the Mex crowd right away," says the deputy, raising his voice and turning his head slightly toward Royal and

Junior. "See, what we got here in El Paso is just a *col*ony, handful of decent white folks sandwiched between thousands of them bean-eatin sonsabitches on both sides of the Rio." He looks Royal in the eye for the first time. "Now and then you got to make a dis*play*."

The prisoner is Cooper, barefoot and without his hat.

"Get him out of town," says the deputy to Junior. "And tell your colonel to keep better track of his niggers."

Cooper sits alone in the bed of the wagon as Royal eases past the courthouse.

"Where are your boots, soldier?" asks Junior, turning back to glare.

"Talk to me like that, you sididdy little butt-wipe," says Cooper, almost calm, "I cut your heart out."

"You're a deserter."

"I only got two goddam days left on my hitch—what the hell I want to desert for?"

"Then what were you doing out on the International Bridge at midnight, out of uniform and—"

"I been to the Chinaman."

Cooper says this quietly, looking away from Junior, as if it explains everything.

"That where you left your boots?" asks Royal, pulling the reins to take them right.

"Maybe. You know how it is—puts you in a different *mind*."

Royal doesn't know how it is, has never gone with the few that smoke it, but did pass out drinking mescal one night and wake to see his father, ten years dead, tipping one back at the other end of the bar.

"I come out and it was dark," says Coop. "All that nice music they play comin out from the cantinas, and it hit that they wants me, they *needs* me to come over to Juarez."

"To do what?" asks Junior.

"You ever been?"

"No. It's off limits—"

"Then I can't ex*plain*, can I?" Cooper looks around to get his bearings, sees the post office. "That Alligator Plaza just up here, Roy. Got to get something before we go back."

Royal steers the pair over the Southern Pacific tracks and into the plaza, pulling the wagon up beside the gazebo. There are a couple dozen people scattered around, all colors, and the fountain in the middle of the circular moat is spilling halfheartedly.

"He's our prisoner," Junior protests. "We can't—"

Royal giving his friend a hard look. "I can do any damn thing I please."

Coop laughs and hops down, crossing barefoot to the low wall around the moat. Royal ties the horses off to a post on the gazebo and follows with Junior. There are two alligators, six-footers, sleeping on the ground just inside the low wall, so still they might be dead and stuffed, and another slowly swimming, eyes just above the surface of the murky green water in the moat. A metal statue of a little boy stands by the fountain on the little island in the center, right leg bare and holding a boot up with real water running out of the toe.

"Look like that boy found *his* boots," says Coop, rolling his pant legs up.

"You left something here?"

Coop looks about to see there is no one near with a badge or a stripe, then high-steps over the wall. "First thing into town I got my ashes hauled over on Utah Street," he says, passing between the two sleepers, "then I come down here to set a spell. Bought some chicken necks in case they still hungry." He steps into the water, begins to move in a slow zigzag, head cocked, searching with the bottoms of his feet.

"Junior," he calls, "you see that gator make a rush at me, I needs you to shoot it." He touches an eyeball. "Right here."

Junior turns, scanning the plaza for somebody who might disapprove, but the noontime idlers seem to be used to people wading in with the reptiles.

"I was carryin my pro*tec*tion," says Coop, moving sideways now, "which a man be crazy to do without in this town, no matter what the damn post regulation say, and these two police start to pass by me, up and down, three-fo times, and I figure it's either have it out with the crackers right then and there or put it where they can't find it on me."

Junior turns back. "You had a *pistol*?"

Coop shows all his teeth in a smile, reaches up to his shoulder into the water and comes up with a slime-dripping, short-barrel Bulldog.

"Just this little ole thing. Don't look like much, but she bite you."

The alligator floats just in front of Cooper's legs then, not more than two feet away. He watches it pass.

"They don't care for the dark meat."

*　　*　　*

Royal has Cooper's revolver tucked in his boot when they come back to Bliss, Junior dealing with the sentries, the armbands and the colonel's name getting them onto the parade ground.

"So what do you think?" he says to Royal. "They're making the pay up, and once you're off the books—"

"Give me one more reason," says Royal, easing the pair to a stop in front of the stockade. "One good reason."

Junior leans in and speaks quiet enough that Cooper, brooding in the back of the wagon, can't hear.

"Because you're my friend," says Junior. "And I can't do it without you."

Sergeant Jacks is in the little guard shack with Lumbley, the duty officer.

"You didn't make it to the other side," says Jacks, looking Coop up and down.

"I was about to the middle of the bridge when I trip over them trolley tracks," Coop shrugs. "And then it feel so good, layin on them boards, my head in Old Mexico and my feets in the United States, I just decide to take a nap."

Jacks steps close and looks into Cooper's eyes, searching. "You wonder what could put an idea like that in a man's head."

Junior makes a noise to get his attention. "I've come to a decision, Sergeant," he says, straightening up and locking his eyes forward the way you only need to do with captains and higher. "I'll be reenlisting."

"I'll call the War Department," says Lumbley. "They been holdin off on their plans."

Cooper starts to laugh. "Me too, Sarge. I mean after I does my little stay in here, you can sign me up."

Jacks shakes his head. "*If* you survive the next three weeks' punishment, and *if* the 25th Regular Infantry, Colored, in its ill-advised generosity, agrees to accept your petition," he says, "you will have to *earn* those boots back, Private." He turns to Royal. "How bout you?"

Fort Bliss is like Huachuca, is like Missoula. Some mountains on one side and then just open land with hardly a soul upon it. Nothing out there. Royal sees himself walking in the great emptiness, on and on, no uniform on his back, a part of nothing with nowhere to go.

Junior won't look at him but is listening hard.

"Yeah," says Royal. "Count me in."

INCENDIARY

This is not the first time Tondo has burned. Twice while he was at the Ateneo the chapel bells rang and the Manila firemen stumbled over each other and the British sent their shiny wagon into the streets and the sky was alive with floating embers all through the night. Diosdado ducks low and zigzags through the maze of nipa huts, thrusting the torch to anything not already ablaze. Men and women and children scatter before him, barefoot, carrying whatever they value most and searching for a pathway through the flames. The plan is to move from east to west, advance runners warning the people and the next wave firing their homes, driving everyone before them to the sea. But the wind has shifted several times, torch-men have run ahead of the ones crying the alarm and there are screams now, lifting above the crackle and roar of the conflagration, screams of fear and more hysterical screams that Diosdado doesn't want to think about and bamboo timbers exploding like rifle shots and the *pop-pop-pop* of real rifles to the east as their snipers engage the first of the Americans to respond. He has to backtrack quickly as a nipa hut ahead erupts into flame, a burning dog squealing as it scampers out, tail on fire, the rush of heat like a blow to the side of his face and there is panic in the firelit eyes of the scattering people, panic in their shouts to each other and the *pop-pop-pop* closer now with what must be every chapel bell in Manila ringing at once. The local firemen are out there somewhere and the British, no doubt, never miss a chance to show off their new steam pumper, and the Americans with whatever equipment they've loaded off their great ships—but when Tondo burns it burns to the ground.

A small boy is staggering under the weight of the plaster statue of Saint Joseph he carries on his shoulder, trying to escape but driven back from a wall of heat in each direction. Diosdado shouts and the boy whirls, sees the torch in his hand and backs away from him, terrified, before turning to disappear into the thick black smoke rolling in from the west.

Diosdado edges away from the smoke and tries to gasp a clean breath, the scorched air searing his lungs, worrying that his clothes and hair, despite their dousing before the raid, will burst into flame. He is trapped. The burning is only a diversion, meant to draw some of the Americans away from Binondo before General Luna's attack on their northernmost lines. It is the last hope, more desperate even than the defense at Caloocan when the enemy first pushed north from the river, Diosdado's company among four thousand dug in by the chapel and the Chinese cemetery, lying in the muck of the rice fields with the American artillery raining down from La Loma and the Gatling gun tearing the sod off the ditches and the *yanqui* infantry advancing like a murderous flood tide as the colonels flapped and postured and squawked at each order from Luna saying Aguinaldo, Aguinaldo was the *supremo* and they would obey only him while their men fought bravely, desperately, uselessly and the railhead and the five locomotives with all their cars sitting on the tracks were lost.

Diosdado tries to strip his uniform tunic off but the buttons are too hot to touch. Luna insisted the officers keep them on for the raid—"So they know we are not *tulisanes*," he said, "not a rabble of bandits but the Army of the Filipino Republic, saviors of the nation." Saviors, Diosdado thinks as the shifting curtains of flame drive him one way and then another, of the very people whose homes we have put to the torch. He is afraid, more afraid than he was on the night the fight with the Americans started, buried in the wet earth as the shells burst above him, or at Caloocan trying to keep his face toward the enemy as he stumbled backward over the paddies, firing his pistol methodically till his ammunition was all gone, the huge Americans in their blue uniforms pausing only to chop and hack with rifle butt and bayonet at the wounded men he'd left behind, Diosdado finally turning and running to catch the ones still living and gather them back into some kind of coherent unit.

The Lake of Fire. Every story Padre Inocencio terrified them with in the *primario* ended with the Lake of Fire and the agonies of the sinners cast into it, their shrieks of anguish unheard in Paradise, their flesh rendered from their bodies, limbs twisted with spasms of pain, bones blackened and cracking in the molten inferno but not dying, no, doomed to endless torment. Once he held Diosdado's hand over a candle flame till the skin of his palm blistered, reciting the litany of tortures reserved for the damned and holding a scapular with the image of a woman engulfed in flames close to his face. "Imagine this pain a thousand times hotter, all over your body," he hissed into the little boy's ear. "Hour after hour, day after day, year after year, without hope, without release. This is Eternal Damnation."

Burning to death has always been his worst fear, the nightmare that wrenches him awake in a sweat. Diosdado drops his torch. The leather of his holster feels like it is melting, the metal butt of his pistol like a sizzling griddle as he forces his hand closed around it. I will not say a prayer, Diosdado thinks, cocking it. And if there is a Hell, Padre Inocencio will be there to greet me.

He is lifting the pistol toward his head when Sergeant Bayani emerges from the black smoke, a torch in each hand, eyes gleaming with flame, a lunatic smile lighting up his face. There is *vino* on his breath as he shouts over the crackling of the nipa and the screams and the bells tolling everywhere and the rifle fire on all sides now, Bayani who threw Diosdado unconscious over his shoulder on the first night of the war with the *yanquis* and carried him halfway to Malolos, who was waiting for Diosdado with the survivors of the rout at Caloocan, dug in and ready to resist again, on the outskirts of Tinajeros, Bayani who the men say is insane and invincible, the *anting anting* sewn beneath the skin just over his heart protecting him from evil thoughts and enemy bullets.

"This is one *baryo*," he shouts gleefully, "that the Americans will not get to destroy. *Sígame, hermano!*"

Bayani hurls his torches into the hottest part of the fire blowing toward them, then turns and strides again into the black smoke. Diosdado fights the urge to shout an order to him, any order, before holstering his pistol and hurrying after.

He holds his breath and runs till they fall out of the smoke, coughing, eyes streaming with tears, into what is left of the mercado. Only charred bamboo uprights are left where the stalls once stood—shops gutted and roofless, a pile of cocoanuts blackened and cracked and oozing, chickens crisped in a cage no longer hanging, bundles dropped by the fleeing residents burst open and littering the street. Diosdado has been to Tondo only once when it wasn't burning, a long drunken night in a rented *calesa* with Scipio and Hilario Ibañez from Santo Tomás, Hilario who wanted to achieve in epic verse what Dr. Rizal had in prose, improvising stanzas about the true soul of the nation residing in this hodgepodge of narrow, blighted streets along the fetid Canal de la Reina as its residents sullenly spit and muttered and moved aside to let their carriage pass. Bayani seems to know it, though, leading Diosdado at a trot through the smoldering maze till they reach the swampland to the north of the *colonia*, flattening themselves in the cogon grass to let a platoon of fire-addled *yanquis*, volunteers by their uniform, hustle by. They catch their breath, then struggle wordlessly through the bamboo thickets and mires and tangling brush, fat embers blown over their heads and settling in the tops of the cabonegro palms to glow like fireflies. They hear noises to the left, Bayani pausing to call in Tagalog and answered with a curse. It is Kalaw and Rafi Agapito, blackened with soot, and the four of them continue for an hour before anyone speaks.

"Did you see any of the others?" Diosdado asks when they stop to rest, Bayani scouting ahead.

"Once or twice in the fire," says Kalaw. "There were so many people running. And I saw the sargento." He lowers his voice as if Bayani might be near. "He was in front of a liquor warehouse he set fire to."

"Drinking."

Kalaw shrugs. "It would be a sin to let it all go to waste."

"I saw Ninong Carangal get shot." Agapito has a sandal off, poking at his bleeding foot. The bamboo poles towering over their heads knock together in the early-morning breeze, and there is distant gunfire. "He ran out with an ax to cut the fire hose and the Americans saw him and shot him dead."

Sargento Bayani reappears and squats by them, his manner completely sober now, calculating. "Our battalion is just ahead at Balintawak, but there's trouble."

"*Yanquis?*" asks Agapito, wincing as he pulls his sandal back on.

"Worse. Filipinos."

They step out of the bamboo forest to find four companies of Caviteños seated on the ground by the side of the road, disarmed and under guard, while Colonel Román tries to convince General Luna it is a poor idea to fire a bullet into the skull of their capitán.

"He'll be punished, he'll be made an example," says Paco Román, his long criollo face tight with apprehension, speaking as calmly as possible. "But not here, General, please. Not now."

Luna's men, rifles leveled at the Caviteños on four sides, look more frightened than the sitting troops. Diosdado and his survivors halt a few yards away, Kalaw and Rafi Agapito looking from officer to officer with anxious incomprehension as the Ilocano general and the kneeling capitán argue in Spanish.

"There is a gap in our line of attack," says Luna, spitting his words. "I need to reinforce it."

"My men will go nowhere unless I lead them," says Capitán Janolino, so Spanish-looking his friends call him Pedrong Kastila, his voice strained but his gaze steady.

"I'll have them all shot!"

"Whatever you do," says Janolino, "it is not as my commanding officer."

There is a battle raging to the west of them, rifle fire steady and deep from the Springfields of the *yanquis*, higher and more ragged from the British Mitfords and captured Mausers of their own troops, and suddenly the whistle of shells overhead and the solid *whump!* as they reach their killing ground in the Binondo cemetery.

Luna gives the capitán's head a final shove with his pistol and then lowers it to his side. Luna stood firm throughout the day at Caloocan, exposed to the murderous fire, running forward to protect the wounded till they could be carried away, coolly sighting and firing his pistol as if it was one of his target-shooting exhibitions. It was thrilling to fight beside such a leader, and then, as the church was shelled to ruins and the rice fields plowed with explosions and the *yanqui* horde advanced, it was suicidal—General Luna determined to fight to his death and expecting the same of the men around him.

"Take a company," he barks to Colonel Román, "and march these traitors to Malolos."

He turns then, and there is fury in his eyes as he discovers the torch-men.

"Who are you people?"

Diosdado salutes. "Incendiary squad, *mi general*. One dead, seven unaccounted for."

"Tondo?"

"Tondo is burning. Santa Cruz and San Nicolas are burning."

"There are two hundred of our people entrenched by the bridge, waiting for the *yanquis*," adds Sergeant Bayani. "And all the *chinos* have gone to hide in their embassy."

Luna grunts. Behind him one hundred forty scowling Caviteños are rousted to their feet and herded into formation.

"Grab a weapon and join us," orders the general, jerking his head toward the stacks of rifles Janolino's companies are leaving behind. "There are plenty to choose from."

AN EXECUTION

The officer walks rather casually before the others. He doesn't look Spanish. They march out of the trees, parallel to the abandoned building, till the Spaniard gestures and the prisoners, four of them, are halted and told to face the stone wall. The prisoners are all dark-skinned men, in motley combinations of clothing. Insurgents. The officer draws his sword as the firing squad, four soldiers, fix their man in place with a hand on the left shoulder, then step back five paces. The officer runs across in front of them and stands parallel to their row, then brings his sword down. A crackling volley from the four rifles—smoke fills the air, and the insurgents drop to the ground.

Harry looks over to Mr. Heise, who nods and steps away from the Beast.

"You can get up now!" Harry calls, and the sprawled insurgents roll slowly to their knees, grinning at each other and at their executioners.

"That's it for today," says Mr. Heise to Harry. "We can pull the film back at the shop."

Harry signals to a pair of the colored boys and they come trotting over from the wall, swatting dust off their clothes.

"I hold my breaf just like you tole me to," says Zeke, smiling.

"You looked perfect, all of you." Harry nods to the wagon. "Time to pack the instrument up."

He supervises as the boys lift the heavy camera on the carry-boards they have rigged up and stagger back to hoist it onto the wagon bed. Stempl back at the shop is the one who started calling it the Beast, though never if the

Wizard is close enough to read their lips. No wonder that Paley's mission to Cuba was a fiasco. With the camera weighing as much and requiring far more maintenance than a field-artillery piece he managed only a few shots of swimming mules and one scene of a very small horse suffering under the enormous General Shafter before rain fouled the apparatus and tropical disease forced his return.

"My people see this, they gone get a start," says Zeke, still excited by his acting debut. "Aint noner them ever been in no photograph, movin or not."

The movement, of course, is an illusion. Inside the Beast there are cylinders that move in concert with other cylinders, celluloid coated with chemicals cranked on a spool and held in its groove by a claw mechanism, and passed, hopefully at a consistent rate, in front of an aperture that allows a finite flash of light to hit it before being wound back into darkness. The image borne by that light and captured in the chemicals is only a photograph, as still as any other. But rolled in succession with the other photographs caught on the strip of film, the human eye is fooled—

"They gone think this real? I mean the other people who don't know me that sees it?"

Harry helps guide the body of the Beast as they slide it forward on the wagon bed.

"That depends on who displays it," he says. "We'll send this out as a facsimile, but as to how it is presented in the halls—" he spreads his arms. "It looked very real."

"That's what I was thinkin," says Zeke, securing a rope around the camera body. "They was just a second there, before the man yell 'Fire!,' where I got to feelin they might be real bullets in them rifles." He touches his chest. "Made my heart skip a beat."

"You were very convincing."

Zeke nudges the other boy with his elbow, winks. "Skeeter here done wet his nappies when they shoot."

It is not so different in principal from the Gatling gun, Harry thinks, though one device makes itself repeatedly vulnerable while the other deals out lead with precision. At the moment of the execution volley he had been struck by the notion that if Heise's arm were quicker, four cranks per second perhaps, or the instrument driven by a dynamo with sufficient speed, one could capture motion faster than the capacity of the human eye. One could slow down time itself. The bullets could be seen in their deadly trajectory, the instant of their penetration into the skulls of the insurgents—but of course that would give away the illusion. There were no bullets, only the wadding from blank cartridges, and there was no smashing of bones, no spilling of brains.

When the equipment is secured Harry joins Mr. Heise and Mr. White in the coach to take them back to the shop. The old stone house, windows missing, overgrown with creepers, is quickly left behind them.

"The Spanish-atrocity theme is wearing a bit thin," says Mr. White. "Given the turn of events."

Before this the only view they've let Harry take part in was *Did Somebody Say Watermelon?*, and that had been done in the Black Maria with Skeeter and another of the boys from today.

"One of them moved," says Mr. Heise. "One of our *insurrectos*. After he was shot."

"The throes of death."

"He looked at the camera before he did it."

"We'll cut it short. The view is over when they hit the ground. No use in being morbid about it."

They ride silently through the Jersey woodlands. There might be some great use, thinks Harry, in being morbid. If they'd been able to mount the Beast on some sort of runner or sled apparatus and push it forward to see the bodies of the executed men more closely at the end, or if the camera were not such a behemoth and could be thrown over the shoulder and transported, like a Kodak on a tripod, as easily as a rifle, think of what Paley, or perhaps an operator less portly, might have captured at Las Guasimas or Kettle Hill or in this new Philippine nightmare that Niles has gotten himself embroiled in. Harry thinks again of the image of a bullet leaving a rifle and followed directly to the spot between the eyes of its victim, a handsome Southerner with a constant smirk of self-love on his countenance—

The ladies could not bear to view such a thing, of course, but ladies are not the advocates or perpetrators of war, and cannot be expected to be its *aficionados*.

The coach passes the wagon bearing the Beast, and Harry leans out to look. To any other eye it is only a bulky and seemingly purposeless piece of furniture.

"I thought our Dago capitán was awfully good," says Mr. Heise. "Haughty and officious."

"And without a moustache to twirl," smiles Mr. White. "Quite an accomplishment."

Harry's mind is racing. If you staged it, he thinks, interrupting the wide view with a closer one of the condemned men's faces, then sighting down the line of pointing rifles, perhaps a little stage blood to increase the impact of the sledding shot of the insurgents' bodies—or if you could be there, be there on the actual battlefield to capture forever that horrible moment, one man murdering another in the name of the flag—how could they go on with it?

If they want war, he thinks, first make them watch it up close.

TURKEY SHOOT

Mariquina has to go. Captain Stewart and Phillippi from Cripple Creek and Pynchon, the bicycle racer from Company K, and Maccoe and Danny Donovan killed in four different fights here and enough is enough. Hod trots with a torch made from a length of bamboo and a googoo's abandoned shirt soaked in kerosene, touching it to the dry thatch roofs of the nipa huts that catch fire with a hiss like that's what they're made for. The church is already pouring smoke. This is how it goes, he figures, maybe not so many of the people in this town want to fight them but there's ones who do who keep coming back and pretty soon the details don't matter—if it shoots at you, you kill it and tear down whatever it was hiding behind.

The people are all gone, run off into the hills around them, and tonight they will come back and dig for whatever they've hidden in the ground and maybe just the church steeple will be left standing and maybe not even that. Lots of the other boys are whooping, eyes bright with the blaze, throwing the wood stumps the locals use to husk their rice into the burning huts and smashing their water jugs with the butts of their rifles and Tutweiler running in and out adding to his collection of statues and pictures of the Virgin and Grissom's monkey tormenting a fighting cock that has been left pegged to the ground, its feathers starting to singe, but Hod is just trying to get the job done. The quickstep has eased off finally, but now he has the other problem, needing to piss all the time and when he does it's like acid coming out. This Philippines is trying to kill him.

It is the most beautiful place he's ever seen, Mariquina, looking at it from the heights by the waterworks, set in between the dark green patches of trees and the lighter green of canefields and corn and rice and bananas and sweet potatoes and watermelons that the fellas would swipe and eat on the road after cleaning the *insurrectos* out of town yet again and now it is burning, burning—nothing to see from the heights if you were up there but black smoke.

He comes upon Big Ten with nothing in his hand to set fire with, the Indian just standing in the middle of it all, watching moodily. The huts crackle and pop around them, black smoke blowing to the west.

"Some party, huh?" he says to Hod, a strange little smile on his face. "All we need is the regimental band."

Later, back up on the hill, there is distant shelling, a hotter engagement just to the north, and the captain lets them stand and watch for a moment before they march off to help. Hod feels it coming and turns his back to the far-off battle and opens his fly and out comes a too-yellow stream of it.

Burning.

Nilda squats with the others in the cogon grass, mosquitoes feeding on them all. Her cousin's little *bahay kubo* in Mariquina is in flames and there is another battle ahead of them, gunfire and explosions, so they hide and wait. The *yanquis* usually leave before it is dark, but this time there will be nothing left.

It isn't her town, just a corner of the room in a tiny hut where she has curled up since they killed Fecundo, washing and cooking for the wife of the *capitán de barangay* and hiding under the copra shed whenever the *yanquis* come through. There are others like her, floating people, on the run back to their home provinces or with nowhere left to go, and she supposes she will join them on the road in the morning, heading north ahead of the Americans, feeling bound to tell Fecundo's mother of his capture and execution. Many of the wanderers are children, sick with hunger, heads too big for their bodies. Too many of them to be cared for. The ground shakes beneath them as the *yanqui* bombs explode. The sun has a good while left in the sky and then they can creep back to whatever is left of Mariquina. Sometimes there are animals burned, cooked, after a town is razed, and Nilda hopes to find one for her journey.

*   *   *

You got to give the little monkeys credit—they dig a hell of a trench. Maybe not so deep as the vols with their longer legs, but deep enough to fit a lot of bodies in. Big Ten grabs the arms on the ones that still got both and Hod takes the legs and they swing them down onto the pile.

"Artillery tore these people up," says Hod, wiping his hands on the sides of his pants.

"Some of them." Big Ten rolls a man over and indicates the hole in his forehead. "This one, you got to say it's superior marksmanship."

"Stupid bastards try to fight us nose to nose. Your outfit never did that."

"My outfit."

"You know—"

"Sure they did, way back. Never turned out too good, though, so they gone back to Indin tactics."

They heave the body. There is still gunfire to the north, just potshots from the sound of it, and Lieutenant Manigault is over with the brass, all of them waving their sticks around.

"Here's another one."

Big Ten squats to examine the hole in the man's head. Not one of his. He is one of two dozen in the company they give a Krag to the other day for "outpost duty," but really cause he shoots better than the rest. "Chief got them eagle-eyes," the fellas say, "like all Indins." Only his father had to wear glasses he bought over in Bemidji and his brother Laurent couldn't hit a chestnut tree at ten paces. It's either you got the feel for it or you don't, and Big Ten knows for a fact he didn't shoot nobody through the head. If they were squared off to fire he snapped their collarbone opposite the rifle side and if they'd started to run he put one in the thigh. What the other fellas done when they come upon these wounded wasn't his business, he figures, it's just one more little monkey I don't have to deal with tomorrow.

They heave the body.

"What's that, thirty-four?"

"I just shoot em," says Big Ten. "Don't ask me to keep count, too."

He used fourteen rounds in the fight, hit fourteen men. The other fellas say they just shoot into the crowd, sitting ducks, they say, but Big Ten can see what kind of weapon they've got and if they're an officer or not and whether they close their eyes when they fire. An awful lot of them, and this is supposed to be their best people up on the line, shut their eyes just as they pull the trigger. Plus their artillery is a joke, old cannons off Spanish ships that blow apart as often as they send a ball flying.

"We're supposed to be counting."

"Make up a number. Manly Goat aint gonna climb down in here and check."

The next one they got to toss in pieces.

"Shell must of fell right on him." Hod is looking queasy.

"He's not any deader than these others. Grab them feet."

Big Ten can knock down a squirrel in mid-leap at a hundred yards through a stand of yellow birch. The rounds run smooth through the Krag, and make half the mess the Springfield .45s do when they hit somebody. Not fit for the stewpot, as his father used to say of birds they brought back too full of pellets. Big Ten has never, he thinks, been as good at anything as he is at this soldiering business.

If only he liked it more.

"You think they'd of learned by now," says Hod, using his feet to position a body so they can get a grip on it. The Filipinos don't weigh much more than a middling-sized Ojibwe child, his brother's son René maybe, and don't carry money into battle, which has pretty much scotched the likelihood of getting volunteers for clean-up duty. "They ought to fight shoot-and-run, like your outfit."

"Sure," says Big Ten, heaving. "Just look how good we come out."

"Well, if I was their general," says Hod, wiping something sticky and yellow off his hand onto the side of his pants, "I sure wouldn't waste any more people in these trenches."

Corporal Grissom wanders back and looks at the jumble of bodies in the pit.

"How many we got in there?"

"Forty-one," says Hod without blinking. Grissom looks to Big Ten.

"We got a smoker goin ahead at the river, Chief. Lieutenant wants you up there on the double."

"What about me?" asks Hod.

The corporal shrugs. "Didn't say nothin about you."

Hod picks up his old Springfield. "Well I aint draggin these dead men around on my own."

"Suit yourself."

They pass more enemy dead on the walk to the river, a few on their bellies with triangular bayonet wounds in the back. The flying column wasn't supposed to take prisoners unless they might have important information. From the look of these little monkeys, nobody asked. They pass the porters kneeling in a circle in their cast-off Army clothes, throwing dice next to a small hill of equipment, and Grissom shouts for them to go back and cover the pile of Filipino that Hod and Big Ten left. Chinks will do about anything you pay them for except fight or touch dead bodies.

Lieutenant Manigault and some bigger brass are back in the trees, while the boys are hunkered down wherever there is cover from the snipers on the other side of the water.

"This is the one I told you about," says Manigault. "Never misses."

"Then get him cracking," says a colonel with a big moustache.

The Lieutenant and Corporal Grissom lead Big Ten and Hod to the riverside, where Sergeant LaDuke lies cursing behind a tree stump.

"Every time we send somebody out he gets plinked by those sonsabitches over there. They must be renegade Spaniards."

"Spanish can't shoot worth shit either," observes Corporal Grissom.

"Maybe it's Lenny Hayes from I Company," says Hod.

Hayes fell in love with a Filipina and went over to the other side, and is supposed to be moving fast up through the ranks of the googoo army.

"Can you see them?" Manigault asks Big Ten.

"Not unless they pop up to shoot at somebody."

Manigault looks to Sergeant LaDuke. "Well?"

"Stick your head out there," LaDuke orders Hod.

Hod gives Big Ten a dirty look. Big Ten points.

"Just haul your freight over and get behind the bank where it rises up there. They won't get more than a couple off."

Big Ten sights on the tangle of trees across the narrow river. "Go."

Hod runs and two men rise slightly from behind a downed tree trunk to fire at him. Big Ten sits one of them down with a round through the collarbone.

Crack! a piece of bark flies off next to his face. LaDuke curses.

"That came from high," Big Ten says to Manigault. "They probably got a bunch in the trees."

"Can you get them?"

"Only if they got a reason to show themselves."

Manigault turns to the sergeant. "Take your squad," he orders, "and trot along the bank like you're looking for a good place to cross."

"Like ducks in a goddam shooting gallery."

"On the double, Sergeant."

LaDuke curses and calls his men over. Hod pretends he can't hear but

Grissom goes to get him. As the sergeant begins to run Big Ten rolls into his spot, bracing the Krag on top of the tree trunk and firing, one—two—three—four—five—six—the other volunteers along the bank cheering as they see bodies drop out of trees and then the 1st Kansas is up and whooping, charging into the water.

The colonel with the moustache and some of the other brass and everybody else but the Sisters of Perpetual Adoration come up to congratulate Manigault on having such a valuable asset in his company. Only one of the squad, Clete Standish, was hit by the snipers while running decoy, shot through the hip, and he is being carried back by Hod and little Monroe who used to tend bar at the Arcade in Denver.

The colonel thumps Big Ten on the back. "If your outfit had a few more bucks could shoot like you do," he winks, "I might never have made it out of Arizona."

Big Ten watches the 1st Kansas wading neck-deep under halfhearted fire with their rifles, bayonets fixed, held high over their heads. Never miss a chance, the Kansas, to stick whoever is left crawling on the other side. He knows he hit at least three of the men in the trees, not showing much of themselves, right between the eyes.

"My outfit never crossed an ocean to kill nobody, either," he mutters, and heads off to help Hod with the wounded man.

ROUNDSMEN

You don't like to see a white foot on a dray horse. Hooker got three of them, and Jubal checks them over after he brushes her, getting her to lift each foot so he can look for splits and see how the shoe is wearing. She is a dapple-gray Percheron, seven, maybe eight years old, and been used hard, which is why they give her to Jubal when Mr. White sent him over from the Island. New man get the sorriest ride. Somebody had bob-wire in her mouth, probly back on the farm, she got some scars and don't feel the bit lest you put some boss into it. Call her Hooker cause she always pull to the left but that was only a shoulder sore let go and Jubal has healed it up. He makes sure to do every-thing in the same order in the morning, like you need to with the jumpy ones, which means he lets her eat hay from the iron manger while he looks her over for rub spots.

"You take this to keep her off you," Duckworth said on the first day they moved him onto the city job, handing him a rusty railroad spike, and she did try to crowd him against the stall boards, but every time he just duck under and go to the other side till she give up on it. Horse can't kick back on you when you between its legs and it don't have the patience for mischief that a mule does.

Jubal ties her lead line off to the post, hangs the collar over her neck, straps it shut, and then fixes the hames in the groove.

"Gone be a good day for us, Hooker," he croons, crossing the trace lines over her back to keep them out of the way. "Get out and see the world some."

He is only started laying the harness saddle on her when her tail goes up. He steps back and lets her pee like she always does, still got the nerves even with how he treats her. He waits for it to soak into the straw a bit, then cinches the harness saddle, keeping it loose. Horse like her only got one question in its head—how they gone hurt me next? She'll bloat on you at first so it's no use pulling that cinch too tight. Jubal lays the britching over her rump, lifting her tail gently to fix the backstrap and then buckling the cropper down to it before snapping the top strap onto the saddle. This was the hardest part when he first come, maybe somebody twist her tail or put a stick up her behind before. Lots of ignorant people think they know how to make a horse act right.

He replaces the halter with the bridle then, slipping the nose band over, working his thumb into the space between her front and back teeth to get her to open and pushing the bit into place. He gets the crown piece over her ears and snugs it all up, being sure the blinkers don't rub on the eye and tightening the throat latch strap. She holds nice and still for him, lazily switching flies with her tail, not twitching under the skin like she done the first week. He had to come in a hour early those days, but now they know each other and got a understanding.

"Gonna be a hot one," calls Jerrold Huxley, walking past with Spook, who is a light sorrel Belgian. "Be quite a number of em fore it's over."

"Spect there will."

It was Jerrold he rode with to learn the job, Jerrold who helped him find the room on 27th. There is colored from just about everywhere in the building, from the Carolinas and Maryland and Virginia and up from Georgia and Mrs. Battle from the country of Jamaica and even one big-headed boy says he was born right in the City, that his people go back here from before it was United States and didn't never belong to white folks. Rent is more than on Barren Island but it smells better and there is something to do at night.

Jubal runs the narrow end of the reins through the terret ring on the saddle, pulling them back through the horse-collar guides and then up to the bit rings on the bridle. He tucks the loose ends of the reins under the back strap and backs her out of the stall.

Tiny Lipscombe is on the ramp ahead of them leading Pockets, a beautiful bay with black points who will bite you if you come at him from the right. At the bottom they pass the grooms throwing dice on a blanket and move on to the wagons.

He backs Hooker up between the wagon shafts, then loops an arm's length of rein around a post to keep her in place. Butterbean comes over from the dice game and holds the shafts up for Jubal to get the tug loops over them. He threads the traces back through the belly-band guides and hooks them to the wagon body, Butterbean stepping away the minute he's not needed. None of the stable boys like to deal with Hooker. Jubal tightens the cinch another few inches and checks the traces for twists. Jerrold is doing the same at the next wagon over.

"Mulraney in yet?"

Jerrold shakes his head. "Aint seen the man, but he might be about. Likes to tip up on people when they not looking."

Mulraney is the dispatcher and is always out to catch you with a bottle. Duckworth says it's cause he can't drink no more, doctor's orders, and can't stand the idea of somebody getting away with a nip under his same roof.

"He catch a sniff of liquor on your breath when you come back to the stable," Duckworth told him the first day, "that is the end of you."

Jubal takes the reins in hand and climbs onto the seat of the tip-wagon, watching Hooker's ears to see that she is ready to go. He clucks and gives the slightest jerk on the lines and Hooker starts them out of the stable.

Mulraney is not in his office when they pass, old Doucette who stays through the night sitting there watching the telephone, afraid he will have to pick it up. They don't really start to drop until noon, though now and then there is one that has laid out all night before somebody reported it.

Jubal gees her out through the doors to join the tail of the line on the Avenue. It is all kinds of horses they got working for White's Sons—Shires and Suffolks and Haflingers and Belgians and big tall Percherons like Hooker. The breweries take up the Clydesdales for their delivery teams, and it seems like all the saddle horses gone off to the Philippines or been sold to the English for their war in Africa. There are six wagons waiting in a row, horses blinkered with their heads down and ears slack, some of them probly asleep, while the teamsters lean back and tilt their faces up to the sun rising over the tenements to the east. He's never known Hooker to sleep in the traces, not even with a long standing spell, too busy worrying what somebody might surprise her with. No telling how many owners she been through to this point. Had her on a farm buggy maybe, mowed some hay, then when she got her size was sold into the City. Before the electric come in they run the streetcar and omnibus teams in all weather, uphill and down, till they were wore out. Every time a horse change hands it got someone new to deal with, someone got a whole nother way of doing to you. It puts Jubal in mind of his Mama's stories about slave days and people being traded out for livestock or stores. Hell, he thinks, I'd balk plenty you put a hand to me. Get away with whatever I could.

Jerrold calls out as a couple of the shitwagon boys roll by, bringing their street manure to the pier.

"You boys had a busy night."

"Yeah, we gonna lose these road apples and put the nags away," answers the lead driver. "Then I'm gonna look up that gal you been keepin with."

The teamsters laugh. Jerrold's wife is a big, rawboned woman who scares the daylights out of everybody but him.

"Aint no woman got a nose will let you near em," calls Duckworth after them. The shitwagon boys ride all night between sanitation stations and then ship it out at dawn. White's Sons sends a dozen wagonloads upstate every day, stable manure bringing a price while the road puckey just gets dumped somewhere. "You boys is *ripe*."

Mulraney shows up then, nodding sharp at them all. "Gentlemen," he says, like always. Mulraney is not so bad for an Irish, he don't call you nothin or tell you how to do your job if you do it right. Knows his horses, too, and word is he trained racers before the bottle got the best of him. He's the one who says when it's time to sell a horse out or send for the Cruelty people and put it away. You need a horse doctor to say it's an accident and shoot it if you want insurance, but the Cruelty people are free if you say it can't work no more and will suffer. Hooker was almost out the door to whatever ragpicker would buy her when Jubal came.

"She's found her man, she has," the dispatcher says whenever he sees her back in the traces. "It's a remarkable phenomenon."

The sun is two fingers over the rooftops when Jubal's turn comes up, one of the stable boys ducking his head out the doorway.

"Thirty-eight between Nine and Ten," he calls, and Jubal puts Hooker into motion.

He tries to keep to the streets with paving block, cobbles dealing hell to a white-footed horse, and keeps her to a slow trot. Hooker likes to run, which makes him think she was maybe once on a fire truck, and you got to keep some drag on the reins. Ninth is already crowded with traffic, hacks and delivery wagons and ice carts, a few pony phaetons and fancy carriages and the streetcar sparking up and down the middle. The hacks you have to watch out for, and the two-wheel cabs are even worse, cutting in and out of the flow to pick up or leave their fares, drivers waving their sticks and yelling at each other to stay clear. On the busiest day of the year in Wilmington it was nothing like this. When he first came, on foot, Jubal made his neck sore staring up at the buildings, one taller than the next, but driving you have to watch the cross streets, watch the rig ahead of you, watch for little ones trying to get under your wheels and you don't dare look up at anything. At the end of the day he can barely open his hands, which never happened back home no matter how long he drove.

White's Sons has the Board of Health contract and guarantees removal within three hours of notice, which is usually by a police from a callbox. But there is no police at the location, only a handful of little ones, Irishes they look like, daring each other to go up and sit on the dead horse's rump. Jubal walks Hooker past it, the little ones, mostly boys and one little girl sucking on her fingers, moving away to watch. He stands in the seat to look behind as Hooker backs the wagon up to the horse's head.

"The Dago left it," says the oldest of the boys, stepping closer. "The one that sells melons. It wouldn't go no more and he whips it and hollers at it in Dago and it still won't go so he jumps off and hits it on the nose and it just kneels down on its front legs and stays that way. So he grabs some crates from the alley here and busts em up with his feet and sets a fire under its back end. Only then it just falls down on its side and don't move no more."

"I seen one explode once," says a boy who keeps putting his thumb up his nose. "Back when we lived by the river. Its belly blowed up like a balloon and then *kablooey*—all over the street. My old lady wouldn't let us outside till they come get it."

If you're lucky the owner is still there and the harness is on and you can use that to pull it up. But this horse has been stripped clean, a dusty chestnut mare that maybe has the glanders, nose still running snot. Have to wash the wagon bed out good when he's shed of it.

Jubal sets the brake and hops down to the street. The rest of the boys step up, leaving the little girl staring from the sidewalk. Sometimes the street children will cut the tail off before you get there, twisting horsehair rings for each other.

"Can we help?"

"You stay clear of her," he says, pointing to Hooker. "Come too close she maybe kick your head in."

The boys look at Hooker with new respect and a few take a step back. Jubal unwinds the cable and pulls it down to the carcass, then lets the tail ramp of the wagon down. He ties the forelegs together just above the knee, yanks a leather strap tight around the neck and then links the two together with chain, slipping the cable hook through the middle link. The boys squat to watch him work.

"You want to get these off the street before they go stiff," he explains, "or else they maybe don't fit on the wagon."

The tip-wagon is low-sided and extra wide, with a pulley block bolted to the frame behind the seat, and the ramp has skid boards that he greases every morning. Jubal runs the free end of the cable through the pulley and then unhitches Hooker, knotting the traces together and then clipping the cable to them. More little ones come down from the stoops to watch, and women stick their heads out from the tenement windows all around. He leads Hooker away from the wagon, waiting for a furniture van to rattle past before heading her on a diagonal across the street till the cable is taut.

"Hold," he says to the horse, using the reins like a lead line to keep her grounded, and goes to check that the carcass is lined up right. Even hooked to a load you never know what a horse might get up to—a loud noise or a bee in the blinkers and they can go off trompling people till they run into a wall. He comes back to her, holding the reins a couple inches from the bridle bit.

"Yo!"

He doesn't have to yank on her or even slap with the reins, Hooker pulling steady and straight and the pulley squeaking and the carcass dragging up the ramp onto the wagon bed. A couple of the boys clap their hands when it is done.

"Where you gonna take im?" asks the second boy.

Jubal grins as he backs Hooker between the wagon shafts. "Straight to the butcher shop. This gone be your supper."

The other boys laugh and call out Kevin eats horsemeat, Kevin eats horsemeat, pointing and dancing around the boy.

"We eat nuttin but cabbage," he answers them, face going red. "Cabbage and beans."

He has almost got Hooker back in the traces when a panel wagon pulled by a hackney horse, half lame and too small for its load, stops alongside him. The panel is new-painted in red and black and gold and says—

EDISON COMPANY PICTURES
HIGHEST-GRADE SPECIALTIES

The white man sitting next to the driver leans out to talk to him.

"There is another one that wants dealing with," says the man, who wears a straw boater and looks like somebody Jubal knows. "At the corner of 39th."

Jubal lifts his hat off. "Can't carry but one at a time, suh," he says. "But I thank you for the lookout."

The man frowns at him for a moment, then points. "I know you."

White folks always think they know colored because they don't look so close, but then it comes to Jubal and he smiles. "That's right, suh, you Judge Manigault's boy."

He does not add "The one who don't walk right" which is how most of the colored in Wilmington know them apart, the ones who don't say "the good one" or "the nasty one." This is the good one.

The white man narrows his eyes, starting to smile. "And you are—?"

"Jubal, suh. Jubal Scott."

"Of course." The white man almost reaches down to shake hands, then catches himself. "What brings you up here, Jubal?"

Jubal keeps smiling. "How things come out, there's a whole lot of us come north."

It sits between them for a moment. As he remembers it this Manigault didn't have no part in it, always being left out from what the big white folks was up to.

"Of course," Harry says, smile fading. He points at Hooker. "I remember you now—you were a drayman."

"It got four legs and a tail, I can make it move."

The white man smiles again. "You own this horse?"

"Nawsuh, this belong to Mr. Tom and Mr. Andrew—that's P. White's Sons what keeps the street clear. They got three, four hundred horses."

The good Manigault nods his head, figuring something. The colored man beside him squirms in his seat, eager to get going.

"Do they have horses for rental?"

"Don't know but they might. Horses to do what?"

He waves a hand at the wagon panel. "To be in a motion picture. They should look like cavalry horses."

Jubal shakes his head. "Don't have none of that kind. Maybe you try the police, they always got some for auction."

The man nods, pulls a small card from his vest pocket and hands it down to Jubal. "If you ever tire of this service, I might have some employment for you. Feel free to call on me."

Jubal takes the card, squints at it. "Thank you, suh."

"Harry Manigault."

The name would have come to him sooner or later. "Like it say on your card."

The man smiles again, just about the first real smile Jubal has seen since he's been in the City. "Good day, Jubal. It is nice to see a familiar face."

The driver smacks the hackney with his stick and the panel wagon jerks away. Jubal sticks his hat back on.

"We get that horse off the street, Mr. Harry," he calls. "Three-hour guarantee!"

Dr. Bonkers' does no harm. It would take a detailed chemical analysis to discover the specific ingredients, but the taste indicates that it is mostly vegetable oil with a dose of cayenne and some camphor to impart a suitably medicinal smell. The recommended dosage is small enough—a teaspoon before retiring—and the taste sufficiently off-putting that subscribers are unlikely to make themselves ill ingesting the Brain Food. Until the licensing imbroglio can be resolved it affords him access to people's homes, and perhaps more importantly, a shiny black-leather physician's bag with which to impress and intimidate them.

Dr. Lunceford is not a gifted traveler, his "spiel" limited to inquiries surrounding the prospective purchaser's ailments and those of their loved ones, and has thus far moved only enough of the product to avoid being discharged and losing the totemic satchel.

"Do you suffer from epilepsy, spasms, convulsions, insomnia, hysteria, dyspepsia, paralysis, alcoholism, St. Vitus' dance or other nervous disorders?"

The woman looks at him blankly, her door open only enough to see him with one eye. "Aint got none of those."

"And how is the general health of your family?"

The woman looks behind her into the dim-lit room, then back to him. "Got a boy bust his arm."

"Ah. Perhaps I can be of some assistance."

Her eyes flick down to the leather bag. "You a doctor?"

Technically, at this time and in this state, he is not. "Madam," he assures her, "I have set countless broken limbs. Countless."

She looks at him suspiciously. "How much it gone cost?"

He is pushing, gently, against the door. It has been the most difficult lesson for him in this great city, that aggressiveness is valued, required, in fact, instead of being considered poor manners. "You should think about what you can afford. Is the young man in pain?"

He is by her then, surrendering to the now-instinctual New York habit of evaluating the apartment in relation to his own. There is light only from the street, coming in through a pair of dirty windows, revealing walls with patches of lath showing through and the remains of two layers of wallpaper in patterns that disagree with each other, wrinkled with moisture. They have pinned up a few color pictures torn from magazines, drawings of white people doing pretty things. No, thinks Dr. Lunceford, ours is not as bad as this.

The boy is small and dark-skinned, a permanent dent, most probably the work of forceps, in one side of his head. The injured arm lays slack in his lap as he sits on the only chair with upholstery in the two rooms, his legs sticking out straight from the seat. He looks up and Dr. Lunceford can read his thoughts—*What is this man going to do to me?*

He sits cautiously on the arm of the chair. "What's your name?"

"Cuttis."

"Curtis?"

"Cuttis."

"How did you injure your arm?"

"Gettin co'."

"In the basement?"

"On the train. When the co' train come by slow enough I climbs up an thow some down to Montrose and James."

"And you fell off the coal car?"

"Naw, I ain that stupit. After all I thown down Montrose and James wouldn't gimme my share an we commence to fightin." The little boy touches his arm, as if to bring back the memory. "James thow me down on the rail."

The mother looks on, standing, waiting to see what he will do next. He has had women, back in Wilmington, repel him at gunpoint to keep him from vaccinating their children.

"Never forget," Dr. Osler used to say when he took his students on city rounds, "that when you are in a person's home, you are a *guest*."

"I'm going to touch your arm, Cuttis. This one first."

The boy reluctantly offers up his good arm, and Dr. Lunceford pushes his fingers to the bone, getting a feel for what should be. There is no way to be precise without a Roentgen, of course, but a few generations of cotton loaders who can still bend their arms will vouch for him.

"Now I'm going to straighten out the arm that you've hurt and have you try a few things."

The boy looks at his face as he supports the broken arm under the elbow and slowly, gently straightens it.

"Can I see you make an o.k. sign with your fingers? That's good—now push your fingers against mine—"

"It hurt."

"But you can do it, can't you? Now I'm going to hold around your fingers and you have to try to spread them—that's good, this is all very good."

He runs his fingers lightly up from the elbow to the wrist several times. "You were in this fight, what, two or three days ago?"

"Three days," says the mother. "But we aint got nothin to pay a hospital."

Dr. Lunceford ignores the statement, looking into the eyes of the boy. "Now I want you to pretend that your pain is a voice. When I touch a certain part, you tell me if the voice is humming, talking, talking loud, shouting, or screaming."

"It hummin all the time."

"I'm sure it is. You've been very brave about it."

He begins to pinch around the bone, very slowly, moving toward the hand. "She talkin now."

"Uh-huh—"

"Louder."

"How about here?"

Tears come to the boy's eyes and he can't speak. Dr. Lunceford eases the pressure, turns to the mother.

"I'll need one of your stockings—it can be old but it must be clean. And if you'd boil a panful of water, please."

She looks at him for a moment, as if the words take time to penetrate, then steps into the other room. He knows he should have phrased it differently—"something you've just washed" instead of implying that most objects in here are filthy. Which they are. There is a thin blanket hung over the back of the chair and he imagines the little boy stretches out on it and the threadbare ottoman to sleep, perhaps sharing the chair with a sibling. He waits till he hears pots banging in the kitchen.

"Your arm is broken up near the wrist, Cuttis, and if I don't set it it's going to heal but in the wrong position—"

"It be crookit."

"That's right. Now you're going to have to help me—"

If it was a Monteggia fracture he'd insist they see a licensed doctor, some-body with a fluoroscope, but this is relatively standard—a distal fracture of both bones, the radial fracture complete and displaced, the ulnar of the greenstick variety, no obvious neural or vascular damage.

He gets a grip above and below the radial fracture. "I want you to take a deep breath now—"

The reduction is simple, rapid traction and torque, the boy crying out sharply and the mother rushing back in with a black cotton stocking in her hand.

"He ain counted to three," complains the boy, tears running down his cheeks.

But Dr. Lunceford has the bag open, fishing in it for the can of rolled bandages. Most of the space is taken up with bottles of Dr. Bonkers', but he manages to crowd a few useful articles between them, most of them pur-chased from a notorious thief on Tenth Avenue, a young Irishman who had never seen or heard of a colored physician.

"Barbers, I knew you had them," he said, laying out his wares on a table-top. "And the ginks who soak you to plant you under the ground. But a colored croaker, who'd a thought that?"

The bandages, already permeated with plaster of Paris, must have been prepared in a hospital, and Dr. Lunceford assumes the crime was perpetrated during a sojourn in one of the city wards, the thief making his rounds while still convalescing. "The quicker the patient can return to preferred activi-ties," Dr. Osler used to say, "the speedier the recovery."

"I could use that water now," he says to the mother.

She hands him the stocking and backs out of the room. He has the boy slowly supinate and pronate the wrist, feels the bones to make sure the reduc-tion is holding, then helps the boy off with his shirt and slips the stocking over his arm, attempting to smooth out the wrinkles. A long-arm cast is not specifically called for, but with young boys the more immobilized the limb the better, discouraging their more rambunctious instincts.

The mother returns with a pan of hot water and he asks her to set it on the floor.

"The break will hurt quite a bit for the rest of the day," he tells the boy as he wets the bandage and begins to wind it around his crooked arm, "but tomorrow most of the pain should be gone."

He has seen no facility in the apartment, perhaps everybody sharing an outhouse in the alley, or common toilets, tiny closets, placed on every other floor. He has seen every possible unsanitary solution as he has moved Yolanda and Jessie from building to building, structures thrown up to maximize profit per square foot, not to house human beings.

"Do you have any sort of medicine you use for the children? For toothaches or that sort of thing?"

The woman frowns, then walks to a rickety cupboard and pulls out a box of baking soda and a bottle of Mrs. Pinkham's panacea.

"I got this for bad stomach," she says raising the baking soda, "and the other for my lady problems."

He nods to the Vegetable Compound. "Give him two tablespoons of that before he sleeps tonight."

The potion is largely alcohol and will certainly have a soporific impact on a small boy. Kopp's Baby Friend, basically morphine in sugar water, would be more effective, but Dr. Lunceford has refused to represent it.

"I got to buy your bottle too?"

He smiles. "Dr. Bonkers' Brain Food is a tonic for a remarkable panoply of afflictions. A broken arm, however, is not one of them. I shall visit, if you don't mind, in a week to be sure this cast is not causing problems. If you can't spare anything now, perhaps at that time—"

The return visit is both responsible and good commerce, as only the most indigent or unembarrassable will allow you to walk away empty-handed more than once.

"I get you something."

She steps out and Dr. Lunceford turns to the boy, who is watching his arm as the bandages begin to harden around it.

"Which arm do you throw with?"

"One that's bust."

"If you can be patient it will get strong again. Strong enough to bounce a lump of coal off this James's noggin."

The boy smiles. He has a beautiful face, really, and Dr. Lunceford vows to carry that smile, like a talisman, with him through the rest of the day's adventures.

Dr. Lunceford knocks on every door in the next two buildings, then navigates through the crowd of humans and vehicles to begin on the structures across the street, the stairways unlit and coffin-like, each with its own particular odor, none pleasant. A few people answer, more just call and ask who he is, and none are in need of Brain Food. It is a wonder, given the conditions they live in, that the denizens of Hell's Kitchen are not in a constant state of epidemic. Many people down home are poor, yes, certainly with less to their names than these urban colored, but they are not crushed into narrow, disease-breeding dwellings in such numbers, not part of an anonymous and vaguely threatening multitude. Dr. Lunceford finds himself, when on the more peopled avenues, walking in a kind of protective daze, eyes focused just beyond any approaching stranger, whereas in Wilmington each pedestrian requires a greeting tailored to their status and circumstance. Once, in their second week on 47th Street, he walked past a throng, taking only fleeting notice of a young pregnant woman, only to have Jessie call him back from his daydream. It troubled him to see her in such a context, his daughter only one more dismissable face among the millions. There is a harmony of purpose, despite its seemingly frantic activity, in a beehive or a colony of ants, but so much of the busyness here resembles nothing more than poultry overcrowded on their way to slaughter, each animal climbing over its neighbor for the last breath of air.

There are young men, and some not so young, lolling on the stoop of the next building. There are layabouts in Wilmington, most notably in the dead season between cotton crops, but there the men tend to congregate at a handful of drinking resorts and barbershops. In this city the front steps of many buildings are draped, by noon, with the unemployed, colored or white depending on the dominant population of the street.

"Bout time somebody come for that girl," says one of the loungers as Dr. Lunceford steps carefully over his outstretched legs.

"She aint passed yet?"

"You know that she aint if you been hearin her Mama boo-hooin on the landing every night. 'Oh my po' daughter, Lord Jesus help my po' daughter!'"

"We in the back. Don't hear nothin but cats."

"She enough to drive a man to bad habits."

"Like you got none of them already."

The men laugh.

"May I ask," says Dr. Lunceford from the doorway, "where I can find this afflicted individual?"

The men eye him without respect or annoyance. He is a passing phenomenon, to be commented on when he is gone, a part of the meager entertainment afforded by the street that lays before them.

"Up five an in the front," says the first young man. "And mind them steps by the second flo'."

The steps just below the second-floor landing have fallen through on one side, Dr. Lunceford stepping carefully on the risers and supporting himself by pressing the wall rather than trusting the treacherously loose banister. He wonders how long they have been in this state, wonders that none of the men relaxing in front has access to a hammer and nails or the inclination to borrow such items. In their first apartment after the move from Philadelphia, in the tenement near the corner of 51st and Ninth, the toilet that served their floor was a swamp. After futile entreaties to the landlord's somnolent representative, a hunchbacked Pole who dwelt in the basement, and marked indifference from the tenants who shared the level, Dr. Lunceford spent a day cleaning, scraping, painting, and doing his best to repair the rudimentary plumbing. When finished he could bear the idea of his wife and pregnant daughter employing the facilities, but within a week the room was back to its former squalid condition.

The woman who answers the door seems frightened at the sight of him.

"Who send for you?"

"No one, but I—"

"She not dead."

"I am a medical man, not an undertaker." He holds the bag up where she can see it. "If you'll let me in perhaps I can be of some service."

There are lighted candles in the first room, one placed carefully next to a tiny chromo of the Virgin Mary. The woman wears a red cloth wrapped like a turban over her hair and sports a large crucifix, carved from yellowish wood, outside of her housedress. Catholics, Dr. Lunceford guesses, up from somewhere in Louisiana. Two very small children, a boy and a girl, play on the bare, sticky floor with a stewpot and a wooden spoon, while a child not yet a year old squats half-immersed in soapy water in the stone basin that also serves for kitchen needs. A girl of perhaps eight years stands by the half-open curtain that separates their two rooms.

"You wash the baby," the woman says to this girl. "This man gone look at Essie."

Essie lies on the larger of the two beds crowded into the back room, a cracked window affording her a view of the grimy brick airshaft and the trio of pigeons nodding sleepily on the sill. Sound asleep, on the other bed, is a fully clothed man of about thirty.

"That Mr. Ball," says the woman softly. "He work nights, so we rents a bed to him."

Dr. Lunceford feels very tired, though it is only eleven in the morning.

Too many stairs. "Hello, Essie," he says.

The girl, possibly as old as twelve or thirteen but wasted with disease, does not respond, her huge, frightened eyes following as he squeezes between the beds and steps to her side. She is propped on a pair of yellowed cushions, her neck swollen, breathing noisily and with extreme difficulty. Dr. Lunceford lays his palm on the girl's forehead.

"How long has she had this fever?"

"She been po'ly more than two weeks now," says the woman. "Her daddy, he work loadin the boats, he been to the hospital but they won't send nobody."

"There are visiting physicians."

"Suh, we just come up here. We can't affo'd none of that."

Dr. Lunceford nods. "Would you bring the lamp over, please?"

The woman squeezes in next to him, holding the oil lamp. "First she tired all the time, then she coughin, and then she can't even swallow."

"Would you open your mouth for me, Essie? Wide, like when you have to yawn—"

It clearly causes the girl some pain to open.

"And could you hold the light closer, please?"

The next time I see that thief, thinks Dr. Lunceford, I'll have to ask him to purloin a laryngoscope. He pushes her tongue down with a depressor and inserts the little ball of a mirror as far in as he can get it. The tonsils, uvula, and pillars of the fauces are all swollen, covered by the grayish pseudo-membrane, which extends up to the posterior nares and down over the epiglottis and into the larynx. The membrane is relatively thick, adhering tightly to the mucous membrane in most places, the windpipe nearly completely occluded. It is a wonder the girl can breathe at all.

There is only one course open to him. Her pulse is weak and irregular, the exudation, though not yet gangrenous, beginning to slough off and spread the sepsis. Five years ago she would be doomed, his role limited to supplying enough opiates to allow her to leave on a cloud. But there is an anti-toxin now, manufactured by the Board of Health itself, a serum he has no access to.

Dr. Lunceford touches the girl's cheek lightly. "You can close for a moment, Essie. Thank you."

"That look bad, don't it?"

He turns to the mother. "I will need some alcohol—three inches' worth, in a glass. It doesn't matter what sort."

The woman leaves and Dr. Lunceford sits on the side of the bed. There is an illustration of Christ on the cross, torn from a newspaper and at some point folded many times, tacked to the wall over the headboard of the bed. The folding has left the image divided into many squares, each one featuring an isolated locus of agony—a spiked and bleeding palm in one square, a section of thorn-pierced hairline in another. The effect makes it seem as if one of the Savior's eyes is raised to Heaven and the other, with a glint of challenge rather than supplication, squarely fixed on Dr. Lunceford.

And what shall you do for My lamb?

"It's hard to breathe, isn't it?"

The girl nods weakly.

"We'll try to do something about that."

The smallest boy is out of the basin, being wrapped in a blanket by his sister, and the woman is pouring gin from a square bottle into a glass. A hinged wooden lid has been lowered over the washbasin and there is a huge pile of dusty field greens spread out on it.

"She gone die?"

"Your daughter is very ill, but there are things that can be done for her. The first and most vital is to make sure her breathing is unimpeded. There is a procedure I will need to perform, and I need your permission to go ahead with it."

It is a matter for the Board of Health, of course, but by the time their representatives arrive the girl will be gone. In a race between the Klebs-Loeffler bacillus and city bureaucracy, there is no question as to which will win.

"You gone cut her?"

"No, M'am, but she will be made very uncomfortable for a short while."

The woman holds out the glass of gin to him, which he takes as acquiescence. Dr. Lunceford stacks several bottles of the Brain Food on the table in order to gain access to his instruments. The woman stares at the bottles. Women such as these, feeding their children on pork fat and road-clippings, are the principal consumers of the Bonkers elixir, and for an instant he feels ashamed to be associated with it. He slips the metal instruments he'll need from the pocketed canvas roll and stands them up in the alcohol. He has only one O'Dwyer tube, medium-sized, something the hospital thief threw in for free with no idea of its purpose.

"We just come up here," the woman says again, shaking her head. "Didn't count on nobody getting sick."

He has performed the intubation dozens of times, often on infants, in the days before the serum. Very few of those children survived. He pushes the tongue to the side with his curved forceps, then uses them to help guide the tube past the epiglottis and into the larynx, the girl heaving and gagging despite his care not to press on the vagus nerve. Her sputa, fine and poisonous, spray upon the lenses of his spectacles. The tube is brass covered with rubber, not very flexible, and when it is in place he tugs very slightly on the thread to be certain that the retaining swell is anchored below the vocal chords. When he leans away with the device in place the girl is soaked with sweat, but her dyspnea has been vanquished, her chest expanding and contracting heroically.

"Just breathe normally," he tells her, tying the thread around the stub of a pencil. "There's plenty of air for you now. And if you should begin to swallow the tube, which can happen sometimes, you can pull on this and cough and it will come out." He hands her the pencil, then touches her face again. "You're going to feel better now."

In the kitchen he scrubs his hands with carbolic soap, gargles with Condy's fluid and carefully cleans his spectacles. He explains to the woman that her daughter should be fed in a supine position with nothing more solid than rice with milk, that she will likely fall asleep immediately, her body sensing that strangulation has been circumvented. He does not tell her the rest. If you warn them the authorities are coming they are likely to hide things, and the bacillus continues to travel. She makes the sign of the cross in the Catholic manner, thanking God several times and Dr. Lunceford once.

"Antoine come back near seven," she tells him, "but he don't get paid till Sa'day."

As he leaves the young men stare at the bundle of greens under his arm.

"Doctor got him some groceries," calls one of them as he heads east. "Maybe he got a ham in that bag."

It is a long walk to the apothecary on Broadway. There is only a young white man in a white apron inside, dusting bottles on one of the half-dozen shelves. Dr. Lunceford lays his bag heavily on top of the pharmaceutical counter. A gaudily painted sign on the wall proclaims that the establishment sells his celebrated Brain Food.

"May I use your telephone?"

The young man frowns. "Telephone is a nickel."

Dr. Lunceford digs a coin from his pocket and lets it spin on the counter. The greens will not be especially filling, but excellent nutrition for a woman in Jessie's state.

"The City Board of Health, please," he says when a female voice comes over the wire. "Pathology, Bacteriology, and Disinfection."

Everyone in the apartment will be quarantined, most likely, the poor dockworker and the snoozing boarder likely to lose their employment. Clothing will be destroyed, the rooms fumigated, but there is no other course if epidemics are to be controlled. They will ask, even before they administer the anti-toxin, who performed the intubation, and the mother will pass on the name he gave to her. The official who informed him of the licensing difficulties clearly did not believe he was a physician, even with the references from fellow McGill alumni, and went into detail outlining the punishments that would ensue if he were caught impersonating one.

"I'd like to report a case of diphtheria," he says when a male voice asks why he has called. "This is Dr. Bonkers, Dr. Jeremiah Bonkers—"

THE WILL OF THE PEOPLE

Diosdado tries to read their smiles. The people, old men and women and children, have come out to greet their army, standing in clusters in front of sawali-grass huts, a few pulling the *salakots* off their heads in respect. A dozen of the more prosperous-looking citizens flank the *capitán municipal* in front of the little church.

"This is a great day," beams the capitán, who is wearing his best *camisa* of Canton cloth, shoes shined and hair slicked back with brilliantine. He is missing several teeth. "We have been expecting your arrival."

Diosdado nods toward the northern calzada, down which Sargento Bayani and his squad herd eight or nine young runaways at rifle point. "It appears that some of you couldn't wait."

The capitán's face darkens. "Those men are not really from our town." He speaks Spanish with some difficulty, eager to impress.

"Don't worry," says Diosdado as the rest of his men spread through the village to flush out the chickens that have run under the houses and search for hidden stores of food. "Nobody will be forced to fight. But everybody has to help dig."

General Luna's latest directive is to present to the enemy a series of trenches, one behind the other, making it less likely that they'll be over-run and forcing the Americans to bleed for each foot of ground. Strategic withdrawal.

"Nine captured, one escaped," calls Sargento Bayani in Zambal, grinning as he approaches with the conscripts. "I shot over his head but he didn't stop running."

"Waste of ammunition. Get them started." Diosdado frowns as he recognizes one of the young men, a barefoot *tao* in kundiman trousers with a face cratered by smallpox.

"I've seen you before."

"Yes sir." The young man dips his eyes to the dirt. He is missing two toes on his left foot. "At San Francisco del Monte and at Novaliches and at Malabon."

"You should enlist," says Bayani. "Save us the trouble of catching you every time."

The capitán, who has not stopped smiling, supervises two boys trying to hang the banner of the Republic from the flagpole by the *convento*, which seems to also serve as the municipal building. Diosdado steps over and helps untangle the lines.

"Do you know what this flag means?" he asks.

"That Padre Wenceslao is gone," says the older boy, "and he won't be coming back."

"It sticks on the wheel," says the other, pointing to the pulley above them.

"As long as you can get it down fast," says Diosdado, pulling the line and tying it off. There is a ragged, scattered cheer from those in his company who see the flag hanging limply above.

"Papi has a place to hide it if the Spanish come back," says the younger boy. "Under Auntie Dalisay's house."

Diosdado has forty-eight men left, twenty of them with rifles that still work, and more importantly, two dozen shovels saved from the equipment shack at Malinta. Private Ontoy, who can sew up a spur-shredded gamecock so it is almost new, is the company *médico*. Sargento Bayani controls the ammunition, issuing each man fifteen rounds and no more before an engagement, making sure the caliber fits the rifle, reminding them to aim before they fire. It is Bayani who hurries along the lines during the fighting, awarding more bullets, five at a time, to those who need or deserve them, bolstering their courage with his deranged smile and disdain for the *yanqui* sharpshooters.

"The Spanish tried to kill me since the day I was born," he explains to the men, tapping the place on his chest where his charm is embedded. "What hope do the *americanos* have?"

Kalaw and a few of the others bring out small sacks of rice and some potatoes and squash hidden in the huts. Three chickens have been cornered and bayoneted, General Luna's order against wasting ammunition on live-stock observed whenever possible, though the general himself is fond of demonstrating his pistolwork by shooting live birds off the heads of junior officers. The cooks, two brothers from Pampanga whose military skills begin and end with scrounging firewood and boiling water, have set up a *tunco* over a fire and are already tearing handfuls of feathers off the chickens. It has been a week since they've eaten anything but cold rice supplemented by the few minnows and frogs Kalaw has been able to scoop from the paddies with a dip net.

"We thank you for your generous contributions to the Republic," Dios-dado announces in Tagalog to the gathering crowd. Anything his men have not found the *yanquis* will not find either. "We will fight the enemy here, and defeat him. However, once the battle has begun it will be best for you to carry what you value most and seek shelter somewhere to the north."

They will leave tonight, he knows, only the dogs who are not afraid of being eaten and the handful of men he's impressed for the *polo* left in the morning, and the flag with the glorious many-rayed sun will be respectfully folded and buried under the old widow's hut. The church here is too low to give the snipers much range, and if the *yanquis* don't lose too many men or are in a hurry there is a good chance they won't burn the village down like they did at Malabon.

In Malabon the *yanquis* had a fright, not knowing that fireworks were manufactured there. Even his own beaten and wounded soldiers turned from their retreat to watch the display in the night sky, cheering each colorful bomb-burst.

A runner trots in from the west, looking exhausted. He sees Diosdado's uniform, approaches and salutes.

"*Mi teniente,*" he gasps, catching his breath. "You have a man who speaks *americano?*"

"I am that man."

"They need you right away." He points back the way he came. "Just down the road, *una media liga*, at the great tree."

Diosdado nods. "Stay and eat something before you go back."

"*Gracias, jefe.*"

He leaves Sargento Bayani in charge and heads down the road to the west, refugees from Marilao eyeing him uneasily as they pass on their way to Bulacan. Hererra, who is head of intelligence under General del Pilar, stands with a squad of bored-looking *fusileros* guarding an American prisoner under a huge *kupang* tree. The soldier is very young and very blond and very sun-burned, looking scared and defiant at the same time as he sits with his hands bound behind his back. He doesn't seem to be wounded.

"Bring him out here."

Hererra's men pull the boy to his feet and drag him out into the midday sun to face Diosdado.

"You know what we want?" asks Hererra.

Diosdado nods and walks around the soldier, who tries to keep a steady gaze but has to blink as the sweat rolls into his eyes.

"Your name?"

"Winston Wall."

"What regiment are you in, Winston Wall?"

The boy squints, frowns. "I don't have to tell you nothin."

Diosdado examines Wall's uniform. They have good boots, all of them, and go into battle with belts spiked full of ammunition.

"You are a private in the Kansas Volunteers," he says, "under Colonel Funston."

Wall tries to hawk on the ground but can't make enough spit.

"Maybe I am, maybe I'm not."

Diosdado speaks to Hererra in Tagalog. Some of the *yanquis* understand Spanish. "How was he captured?"

Hererra smiles. "This *yanqui* cannot swim. We pulled him out down-stream from the fight at Marilao."

Diosdado turns back to the private. The Kansas soldiers have already made a reputation. "It seems your *cupadres* have abandoned you."

"I just got separated, is all." The boy, taller by a head than Diosdado, lifts his chin and tries to look indifferent. "So you people gone shoot me?"

Diosdado shakes his head but doesn't smile. "Not now. Not here."

Before they would send this boy on to Malolos for questioning, would hold him for a prisoner exchange, but headquarters is preparing to leave Malolos and haven't told anyone where they will set up next.

"You gone feed me, then? I haven't et for two days."

Diosdado nods at the *fusileros*, tiny-looking near the American, who follow their words with rapt incomprehension. Most have never seen a *yanqui* who wasn't charging them with a Springfield in hand.

"When these men get to eat," he says to the private, "I'm sure they'll give you something. Did you fight at Caloocan?"

The boy can't help but grin. "That was one hell of a scrap. You boys give it to us pretty hot for a spell till they brung the artillery down on you, tore the hell outta that town. Then it was pretty much butt-and-bayonet drill."

"You executed prisoners." A few men who submerged themselves in the water of the ditches saw and crawled back after dark to report the slaughter. The boy seems perplexed, frowning again.

"I don't know as how we held on to anybody long enough for them to be a prisoner," he says finally. "Int there some kinda rule about that?"

"If a man is unarmed and surrenders, he is a prisoner. Such actions have their consequence."

"So you *are* gonna shoot me."

Diosdado looks up into the boy's sunburned face. His nose has begun to peel. "That depends on what you can tell us."

The boy looks as if he will cry. "But I don't *know* nothin. I don't even know where this is."

"We are on a road between Marilao and Bulacan."

"I mean where this whole island is, like on a map. I never been out of Kansas till they shipped us out west, and I was sick on the boat the whole damn trip over. We come to that Hongkong they wouldn't even let me ashore."

There isn't much to know. The Americans are driving north and east from Manila and they have better rifles and better training and officers who speak the same language as their men and aren't threatening to murder each other. There is no great mystery to their tactics, MacArthur's division moving parallel to the one commanded by Lawton, fighting up the Dagupan line till they can move their troops by rail. The boy knows less than Diosdado's own ignorant *soldados*.

"You had better think of something," he says to Private Wall. "The people where they are taking you are very angry."

"I can tell you one thing." The boy is shifting from one foot to the other and sweating heavily now. The *yanquis* have been in the country long enough to have the sprue and if they stay through the humid months many will die. The Spanish cemetery in Manila is full of boys who wasted away with disease and weren't worth the trouble to ship their bodies home.

"I can tell you one damn thing," he continues, "and that's that you googoos don't hold a prayer in this deal. Once Uncle sets his cap for something you can't chase him off from it. We got an Army full of Indin fighters and wildass country boys and there aint a thing we like better than a old-fashioned rabbit hunt." He jerks his head at Diosdado. "You're as near to a white man as they got here—you ought to tell em they don't have a show."

Hererra, curious at the boy's outburst, steps closer. "What is he saying?"

Diosdado wonders how he would act if captured by the Americans, what posture of resolute defiance befits an officer of the Philippine Republic. "He tells me that we're losing the war."

The capitán smiles grimly. "I'll pass that on to my superiors."

Diosdado gives Private Wall a last appraising look, then starts back to Bulacan. "Your prisoner is going to shit his pants," he calls, "and then you are going to have to smell him all the way to headquarters."

"*Cabrón!*" Hererra shouts, grabbing the private and shoving him toward the stream that parallels the road, yelling at his men to pull the boy's pants down.

The first line of trenches is dug at the south end of the village, women and boys running with water held in joints of bamboo for their own men and for the soldiers who toil beside them. The Pampangano brothers have something resembling a *tinola* cooking and many of the men are chewing on unripe mangos they have knocked down. It is the time of day when Diosdado feels like he would resign his commission and surrender to the enemy in exchange for a *café con leche* and a *buñuelo* at La Campana on the corner of the Escolta and San Jacinto. He did not appreciate the sweetness of his student days, the dreamlike quality of life in the Walled City, and now it is gone forever.

"What was he like?" asks Sargento Bayani, helping the men reinforce the trench walls with lengths of bamboo and palm trunks. "The prisoner?"

"Big," says Diosdado. "Like all of them. Giants." He sits on top of the piled earth. His uniform pants can't get any filthier. "Above all else, the *americanos* are not the Spanish."

"You still believe that?"

"The *peninsulares* are capable of wickedness. And they're weary—three hundred years of fighting us here."

"And the *americanos*—?"

"The *americanos* are—innocent. The way a crocodile is innocent."

He has seen them shoot unarmed men, men begging to live, has seen them set fire to a palm-thatch hut to drive whoever is inside out onto their bayonets. But still they seem guileless, childlike in their murder.

"Innocent and hungry," he says.

Bayani spits. "I grew up hungry."

It seems that he is from Zambales like Diosdado, though they have avoided speaking of it.

"I mean hungry for everything. Hungry for our lands, our souls, hungry for the world. These people," he waves to the south, to where he knows the Americans are marching, steadily moving forward, "they could devour every one of our islands and never be satisfied."

The *capitán municipal* shuffles up to Diosdado, bowing twice as he approaches, and holds something out to him. It is a flintlock pistol from the time of the Peninsular War and smells like the cigar box it has been kept in.

"My grandfather owned this," he says. "He fought against the Spanish."

"All alone?"

"Whenever they turned their backs. I offer it to the Cause."

"Do you have bullets for it, *hermano?*" asks Bayani.

The man scratches his head. "My grandfather kept them hidden in a different place, so we wouldn't be tempted to shoot each other. But he is dead now."

"After the battle has passed and you've come back," says Diosdado, gently pushing the pistol back into the capitán's hands, "send the children out onto the field to pick up the shell casings. We have a *factoría* in San Fernando where they are filled and become bullets again."

"*Por supuesto, mi tentiente.*"

"And when you talk to the *yanqui* officer, tell him that you were forced to help us dig, that there were hundreds and hundreds of us and you were afraid."

"If you wish, sir."

"And when those boys who raised the flag are a bit older—"

"My sons?"

"When your sons are a bit older, send them to join with us."

The *capitán municipal* is clearly troubled by the idea that the war may last so long. "But where will you be?"

"With the Igorots," smiles Bayani, "in the Cordillera. Sharpening our spears with the true Filipinos."

CONEY ISLAND

"It's a poor cut of meat that wants special wrapping."

Brigid tries to pull her stomach up under her ribs as Grania laces from behind. When she bought the corset, the shopgirl called it an investment in her future.

"Ye should wear it more often," says Grania. "It wouldn't hurt so much."

"And trussed up at work as well? On my knees scrubbin the boards with this takin me breath away?"

Maeve holds the pitted mirror she salvaged before the trash man got it. "But look at the shape it gives you."

"It isn't natural."

"All the girls will be lookin the same," says Grania.

Grania is an authority on what all the girls are wearing, what all the girls are saying and doing. Not a thought in her head but boys and how to get them to pay mind to her, impatient to escape from school and begin what she likes to call her "proper life."

"None will hold a candle to our Brigid," says Maeve. Brigid has hope yet for Maeve, who is sweet and clever at books and speaks like an American and still has her hair in braids.

"None will be my age, either."

"Ye look no older than ye are," says Grania, pulling the laces taut and tying them off. "Turn sideways—there, d'ye see?"

"Hand me the waist."

"Yer not wearin the plain one—"

"And why not?"

"Because yer going to see the Elephant, not to a temperance meeting." Grania pulls her own striped blouse from the peg beneath Father's fading portrait of Parnell. "This might fit ye."

"The Elephant burned down, and I'll not wear that, whether it fits me or not."

"Ye liked it when ye bought it for me."

"It's too flossy for a woman of my—" she is about to say age, but that isn't it. They bought it from a jewcart because it looked like the one Grania had admired in a store window on Grand Street, the three of them out dream-shopping together one night when Brigid wasn't too tired. But the material is not the same and up close you can tell that it is only an imitation.

"Ye have to wear somethin."

"Give me the black."

"That ye wore for Father's funeral?"

"It's the best I own."

"But—"

"Black will set her hair off," says Maeve, putting the mirror down and hurrying to the dresser. Trying to spare her feelings, it's clear, but Brigid appreciates the effort. Maeve jiggles the broken drawer till it opens, then pulls out the blouse, black bombazine with vertical pleats that Mother brought from Donegal.

"And it goes with my skirt—"

"He'll take one peep," says Grania, sighing with exasperation, "and offer his condolences."

"One more word," says Brigid in the tone that Mother would use when she'd had her limit with them, "and I'll jerk a knot in ye." She feels a fool, standing there in corset and gauze stockings, girding herself for an excursion with a man she hardly knows, and her sister's mockery on top of it—

Maeve has to climb on a chair to deal with her hair, plaiting it first then artfully piling it over the pompadour frame on the crown of her head. She does it with the same nimble care as when she hung the cloth to cover the grimy walls, as she applies to the funeral wreaths assembled by lamplight each evening after school. *"A dexthrus hand,"* Father used to say. *"She'll earn a handsome wage someday."*

"If ye had a poof," says Grania, "ye could wear it higher."

"Any higher and I'll topple from the weight of it. And I haven't even got the shoes on yet."

Rivka who scrubs with her at the Musee has loaned her the shoes, calf-high leather with a heel as long as her middle finger.

"They'll shape up your legs," she said, winking. "Just in case he gets a gander at em."

Brigid can't bend over with the corset on so Maeve kneels to button them up.

There is much discussion over the hat, ending with Grania allowing her the simple black straw as long as Maeve is allowed to decorate it with ribbon and rosettes. Grania studies Brigid's face as she buttons her collar tight.

"Ye should do yer lips over."

"I'm a working woman," says Brigid, "not a streetwalker."

"It's not who ye are, it's the idea of ye they carry in their heads."

"And what do you know about men?"

Grania sneaks out with older ones, girls sixteen and seventeen with money from their shops and lunchrooms, and Brigid has warned her and threatened her and pleaded with her not to be so fast, to enjoy what she can of life before giving up to the hard weight of family the way that Mother did, just a girl herself when Brigid was born. Mother who was wore out at thirty when they took the boat, and dead within the year.

"I know enough," says Grania. "Take a few steps and lookit yerself."

Grania holds the mirror for her and she totters around a bit, getting used to the shoes.

"You look lovely," says Maeve, on the chair again to pin the newly adorned hat to Brigid's hair. "Like a queen."

Brigid turns to kiss her cheek. "Yer a darlin to say so. But I don't feel like meself at all."

"It's only a different you," says Grania, taking her hand. "A special you."

"You'll have a grand time," says Maeve. "Ride the wheel, shoot the chutes—"

"I'll do no such thing."

Neither of the girls has ever been to Coney, and Brigid only the once with Mick Cassiday the bricklayer who was so full that halfway through the day he pulled her out on the crowded beach and proceeded to fall asleep right on the sand, herself sitting on his little square of a handkerchief till his snoring attracted a gang of little mischief-makers and she took the steamer back alone.

"It'll be loads of fun whatever you do."

Brigid turns her head this way and that, studying the damage in the ancient looking glass. "Fun," she says, "has nothing to do with this."

The girls accompany her down the five dark flights and watch from the stoop as she starts down 38th toward the river in her borrowed shoes. Father stood that way, watching them when Maeve went to make her First Communion, chuffed with pride but firm in his promise never to set foot in a priest-house again after the way they'd banjaxed the great Parnell. A trio of cadets lounging at the corner make their kissing noises at her but stay where they are. After the one incident when Grania was little, words mostly, but words a young girl shouldn't be hearing, Father had asked a few of the lads from the Clan na Gael to come by and remind the gang they weren't the only Hibernians in the city with some clout behind them. Since then it's been the occasional dirty-mouthed pleasantry, but never a hand laid on any one of them.

Harry offered to come for her, of course, gentleman that he is, but if the sight of her wreck of a tenement on Battle Row didn't chase him the Gopher boys surely would. He'd have given her trolley fare too, if she'd asked, but the boldness of it, asking a man for coins in the hand, made her blush at the thought. American girls could manage such things—Grania was full of stories how'd they'd get this one or that one to treat them, how they did the town and never parted with a cent. Brigid turns left on Ninth, weaving through the crowds and pushcarts of Paddy's Market, trolley cars rushing overhead, each shopkeeper with a barker in the doorway shouting out wares and prices, scullery maids searching for bargains for their mistresses, dray wagons empty and full rattling up and down the Avenue. The shoes aren't as bad as she thought, only a matter of leaning forward on her toes, but the corset is a mortification. It is a warm day, and even in the shade under the shop awnings or the Elevated tracks Brigid is soon damp all over, sweat running down her forehead, and begins to feel resentful. This is it, she thinks. Our only adventure, our great single drama in life over in a flash, and then motherhood and the labor of home until the grave. Mr. Manigault is stepping into a hack about now, she imagines, comfortable in his clothing and not a worry on his brow. No wonder the men in Bunbeg were known to wait till their first gray whisker before they married, no wonder the silver-haired gents in the offices she cleans are full of laughter and boasting. Even Rivka's own intended, a Second Avenue sport Brigid has never liked the look of, nipping off to this new war as if it is a weekend excursion. Her collar is choking her.

Brigid pauses a moment at the corner of 24th Street. Father died here. Scraping horse-pies off the stones, the job his cousin Jack Brennan high in the Twentieth Ward Democrats had secured him, and a pair of university boys racing their phaetons, Father able only to stand and face them and hope they'd pass on either side. The Brotherhood had paid for the funeral, so the eulogies quickly turned to calls for Home Rule and the expulsion of Tory landlords.

"Saint Patrick drove the first nest of serpents from Ireland," said Jack Brennan, mourning band on his arm and golden harp pinned to his lapel, "and it's our lot to finish the job!"

Brigid has gone to a few of the IRB dances and thrilled to hear Maud Gonne, tall and elegant, scold the British in her triumph at the Grand Opera Hall, but the blighted nation's problems are not hers anymore. If she woke tomorrow with Mount Errigal itself looming outside the cottage window she'd throw the blanket back over her head and pray for the nightmare to end.

"The most beautiful spot in the world," Mother would sigh. *"But beauty never filled a stomach."*

He'd been trampled into the stones, Father, first the hooves and then the carriage wheels. Brigid had been called away from work to identify his remains.

She turns west, breathing through her mouth as the stench from the slaughterhouses thickens the air, hurrying now, afraid he'll be there early and give up on her, looking out for the Tenth Avenue cowboys, young lads who ride up and down ringing their bells to warn of an approaching freight train, then high-stepping over the tracks and there are others now, the girls all putting on style in bright colors and gaudy hats, American girls by the ease of their movement, people joining in streams from north and south, a human flood driving shoulder to shoulder toward the pier, crowded like the flocks of sheep that follow their belled Judas to be butchered at 42nd. Grania was right, she thinks, among this lot I look like a grieving widow and an old one at that. There are some couples, but more groups of girls and groups of young men, pairs, trios, quartets of them, laughing and shouting from group to group and now the smell of the river and thousands on the pier, it must be thousands.

"I'm an eejit," Brigid says out loud, too late now to turn and fight the current of bodies. She can tell that every eye that falls on her sees nothing but a poor Irish scrubwoman from Hell's Kitchen itself, an ignorant country *cailín* tarted up like a spud in a silk handkerchief.

"An eejit," says Brigid McCool out loud. "And when he sees me he'll know it for sure."

*   *   *

It is more people in one place that he's seen in his life. Harry is not a small man, but his view is blocked by any number of young giants with bowlers tilted high on their heads, and the hot, indecent human crush of them all, men and women together, has him anxious and wet-browed, struggling to keep his feet. This is not his crowd. Many, if not most, are younger, loudly dressed and raucous in their speech, a half-dozen foreign tongues as well as the grating New Yorkese shouted past him as he pushes through with his uneven gait and tries to locate her in the multitude. I'm the freak attraction they've come to see, he thinks, or merely an annoyance to be trodden under-foot in their rush for the pleasure boat.

And then there she is, striking in satiny black among the garish stripes and dots of the shouting girls, her glorious red hair pulled up on her head, a calm watcher amid the frenzy. Her smile when she sees him seems reserved and he feels his knees go watery with uncertainty. What can a woman like this see in hapless Harry Manigault?

"I'd almost given up on you," she says when he reaches her.

"Next time I'll come for you in a carriage," he says, stomach tightening at his own boldness. As if he assumes there will be a next time.

"We'd better get on board."

Harry holds up the tickets he's bought, limp from the wet of his hands. "They said there's another in twenty minutes."

"It won't be any less of a mob then."

They walk side by side toward the gangplank, ropes narrowing into a chute, the crowd pressing in on them and Harry takes her arm, trying might-ily to even his step and be the leader. The bored-looking ferryman yanks the tickets from his hand—

"Step to the rear, keep moving, step to the rear—"

They push their way to a spot on the starboard rail, bodies and noise all around them, and Harry is twisted with a sudden shyness.

"And how was your week?" he asks finally.

She gives him a sideways glance. "Thursday we polish the glassware," she says, "and ye can stand or sit. I do look forward to a Thursday."

He feels chastened by her tone. A cheer goes up, then, as the ferry horn blasts and the boat begins to churn the water, backing out of the slip.

"And yerself?" she asks.

"We made a story. Little boys fool their grandfather with a garden hose."

"I think I've seen it."

"That would be the French version."

"Ah," says Brigid, nodding her head. "If I had any French I would have known."

She is mocking him, he knows, but in a gentle way.

"And yer machine is well?"

"I've been working on a swivel mount for the tripod. It would allow the camera body to be moved—"

"From side to side," she interrupts, swiveling her head to take in all of the far shore, "like this."

"Yes, actually, that would allow us to—"

"It would be grand," she says. "I saw one that was the general who led the byes in Cuba, the fat man—"

"General Shafter—"

"—and he rides on the poor little horse across the variety screen and off into nowheres, not more than a few seconds—"

"Bill Paley shot that before he got sick and the device was damaged—"

"But where is he riding? *That's* what we want to know. If you could turn the head—ye told me ye call it that—"

"We do—"

"—ye could follow him along the trail. Even—" and here she raises a finger, imagining the scene, "—swinging the camera view *ahead*, and see if there's any Spaniards up in the bushes waiting to do the man harm. I'd have me heart in me throat to see that."

It shocks him sometimes, how much she understands his work, how interested in it she seems, and then he chides himself for seeing the cartoon and not the woman.

"I'll have to bring you to the shop sometime," he offers.

"I'm sure it could use a good cleaning."

"I meant," he has to look away, suddenly embarrassed, "I meant to talk to the boys. Your ideas."

She says nothing, but slips her arm into his again. "Will ye look at Herself, now."

They are chugging past Liberty, gulls swooping around her handsome face.

"I saw the photographs when I was a boy. Postcards. But I must say, close up—"

"She came out of a fog." Brigid turns to look after the statue. "We were all of us sick with the waves and sick with not knowing what was here for us and then Herself—" She shakes her head. "If it had been your eagle, or a man with a rifle in his arms—but one look at Her and I felt, all right now, Brigid McCool, this might turn out well. And then they took us there," she points to the brick buildings on the low island beyond the Statue, "and they put a hook in me eyelid and peeled it back and asked Father a thousand questions, each one I was sure would be our undoing."

"You coming on your boat."

"Yes."

"I wish I'd been there to greet you."

She turns to study his face. The ferry churns past the Battery.

"And what would ye have said to me then, a great Donegal brute of a girl in a dress made of sacking and her father's old brogans?"

Harry feels himself blushing, her bright emerald eyes digging in to him. Niles would have something clever to say, some *bon mot* to win a girl's heart that he'd refined through a dozen flirtations. But he is Harry, the quiet one, the lame one, and can only say the first thing that comes to his head. Which might be the truth.

"I would have been made speechless," he says, "at the sight of you."

They are quiet then. Brigid squeezes his arm in hers as they lean on the rail together and watch the wheeling seabirds and the river currents clashing and the other boats speeding to and fro, marveling at the great newspaper towers visible from the water, at the structures being built that will soon dwarf them, steaming around the point of Manhattan and churning giddily, if a boat can be allowed an emotion, toward the Brooklyn shore.

They are nearly to the Island when a group of young sports begin to sing—

I've seen the Tower of London
The lights of gay Paree
Now I'm off to see the Elephant
Though it mean the end of me

When the Judge speaks of going to see the Elephant it is stories of slaughter from his service during the Great Lost Cause. But these singers are too young for that War. Harry has been told that in the years before he came to New York there was a hotel on Coney, built in the shape of an enormous pachyderm. The rooms in the creature's head, with their eye-windows and view of the beach, were more expensive than those in the legs, and for a small fee a non-guest could ascend to the observation deck in the howdah on the elephant's back. But as the immediate neighborhood grew less wholesome the significance of the term was debased until it could be applied to a visit to any house of ill repute—

You may be wise and worldly

They sing—

A rambler bold and free
But until you see the Elephant
You're as green as green can be!

Brigid, unaware of this darker connotation, trills along gaily.

There are an unthinkable number of people already on the sand and board-walk at West Brighton.

"Will ye look at us?" says Brigid as they are swept down the gangplank, bright-eyed and pulling him forward into the crush. "It's the whole city here to throw off their cares."

Their feet are no sooner on firm ground then a half-dozen touts begin to chatter at them, vaunting their amusements. The West Brighton Hotel is the only solid body in a Bedlam of activity, the rides ahead gyrating and rolling and tumbling and swooping, a cacophony of musics blaring out from them, leaving Harry stunned and looking to Brigid for guidance.

"I've never been to the sea creatures," she says.

The "park" is fenced in, next to the lot where the Elephant Hotel burned. Captain Boyton's sea lions leap and dive, balance on balls, play the xylophone with their flippers, juggle objects on their noses and pause frequently to gulp down whole fish thrown into their sharp-toothed maws. There are lots of children in the gallery, their wails of wonder and delight mixing with the screams of the adventurers risking life and limb on the Flip-Flap Railroad behind them, whipped completely upside-down for a terrifying moment. The bodies of the sea lions are shiny and supple and Harry cannot keep him-self from thinking how beautiful they would look on film.

"I've only seen them dead on the strand," says Brigid, holding a hand to her chest in awe. "Our fishermen kill them with gaffs when they can." She looks to Harry, apologetic. "It's that they tear the nets."

One shoots up from the depths just in front of Harry, flinging water, twisting to stare at him with liquid black eyes. "They look frantic," he observes, "but not happy."

"The sea lions or the spectators?"

Harry smiles, but is not sure if she's being ironic or not. "I meant the animals."

Brigid watches as each of the dozen clap their flippers together, then dive backward into the pool. "Content, I would say," she judges, "but no, not happy. Happiness is only something in the human mind, poor creatures that we are."

The sea lions scoot away through an underwater passage and are replaced by Captain Boyton himself, demonstrating his famous life-saving suit. He lays on his back in the rubber suit, feet forward as he employs a double-bladed paddle to move himself about the pool.

"There are air-pockets in the suit—" Harry explains.

"No doubt."

"He had the idea of transatlantic ship passengers wearing it. In case of an accident."

"The women as well?"

"Of course."

Brigid watches as the Fearless Frogman paddles below them, a small circle of his face visible within the tight rubber hood.

"They'll never put it on," she decides. "To be seen in public dressed like that—"

"Death before dishevelment."

"If my corpse is to be pulled up from the cold ocean, it will be in decent attire."

Captain Boyton emerges from the water and gives a very brief lecture, finishing with an invitation to observe the celebrated Diving Dobbin perform in the Lagoon behind them. Harry and Brigid make their way with the others, standing together craning up at the platform where a riderless horse steps cautiously to the edge, head low as a boy raps a rolling tattoo on a snare drum, then at the clash of a cymbal gathers itself and leaps splay-legged into the air. Harry feels himself gasp with the others and then the huge splash and the beast churning its legs to reach the ramp at the far end of the lagoon and he can only think of the haunting Biograph view they've been showing at Koster and Bials, mules and horses swimming in the waves off Cuba. Niles and some friends had unhitched an old negro's carriage horse on an excursion to Lake Waccamaw when they were boys, driving it deep into the water by throwing stones, the horse snorting spray out of its great nostrils as it tired, eyes rolling white in panic, treading desperately till some white men came to chase Niles and his friends and catch Harry, too lame to outrun them, and yank him by the ear to where the Judge sat in the shade telling war stories. The Judge had not whipped him, saving that for Niles later, but forced him to apologize to the old uncle.

"That's a mean way to do him," the negro kept saying, shaking his head and dabbing at the cuts the stones had opened on the horse's hide. "That's a *mean* way."

Once Diving Dobbin has climbed out and been led off, shaking himself dry, the Shoot-the-Chutes is back in business.

"Would ye like to try it?" asks Brigid, squeezing his arm and with a hopeful glint in her eye. He hesitates, a lifetime of embarrassments holding him back, and she senses it, adding, "But of course I'd hate to get wet, wouldn't I?"

They settle for the bleachers and watch the flat-bottomed skiffs sluicing down the channels then flying off the final lip to smack and skitter across the surface of the Lagoon, passengers shouting and laughing and sprayed with water as they desperately grasp the sides and try not to spill out.

"They must have made quite a number of tests for this," says Harry. "Deciding on the slope of the chute, the design of the boat."

"Dangerous," says Brigid, "but not fatal."

"I've never been much of a dare-devil," Harry admits, then regrets pointing it out.

"There's not many who are," says Brigid, rising to leave. "Which is why your fillums are such a sensation."

They pass under the obscenely grinning Funny Face then, demonic eyes and tombstone choppers gleaming, and into Steeplechase Park. It is another machine with too many moving parts, thinks Harry, and at first he is frozen with indecision, finally allowing Brigid to tug him to a booth where a nickel buys you a dozen chances to break a china plate by throwing a hard black ball. They are a far cry from actual china, of course, but Brigid squeals with glee at each of the three she manages to shatter.

"I knocked one over in a lady's cupboard last year," she says, "and it was a day's wages lost."

He had thought at first that the plates were prizes, not the object of pleasurable destruction, and is impressed with her skill. "I'd never have hit as many."

"Oh, we Irish are known for our hurling," she says, teasing him. "It's bricks through the landlord's window and on from there."

The Steeplechase horses come whizzing around a curve in the track above them, trailing excited screams from the riders. Harry is still smarting from his cowardice at the Shoot-the-Chutes. "There's not much of a line," he says, pointing. "We should go."

Brigid stops to look at him. "Are ye sure?"

"*A half a mile in half a minute*," he says, quoting the painted advertisement at the entrance gate. "We have to experience that."

They climb the stairs, Harry pulling himself up the railing, and are in the second group of eight couples waiting to mount. The height and the steep decline of the first section of track begin to work on his nerves, and he calms himself by imagining what alterations would allow a camera operator to ride with the device in hand and crank film through the aperture. Certainly an assistant behind to keep him from falling off, and a special housing to reduce the bulk of the apparatus. But would the image be only a blur? Would the spectator in the theater grab his hat, gasp in fear, suffer a queasy stomach?

"Who's first?" barks the loader, a slightly cross-eyed man in shirtsleeves.

"Oh, I couldn't possibly," says Brigid.

"But I'll block your view."

"Ladies first, then," says the loader and taps his foot with impatience as Brigid anchors her hatpin securely, then steps onto the box and takes his hand, deftly arranging her skirt to throw her leg over the back of the hobbyhorse. Harry has a moment of panic but the loader squats down without comment, offering his shoulder for leverage, and he is able to drag his bad leg over the saddle and get himself centered as the other couples arrange themselves. He feels ridiculous for an instant, a grown man on a wooden horse, but then the starter yells "Ready?!" and he puts his arms the only place they can go, snug around her waist, and the nape of her lovely neck close to his lips, the smell of her hair—he has half closed his eyes with the rapture of it when the bell rings and the horses are released, eight across, eight couples screaming as they plunge down and veer sharply this way and that, Brigid clasping his wrist with one of her hands and he can't tell if that's her heart beating with excitement under his fingers or his own, pounding his blood out into his extremities, bits of track and safety wall and sky whipping across his eyes, his hat blowing off his head, squeezing the wooden horse between his knees to keep from being flung out into space and then they are falling abruptly and speeding down the final straightaway, second across the finish line and coasting hoarse-voiced to a stop.

They are helped off the wooden steed, Harry reeling with dizziness and taking her hand as they step through the exit tent and all of a sudden there is air blasting up from the floor lifting Brigid's dress up over her stockings and a negro dwarf in clown paint and horns poking him with a staff that gives him a jolt while a taller white clown jabs a pitchfork at him, trying to separate him from her, Brigid holding her skirt down with her free hand and the other couples around them now receiving the same, the blowholes flouncing colorful lacy undergarments and the men's hair shooting up at the dwarf's electric prod and then Harry hears the laughter and realizes they are on a raked stage, being tormented for the jollification of the people who have just come through the ride themselves.

They escape the Blowhole Theater to the bright outdoors together, both blushing, Harry not letting go of her hand and Brigid not asking him to.

"We almost won," she says finally.

"All else being equal, the heaviest couple will always win."

"Well, then I certainly did my part."

She is perhaps an inch taller than Harry, with broader shoulders, but slender of waist and ankle.

"It felt like more than half a minute."

"If ye hadn't been there to hold me," she says, talking loudly over the shouts and music from the Wonder Wheel to their left, "I'd have fainted dead away."

There is a bin full of hats by the exit gate, and Harry recovers his own.

They wander then, hand in hand, past the pushcart vendors with their clams and corn, their pretzels and red hots, through the Bowery with its penny arcades and Kill the Coon games, its slot machines and dime museums and kinetoscope parlors, Harry cranking the machine to demonstrate how it is the same but different than his motion-picture camera, past the side show with its lackluster freaks of nature slouching out front, settling finally at a restaurant deck overlooking Tilyou's Bathhouse and the crowded beach beyond. Harry orders clam chowder and crackers for them and they watch the bathers cavort in the waves.

"One of our earliest numbers was taken here," says Harry. "*Cakewalk on the Beach*. There are new copies going out every week."

"You turned a camera on the poor souls."

Women and men jump and somersault and splash each other in their wet wool costumes, shrieks of joy carried over the steady crash of the waves.

"They were enjoying themselves. You can see that in the view."

"But they're being photographed while they're at it. That changes everything."

"Does it?"

"Without a doubt. People become shy or they prance about like fools. But they don't act naturally."

"Then I suppose we should use a lens that can see from a great distance, like field glasses. Or hide the camera somehow—"

"That would be indecent."

"To share the joy of these bathers with those who live far from the sea—"

"The story you showed me in the box just now—"

"The kinetoscope."

"Peeking through the boo-dwar door at some poor woman getting ready for bed."

"She was an actress."

"An actress pretending not to know there's a man grinding his camera-box not four feet away, that's bad enough, but if it really *had* been hidden and the girl a normal, innocent person—"

"We wouldn't do that."

"Somebody will."

She hadn't wanted to stay and watch the others prodded through the blowholes and neither had he, but all day long much of the fun has been to watch other people swept off their feet and tossed about, to see them drenched or frightened into hysterics.

"Then I suppose," ventures Harry, "that the picture tells you something about the person who photographs it."

"So it does," she says. "Until yer camera learns to crank itself."

There is music drifting from a dance pavilion behind them and after they've eaten Harry follows Brigid over to watch from the edge of the floor. The band is small—a piano, bass, drums, and cornet—but skilled enough to hold a hundred dancers in thrall amid the competing noise of the rides and variety halls. Harry watches Brigid watching the dancers, often two young women together till a pair of sports gather the nerve to break them up and partner off, a semicircle of males observing from one side and a semicircle of their opposites on the other. The band shifts into a livelier tune and a few of the bolder couples begin to spin, pressing their faces and bodies tightly together, one arm extended stiffly outward, pivoting around and around at twice the tempo of the music, other couples dancing away to give them room and goad them to even greater speed.

"Spielers," says Brigid, smiling and shaking her head. "My sister Grania is mad for it."

It is the moment he has dreaded, the place where he can't follow her. He feels other men's eyes on her, bold as wolves, waiting for him to step—to *limp* away only for a moment and provide them an opening.

The spielers wind down, laughing and hugging, the women repinning their fascinators on their heads, a few couples kissing openly on the crowded floor and here it seems natural, it seems proper, as if in a place where gravity itself is defied all other rules are suspended.

The piano player leads into a slow waltz then, and Brigid pulls at his arm.

"I can't," he says, resisting. "One of these other fellows—"

"I'm not *with* any of these other fellas, am I?" says Brigid, and leads him onto the floor.

Harry stands while Brigid holds his eyes and waltzes around him, taking first his right hand in hers and then his left, stepping in and away, and he loses sense of the others, only the music and Brigid, the grace of her, her hair framing her face, Brigid light in his hand as if she is floating.

At the end of the waltz one of the floormen gives him a nudge.

"A drink for the lady," he says, "and one for yourself and you can dance your shoes off."

They step to the concession and he buys a Horse's Neck, without the whiskey, for Brigid and a Mamie Taylor for himself. He has not told any of the men at the boarding house about her, unable to bear their joking. She is a scrubwoman and he, despite all his education, a tinkerer for a penny vaudeville concern. He can imagine the stock actors who would portray them in a Vitagraph story—a bug-eyed degenerate for him and a man, preferably fat and unshaven and stuffed into a dress, for the Irish maid.

Here lies Molly O'Keene—reads the epitaph on the gravestone at the end of one popular comedy view—*Lit a fire with Kerosene.*

"It seems we have to pay for our pleasure," she says, bobbing the spiral of lemon peel in her drink.

"Paradise for a nickel."

They take their time strolling on Surf Avenue, people still arriving from the excursion ships at the pier, Harry's heart full to bursting with the wonder of it, this woman who is who she is and chooses to spend a day with him, and finally they take the steam elevator to the top of the old Iron Tower next to the train station. They stand at the rail of the observation deck, three hundred feet high in the sea air, and are watching it all from above when the sun dips below the horizon and they hear a gasp from a quarter million people below. The electric lights are coming on, white lights, colored lights, lights that spin and blink and cycle in undulating patterns, more than you could count if you made a night of it.

"Will ye look at us now," says Brigid, leaning her head against his shoulder. "Gazing *down* at the stars. And we haven't even left the city."

WAGES OF SIN

Once you know the drill they let you do it in private. Hod pulls the canvas across the opening, which always reminds him of the lowest of the cribs in Leadville, the girls standing outside, smiling and deadeyed, beckoning you to come have some fun, Honey-pie. The cleaning basin is there on a stand, with the Protargol solution and a fresh syringe beside it. He is glad he can do his own now cause it still hurts like hell and the mean prick of an orderly, Corporal Spinks, shoots it up in there fast and hard on purpose.

"What she call herself?" Spinks says, looking you in the eye with that nasty idiot grin of his. "Esmeralda? Trinidad? Consuela?"

"What's your mother's name again?" half the men respond. "She was squealing so loud I forgot—"

Then Spinks grins and jams the plunger in.

There is not as much gleet come out as there was yesterday. This is supposed to be a good sign. At first when he saw it, yellow and cheesy-looking on the end of his pecker, Hod was afraid it was one of the tropical diseases the men joke about and exaggerate, or even the start of leprosy which you can see people rotting away with it all over Manila, finger-missing hands out to beg for your loose centavos. The doc says the signs show up between a couple days to a couple weeks after you get it so it has to be the one night with him and Big Ten and Runt and two of his friends from the Minnesotas drunk out of their skulls over to Sampaloc. The Minnesotas have the provost with the Dakotas, wearing white and acting like company bulls, so they know where all the rum and women are kept. It was a slick-looking parlor, with red satin covers laid over the furniture, and Runt's buddies made a show of chasing the couple Spanish soldiers out.

"You fellas lost the war," said the big squarehead-looking one, "and got no business enjoyin yourselves. Skedaddle."

Hod washes it carefully, gingerly, with the yellow soap and tepid water, squeezing the head to get the last of the discharge out.

"Aint handled it this much since I was twelve," says Corporal Blount from the next enclosure. "Settin in the backhouse, thinking about Mary Jane Riley—"

"Whose name you should not be allowed to speak," Hod calls back, "in light of your present condition."

The fellas who only got the clap like Hod are a good deal more whimsical about it than those the doc has condemned with the pox. Medical speculation is bandied about when there are no officers present, and the accepted wisdom is that the whole mercury deal is only a way of further punishing the syphilitics and in the long run won't cure a hangnail.

"Oh Lordy!" Blount exclaims in pain on the other side of the panel. "The consequences of moral turpitude."

Hod lowers the syringe into the brown bottle and draws it full of Protargol. They say it's silver in the solution that kills the bugs, fine silver dust stirred up so you can't see it, and Hod wonders if he could have dug up any of what he's pumping, slowly, very slowly, damn that hurts, into what the doc keeps calling his urinary meatus.

If the girl, Corazón, who seemed nice enough, had told him he was going to have to stick a needle up his peehole every day for two weeks he might have had second thoughts. Runt passed out on a couch, sick as a dog from the rum, but the Minnesotas said he always does that, can't handle it, and them and Big Ten went too, each with a different girl, yet he is the only one of them here in the clap shack. He wasn't even that keen on it, only full-on drunk for the first time since San Francisco and doing what the others wanted, and it is just the odds caught up to him, like how he figures it must be on the battlefield.

"Don't hardly make sense to duck or hide," says Corporal Grissom in his platoon, whose daddy chased Cheyenne in the regulars. "Bullet got your name on it, it's gonna come find you."

Hod pulls the works out and wants to pee right away, the burning and the pressure just awful, but you got to hold it five minutes.

Spinks is waiting when he pulls the canvas curtain open.

"It fall off yet?"

Hod ignores him and hobbles off toward the shitter. They give you some little woven-straw slippers that got nothing behind the heel, so the whole ward of them are shuffling like the old whiskey-soaked paretics he's seen on Skid Road, the pox gone to their brains.

He crosses paths with the chaplain, who hangs a glare of disapproval on his mug before he comes into the ward most every day to gloat over the ones so far gone they can't get out of bed. "Malingerers" is the nicest thing the chaplain has called any one of them, but you suppose it's part of the treatment, Uncle paying you to shoot at Spanish boys and now the natives and not to get infected by the local *queridas*. Manigault has been riding him since Denver, like the rest of the company won't figure out their lieutenant is a poker cheat and a humbug without Hod telling them, so it is something of a relief to be in here, now that he's sure it's nothing that will kill or unman him. The doc isn't so bad as long as you hand over a glass of your pee now and then for him to ogle at under his microscope, and the chuck is passable even with meat crossed off the diet.

The clap patients outnumber the syphilitics three to one and there are a couple fellas who got other problems with their kidneys that they put up right next to the shitter. Hod nods to one of them from his company, Loftus, who is propped up to almost a sitting position.

"How's it going?"

Yesterday Loftus said "Not so good" but today he is a bad color and just looks at Hod like he's somehow at fault for it all. There is white folks and black folks, thinks Hod, rich folks and poor folks, Spanish and Filipinos, but there is no greater gulf than the one between the sick and the well.

And he's not that well.

There are maybe a half-dozen of his fellow sinners, what the wags in the hospital have taken to calling "Rough Riders," lined up at the trough, a couple of them with their pocket watches swinging in front of their faces. Every few seconds one will let it go and moan in anguish or curse or just gasp a quick deep breath as the Protargol and what it carries splashes down onto the metal. Hod is careful not to stand too close to any of them.

"Back on the firing line," says Blount, shuffling up beside him.

"I figure another minute."

"Yeah."

"You wonder who she got hers from."

"We are all brothers under the foreskin."

"What's that mean?"

"If you follow the chain, somebody gives it to somebody else, they pass it on—hell, it could go back to Moses."

"Moses had the clap?"

"No, but I bet a couple them old boys dancing around the Golden Calf had it. Only they had to persevere without the wonders of modern medicine. Half the damn population must have been in tears every time they took a leak."

"I say it's five."

"Feels like ten. Ready, aim—"

Blount makes a high whine that comes out through his nose, while Hod grunts an "*ah—ah—ah—ah—*" as he urinates, both men tilting their heads back and squinching their eyes shut. Afterward there is water and soap set out to wash it again and towels for drying and then a fresh-cleaned sock to pull over it and keep the new discharge from staining your hospital togs.

"I'd have worn this sock over it when I rolled that señorita," Blount observes, "I wouldn't be in this fix."

She wore a lot more powder than Addie Lee ever did, this girl who give it to him, but seemed nice and friendly and not in a hurry. She was rounder than Addie, too, round in a nice way, and looked to be some kind of mix of Spanish and Filipino, though the people here look so many different ways it's hard to get a handle on them. She called him "Yankee Boy."

When he's finished Hod goes to look for Lan Mei. The corpsman, not Spinks but the other who doesn't seem to want to be there, says that she was left behind by a pack of nuns who used to run this ward till they set sail for the motherland. Some of the fellas say she was a whore like all the Chinese girls who come from Hongkong and the sisters brought her to the light and give her a job dumping bedpans, but that is only a rumor. There are no women allowed on the venereal ward at all but they've seen her in the hall-way and one sergeant from the Nebraskas who has since been shipped home smuggled a pint in and got pickled and started railing about how she sneaks in at night and smothers white men with a pillow.

Hod finds her in the little room just off the kitchen, wearing gloves and using tongs to drop the syringes from the morning irrigation into a large kettle of boiling water.

"Mei."

"You still here, huh?" She shouts a little when she is teasing him, but otherwise has a nice voice, soft and deep for a woman.

"I could go back to my unit any time," says Hod, "only I'm stuck on you."

"Stuck."

"Enamored." He is a little embarrassed to use the fancy word and wonders if she understands it. Their eyes don't show as much as a white girl's, and maybe that means they can't pretend so much.

"You don' think right," she says, attending to her work. "Too much time inna sun."

She knows that is not what is wrong with him, knows which ward he comes from, but doesn't seem to care. The steam from the kettle turns to a thin film of water on her face and her hair is wet where it peeks out of the cloth she has tied it back in. He's seen the other fellas say things at her or about her but none ever really stops to talk and she seems alone, alone as a person can be, though this is more her country than his.

"So where you come from, Mei?"

"Born in Guangxi."

"What's that like?"

Mei looks up at him, wipes the wet from her face with the back of her sleeve. "Work in a field. Leave there when I'm a little girl, go to Hongkong."

Hod decides not to ask her what she did in Hongkong. She is skinny like Addie Lee but not from the consumption or they wouldn't let her work in a hospital.

"We stopped by there for coal," says Hod. "But they wouldn't even let us off the ship."

"You pretty sorry bugger, then, huh?"

He has to laugh. "Yeah, that would be me." Disgrace to his uniform or no, Hod thinks, before I go back to the company I am going to try to kiss this woman.

One of the doc's adjutants steps in then and asks what he is doing there.

"I found a syringe on the floor," Hod tells him. "I just brung it in."

The officer looks at the black mark on Hod's sleeve and makes a disgusted face. "Get back to your ward."

"Yes sir."

He pauses in the kitchen to listen and is relieved when the adjutant has nothing to say to Mei. A sad-eyed private who looks sicker than most of Hod's bunkies is stirring a huge cauldron full of bubbling oatmeal with a wooden paddle.

"Got any bacon loose?" Hod asks.

"Venereals don't get bacon," says the mess private. "Scramble, pal."

*　*　*

Baba always blamed it on her clown feet. Baba was his father's only son and started with twenty *mu* to plant but liked to drink and liked to gamble and by the time Mei was born he had lost half of it. Her mother was very beautiful and had the lotus feet and gave him two sons, but the winter Mei was old enough to have hers bound Ma was under the influence of the *yang gweizi* and only got as far as cutting her toenails. She had a bowl of pig's blood and the bandages ready but when Mei came in from numbing her feet in the snow Ma said "No, this is why the *yang gweizi* say we are stupid people and I will not do it to her." It was the first time she saw Baba hit her mother, chasing her out in the yard with a stick of firewood and Mei crying, crying because he was beating her mother and because now she would never have lotus feet. Baba came back in alone, saying "What do these *yang gweizi* have to do with us?" but he had no idea how to bind feet and when Ma came back later, her face bruised, she threw out the pig's blood and gave the bandages to Mrs. Hong for when her daughter turned four. When Mei's brothers came inside they sensed that something was very wrong and did not speak. Nobody spoke for days.

Baba never liked Mei after that. Before, he would let her walk behind the donkey to the market to sell their sweet potatoes and then let her ride in the side basket on the way home. After, he would only look at her and say that she was born in the year of the Great Famine and was a curse on the family, and if she was going to have clown feet she would have to work in the fields with the boys.

Ma had followed the White Lotus way until the governor started putting those people in prison and many of them went to join the *yang gweizi*, who were yellow-haired beings from a land in the north where there was always snow. At that time if you bothered their followers they would complain to the other *yang gweizi* in Pekin, who would tell the Empress who would send soldiers to whip you. Even though Ma was a Christian she still bowed to the sun once every morning, noon, and evening and when she went to her knees to pray it was the old *sutras* she repeated over and over.

"What good is it for you to be a Christian," Baba said, "unless they give us food in the winter?"

"They have taken a vow of poverty," Ma would explain. "And besides, the *kalpa* is about to end and we cannot know what will follow."

When she was eight, Baba gave Mei a basket to collect dung. She spent most of her day by the road that passed the *sheng-yuan*'s fields because he had more land than anybody, more than one hundred *mu* that he planted with *giaoliang*, and more animals to work in it. She hid in the ditch by the edge of the field, watching the mules or the oxen being driven, and when one unburdened itself she would wait till the man driving the beast had moved it past a ways and then run to gather the dung, scooping it into the basket with her hands and running back to the ditch before he could turn the animal around. The best were the days when a caravan would pass by on the way to Qingdao and she could follow the camels. It only took a few camels to fill the basket. Ling-Ling, who was the *sheng-yuan*'s puppy, would find her in the ditch some days and they would play. Sometimes he would try to follow her home and Mei would have to throw a ball of dung as far as she could for the puppy to chase and then run away with the basket. Eldest Brother said she was the fastest girl he had ever seen, but of course that was because even the other Christians in the village let their daughters have lotus feet.

Ma was always pleased if it was camels, especially in the winter when fuel for the fire was scarce. Mei hated winter because there was no hired work for Baba and he drank more and because it was always smoky inside their hut and freezing when she had to go out and squat to make her own dung on the pile next to the door. She didn't like it in the summer either when the flies tickled your bottom but the cold was worse.

One day in the winter when she had a basketful from the camels and it was almost dark and she was hurrying home there was a wolf eating something in front of the Chans'. The Chans were very poor, only straw on top of their mud hut instead of reeds like at Mei's, and at first she was afraid because Mrs. Chan had just lost a baby and the poorest people would throw the little bodies outside for the animals. But when the wolf stepped away to look at her Mei saw that it had killed a pig, black bristles stained with red. The wolf's eyes were like ice watching her. Mei circled around in the stubble on the far side of the road, but when she came back to the path the wolf began to walk after her. Mei walked backward. She used to practice walking backward sometimes because Second Brother said it was a good way to confuse evil spirits. The wolf began to catch up and she tossed a handful of the camel dung, which was still warm, onto the road and kept backing up. The wolf stopped to sniff the dung for a moment and she walked faster but still didn't turn her back to it. As terrifying as the wolf was to look at she knew it would be worse if it was behind her and she couldn't tell how close. It began to trot toward her, making up distance, and this time when she threw dung at it the wolf only shied away and kept coming. They were only halfway to her home, which was at the edge of the village, and it was winter so there were no men in the fields. Even the fastest of girls cannot outrun a long-legged wolf.

That was when she heard Ling-Ling barking. The dog was in the last of the *sheng-yuan*'s fields, ears back and shaking all over, taking three steps forward and three back as she barked, her little paws nearly lifting off the ground with each high-pitched yip. The wolf looked at Mei, then took a few steps toward Ling-Ling and Mei began to run backward, dropping the basket to the road. The wolf turned and started after her again, loping, and Mei turned toward home and ran faster than she had ever run to gather dung.

Mei could hear her own breath and hear the feet of the wolf on the dirt of the path behind her and Ling-Ling running parallel to them, barking, and then she could hear the wolf getting very close and Ling-Ling too, barking hysterically, and then a low snarl and Ling-Ling yelping and Mei ran, hollering now, hollering for her mother and there was Ma coming out into the yard tottering with her lotus gait, arms spread wide for balance and screaming, picking up the rusty ax with the split handle that Baba used to cut wood if there was ever wood and Mei hearing the wolf after her again, Mei running, running straight past her hobbling mother into the hut to leap on top of the *k'ang* and shake, breathless and crying, and Ma scolding the wolf as she backed into the hut with the ax in her hands, the wolf stalking her on one side and then the other with its head so low it almost touched the ground until Ma backed inside and slammed the door shut.

Mei was still shaking when Ma put a new pile of sticks and grass into the fire under the *k'ang*, still shaking, even with Ma holding her, when both her brothers came home, surprised by the story, and said there was no sign of a wolf outside. And shaking still when Baba came in, drunk from the *baijiu*.

"A wolf is a very bad omen," he said, reeling around the smoky room. "A very bad omen. She has cursed us again."

"If I listened to you about her feet," said Ma, "we would have no daughter."

Mei waited for him to say that was right, that they were all very lucky, but he only snorted. Her brothers went to sit in the far corner and scowl then, because they knew there would be no dinner tonight. Ma sat on the *k'ang* holding Mei, rocking her, not even looking at Baba while he paced the few steps from wall to wall and complained that the foreign devils had cursed them all.

"They dance naked to stop the rain," he said. "They poisoned our donkey and called the locusts onto the field. They steal the part that comes out after a baby is born and keep it in a jar to make potions, and they dig up the dead to steal their eyes."

Ma only looked away and rocked Mei, waiting to see if he would tire and lie down first or if she would be beaten, but then there was shouting outside and someone banging on their door.

It was the lantern-bearer for Zhou, the *sheng-yuan*. Zhou himself was behind, sitting in the wheelbarrow that Mr. Chan's eldest son wheeled him around in. Baba could not speak at first, the *sheng-yuan* never having stopped at their hut before, certainly not on a winter night, and could only kowtow with his mouth hanging open.

"The *sheng-yuan* is looking for Ling-Ling," said the lantern-bearer.

Baba only stared, not understanding, as smoke from the fire poured past him out into the dark night.

"Ling-Ling is his dog," Ma hissed softly from the *k'ang*.

The *sheng-yuan* pointed through the doorway at Mei.

"I am told this girl plays with it. And steals dung from my fields."

Mei still trembling, chilled to her bones with fear, could only shake her head. The *sheng-yuan*, who could barely read and had bought his position, had eyes like the wolf.

"She has not seen it," said Ma softly, not looking at anybody.

"She says she has not seen it," said Baba, his voice shaking. "I am sorry."

The *sheng-yuan* made a grunt then, and immediately the lantern-bearer was trotting away in front as Mr. Chan's eldest son hustled Zhou away in the wheelbarrow.

Baba shut the door and sat heavily on the floor and began to weep.

"Now we are ruined," he said between sobs. "He thinks she has killed his dog."

After that there was no more Ling-Ling to play with in the ditch and at night when they rolled their mattresses out on top of the *k'ang* Baba was always on the far side and then Eldest Brother and then Second Brother and then Mei and then Ma. Ma's legs started to hurt her more than ever, though she never complained about it. Sometimes before Baba came home she would sit on the *k'ang* and stretch them out one at a time for Mei to rub.

"I used to feel bad," she said to her daughter, "and sometimes I wondered if it was not too late to turn your toes under. But now I know. If we have lotus feet the wolves will catch us."

For two years there was no rain and the next year there was too much rain and there was only boiled millet to eat with no salt or soy and sweet potatoes that were rotten by the end of the winter and even the *sheng-yuan*, who grew his sorghum to brew into *baijiu*, began to look hungry. He was the only one in the village who lived in a house behind walls like the *yang gweizi* in Weifang did, the only one who wore clothes of cloth that was not spun at home. There were mulberry orchards in the next village, and oak for *pongee*, and years ago Ma's family had all been silk weavers, but now nobody had the money to buy silk unless it was for a wedding. For a wedding people bought it to make a dress and hired a boy as a crier to warn you there was a bride coming by and Mei would stand out front of the hut with her mother, her mother's hand on Mei's shoulder for balance, and watch the bride be carried past in her chair. Mei would always look first to the red veil, trying to see through to the girl's face and know if she was crying or smiling, and then her eyes would go to the tiny feet, delicate triangles in beautiful beaded slippers. The men carrying the brides were professional porters, paid by the number of *li* they had to travel, and kept the chair as steady as if it was floating down a peaceful river.

"Don't worry," Ma would always say, reading Mei's thoughts when the procession passed out of sight. "When this *kalpa* ends things will be different. Men will want girls with feet like yours."

At the rumor of the next spring Baba kicked her awake and told her she was coming with him and her brothers to work in the field. The field was full of weeds and every one of them had to be pulled and burned before the ground could be broken to receive the seed. Baba stood over Mei, scolding whenever she missed a weed or broke the stem without pulling up the roots.

"If you are going to look like a man," he said, "you will learn to work like one."

Mei didn't mind the work, which was different than what Ma did in and around the hut. You breathed less smoke. She only felt bad when people would stop on the road to stare at her.

"You have a mule there," said Yip who did not own land but lived in a hut where men went to drink *baijiu* and gamble and meet with wicked women. "Neither a horse nor a donkey."

A week later Baba hired her brothers out to work in the *sheng-yuan*'s fields. Most days after that he would just sit and smoke tobacco and watch Mei work, shouting if he disapproved of something she did or did not do. Mei missed being with her mother and wished she had a puppy like Ling-Ling to walk along with her and chase butterflies while she was pulling weeds or driving the young ox rented from Mr. Hong around the wet field with a switch or poking holes with a stick and planting seed or spreading the dung from the pile next to the door or pulling up the next growth of weeds. But when there was not too little rain nor too much and the locusts decided not to come, the millet began to grow, and Mei was proud. She had made that happen. She began to watch the sky and smell the air like the other farmers did, began to search the stalks for insects whenever she walked in the field, began to dream about things that might hurt her crop. Sometimes, if she watched very carefully, she could see it growing taller.

One day while she was pulling more weeds and Baba was sitting on the little stone wall smoking tobacco, Feng, who hired men for the *sheng-yuan*'s fields and supervised his harvest, stopped to talk to him.

"This soil is weary of millet," he said looking out at the crop, which was then no more than two feet high. "It will yield very little."

"I would grow pearls," said Baba, who according to Ma had been a clever man when he was young, happy even without drink, "if only I could afford the seed."

"There is something better than pearls," said Feng. "Everybody in Dang-shan is planting it."

Baba tried not to look the foreman in the eye, instead staring out past Mei to his little ten *mu*.

"Is the *sheng-yuan* going to grow it in his fields?"

Feng shook his head. "He is not so hard-hearted. He would not deprive his neighbors of their sorghum wine."

"Growing poppy flowers in forbidden," said Baba, looking into the sky.

"What is forbidden here," smiled the foreman, "is determined by the *sheng-yuan*. If you decide to change your crop, as many here are doing, I can give you the seeds without charge. But when you gather the gum you must sell it to me."

"How much is it selling for?"

Feng put his finger to his lips. "We must not speak of such things. I only wish to leave you something to consider."

Baba left the field in millet and it was the best crop in years. But the men who had grown poppy flowers were boasting and wearing real metal coins strung around their necks after their harvest and every night there was noise from the crowd at Yip's hut.

"Pay no mind to those people," Ma told Baba. She was saying her *sutras* more than ever and calling on the Eternal Mother even though she could no longer kneel like a Christian. "What is won too easily does not last."

"They do not work as hard as I do," said Baba, who only helped Mei during the harvest when he was afraid the grain might shatter if left too long on the stalk. "But they have twice as much in their palms at the end of it."

There was enough to eat that winter. Ma made noodles once, and once Baba brought home a chicken he had won gambling.

"Too bad you don't eat meat," he said to Ma. "It will be torture for you to cook this."

Most years he only got to tease her about being a White Lotus at New Year, when they spent their savings to buy pork buns and Ma would only eat the outside.

The next year Feng came to talk to Baba even before planting, but he had Mei put in the millet seed again. That was the year Quan Chuntao, who was Mei's age, was taken as a bride by a young man in a village outside of Weifang and Eldest Brother was taken by the soldiers to fight against the Dwarf Bandits. Once again there was not too much or too little rain and only the usual insects and the crop was nearly up to Mei's chin when Second Brother came home to say he had been let go from working in the *sheng-yuan*'s fields.

That night they were already asleep on the *k'ang* when there was a banging on the door and Baba went to it holding the rusted ax. It was poor Mr. Chan, who had taken to begging and sleeping outside since his wife died, shouting that there was a fire in Baba's field.

There was a big moon and if Mei had not weeded and planted and weeded till her hands bled she would have thought the fire beautiful. As the night breeze swept it across the field, grasshoppers, some of them on fire, buzzed into the air just ahead of the flames. The breeze pushed the fire to the stone wall by the road and soon there was nothing left.

"We are cursed," said Baba, his face black from the blowing soot, flecks of ash in his hair. "She has cursed us."

The next day Mei was with Baba in the charred field, looking for burned animals they could eat, when Zhou stopped on the road. He had a sedan chair now, with silk curtains and four porters wearing a kind of uniform who carried it, and he wore a long silk vest and a hat that had a jeweled button on it to signify that he was a *sheng-yuan*. Mei stood by the wall while Baba climbed over to squat by Zhou's chair and be spoken to.

"You are an unlucky man," said the *sheng-yuan*. "We will have to discover who has done this to you and see that they are punished."

"I have nothing," said Baba, looking at the ground.

"Nobody starves in my village," said Zhou. "I will have Feng bring you some seed, and you will plant again. They say a fire is good for the soil."

"You are very kind."

The *sheng-yuan* looked at Mei then with his wolf's eyes and gestured for her to come forward. When she put her leg over the stone wall he began to laugh.

"What clown feet!" he said. "Your daughter is very beautiful—above the knees. You are truly an unlucky man."

When the sedan chair and its passenger had passed Baba slapped Mei in the face.

Mr. Chan was arrested then and charged with setting the fire, worse, accused of lighting it with a match he had been given for that purpose by the *yang gweizi*. The village was told to gather by the gate in front of the *sheng-yuan's* house, gathering obediently to watch Mr. Chan beaten one hundred strokes with the bamboo cane before he was taken away with a yoke around his neck. The *sheng-yuan* came out to warn all of them to be wary of the foreign devils, who were all spies for the Dwarf Bandits who were making war on the Empire. He offered free *baijiu* for the men then, and when Baba finally danced home he was with a half-dozen others, all of them ready to go to war. Ma was having her bleeding and he held her down and yanked away the rag and went out to the others saying they were going to Weifang to wipe the dirty blood on the house of the yellow-hair *yang gweizi* and break their spells.

It took Mei a week to rake the ash in the field till it was even. Then after a little rain Feng came with the seed and watched her plant the first handfuls.

"Not so deep as the millet," he said. "Put it in rows with space to walk in between. This is gold you are planting."

Ma's left foot had begun to smell, and soon she could only walk on one leg using a crutch that Second Brother made for her.

"I was as pretty as you," she said to Mei one night before either of the men had come. "Would you believe that? And then I was married. Mei, your feet have saved you again."

"If I don't marry," Mei asked, "what will I be?"

Ma thought a long time about it. She was in less pain than usual but weaker, her eyes growing cloudy, and she smelled too sweet, like fruit fallen to rot.

"When this *kalpa* ends," she said finally, "and it will be very soon, there will be a way for you. It will be a difficult way, terrifying, but you must stay on the path and never despair."

"Like when I ran from the wolf."

Ma squeezed Mei's arm then. As Mei's arms had grown stronger Ma's had turned to sticks.

"Running may not be possible."

Baba was very worried about the new crop, never having grown flowers before. Every day he scolded Mei, telling her not to crush the new plants under her big feet as she searched for weeds to pull. In only two weeks the sprouts came out, and after a month and a half it looked like they were growing tiny cabbages. And then the plants began to rise. Baba would brag to Second Brother, who had been taken on again in the *sheng-yuan*'s fields as an act of charity, that he was going to have the finest poppy-flower crop in the village, and Ma would cover her ears so she wouldn't hear. Most years she put a smear of honey on the lips of their kitchen-god statue so in the New Year it would say sweet things about them when it flew to report to the Jade Emperor. Now she covered his whole head with clay so he could not see or hear what had become of her family.

"The four walls that we must escape in this life," said Ma, who was more of a White Lotus than ever now that she could barely walk, "are liquor, lust, anger, and wealth."

Baba and Second Brother laughed.

"We have escaped from wealth thus far," said Baba. "Maybe this year we will let it catch us."

Three months after the sowing, Mei's plants began to blossom. The petals were crimson red, the color of happiness, and more beautiful than anything she had ever seen. But in only a few days they began to fall off the plants, carpeting the ground in red and leaving a little green ball on top of the stem.

The balls were growing fatter each day by the time Eldest Brother returned from fighting the Japanese. Everybody in the village knew that the Imperial Army had failed, had somehow been defeated by the Dwarf Bandits and their *yang gweizi* weapons, and so the family could not have a public celebration. Baba and Ma were excited though, even if Eldest Brother looked like a different person and was not at home in his body anymore, as if the Imperial officers or the Dwarf Bandits had stolen his spirit. He was going to be an escort, he said, a guard for the caravans passing from the mountains to the sea, but most days he only sat around drinking and gambling with the *pu hao* at Yip's and people in the market said he was a salt smuggler. Then he joined a group called the Obedient Swords and on market days would appear with them to demonstrate how they could whip their swords at each other but always duck or leap over the blade and never be cut. Eldest Brother was the one who had to pass through the crowd with a rice bowl, asking for the audience to contribute money for their further training. He never came home to visit.

"The foreign devils have put a spell on Ma," he told Second Brother when he saw him at the market. "They are making her rot while she is still breathing and it is unlucky to look at her."

The plants were as high as Mei's breasts and the green balls the size of hens' eggs when it was time to harvest. Feng came to show them how to do this, bringing Mei a special slicer, a wooden handle with three slivers of glass stuck in it.

"Choose only the pods that are standing at attention, like this one," he said, demonstrating. "Then make a cut, up and down, on three sides. Wait until the sun is three hands from the ground before you do this, or the nectar will dry too quickly and not flow out. In the morning you take this other blade and scrape off the gum, but be careful not to hurt the pod, because it can be milked many times."

There was so much work to be done that even Baba had to help every morning, scraping the pods that had been scored and then slicing the newly ripe ones in the late afternoon. Ma refused to help drying the gum they collected, so he had to tend to that as well, even boiling some down to a brown paste in the cooking pot and then drying it more. Ma only watched him with her cloudy eyes, sitting on the *k'ang* all day, unwilling to help him keep the fire going for his business and unable to cook because he always had opium boiling in the pot. Mei came in late from the field, sticky with poppy gum, and had to help Ma outside to relieve herself on the dungpile. Second Brother came to say he was moving to the barracks the *sheng-yuan* kept for his workers. At night it was only the three of them, Mei trying to rub the gum off her fingers and Ma sitting on the *k'ang* looking into the next world and Baba sitting on the floor under the window smoking opium in his pipe, his eyes as cloudy as Ma's.

The pods were milked out in two weeks and then Mei had to cut them off and leave them in the sun to dry. The day she cut them open to take the seeds out was the day that Ma died.

The hut was ripe with the sweet smell of her. Mei came home just as the sun hid behind the earth and Baba was already on the floor with his cheeks wet with tears, smoking opium, Ma laying flat on the *k'ang* with a white cloth laid over her face.

Eldest Brother took charge then because Baba could barely breathe without weeping. He came home from the swordsmen and burned spirit money in front of the hut and poured a ring of sorghum wine around it. Feng sent word that the *sheng-yuan* would offer credit on the opium paste that was still drying, and a coffin was ordered and a new set of white clothing for Baba and Mei and her brothers and even for Ma. Mei was allowed to help prepare the body with Mrs. Hong, taking Ma's old clothes off to burn and cleaning her and dressing her in the new white clothes and the beautiful beaded slippers from the day she was married. Mei had never seen her mother's feet naked before, and they were not beautiful. Mrs. Hong held a cloth dipped in jasmine water over her nose because the smell was too powerful, and put the powder on Ma's face and put her brass earrings on and covered her face with a yellow cloth and her little wasted body with a sky-blue one.

Eldest Brother lifted Ma into the coffin and put up an altar at the foot of it. Because Ma had a bad ending very few people came. Mei remembered only a paid monk chanting prayers and Ma's older sister crawling into the hut on her knees. Eldest Brother broke Ma's comb in two pieces, putting one half into the coffin and giving the other to Mei, and then Ma was gone from the earth.

Feng did not wait the forty-nine days of mourning, incense still burning at the altar, before he came to sit with Baba.

"A death in the family is a very hard thing," he said, sitting cross-legged on the *k'ang* and drinking the tea Mei had served him. "Very expensive. The coffin, paying the monk, clothing—with all that the *sheng-yuan* has advanced to you, I can only pay twelve *tiao* for what you have harvested and what you have cooked."

Baba only nodded. Twelve *tiao* was more than he had had in his palm for many years. The foreman sighed.

"But now you have no real woman to tend to this house," he said, as if Mei was not squatting on the floor only a few feet away from him, "and no son to work in your field. It will be difficult. You will have to hire someone to do these things, and that costs money."

"I have seed drying," said Baba, picturing the twelve *tiao* disappearing into the hands of strangers. "And my Second Son will come back."

Feng shook his head sadly. "He is contracted to the *sheng-yuan*, and owes him money for food and shelter. A contract is a sacred obligation. However,

I know people in the South," and here he glanced at Mei, "who are looking for girls to work for them. People willing to pay a good price."

She wanted Baba to say he would not sell her, that she was too good a worker, wanted at least to hear him say her name out loud, but he only nodded and said, "This flower-growing is not so easy as it looks."

Later he filled his pipe with opium and sat on the *k'ang* and smoked, silent as always, staring at Ma's altar while Mei tended the fire. It was beginning to be winter, wind moaning outside their hut, and Mei thought she heard barking and wondered, as she never had before, if dogs might have spirits and if Ling-Ling might come back to haunt her.

One day all the opium paste was gone and Baba came home drunk like he used to, singing to himself and jingling coins in a sack. Mei did not speak to him, did not even look at him. When he fell asleep he lay on top of the sack and Mei had to stay awake watching him, her breath showing in the cold hut as she waited. It was almost light when he stirred and rolled over and she eased the sack away and emptied it on the floor and counted the coins. She was worth less than thirty *tiao*.

My feet will save me again, Mei thought as she pulled all her clothes on, layer after layer, and started out into the village. Nobody was on the road. Nobody was awake in Yip's hut, but the door was unbarred, and she stepped over the bodies of the sleeping *pu hao* until she found Eldest Brother in the arms of a wicked woman. He was not pleased to see her.

"Why would you want to stay with Baba when he treats you like a dog?" he said without sitting up. The wicked girl lying with him was named Ai and was only a year older than Mei, a third daughter who had been sold to Yip when no husband could be found for her. "Go with Feng—the people in the South aren't so bad."

As she left, Yip woke up and cursed her for leaving the door open.

Mei began to run as she passed their hut again, worried that Baba might wake and find his coins melting in the fire. The workers were just coming into Zhou's fields as she passed, cutting the last of the *giaoliang*, which was twice as tall as Mei. She asked for Second Brother, who she had not seen since the burial, and when she found him he was on his knees chopping the stalks with his knife. He turned and smiled when she called his name and she saw that his teeth were blackened like the other workers', blackened from chewing opium paste.

"Is something wrong with Baba?" he asked.

"I have only come to say goodbye."

She ran down the road then, away from the village, away from the *sheng-yuan*'s fields, vowing that she would not stop until she was in a place she had never seen before, running even faster as she passed through the market. It was not market day but there was a caravan, the porters pulling down the tents where they had spent the night. Feng was with them.

"Ah," he smiled when he saw Mei and caught hold of her arm, squeezing tight. "We were just coming for you."

Niles says he is there to visit Private Burns and is waved through.

"He's in isolation," says the orderly, lowering his voice meaningfully. "Doesn't look like he'll see tomorrow."

Burns and a half-dozen others from the company are in with the typhoid, no surprise in this pesthole, and the flux is ubiquitous within the volunteers, not to mention the growing number sidelined by the wages of sin. The life of a soldier. Niles checks to be sure the orderly is not watching after him and then cuts left toward the dispensary. The air is laced with ammonia and carbolic acid, stinging his eyes and the back of his throat. No telling in what manner the Spaniards, never the most hygienic of races, operated the hospital, but the Medical Corps have obviously given it a thorough scouring. Niles pauses at the doorway of one of the ambulatory wards, men chatting in groups or with playing cards laid out on the beds between them, the legs of the beds standing in small pans of liquid, kerosene most likely, to keep the marauding squadrons of biting ants from climbing up onto the patients as they sleep. Plain water had been used for this purpose in Cuba until it was found to breed mosquitoes, which proceeded to torment and re-infect the quarantined unfortunates. One of the ambulatories looks his way.

It is the hard-rock miner, late of Skaguay, dressed in Army-issue pajamas and slippers.

"Enjoying yourself, Private?"

The miner, who was Brackenridge and then McGinty and now something else, is not happy to see him.

"The chuck's no better in here," he says with an insolent tone, "but I prefer the company."

He is a chronic kicker, this one, not so much in words as with his attitude—the way he looks at you and moves his body a challenge to every order. Harboring some grudge, perhaps, or just incorrigible. Niles looks beyond him into the wardroom. "So this is where they house the slackers."

"Venereals," says the private, turning to walk away from him. "Watch out you don't catch something."

Supply Sergeant Slocum is in the solarium, talking with a mopey-looking artilleryman who slumps in a rattan-backed rocker. Slocum sees Niles, nods almost imperceptibly. The sergeant is something of a wizard with figures, and like many similarly afflicted, believes this increases his ability to fill an inside straight. A fantasist, doomed to be mulcted even without Niles's dexterous mastery of pasteboard royals.

"In the morgue," the man mutters as he brushes past. "Give me five minutes."

Slocum's camera, an old Turner Bull's-Eye forfeited in the same poker game, hangs from a strap around Niles's shoulder. There is a handsome slant of sun coming into the high-ceilinged room from the east windows—he pulls the device out and kodaks the long row of convalescents in their rockers, hoping the light will be sufficient. A Chinaman he's found in Binondo makes prints most reasonably, and the Judge has written that he is eager for views of "the Pearl of the Orient" and the American boys who have liberated it. Harry was always the photo bug, even learning to develop his own snaps, but never goes anywhere interesting enough to record.

Corporal Grissom, who shilled for Niles in the game, was rewarded with Slocum's pocket watch.

The morgue is at the rear of the building, cool and windowless, with its own peculiar smell. There is a body on a draining table, rigid beneath a rubber sheet.

"Passed this morning," says Sergeant Slocum when Niles arrives, his voice echoing under the vaulted ceiling. "Infection. He was shot through the lungs the day we took the city."

"War is hell," Niles intones. To be killed in a mock battle engineered to salvage the honor of some peacock Dago general—a dismal hand to be dealt. Slocum lays a heavy wooden box on the table next to the dead soldier, snaps open the brass fastenings and lifts the lid.

"They accidentally shipped a double order," he says, fixing Niles with a look. "Which I have not made record of."

The box is segmented into dozens of compartments, each containing a vial cushioned with cotton wadding. Niles pulls several bottles out to examine them. Mostly quinine, with some tincture of chloroform, laudanum, ipecac syrup, and a quantity of strychnine.

"No medical supplies besides ours have entered the city since the Filipinos began their siege months ago," says Slocum. "This might as well be gold."

He is eyeing the camera. If he had been a gracious loser, a gentleman, Niles might entertain the idea of returning it as part of the present transaction. But no, the man is a boor. An egotist, a yankee, and a boor.

"You should be able to sell these for far more than the amount I owe you," he continues. "The anti-malarial alone—"

"But I shall be the one incurring the risk," says Niles, and closes the case.

Slocum hands Niles a form in three pages, white copy duplicated in yellow and pink.

"In that case you are transporting these to Brigade in Cavite," he says. "In the event anybody inquires."

The supply sergeant opens a somewhat battered leather satchel, carefully places the wooden box into it.

"The luggage belonged to a missionary gentleman from Nebraska, a Presbyterian, I believe. Sampled a bit too much of the local water." He closes and fastens the satchel, placing it at Niles's feet. "Gentle with this," he says. "And give me the whole five minutes this time."

Slocum leaves Niles in the morgue. They've only had a few fatalities in the regiment so far, and unless the natives learn to shoot, disease will be the greatest enemy. If Burns succumbs Niles will be forced to write his first letter of condolence. He lifts the rubber sheet to view the dead soldier's face. His skin is blue-gray, and they have tied a bandage from the top of his head under his chin to hold his jaw closed. Niles does not recognize the boy, not from his outfit, and wonders if his mates have begun the collection to send the body home. He has visited Paco, the most celebrated of the local mausoleums, viewed the circular wall of cement with niches for the deceased one atop the other, rentable for five-year residencies. Cracked skulls and jumbled bones of the evicted lay heaped in one area, while domesticated turkeys and a small, bristly pig patrolled the grounds. The dead rest here, but only if they can make the rent.

Niles does not plan on dying in the Philippines.

In Hongkong Mei lived in a house on the steep hill behind the Victoria Barracks. Madame Qing was in charge of the house and the first thing she did, before learning their names or giving them new clothes, was to have each new girl demonstrate how to use the water closet. The house was made of wood, with wooden floors and stairs leading to a second set of rooms with windows that looked over past the Victoria Barracks to the harbor. Mei had not eaten much on the road and was sick on the steamboat ride, so it was a long time sitting on the hole in one of the three water closets before she could shout to Madame Qing and show her what she had done.

"Pull the chain," said Madame Qing, and they both watched. It seemed like a waste of both dung and water. "Now pull your pants down."

Mei was afraid because Ma had always done everything in the household while she had worked in the field and soon they would discover how useless she was. She turned and pulled her pants down.

"What did I tell you the paper was for?"

There was white paper rolled up beside the hole, softer, but the same width as the paper on which she had written the characters Second Brother showed her, the paper she had hung as a banner outside their hut when Ma died.

"You are a stupid, dirty girl," said Madame Qing. "Now show me how you clean yourself with the paper."

Mei reached into the hole for water to wet herself and Madame Qing slapped her and said she had to do it only with the paper and then wash her hands in the basin with the slippery cake.

"You girls from the North are not worth the trouble," said Madame Qing.

There were girls in the house who weren't new, mostly Southerners, and three Dwarf Bandit girls, who woke up late in the day to look over Mei and the other arrivals. Mei couldn't understand most of what they said but a lot of them pointed at her feet and laughed and that was more shameful than Madame Qing watching her clean herself.

When it began to get dark each of the new girls was given a ball of rice and then locked in a room with mattresses laid on the floor. Mei thought the rice was very sweet compared to millet and it made her feel a little sick. After the candles were put out they lay and listened to the music on the other side of the door, and to the laughing and men's voices braying in another language Mei could not understand.

"These are wicked women who live here," said one of the girls from the boat, who was from near Jinan. "They lie with *yang gweizi*, and we are going to be their servants."

They were there nearly a week, Madame Qing teaching them more about cleaning themselves and not eating with their hands, until late one afternoon they were ordered to take all their clothes off and pile them in the middle of the room. A servant woman—all the servants in the house were older men and women—gathered the pile and carried it away and it was too late when

Mei remembered that her half of Ma's comb was still in her pants. Basins filled with a sharp-smelling liquid were brought in and they were told to wash their hair in it and then sit while the servants picked the bugs from their scalps. Their hair was dried after that, servants rubbing it with towels, and then the wicked girls came in with a trunkful of beautiful clothes and began to dress them up like dolls, chattering and laughing the whole time. The silk felt slippery against Mei's skin and when the old girls began to powder and paint her face she understood, finally, that it didn't matter if she could not cook or sew. It took a long time for the Southern girls to find a pair of slippers that would fit her feet.

The old girls went out then and Madame Qing came in to explain that Mr. Wu, who owned the house, was coming tonight to entertain some of his friends and that they were to do whatever they were told or they would certainly be beaten and possibly thrown into the harbor for the sharks to eat. The girl from near Jinan began to cry then and Madame Qing slapped her for making ugly tracks in the powder on her face.

"If they ask your name," said Madame Qing, "you must tell them something beautiful."

"I will be Jade Lily," said one of the girls, quickly.

"I will be Morning Dew," said another.

Mei thought of Poppy Blossom, but it only brought pictures of Baba smoking his pipe and Ma dying on the *k'ang*.

Mr. Wu was an older man with eyes that watched everything, and his friends were all very rough men from the South. The new girls were supposed to serve them rice wine and then sit with them and answer questions if they were asked. The man next to Mei, who had drawings inked into the skin on the backs of his hands, kept shouting the same words at her till she decided he was asking for her name and she said Ling-Ling.

The men stayed for three days. They made her drink wine and they used her and the other new girls whenever they wanted, sometimes taking them into another room and sometimes using them in front of all the others, who laughed and shouted things. Mei hurt everywhere they touched her but was not ashamed. They were doing these things to Ling-Ling, and that was only a dog after all.

When Mr. Wu and his friends finally left the old girls came back.

"Now you are our sisters," they said. "We can teach you what we know."

Some of the new girls were bleeding and some were still trembling and the girl from near Jinan, who had decided to call herself Silk Whisper, tried to drown herself in one of the water closets but there wasn't enough water.

None of them were ever let out of the house. In the daytime, if they wanted, they could go out onto the balconies from the rooms on the second floor and look down past the barracks to Hongkong and the harbor. Even from that distance Ling-Ling could see that there were more people in Hongkong than she had imagined there were in the world. Mr. Wu's friends had only been there to "break the soil" said the old girls, Ling-Ling's new sisters, and most of the time the house was for entertaining *yang gweizi*, "officers and gentlemen" as Madame Qing called them. They had to learn to smile and be gracious and please the English men, and even learn some of their words.

Ling-Ling decided that it was not knowing that made her the most afraid. Not knowing what the Southern girls were saying, not knowing what Madame Qing was planning to do to them next, not knowing what was in the minds of the English foreign devils.

"Sister," she said to one of the old girls who was called Radiant Star and had originally come from the North like herself, "I want you to teach me everything."

Radiant Star taught her how to put a vinegar sponge up inside herself so she would not make half-human babies with the *yang gweizi*, taught her to sing some of the dirty songs the men liked and how to talk like South China people.

"You are like Fan-tail," she told Ling-Ling when Ling-Ling would try her South China talk out. Fan-tail was Madame Qing's parrot, who repeated phrases from all the languages spoken in the house. "Everything you hear you say it the same."

She also began to learn English from one of the *yang gweizi*, a young man who was not an officer, not a soldier at all but some other kind of official sent to work in Hongkong. Nights that he came, two or three times a week, were easy for Ling-Ling because he always asked for her and paid extra to stay the whole night and wore a rubber bag on his penis so she did not need the sponge, which sometimes got lost inside her. He would use her in one of the usual ways and then sit with her in the bed or out on the balcony if it was hot and want to talk. He already knew how to talk Southern, would joke with the sisters in that language, but wanted to learn to speak like North China people too. Ling-Ling was his "sleeping dictionary," he said, and insisted that she learn how to say his name, which was Roderick Hardacre.

As good as Ling-Ling was with South China talk, this was almost impossible to do, her tongue unable to imitate the sounds. Fan-tail was much better at it, mastering "Well I'll be buggered" after only a few visits from Roderick Hardacre. He would have her say his name again and again, correcting her patiently, and then ask her questions in South China talk while she answered in what he called Mandarin. After a while he would get tired of that and try to teach her things in English that weren't his name.

This is how she discovered that the *yang gweizi* know nothing about the sky. They would stand on the balcony and Roderick Hardacre would point to the stars and make her try to see shapes of animals or people and tell her long stories about their adventures. When Ling-Ling began to understand the words she discovered that he was not talking about the Three Enclosures or the Azure Dragon or the White Tiger of the West or the Cowherd and the Weaver Girl but something completely different, either something he was inventing to mock her or strange beliefs of the *yang gweizi*. If it was overcast or too cold to step out he would teach her poems, having her repeat them line by line and then explain what they meant.

Roderick Hardacre was very red on his face and hands, almost crimson, and very white everywhere else when he took his clothes off.

"I am so relieved about your feet," he said once. "The other girls, the mere thought of it—it puts one off."

All the sisters were allowed to sleep till noon and their meals were prepared for them. The three Japanese girls were called *karayuki-san*, which they said meant "Miss Gone-to-China" and were the most obedient, never complaining if they were awakened to entertain an early visitor, never sticking their tongues out at Madame Qing when her back was turned. It was being inside all the time that bothered Ling-Ling the most, always a dog that loved the fields.

Some of the sisters smoked opium when Madame Qing allowed it on slow days and some drank too much when there were parties with men and some embroidered and Silk Whisper got into the kitchen even though it was supposed to be locked and cut her own throat and bled to death.

At New Year they celebrated inside the house and there was lots of food and they dressed in their best clothes and went out onto the balconies to watch the dragon come up the hill and waved to the young men hurling firecrackers. For an hour or two Ling-Ling was as happy as a dog can be, happy to be warm and well-fed and with her many sisters. That night Roderick Hardacre came with a friend, another young Englishman who was not a soldier, and had her stand before him.

"This is my linguist," said Roderick Hardacre. "My Ling-linguist."

"I fancy a bit of tongue," said the friend, who was already drunk.

Ling-Ling was afraid they were both going to use her at the same time, which had happened with Mr. Wu's friends.

"He thinks I've been telling tales," said Roderick Hardacre. "You're going to make a believer out of him."

Other of the English men gathered around her then, Ling-Ling smelling the starch in their uniforms, the tobacco on their breath, and it made her face burn.

"You know what I'm after," said Roderick Hardacre. "You know the one I want."

Ling-Ling took a deep breath and said it to them, trying to make the sounds exactly the way Roderick Hardacre did when he taught it to her, not using his own voice but a different one, rougher—

Ship me somewheres east of Suez—

—she said—

Where the best is like the worst
Where there aint no Ten Commandments
An a man can raise a thirst
For the temple bells are callin'
An it's there that I would be—
By the Old Moulmen Pagoda
Looking lazy at the sea
On the road to Mandalay
Where the Old Flotilla lay
With our sick beneath the awnings
When we went to Mandalay!
On the road to Mandalay
Where the flyin' fishes play
An' the dawn comes up like thunder
Outer China 'crost the Bay!

The *yang gweizi* smacked their hands together and cheered and the sisters in the room laughed and Fan-tail said that he would be buggered. Later Roderick Hardacre's friend passed out from the wine and Roderick Hardacre took her upstairs to one of the rooms and used her like he always did but looked at her with his strange blue cat's eyes the whole time. After that they wrapped themselves in blankets and stepped onto the balcony to see the fireworks explode over the harbor. At one point he watched her face for a long time and then shook his head.

"Life is bloody strange," he said. "Bloody strange."

Niles summons a *carromata* outside of the hospital, satchel held tight between his knees on the two-wheeled buggy while the little horse—a pony, really—navigates the streets of the Walled City. It is a low, somewhat somber metropolis, squarish stone edifices set in a grid between the ancient, moss-covered walls, everything low and heavily buttressed in deference to the frequent earthquakes, the barracks, post office, treasury, *ayuntamiento*, and customs dwarfed by the larger and grander church buildings, a fair representation of the relative stature accorded by the citizens to the still-present Archbishop and the erstwhile Governor General.

The Minnesotas are on provost today, showing no interest as he is trotted past, their orders to detain suspicious natives or the disarmed, loitering Spanish soldiers who seem to infest the city looking for a handout. Niles passes the Church of San Ignacio with its breathtaking woodwork inside and a covered walkway connecting it to the Jesuit-run Ateneo, the minions of Loyola within no doubt up to their habitual scheming. The private houses in the shadow of the cannon-bedecked parapets and bastions are impressive, two-story affairs with space for a carriage below, living quarters on the second floor, with balconies rimmed by elaborate wrought-iron hanging over the sidewalks and the red-painted galvanized-tin roofs that have mostly replaced the tile which becomes so hazardous when blown asunder by their incessant typhoon winds. The driver pauses to let an overloaded, pony-drawn tram pass, people crammed not only inside the car but hanging on to the front and rear platforms, the standees all smoking while one determined *hausfrau* plucks feathers from a live and understandably distressed chicken that she holds upside-down by its feet, tossing the feathers in the wake of the conveyance. When they have passed, the driver turns onto the broad Avenue Real. They pick up speed, weaving around elegant landaus and barouches and tottering *calesas*, past Chinamen waving switches to drive oxen hitched to wood-wheeled carts filled with furniture, avoiding the occasional bicycle enthusiast, the wheeling mania having arrived only recently on this island. A sentry snaps him a salute as they roll under the ornately decorated portico of the Parian Gate. The moat that lies beyond the thick earth-and-stone wall is a cold, scum-covered porridge, rampant with weeds and piled with refuse, from which there exudes an unholy stench. When the googoos cut off water to the Intramuros during the siege the Spaniards' sanitary response was to collect their excrescence and hurl it over the parapets. No great wonder that the more well-to-do residents are offering fortunes for medicine.

They turn right and cross the Bridge of Spain, rafts of cocoanuts and slender *bancas* laden with fodder being poled upriver beneath them, the driver flipping a centavo to the tollkeeper and being rewarded with a box of matches in lieu of a return stub. Every Filipino man, woman, and child Niles has laid eyes on in the capital has the smoking habit, and the boys in his company have stocked up, buying packages of thirty cigarettes for a pair of coppers. Niles prefers a cigar, and these are manufactured in the area as well, the Montecristos comparing not unfavorably with their Cuban counterparts. There is excellent rum available for those with valuables to trade, and a passable local moonshine the men call *beeno*. If only the females were more attractive.

Several classes of them are on display as Niles descends from the buggy at the base of the Escolta. It is a full hour before siesta, the mercantile street clogged with all the mongrel races produced here, freight vans bumping over the cobblestones while a mix of near-naked coolies, Spanish Peninsulars, and white-suited Filipino dandies compete for space. The Spanish ladies are in white muslin, carrying white parasols to match, pointed in their refusal to meet an American's eye, while the wealthier Filipinas either ape this Western garb or sport pineapple-fiber gowns with exaggerated butterfly sleeves, their ebony hair slick with cocoanut oil and held in place with ivory combs, their upper bodies held elegantly straight as they shuffle along in the little heelless slippers they call *chinelas*. None of these ladies walk alone, of course, while the less fortunate native women often appear so, selling trifles or begging with filthy palms extended, barefoot women in long red skirts and white waists, often with their equally scruffy pickaninnies in tow. Niles steps around a trio of wizened crones squatting on the walk operating foot-pump Singer machines, gabbling with each other and expectorating without regard to passersby, their teeth dyed red from the concoction they chew. He takes a firm grip on the satchel, then plunges into the morass of humanity, reminding himself that he is a uniformed lieutenant of the victorious army.

The shops here are mostly operated by Spaniards, with the occasional Frenchman or Hindoo, shelves bursting with European goods arranged behind the only glass windows Niles has seen on the island or spilling out onto the walk in front of the stores, laid on the ground or displayed on mahogany tables and desks looted after the fall of the Dons, awnings over-head affording some shade on the east side of the street. A pair of native lotharios, resplendent in white and deep in conversation, approach in the opposite direction, each with a carved walking-stick in hand and straw boater tipped on the head. The recent hostilities seem not to have affected this strata of the local gentry, Niles resentfully aware of their lack of either gratitude or deference. He looks through them and strides down the center of the walk, the gesticulating niggers acknowledging his presence only in time to veer awkwardly to each side, the one stumbling off the curb into an unfortunate encounter with a hustling rickshaw artist that sends the dandy ass over teakettle onto the cobbles. Niles takes a few more steps, then very deliberately halts to unsheathe his camera and photograph a gang of bare-chested coolies transporting a medium-sized piano perched upon a pair of thick wooden poles.

The pistol he has his eye on is in a curio shop—telescopes, old sailing charts, stuffed lizards and fruit bats, carved bookends of various exotic mate-rials, forbidden etchings shown on special request. The proprietor, a Señor Ocampo, claims that it has only recently come into his hands from a Spanish officer of exalted lineage with a particularly avaricious mistress in Santa Mesa. It is a gleaming "Chinese" Webley, displayed in a velvet-lined box that Ocampo, forbidden now by the Occupation Authority to sell firearms of any sort, pulls from behind the counter.

"A pity," Niles muses as he turns the revolver over in his hands. "They'll probably confiscate this now that your *indios* have gone on the warpath again."

Ocampo moves, as always, to put his body between the customer han-dling the merchandise and the door to the bustling Escolta. "Is yes a pity. You wan to buy him now?"

"We would be in violation of the decree."

"This is true."

"But if purchase is out of the question," says Niles, sighting the .45 at a panther crouched to spring off its pedestal, "perhaps an exchange of gifts might be arranged."

"Gifs?"

"Tokens of friendship. There are many things which we in the military have in abundance, which, due to the vagaries of the present conflict, the average citizen lives in want of."

The proprietor is mute with calculation for a moment, staring at the pistol and trying to gauge its equivalent in various commodities.

"This might happen, yes."

If his company were assigned the provost it would be simple. A search for contraband up and down the street, Ocampo eagerly giving up the Webley to avoid too thorough a going-over of his premises. As it is, a crate of tinned beef, to be delivered within the week, is equal to the task. Niles slips the pistol into his empty holster, stuffs the proffered ammunition into his pockets, and bids the Spaniard a good day.

He steps out into the fetid press of the Escolta at noon.

It wasn't long after New Year that Madame Qing said some of them were going to be sent to Manila. The *karayuki-san*, who had been there, said this was a city on an island across the sea, full of *yang gweizi* with black hair and dark eyes and little brown Monkey People, and only one section where all the China people were crowded together. When Ling-Ling was picked among those to go Radiant Star hugged her with tears in her eyes.

"Don't worry, sister," she said. "Soon you will know the poems of the Monkey People."

But once she was out of the house, riding down past the Victoria Barracks among the real people, she couldn't be Ling-Ling anymore, only Lan Mei, who was a disgrace to her poor dead mother and to all the Lans who had gone before, a wicked woman who could be sold or traded like a sack of salt.

Mei and the other ones being sent to Manila were brought up onto the steamship after all the coolie-brokers had loaded their men into the hold, the sisters herded into a cabin by two of Mr. Wu's friends. There were other people on the deck, China people and *yang gweizi*, and one man dressed all in white who didn't seem to be in mourning and held the hand of a little girl with beautiful hair and a lacy white dress. When the little girl saw Mei's face watching her from the round window of the cabin she smiled and waved.

In the morning the sun was out and Mr. Wu's friends brought the sisters onto the promenade deck, one standing guard at each side of the little group, and they watched the flying fishes from Roderick Hardacre's poem. Mei had thought he'd made them up, like the jabberwocky in one of his other verses. These were creatures that could not decide whether they were birds or fish, but were in a hurry to get somewhere, speeding in a pack parallel to the big ship, skipping from swell to swell with their wings held wide.

The swells began to rise then with the wind, and the sun was swallowed in black clouds. The sisters and everyone else on the promenade were herded back below as the deckhands scurried around tying things down on the wildly tilting deck and then breaking waves began to heave over the sides of the ship and slam against their cabin, only Mei standing at the round window still, holding tight to a side rail and then she knew that the steamship was not so big when tossed on an angry sea, that it was a paper toy, it was nothing, and her tiny life inside of it was less than nothing.

Even Mr. Wu's rough friends, one of them the man with the pictures inked on the backs of his hands, were crying when the ship listed to one side and did not right itself and a man from the crew wrestled the cabin door open to shout that the ship was going down, that their only hope was to get into the lifeboats.

Mei tried to remember one of the *sutras* that Ma used to chant but the words would not come, so she only repeated My life is nothing, my life is nothing, my life is nothing as they held a rope and moved along the storm-battered deck, two of her sisters knocked off their tiny lotus feet and swept over the rail into the sea.

My life is nothing.

There were rope ladders to climb down onto the lifeboats, which were being smashed against the hull of the sinking ship and some people were falling and some were jumping and Mei had the quick thought that she saw none of the coolies and wondered if they had been locked in the hold. Hands grabbed her and yanked her into a boat and she saw the little girl a ways down in it but without her father. The men in the long boat pulled their oars to row away from the ship then, the ship that was about to roll on its side, that disappeared from sight whenever they slid into the trough of a swell. The men rowing shouted and cursed at each other, disagreeing on which way the nose of the boat should face and then they were swamped from the side and Mei saw the little girl go over and because her life was nothing Mei rolled into the sea to find her.

Mei did not know how to swim and her clothing dragged at her but she thrashed with her arms and legs and her head stayed up enough to gasp a breath of the air that was full of whipping water and then a wave smashed the little girl against her, Mei ducking under so the girl could ride her back, arms around her neck almost choking her, Mei thrashing with her arms and legs with no thought of salvation only that this little girl should not die alone, nobody should die alone, and then they were smashed against a boat, Mei clawing for it and catching hold of a trailing rope that she pulled on hand over hand, a strong girl, almost a man from wrestling crops out of the stingy ground, and got her shoulders lifted out of the water, the wind roaring full of rain and no sense to keep shouting when she couldn't even hear herself, and when she felt the little girl's arms weaken around her neck Mei clamped her teeth around the little wrist and held on that way, like Ling-Ling used to do when they would play in the ditch beside the *sheng-yuan*'s fields.

The sea was still furious, though, and tried to wrench her away from the boat and smashed her against its side and covered her head with water again and again, but Mei held on, held on with her two hands and her teeth because her life was not nothing, she was the raft this little girl was going to ride to safety.

Then the sea began to tire of its anger and the black clouds skulked away and left the sky purple and gray and ashamed at what it had done. People on the boat saw Mei then and strong arms began to pull at her, but she didn't unclamp her teeth from the little girl's arm till she was lying face-down across the laps of the men on the boat.

The little girl was not alive. She had drowned maybe or had her neck broken, they said, and thought Mei was her mother.

"I am so dreadfully sorry," said an English man.

They spent the night huddled together in the boat, a dozen people with the body of the little girl wrapped in canvas, wet, freezing, the men bailing water out with their hands. When the sun came out of the water again there was another steamship in the distance and the men stood and peeled their shirts off and waved them in the air, shouting.

The people from the lifeboats that did not go under were gathered together in a warehouse on the dock in what they said was Manila, sitting on benches, wrapped in blankets. The officials, *yang gweizi* with black hair and moustaches and a few Monkey People, had not yet reached Mei when Mr. Wu strode in with two men in uniform beside him and walked along the benches looking into the faces of the women who had survived.

"This one is mine," he said when he came to Mei.

Two of the port officials came over then and one of them tried several languages she didn't know till he asked her in very poor South China talk, "Do you know this man?"

"My life is nothing," she answered.

Niles stops at a bakery for a *buñuelo* and a cup of the hot liquid mud they sell as chocolate, watching the last of the chaperoned young ladies hurry to shelter themselves from the blaze of noon. They are flat-nosed, like a lot of the darky gals back home, and rather meager in the hindquarters. The cream of the city's courtesans will become available, he suspects, when the last of the Dons are packed off, but by that time he may be relegated to the hinterlands with nothing but barefooted, betel-chewing peasant maidens for comfort. As he leaves the bakery a funeral procession rolls past, the brass band in the van playing a dirge-like version of *The Star-Spangled Banner* that they have no doubt picked up from the nightly military concerts on the Luneta, the driver of the wagon bearing the coffin dignified in top hat and bare feet, the pair of scrawny Filipino equines supplying the motive power barely coming above his hip. Niles uncovers and stands watching with hat over heart as the mourners' carriages rattle by, trying not to smirk.

Many of the Celestials do without a siesta. Niles passes through the Plaza Moraga and onto the narrower confines of Rosario Street, John Chinaman's bailiwick, and they are out in abundance, hawking, hustling, shouting at each other in their harsh singsong, a teeming yellow horde fairly crawling over each other in their frantic quest for sustenance. Shriveled roots that resemble mummified animals are offered at one stall, whether for food or medicine he does not dare wonder, while another vendor presides over arm-thick live pythons wrapped around poles, their heads bound to the bamboo with wire, and a third sends lung-splitting cries into the air as he waves a pair of flapping chickens like a signal corpsman wig-wagging his flags on a ship's bow. Niles takes a deep breath and attempts to hold it all the way to An's.

A sullen-faced Chinaman slouches with arms folded inside his sleeves next to the door, seeing all and reacting to none, a caution to any highbinders contemplating pillage within. The interior reeks of sandalwood and incense, walls laden with silken tapestries, the narrow space a forest of intricately worked statues and figurines in porcelain and rare stone, banners with Chinese characters in thick black strokes hanging from the ceiling. A small boy wearing only a shirt that barely covers his shame squats near the door, pulling the cord to operate a punkah fan overhead, and An, with his cold abacus eyes and billygoat wisp of chin hair, sits back on a carved throne of zitan wood he claims once cradled the posterior of the Ming Emperor.

"The handsome lieutenant," he observes, his accent that of a British tea merchant. "To what do we owe the honor?"

Niles lifts the satchel to his chest. "Western medicine."

An smiles and rises from the throne, crossing to a beaded curtain, where he barks a few instructions in his native tongue. Niles caught a glimpse through the curtain on his first visit—Oriental gentlemen and at least one well-dressed Spaniard recumbent on divans, languidly sucking at hoses attached to smoke-filled globes. A scene he'd love to capture with a snap, but woefully under-illuminated.

An pulls a lacquered miniature pagoda off a table to make room and Niles lays the satchel on it. The Chinaman is silent as he lifts each of the vials to the light bouncing in from the street, reading the etiquette with a jeweler's loupe.

"These might only be bottles filled with water," he says.

Niles picks up a golden, ruby-encrusted scabbard. "And this may be nothing but paint and paste."

"You distrust me?"

Niles bows slightly, lays the scabbard down. "I think you are a master of your trade. It amounts to the same thing."

An smiles and carefully replaces the last vial. He writes a figure on a slip of paper, hands it to Niles.

"Twice this," says Niles after a glance. "At the least."

An looks over the medicines in their compartments, methodically clacking a pair of ivory mahjong tiles together in his hand. "I believe we can come to terms," he announces finally, "but gold—"

"I can't accept coins," Niles avers. "And neither can my client."

Paper money is distrusted, quite properly, at the moment, and nobody carries more than a few of the heavy Mexican cartwheels in their pockets, preferring to do business with letters of intent, coolies crisscrossing the streets with sacks of gold coins in wheelbarrows to settle the account at the end of each month, pistol-wielding guards trotting alongside them. Niles looks around the shop.

"Surely you have something of equal value but lesser magnitude?"

An strolls past a few of his display cases, clacking the tiles, before selecting an ornately carved dragon about the size of a ferret and holding it up for Niles's inspection. It has a pleasing weight, a deep, translucent emerald color with reddish-orange highlights on its dorsal spines.

"Kingfisher jade from Burma," says the trader proudly. "From the time of Han—when your Jesus Christ was alive."

Niles bristles inwardly at the heathen's mention of the Savior, but allows it to pass. He scratches at the dragon's scales with a fingernail. "This will very likely do," he says.

* * *

The *ama* of the house in Sampaloc was Señora Divinaflores and she did not ask Ling-Ling to demonstrate the use of the water closet. She was a moody woman even when she wasn't drinking, and had a lover who was in the *guardia civil* who did not treat her well. There were only five other girls in the house—Eulalia, Dionisia, Carmen, Ynés, and Keiko, who was a *karayuki-san.* The Filipina girls all came from different villages far from the city and spoke at least three different languages as well as some Spanish, which Señora Divinaflores insisted they talk with the visitors, who were mostly from the army and the government, *"oficiales y caballeros,"* as she described them. These were more likely to sing than the English, and spent more time in front of the mirrors in the rooms, but they were only men. Ling-Ling opened herself up to their words, love words, some of them, and *joder* words, and to the words of their songs and poems and stories. There was one young man who was a junior officer of the *fusileros* named Rodrigo Valenzuela who always asked for Ling-Ling and came twice or three times a week, staying the night if the other visitors weren't too noisy. He made Ling-Ling say his name over and over until she could pronounce it, but was not interested in learning the North China talk. The sisters were allowed outside at this house, a house like many others on the street, and if she woke early Ling-Ling would sit on the sill of the front window, underneath the huge red-and-yellow Spanish flag hung on the outside wall, and watch the coolie gangs hurry by on the Calzada with their loads. They looked like South China men, stripped to the waist, running with knees bent and poles that supported large and heavy objects in their hands or on their shoulders. She sat watching them pass for hours sometimes, but they never seemed to notice her, as intent on their next step as the oxen pulling carts they sometimes drove, whipping their massive flanks, running to their great meaty heads to splash water on them. She wondered if there was a South China girl for every one of them, waiting for her man's contract to be up and for him to brave the ocean crossing with the gold he had won in his hands. To work like beasts and have no one to dream of, no one to suffer your labor for—she did not want to imagine it.

Señora Divinaflores had lost a girl to infection who was using sponges and beat Dionisia with a strap when she discovered the girl was pushing half of a cut lemon inside herself before each *visitante*. Instead, each week she made them all drink a tea made with *hierbas* prepared by her ancient friend

Doña Hermanegilda, who even shy Keiko agreed was a witch. It tasted almost as bad as China medicine, which tastes like the ugly disease you are trying to kill, and Señora Divinaflores watched them swallow every drop.

"We are here to entertain the *caballeros*," she said, "not to produce their bastards."

In the slow afternoons the Filipina girls liked to play cards together and Keiko embroidered handkerchiefs with flying sparrows, always sparrows, and Ling-Ling would sit out on the sill of the window under the Spanish flag, watching the world pass by. Señora Divinaflores allowed this as long as Ling-Ling dressed up in her working silks and wore makeup and oiled her hair so people passing would know hers was a high-toned establishment. The Filipina girls taught Ling-Ling to comb the cocoanut oil through her hair and her favorite part of the day was early afternoon when they would sit and do it for each other. Only Ynés, who was *mestiza* and had curly hair that was almost red, was left out of this pleasure, but she was the one the *caballeros* asked for the most. There were *yang gweizi* women in Manila doing the same as them, said Eulalia, but they could afford to entertain alone in their own houses.

It wasn't long after Ling-Ling arrived in Sampaloc that the *Comisaria de Vigilencia* man came along with Señora Divinaflores's lover, who was called Sargento Robles, to tell them that they had to be registered and inspected. They were brought to the Office of Public Hygiene and their photographs were taken. When the *oficial* asked her name she said Ling-Ling, just Ling-Ling. She was given a card that had writing on it and her photograph in the corner, and the *Comisaria* kept an identical card. Ling-Ling had never had her photograph taken before and did not like to look at the girl in the picture. At least it was only from her shoulders up and did not show her feet.

Twice a week they were supposed to either go to the hospital or let Dr. Apostol look inside them when he came by on his rounds through Sampaloc. It cost a Mexican silver if you went to the hospital or two if you waited for Dr. Apostol, money taken out of your pay by Señora Divinaflores.

They were paid in this house in Sampaloc, though after their food and lodging and *hierbas* and clothing and now medical examinations were taken out very little was left. The Filipina girls bought themselves things, sweets, pretty things, things you could buy on the street or from vendors who came calling under your window and would send your purchase up in a basket. Keiko gave her coins to a Dwarf Bandit man who came by once a week and who, she said, was sending it home to her parents. Ling-Ling kept hers in a wooden jewel box Eulalia had given her and never counted them. Eulalia had given her some gold earrings, too, and an ivory comb and a small icon, carved out of black stone, of a naked man with his hands and feet nailed to crossed planks. Ma had had something like that but one night when Baba was drunk and angry at the *yang gweizi* he threw it deep into the fire and wouldn't let her reach in to pull it out. Sometimes in the mornings when Ling-Ling was lonely and sad Eulalia would come into her bed and hold her. Eulalia always smelled of cinnamon and cocoanut oil and gave Ling-Ling sarsaparilla wine to drink.

"The *hierba* tea only protects you against babies," she said. "This will keep you from being infected."

But even though they always drank a small bottle of it to make their mouths forget the taste of Doña Hermanegilda's brew, one week Dr. Apostol said they had to go with Carmen to the Hospital San Juan de Dios to be cured. They were marched there by Sargento Robles and one of his fellow *guardia* and locked in a ward full of infected girls from all over Manila.

They had to lie on their backs three times a day and pour a cup of something that stung into themselves, holding it in till they could hold it no more and were allowed to run to the bench full of holes and pee it out. There was not much else to do and sometimes there were fights between the girls.

"Stay away from that one," warned Eulalia, pointing to a hard-faced *mestiza* across the ward. "I was in Bilibid with her once. She hides a razor in her hair."

"Why were you in prison?"

Eulalia raised her shoulders. "I argued with the *ama* at the house I was in before I came to Señora Divinaflores and she had me arrested. And even before that, on Thursdays and Sundays they let visitors into the cells, so we would go and entertain the prisoners who had money but no wives."

In the evening the Daughters of Charity came in with their white hats spread out like the wings of flying fish, to pray for them and remind them that they were wicked women. The only one Ling-Ling liked was Sor Merced, who was young and would sit by her with her hands folded inside her robe and ask in Spanish what life was like for North China people. The robe was bluish-gray, the exact color of the cloth that Ma had woven so skillfully when she was still able to work a loom. Sometimes Sor Merced would tell stories about the life of San Vicente and sometimes even stories about herself when she was a girl and had a different name that Ling-Ling never asked her to reveal.

"Your sickness," Sor Merced said, "is God's warning that you are in peril. If you wish to lead a different life, perhaps I can help you."

The Daughters of Charity were supposed to help the Poor and the Sick, and Ling-Ling was both of those. "But Sister," she said shyly, "I am a *pagana*."

Sor Merced looked at her for a long moment. "That does not mean I won't help you," she said.

But they were only at San Juan de Dios for a week when the doctor said they had been cured and something was written on the registration card with her photograph on it, both on hers and the one they kept, and she and Eulalia and Carmen were sent back to Señora Divinaflores.

"I kept your beds for you," the *ama* told them. "You are in debt to me."

Then there was a war between the government and the *insurrectos*, who were all Filipinos from Cavite, said Eulalia, who was from Ilocos, but after the very beginning it didn't come too close to their house in Sampaloc. On the night before they were to be sent to fight, Rodrigo Valenzuela and many of his fellow junior *oficiales de fusileros* came to drink and sing and be entertained. Before he went to the room with Ling-Ling he pulled her out in front of the others.

"We have a wager," he said. "A wager between *caballeros*. They say there is no *china* capable of this, that I am only a braggart and a fabulist."

Ling-Ling stood looking down at her clown-feet, never happy to be the focus of so many eyes.

"Go ahead, *querida*. You know which one."

And then Ling-Ling raised her head and covered her heart with her right hand and recited, trying to say the words with exactly the tone and exactly the rhythm that Rodrigo Valenzuela had taught her.

A mi alma enamorada—

—she cooed—

Una reina oriental parecía
Que esperaba a su mante
Bajo el techo de su camarín—

—the *caballeros* standing with their mouths hung open like carp in a too-small bucket—

—O que, llevada en hombros
La profunda extensión recorría
Triumfante y luminosa
Recostada sobre un palanquín

The *caballeros* smacked their hands together and the girls squealed with laughter and even Señora Divinaflores gave a bitter smile before she swallowed another glass of *jerez*.

Later on, after he had used her and lay curled up with his hand on her stomach like a small boy, Rodrigo Valenzuela began to cry. "I'm going to die," he said. "I'm going to die in this *hoyo de mierda*."

The war was still being fought when Ling-Ling started to feel sick all the time, like she had on her first voyage at sea, and her body started to thicken.

"Drink this," said Doña Hermanegilda when the *ama* called her in to consult. "There is still time."

These *hierbas* made her sweat and have cramps and feel sick in a different way, but her bleeding had stopped and nothing else came out and then it came into Ling-Ling's head that the being inside her was determined to live.

"She's just getting fat and lazy," Señora Divinaflores said to Lao, who came to collect money for Mr. Wu. "I think you should send her on to Singapore."

Ling-Ling still had to entertain, so many new soldiers being sent to Manila from Spain to fight the *insurrectos*, and most did not even notice or care when her stomach began to push out. Dr. Apostol examined her for the disease and said she was at least a month away.

"Doña Hermanegilda is coming today," said the *ama* the next morning. "She can make it come out sooner. The sooner it comes the sooner you will be able to go back to work to support it."

The old lady came and began to lay out her needles and Ling-Ling saw Sargento Robles and one of his *guardia* very pointedly lounging out in front of the house in their lacquered hats, smoking cigarettes and telling jokes and looking as if they would be there till it was finished.

"Hermanegilda is an *abortista*, not a *partera*," said Eulalia, so she and Dionisia and Keiko, who were already awake, made a rope of sheets that they wet and knotted and lowered Ling-Ling down on in the back, waving but not calling as they watched her hurry through the alley to Calle de Alejandro.

The man at the cigar factory next to the church in Binondo said that they did not hire *chinas*, pregnant or not. The *mestizas* who sold cloth from their narrow stalls said they needed no help and even the woman who hired for the *lavandería* by the barracks inside the Walled City said there was no work for her, that she should go back to her own neighborhood north of the river. Ling-Ling knew that if she tried to sell mangoes or milk or *dulces* on the street the *guardia* would soon arrest her, a *vagamunda* with her photograph on a card, not living at the house where she was registered. She spent the first night crouching under the Puente de España, not sleeping, and the next day was told they would not hire her at the *fábricas* in Tondo and Meisic, not hire her even to wash the long tables at night after the *cigarreras* went home. It was late afternoon when Ling-Ling passed through the Parian Gate and talked her way into the hospital, saying she had come for her examination this time to save a dollar. When they forgot her on the waiting bench she left and wandered the long hallways till she saw a sister wearing the cornette, and asked for Sor Merced.

"*Soy puta y pagana, y eso es hijo de quién sabe,*" she said to Sor Merced, touching her swollen belly, "*pero pido su ayuda.*"

"Every child is a child of God," said the sister, and found her a bed to lie in.

It was mostly poor Filipinas in the ward, women who did not care to talk with a *puta china*, but Lan Mei did not mind. The doctor said there was something bad in her blood and that she would have to lie flat on the bed and not get out of it even to pee or make dung. She had never lain in bed so long with nothing to do, nobody to entertain, and relieving herself in the cold pan the nurse slipped under her was difficult at first. After about two weeks Eulalia found her. She had Ling-Ling's money from the jewel box in a sack and the little idol, attached now to a thin golden chain.

"You have to wear this now," she said, hanging the idol around Mei's neck. "But the money—I'm afraid one of these *sinverguenzas* will steal it while you're asleep."

"Sor Merced will keep it for me."

"As long as she doesn't show it to any fucking friars." Eulalia moved close to whisper to her. "They're looking all over for you. The *guardia* and the people from Mr. Wu's Society."

"I am safe here, I think."

Mei's friend embraced her before she left.

"If it's a girl," she said, "think about naming her Eulalia."

"Do you know why they did that to Him?" asked Sor Merced when she came to sit by Mei and saw the icon on the chain.

"He must have disobeyed the authorities," said Mei.

"Yes, He did that," smiled Sor Merced, who had a similar icon, carved in white stone. "And why do we wear this around our necks?"

Mei held her icon close to look at it, turning it this way and that, the man's body twisted, spikes driven through the palms of his hands and both of his feet. "It is a very good warning," she said.

When it was her time, the hurt was worse than anything she had ever felt before, and she thought then that women were given the icon to remind them that some men suffered almost as much as they did. Mei refused to cry out, though, holding on to Sor Merced's plump arm as if it was a lifeline, as if she would drown if she let go. Her life was not nothing, it was the raft on which her child, whoever it was, would be borne above the waves. Sor Merced was shaking the whole time, praying and shaking and trying to keep her face averted from whatever the doctor was doing behind the curtain that hung over Mei's swollen breasts.

It was a boy baby, and she told the *oficial* his name was Lan Bo, son of Lan Mei.

The Mother Superior arranged a job for Mei when she was well enough to walk, wearing rubber gloves and a mask and boiling the metal cups and bowls used to feed the patients infected with malaria or typhus or smallpox or cholera or tuberculosis or diseases the doctors had no names for. With this job came a little room behind the laundry, and, during Mei's work shift, a *niñera*— a sweet-natured woman named Paz who had lost a leg to diabetes, and who stayed with Bo and the other babies of poor mothers who were recuperating.

The war was over for a while but there were still the Sick and the Poor for the sisters to care for, always the Sick and the Poor, and even if he had gorged himself on Paz during the day Bo would take some from Mei's breasts when she came back to the little room, looking up at her with his hand resting on her throat. She slept with him on her chest at night, loving the weight of him, the warmth, and each morning she would bundle him up and carry him out through the gate of pariahs to greet the sun, its first tentative rays like gold thread on the surface of the Pasig.

The war started again after a year or so, thunder of cannons in the bay and then some very bad days inside the walls while they were under siege from the *insurrectos* and then the *americanos* too and suddenly there was no more water to boil the metal in or mop the floors with or to flush away the dung of the patients or even to make a bowl of tea.

"If this keeps up," said Paz, who somehow remained fruitful through it all, "I'll have half the city at my *tetas*."

Mei could no longer bring Bo out through the Parian Gate because people were throwing their dung over the wall and into the moat beside it and because there were snipers outside and every evening she knelt with the Daughters of Charity to pray for Spain's deliverance from this menace, to pray for the poor Filipinos whose souls would surely be lost along with the islands. On the last day, when there was thunder from the bay again and shooting over the walls,

Mei helped the sisters with the wounded men who were carried in, blood staining the clothes that Sor Merced had given her, clothes that had belonged to a poor local woman who had joined the Order and was sent to Mindinao. Mei searched for Rodrigo Valenzuela but didn't see him, only dozens of young soldiers who looked like him. It was dark when the first of the *yanquis* came into the hospital, candles lit because the electricity and the gas had both been cut, an officer with a yellow bush on his lip and four soldiers carrying rifles. None of the doctors and none of the Daughters of Charity spoke any English and the officer had not a word of Spanish or any of the Filipino tongues.

"Goddammit," said the officer, "what's their word for surrender?"

"*Entregar*," said Mei, without thinking. The officer looked at her as if she was a sniper.

"In Chinese?"

"Espanish."

"And who the hell are you?"

"We need water," she said, indicating the wounded soldiers laid out on the cots and on the blood-slippery floors. "Or alla these people die."

When the sisters were told to come back home to Spain their Mother Superior said they could not bring a *china caída* and her bastard child with them, so Sor Merced had the only Filipino doctor, who was staying, tell the Americans to give her a job. Most of the Poor and Sick were gone by then, and the infected girls from all the houses were being sent to San Lázaro with the lepers, and the beds were filled with young American soldiers who were sick with all the same diseases or torn by bullets.

"She is clean and she speaks English," the doctor told them, "and she bears no malice toward your flag."

There are always things to boil in a hospital.

When Hod gets back to the ward Runt is sitting on his bed, oversized pistol and billy club lying beside him.

"Jeez, I feel bad about this," he says, looking Hod over.

"I didn't get it from you."

"But I steered you to those girls."

"And three of them were just fine," says Hod, sitting on the wicker chair beside him.

My Son, if a maiden deny thee

—Runt proclaims—

—And scufflingly bid thee give o'er
Yet lip meets with lip at the lastward—
Get out! She has been there before

At the end of the fight is a tombstone

—Blount chimes in from across the aisle—

With the name of the late deceased
And the epitaph drear, "A fool lies here,
Who tried to hustle the East."

"What's that?" asks Hod.

"What they'll write over your grave if you go back to that parlor," says Blount. "There's not that many a rose that don't have a thorn on it."

"I brought some provisions," says Runyon, pushing his glasses up on his nose and looking around for officers. He shakes a small cotton sack and there are metal sounds. "Sardines, crackers—real crackers, none of that wallboard they give us to march with—gingersnaps and a couple fruit I can't remember what they call them. Fruit is supposed to be good for it, I think."

Blount is staring at him. "They recruit in the grade schools in Minnesota?"

"He's from Pueblo."

"No shit. You know Vern Kessler?"

"I worked for him."

"Selling papers—"

"Writing for the *Evening Press*."

"So did I," Blount grins, "back when it had a little snap. Now I wouldn't line a birdcage with it."

"So where'd you get yours?" Runt nods toward the corporal's crotch.

"A rather overdecorated establishment in Binondo."

"Silk wallpaper with nymphs and satyrs?"

"You've been there."

"We hit em all. Encourage the ladies to be examined, shut them down for a day or two—looking after the physical and spiritual welfare of our fighting men."

"So you know where the best—"

"The best," says Runyon, "is Nellie White's on First Street, Pueblo Colorado."

"The playground of my misspent youth," smiles Blount. "But here?"

"I have ceased to be involved with the trade girls, having given my heart to Anastacia Bailerino."

"A lady of some quality, no doubt."

"Raven hair, skin like coffee and cream—"

"No itching or pain on urination yet?"

Runyon narrows his eyes at Corporal Blount. "If you weren't a fellow newspaperman I'd demand satisfaction."

Hod slips tins of sardines under his pillow. "What's the news from the world, Alfie? When are we going home?"

Runt gives him an exasperated look. "You're pulling my leg."

"What—?"

"McKinley says we're holding on to the joint."

Hod feels a twinge in his testicles. If you let it go too far, the doc says, your testicles get inflamed. "Manila?"

"The whole shebang. They posted the Proclamation this morning. The googoos aren't too thrilled."

"How can he do that?"

Runt grins. "God told him to. 'Benevolent Assimilation,' he calls it. He says he got down on his knees and petitioned the Lord for guidance—"

"It would be easier," Blount interrupts, "for a camel to pass through my urinary meatus than for a Republican to enter the Kingdom of Heaven."

"A Bryan man."

"Me too," says Hod. "As far as voting goes. Free Silver!"

"Free Silver Nitrate!" echoes Blount. "Venereals of the world unite!"

"They got the volunteers putting out brushfires all over the islands, chasing after Aguinaldo, challenging every *amigo* they meet on the road," says Runyon. "The order is 'shoot on suspicion.'"

"Suspicion of what?"

Runt shrugs. "Suspicion of not assimilating benevolently." He stands to pose with his hand over his heart—

Ride with an idle whip, ride with an unused heel

—he recites—

—But once in a way there will come a day
When the colt must be made to feel
The lash that falls and the curb that galls
And the sting of the rowelled steel!

An orderly comes around then with the rolling table and Hod and Blount drink their hourly glass of water.

"Sometimes they put a little sandalwood oil in it," Hod tells his visitor. "Improve the taste."

"Manila water, *Christ*," says Runt. "They trying to kill you people?"

The *convento* is just a bit farther east along the Pasig, attached to one of the less ostentatious of the Catholic churches Niles has seen here. A barefoot boy leads Niles past the sacristy and up the polished wood stairs to the living quarters. Brother León is playing billiards.

"A superior pastime for developing the mind," says the Franciscan, laying his stick on the table. He is tall, with a narrow, hawklike face, only a trace of the Spaniard in his diction. "It requires steadiness, concentration, and the ability to foresee the consequences of one's actions."

"I prefer cards." Niles lifts the satchel onto a table that has tiny wells to hold gaming chips at each station. The friar steps over to watch as he opens it. On closer inspection, the cloth of his brown robe is not so rough as Niles imagined. Brother León's face registers disappointment as he sees the medicines in the wooden box.

"I cannot do anything with these," he says.

"Merely to acquaint you with my end of the transaction," says Niles. "You are familiar with An Chao's emporium?"

"Of course."

"He has a dragon. Emerald green with red-tipped scales—"

"I know it." The Franciscan's eyes narrow shrewdly. "If I have learned one thing in this dark corner of Our Lord's domain," he says, "it is the unwavering value of precious stones."

Niles wonders which of the three knots on the friar's rope belt designates poverty. "And you would accept it as recompense for a sizable parcel of your land?" he inquires.

Brother León places the lid back on the wooden box. "You have me at a great disadvantage."

The religious corporations have petitioned the military authority to return the lands and privileges usurped by the native filibusters, but no promises have been made, and given the average American's distrust of papists, none are likely to be forthcoming. All over the city Spaniards are offering for a song that which they cannot carry with them, and the holy men are no exception.

"We adjust to circumstances," says Niles, smiling politely. There is a portrait of the order's namesake in his rough garb hung on the wall, a sparrow perched on one shoulder, a wolf curled peacefully at his feet, a lamb, unafraid of the predator, tranquil under his open hand. "Where exactly—?"

"Pampanga. North of here, not far from the rail." Brother León crosses to a rolltop desk and extracts a folio of papers. "Your troops have yet to occupy this area, but given your superior force and the volatility of the situation, it is inevitable." He lays the folio on the billiard table in front of Niles.

"And if Mr. McKinley loses heart and chooses to leave these fair isles to their natives?"

The friar smiles now, hawklike. "We adjust to circumstances." He hands Niles a pair of deeds. "Much of the land still belongs to the order, of course, but the properties described here are in my brother's name."

"Your brother—"

"Who does not exist." León wiggles his fingers. "His signature is amazingly similar to my own."

Niles has already considered using Harry's name for some of his acquisitions. "Pampanga is mountains, if I'm not mistaken."

"With a broad plain at their base. Hemp, sugar cane, rice, mangoes—"

"My people were in tobacco before the War," says Niles. The first deed is for 150 acres situated near the city of San Fernando. "We understand how to operate a plantation."

An underdeveloped land, a soon-to-be advantageous labor situation—a man could do quite well for himself.

"I'll need to have these gone over," he informs the friar.

"Naturally."

The art of commerce, he muses, lies in recognizing desires and seizing opportunities. There are countless citizens who need medicine and have been denied their usual access. There are the suddenly deposed, such as Brother León, who wish to recover some value from what they will be forced to leave behind. There are those like An Chao and Niles, who assure that the flow of goods and services continues despite the uncertainties of the present situation.

And suddenly, there is a Filipino in the room.

Well-dressed, nose in the air, nervously tapping his walking stick against the floor as he glares at Brother León. A *mestizo*, the term they apply to their half-breeds, from the look of him.

"Ah, Ramiro—"

The young man says something in Spanish to the friar. Niles closes the satchel and lifts it off the table. If he hurries his lawyer friend at the Hongkong and Shanghai Bank will be able to verify the deeds during his tiffin and set the affair into motion.

"This is Ramiro, my *sacristán*," says Brother León. "I have known him since I arrived from Gibraltar, since the day of his First Communion."

Niles recognizes the young man, who is glaring at him now with undisguised resentment, as one of the sepia dandies he forced off the sidewalk on the Escolta.

"He is also, when we come to that moment, our notary."

Niles offers the sullen googoo an ironic bow. "How very convenient."

When Mei comes down from the wards at night Bo is waiting, squirming to be out of Paz's arms and into hers, and if the sky is clear she takes him out away from the walls and she points to the stars and tells him stories about them. At first she wondered if they should be Chinese stories about the Three Enclosures or the *yang gweizi* stories about hunters and flying horses that Roderick Hardacre told her, but decided that nobody knows what takes place in the heavens, or how the world works, that even the most powerful are only guessing at how one thing is connected to another, pointing at dots in the distant sky and making up stories about them.

"Do you see those over there?" says Mei, pointing, talking the talk of the North China people to her little boy who starts to shake with happiness whenever he sees her, who calls her Ma and hugs his arms around her neck so tight it almost chokes her. "See those ones that make the head, and then those three, that are the tail? That is called Ling-Ling, the Brave Dog, who once saved a little girl from a wolf, and tried to save another from drowning—"

ADVANCE OF THE
KANSAS VOLUNTEERS

All yesterday they were at it with shovels, the boys digging and Jubal hauling it off in a wagon. He ask why don't they just pile it up in front like the
real soldiers do but Mr. Charles who is Mr. Harry's boss says it would get in
the way of the volunteers and spoil the shot. So they dig it deeper and carry
the dirt away, and Jubal can just see over the top when he stands tall.

The volunteers, which is really New Jersey National Guards, are having
a time over in the pines, laughing and calling out how maybe they put real
bullets in their rifles. The one being Colonel Funston is up on his ride, a big
bay Morgan horse that got its ears up for what happen next. The white boys
can play the fool cause the camera pointed elsewhere, looking right down
the line of all the colored being Filipinos. Jubal has put himself as far away
from it as he can get, worried lest he mess up somehow and get Mr. Harry
in trouble. There is no snow left on the ground but it is cold, colder than it
ever get in Wilmington and he bets the Philippines either. They only got on
white pants and white shirts but just now Mr. Charles tell them to take their
hats off and leave them out of sight. Royal is headed over there right now,
where the real Filipinos stay, and if this is what they look like, just colored
men without hats, it's good they all in white and he'll be wearing blue.

"Remember it's two shots and then we scatter," says Zeke, who has been
a Filipino before and act like he's the sergeant here. The National Guard who
is being Colonel Funston has run them through the drill over and over—how
to load and shoot, load and shoot, not to point at anybody too close. He show

them how it's only paper inside the cartridges and won't hurt you at a distance. Jubal has it all in his head and wishes they would start and get it over. Got him so riled up waiting in the ditch for them to charge and it's only for the camera, you wonder how can Royal abide the real thing. He hears Hooker nickering, tied back by the camera wagon and wondering where Jubal is. She maybe fuss some when the shooting starts, but her making noise don't matter none.

Mr. Harry come out in front of the ditch and lean on his stick to talk to them.

"The key principle to keep in mind," he says, "is not to look at the camera. There is the enemy before you—" he points with his stick, "—and there is your route of escape. Remember that you have been instructed by your officers to hold this position at all costs and should not abandon it lightly. And—if you have been selected to die—please do so before the volunteers enter the trench."

Zeke raises his arm. Zeke got himself closest to the camera, nothing between him and it.

"Suh?"

"Yes, Zeke."

"Them of us that got to run, how far we spose to go?"

Mr. Harry points past them with his stick. "You see the chestnut back there? Run behind that and then take up your firing position again." He smiles. "Consider those trees your second line of defense."

He tells them to check one more time they got a round in the chamber and one in their back pocket, then limps out of the way. Mr. Harry takes care of the camera but doesn't turn the handle.

Jubal looks over at the volunteers again, searching out which one he will aim at. If he really do it like he got to kill the man before the man kill him maybe it will take some of the nerves away. The one that carry the flag is the easiest to spot, but that don't seem right, shooting the flag, so he picks out the man next to him. You dead, Mister Volunteer. Mr. Charles calls are they ready and it gets real quiet, Colonel Funston's ride side-stepping some like it be nervous too, and then Jubal hears the camera winding and Mr. Charles calls "Charge! Fire!"

The white men come ahead, hooping and hollering as they run and Jubal gets a good one off, dead center on the man but then there is so much smoke from their rifles shooting you can't see a thing. He digs the second round out, trying to stay calm, and loads it up. He is looking for a body through the smoke when Ernest and Tip fall beside him and he remembers he's been tapped to die. He fires high into the smoke and tosses the rifle clear before dropping straight down holding his chest like he always done when Royal pretend to shoot him when they were boys playing blues and grays. The volunteers, not so many as there are Filipinos, stumble down the front of the ditch and each fires once at the men running away before they chase after. The smoke hangs over and then there is Colonel Funston on the Morgan prancing along the front of the ditch and then down into it, coming way too close and before he can think Jubal has jumped up and dove away from the hooves.

If he was dead his eyes should have been closed and he just get trompled, but it is too late now, the camera has seen him and remembered it. So now maybe he is a Filipino been wounded a little or faking and when Funston trots back at him with his pistol drawn he hops up and lights out for the trees. He runs a few feet and there is the pistol shot but he is not hit and he keeps running till he comes to where everybody has stopped around the chestnut tree and one of the volunteers points a rifle at him.

"Hands up, boy," says the volunteer. "You been nabbed by Uncle Sam."

They all laugh, the volunteers and the Filipinos, and then Mr. James shouts for them to come back. He is smiling and Mr. Harry is pulling the roll out of the camera, so maybe he didn't mess up too bad.

"Excellent, gentlemen. Just excellent," says Mr. James. "Stirring. And you," he points to Jubal, "the terrified insurrectionist—that was *inspired*."

This must mean good because Mr. Harry is taking the camera off the sticks and the one who does the cranking is writing something on a pad of paper, both of them smiling too.

"Now if our Filipinos will don their hats and reclaim their rifles, we will move on to the *Capture of Trenches at Candaba*." He points up to the one playing Funston. "Captain Ditmar, be advised that in this film you will be required to fall from your mount. Quickly, gentlemen!"

Jubal climbs into the ditch to find his rifle. His heart is still racing. This time, if he is wounded, maybe he'll remember to drag a leg.

OBSTETRICS

He hopes it was only the stairs. Jessie breaking her water halfway to the fourth and calling in a panic until he and Yolanda could carry her up, and now writhing on the bed with a blood-tinged mucous plug on the floor. *Placenta previa* is the worst of the catalysts he can think of, the hemorrhaging so likely to carry the mother away during or after the delivery, but there is also *eclampsia* and *endometritis* and *hydramnios*—so many possibilities for preterm induction, and obstetrics never his strongest suit, if only for the lack of opportunity to practice. Only the wealthiest of colored women in Wilmington choose to engage a physician rather than one of the city's half-dozen midwives, even in emergency situations.

The idea of attending his own daughter's first parturition has never, until this moment, occurred to him.

Dr. Lunceford forces himself to concentrate on his preparations. Yolanda is trembling, cold as always, her own harrowing experiences no doubt weighing on her thoughts. And Jessie, his little Jessie, lies back on the pillows breathing deeply and studying his face for clues.

"It's coming, isn't it? It's coming now."

The arithmetic is not difficult. The one incident she confessed to, on the night of Junior's final visit, then counting forward—it is twenty-eight weeks.

"We shall see," he says to his daughter. "The vital thing is for you to remain as calm as possible while I see what we have here."

"What can I do?" Yolanda asks, standing as far back as the room allows, terrified. She has never observed him in practice, Yolanda, has demurred even when close friends have asked her to be present at their own birthings.

"I need you to clean the stove, as thoroughly as possible."

"The stove?"

"Just the warming compartment, the larger one." He looks deeply into her eyes. "Please."

It is an unlikely possibility, but he needs to spare her the sight of what may come next. Yolanda crosses quickly to Jessie, bends to embrace her and kiss her on both cheeks.

"You're all right now, baby," she says. "Your father knows what to do." And then hurries into the kitchen.

It is near freezing in the room, Dr. Lunceford in his overcoat and Jessie with her top half weighed down under all of their blankets, little puffs of condensation from her mouth as she breathes irregularly now, the landlord untraceable whenever the radiators fail in the building. Jessie's eyes are bulging slightly as she watches him. Blood pressure elevated. In Wilmington, even with the home births, there would be a curtain or a kind of tent structure blocking the woman's view of his actions and his view of her face. Better to concentrate on the organs involved in the procedure and nothing else. But there is no time for that now, and he seats himself at the bottom of the bed to stare into the vagina of his only daughter, who he has not seen naked since she was four years old.

It helps that there is no footboard. Jessie is frightened, perspiring, the pains having come twice, some five minutes apart. She is barely dilated.

That was the problem for Yolanda the second time, with Jessie and what would have been her sister. Dr. Tinsley reaching for the dilator, eyes apologetic as he glanced to Dr. Lunceford, allowed in the room as a professional courtesy. Many physicians preferred to perform their *accouchements forcés* digitally, but at the Freedman's Hospital they had the latest of instruments. It was shiny, polished steel, he remembers, four blades with a screw mechanism at the top. He remembers the tearing, remembers his wife's screams, the chloroform ineffective in the dosage they regarded as safe, remembers the sister, never named, coming out first and then Jessie, identical except for her color, her faintest bloom of life.

"I want to hold them both," Yolanda said, coming up from the morphine when her condition was stable, when the bleeding had finally been halted. "I must hold them."

"The one has been buried," he had to tell her. "Two days ago."

There are so many things that can go wrong. A girl in her teens, first delivery, preterm—he tries not to imagine any of them. Let it present itself, he thinks, and I will choose whatever remedy is available.

"It hurts, Daddy," Jessie says, tears streaming down her cheeks. "It hurts so much."

She hasn't called him Daddy for years. It is what common girls, white and colored, call their fathers, and Jessie has not been raised to be a common girl.

"I can't give you anything yet, Jessie. It would interfere with what you've got to do."

There is ether in hospitals, and even without his license he could obtain chloroform tablets and an inhaler, but he is convinced that as commonly employed such anesthetics are unsafe for both mother and fetus. The Twilight Sleep advocates to the contrary, a comatose mother is unlikely to experience normal contractions.

Jessie arches her body, clenching her fists and crying out. Yolanda appears in the doorway.

"Go," says Dr. Lunceford, and she returns to her scouring.

He shifts the oil lamp closer and pushes the labia apart with his fingers. He has only an ancient Sims speculum in his bag that at the moment seems a device of torture rather than diagnostics. She is beginning to open.

"I want you to breathe somewhat rapidly in between the cramps," he tells Jessie. "Rapidly but not deeply. If you start to get dizzy, slow your breathing down."

"It's coming, isn't it?"

He doesn't want to get her hopes up, not at her age, not when it is this early. His first delivery, the one that soured him on obstetrics, was a girl about Jessie's age. She was long overdue, her mother said, but had had no contractions and now was sick with a fever.

The baby was very large and beginning to decompose. He insisted on the curtain that time, insisted that the mother and the aunt and the girl's best friend stay on the other side of it to comfort her while he worked. There was enough swelling that neither the blunthook nor the cephalotribe were of any use, no way to insert them without further damaging the vagina. He was forced to use the trephine perforator, asking the women to sing a hymn to distract from the sound of it, and then hook in and yank the tiny body out with a crochet. At least it came out in one piece.

So many possibilities, so many pitfalls.

"You're going to have to help me," Dr. Lunceford says to his daughter.

"Do you think you can do that? You have to be very brave."

"I'm only a girl," says Jessie in a very small voice.

"You have been married, you have been widowed, you have been exiled." It is the first time he has ever said the word aloud. "You only have to do what all women do."

"I'm not ready."

"I'm sorry. It won't wait."

They speak very little these days. Yolanda pleads with him to forgive Jessie and he maintains that their acceptance of her, living with her and what they all know to be true of her condition, is forgiveness enough.

This time she cries out louder, and Dr. Lunceford has a momentary twinge of concern for their neighbors on the fifth floor. Their neighbors who engage in screaming matches twice a week.

A tiny knob of skull is pushing through now.

"Aaron?" calls Yolanda from the kitchen.

"Is it clean?"

"As clean as I can make it."

"Take some of my handwash, the antiseptic," he calls, "and wipe the inside with it."

Jessie is huffing now, balling handfuls of the bedsheet in her fists, pushing down hard enough with her feet that her buttocks raise off the bed from time to time.

"It shouldn't be coming now, should it?" she says to him when she can catch her breath. "I'm not ready."

"We won't know anything till it reveals itself," he says. It is not true. He knows it will be undersized, discolored, the digestive tract not finished, the lungs prone to atelectasis, susceptible to infection—if it is viable at all. "You just have to concentrate on helping it come out. When the next cramp happens I want you to try to breathe in and make your chest and stomach rise up. You've been clamping down."

"It hurts so much."

"The pain will be there no matter what you do, Jessie. But if you lift up with your stomach it will allow the baby to come out."

He is careful to call it a baby and not a fetus. Dr. Osler once presented a lecture that concerned nothing but Terminology and the Patient—when the lay terms should be employed, when a bit of scientific Latin was not amiss to either obscure a harsh reality or impress a skeptic. But in his mind this is no baby.

The membrane on the cervix is appropriately thin, and it has opened to nearly five centimeters. Dr. Lunceford's pitiful collection of instruments, just sterilized, is laid out beside him on a clean towel. He will have to cut and sew, there is no way to avoid it, with the attendant risk of sepsis. He wonders what the midwives do, women with their herbs and potions and folklore. That so many of their charges, mother and child, survive, is either a testament to their common sense or to the inherent hardiness of the species. That something so vital to our existence should require the ministration of others—

"Ah, ah, ah, ah!" cries Jessie.

"Lift your stomach—"

"*Do* something! *Give* me something!" she shouts at him, red-faced, furious in her agony.

Dr. Lunceford flushes as he stifles his first response. This is the consequence, he thinks, of her own actions. And then anger, at his own arrogance, at Nature itself for contriving to allow his sweet little girl to hurt like this.

"When we get it out," he says to her soothingly. "We just need to get it out and then I can give you something."

The veins on Jessie's temples stand out as she strains, crying out each time she exhales, but he sees that she is trying, chest and stomach pushed up spastically with each convulsion.

"That's my girl," he says. "That's my Jessie."

"Aaron?" calls Yolanda from the kitchen. Her voice wavers, he can hear that she is crying.

"Feed the firebox," he says. "But keep the door to the warming compartment open."

She had nightmares, Yolanda, for years after the birth, waking in a sweat and then insisting on going into the children's rooms to be sure they were both still breathing.

"Daddy!" Jessie calls. "I feel it moving!"

Another contraction grips her, her little face contorted with pain, Dr. Lunceford holding tightly to her ankles to keep her on the bed and it is fully crowned now, purplish with fluid-slimed hair on top of it. Not breech, thinks Dr. Lunceford thankfully. Not transverse.

Jessie slumps back into the mattress, wheezing for breath, and he quickly injects cocaine solution into the perineum. This late in the procedure there is little chance of it passing into the fetus. He lifts the scalpel, stretching the cervix away from the cranium with his other hand, counting. He wants to give the drug time to dull the nerves, but to cut before the next contraction. Just a little nick, enough so it won't tear.

"We're halfway there, Jessie. A little sting now—"

He slices, less than an inch, and immediately she spasms and there is blood and amniotic fluid and the nose and mouth are pushed out, a vertex presentation, and he reaches under and quickly clears its tiny mouth with his little finger.

"A couple more, Jessie," he urges. "Push from your diaphragm. Remember your singing lessons."

He misses her playing. He never thought too much of it in Wilmington, something the women liked to occupy themselves with and Jessie apparently a prodigy, but here, in these dingy rented rooms, he feels its absence. He hears Yolanda in the doorway again.

"The shoebox," he says.

"That I keep my jewelry in?"

"Empty it out and line it with cotton batting. There's some in my bag."

He hears her move away. His eye falls on the forceps lying beside the bloodied scalpel. No, he thinks. We're past that. Jessie starts to growl, the growl raising in pitch till she is shouting, one long agonized howl and she is pushing from her diaphragm as he asked and more of it is revealed and he is able to hook his index finger in and get a purchase on something, perhaps beneath an arm, and when Jessie goes slack this time she is weeping, her shoulders shaking and her head rolling from side to side on the pillows.

"I can't, Daddy. I can't anymore."

"You would be surprised," he says, "at how strong, at how *will*ful my daughter Jessie is. Come on now—one more big push when it comes—"

Her scream this time is not the noise a girl makes. She strains and contorts her face and mucous blows out of her nose and Dr. Lunceford pulls gently and it is free, tiny thing and fluid and blood and black meconium and the cord exactly where you want it to be, the cord purple and red and blue and with the faintest of vibrations, a pulse, when he squeezes it with his fingers.

"Yolanda!" he calls. "I need you now!"

She is beside him, holding the shoebox, as he turns the tiny, wrinkled thing in his hand to rub its arms and legs. The color begins to change and it makes something like a hiccup.

"Oh my," says Yolanda. "Oh my."

"It's still in me, Daddy," says Jessie, her hot breath turning to steam in the freezing room. "I can feel it."

"That's the placenta," he tells her. "Just push with the cramp and it will come out."

He holds his rubber-gloved hand out toward Yolanda. "Alcohol."

She splashes the alcohol over his fingers and when they are relatively clean of effluvia he pulls down on the lower eyelids, black bead of a pupil swimming, and squeezes a drop of silver-nitrate solution into each. More than a precaution, considering the father.

"Can I take it?" Yolanda asks.

"Not yet. You see those pieces of string?"

"Yes."

"Clean your hands with the alcohol. The length of your finger from the body—tie the cord off there. Don't pull tight. Then another knot an inch farther."

Jessie's cry is exhausted as she stiffens and pushes again. The placenta presents itself in a drooling of fluid.

"Jessie, I'm here, baby," Yolanda calls, concentrating on her tying. "Everything is just fine."

"Is it alive?"

Yolanda flicks her eyes up to his. "We're going to do our best," he says. "It's so early—"

"It's a girlchild," says Yolanda. "I think."

The body is limp in his hand, veins showing through in the places where its skin is unwrinkled, its abdomen extended, extremities a purplish blue, its respiration shallow. The few little sounds he can induce from it are low and weak. There is the tiniest spark of life glowing within.

"What do we need to create and maintain a fire?" Dr. Osler used to say. "Heat, oxygen, and fuel. An infant is no different."

Dr. Lunceford waits for the pulse to end, then slices the umbilical between the two knots his wife has tied. "Tear the short side of the box down so it's open at the end—that's it—" He folds a gauze pad over the cord end and fixes it with a clamp. "Now let's put it in the cotton—"

"I want to hold her," calls Jessie.

"You can't, baby, not yet." Yolanda cradles the creature in her two hands and holds it close. "But look—"

Jessie looks horrified at first, then tears pour from her eyes and steam on her cheeks. "It isn't finished."

"It's just *little*, that's all. We'll have to take special care."

Jessie stiffens involuntarily, the rest of the placenta sliding to where Dr.

Lunceford can pull it out. "Get it in the cotton," he says, impatient, "and into that warming compartment."

Yolanda lays the creature gently into the shoebox, pushing the cotton tight around its tiny listless body, and hurries from the room. The Sloane Maternity Hospital has at least one Tarnier couveuse, and if there is room will place infants from the charity ward inside. But transporting it in this cold—

"You can relax now," he says to Jessie. "Close your eyes, breathe slowly and deeply."

He drops the placenta onto the newspaper spread on the floor, quickly sponges her as clean as possible with the alcohol and then begins to suture the perineum, the cocaine obviously fully in effect as Jessie seems not to notice. She is looking over his shoulder to the kitchen.

"I'm going to call her Minnie."

Dr. Lunceford sighs. It is hard to make the stitches close enough with only the meager lamplight to see by. "Minnie is a nickname, not a name," he says. Her own is Jessamyne Root Lunceford, Root being his mother's maternal surname, but Junior never called her anything but Jessie.

"Minerva," she says, shifting her eyes to him. "Minerva is Minnie."

It is the name of the most popular midwife in Wilmington. The name of the woman who, if by some miracle the creature in the oven survives, will be its other grandmother. He refuses to be provoked.

"Plenty of time to think about names. Try putting your legs down."

It costs her some pain, and he steps to the head of the bed to help pull her into a more comfortable position. She takes hold of his hand.

"I'm sorry, Daddy," she says.

"We don't have to continue to—"

"I mean sorry that you had to do this."

Her eyes look clear, her color good. He pulls the blankets back up over her shoulders. "I consider it a privilege."

She gives him a little smile then and asks that he send her mother in. It means she wants to be alone with her. He steps carefully over the mess on the floor. It looks like there has been a slaughter.

"The bread won't rise if you keep the door open," Yolanda says. "It keeps bothering me."

"In an hour, if—in an *hour*, we'll heat some mineral oil and then clean it off. I'll put a cup of water in there, keep the air moist. And I'll have to buy a breast pump—" as he says it he is not certain he has enough money, "—and see what Jessie can provide. Until then we'll see if it will take some sugar water from the eye dropper—"

Yolanda stands up abruptly. "She's not going to die," she states, and goes to sit with Jessie.

He can see his own breath by the light of the oil lamp. The wind is howling outside, a storm, and he imagines it has been going on for some time without him noticing. His wife's jewelry has been dumped out on the peeling kitchen table, a jumble of the rings and necklaces the pawnshop owner would not accept. We are not helpless, he thinks, sitting alone in the kitchen. With Yolanda's will and his experience, his training—we are destitute, but not helpless. Dr. Lunceford scoots the chair closer to the coal stove and brings his face close to look into the warming compartment at it, at her, wrinkled barely breathing handful of a creature out where she has no business being yet, and he is suddenly filled with a rush of something that is neither rage nor relief nor despair.

It is defiance. They have taken everything else, money, home, pride, but they will not take her. They will not take her.

Little Minnie.

WHITE HOUSE

He sits on a wooden chair in a hallway lined with other petitioners on wooden chairs, backs to the wall, hats in their laps, all turning to look whenever somebody comes out from the room. Directed by the secretary, Mr. Cortelyou, he has made his way from the central hall past the stairway landing to the east sitting hall, shifting from chair to chair closer to the desired audience, warmed now by the mid-morning sunlight spilling through the enormous fanlight window at the end of the corridor, sitting directly across from the President's study. He is still discomfited by the aspect of the residence—not shabby, exactly, but worn in a rather neglectful way. The building, beyond the magnificent Tiffany-glass doors of the vestibule, suggests a once-resplendent hotel long past its glory days more than the symbolic centerpiece of a nation's government. There are cracks in the ceiling, carpets faded past respectable use, a curious smell. The bottom floor is crowded with tourists and curiosity seekers, the stairs lively with clerks and household retainers carrying the implements of their station. He expected something more august, more Olympian.

The interview has been difficult enough to obtain. George White, now the last of his race in the House, imposing on a number of his prominently placed sympathizers, keeping the particulars vague enough to escape alarm, hinting at political capital to be earned in the South. It is a surprise to be here at all.

"I have chosen not to run again," White explained to him, "because I value my own neck, and because I value the safety of my constituents. Even great armies retreat when the vagaries of the day presage a disaster."

"But we outnumber them in your district."

White smiled then. "The Black Second is that in name only. Our vote was our only weapon, our only tool. It has been taken from our hands."

A trio of men, beefy and laughing, step out from the study. Mr. Cortelyou appears at his side, pushing his spectacles back onto the bridge of his nose and speaking softly in his courteous manner.

"He'll see you now."

He is led, surprisingly, not to the study but to the office beside it.

"Mr. Lincoln used this room as his office," says Cortelyou, opening the door. "The Cabinet have their meetings here now."

The room is empty. The secretary indicates a chair at the end of a long table of polished dark wood. "If you'll have a seat, he'll be right in."

To his right there is a huge globe mounted on a heavy metal floor stand, a glass-fronted case, a cherrywood rolltop desk. The walls hold a dozen smallish portraits in oil, many of them presidents. There is a brass chandelier overhead that has been converted to hold electric lights. The long table is divided by a dozen leather-bound books propped in a row in the middle. A large bouquet of fresh flowers sits just in front of his seat. He looks at the other chairs, imagining them occupied by the Secretaries of Navy and War, by Hay, Alger, Long, Griggs, and the feeling again percolates through him that he should not be here, followed by the smallest twinge of hope, of exhilaration that the quest for justice has penetrated so close to its duly elected guardians.

He nearly jumps to his feet as the President enters from the door to his study.

McKinley is shorter than he had imagined, though he is a fleshy, sturdy-looking man, clean-shaven, with the large head and noble profile of the newspaper illustrations. He holds out his hand.

"A pleasure to meet you."

They shake hands. "Thank you for seeing me."

The President sits in a wooden swivel armchair at the far end of the long table, surrounded by inkstand and pens, a wooden stationery holder, wearing a vague smile on his face.

"And how may I help you, Mr. Manly?"

He has rehearsed this over and over, Carrie serving as coach and audience, searching for the proper balance between his respect for the personage and his outrage over the offense.

"I imagine you have been informed of the events in Wilmington over the past election—"

The vague smile does not change. The President's eyes, expressionless, seem empty of thought, of emotion—

"—voters intimidated, killings and expulsions, my own press burned—"

"You are a newspaper man."

If he has in fact heard of the riot, the President is an excellent actor.

"I was, until my property was destroyed and my life threatened."

"This sounds like an obvious legal complaint."

"A futile one, I'm afraid, Mr. President, in the courts of North Carolina."

"North Carolina."

The President says the words as if they are the key to a room he does not wish to enter.

"I believe the outrages fall under the purview of the federal government. Constitutional rights have been violated, property illegally seized—"

"This was on Election Day?"

"On the following day. An armed mob, led by members of the political faction that has since gained power, fired indiscriminately into several neighborhoods, killing an untold number of citizens. Men were rounded up and forced to leave their homes and families without legal proceedings or even complaints, women and children forced to cower in the woods overnight during a rainstorm—"

A small frown creases the President's forehead. The interview has veered into territory he has not been prepared for. "You saw these things with your own eyes?"

"Not personally, no—"

"Ah—"

"I was forced to flee just before the—"

"I see—" Losing him, fleshy hands on the arms of his swivel chair now, ready to rise, to bequeath him to the appropriate supernumerary—

"I only escaped because my skin is so light."

Confusion on the President's face.

"But I have the testimony of dozens of eye-witnesses, many who have suffered more than I. This was mob rule, highly organized and specifically targeted at bringing the Democrats, despite their numerical disadvantage on the voter rolls, back into power in Wilmington. As my people have been among your greatest supporters in the past, they naturally hope that you, as a last resort, could offer some sort of just response to this—"

"You're a negro?"

He asked no subterfuge of Congressman White in setting up the audience, and assumed none had been necessary.

"Of course."

The President flushes a deep pink, like a gulf shrimp suddenly boiled. His fingers tighten on the arms of the swivel chair.

"You'll have to leave."

He is angry, and what is worse, what is more disappointing, he is afraid. This white man at the far end of the long, polished table, is visibly shaking.

"I am an American citizen," says Alex Manly, "a registered Republican, and, until recently, the editor of a—"

"You must leave this room!"

The voice much louder now, though not firm. On the other side of the door, leaning against the wall reading newspapers, were a pair of men who Manly had taken for Pinkertons, involved somehow with the President's security. He stands slowly, hands spread slightly in a placating gesture.

"Thank you for seeing me."

The President does not answer.

Mr. Cortelyou frowns at him as he steps out, and one of the security men flicks his eyes over the newspaper, suspicious. The floor beams seem to shift under his feet, he feels unsteady. The petitioners, nearly in unison, move up a seat. He passes an older colored man mopping the stairway on the way down.

"We will now enter the Public Audience Room, often referred to as the Banquet Room or East Room," says the young man leading a dozen visitors along the Cross Hall past the foot of the stairs. "Mourners gathered here to view President Lincoln's body after his assassination, and it has provided the setting for many a gala affair. This room, more than any other in the residence, belongs to you."

Manly exits through the North Portico, perspiring now under his suit as he hurries past soldiers rigid on either side of the doorway, their eyes fixed on an invisible locus. He does not look back.

DREAM BOOK

NOTICE
TO RESIDENTS OF ILLINOIS ONLY
*If you live in any other State
you do not have to send the "Sample Letter."*

It seems Illinois is worried about minors buying firearms through the mail. But if you write the catalogue people a letter saying you are twenty-one or older, they will send whatever you order. It makes the Assassin wonder. Is there some way they can check to be sure? Do they bother? His name is on lists, he has had to change it more than once.

But outside of this one state, they make it so easy—

REVOLVERS
The following quotations do not include cartridges.

42033   Eclipse vest pocket single-shot pistol,
Nickel-plated, wood stock, 2½ inch
Barrel; weight 5 ounces; for BB and
conical caps and .22 caliber short
cartridge, safe and reliable, barrel
swings to the right to load.

Each............................... $0.50
By mail, extra......................... .05

So easy to conceal, but only that one shot. You have to be close, close enough to put it to the temple. To look the man in the eye.

BIG BARGAINS, AMERICAN BULL DOG REVOLVERS

This line of revolvers are strictly first-class in every respect. The quality of workmanship and material is best; all have rifled barrels and are good shooters. All 5 shot. These are not toys but good big guns. We can sell them at these prices because we buy them 5,000 at a time. American Bull Dogs, all double-action, self-cocking, all have rubber stocks, all beautifully nickel-plated, all have saw handles, all have fluted cylinders, all have octagon barrels—

There are so many to choose from. Forehand and Wadsworth, Harrington and Richardson, Hopkins and Allen, Colt, Smith and Wesson—it is hard to know. The higher calibers will do more damage, of course, but the pistols that deliver them tend to be bigger, longer, harder to hide—

HANDSOME REVOLVERS
ACCURATE   RELIABLE

47146   **Colt's New Navy**

This revolver has been adopted by the U.S. Navy and every one has to pass a rigorous inspection.

Double-action, self-cocking, shell-ejecting revolver, nickel-plated or blued finish, rubber stock, beautifully finished, finest material; length about 12½ in., 6 shot, weight 2 lbs., 4½ or 6 in. barrel, 38 caliber using 47981 cartridges.

Each............................... $12.00
By mail, extra......................... .35

The Assassin is a metalworker but not a gun person. He looks at his hand, tries to imagine it holding something with a six-inch barrel. Military men shoot to kill all the time, they are trained for it, but the military belongs to them, it is the whip hand of the State. In all the strikes the military and the police have had the guns, have had the power—

52338 **Iver Johnson "Safety Automatic"**

"A Sure Shot"

Small-frame double-action top break
revolver; nickel-plated, hand-checkered
wood grip, exposed hammer, 3 in. barrel.
6 shot, chambered for S&W .32 cartridge.

Each.............................. $3.10
By mail, extra....................... .17

It is no bigger than the palm of his hand. The Assassin has seen them for sale in hardware stores, short and heavy-looking. He has even lifted one in his hand, pretending to consider buying it. Even without the cartridges loaded he felt a different man. A man who could make some difference in the world.

A man of destiny.

HOW TO ORDER—

A DEATH
IN CABANATUAN

Diosdado carries his uniform in a sack, easy to toss away if they encounter the Americans. No point in drawing more fire than you need to. The men, remnants of four companies, walk on ahead and behind him through the head-high cane, ducking away from the razor-sharp leaves, rifles slung over their shoulders, silent, listening to the terrain in front of them. A pair of hawks wheel slowly overhead, hoping the troop will flush something edible into the open. With dead, wounded, and deserted it is only twenty-five of them left plus the boy, Fulanito, who appeared one day carrying a Spanish Mauser nearly as tall as he is.

They pause at the end of the cane, Sargento Bayani crossing the road first as always, moving unguardedly into the rice paddy with a bolo resting on his shoulder. The enemy is too confident to bother with ambush, impatient to fire at anything that moves, and Bayani insists he is an irresistible target. He walks for a full minute, then turns to wave them ahead.

There is no telling what the reception will be in Cabanatuan. General Luna has ordered every telegraph line in the province cut and by the time runners have traveled back and forth the situation may have changed completely. General del Pilar, busy gathering his own men for a forced march to Bayambang, only nodded when Diosdado informed him that the men had voted to stay together rather than be split up and reabsorbed into other units.

"Go to headquarters," he said. "They'll find something to do with you."

Diosdado's troop is a mix of Zambals, Ilocanos, Pampangans, and Tagalos, bound now by blood and suffering. The rumors—that the *ilustrados* are selling the country to the Americans, that General Luna is secretly forming his own army, that the Jesuits are behind it all—do not seem to concern them. They talk about food and women and gamecocks, they make fun of each other, play *liampo*, gripe about the rebuilt shells jamming in their rifles and the true provenance of dried beef. They are good Catholics, kneeling for a quick *Jesus, Maria, y José* even in the roofless shell-blasted churches, and believe deeply in the miraculous power of the saints. Kalaw who writes an *oración* on a circle of paper and puts it in his mouth before a battle, careful not to swallow the *hosta redentora* till the danger has ended, Rafi who wears a vest with a red-eyed, sword-wielding angel embroidered on the back, the Pampangano brothers who empty their pockets of all metal when the shooting starts and say that Dr. Rizal is not really dead, that he will be resurrected on the day the *americanos* are driven from Luzon.

The boy, Fulanito, carries messages and brings water and spies on the *yanquis* but does not speak. It is not clear whether he ever could.

The cane fields give way to a series of hills, Diosdado keeping the troop off the main road as they begin to climb. It is morning still, but the men are careful when shifting their rifles on their backs not to touch sun-heated gunmetal with bare skin. He wonders if his boots will give him away as an officer if they are captured by Americans. Goyo del Pilar looked immaculate as they left San Isidro, a warrior in white astride his steed, breaking hearts in every *barangay* he rides through. Diosdado can't imagine Goyo hiking through the mountain passes in rags and a straw hat, no matter what the danger.

Sargento Bayani drops back beside him, using the bolo now and then as a walking stick as he climbs. He has taken to carrying it instead of a rifle as an example for the men, saying that this is their future, that before long they will have nothing left to fight the Americans with but their bolos, and on that day they will be true Filipino patriots.

"Maybe they'll send us to General Tinio in Ilocos," he says. "Somewhere they know how to fight."

Tinio is younger than Goyo del Pilar, only Diosdado's age, but already making a name for himself around Vigan.

"Why would they send us away from the front?"

Bayani shrugs. "Because we're not Tagalo and they don't trust us."

They climb silently for a while. Diosdado had been thinking the same thing, but resists seconding his sargento's cynicism. An officer must appear to be above politics—

"Maybe to Zambales, *di ba?*" Bayani smiles. "It would be nice to see San Epifanio again before they kill us."

Diosdado shoots his subaltern a look. "How do you know my *baryo?*"

"Because I'm from the same place."

Diosdado feels a chill. He studies the man's face as they climb, sees no one from his past. "There was no Bayani in—"

"A name I took after I left. My mother was Amor Pandoc."

The sargento says it lightly, eyes on the faint trail through the rocks, waving his bolo at his side like he is on a stroll in the country. Diosdado can think only of a day riding back from Iba with his father, passing a tiny patch of ground about to be swallowed by the jungle, a woman with dark skin and fierce eyes rising up from her sweet potatoes to stare, and a sullen boy some years older than him on his knees in the mud next to her. Don Nicasio kept his eyes forward and did not speak for the rest of the ride home. Diosdado had seen the woman in town for holy days and at the *misa de gallo* while he yawned through his duties as an altar boy, always a hushed tone in the churchwomen's voices when she was spoken of, some scandal that, like the countless others in San Epifanio, was never revealed to him. His first year back from Manila he heard that this woman, this Amor Pandoc who never had a husband mentioned with her name, had died of tuberculosis and that her son had run away to join the *tulisanes* in the mountains.

"I remember there was a celebration when you left for school," says Bayani, deadpan. "A feast for all of Don Nicasio's laborers, with fireworks and everything."

"You were there?"

Bayani looks away. "I heard about it. People were very proud."

Diosdado scowls. "Rich men send their sons to university because they're not fit for anything else."

"But you learned."

"Nothing of use here." He indicates the rocky path, the line of straw-hatted soldiers ahead of them.

"You have languages," says Bayani.

"So have you."

"I have the languages of ignorant people. You have proper Spanish—"

"Which my father spoke in our house. English is from our trips to Hongkong. At university I learned only Latin—"

"You know sciences."

"The theories only. Nothing practical, like how to make gunpowder—"

"You know history."

"So do you."

Bayani snorts. "I know stories—"

"History is only stories written down."

Bayani looks disappointed. "Then how do the young *ilustrados* occupy their time in Manila?"

Diosdado sighs. "Some drink and gamble. Some put on their *frac* coats and bowler hats and spend their nights attending the theater and courting young ladies. My friends and I spent most of our time trying to impress the padres with our intelligence and our cultivation," he says, "and the rest of it plotting their destruction."

"You wanted them to like you?"

"We wanted them to love us like their perfect children. We wanted them to respect us. But no matter how we parroted their language, no matter how much we learned from their books, we were never more than *indios* to them."

"They insulted you."

Indios sucios. It is what his father had called the majority of the people who lived in San Epifanio, people who cut his cane and processed his hemp and picked his mangoes in the orchard, *indios descalzados*, *indios tontos*, *indios sinverguenzas*, and Diosdado had spent his young life striving not to be anything like them. But even with Padre Peregrino, whose pet he had been at university, he was never more than a curiosity, an *indio* who won honors in Latin, a talking monkey.

"We were so full of hope," he says to the sargento, "so full of energy and *patriotismo*. We would not become rich and corrupt like our fathers, we would fight and fight and never sell ourselves, we would never—"

"Take money from the Spaniards and run to Hongkong." Bayani looks up the hill to the summit, speaking casually.

"That was a strategy, carefully thought out by General Aguinaldo. A chance to heal and to plan—"

Bayani turns to look him in the eye. "If the *americanos* had not come, you would still be there."

They have stopped moving, as have the men behind them. Joselito runs down to them from the top of the hill.

"*Yanquis* ahead of us, Teniente. On the other side."

Diosdado gestures and little Fulanito rushes forward with his binoculars. The boy loves to carry them, the strap around his scrawny neck, bumping in their leather case against his knees. The men ahead are already sitting, eyes following Diosdado as he hurries up past them with Sargento Bayani.

The uniform shirts are a beautiful bright blue against the brilliant green of the rice paddy on the plain below. Two full companies, most resting on the side of the plantation road, a dozen standing stretched in a firing line. Diosdado twists the focus ring on the field glasses until the others come clear.

There are ten of them, in the simple white cotton with blue stripes, straw hats scattered on the ground behind them. Their arms are tied behind their backs, their bare toes curled over the stone of the low dike they stand upon, facing a shallow trench they have just finished digging. The Americans raise their weapons in unison and there is a dotted line of smoke puffs. The Filipinos have toppled out of sight into the ditch before the rifle report echoes up from the plain.

Diosdado puts the binoculars down. Sargento Bayani lies on his belly beside him, his face impassive.

"If we cut around the hill to the north we should be able to miss them. Unless you want to try an ambush."

"General del Pilar told us to report to headquarters, nothing more."

The sargento fixes him with a look. "*A sus órdenes, mi teniente.*"

They crawl away from the top, then stand to head back to the men. "We swing to the north," says Diosdado. "General Aguinaldo should be informed of how close they are."

It is a hot, airless, dusty march around the hills, past noon when they reach the outskirts of Cabanatuan to be greeted by dogs in an ugly mood. There are dozens of them, scabby, ribs showing, shifting around the troop in a loose pack that seems to have no leader, snarling with their ears laid back. The men throw stones but the dogs only scamper away a few feet and then regroup. Diosdado halts the makeshift company by the first decent-looking dwelling they come to, and asks the betel-chewing old woman in front if he can go inside to change clothes.

The tunic is not so white now, hanging loose on him, buttons unpolished. His friends at the Ateneo called him *flaco* sometimes, and he hadn't thought he had any weight to lose.

"*Por favor, mi teniente,*" jokes Kalaw when Diosdado steps out of the hut dressed to report to Aguinaldo. "Ask the General if we can have a week's leave in Manila. They say the *americanos* have the lights working again."

Bayani walks with him into the town. There are more dogs, growling low as they pass, and dozens of the Presidential Guards lingering in the plaza, eyeing them suspiciously.

"Something bad happening here, *hermano*," says Bayani.

Sometimes it annoys Diosdado when the sargento calls him brother, and sometimes it seems like a compliment.

"They've probably heard the Americans are close."

Bayani shakes his head. "We've seen these Caviteños before. This is the bunch that Luna disarmed after we burned Tondo."

"I don't think so."

"You can wash their faces and stick them in red pants," says Bayani, "but they're the same *putos tagalos*. You better be careful."

"Go see if you can find the men something to eat." Diosdado wishes there had been a mirror in the woman's hut to comb his hair. He wonders if General Aguinaldo will remember him from Hongkong.

Scipio Castillero, wearing a spotless white suit and polished leather shoes, is lounging by the entrance to the *casa parroquial* next to a pair of sentries. He grins when he sees Diosdado.

"It's Brother Argus, all dressed up like a soldier."

Diosdado is too tired to smile. "Look who's visiting the war."

"I'm here with Don Felipe," says Scipio, pointing upstairs. Don Felipe Buencamino is Secretary of War, one of the old guard who are said to be *autonomistas*, willing to trade Spanish domination for that of the *yanquis*. "How about you?"

"Reporting to General Aguinaldo."

"Miong isn't here."

"We were told he was."

Scipio shrugs. "This may not be a good day for you to be here, *compa*. Something in the air."

Scipio has always been the one with the inside information, the one at school to steal the answers to the history examination, the first one in their class to start spying for the junta. He wears the smile of a man who knows what you don't.

"I have to take care of my company."

"The best thing you can do," says Scipio, not smiling anymore, "is march them far away from Cabanatuan until things settle down."

Diosdado steps past him into the building. "Politics must agree with you," he says. "You're getting fat."

It is hotter, if possible, inside the *casa parroquial* than in the plaza, and there are flies everywhere, crawling on the walls and windows, buzzing lazily in the air, dead flies littering the tile floor. The *encargado* behind the desk, a nervous-looking sargento, also tells him that General Aguinaldo has left Cabanatuan, and does not know when he will return.

Diosdado sits on a bench by the wall to wait. The next superior officer who comes in can give them orders. He sits with his back straight and concentrates on keeping his eyes open, occasionally wiping at the sweat rolling down his face with the back of his hand. His stomach is making noises, low rumbling under the drone of the flies and the squeaking of the lopsided fan that turns overhead, barely managing to stir the air. Better that the *supremo* doesn't see him in this state. He has developed, if not patience, the talent for waiting that is vital to a military career. He counts flies, living and dead. A Presidential Guard *teniente* sticks his head in the door, glares at Diosdado, then disappears. Diosdado hears some pacing upstairs. He guesses it is near three o'clock when there is a chorus of barking from the plaza, then angry shouting just outside and a slap and then General Antonio Luna stomps into the room. Diosdado jumps up and snaps to attention, but the *encargado*, surprised halfway to his desk with a wastebasket in hand, can only freeze with his mouth hanging open.

The general is in his usual fury. "Have none of you people been taught how to greet an officer?"

The sargento drops his trashcan and salutes. Colonel Román and Capitán Rusca step in behind Luna, looking around the room. Paco Román nods to Diosdado.

"I have come to see the President," Luna announces.

"He is not here, *mi general*," says the *encargado*.

Luna yanks a folded paper from inside his jacket, waves it in the air.

"Then why has he summoned me, in his own hand, to report to him at this place and time?"

"I don't know, *mi general*. I only know that he is not here. He has gone—away."

Luna, seething, suddenly turns to fix his glare on Diosdado.

"I was told the same," says Diosdado. It does not seem the moment to ask if the general will give his bastard company an assignment.

Luna snorts, then steps up close to the sargento. "This is the seat of our government. The headquarters of the army of our nation. This paper says I am to head a new Cabinet. Is there anyone here who can offer me an explanation?"

"Only Señor Buencamino is upstairs, sir."

The general's face turns a deeper red, almost purple, as he turns to Román and Rusca. "We are engaged in desperate battle," he says in a barely controlled voice, "and they leave a traitor in charge of headquarters." He pushes past the sargento and bangs up the stairs. Paco Román rolls his eyes toward Diosdado before he and Capitán Rusca follow.

There has been more bad blood and trouble. Another officer refusing, at Bagbag, to honor Luna's authority, the general pulling two companies off the line to confront him and his troops, and Bagbag falling rapidly to the *yanquis*.

"He was almost killed at Kalumpit," whispers the sargento as Diosdado sits, uneasy, back on the bench. "Shot off his horse with the *yanquis* all around him. The say he was like this when the colonel saved him." The *encargado* points an imaginary pistol to his skull. He seems disappointed by the outcome.

There is shouting from upstairs then, two voices. Luna's is the louder, cursing. Diosdado hears the word *traitor* more than once. Buencamino has no place here, shouts the general, no authority. A capitán of the Presidential Guard strides into the room with a half-dozen of his men, ignoring Diosdado to look up the stairs with a tight face. Diosdado's stomach drops as he realizes that the capitán is Janolino, whose brains were very nearly blown out by General Luna after the burning of Tondo. "Be prepared," says the capitán to his men, "but do nothing without my order."

The men bring up their rifles and *bam!* one discharges, the bullet shattering the glass of a framed photograph on the *encargado*'s desk.

The yelling upstairs stops abruptly.

"*Mierda*," hisses Capitán Janolino.

The flies stop buzzing.

General Luna charges down the stairs, livid, the summons to report clutched in one hand and the other on the butt of his pistol.

"Who fired that shot?"

Before there is an answer his eyes fall on Janolino, also gripping his sidearm.

"You. What are you doing here?"

"I am commander of the Presidential Guard—"

Just as Colonel Román appears at the head of the stairs a pair of the soldiers leap forward swinging their bolos, metal hacking into bone before the general pushes clear of them, blood spurting from the side of his head, yanking his pistol out to fire wildly, chips of stone from the wall stinging Diosdado's face, Luna staggering out the door and down the front steps with Janolino's men rushing after. Román and Capitán Rusca run down the stairs and out past Diosdado and then there is a ragged volley of rifle fire. Diosdado trades a look with the terrified *encargado*, then rises and goes to the door.

Paco Román lies splayed at the bottom of the stairs and the plaza dogs howl as at least a full company of the Caviteño *guardia* surround the stricken general, firing indiscriminately now, Luna still on his feet with eyes blinded by his own blood shrieking *"Cobardes! Traidores!"* and firing his pistol till it is empty and he falls to his knees and immediately the bolomen are in hacking, hacking, as the dogs bark and snarl and nip at the backs of their legs in a frenzy of excitement. Diosdado feels a hand on his shoulder.

It is Scipio, somehow inside the room now. "A very bad day for you to be here, *compa*. Out the back door."

Diosdado takes a last look, Capitán Janolino yanking the bloodied summons from the dead general's fist, then turns to hurry past the weeping *encargado* and out through the rear of the *casa parroquial*.

Sargento Bayani, running, finds him halfway back to the men.

"What is it?"

"They killed Luna."

"Carajo."

"They killed Luna and Paco Román is dead and Rusca I don't know—"

"General Aguinaldo—"

"Was not there."

Dogs are scampering past them toward the plaza. Diosdado has never seen so many dogs in one town before.

"Luna lost his temper, as he always does, but this—"

Diosdado knows he is an officer in the Filipino Army and should not be shaking. He should be calm and clear-headed and decisive. The side of his jaw is wet and there is blood on his fingers after he touches it. He feels dizzy.

"I don't know what to do."

Bayani puts a hand on his shoulder. *"Tranquílate, hermano.* The men are all ready to march."

"But where are we marching?"

"Home to Zambales," says the son of Amor Pandoc, as if this has been their plan all along.

WATER CURE

Hod is happy to sit, even if it is on the suspect's arm. Neely arranges himself on the other arm and Big Ten across the man's skinny legs, holding the ankles and facing himself away from the whole business. Hod is just back on the line and wants to puke from the heat and the recon march and the battle to take the high ground this morning when they hacked Major Moses's arm near off his body. The suspect isn't even trying to move now, just lying there with the *whump* of the shells they're dropping onto Las Piñas from offshore coursing up through his pinioned body and if Hod could manage to spit he knows it would sizzle in the air and burn off before it hit the dust. The platoon is down to twenty with the injured carried back to Manila by coolies this morning, and others falling out on the side of the road and Lieutenant Manly Goat saying if we pass this way again and they're still alive maybe we'll pick them up. He is waving his damn cane around and acting like every fucking shitheel boss Hod has ever hated, the Lieutenant, every company gun thug with a mean streak, like a dog gone bad that somebody ought to put down and Hod would gladly volunteer only he is too jaded with the heat to raise his hand.

"Pry it open," says Niles, pacing and pulling out his fancy new British pistol. "Let's put this show on the road."

Sergeant LaDuke, who even without the heat is no great thinker, tries to ram the sun-heated barrel of his Krag down the suspect's throat, busting a couple of teeth in, which the man proceeds to swallow and then choke on.

"Jesus Hiram Christ," sighs Manigault. "Flip him over."

Hod and the others roll off and Sergeant LaDuke and Corporal Grissom yank the man onto his belly and dig their heels into his back till he coughs out the teeth in a gout of blood. It is the *Monadnock* doing the shelling, Hod able to recognize the pitch of its ordnance whistling in from the sea, and they struggle to get the suspect pinned again, just some poor googoo in a field who waved and called out *"Amigo"* and Lieutenant Manigault said The hell with this *amigo* business, grab the yellow son of a bitch. Vásquez, who interprets from Spanish for the Macabebe scout, just stares down the road, and the Macabebe, looking disgusted with them all, kneels beside the man's head and works the tip of the buffalo horn he carries into his blood-smeared mouth.

"Let it pour," says Manigault, and Corporal Grissom carefully tips the kerosene can, filled with muddy water at the creek they just crossed, into the wide end of the horn. The suspect's arm begins to jerk underneath Hod, the man making strangling noises and arching his back, and Hod looks away trying to concentrate either on his plans for Mei when they get back to Manila or how to shoot Manigault the first chance he gets, anything but thinking about the heat that cooks off all the air before you can breathe it, that is like a hot poker down your nose and into your throat, that the Spanish and the natives are smart enough to hide out from and only volunteer lieutenants and the half-wits above them would expect you to march or fight in. They said in the clap shack how if you have the pox and let it go you might look almost normal as you get older but your head will never be right, which goes a long way to explain the folks running this army.

A good deal of the five gallons gurgle out before Sergeant LaDuke says stop and has the Macabebe pull out the horn so he can stomp hard on the googoo's distended belly. Hod lets the arm go so the suspect can half roll and puke up water, pink with blood, mostly onto Neely.

"What the hell you doing?" asks Neely, offended.

"He's got to get it out or he'll drown."

"Well he don't have to get it out all over *me*."

"You pin this suspect down, Private," the Lieutenant growls to Hod. "And *keep* him down."

Manigault has always been shit, a card-cheat and an errand boy and a faker, and he knows that Hod has him pegged, all the way back to Skaguay. But there is a different look in his eye today, wild and fry-brained, and there is that pistol—

The Macabebe says something to Vásquez, who turns to the Lieutenant.

"What do you wish to ask this man?"

"Ask him?"

Vásquez sighs. He seems like an educated man who, for whatever reason, is not so welcome back home. "The suspected one. You wish to ask him something. That is the reason for this—" he indicates the writhing, choking googoo.

Manigault stares at the Spaniard for a long moment, having clearly forgotten what he wanted to know, if in fact he ever had anything in mind.

"Ask him if they got as many pin-head officers in their outfit as we do in ours," says Big Ten.

Manigault glares at the Indian, then makes sure the suspect is back to his senses before sticking the barrel of his pistol to the man's forehead.

"Ask him how many troops they have waiting for us in Las Piñas," he says.

Vásquez says this to the Macabebe in Spanish and the Macabebe repeats it in whatever lingo he thinks the suspect talks and the suspect manages to croak out a few words before the scout slaps him and barks something to Vásquez.

"This man asks who would still be in Las Piñas," Vásquez reports to Lieutenant Manigault, "when your navy has been shelling it for six hours?"

Blam! Manigault fires the pistol into the baked dirt just to the side of the suspect's ear, causing him to urinate in his trousers and startling Neely so bad he rolls onto his side and covers his head.

"Jesus, Lieutenant," he complains, rolling back onto the man's arm. "How bout a little warning?"

"Ask him something else," says the Lieutenant.

"If they are going to make a stand," the Spaniard explains, "it will be at the Zapote Bridge. We fought them there many times before you arrived."

"Ask him about that, then."

"But if we know this already—"

Manigault points the pistol at Vásquez. "Ask him!"

Vásquez does not take his eyes off the shrill-voiced Lieutenant as he speaks to the Macabebe scout. The scout shouts into the ear of the suspect, who sobs something back. Hod doesn't want to look in the suspect's face. The Macabebe says something to Vásquez in Spanish.

"He says he has not been across the Zapote Bridge for many days."

"Well—that is very unfortunate for Mr. Nig." Manigault nods to the Macabebe scout. "Give him another drink."

The scout pinches the suspect's nose shut till he opens his mouth to breathe and then pushes the tip of the buffalo horn back in. The Macabebes don't look so much like the other natives here, the rumor going that they're Mexican Indians brought long ago by the Spaniards to work the crops, and of course the fellas expect Big Ten to be able to palaver with them.

"C'mon, Chief," they say. "You're holdin out on us."

"You know how many Indin languages they got back home I can't say a word of?" he tells them. "I barely remember any Ojibwe after a year with you people."

Corporal Grissom yanks the suspect's head to the side so he sees, then pisses loudly into the mouth of the kerosene can while Sergeant LaDuke giggles. After I shoot Manly Goat, Hod thinks, these two will have to be next. And maybe the Macabebe too, though this is his country after all and he is entitled to play his cards the way he wants. Corporal Grissom, who has been on the warpath since his monkey disappeared, convinced that the Chinese porters ate it, rebuttons his fly and begins to dump the liquid into the buffalo horn, splashing far too much of it onto Hod.

Shoot him in the belly, thinks Hod, wiping sweat from his eyes, and leave him in a ditch.

The suspect makes more strangling noises and tries to jerk himself out from under them and the barrage continues to the south, *whump! whump! whump!* and when the can is empty Sergeant LaDuke drops with both knees on the googoo's belly and what comes up smells like bile. There is a series of words between Vásquez and the Macabebe and the half-dead suspect, with Manigault pacing back and forth, back and forth.

"Let's hear it."

Vásquez turns to him. "He will admit to anything you wish."

"Very prudent of him."

"But you must first say what it is. He confesses that he can no longer reason."

"I don't understand."

The Spaniard speaks slowly, softly, as if to a small and not very clever child. "If you wish there to be an ambuscade waiting at the Zapote Bridge, he will confess to it and we may return with this information."

"So they are waiting—"

"And if you accuse him of being a general of the *insurrectos*, he will not deny it."

Again it takes a long moment for the meaning to penetrate the Lieutenant's overheated skull.

"You're saying the man is lying."

"I am saying nothing," Vásquez replies. "I am merely translating his words, as passed on by this *indio*, to the best of my ability."

And I am merely sitting on some unlucky fuck's arm, thinks Hod, while my comrades in arms, the kind of people who tried to smash my head in with clubs back in Montana, torture him to death for no fucking purpose.

"We're wasting time on this *amigo*," says the Lieutenant, kicking the suspect hard in the ribs and eliciting another heave of blood-tinted water from him. "Everybody up!"

The moaning is general as the rest of the platoon drag themselves to their feet, faces stupid with the heat, the suspect's torture being the only rest they've had all day. Big Ten crawls to his Krag and climbs up it to his knees, then stands, wobbly and soaked through with his own sweat. He wears the straw hat shaped like a pith helmet that many of the volunteers have adopted, their campaign hats worn out, and has lost a good deal of his bulk to the shits.

"We get to this bridge," he says, "there damn well better be a river underneath it."

As Hod reaches for his own weapon the Lieutenant appears in his face. "I know what you're thinking," he says, loud enough for the others to hear. "If I catch you skulking behind me, I'll have you shot."

The lead dog can never relax. He can never, once they're all out of the traces, let the others slink behind him. Niles has seen it more than once here in the Yukon, the other curs waiting, watching, hatred building with every shock of leather cracking on their hides, with every deep, freezing snow they have to struggle through or die, with every scrap of fish jerky the lead dog chases them off of, till the moment the scales tip—the lead dog coming up lame or finally too old or too weakened from the trek or just not savage enough to dominate the three or four who jump him and get him on his back and eviscerate him before fighting among themselves to be the new leader. Men with guns are ever more devious, the courage to pull a trigger available to the weakest if you pour a half bottle of whiskey down his craw or place a subversive thought in his hate-crazed mind. It is such men, drunkards, cowards, who cut Soapy down in Skaguay, Don't go, don't go I said and Doc and Rev Bowers and Old Man Triplett all said Don't go but him hot-eyed with pride saying that nobody, *no*body tells Jeff Smith where he may go and what he may do in this or any other town, marching to the pier with his Winchester in hand, ready to discipline the pack as he's done so many times before, keep them in line, all of us from the Parlor following to the base of the pier saying Wait, Jeff, at least wait till sunup when they have to look you in the eye but Jeff striding, striding tall and proud as he'd been on his mount in the 4th parade till out steps Frank Reid who thinks because you've drawn a map of a town you ought to own it and knowing he has Si Tanner and a dozen other guns ready behind him grabs the barrel of the Winchester and tugs it down and draws his Colt on Jeff. "For God's sake don't shoot!" cries Jeff, knowing a standoff when he sees one and they fire into each other so close each can smell the whiskey on the other's breath and then the rest of the dogs pile on and Jeff Smith, who'd be Emperor of Manila by now, Army command or no, is on his back and the rest of us are running out of Skaguay like greenhorns before an avalanche.

The Macabebe catches up with Niles, walking silent and fast, not even a footcrunch on the snow, not even nodding as he passes to join the platoon ahead, and one assumes he has dealt with the suspect in the appropriate manner. The lead dog should barely have to growl. They are skirting wide around Las Piñas, no reason to give the boys on the *Monadnock* a chance to misfire and tear them apart, smoke rising from where he expects the native village to be, and he half hopes there will be an ambush ahead to dispose of the worst of this band of assassins he has been placed in charge of.

It is cold, killer cold, a cold that makes the thoughts freeze and snap off before you can form them in your mind, and the only remedy is to keep moving, keep pacing, keep the blood flowing in your extremities while the dullards all around you flop in the snow and let the cold creep into their bodies.

They have stopped ahead, crouching in a drift. Niles draws the Webley from its holster, cold metal stinging his hand. Bare the teeth and raise the hackles, he thinks as he steps forward, and don't let them out of your sight.

Hod is on a knee next to Vásquez as the Lieutenant comes up, crouched low, the pistol out and ready. Please let there be shooting, he thinks, shooting and running and confusion like this morning on the heights and bullets winging this way and that and anybody likely to get plugged in the heat of it. The best would be to pick up a Mauser from the googoos once they're overrun and do it with that, a tidy hole between the peepers that nobody will question, only they leave their dead and wounded sooner than they leave their weapons, two bolomen behind each soldier with a firearm, ready to scoop the rifle up and continue the fight. I want him to be looking at me when I do it, too, so a stray round from behind is out, though there'd be a dozen men in the platoon they'd have to consider as its author. Manigault kneels by the Spaniard.

"Why have we stopped?"

Vásquez points. "The bridge is down there."

The Lieutenant rises to gaze over the top of the razor-edged grass and sees what they all have seen, googoos in number on both sides of the river at the base of the stone-span bridge, working in spite of the brutal heat to reinforce their breastworks, digging in for a serious smoker.

Manigault kneels again, turns to stare at Hod. "You," he says. He hasn't called Hod anything else since his return from the clap shack. "Get up there and take a look."

They have been spotted by now, the lack of gunfire meaning only that the googoos know they're just out of range, and this demented cracker wants to waste time just to get him killed.

"I can see well enough from here," says Hod, not moving.

Niles brings the pistol up into his face. Ever since he got the Webley he has been overly free with it, as if the pistol alone bumped him up a few bars in the pissing order. "Are you refusing an order, Private?"

Big Ten is off to the left and Hod hears the bolt on his Krag first, followed by several others. No telling who will take which side in the disagreement if it comes to blood, but if he goes forward now the googoos will shoot at him and miss high like they always do and then start running and waving their bolos and it is too fucking hot to run, even to save your own hide. So he might as well just settle it here.

"If that's the way you want to hear it, Lieutenant," Hod answers him, "sure."

He can't tell from Manigault's eyes if he is too sun-baked to know he will be the second one to die, and damn quick too. They are still pounding the hell out of Las Piñas, the *whump! whump!* north of them now, and the shellbursts punctuate the long silence between the men.

"When we return," says the Lieutenant finally, "you shall be court-martialed."

"Fair enough."

Manigault turns to eyeball each man in the platoon. "You all witnessed what has just transpired. Sergeant LaDuke, relieve this man of his weapon."

LaDuke takes Hod's old Springfield, then gives it to Corporal Grissom to carry, who lays it off on Neely as they come out from the tall grass and back onto the road, Hod walking ahead with the Macabebe scout, who seems unperturbed as usual.

"Son of a bitch," gripes Neely behind them. "You done that just so's you wouldn't have to lug your damn rifle comin back."

They have not gone too far when Lieutenant Manigault starts to weave on the road, drifting from this side to the other and muttering to himself.

"I can't feel my limbs anymore," he says. "They must be frozen."

And then crumples to the ground.

There are no oxcarts around to commandeer and for a moment LaDuke stares at the heap of lieutenant like he might just leave it there in the road. Finally he has Tutweiler take Big Ten's Krag and tells the Indian to help Hod carry. Big Ten hefts Manigault up under the arms and Hod takes his feet and it is awkward and still scorching and no way to wipe the stinging sweat out of their eyes.

When they stagger past the mutilated body of the suspect there are already buzzards, three of them, picking at it without enthusiasm, as if the heat has ruined their appetite.

DEVOLUTION

Cross-hatching won't do for it. To set off the white of the bone in the nose, the white of the rolling cannibal eyes, the hanging shell beads and stiff fronds of thatch around the waist, you need pure black, midnight black, so much ink that it soaks through the pad to stain the desk beneath. The photos of the little nignogs coming down from the exposition in Buffalo have been useful—who knew they had their own pygmies?—but it has been necessary to blend the googoo with his Ubangi cousins, also well-represented at the Pan, in order to convey the true, primitive horror of what our boys are threatened with on that Godforsaken splatter of Pacific islands.

Amok, they call it, this state of blood-lust, this disregard for your own body's vulnerability to shot and shell, that hurls the ink-black savage forward with razor-edged bolo in hand to wreak havoc on American boys in their shallow trenches. To run *amok*. How does one defend against a foe with no care for his own well-being, who sweeps forward though thoroughly drilled with pistol shot, who, like the fanatic Chinese Boxer, believes himself invulnerable in his rush to murder and mutilate? If this be, indeed, the White Man's burden, to civilize, to Christianize this creature of darkness, we have accepted a task far greater than that of our forefathers who confronted the red-pelted tribes of wood and plain, and face an opponent too base to elevate and too numerous to exterminate.

The bolo is suspended from one sinewy arm, the wooden spear held ready to launch in the other, the kinky locks, a maddened squirrel's nest of hair, springing in every direction.

Behind this apparition sits the humble Cuban Peasant, brim of his straw hat turned back to reveal an honest if uncomplicated face, building a sand castle with the ripe-breasted, silken-haired Hawaiian Girl, the grass of her skirt fuller, looser than the googoo's spiky fringe, simple, but elegantly becoming to this daughter of Nature. Uncle sits on a beach chair, sleeves rolled up, arms crossed, balefully staring down at the wretched, threatening Filipino, who comes only to his shins.

AMERICA'S PROBLEM CHILD

—says the caption. Horrible as the Tagalo bandit is, the petulant futility of his resistance must be kept in sight.

And no, cross-hatching will not do for it. The Cartoonist opens the top of his pen, and the ink spills forth.

PEARL OF THE ORIENT

Even the coolies are staring. Sergeant Jacks leads the company along the north side of the Pasig, a hodgepodge flotilla of hemp barges and shallow-draft boats covered with curved, palm-thatched roofs bobbing to the right. Barefoot Chinamen balance on long planks leading from the boats to the cement dock, each pair with a huge basket filled with fish hung from poles over their shoulders, pausing to gape at the smoked yankees of the 25th. Small boys snap their switches against the flanks of water buffalo pulling wood-wheeled carts full of bulging rice sacks, the boys giggling and shouting to each other when they see the soldiers file past the steep-roofed warehouses where Filipino brokers in white suits sit on crates to watch, holding parasols over their heads to block the suddenly brutal sun, even the towering crane arms throwing no shadow at this hour. There are boat horns and steam whistles and tethered goats bleating and the shouting of the boys and the brokers and the coolies, none of it in anything Jacks can recognize as Spanish. The dock is puddled from the downpour just ended, what they call an *agua-cero* in El Paso, and another threatening in the sky behind.

Jacks looks across the wide, placid river to the Walled City and just from what is visible over the parapets he can tell Manila is a bigger deal than Juarez could ever hope to be.

Company E, just ahead of them, cuts left up a street along the side of the customs building. The boys don't have the usual strut, legs still wobbly from the choppy trip on the launch from the anchorage and their two weeks at sea out of Hawaii on the *Valencia*, but orders are to march them without pause through what is supposed to be secure territory all the way out to the reservoir at El Depósito.

"Companyyyyy—*left!*" calls the sergeant and they follow him up the side street. Like most folks, he never heard of the Philippines before Dewey steamed into the Bay. There was some possibility, just before climbing aboard in San Francisco, that it would be China to fight the Boxers, but it looks like they got their share of Celestials here, doing all the nigger work with their long braids hanging down their backs. He wonders if they speak the same brand of Chinee as the ones on St. Louis Street in El Paso.

"Let's pick us up a couple of these yellow men here, Sarge," calls Cooper from behind him. "Leave them Army mules behind."

There seems to be no glass in the windows, just panels with a lattice-work of little pearly squares set in them, oyster shell maybe, ground thin to let the light through. The panels slide back and forth in grooves and are pulled open now for the break in the rain, what he figures must be more Filipinos sticking their heads out to stare at them. So far they seem to come in as many shades as his troopers, only straight-haired and pint-sized. Old women and near-naked children have come out to try to sell something like a *tamale* wrapped in a leaf, walking alongside and calling to them and Jacks feels like he's in Mexico again only the heat, thick and liquid still despite the hours of rain dumped this morning, is more like Cuba. Like Santiago just before they left, half the outfit down with fever and feeling like you could drown on dry land. The white folks still call his men all the same things they ever did, good and bad, except for "Immunes."

They follow E Company to the right now, old women with red teeth setting up shoe-shaped earthen ovens on the ground, feeding sticks to the fires within and arranging kettles filled with anybody's guess above, and then they pass between a stand of bamboo with leaves like spearheads and a huge, oak-looking tree covered with red blossoms and Sergeant Jacks asks himself for the thousandth time how else a narrow-ass little cane chopper from the Texas border get to see all this?

And maybe when the brushfires here are all stamped out, on to China.

They come to an estuary of the Pasig, more like a canal from how they've built along it on both sides, and head toward a little bridge Jacks can see to the north. Good we're here, he thinks, nothing for the boys to do at Bliss but get into trouble, the Army like a horse that needs to be rode or it gets sullen and ski-footed. He knows they've been talking on the ship about Indian-fighting, but this far behind the lines it looks like a fairly peaceable tribe, nothing a steady flow of government beef and some vigilance over the firewater can't control. There are lizards skittering on the walls of the stone buildings, the little thumb-sized ones Mingo Sanders in B Company always calls "Apache breakfast sausage." It is puddled up pretty deep here and the boys enjoy splashing through it, *one-two-three-four, one-two-three-four*, but slogging all the way out to these waterworks in wet socks isn't a good start for troops penned up sitting on a ship for a month. Jacks is sweating from everywhere now, blue shirt stuck to his back, but smiling. Beats Missoula in fucking January any day.

He leads the company over the bridge, a pair of local sports in white linen outfits gawping at them from some sort of high-wheeled pony carriage stopped in the middle—that's right, fellas, there's people darker than you in this world—and then they jam up behind Company E and the rest in a little plaza.

"What's the deal, Sarge?" calls Hardaway. "What we waitin for?"

Hardaway has a burning need to be informed, a hopeless business for anyone pursuing a career in the military.

"We are waiting," Jacks answers, "because we stopped moving ahead."

"Oh," says Hardaway, for the moment accepting this as an explanation.

There are shops and stalls all around the plaza and the proprietors, mostly Chinese, come out to stare.

"Where this is?" asks Cooper.

Sergeant Jacks looks at the map they've given him. "Binondo," he says. "Does it matter?"

"We gone billet here?"

"No."

"Then it don't matter."

When you come into a place like this you never know if you'll be back. Jacks waits for what feels like ten minutes of being steamed, then breaks rank and saunters forward. Take a look, at least.

"Where you going, Sarge?" asks Hardaway.

"General MacArthur is supposed to be somewhere up ahead," he calls back. "Figure I ask him what's for supper."

"I don't like the look of it," says Royal.

"You didn't like the look of Hawaii either," Junior reminds him.

"I saw a rat in a palm tree."

"All the places in the world you could be a rat," says Too Tall, "up a palm tree in that Honolulu would be my pick."

"They don't want us here."

"Didn't want us in Missoula at first, neither," says Corporal Pickney, who has been in since before the Pullman strike.

Royal turns a full circle. They are supposed to stay in rank and be ready to march but Jacks is gone and there is no brass in sight. He meets the eye of a red-faced Chinese pacing in front of his storefront. The man gets even more agitated, yanking his broad-brimmed white hat off then slapping it back onto his head several times. A pair of white soldiers, volunteers from their uniforms and drunk from the wobble in their progress, come past them heading for the bridge. The two stare like they've never seen such an apparition in their lives. The dirty sky that was hanging offshore has crept forward and hangs over them all now, low and threatening to rain.

Coop, grinning from ear to ear, calls out to the vols.

"Where you boys from?"

"Oregon," says the shorter one, tapping an insignia on his arm like it should be clear to anybody.

"Damn," says Coop, acting impressed, "did we win that in the war too?"

The Oregons glower at him as the other boys laugh, then change their direction and go to join the red-faced Chinese, all three disappearing into the shop. Unlike most of what they've passed, this building has a proper glass show window, full of brightly painted gimcracks that Royal can't make any sense of.

"What I'm saying is," Royal continues, turning to scowl at the plaza, "this here must have come to a sorry state if they bringing *us* in."

"You don't like the duty," says Pickney quietly, "you shouldn't of signed up for it."

Junior gives Roy a look. Junior has been coaching him all the way from San Francisco on how you have to apply yourself to the task and be an example everybody can be proud of. Only there's nobody here, Royal thinks, who I give a damn what they think of me. If we get into a scrap, sure, you got to fill out your end of the bargain, do what you have to for the sake of the others, but none of it, not even Cuba which everybody wants to write a song about them for, makes any sense to him now.

"It aint just we're a new color they're seeing," he says. "This is their country and they don't want us here."

"Man been on shore twenty minutes and he got the whole deal figured out," says Cooper.

"What it is," says Too Tall, "is that folks here been dealing with these volunteer outfits, can't find their dingus in their own trousers without a Manual of Instruction and a drill sergeant to turn the pages for em. We can't expect no parade from people been puttin up with them jokers."

"Runty little bastids," says Willie Mills, watching a trio of Filipino men pass by. "Aint gonna make much of a target, once we get into it with em."

"They learn fast, though," says Coop, pointing.

The red-faced Chinese is in front of his shop again, pasting a sign that says WHITE ONLY, in fresh ink, onto his show window.

"Aint that nice? Make us feel right to home."

And then the sky opens and they are soaked in an instant.

NEWS FROM THE FRONT

Father—

    My sincere apologies for the tardiness of this missive, but writing paper has been in short supply again and prone, in this wet and unconscionable heat, to dissolve in one's hand. We arrived with Company E under Lieutenant Caldwell somewhat in advance of the rest of the 25th, and were immediately put to work guarding the reservoir to the northeast of Manila. This is a vital position, of course, and the rebels' former control of it a key to the eagerness of the Spanish garrison within the "Walled City" to surrender to our volunteers. Though there was little glory to be had in this transaction, one cannot but laud the relative paucity of casualties resultant on both sides. The volunteers, mostly units that never set foot in Cuba, are overly impressed with themselves for this and subsequent engagements that would have been "business as usual" for our fellows, and are in general quite insufferable. Most are from the Western states, with the predictable lack of discipline and prejudice against our race. There have been times when we profess to miss the "crackers" we camped with in Chickamauga and Tampa, who at least share a long and contentious history with us.

    Junior on the groundcloth in the airless little tent, paper laid flat on the top of an empty wooden ammo crate, pen hot in his fingers. The boys not on leave are throwing dice outside on a poncho thrown over the mud, argument between them almost constant as to which way the die is leaning against its folds and wrinkles. He is stripped to his underclothing, his uniform draped over the top of the tent to dry. The mosquitoes that seem to come every time the rain lets up for a day have discovered him, and he keeps his hat by his side to wave them off.

The duty at El Deposito, where the waterworks are located, was mostly uneventful, the rebels there nocturnal creatures satisfied with the odd sniping "potshot" that does more to disturb the sleep than to penetrate the epidermis. The only scrape with destiny came when Royal Scott and I, on a rare afternoon without assignment, endeavored to take advantage of some rock tanks nearby for a bath. Personal hygiene is a constant struggle in this heat and filth and wet, and I never pass up an opportunity for ablution, a habit which has earned me the sobriquet of "Waterboy" among my cohorts. There were a number of Chinese, who we and the other units employ as bearers when on the march and general factotums when in camp, engaged in cleaning cookware at the other end of the man-made pond, so Pvt. Scott and I resolved to keep an eye on the clothing we had just shed (the Chinese being notorious filchers) and entered the water. We had only just begun to employ the abrasive bricks of what the Army issues as "soap" when we spied a serpent of at least four yards' length (this is not an exaggeration) undulating rapidly across the surface in our direction. Needless to say, Pvt. Scott and I quit the water with extreme haste, then, dismayed to discover that the creature's mate (more than its equal in size) had curled up to nap upon our uniforms, we continued at a gallop to the encampment. There was a good deal of merriment provoked by our naked condition, as well as skepticism voiced as to its cause until a pair of the Chinese appeared, clutching, head and tail, one of the writhing snakes and recommending that it would make excellent "chow." Luckily a third coolie followed with our clothing and dignity was restored. Our boys left the feasting to the bearers, all but Pvt. Cooper, who claims to have partaken of a good deal of "rattler" in his former life and declared this Philippine delicacy its equal.

Junior has not dared to mention his disappointment with Father's handling of the affair between Royal and his sister, has in fact barely alluded to that "unfortunate business," but is not going to pretend his friend is no longer with the company. For his own part, Royal still feigns an annoyed disinterest in Jessie's whereabouts and welfare, often walking away in a funk halfway through a sentence when read the news from the great metropolis that Junior strives now to think of as "home," and speculations as to paternity are clearly unwelcome.

He has remained in a state of abstracted distemper, Royal, since his reenlistment at Fort Bliss, and the others tend to steer a wide passage around him. "Only one thing more useless than a cripple-leg pony," says Too Tall Coleman, "and that is a moody nigger."

The food here is superior to that available either in Cuba or at our Southwestern postings, Army fare supplemented with rice (a godsend for the Carolinians in uniform) and the occasional stray chicken that runs afoul (a fowl?) of our bayonets. This latter is a great sport among the fellows, one of the few pastimes than can rouse them from heat-induced torpor, and the order to "propaganda" with the natives is obeyed after a fashion. After a bird is successfully skewered the nearest Filipino man, woman, or child has a handful of centavos pressed upon them, whether they are the owner of the recently deceased or not. None has ever refused the compensation.

They are a peculiar race, the Filipinos, mixed to a high degree, though this is more apparent in the larger towns than in the "boondocks" where we have been relegated. Relations being dodgy as they are, I have not been able to pick up more than a few words from their frustratingly large repertoire of dialects, and thus can be no judge of the level of their intelligence. They are, however, amazing mimics, and with only brief exposure begin to parrot the more colorful of Army expressions and sing our songs with uncanny accuracy and brio. I witnessed a touching scene in the "Luneta," a kind of city park by the sea, when the better class of natives gathered there for a concert our regimental band presented stood and doffed their hats upon the playing of the ubiquitous "Hot Time in the Old Town Tonight," believing it to be our national anthem!

We were, of course, a great novelty to them at first, the children maneuvering to touch our exposed skin and see if the color rubbed off, but with time they have become quite accustomed to the "yanquis negros" and seem, though I cannot swear this as a fact, to prefer us to our paler compatriots.

This is not to say that we hold a warm place in the hearts of the insurgents. At the beginning of August, as the typhoons began to blow, we were sent to join Companies B, F, I, K, L, and M, just arrived under Colonel Burt, to form a defensive line stretching from the town of Caloocan (site of much fighting and the heroics of the 1st Kansas) to Blockhouse #5 at La Loma, some four miles to the east. This at the time constituted the front line in the North, and there were daily patrols in the vicinity to ascertain the presence and strength of the enemy. These resulted in quite a few damp outings for our squad and a series of inconclusive encounters, shots fired from cover and returned with our characteristic dispatch, the rebels often fleeing before we were able to catch a glimpse of them. We are quite a phenomenon in the field, Father, and I wish that there was some manner to transport you here for one day to witness it. A body of men of color (albeit still under white officers) who function with a discipline and spirit under fire that is a sterling example to regular soldiers and volunteers alike. I am reminded during our "smokers" with the enemy that despite the privations of Army life and the absence from those I love that this has been the proper decision, and that any self-respecting colored man needs be envious of my good fortune to play a role in this great venture.

Our mascot, a spaniel with white body and black ears who answers to the name Snaps, is the only member of the regiment consistently "dogging" it—laid absolutely low by the heat and outnumbered by inhospitable packs of native curs, he spends his days seeking a parcel of shade and dreaming of the snowy vistas of Fort Missoula.

Yesterday we were put to the first serious test of our tenure here. Just past noon the rebels made a desperate attack all along our line. They seemed to materialize in number and the action was exceedingly "hot" for the greater part of two hours. I must say that our fellows remained cool and professional, and though it was certainly no turkey shoot I doubt the enemy will again consider such a frontal assault on the 25th. I was at an especially isolated section of our position when the attack began, and as our artificer, Bryce, had just been overwhelmed with intestinal cramps (a not infrequent occurrence here) and required two soldiers to carry him to the rear, and a good number of others were away on leave, we were somewhat undermanned. Our sergeant was engaged in a matter of resupply some distance down the line of defense, so when the onslaught erupted we were without leadership. Realizing that the rebels had crept up undetected and held us in something of a crossfire, I suggested a quick dash to overrun their position on our left, and subsequently found myself leading the men in this tactic. The Filipinos, surprised and I must say outmaneuvered, fled instantly, and our new position gave us superior ground from which to trade fire with the remainder of their party. When they finally broke off the fight they left several dozen killed and wounded along the line, while the regiment's only fatality was Pvt. Parnell, a musician with Company E who succumbed to a heart failure during the engagement. He was young and fit, and his demise must be due either to a congenital weakness or to the combined effect of overexcitement and murderous heat. You cannot imagine the thirst experienced during such an extended battle, or the impression that the sun is working harder to undo you than your opponents.

Sergeant Jacks squats by the opening of the tent to look in.

"Patrol in twenty," he says. "Two squads. They want us to check out the track to the north."

The rebels infiltrate to cut the telegraph wire along the Dagupan line every few days, or pull some iron hoping to derail a troop train.

"They just attacked in force—"

"And had their tails whipped. Two squads. You pick the men."

"Me?"

"You, Corporal. It comes with the chevron."

Jacks stands and walks away across the hardening mud. Junior can hear Too Tall, talking to his dice.

"Be good to your Daddy," intones the private, "and show me a seven."

Please do not share this with the ladies—

Junior holding his arm out to let it drip sweat and then writing again—

—but I killed my first man in the engagement. Perhaps I have done so before in Cuba, but at El Caney I fired my weapon no more than twice and that hurriedly, intent on not being left behind as we clambered up the slope under fire. I looked into this man's eyes as I shot him, bravely holding his ground or merely rooted to the spot in terror as we overran their ditch, and I must have pulled the trigger automatically as I have no recollection of doing so. He fell backward without a cry, but when I drove my bayonet through him, as we have been endlessly trained to do, there issued from him a sound I shall never forget. War is not a business for children. This man I am certain was fighting for his flag, for his dignity, no less than I, and I can only trust that Providence holds the answer to why we were fated to meet in such a way. The men don't speak of the whys and wherefores of our presence here, but I sense an uneasiness that was not in evidence when we were outside Santiago. We must, as always, trust our leaders and our faith in God, but I have seen and done things here I fear will haunt me forever.

He was as small as a boy, hard to determine his age, and wore a gold cross (as many do here) hung around his neck. I insisted this not be taken from his body before it was laid in the common grave and covered over.

Junior takes a moment to allow a half-dozen mosquitoes, one by one, to settle on his body and then swats them dead. They cannot help themselves, he thinks, though their only chance of escaping with your blood is to attack while you sleep, to do their business and fly away. There is speculation now, maybe even solid evidence from what his father writes him, that the mosquitoes play a part in the spreading of both malaria and the yellow fever. He wonders if the natives, insurgent or not, are immunes, or if they, out there crouching in wait to kill him, are just as queasy and feverish as their American tormentors. He watches one of the insects on his arm, carefully spreading its feet to drill, then crushes it with his palm. A common enemy, like the Spanish, that should draw the opposing sides together.

I am understandably distressed to hear of your present situation in the North. There are no New Yorkers in our company, though from your description of conditions there it is a wonder more of our people have not fled it for the military life. There is overcrowding in sections of Manila, and terrible poverty, but nothing of the magnitude that you report. We have been for the most part kept from that municipality, and the suspicion is that the powers that be believe our presence, in numbers, might offend the wealthier, more educated class of Filipino who are in the assimilationist camp. These people, labeled Americanistas *in the local press (and no doubt as* traitors *by their Tagalo brethren still in arms against us), with their innate tendency to ape the manners of their conquerors, have been quickly taught that they should despise the colored man.*

I can only hope that you find a way to prosper in your new surroundings, foreign and chaotic as they may be, or that reason prevails and enables you to return to W *with your rightful property and position restored.*

In the meantime, give my love to Mother and to Jessie (and to her little one— I am an uncle!) and tell them I think of them constantly.

Oh yes—I have been raised to corporal due to my actions in yesterday's fracas. It is a small enough accomplishment, but evidence that merit, regardless of the obdurate prejudices of the world, may sometimes be rewarded.

I shall send what money I can when you have a more reliable address.

Ever your son,

Aaron Lunceford, Jr.

Junior steps out under the oppressive sky. The Filipina who washed his overshirt got all the blood out but sewed the new chevron on crookedly, so that it does not line up evenly with the one above it.

"You done writin to you Mama and Daddy—*Cor*pral?" Too Tall calls to him from his knees, mocking.

Junior steps into his pants. "Indeed I am," he says. "And now perhaps you gentlemen will join me for a little stroll?"

ON THE HIP

For at least half a day nobody will tell him what to do. Coop wanders the crowded streets, the *amigos* and the pigtails taking no special note of a colored man by now, feeling like the rum has done his insides no good. He could spend his leave in the sick ward, squirming on a bench, waiting his turn to get probed, or be out here a free man looking for a better cure.

They call at him from their shops and stalls, "You buy! You buy! Yankee soja you buy!" but none are selling anything he is hankering for. There is even one Chinese, wearing smoked glasses, who follows him grinning down the street riffling a paw full of playing cards and hissing his come-on and Coop has to laugh out loud, the idea you would play a man at his own game with his own deck in his own lingo and expect to leave with your pants on. There must be some greenhorns that fall for it, drunk or stupid or both, but Coop isn't one of them.

"Yankee soja no *tonto*," he says finally to be rid of the little sharper, turning and waving a finger at him. "You go way yankee soja."

But the hands that were played—

*—*Big Horace used to recite from his cell after lights-out in Greenville—

By that heathen Chinee
And the points that he made
Were quite frightful to see—

Where a geechie no-count like Horace ever run into Chinese was a question, but all he ever answer was with another verse from one of his stories.

The cowboy slept on the barroom floor—

—went everybody's favorite—

—*having drunk so much he could drink no more*

The gambler fades and then there is a pair lugging a pig on a pole, tied by its trotters hanging upside-down squirming and squealing just like Coop's guts and he has to bend over for a moment, head held low and hands on knees, while his stomach does some tricks. Like a tug of war going on down there. He's had the quickstep for a couple weeks now like a lot of the boys, but now there is blood in it and there is only one cure he knows for that.

A half-dozen pigtails hustle past, each loaded down with something Coop doesn't want to think about lifting. Just what they want back home, he thinks, niggers who don't know how to stretch a job out. Way they hop around and jabber so fast it's no wonder they got to burn some poppy at the end of the day, just to catch a breath.

He is able to straighten and take a few steps and right ahead there is a pair of provost guards in their white uniforms staring at him, so he flashes a big melon-eater and steps up to where they can hear and salutes, though they are both only privates.

"You gentlemens know where Division Hospital at?"

They give him directions, very polite and proper, and he heads away in that direction till he can cut out of their sight. Always somebody to throw a shadow on you, no matter where you are, and he wishes he had took his chance and run off when he got the notion in San Francisco. Not like they got his proper name or got time to go chase one darky trooper while they got so many dog-eaters to kill and such a big passel of islands to take over. Morning roll-call before they climb up that gangplank—"Where's Coop?"

"Aint seen him, Sarge."

"We better off without that trash. Let's march."

Only he let the chance slip by and here he is surrounded by *amigos* that want to slit his throat open and pigtails after his pay and a stomach knotted up like a mule-hitch and hot, Lord, even Shreveport in the dead dog of summer got nothing on this mess.

There is a pair of pigtails shuffling after him and waving, one of them lugging a stool, and hell, poorly as he feel right now he might as well sit down. He settles on the stool and the younger one outs with a pair of scissors.

"Takee hat off."

Coop laughs and loses his topper. "Brother, you aint never cut this kind of wool."

The pigtail frowns and grunts and walks in a circle around him, studying the problem, while the other squats on the dirt street and lays out a little wooden case full of all kinds of truck that looks like a doctor's tools only made from bamboo.

"What's all that?"

The barber grabs an earlobe and wiggles it.

"Takee out dirt."

"From my ears?"

"You hear everything better, ha?"

Mostly what there is is people giving him orders and blowing the damn bugle and he hears that just fine, but there was that boy from Company L had a bug crawl up in his ear and get stuck there and he near went crazy with it.

"Guess it can't hurt," says Coop, giving the ear-cleaner a hard look. "But you better be damn careful about it."

The crowd on the street keeps flowing past them up and down, paying no mind, while the barber snips away at the edge of his hair with the very tip of the scissors, cautious, and the other one slips a long, bendy strip of bamboo into Coop's left ear and begins to slowly dig and wiggle. Coop tries not to laugh thinking of what the boys would say if they seen him here. His mama always told him to clean his ears but he never did and then she'd catch him and scour them so hard with a lye-soaked rag they'd burn for days.

The cleaner goes in with a set of pinchers and plucks something out—a dirty chunk of wax near as big as a shelled peanut—and Coop wonders if it really come from him or if the pigtail just palmed it from his kit to have something to show for his pay, some heathen Chinee trick the two of them will laugh about when he's gone.

At least it's not a bug.

The cleaner goes in again with a long stick with a little scoop on the end then, scraping out the smaller bits, while the barber gives up his snipping away a hair at a time and lathers the back of Coop's neck to shave beneath his kitchen. Coop gives a listen to see if he can hear any clearer. Somebody is playing a guitar not too far away, got to be a colored man from the sound of it, only when the ear-cleaner pulls the scraper out and he can turn his head to look there is only a little *amigo*, barefoot and in rags, with a guitar nearly half his size hung over him. Coop watches the boy's fingers, one with a piece of curved sea-shell around it that he uses to slide up and down the strings on the neck while he picks with the other hand. The music is too familiar to be Filipino.

Coop's stomach suddenly tries to climb out of his body through his asshole. He grabs his sides and holds himself together till it passes and then takes the barber by the wrist.

"I needs smokee," he says and mimes a long draw, sucking air in and closing his eyes.

The barber looks to the ear-cleaner, who holds out his hand and wiggles the fingers like a bug crawling and says something in Chinese.

"Plenty smokee, Olmigo Street," says the barber.

"Olmigo—"

"*Hormiga, Señor*," says the little *amigo*, who has come over with his hand out. He makes the bug wiggle too. "*Es muy cercano.*"

Coop digs out a handful of centavos and the pigtails take some and he flips a couple to the boy and says Take me to Hormiga Street.

The boy smiles from ear to ear and takes off up Analoague where the carpenters are out working on chairs and tables with the little dogeater calling proudly to the other boys selling candy or shining shoes or hawking the *lotería* which is supposed to have been shut down, showing off the *americano* he's hooked, the guitar making a little hollow sound as it bumps against his body and damn if that ear business didn't work, the whole racket of the streets like it's right inside his skull now, like it or not.

Hormiga Street cuts off to the right, short and narrow and leading to the bustle of Rosario, with its street hawkers and tailor shops and painted portraits of Jesus, the Virgin Mary, and Admiral Dewey. Coop flips the little *amigo* another coin and does his viper again.

"*Fumar*," he says. "*Dónde?*"

The boy giggles and points out a shop with scrawny plucked ducks hanging by their necks on either side of the door. "*Al bajo*," he says and runs off with the big guitar slapping against his backside. Coop steps in between the ducks.

A pigtail with pox scars and a moustache nods to him from behind a counter where he is chopping apart a small pig, then waves a bloody hand toward a beaded curtain that leads to the back. Coop can smell the bitter smoke already.

The place behind the laundry in San Francisco was tiny compared to this, just a few bunks in a storeroom. This joint could hold a dozen fiends, with narrow shelves built into the wall, woven mats and pillows in red silk covers on them, every nook with a spirit lamp and pipe layout ready to go. A silver-haired man in the loose blue suit they wear seems to be in charge, while the chef sits carefully scraping ashes from the bowl of a pipe into a small lacquered box. There are four or five already here on the hip, glassy-eyed, mostly Chinese with one well-dressed white-looking man who might be Spanish.

"You lie down," smiles the silver-haired man, "you feel better chop-chop."

"How much for a pipe?"

"Fittee centavo."

Coop has a couple American, a couple Mexican in his pocket but knows you have to jawbone them a bit.

"Twenty centavos a pipe."

The man smiles. "Twenty centavo, fuck you."

Coop laughs. "All right, six pipes for an eagle."

The man holds out his pudgy hand and Coop lays a gold dollar in it. If he was a white boy he could say he was military police and threaten the price down some, but even the pigtails know there's not any colored provost. Coop pulls his boots off and climbs onto one of the shelves, lying on his side and resting his head on the pillow. The chef sits on a stool by him, working an iron wire into a little pot of the sticky stuff till there is a gob big as a blackberry on the end of it, which he holds over the open flame of the lamp by Coop's side, turning it this way and that till it starts to blister and crack with the heat. He used to watch his mama make johnnycakes with the same attention, his mouth watering and hoping his other brothers wouldn't smell and come in to eat them all. The chef takes the bubbling ball of dope and pokes it into the center of the clay bowl on top of the end of his pipe, then moves away to deal with one of the other guests.

Coop takes a long draw, pulling it in through the pipe and into his lungs and then slowly letting the bluish smoke escape through his nose. Got to give it time to soak in.

He has to reheat the ball after every draw, tilting the bowl toward the open flame and then sucking the bitter heat into himself, but the knots in his belly begin to unravel and at the end of four long pulls the ball of dope is nothing but ash and he can't feel any of it.

The chef cooks another up for him. The first time he got the quickstep was in the Memphis lock-up, from the food, and when he and Tillis got out they broke into a pharmacy but could only find some bottles of paregoric which they drank down even with the awful camphor smell and then some of Mrs. Winslow's Soothing Syrup which made Tillis, who didn't even have the dysentery, chuck the whole mess up.

You are supposed to have these crazy dreams but really for Coop it's just peaceful, nobody blowing bugles at you and now with his ears unstopped all the little sounds, the crackling of the dope ball in the flame and the in and out of the others as they breathe their smoke down and the scratch, scratch as the chef scrapes the ash from the bowls to save in his lacquer box and Coop's own heart, beating long and easy now like waves on a broad beach and more pipes come, hard to keep count, and the thought floats through his head that the heathen Chinee are maybe shorting him but then the thought goes curling up to the yellow-stained ceiling and who cares when you are so high above them all? Floating, with them all below, white and black and Spanish and Cuban and *amigo* and pigtail looking up as he floats over like the observation balloon that morning at El Caney, above it all, but no, no, they shot that down and all of them are shooting at him now, pointing and shooting but he is too fast for the bullets that rise up slow like bubbles from the muck in Silas Tugwell's bog where they used to swim, why are they even bothering to shoot when he is so high, a hawk soaring, Cooperhawk that he took his name from, Cooperhawk that catch all the other birds in its claw and take them away, that fly so fast even through the thick woods and somehow don't ever hit a branch and how can bullets hope to reach him? But then the ants start coming out, out of his ears, going in the right direction at least but so many of them, tickling his neck where it was just shaved but there's a reason they are leaving, it's to make room for the music, the notes from the little *amigo* sliding back to him, so familiar, so like the music he heard the Mississippi boys playing on the rail gang down south, a new kind of music but familiar, simple on top but bubbling and twisted underneath, who knows what be hiding in that muck at the bottom, can't see the end of it from the surface and it wants words, the music, words to make it a story—

Ashes from the smokestack

—he thinks, and can hear someone, maybe himself, singing along—

Cloudin up my brain
Can't believe my woman
Leavin on that train
Blow your whistle, captain
All my dreams in vain

—and then he dives, Cooperhawk, into the black water.

*   *   *

When he wakes his mouth is full of ashes and he is looking into the bottom-less black holes in the eyes of the old man on the shelf across from him. The old man is the color of what they pulled out of Coop's ears, with long twigs for arms and legs, body withered like a persimmon been left on the ground so long even the bugs don't want it and with a look on his face that is no more solid, no more really here, than smoke.

"You and me, brother," Coop says softly to the old Chinese man. "We been there, aint we?"

The old man stares toward him but not really at him, his eyes all black pupil, his mouth only inches from the pipe gripped feebly in his bony hand. Coop smiles at him. Coop loves him.

"Only difference is," he says, "you aint comin back."

OUR MAN IN PAMPANGA

It is not, at this juncture, the sort of conflict the Correspondent cares to report on. The indigenous forces remain maddeningly elusive, assembling in number as if to make a counterattack, then melting away so rapidly that the engagement is barely worth giving a name to. Diligent as his fellows in the ink trade have been to inflate the skirmishes at San this or Santa that into something newsworthy, the countryside north and south of the capital remains infested with communities never to be immortalized in military history. And then the deuced luck of his diminutive, hastily purchased mare perishing beneath him on the way to the Zapote Bridge. Even Creelman of the *Journal*, recovered from his blooding at El Caney and screwed to Colonel Funston's hip all these months, was there for the festivities, the signalmen obliging him by steadily unrolling their spools of wire behind the heat-addled column so he might telegraph his despatch immediately upon the taking of Bacoor. And Creelman is not the most insufferable of the lot. The Correspondent had hopes that with Crane *hors de combat* and Dick Davis chasing the Boers there would be a clearer field in this pestilent backwater in which to distinguish oneself, but his competitors, toiling for periodicals of greater circulation than his own, are free to spend money like fresh air to corrupt the cablemen and thus beat him onto the wire even when his report is on their desks hours earlier.

Not that they refuse what little gratuity he offers them.

Manila, though the climate is beastly in the dry season and unspeakable in the wet, is all right in a Spanish-gone-tropical sort of way, offering livelier diversions than the worthy Davis can be enjoying in Ladysmith or Pretoria. The local seegars are cheap, plentiful, and surprisingly smokable, while the chief industry seems to be making a racket and selling rides in their unstable two-wheeled outfits (the Spaniards having taxed vehicles per axle) from one side of the pitiful excuse for a river to the other. The horse races are colorful and pleasant, the wealthier caste of Filipinos no less sporting than their Celestial cousins, and there is no end to religious pageantry despite their purported disaffection with the Roman Church and its representatives. But the inequality of the two protagonists has left this conflict nearly devoid of heroic feats and consequently uninspiring, if not undeserving of heroic prose.

Not that an adept such as the Correspondent cannot cobble something together.

Serving as he is for a northern publication hungry for "American color," the Tarheel Lieutenant has been a find. Gifted with the charming accent and fecund locutions of his section, Manigault also boasts an ancestry steeped in military tradition and dedicated to the Great Lost Cause, having no compunctions, as the rare Southerner displaced in Colorado's volunteer contribution to the effort, to find fault with superiors both immediate and of greater stripe.

"General Otis would be better employed anchoring a deck chair on the verandah of an establishment catering to the elderly," remarks the Lieutenant as they clickety-clack north past the earthquake-baroque church and much celebrated ruins of Caloocan, "than put in charge of a body of fighting men. My old Granny, rest her soul, was of a more decisive nature than he. When one encounters an inferior and hysteria-prone foe such as our present antagonist, one does not retreat, one does not pause, one does not *rest* until he is vanquished. They are the hare and we the hound, but we have been kept on a damnably short leash."

"You believe that if MacArthur—"

"If either General MacArthur or General Lawton were given free reign, Mr. Nig would have received his much-deserved thrashing, contritely cast away his arms, and we'd all be home by now, amazing our loved ones with the ease of it all."

"There would no doubt be holdouts—"

"Driven to the farthest and most forsaken outposts of these isles to live as mere *banditti*, as was done to the worthy Geronimo and his cutthroat band. But in lieu of that, we, and I use the term in the national sense of course, shall remain here, exposed to the diseases rampant in these latitudes, for at least another year. Not to mention the followers of Mohamet—"

"In the southern islands—"

"They have a custom in which their men who are hopelessly mired in debt appear before a wily *imam*, shaving their eyebrows and swearing an oath to the Mighty One that they will proceed to murder as many Christians as possible until they are themselves destroyed. These *juramentados*, these pledged assassins, then go about their bloody work assured that not only will all that they owe be forgotten but that upon their ending they will sit at the right hand of the Prophet, with a gaggle of black-eyed houris to attend them. How do you fight people for whom death is an improvement on their condition?"

"But your volunteers have finished their service."

"So the General Staff informs us. The Regular Army is more than welcome to the travesty of a war we leave behind."

They met in the hospital ward in Manila, both recovering from an overexposure to the sun on the day of the Zapote affair, the Lieutenant spouting his theories, many quite fantastic, and the Correspondent overcoming a vicious migraine to get it all down on paper.

"And your mission—"

"Has been fulfilled with honor and alacrity," chuffs the Tarheel Lieutenant. "The Colorados, despite a handful of incorrigibles I have had to deal with sharply, have the blood of frontiersmen in their veins—it is their nature to contest the savage on his own ground, and to conquer him."

The train slows, passing through an orchard that has been cleared back only far enough to give the troops on board the flatcars a clear field of fire at any snipers. The rains have stopped but the vegetation is still very green. He has tried *hellish green* and *bilious green*, only to settle on *interminable green*, although at this time of year it is often interrupted by splashes of *death's bed yellow*. He tried *jaundiced countryside* during the first dry season but Cheltingham in New York has let him know his *double entendre* was blue-inked every time he wired it. Crane has a patent on *red*, of course, any journalist employing it suggestively (*the bloodshot eye of the Tropics*) mocked brutally by his cohorts. The Correspondent's own strength is not in description, literal or baroquely impressionistic, but in his snippets of "overheard" dialogue, some of it actually transposed from interviews with the warriors themselves. That and a knack for the comical pidgin-speak of the natives, developed in his days as a cub enduring the exotic odors and sullen yellow glares of Pell Street.

He scribbles *sullen yellow glare* into his notebook.

"This land is a veritable cornucopia," announces the Lieutenant, gazing moonily out at the fruit trees. It is gloomy inside the passenger car, the windows taped over with cardboard to discourage target practice by the locals, each mile of the railway bought with American lives and still vulnerable to sabotage, but Manigault has peeled one of these blinders away so they can admire the countryside. The two privates he has impressed to accompany them sit glumly in the seat behind, terribly dull souls who seem as resentful of each other as they are toward their officer.

Manigault is a bounder, of course, but except for the redoubtable and ever loquacious Funston, remains the most inexhaustible fount of material the Correspondent has discovered in the Philippines. And though the Lieutenant's outbursts and observations retain a tinge of hysteria, he was pronounced fully recovered by the worthy *médicos* at San Juan de Dios and put on the street.

"Once we have opened it up for white men of boldness and industry—"

"But that pestilence you mentioned—" the Correspondent interjects in his not-for-the-record voice.

"The Anglo-Saxon brings many blessings on his march to glory," winks Manigault. "Paramount of these is the concept of hygiene."

"But the very soil seems to breed these scourges."

The orchard gives way to a miasma of murky standing water and rotting plant life, the roots of the stunted trees writhing up from the ground as if in a desperate attempt to escape it before being wrenched under again.

"The soil responds to its master. Before the War, my people were in tobacco," proclaims the Lieutenant for the hundredth time, and the Correspondent can only picture these ante-bellum Manigaults lying in a warehouse, dried and rolled in enormous leaves of white burley. "They could expectorate on an anthill and raise a cash crop from the result."

The Lieutenant waits for him to finish writing, the mark of a born newspaper source.

"Unless my presence is urgently required back in Wilmington," he says, staring unimpressed at the festering swamp without, "I shall embellish my new properties with that tradition."

The Correspondent attempts not to snort. "Have you seen any of it?"

"As of yet, only in description. But this," and here he waggles a much-folded survey map in his hand, "though only recently liberated, should prove the most developed of my holdings."

Cheltingham has been cabling that the subscribers are not so much bored with the conflict as confused, "Why are we there?" rapidly deteriorating into "I don't care to read about it." It was no problem after the treacherous attack in February, the Tagalos begging for chastisement, but as the fury of battle has dissipated into the grinding trudge of skirmish and evasion, a chess game where the opponent has only pawns and hides them under the table, the purpose of the adventure falls further into question. The Indians had at least their Fetterman massacre, their Little Big Horn, ambushes of a scale and barbarity to rouse the public's sporting blood, but this—

Not that he is wishing slaughter on American patriots.

He arrived in Havana rather too previous for the fireworks, a terrible case of the sprue forcing him to return to New York and sit out the siege of Santiago in an isolation ward on Long Island. American shooting wars, and the opportunities for rapid advancement they afford men of print, are in short supply. The Otis angle has been fruitful, the Correspondent using the Tarheel Lieutenant's pungent observations to hint, nay, to declare that swifter progress (and greater pyrotechnics) should be had if the general were replaced by a younger, bolder commander. And perhaps this plea to the American spirit of adventure and commerce, plus the suggestion that the next Klondike is festooned with palm trees, will reawaken their interest.

A paradise, he writes, *waiting for Anglo-Saxon angels to reap its bounty.*

The train slows, stops, and they disembark at what the freshly painted sign announces as San Fernando, taken two weeks ago by Hall's flying column. The sun makes its sudden and cruel assault on the Correspondent's epidermis and spirit, seeming to drill through the woven palm of his Panama to blister his cranium. They walk through the artillery-blasted stone buildings, the morose privates dragging behind them, to the stick-and-mud village beyond, the dwellings comparing unfavorably with his boyhood treehouse, the requisite coterie of louse-ridden canines harrying their steps (the poorer the man, the more dogs he is bound to own) as Manigault smartly salutes the garrison sentries. Filthy children abound, a few clothed only in Nature's costume, and he witnesses one old woman entering the rubble-strewn, roofless shell of what was once a small church and pausing, even in the absence of holy water (or the basin that once held it) to sign her wrinkled forehead.

"Ninety percent of war is character," says the Lieutenant, *apropos* of nothing. "Character and will. The googoo shoots badly because he is untrained, yes, but he remains so because training would be wasted on him. Your mongrel races do not possess the mental stamina, the powers of self-abnegation to apply themselves to any endeavor requiring concentrated effort and under-standing. When faced with an enemy greater not only in stature but also in force of will and character, he senses the futility of direct resistance and either flees in panic or resorts to a more skulking, treacherous type of aggression."

"So you do not esteem the *insurrecto* as an opponent?"

"Our chief opponents here are ignorance, superstition, and savagery. Where the lower races have polluted each other to the degree we have encountered here, their effect is legion. But we shall prevail."

"*'Their silent, sullen peoples shall thank your God and you.'*"

Manigault gives him a wry smile. "As your Mr. Roosevelt has observed, indifferent verse, but noble sentiment."

The Correspondent smiles, never having thought of the bucktoothed Rough Rider as *his* before, and noting again that to a son of the South all yankees are as one.

It is early afternoon when they leave San Fernando, walking eastward toward solitary Mount Arayat, Manigault holding his survey map at arms' length and turning it this way and that as he strides down a dried-mud thoroughfare much pitted by buffalo hooves, occasionally checking the unrelievedly flat horizon for some reference point while one of the privates, embarrassed, lets the woven basket holding their supper slap against his leg every other step. They cross a tiny stream, a trio of young women with the surly aspect of the Malay flogging wet clothing on the rocks while their offspring, barely old enough to walk, gambol in the listlessly flowing water, then rediscover the sorry excuse for a road. They pass vast grayish squares of harvested rice interrupted by desultory stands of banana trees or indigo, then one irrigated field in which a lone water buffalo, one of the ubiquitous *carabao* glistening like polished steel from its recent wallow, treads snuffling for edibles with an equally solitary white egret following after, feasting on the crawly things brought to the surface in the great beast's footprints. That is me trailing the Tarheel Lieutenant, thinks the Correspondent, with the crawfish and cutworms replaced by quotables. The soggy patch gives way to desiccated plain, some sort of ground crop with a scraggle of green leaves planted on both sides of them. The few rustics they pass, out chopping at weeds in the vicious sun, studiously avoid taking notice of their procession. *Thus it was for the conquering Roman*, the Correspondent writes as he walks, perspiration burning his eyes, *in all venues the focus of a dull hatred cloaked with indifference.*

"Where you grew up," he asks the Tarheel Lieutenant, "were there still Union soldiers in uniform?"

Manigault stops and gives him the frankest gaze he has ever received from the man, as if he were just pondering that very image.

"There were indeed," he answers softly, "but my father instructed us to pay them no heed."

They continue in silence, the burden of the heat robbing his limbs of their vitality, and he begins to feel sorry for the poor, obdurate devils sentenced to be born and die in this crucible. He does not wonder that the Spanish who ruled it slid so quickly into a mean-spirited decadence. As Mrs. Jefferson Davis and Senator Tillman of the anti-Imperialists so eloquently state it, the worry is not what shall we do with the Filipino, but what shall our association with him do to *us*. He writes the word *decay* into his notebook, underlining thrice, and then the Lieutenant halts again and spreads his arms.

"I believe this is it."

There is no signpost, no marker, not one stone laid upon another to indicate a boundary, only the same fields extending on both sides of the road broken here and there by outcroppings of thorn-brandishing greenery.

"You're certain?"

Manigault points across the planted rows to a structure at least a half mile away. "The house comes with it."

They set off diagonally across the field then, the new proprietor fairly leaping over the shabbily cultivated rows, the Correspondent quite done in by now and staggering in the rear. The boots he purchased in San Francisco make a bully impression in photographs but are not equal to the terrain, and the white suit built in Hongkong is stuck to him like a second, repulsively slimy skin. His collar is a rag. There will be nothing cool in the basket when it is opened, no rum cock-tail with ice waiting at the *hacienda*. He has partaken only sparingly of the native cuisine since arriving, the spices overstated and the indiscriminate mixing of fleshes so favored by the Spanish—beef, fowl, and fish more than likely to cohabit the same dish—seems less than wise given the extremities of the weather. As for what is fed to the column on the march, the less said in print the better, the charges leveled at the much-maligned war secretary Root after the sickness that followed victory in Cuba still a sore point with Army censors. Home again, carving a slab of prime at Rector's or enjoying the delectable ice cream at Louis Sherry's establishment, he may confess to having eaten canned bacon, but at the moment the mere thought of that delicacy causes his insides to somersault.

The *hacienda* house is much larger than it appeared to him from a distance, a few outbuildings half-hidden behind it. It seems a rather stately pile to belong to the purebred Malays who Manigault has so colorfully described as being no distant removal from the "missing link." Four massive posts support the tile roof over the two stories, the lower floor of bullet-scarred adobe masonry and the upper of wood. The façade of the lower is dominated by a huge door arched high enough to admit carriage and passengers, with a normal-sized rectangular door cut into it for pedestrian traffic. Vertical iron grilles cover the tall windows that flank the carriage gate, some sort of flowering creeper vine half-covering them.

A kind of gallery runs around the front and sides of the upper floor, repeating sets of wooden louvers opening to reveal sliding panels of hand-sized capiz-shell "windows" of the sort seen in the Walled City. Beneath the bottom sill of these runs what the Correspondent has been told is a *ventanilla*, perhaps a foot high, fronted with wooden balustrades, to allow the air to flow even when the larger openings are shut fast. Another opening just beneath the eaves serves the same purpose. If it were a boat, thinks the Correspondent, it would sink in an instant.

The *hacienda* compound is deserted when they arrive, not even one of the scabrous fowl that seem everywhere underfoot in this country gracing the yard. Manigault calls up to the living quarters, but there is no response. The pedestrian door, however, is unsecured, and they venture into the *zaguan*.

There are no partitions in this lower level. The space the family *carroza* would normally occupy is empty, as are bins that appear to once have been filled with grain, set upon large square slabs of stone flooring. Nearly half the room is piled with furniture, some broken, some appearing to be perfectly serviceable. An ornate stairway invites them to ascend.

"I imagine they've sacked the place," says the new *dueño*, starting up, "but we'll have a look anyway."

The drawing room that greets them is remarkably intact, chairs and tables haphazardly placed but still present, a lovely design painted on the ceiling of stamped tin, and only a few of the somewhat garishly colored chromolithographs these people seem addicted to hanging on the walls. Large double doors draped with damask curtains open to the *sala mayor*, which seems to have hosted a dance party immediately before the departure of the former owners, the numerous rattan chairs all pushed against the walls. The floor is of a highly polished native wood held together with pegs, as these materials are generally impervious to nails. A frieze of intricately carved *molave*, reminiscent of the stunning altar of the Jesuits' San Ignacio church in the Intramuros, crowns the walls, which are painted with gilt trimming and designs markedly Chinese in character. A massive upright piano dominates the near end of the room, Shubert's A-minor Sonata still propped on the music shelf. The west wall sports two large oil portraits of the erstwhile *hacienderos*, a man and woman, in their late fifties perhaps, each in semi-profile facing toward the other. Though the features of the couple are what the Correspondent characterizes in print as thoroughly "Asiatic," the effect of their bearing and European finery and the artist's *chiaro oscuro* is of a Spanish grandee and his *señora*, a kind of Tagalo nobility.

"Most of my lands were purchased from the friars," says Manigault, strolling around the room, careful to avoid the scattered leavings of some bird that has found its way into the house. "But Mr. Impoc here was evidently as afraid of the *insurrectos* as he was of our own forces, and decided, through my intermediaries, to take the most prudent course of action."

"You bought this palace on a lieutenant's pay?"

Manigault remains unfazed, smiling enigmatically and continuing farther into the dwelling, trailed by the Correspondent and the unhappy troopers.

The avian intruder has been even more destructive in the dining room, his presence recorded not only on the floor but on the long table and ornately detailed sideboards of red *narra*. The china and silver have been removed, of course, but the impressive cut-glass chandelier, though slightly atilt to the Correspondent's eye, remains overhead. The privates slump onto chairs and begin to lay out the items from the picnic basket. The Correspondent wishes nothing more than to throw himself prone on an unsullied patch of floor while someone gets the punkahs turning. But his interlocutor is moving ahead to explore, and he, duty bound, must follow.

The kitchen seems also to serve as a laundry, a pair of flatirons left on the chopping block. There is an earthen oven shaped something like a beehive and a wooden rack hung from the tiled wall that must be employed for drying dishes. The Correspondent pushes a shutter back and a breeze suddenly whispers through the vertical bars in the minaret-shaped window that looks down on the *azotea* below, an aromatic, lushly planted hanging garden with stone benches and a pathway bordered by a split-bamboo rail that leads to an even greater collection of exotic flora.

Manigault finds the bird, a large, glossy-black crow, dead on the floor. He lifts it up by the tip of one wing.

"I'm afraid the intelligence of these creatures has been overrated," he jibes.

"This fellow managed to find a way in, but evidently forgot where it was."

The back of the Correspondent's neck begins to prickle, usually a presentiment of unfortunate events, and he turns to find the room filled with intruders, barefoot *insurrectos* with bolos in hand.

The Correspondent reels, dizzy, while Manigault's free hand drops to the butt of his holstered Webley but freezes there as the one man wearing boots jams the barrel of his antiquated rifle against the lieutenant's chest and begins to scream in one of their many confusing lingos.

The demon with the rifle gestures to the floor. Manigault gently lays the unfortunate bird on the painted clay tile before prostrating himself. The Correspondent keeps his eyes fixed on the blade of the nearest insurgent as he kneels, relieved to see no blood staining its edge. The voices of the men above as they argue with each other are high and nervous, like parrots screeching. He smells urine. The tile is cool against his sunburned cheek.

Dead or alive, he thinks as his heart gallops, unharnessed and wild in his chest, they'll give me four columns at least.

BILIBID

They send a captain he's never seen before. Big Ten has been in Bilibid since the dust-up at the bridge, sharing a bullpen with a dozen goldbricks, thieves, and deserters in a building reserved for Americans. The poop is they've got Hod somewhere in isolation, the long rectangular cellblocks spreading out from the central hub of tower and chapel, more than half of them filled with locals. On the far side of the wall that splits the prison is the *presidio* where they keep another five hundred and you get to walk around a little more. The guards haul him out just after reveille and march him across to the office building by the warden's quarters. In the room there is nothing but a plain wooden desk with the captain he doesn't know planted behind it and Corporal Schreiber beside him ready to go with pen and ink.

He stands at attention.

"McGinty."

"Sir."

Corporal Schreiber starts scratching on his paper.

"You were in Company G on the tenth of June."

"Yes sir."

"I'd like to hear your version of what took place on that day."

"The scrap in the morning or what happened later?"

"Start at the beginning."

He thought there was supposed to be a judge and a jury, lawyers. How dumb, he wonders, does this fella think I am?

"It was hot," he says.

The captain is dripping sweat. There is a ceiling fan turning lazily above them but Big Ten, standing with his head right under it, feels no stirring in the air.

"We're in the Philippines, Private. It's always hot."

"Not like that day it isn't. We mustered up in the morning and you couldn't breathe, it was already so hot. Men started falling out right away, marching to Parañaque, and then there's the shoot-out, charging up the hill at their trenches, and they get Major Moses—"

"And you and Private Atkins—"

"We're in the thick of it. Sometimes the googoos just shoot over your head and run, it's a joke, but these ones were holding high ground in the woods and knew what they were up to."

"Lieutenant Manigault took part as well?"

"Oh sure. Don't anybody have a problem with the Lieutenant when there's lead flying."

"No contretemps between the Lieutenant and Private Atkins?"

He figures that means something bad.

"No, nothin between them. We been in a lot of these smokers, sir. The fellas pretty much go to it, orders or no."

"And then later in the day—"

"They sent what's left of our company ahead to scout, marching wide around Las Piñas while they shelled it, and it's even hotter and more men start to fall out, which puts the Lieutenant in a mood. He's feeling the heat too, I suppose, like anybody would, and then there's this googoo fella out in a field—why he don't have the sense to go lie down in the shade I don't know—but he waves and grins and calls out that he's *muy amigo* the way they do, and like I said it's hotter than hell and Lieutenant Manigault takes offense at this and—"

The captain cuts him off. "That's not the incident I'm interested in."

"Oh."

The thing about the Army is when an officer asks your opinion that means he don't want to hear it.

"When you reached the Zapote Bridge—"

"Well, sir, we was operating as a recon patrol by that time, so we never got right up *to* it—"

"Lieutenant Manigault issued an order—"

"He issued a good number of them, all day long—"

"He issued an order to Private Atkins."

"Atkins was still there, I do remember that. We'd had all kinds of fellas fell out on the way, left a trail of em behind us, but Atkins kept up till the bridge. It was around then that the sun got to the Lieutenant—"

"*Got* to him."

"Yes sir. He went down like a sack of spuds."

"But before that, was the Lieutenant acting erratically?"

Big Ten has been staring at a brown lizard twitching in a crack in the stone wall behind the others. He looks down into the captain's eyes.

"I'm just a private soldier," he says. "It aint up to me to judge whether an officer is bughouse or not, is it?"

The captain meets his gaze for a long moment.

"Did Private Atkins refuse an order from the Lieutenant?"

Big Ten ponders it. "There was some debate on tactics."

"Lieutenant Manigault gave an order and the private refused to carry it out."

The way the captain says it Big Ten realizes it is an offering. One day here is worse than a month in the Leadville box and there is no telling how much time they can throw at him. All he has to do is say yes and his part in the deal will be over. He'll walk out of Bilibid and leave this shithole island with the rest of the outfit. As for Hod—

"The way I remember it," he says, carefully, "and none of us was thinking too clear on account of the heat, the Lieutenant said something that didn't make no sense and then Atkins asked if that's what he really meant and the Lieutenant he jumped to conclusions. Such as that his own men, starting with me and Atkins, were fixing to do him in."

"And were you?"

He shakes his head. "Who'd believe a thing like that, Captain?"

The officer considers for a moment and then grabs the paper Corporal Schreiber has been writing on and crumples it.

"You lose two months' pay," he says to Big Ten, "and when you go back to your company you keep your lip buttoned."

Big Ten feels a little dizzy. The chuck in Bilibid is about what you'd expect it to be and his stomach hasn't been right from the second day inside.

"I don't know, Sir—what with Lieutenant Manigault thinking I'm out to—"

"Lieutenant Manigault," interrupts the captain, "is no longer with us."

* * *

Big Ten comes upon Hod out in front of the prison, looking pale and skinny and staring up at the Teatro Zorilla, which is presenting something called *Bodabil*.

"Look who else bust out of the hoosegow today."

Hod sees him and grins. "What you tell him?"

Big Ten shrugs. "All a big misunderstanding. Plus Manlygoat's gone and they don't know if he's coming back."

"Yeah. I guess it's been LaDuke trying to put the screws to us." They walk toward Calle Iris.

"Lose your pay?"

Hod nods.

"So we're back to where we started in Denver, aint we?"

"I spose so."

Hod turns, walking backward to watch some coolies putting up wood and bamboo bleachers for a parade. There has been a parade near every day they've been in Bilibid, music drifting over the walls, the goldbricks and thieves and deserters singing along to the ones that have words. Hod turns back to him and grins again.

"As I remember it, back in Denver, we were set to have a fight."

No woman who wasn't a whore, any color, has ever asked Hod in before. Mei seems nervous, looking around corners to see if anybody is watching, and then waving him up to join her. He is excited in his stomach, his eyes still smarting from the bright light after the months of prison gloom. They go past the ventilators of the hospital laundry and then there is a little shed that probably once had supplies in it. Waiting outside is a very round Filipina gal holding a little boy who the minute he sees Mei spreads his arms wide and smiles and starts hollering "Ma! Ma! Ma!"

Something she never told him.

The Filipina gal says some things in Spanish and hands the boy over and then Mei gives her a few centavos and she makes herself scarce, giving Hod a quick once-over as she leaves.

"Bo," says Mei to Hod as she bends to open up the shed.

"Hey, Bo," says Hod, trying to hide his surprise as the little boy shyly stares at him over his mother's shoulder. "How's it going?"

Inside there is a cot for a bed and a single wooden chair and a washbasin and not much more. He wonders how she cooks. Mei points to the chair.

"You sit."

Mei sits across from him on the edge of the cot and the little boy, Bo, who is half crawling and half walking when he can get a hold on something, moves around the floor making noises, sneaking a look at Hod now and then and with each pass coming a little closer to him. He doesn't look all Chinese.

"How old is he?"

"Almost two year."

"And his father—?"

"Bo never gonna know his father," says Mei flatly.

The boy definitely doesn't look all Chinese, black hair that sticks straight up on his head but big round brown eyes and a coloring that is lighter than Mei, who is the color of Kansas soil after a drought. He's never seen why they call them yellow. In this country there are all kinds of mixes and all kinds of shades, like the House of All Nations in Leadville, and you've got to look more at the clothes and how people carry themselves than their skin color to know who is a big cheese and who is not.

"They give you this place with your job?"

"Spanish people give it to me. I think the American forget."

"Yeah," he says, looking around. "It is kind of forgettable."

There is a crucifix on a gold chain hung from a nail over her bed and one of the little fat gods they sell in the Binondo shops, big smile and all belly, sitting on the ledge of her only window. Bo gets close enough to stand by climbing up Hod's leg and then yells something over and over, pointing at his face.

"He want something?"

"He points at your nose. He never see one like that."

"Well—spose you need a closer look."

He picks the little boy up under his arms and sets him standing in his lap and right away Bo latches on to his nose, squeezing it on the sides with a little frown on his face.

"I bust it a couple of times in the ring," Hod says to Mei, as if she is the one who wants an explanation. "Fighting."

"You a boxer?"

"More like a punching bag." If he and Big Ten can pull it off there will be enough money for a start. He had a speech all planned out, practicing over and over in the cell, sure that Mei could not resist if he put the idea right. But this, this Bo all of a sudden, is a whole other deal. It wants some thought before he sticks his neck out.

The little boy butts him in the chest with the top of his head then, over and over, till Hod turns him around and sits him down in his lap and hugs him tight with his arms.

"He never have a man hold him," says Mei, watching him carefully. "He like to wrestle."

"Sure," says Hod. "All boys like to wrestle."

He decides not to ask her more about the father. There are hundreds of boys Bo's age and size out on the streets in Manila and in the villages, cute little monkeys with dirty faces and bare feet and their naked keisters showing under the rags that have been thrown over them, eye-to-eye with the pigs and chickens and turkeys that run free here. Some have bellies like the god on the window ledge, but theirs sticking out from hunger, and some have sores on their heads or flies crawling on their faces or legs and arms that aren't straight and the ones a little older chase after you calling "Hey you Joe!" or "Yankee soja looka me!" hoping you'll flip them a centavo or a cigarette and maybe in a few years they'll have a gun or an old rifle in hand and be out running with the *insurrectos*.

"This is a lucky kid," he says to Mei.

"Kid is a baby goat."

"It's what we call little ones. Children. Kids."

Mei smiles. If he can make her smile once Hod figures it has been a successful visit. "Lucky kid," she says.

She stands then and crosses to the window ledge where next to the fat god there are two banana leaves folded in packets. Inside are small loaves of rice with meat and vegetables mixed into it.

"You sit over here now," she says.

Go or stay, he thinks, I need some money.

He sits with Bo still in his lap and Mei puts the food in front of them on an empty fruit crate turned over and brings out the sticks they use, Hod making his into a kind of shovel and Mei deftly snatching up little bits of the food to put in Bo's mouth or her own or even once or twice into Hod's. The food is terrific, still hot and not strange-tasting at all but after a couple months of bread and water and the years of boardinghouse grub and Army chow and mulligan stew on the bum he has a hard time swallowing it, thinking about what she has risked to ask him in here, to show herself like this, close to tearing up from how it feels that instead of being court-martialed and thrown back into the hole it is the three of them here, sitting close together on the cot. No woman, whore or not, has ever asked Hod Brackenridge to eat dinner with her family.

LAS CIEGAS

The soldiers sit on a load of track ballast in the gondola, rolling past cane fields where men crouch with curved knives flashing and past rice fields with barefoot women walking up on the dikes carrying parasols to shield them from the brutal sun and tiny clusters of huts where the people wander out to stare at them but nobody shoots. There are mountains ahead in the distance, a long jagged-top wall of them off to the left, the west, and a big one sticking up all alone ahead to the right. There is one passenger car that the officers ride in, and boxcars full of horses and mules and Chinese and supplies for the Pampanga outposts. Royal fingers a heavy, round ballast stone, angry, but the land is so flat there is nothing to throw it at.

"Got us up here on this rockpile," he mutters to nobody in particular. "Just a load of freight."

"Wasn't no rocks, we couldn't see over the sides."

"They put on some Pullmans, we could ride in style," calls Hardaway.

"Aint gonna let you in no Pullman without a red cap on, nigger," smiles Cooper. "What you think this is?"

They have patrolled along the Dagupan line before but never been this far north. It is almost November but it is still hot. The ballast rocks are hot where there is no soldier to cover them. The smoke from the stack on the little toy-looking engine blows straight back over them and Royal watches the hats of the others turning gray with a layer of ash.

"Treat the damn mules better than us."

Achille points out to a trio of smallish men hacking at a stand of cane. "You want to trade places with them?"

Royal just squeezes the rock.

"Ever chop cane, Roy?"

"No."

"That sugar will eat a man up." Achille frowns out at the field as they pass, their smoke spreading behind them, drifting downward. "Harvest season one year when I was only *un ti boug*, my *maman* say go find your *père* cause it was nearly dark and he not home. I walk out by the field and there I see him, lay out on his face in the red dirt of the road and I know from how he looks he is dead. Not move a thing. But when I come close he is breathing. Just so weary he can't make it home without he lie down and sleep some, right there in the road."

Royal turns to watch the cane-cutters disappear behind the rear of the train.

"So I sit by him and maybe one hour, two hour, he wake up and see me, don't say a word, just stand and start out for home. Let me carry his long knife."

"Them boys not really cuttin sugar," says Cooper. "They just practicin. Sneak up on Corporal Junior here some night and *whack! whack!*" He makes a chopping gesture to Junior's neck.

"Only if you fall asleep on sentry duty," says Junior.

They pass a shacky-looking mill, a single water buffalo plodding in a circle to turn spiked, hardwood rollers while one man jams stalks of green cane in between them, snapping and cracking, the juice running down a bamboo trough the carabao carefully steps over into a huge iron pot smoking over a furnace sunk in a pit, another Filipino pulling the crushed cane out to be spread in the field while a third, a sinewy, sweat-pouring man in nothing but a loincloth, feeds the furnace from a stack of dried stalks, all of them looking like they've been doing this since the beginning of time. The smoke from the pot, smelling of burned sugar, drifts across the track as the soldiers roll by.

"Them people change place with any of us up on these rocks in a minute," says Achille, shaking his head. "Workin that sugar eat a man right up."

San Fernando is a big town or a small city and the train station is the grandest they've seen outside of Manila. The church and the *casa municipal* and some of the nicer houses have been knocked apart by American artillery or burned down by the rebels before they left but life is going on here, market day, women walking with big wide baskets of fruit balanced on their heads, no hands, women plucking chickens to sell while they're still flapping, a band with an accordion and a fiddle and a boy drumming on some kerosene cans on the platform and the people about their business, putting up with the soldiers from different units walking among them like they put up with the typhoons that sweep through or the daily rain showers or the stifling heat, just another unchangeable thing in the world. The soldiers pass their rifles down and jump off the gondola and are lined up in twos with Company F and marched double time through the streets.

"I gots to wee-wee, Sarge," calls Hardaway.

"You can do that when we get where we're going," says Jacks without turning around.

"Where that is?"

"They'll tell us when we get there."

They are marched double time through San Fernando, sweat-sticky and covered with ash, and head away on a wagon road to the northeast. A pack of little boys follow for a while, laughing and pointing excitedly at the smoked yankees, the boldest working up the nerve to dart forward and touch Royal on the back of his hand.

In Cuba after the Dons surrendered, the little boys, skinny and hungry as they were, would lug your rifle for you on a long march, three, four, five miles hoping maybe you'd stop to eat and they get a scrap of hardtack out of it. Raggedy-ass, smiling, every color you could imagine. Here the word has come down that you don't even let them near, any googoo over ten year old as like to cut your throat as look at you.

"Look like we the first colored been up this far," says Too Tall. "Folks don't know what we about."

"Then it's up to me to spread the news," says Coop.

Clouds hang low in the broad sky. Companies H and F in dusty blue march down the red dirt road between deep green rice paddies dotted white with cattle egrets, one hundred twenty men with rifles on their shoulders and two dozen coolies staggering after them under packs and cases. It is rice-harvest time, women in broad hats bending to sickle handfuls of the stalks close to the ground, then binding them into bundles hung on tentlike wooden racks to dry. The Filipinas are careful to keep their faces turned away, but a huge carabao steps forward to get a closer look, chewing, snot running from its nose, a cloud of flies lifting and following, then resettling on its glistening black hide when it stops at the edge of the dirt road.

"Lookit that, Too Tall mama come out to greet us."

"She that good-lookin, Too Tall, how come you so ugly?"

"And what that big ole thing hanging twixt her legs?"

"Googoos come after you sorry-ass niggers," says Too Tall, who is dark-skinned and used to this, expects it, even, "don't count on no help from me."

"Somethin wrong," says Corporal Pickney suddenly, looking up into the sky.

"What that?"

"It aint rainin."

"Got to wait till they not one tree left we can stand under," says Gamble, "then she gonna dump on us. I see one way over there."

"My people had come to these islands, see what the weather is like, they would of kept on sailin."

"Sailin, shit. Didn't nobody in your family ever get let up on the deck to look at no islands, man."

"I'm talkin way back. Story is they sailed in boats, knew how to swim—"

"If they was ever in the water it was with a rope around their ankle, some white man trolling for alligators."

"Couldn't use you for bait. Scare them gators away."

"This enemy territory, less you all forgot," calls Sergeant Jacks. "Might want to keep that noise down."

"We aint sneaking up on nobody, Sarge," Cooper calls back. "Hell, they can see for clear twenty miles across these fields."

"Yeah, right about now they gone to wake General Aggy up from his nap, tell him the 25th is coming to grab his little googoo ass."

"Can't catch nobody you can't find."

"Hey, if we *was* to catch him—"

"Aguinaldo, shit," says Coop. "Aggy aint but just one damn general. These people got more generals runnin around in these boondocks—hell, you own a pair of *shoes* they gone make you a Captain at least."

"What's this?"

Junior steps out of formation and pulls off a square of paper tacked to a telegraph pole.

"Junior mama left him a grocery list."

There is a drawing of a black man at the top of the paper, hanging dead from a tree, his head cocked at an unnatural angle.

"*To the Colored American Soldier*—" reads Junior.

"That be us," says Hardaway.

"*Why do you make war on us, freedom-loving men of the same hue, when at home the whites lynch your brothers in Georgia and Alabama*—"

"And Mississippi and Florida and Texas—"

"*It is without honor that you shed your precious blood. Your masters have thrown you in the most iniquitous fight with double purpose—to make you the instrument of their ambition. Your hard work will make extinction of your race*—it's very well written," says Junior, scanning down the page.

"—and Kansas and Missouri and Indiana—"

"The googoos think we gonna join up with them?"

"Hell yeah. Lookit all they got to offer—" Gamble sweeps his free arm at the rice fields around them. "Give us forty acres and one of these water buffalos that look like Too Tall mama."

"Maybe if they throw in one of these little long-hair gals—"

"This not our country," says Royal.

Too Tall laughs. "That's what old Geronimo used to say bout that sorry pile of rocks where we built Huachuca. But now it *is*."

"That's what old King Cannibal say when the white mens come to take your grandaddy out from Africa. And they took him just the same."

"But what they're saying—"

"What they're saying don't mount to muleshit," says Corporal Pickney. "'Freedom-loving men of the same hue—' that's a laugh. Aint none of these people my color."

"White folks calls em niggers just like they do us," says Hardaway.

"A wolf and a dog may both be referred to as canines," says Junior, folding the paper and slipping it inside his shirt. "But there is no confusing the two."

"Junior—I'm sorry—*Co*rporal Junior—have got that right on the money," says Coop. "Even if he is a in*i*quitous sumbitch. But in this story *we* the wolves." He jerks his head at a pair of the Filipinas across the field, shaking grains loose from dried bundles of rice straw. "And these people just shit out of luck."

They come on the village of Las Ciegas in the late afternoon, the usual cluster of nipa huts scattered around the plaza in front of a tiny stucco church, Jacks sending a squad around to the rear of it to catch anyone trying to sneak away and the rest of them rushing in with bayonets fixed and voices barking.

"Front and center!" they shout. "All you googoos come on out! *Fuera, fuera!*" Two men rushing up each of the little ladders and onto the platforms of the huts and chasing people out, mostly old or women with children but a handful of younger men who scurry out with their hands on top of their heads crying "*Amigo, yo soy muy amigo!*," herding them all into a mass in front of the church and telling them "*Bajo, bajo!*" to sit on the ground and some crying while the search is made, bayonets poked and probed and stashes of supplies dragged out and chickens and turkeys flapping and dogs hysterical at their boots and a bristly black hog tied to a tree with a knotted rope through its ear squealing in panic, squealing and trying to bolt, like to tear that ear right off till Coop puts one between its eyes to shut it up and impress the googoos and Royal biting his cheeks the whole while, hating them for this, pushing a man twice his age who is the size of a middling boy, all bone and gristle, pushing hard enough that the man falls over on his face.

"Get up! *Arriba*, goddammit, don't make me be draggin your sorry ass over there! Up!"

One squad surrounding the villagers while the rest stab their bayonets into walls and floors and bedding, Coop and Too Tall digging with theirs under the hut platforms hoping for buried gold.

And then Captain Coughlin singles out one or another of them, jerked up and slapped onto a beautifully carved wooden chair in the middle of the plaza to face him and the turncoat interpreter whose name is Dayrit but the men call Stubby. Royal is the one supposed to pull them out, stepping over the cowering, crying mess to stand over the one he thinks they're pointing to and saying "This one? You want this one?" and then grabbing hold of skinny arms to yank them up and drag the suspect stumbling over the others, gabbling and crying, to be interrogated.

I am death, he thinks. I am their angel of death.

One musket, useless to fire, is found in Las Ciegas, and a store of rice maybe too big for one family, and, under the mayor's big hut that sits behind a little staked fence, a stack of Mexican silvers buried in a bamboo safe.

"I knew it!" cries Coop when he pries the lid off the bamboo section and pours the coins out on the dirt. "They just pretendin to be so raggedy-ass. Got their whole deal hid away somewhere."

And the story from the ones set in the chair is always the same. This is a poor village. Some of the young men were killed by the Spanish, some have been kidnapped by the *insurgentes* or by gangs of bandits. If you take our food we will starve. We are *amigos*, friends of the Americans, and know nothing about fighting. And then, when it is clear that the *soldados negros* are not moving on, that they are going to garrison this town, they point out the mayor who is the only one with shoes on and can explain how the Spanish used to do it.

There is one young woman who does not cry and sits a little apart from the others. When Royal stands over her she gets to her feet before he has to grab her. He can smell cocoanut oil in her hair.

"She say her husband is died," Stubby tells the captain when she is planted in the chair. "She say the *kastilas* kill him in Manila." He puts his hands around his fat neck and makes a choking gesture. "Some time ago."

"They all say their husbands were killed," growls Captain Coughlin. "There's nothing but widows in this country."

Stubby grins and nods. "Widows, yes. We have many of these."

"Tell her I don't believe her. Ask her where he is."

Royal watches the woman as she answers the shouted questions. She looks like she is maybe his same age. She looks like she is past hurting.

"She say he is *en la tumba*," says Stubby. "He was called Fecundo Magapuna."

Captain Coughlin bends to put his face very close to hers, but her eyes are unwavering.

"Get her away from me," he says and Royal moves but she is already on her feet. He follows her back to where she was sitting, cocoanut oil the sweetest thing he's smelled in weeks, and when she turns to look into his eyes he mutters to her.

"*Perdóname*," he says.

He is not sure if that's right, if it's only what you say if you bump a lady on a crowded trolley, if it doesn't count unless you take your hat off first, but she does not glare back at him, only keeps looking, and for the rest of the questioning he can feel her eyes on him.

Nilda, he heard her say when Stubby asked her name. Nilda Magapuna.

They are bigger than the Spanish, much bigger. And dark, some of them, some as dark as the *negritos* up north and some closer to her color, but the ones in charge are all white men. So it works the same with them. They are men with rifles and do what is always done. At home in Zambales when she was a girl the Spanish did the same, and took everything there was to eat, but these men seem to be staying. If they stay long she will leave, after they relax their vigilance, leave and try to go back to Zambales. There is nobody here in Las Ciegas for her anymore, Fecundo buried and his mother gone to the coast so now they can talk about him openly, how he left owing money to so many, a gambler and a layabout and where did he find that girl?

When she looked into the eyes of the one it surprised her at first. They are just men. Just men with rifles like the Spanish are men or the ones fighting still to the north are men and if she doesn't leave, soon, that will be trouble.

Hilario, the *capitán de barangay*, is pointing her out now.

She really is a widow, he says. She lives in the house of her dead husband's mother who has left for the coast and that house is a good place to put some of your soldiers. If you pay her she can cook and wash your clothes. Hilario's wife is glaring at Nilda because the wife knows Hilario has been after her since the day she arrived from Mariquina. The dark soldiers are all under the houses now, stabbing the ground with the blades on their rifles, looking for treasure. She hopes if they find any more they don't start to fight over it. Some of them are looking at her, too, and the other young women. We are treasure, Nilda thinks, but only for a moment.

WARRIORS

Call it sentiment, but a guy will naturally back a slugger of his own complexion. Of course, if the scrap is a mismatch and his own pile of cocoanuts is on the line it is a different proposition. Which is why I, Private Runyon of the Minnesota Volunteers, give no odds when the mess-hall donnybrook between the Chief and the rock-knocker becomes a public event.

Previous to the incident they go for pals, these two, as much as any pair of one-stripers in the vols—the Chief being as talkative a representative of the feather-and-warpaint outfit as you are likely to bump up against and the rock-knocker, a hard-luck case out of Montana, an area where such individuals are in oversupply, always happy to give him an ear. Before their dust-up you could figure that whither goest one of them the other is never far behind, to the point where when the rock-knocker lands his tail in the jug for nixing his looey in the line of battle, in goes the noble savage as well. Fortunately for them, said officer is snatched by the googoos whilst on an excursion of dubious intent out of town, and charges against the two evaporate.

The exact cause leading to their sudden exchange of knuckle bouquets is difficult to nail down, though the dope which circulates after suggests that Atkins, which is the handle the rock-knocker chooses to be known by, commits the error of revealing a Kodak of his innocent sister back in Bozeman or whichever such burg he hails from, and the Indian, who states that his moniker is McGinty though everyone addresses him as Chief, makes a comment inappropriate to his stripe and hue. What with the mercury popping high and the general boredom served our hitch here in the Pearl of the Orient it is not unusual for rank-and-filers to altercate with each other based on one does not care for the manner in which the other peeps at him over their morning java, and when skirts are involved, no matter what color hide they are wearing, the stakes are likely to double.

Whatever the kick-off, here comes Atkins flung over from where the Colorados are laying on the feedbag, smack down onto our table with tin cups of java flying this way and tin plates of mutton stew flying that way and the Chief right after on top of him like Strangler Lewis attempting to twist his hat-holder off. Threats and remonstrations are traded—dirty savage this and red nigger that and I will kill you you paleface son of a bitch and things of this sort while all of us Minnesotas step back and provide them room to settle their disagreement—Atkins using the opportunity to test a rattan-mesh sitter on the Indian's skull and the Chief lifting the rock-knocker by his shirt several times and throwing him against the floor to see if he will bounce until Captain Sturdevant arrives to spoil the entertainment.

Now this Sturdevant I know from the cow town of Pueblo, Col., a feedlot operator and promoter of contests of skill and science who owns half interest in a sporting club and has parlayed his status in that burg into a position of military importance. As a captain he has his detractors, consisting princi-pally of those of a rank either higher or lower than his own, though I am told he is well regarded by his peers, the fellow captains of Companies A through H. I myself do not personally care for the gent, as he is the one who seconded a certain lieutenant's pegging me as a runt not worthy to risk his hide next to the other stalwart sons of the Centennial State, forcing me to cast my lot in with the Minnesota delegation, who upon arrival in Googooland were made, of all the undignified possibilities, military coppers in charge of the deport-ment of both American fighting men and slant-eyed denizens of our newly acquired Walled City and its surroundings.

The captain suggests very forcefully that we separate the combatants, and it takes three of our huskier squarehead volunteers to drag the Chief back onto the reservation. I decline to participate, judging that after being blackballed from one outfit and wangling my way into the other I have done my share of volunteering and no more is necessary, as they can always find something to keep you busy whether it needs doing or not.

The aggrieved parties stand drilling holes into each other with their glimmers while Captain Sturdevant struts back and forth in between them, which is his specialty. I personally have never seen an officer could hold a candle to Sturdevant in the strutting department, slapping his little swagger stick against his leg and clearing his throat over and over which is the sign he is about to issue a pronouncement.

Since you two cannot comport yourselfs as soldiers, is how he says to them, perhaps you would prefer to settle it in the ring.

This comes as no surprise, knowing myself that the captain has been a steadfast voice to make prizefighting legal in our fair state, staging many of what are loosely termed exhibitions of the manly art in order to prepare our citizens for that happy day and give the sporting men among them practice in the art of the wager, from which he extracts a generous percentage. Plus he already prescribes the same remedy for a couple goldbricks from B Company who were carrying a grudge, on which occasion I am set to make a bundle only the bout is called when one of the stiffs begins to pour blood out of his beezer and the mental defectives in his corner cannot stop it. I myself have only seen so much of the red stuff one time when Private Gustavson and I interrupt a pair of googoo sports carving each other up on the Escolta.

If you do not feature a contest of skill and science, the captain adds, there is always lodgings available back in the Bilibid Prison.

The Dagoes who rule the roost here before our arrival built this accommodation, with little thought to the finer amenities, such as air circulation or plumbing. Atkins is the first to speak up.

I will fight this heathen bastard, is how he puts it, any time and any place.

This promotes a hearty cheer from both the Colorados and the Minnesotas, as we are retired from the googoo-hunting business now and there is not much to occupy our attention until a suitable bucket can be shanghaied to haul us back home.

The captain struts over to the Indian then, gives him a once-over, and asks if he is game for the proposition.

The Chief never lifts his glimmers off Atkins. If this bird should fail to step out of the ring alive, he informs the captain, let it be on your conscience.

Sturdevant's kisser goes from cream to crimson in a second, either because the Chief did not tack a "sir" onto this statement or at the suggestion that a captain of volunteers possesses a conscience for something to weigh upon. He turns and shows both of them the back of his neck, calling out that all will be settled in the riding ring tomorrow night.

This promotes another round of approval from the ranks, the ones in charge of holding back the two opponents forgetting their mission, but

Atkins and the Chief once unleashed only shoot a last skull-splitter look at each other and take a powder in opposite directions, Atkins wearing most of our supper on his back.

Runt! the boys are immediately shouting, Runt! for although in civilian life I go by Alfie this is the moniker they hang on me. Tell us Runt, they query, what is the tilt on this contest?

Now this Atkins has got arms like hawser cables, the kind of grabbers your hard-rock miners often carry, but this is one large Indian he is set to tangle with. The redskins I know from Pueblo, mostly characters from Little Raven's aggregation, are middling-sized and, since they are frequenting the same type of establishments I am, likely to be overly fond of belting the barleycorn. But this Chief is no Arapaho, instead issuing from some tribe of titans in the north woods, and has never once been observed, at least by my searching peepers, to sample the local *beeno*. A sober Indian is difficult to factor in.

I will hold your wagers, I tell my fellow volunteers, because I am known as a reliable hand in matters concerning cards, dice, or creatures that race on four legs, and am expected to do something. But I cannot yet assess the odds.

There is not much time for the rumors to percolate, but I hear some ripe ones in the day that precedes the bout.

The Red Man in general is known for his thick skull, it is said by one expert, and for his weak chin. The Indian has not been born who can take a pop on the kisser without his knees go to water.

On the other hand, counters a different enthusiast, this redskin has caused the demise, through his superior marksmanship, of more rebel googoos than any one-striper in all the volunteer outfits. He is a natural man-killer.

And it is also common knowledge, adds another, that the rock-knocker calling himself Atkins is only just now bounced from solitary and before that the clap shack and has picked up a nail that cannot be pried loose, being presently on death's front door and shot full of arsenic by the croakers.

But do not forget, confides another, from the same company as the combatants and therefore privy to superior dope, that this is the Atkins who goes toe-to-toe with Joe Choynski in the Yukon and lives to tell the tale before he causes the sudden demise of some Swede in a barroom with a single punch and is forced to don the khaki and blue to make his escape.

Rumors feed action, and there is soon a throng rattling their coins and waving their paper in my kisser. I refuse all markers, pointing out that as the smallest member of the regiment I am the last person able to strongarm a welsher. Cash only, I inform them, and scribe each wager in a notebook purloined from the company clerk as the cocoanuts pile up, the action on one slugger instantly covered by the action on the other, there being a balance between the believers in the White Man's Destiny versus the believers in if you get hit by a guy as big as a shunt locomotive, no matter what color hide he wears, you will eat the canvas. I am of the second religion.

There is not much percentage in such a role when the odds are so close, so I extract a Mexican silver peso per transaction as banker, which keeps the pikers and small-change artists at bay, and inform the multitudes that wagering will continue during the contest at odds adjusted for the circumstances. This gives me what I judge will be less than three rounds to snag, before their champion is pounded into jelly, the last of those who profess their inability to bet against a fellow Anglo-Saxon. I am not an individual prone to take risks when hunches of a sporting nature are being wagered upon a contest, but am not opposed to it when the conclusion is of the forgone variety.

In business dealings of this sort one must be firm and fearless, but I am mildly ruffled when the rock-knocker comes to me the morning of the event and wishes to lay down a bundle the size of which will choke an Army mule.

On himself.

To win.

Save your cocoanuts, I say to him, and protect your chin.

Alfie, he comes back to me, calling me thus because we are acquaintances from before the Runt moniker is applied, Alfie, he says, I need to improve my financial standing in the world. While the rest of you are feeding the fish over the side of the bucket that takes you home, I may remain back here with other ones to fry.

Now most of the boys have been faithful visitors to the knock shops and sporting houses that we of the Provost are charged to regulate, and a few have lined up permanent Margaritas for themselves, fronting the scratch for improved lodgings or the latest rags and perfumes, but the brass give us the glare about it and it is greatly discouraged to get in any deeper with these dolls. A little jiggy-jiggy is one matter, shipping a googoo in a grass skirt with a gold link on her pointer back to Mom and Dad in Prairie Junction is another. And so it grieves me to see Atkins standing before me with a wad in his mitt, hinting he will throw it away for the sake of some yellow frail looking for a meal ticket.

Private Atkins, I say, calling him this because in business it is best to remain formal even with acquaintances who know your real handle, Private

Atkins, I say, if that scalp-lifter hits you a clean punch he will not only kill you but do serious harm to your friends and relations in the far off hills of the Treasure State. You can knock a hole through the side of Admiral Dewey's big white bucket sooner than you will put a dent in that redskin.

I understand, he says to me, and hangs his head a little like he is already reading his own obituaries. I understand, which is why I am hoping you can give me odds.

Here I am forced to confess to a certain amount of guilt, being the party who steers Atkins and some of the other boys to one of the knock shops we have recently regulated, and while I am laying about slightly poleaxed by a few glasses of the high-class Spanish *beeno* they keep on hand in such establishments, Atkins picks up the nail that sends him into the clap shack and the clutches of this china doll he is currently attempting to blow all his cocoanuts on.

Odds? I say. Nobody is getting odds.

As you suggest, he replies, all puppy-eyed and resigned to his fate, I do not hold the chance of a snowball in Hell in this contest, but if some miracle should happen could you cover me at two to one?

If you were the favorite, I commiserate, you could profit by a plunge into the tank. However, unless the Indian is willing to—

Do not mention the name of that heathen savage to me again, says Atkins. I mean to whip him on the fair and square.

Guilt, like the clap, is extremely difficult to shake loose of, so I accept his entire bundle and write it into the notebook at two to one. I judge that he is tossing his bankroll to the wind anyhow, so he may as well believe the payoff is worth the risk.

On the evening of the contest my sergeant, who is of the Swedish persuasion and is monikered the Blond Bear, comes to me with a further proposition.

Runyon you sorry sack of shit, he informs me, always one to forgo nicknames and use the proper address, Captain Sturdevant from the Colorados wants you in the riding ring. Put your worthless backside in motion.

It seems that somebody has fingered me to the captain as wise to the fight game, and he enlists me to help supervise the wrapping of the mitts, each man and his second peeping the process to make sure there is no plaster in the bandages or roll of Liberty Head dimes clutched in anyone's pointers to better bash the skull of their opponent with. It all looks jake to me and I share this opinion with the captain, who is serving as referee and both judges for the scrap.

No need to keep track of points, says he. This one lasts till one of the sluggers does not return to his feet.

A platform is built in the middle of the old indoor riding ring where in earlier times the Dago cavalry prance their nags and the brass practice their swordwork, for all the good it does them when Uncle Sammy's boys come strolling up the beach. There is canvas underfoot and real ropes and turnbuckles the captain ships over from Denver that I can tell have seen some action by the blood dried black on them, and wood bleachers are thrown up all around for everybody in the two outfits not on duty to park their keisters. The brass wander in last and plop down on rattan sitters in the front and one of the regimental bands bangs out *Marching Through Georgia* and there is a considerable racket when the sluggers step out between the bleachers and climb up on potato crates to duck under the ropes and take their corners. The band stops then and the racket dips into the kind of mumble you only hear after fatal house fires and lynchings, as none of the assembled throng besides myself and the other characters in the dressing room has seen the Indian's naked torso before. He does not resemble the cigar-store variety so much as something along the Greek model, chiseled in stone, Hercules or Atlas or some such personality with shoulders you could hitch a wheat thrasher to and legs like pillars of oak. They do not feature any follicles on the chest, your noble savage, which adds to the Chief's sculptured appearance, and his neck is just as wide as his hat-holder, a phenomenon seen in large bears and squarehead sergeants. I am surrounded by volunteers wishing to hedge their bets.

That will be an American eagle per wager, I say to them, doubling the ante, and the tilt is no longer even. Just to cover the play I start at three to two for the Indian, and by the time the crowd thins I am up at five to one with only the most diehard of Anglo-Saxons still taking the miner without a hedge.

The boys begin to stomp their feet for action, quieting only when Captain Sturdevant struts to the middle of the squared circle, looking raw without his swagger stick, and raises his mitts for silence.

It goes dead quiet, only Atkins's boxing brogans, also shipped from Denver by the captain and a size too big for the rock-knocker's feet, shuffling nervous on the canvas while he throws little jabs and rolls his shoulders in preparation of having his block knocked off of them, molesting the silence. The Chief stands with his knuckles dragging on the floor, still as a mountain and nearly as big.

This fight, announces the captain without raising his voice, will continue until one man is unable to answer the bell. Throws will be allowed, but gouging, biting, low blows, obnoxious use of hands and elbows, and lollygagging in the ring will be punished—and here he pauses to gander meaningfully at each of the sluggers—will be punished by time in the stockade. I want a show from both of you fellows—come out fighting and may the best man win.

The bit about the throws is a raw deal and I stifle the urge to give it the hoot. Throws have not been allowed since Pegasus was a two-year-old, and it dawns on me that maybe the brass have their own pool going, with the captain down heavy favoring the Chief. I have seen a referee tackle a slugger in Idaho Springs once because he was in the satchel and concerned about his percentage, but tonight I am covered, I am in fact sitting pretty with a pile of Mexican silvers and American eagles already bagged and nothing riding on the outcome.

The bonger is tapped and the melee commences. Atkins steps out sharp, throwing leather in flurries and putting lots of mustard on it, with relish on top, but the Indian covers with his big slabs of arm and the assault does not amount to much. The volunteers are on their feet and shouting in the way of all suckers, thrilled to witness a contest of skill and science and probable slaughter. Atkins wears himself out by the end of the round and just before the bonger sounds again the big redskin decides he is crowding too close and lifts him up under the arms and tosses him halfway across the ring. The rock-knocker lands on his keister and the boys all give this the hoot while the Chief circles around the ropes hollering a war whoop strictly from Buffalo Bill Cody's Wild West Extravaganza. This gets a rise out of the more fervent of the Anglo-Saxons in the crowd and between rounds a few of them come to me and double their bets, which more than covers the five-to-one play on the Chief.

Corporal Grissom is the Chief's second, assigned to the duty by Captain Sturdevant, and he is absent without leave, leaning with his back to the ropes and jawing with a pal up in the cheap seats while his fighter plops on the stool.

Private Neely is busy in the other corner spitting water in Atkins's kisser and then greasing it with lard and yapping strategy at him, though the only strategy available is the one adopted by El Supremo Aguinaldo and his outfit and this Atkins cannot implement because the captain will plug him before he gets halfway to the door. What Private Neely knows about boxing I know about flower arrangement, if you do not count what wreath to choose when a fellow sporting man is planted, and Atkins is not paying mind to him, only peeping across the ring at the Chief like a spring hen peeps a butcher with a meat cleaver in his mitt.

The second and third go pretty much like the first, the lead miner throwing and the redskin catching where it does not sting, only there is no mustard left on Atkins's punches now, arm-weary already or maybe the croakers really did pump some poison into him which they say is the only way to kill the French ache if the quicksilver does not kill you first. In the fourth the Indian goes finally on the warpath, swinging haymakers left and right, sidearm jobs that no matter how Atkins tries to block with his elbows still nearly knock him crabwise off his feet, the boys up and hollering for blood and they will see some only the Chief needs to raise his artillery a notch, happy to bat his former pal around the ring till Atkins ducks when he should not duck and catches one on the side of his noggin that puts him on one knee. The Chief seems confused and backs off, looking around at all the volunteers who have cocoanuts riding on him screaming to finish the job, even the captain waving him in for the kill, but he only frowns like he suddenly does not savvy the white man's tongue and then Atkins is saved, or perhaps doomed, by the bell.

A dozen chalk-eaters crowd me then, desiring to hedge their previous indiscretions and get on the Indian at five to one, but I inform them that the bank is closed. The fifth begins with the rock-knocker looking like his pins are not completely beneath the rest of his corpus and suddenly there is Private Neely pulling at my coat with his mitts full of scratch and wearing a face that will make a hangman weep.

He makes me promise, says Private Neely. He wants to blow the rest of this at whatever the tilt is.

On himself? I query, judging that the whack on the noggin has relieved the miner of what little sense he possesses to begin with. Let us remember that this is an individual who tumbles for a doll he meets in the clap shack.

He makes me promise, explains the second, on my mother's grave.

Inform him that your mother is still living.

Please, he counters, waving the rock-knocker's boodle under my nose. Now this is paper money, the green variety that Uncle Sammy puts the ink on, the variety that is accepted in the sort of San Francisco sporting houses I shall soon be a patron of, the kind that spends plenty but does not wear a hole in your pockets the way a pile of golden eagles will. The miner has been a stalwart companion to me as far back as Denver and I am as sentimental as the next character, crying at weddings of dolls I have a yen for, the christening of screaming infants and the planting of dear friends who die owing me cocoanuts—but this waving green I cannot resist.

It is five to one, I announce, snatching the cabbage.

Could you crank that up to six? queries the second. My slugger is on his last legs out there.

This is not an exaggeration, as I have not removed my peepers from the ring, where Atkins is being pounded like a boardinghouse steak, the Indian unloading with both paws into his barely protected middle, the rock-knocker staggering backward without throwing a counter, the boys hollering their lungs raw and Sturdevant, hands folded behind his back, strolling around them with a little smile on his kisser like he is admiring the roses. I will sit through an evening of Manila googoo chicken fights before I stay put for a mismatch, but I am holding the bank and have my own pile of cocoanuts riding on it now, so I cover the play six to one in the notebook and hold my water.

Private Neely hurries back to the corner and I see Atkins look over to him after he dives into a clinch with the big Indian hoisting him clear off his toes and squeezing the wind out of him, and the second gives Atkins the thumbs up as if to give him heart. As if heart can help a cornered coon against a grizzly bear.

The Chief tries to throw Atkins clear out of the ring and nearly makes the point, the miner snatching the ropes to keep himself out of the laps of the Company D Minnesotas and then sprawling onto the canvas. While he crawls back onto his pins the Chief goes into his war dance again, whooping and chopping one hand down like it is the hatchet he will bury in Atkins's skull. It does not appear to be a good night for Anglo-Saxon progress.

Atkins gets himself steady and when the redskin turns they exchange a look I have seen before on the front range between a timber wolf and a very old fleabag of a buffalo, a look that says This is the curtain, buster, and the miner even nods slightly, as if saying I understand, thus reads the rule of claw and fang, and then the Indian lumbers in.

He lumbers in cocking his sleepmaker behind him but the little worn-out rock-knocker quicksteps forward and whips an overhand right like a base-ball hurler flush on the redskin's beezer, crowding to follow it with an uppercut he starts from the toes, planting it square on his opponent's chin, and then staggers back as if that is all he has.

The Chief's peepers roll up in his head and he totters this way and that and then somebody from the Colorados hollers "Timberrrrrrr!" and he goes down on his face like a hundred-year-old redwood. It is quiet for a moment, all of us as stunned as a catfish on an ice wagon, and then the bell rings and the true-blue Anglo-Saxons start to whoop and holler and stomp on the boards, celebrating the ineffable march of the white man and calculating their haul. Mostly I am hearing the clink of all those silvers and golds I collected rattling down the shitter, the sound of greenbacks flapping out of my pocket, and the Indian does not stir.

He does not stir as a detail of the boys carry his carcass into the back where Major Ruckheimer, our company croaker, slaps his kisser and dumps a bucket of water on him and jams a stick in his jaws so he should not swallow his tongue, does not stir until after the mittens have been untied and yanked off and Atkins has been helped in, looking beat to hell but relieved he is not dead and has earned so many hundreds of cocoanuts to blow on his china doll.

Where am I, ask the redskin then, and Who shut the lights off and things of this nature as he sits up and plops his hat-holder into his big, bandage-wrapped mitts. There is resin on his kisser where it hit the canvas, his beezer scraped a little, but he looks pretty chipper for a guy who has just been coldcocked in the ring.

Who won? asks the Indian and Captain Sturdevant and the other brass crowding around get a laugh out of that but I do not.

I do not laugh when I settle accounts with all the boys, nor when I hand over a sack of my own hard-won cocoanuts to the rock-knocker, as it should be known that the Runt, if that is how you choose to address me, is no welsher. Atkins is bruised and battered but still in possession of all his choppers.

Private Neely informs me you take my play at six to one, he says to me, laying a swollen-knuckled hand onto my shoulder. That is extremely white of you.

I do not laugh either when later, being of a suspicious nature, I sneak back and shake the lumps of sponge from their boxing gloves, the last substance one would expect sworn enemies should be stuffing into their mittens, nor when I see them together in the mess a few days after, chumming around like there is no hard feeling betwixt fellow ring warriors. I judge from his haymakers that the Chief has not previously taken part in a contest of skill and science, but somewhere, perhaps in Buffalo Bill Cody's Wild West Extravaganza, he learns to take one hell of a dive.

And as for sentiment—unless you have got both fighters in the satchel you can forget about it.

SQUAW MAN

"Arizona," he lies.

It has gotten to be a habit, like calling himself Tommy Atkins. If the railroad man has noticed Hod's cheek swollen from the fight he's at least not staring at it.

"Arizona and New Mexico, mostly. Little outfits digging for gold and silver, though the ore isn't as rich there as they hoped."

The recruiter eyes his uniform. "And when exactly do you become a free man?"

"Ship leaves Friday."

"And if I was to check with your lieutenant—"

"Googoos got him about a month back. But any of the other officers—you know—'Service honest and faithful.'" If they bother to check he is sunk, but this is not the minefields and they are pretty hard up for white men.

"We won't be digging tunnels right away. How the line is set up now, it's just maintenance—"

"Hell, I helped build the White Pass Railroad in the dead of winter," he lies again. "Back in the Klondike. And I spent a good deal of time on the Northern Pacific and the Denver and Rio Grande."

The recruiter, who says he is from Idaho, narrows his eyes. "You been all over the damn map, haven't you?"

Hod gives him a smile and speaks softly, thinking how Jeff Smith would play it. "Yes, sir, and I think I finally found a spot that suits me."

The recruiter has an electric fan pointed straight at the back of his head, making his little bit of hair stick up, and does not appear happy to be in the Philippines.

"Your work gangs will be mostly coolies. You speakee any of that?"

"No, sir, but we had em to carry our supplies on the march. You just sing the right tune in American and they'll hop to it pretty good."

Mei has taught him a few words, useful to tell a shopkeeper he is a thief and a liar and you might pay half of what he says but not a penny more.

"Foreman's wage is fifteen a month, which is plenty when you think how cheap it is to live here."

"Bout what I get now," Hod nods, as if agreeing on the salary. "Course nobody sposed to shoot at a section boss. How far up the line you think I'll be?"

It is always good to talk like you already got the job. Make their mind up for them.

"From here to Dagupan, wherever we need a road crew. Till we start to expand."

"And that would be—?"

"Whenever they get the damn bandits under control. You people," and here he points at the single stripe on Hod's uniform sleeve, "been taking your sweet time about it."

"Yes, sir, I spose we have."

Hod pictures the recruiter sweating it out, surrounded by a bunch of *insurrectos* with their bolos in hand. Hearing that guff from the regulars is one thing, but from a civilian—

"And you know we don't give any pay in advance."

"I'll draw a full month when I muster out. That should tide me over."

The recruiter looks like he still isn't sure. "You a temperate man?"

There has been more shooting in Manila lately than any time since the first days of the war, men bored and drunk and dreading the confinement of the long ship ride home. A provost guard got killed the other night by an Oregon crazy on *beeno*, some of the men still preferring jungle juice to anything with a label on it.

"I haven't taken the Oath," Hod smiles, "but liquor don't set right with me in the heat."

The recruiter nods. The front of his face is running sweat. "And you understand the deal with your citizenship?"

General Otis has decreed that volunteers may not remain in Manila to engage in business, forced either to be shipped home or re-enlist for immediate service.

"I think so—"

"Mr. Higgens prefers you go for a British passport, since they own the road. He can help at their embassy—"

Hod grins. It is a big step, he knows, giving up on America, but so far he's surprised at how little the idea bothers him. "Long as they don't send me off to fight them Dutchmen."

The recruiter doesn't think this is funny. "Africa," he says, writing Hod's made-up name onto a list, "can't be any worse than this."

Hod walks out through the switching yard, a boxcar being loaded with crates full of tinned peaches. There are all kinds of fruits hanging off the branches here, pineapples busting out of the ground, but he's never seen a peach tree. That would be an angle if he knew how to farm, growing things that Americans want and don't have here yet. Manila is a boom town, he thinks as he cuts south on Abad Santos, no less than Cripple Creek or Creede or Skaguay or Leadville in its day, filling up now with sharp-eyed Americans dressed in new Hongkong suits looking for the main chance and paying double for whatever they hanker for from home. Jeff Smith would be a millionaire in a year. A man with a lemonade stand—

There are a half-dozen Filipino boys, the littlest only in a dirty shirt that comes down to his knees, trying to play base ball out in front of the laundry. The batter has a wooden bed slat that he holds cross-handed, and the pitcher windmills forward then backward before underhanding a scabby-looking rubber ball toward the paint-can lid that serves as home plate. The end of the bed slat splits as the batter makes contact, the ball thunking off the side of a passing carabao drawing a cart and bouncing unevenly down the street, small boys dodging through hooves and wheels till one catches up with it, runs back and thunks the advancing runner between the shoulder blades with a vicious throw. There have been inter-regiment games on the Luneta, well attended by both Americans and locals, and the boys seem to have picked up the basics.

"You're out!" calls Hod, jerking his thumb up, and steps into Lavandería Hung.

The front counter of the laundry has no wall behind to block it off from the works, though on one side the finished orders, wrapped in brown paper with black Chinese characters scrawled on them, are piled several feet high. Three Chinese men, stripped to the waist, stand over huge steaming vats, stirring a heavy porridge of clothing with thick paddles, their queues dripping water, their skin flushed red with the heat, while another younger one hustles about with sticks in hand tending the fire under each vat. One of the stirrers hoists a steaming mass of clothing with his paddle, swinging it dripping behind him to slap down into a cooling trough. Yet another Chinese lifts one garment at a time from the long trough and cranks it through an iron mangle to squeeze out most of the water. Behind him are two more men lifting heavy irons from the top of a woodstove to smooth out the wrinkled clothing on a plank, while another wrestles a huge skillet-like affair with glowing coals on top of it, using it to press pants flat. Darting between them, a pair of Chinese women run the clothes out through the back door to hang-dry. It is hard to see how anyone can keep the orders separate. An older man, maybe Hung himself, appears out of the steam to stand behind the counter.

"You got tickee?"

Hod shakes his head. "Just come in to look your operation over."

"No tickee," says the older man, "you go scram."

The boys are still playing ball when he steps back onto the street and heads for the Walled City. He feels the grouch bag stuffed with his winnings from the show with Big Ten snug against his belly. Just a little set-up at first, he thinks. Hire a couple coolies, maybe right off the road crew or bring them over on contracts, pay them a little better so they want to keep the job. What he's won and his muster pay and a couple months' work on the railroad should cover the equipment, and then you just need to be near a good supply of water.

If she'll have him.

Working the Dagupan line he'll be able to scout the right location, wherever the Americans plan to dig in and send out east–west rails. Mei would only be up front, with a wall behind her to keep the steam off, running the whole deal with her good English and her head for numbers. Never seen a woman could juggle sums like her—the once he took her to buy some clothes she jawboned the fella down way below what Hod was willing to pay and told him all their business sliding beads around the rack was just for show, that she had the figure in her head way before they got to clicking and clacking.

If he can only lay the deal out right, be sure not to spook her.

He turns down Azcarraga Street. There are more and more shop signs in

English, mostly the ones run by Spaniards and Chinese. Only the Filipinos don't seem to have got the message yet, and they'll be the ones left in the dust. Like back home where the only Indians selling anything are carved out of wood and got a handful of cigars.

Big Ten is sitting on his favorite chair by the trolley terminal in Plaza Santa Cruz, having his boots polished.

"How'd it go?"

Hod shrugs his shoulders. "I'll find something. If they gonna bring this country up to snuff, they be needin some experienced hands. And then when I get my own operation runnin—"

"Hell, you'll make out fine."

"If you was interested—I mean, you go back and it aint any better than it was, I could use a partner—" Hod has no idea if the British will take an Indian for a citizen or not.

Big Ten smiles. "Naw—I can't take the heat."

Hod sighs. "Well then."

"I got no worries," says Big Ten. "I'm a Ward of the State."

The soldier is sitting on the wall outside the hospital, waiting for her. There are a lot of *karayuki-san* selling themselves in Manila now, and she watches as three of these stop to offer themselves to him and then walk on. He has come to tell her he is leaving.

All the sick and wounded ones of the Colorado, and of the Oregon and of the Minnesota and of the Dakota are being prepared to leave on a hospital ship, their time of bondage to the Army over, and they say the healthy ones are going as well. They make jokes about taking her with them.

"If I could fit you in my rucksack," they say, "we'd go do San Francisco together."

He is the nicest one, Hod, a soldier who takes his hat off when he talks with her and bought her shoes and a silk dress she has only worn once so he could see her in it and brings her food sometimes, American food in metal cans that she has kept hidden in her room because she has no way to open them and is afraid the Americans who run the hospital now will find them and think she is stealing. He has even brought presents for Bo, toys that he bought on the street. Radiant Star in Hongkong was taken once and kept for a year by a very rich trader who fed her and dressed her like a rich woman till he was tired of her and found a younger girl. When she came back she told

Mei and the others what it was like, how easy, such a crystal life, and they all tried to imagine this. She didn't talk about what words he used when he told her he had a new girl.

Mei steps out to the soldier, to Hod, and breathes hard through her nose so she won't cry. Her only worry now, really, is that with all the soldiers going home they may change the hospital or close it and to take care of Bo she will have to be Ling-Ling again out walking with the Japanese girls.

He stands and takes his hat off when he sees her, smiles. His cheek on one side is swollen, as if he's been in a fight. She thought he was funny-looking at first, like they all are, but now she likes to see his face. The one time he touched her with her clothes off, in a rented room after she wore the dress for him, his hands were very rough from working and he said he was sorry about that. But her own hands are rough too, a farmer's hands, boiled now in the water every day, and if she has to walk with the Japanese girls maybe she will wear gloves and keep them on till the deal is struck.

He kisses her on the cheek like he does, as if she is a little girl.

"Let's walk."

It is the part that is the strangest for her, this walking in front of everybody's eyes. In the Walled City the other soldiers smile and wink at him and the Spanish and Filipino ladies who walk in twos and carry parasols make faces and turn their heads away and in Binondo the Chinese merchants hiss terrible words at her, acting like she is still Ling-Ling and not just a woman who works in the American hospital, almost a Daughter of Charity.

They walk down Legaspi together, a couple feet apart from each other.

"There are some things I got to say to you," he says, still holding his hat in his hands. She breathes in hard through her nose. She will not cry now, she will wait till she is back in her room at the hospital, till she takes her new shoes off and puts them under the bed with the metal cans of American food.

"You are leaving."

He looks at her. She feels stronger, saying it before he does.

"Well, that kind of depends. What I was thinking, see—" and he sighs like it is hard for him to tell her. Perhaps it is.

"They got a boat for the regiment now, yeah—"

Some soldiers at the corner look at them as they pass and laugh, not a kind laugh, and it makes her angry. She moves closer as they walk, shoulders almost touching.

"So when everybody goes—see, boiling clothes aint so different than boiling anything else. And you got your Chinese and the local lingo and half the time your English sounds better than mine, so it's a shoo-in we could open a shop somewheres up the railroad line."

Sometimes her English is not so good. "Shop?"

"Not a big one at first, just get our feet wet, see how it goes. Or hell, you hate the laundry idea, it could be a lunch counter. Chop suey or whatever. You wouldn't have to cook, just run the business."

He has stopped walking now, looking at her, worried.

"Of course first we got to find one of these Jesus-peddlers showing up here every day who can say the words without choking on em. Or whatever you folks do for it, some Chinese deal, that's fine with me. Anybody don't like it, that's just their lookout."

Mei feels dizzy, her vision blurring, like she is being tossed in a storm at sea and cannot tell which is sky and which is water.

"Bo," she says.

The soldier lifts his shoulders. "Too bad he got to learn his English from someone like me."

Mei thinks of the card with her photograph on it, the one she tore up and burned and the one the *Comisaria de Vigilencia* still has, with all the things about her written on it.

"I am only a no-good China girl," she says.

"I aint much of a bargain either."

He holds his arm out then, bent at the elbow for her to walk with him the way the Spanish men walk with their ladies on the Luneta at sunset.

"So what do you think?"

The breathing hard through her nose doesn't work. Lan Mei takes the soldier's arm and holds on to it with both hands. Holds on to it for her life.

SINGING WIRE

The women cross themselves when they see Diosdado sitting on the dike. They adjust the bundles on their heads and fix their eyes on the road ahead as they hurry past, muttering incantations in Pampangano. Diosdado and his band have become phantoms, haunting the balete forests between Guimba and Malolos, creatures whose existence is understood but whose presence is feared. They are the shadow government, collecting taxes for the fugitive Republic. They are the unwritten law, whispering decrees and punishing collaborators. They are, he hopes, the fabric of American nightmares, the thing the *yanquis* fear most when daylight drains from the sky. It is an intermittent, skulking war that they wage, waiting in ambush for forces they never outnumber, shooting and running with no time to assess the damage inflicted, firing at night-lights and noises in the occupied *baryos*, stealing sleep from the enemy.

And every day the cutting of the wire.

Half the men still believe it is magic, a metal string that goes on for miles and miles and sings its secrets to the *yanqui* invaders. Pressing their ears against the wooden lances to listen the high-pitched keening of the wire, or holding a cut length in their hands, turning it this way and that, trying to divine its power, keeping a few silenced yards to hang their wet clothes from in camp.

"The wire is their mark, their claim on our land," Diosdado tells his men. "Wherever we let it stand belongs to them."

If there is time they pull the lances out of the ground, one every fifty-five paces, then chop the insulators off, cut the wire in several places, and scatter it all in the woods. Closer to the garrisons or in an area with regular American patrols they only stand a nervous guard while little Fulanito shinnies up and uses the cutters Orestes Pulao stole from the signalmen's shed before he ran from San Fernando. The taut wire zings in protest as it whips apart, the flow of coded orders and reports broken off, telegraph bugs up and down the line gone mute. Fulanito backs down quickly, bare toes gripping the wood, and they all fade back into rumor.

Diosdado and his band are phantoms in the minds of the *kasamas*, haunting the orchards and fields between San Idelfonso and Mabalacat, materializing when it is least convenient to demand part of their meager harvests, any contact forbidden by the martial law of the occupiers. And phantoms can never rest—west from Cabanatuan after the murder of Luna but never quite reaching Zambales, ordered to slip below enemy lines in Tarlac, sniping, stealing, scurrying from one jungle hideout to the next, counting their bullets and losing track of their days. They joined General Tinio's Ilocanos for a spell in late November, helping to cover Aguinaldo's flight to the north, then were sent back to Bamban after the Tirad Pass fight, harrying the mule trains hauling supplies to the American outposts. In January it was up to Pangasinan, responsible for the villages along the Agno River, encouraging informants, threatening fraternizers. In March they were part of the larger campaign to tie up the American troops protecting Concepción, Sargento Bayani's monkey-chanting night raids so effective that all the Chinese coolies working for the *yanquis* deserted in terror. In August it was the foothills of Mount Arayat, coming down to ambush the parties of fevered bluecoat soldiers unlucky enough to be patrolling in the heavy rains. And now working their way west again, skirting above Macabebe to Guagua, cutting wire as they go.

The villages were open to them at first, Americans passing through so fast in their chase that food could be hidden, the invaders' dust barely settled before Diosdado's men were there to collect the rice-tithe. Then the *yanquis* began to garrison—ten soldiers for a medium-sized *baryo*, a company or more for the stone-church towns. And now the barbed wire, the concentration camps, the railroad-tie corrals for men caught without safe-passage documents between villages. In many areas the Americans have shot all the carabao, have torched the rice fields and forced people to eat the same tinned meat and crackers their troopers live on.

Diosdado has eaten lizard, gratefully, and made a belt of hemp to hold his uniform pants up when his leather one rotted to pieces in the damp jungle camps. His men are a hollow-cheeked, spindly-limbed band, as phantoms must be, and the droning camp conversation always reverts to meals once eaten. Kalaw is the master of this, his descriptions of his mother's saint's day feasts so detailed they make hard men weep with longing.

And every day they cut the wire.

"The wire is the voice of the oppressor," Diosdado tells his men. "The wire is his eyes and his ears. If we let the wire stand he will never be gone from us."

The best tactic is to cut the line halfway between one garrison and the next, to wait in ambush for the Signal Corpsmen and their escorts, far enough away that the sound of gunfire won't summon reinforcement. The *yanquis* have implemented mounted patrols, though, on the roads that permit it, whooping troopers too big for their skinny Filipino ponies, dashing along with pistols drawn to shoot anything that moves. They've begun to set their own ambushes as well, Diosdado losing a fighter from La Union and three good rifles when they were surprised on the footpath to the Candaba–Santa Ana road.

At the beginning of October a messenger came all the way from wherever General Aguinaldo was hiding out that week, telling them to hold fast and not despair, telling them that the Americans were about to hold elections and that the challenger for president, a great orator named Bryan, pledged to pull their army from the Philippines if he won. The messenger waited while Diosdado explained this to the men, explained just what an election was and that Bryan was a great anti-Imperialist who refused to be nailed to a cross of gold and that no, he wasn't a Catholic, but a fervent believer in the Almighty nonetheless.

"General Aguinaldo says if we can keep them fighting till November," said the messenger, "if we can keep them sick and sleepless and longing to go home, then victory may be within our grasp."

Only Sargento Bayani was not filled with hope by this.

"Whenever the Spanish sent us a governor who considered reform," he said, "the friars would have him recalled. Friars or not, the Americans must have someone who will destroy this great man of words."

Then the messenger told them they were to stay in Pampanga, to haunt the countryside around San Isidro and Las Ciegas, to remind the people that they were still free Filipinos and that if they betrayed the Republic they would be executed.

Diosdado gets up from the dike and crosses the road to the telegraph line. He is hungry and tired and unshaven, a phantom in the remnants of a lieutenant's uniform with a rope belt and boots that have given up the cause. He presses his ear against the telegraph pole, feels a tiny buzz against his skin, hears the singing of the naked wire above. The Americans are talking to each other with electricity. He hopes they're talking about Bryan.

CELEBRITY

They hide Teethadore in the library. Once he is alone he runs his fingers along the spines of the leather-bound Shakespeares, many, no doubt, once pored over by the Prince of Players himself. He is too nervous to read, though, and paces the long rectangle as he waits, employing the character's distinctive strut rather than his own gait. He was unable to stifle a giddy laugh earlier as he stepped between the gas lamps and in through the front entrance. How many times has he strolled around the private, padlocked greenery of Gramercy Park with one eye fixed upon the brownstone façade with its columns and balconies, hoping to spy some adept of the Craft or other notable entering or leaving? And often rewarded—Augustus Saint-Gaudens, his profile chiseled from New England granite, banker Morgan with his angry turnip of a nose, burly, ginger-haired Stanford White who designed the interior of the club, rascally Samuel Clemens with an evil-looking cigar in his mouth, and once, on his very first visit to the great city, Edwin Booth himself passing on the walk. After the shock of recognition, the strange realization that they shared the same diminutive stature, there were the eyes—sad and shy, begging not to be hailed or complimented. He let the great man, appearing old beyond his years, pass unlauded.

Teethadore is well aware that performers of his caste are not ordinarily welcome at The Players. His own father was a lowly Tommer, traipsing the tank towns as Arthur Shelby, the old darky's first owner, a thankless role if there ever existed one. But it was at least a play, not, as he derisively snorted when his son debuted as a joke-spouting juggler, "a carnival attraction."

He certainly felt the freak last night at Proctor's 23rd, with election returns projected on a white sheet lowered over the olio curtain between each act, his turn as TR greeted with cheers and jeers by the house, packed to the rafters with partisans celebrating their affiliations at the top of their lungs. Spectacles off, a van Dyke slapped on with spirit gum, he was able to push out of the theater without being spotted as a performer or misidentified as the bully little candidate. The crowd was just as dense outside, thronged all the way down from Longacre Square to Madison Square where the *Times* bulletin was hung four stories up on the side of their new building, a stereopticon flashing election returns as soon as they were telegraphed to the newspaper. Thousands cheering as the first Massachusetts returns favored Bryan, and thousands more when Queens and New York counties tallied for McKinley. For entertainment in between reports there was the searchlight hired by Croker and the Tammany crowd, mounted atop the Bartholdi Hotel and blazing advertisements for Bryan and several local Democrats, as well as for soap, whiskey, and a remedy for dyspepsia, upon the face of the rapidly deteriorating Dewey Arch at 24th.

Caught up in the good-natured spirit of it, he grabbed the trolley and rattled down to witness the even larger horde assembled around Newspaper Row, citizens jammed together from the bridge to the post office, filling City Hall Park all the way to Broadway. Over a hundred men in blue were needed to clear a path for the trolley to come to a stop, Teethadore nearly losing his feet several times in the crush. Each of the great papers had their own screen hung on the side of their massive buildings, stereopticons mixing hastily scrawled polling figures with photographs, illustrations, and burlesques of the candidates, a few augmenting these with moving kinetoscope views— marching soldiers, steaming battleships, and once, to great amusement and applause, his own shenanigans as TR chasing a bear cub up a tree. It seemed that a full half of the throng, from uptown swells in raglan overcoats and silk hats to entire families of East Side flockies, had purchased some sort of noisemaker—rattles, tin horns, buzzers, bells, and, for the vocally inclined, cardboard megaphones—from the scores of little street fakirs peddling them.

One of these, alarmingly yellow-tinged for one not of the Confucian persuasion, took pause from whirling his rattlers to accost Teethadore directly.

"You look just like him!"

"Like whom, may I ask?" All this shouted, of course, as the multitude demonstrated at great volume its approval, opprobrium, or boredom with the latest despatch.

"Like *Ted*dy, who d'ya tink? I seen him once in person, Tanksgivin at the Newsboy's Home. You shave that chin-warmer off, put on some specs, an yer the spittin image."

"I've never heard that before."

"Then yer deaf as a post or people aint payin attention. Rattler?"

By eight o'clock even Hearst's *Journal* conceded that McKinley was the victor. One fellow, squeezed very close to him, primed with perhaps too much liquid enthusiasm, had tears in his eyes.

"Who I feel bad for is poor Adlai Stevenson," he lamented for the former but not future Vice President. "Where is an old man like that going to find a new job?"

His companion, bulging coat laden with McKinley–Roosevelt buttons, who had obviously already enjoyed his "full dinner pail" and a couple pails of something with foam on it, was in brighter spirits.

"Mac's the man for the new century," he beamed. "Just you wait and see."

The crowd was still in the thousands, a surprising number of them ladies, when Teethadore pushed through and headed north to his MacDougal Street garret. Hundreds of citizens were out with him for the entire walk, passing dozens of huge, crackling political-club bonfires, everybody full of energy and good spirit whatever their affiliation, this on not the balmiest of November nights, and he had occasion once again to be thrilled to be a New Yorker.

Mr. Oettel, Booth's dresser in his later years and now chief functionary at the club, steps up into the library with John Drew. There are voices below, laughter.

"Mr. Brisbane?"

John Drew, *the* John Drew, is offering his hand. A manly handshake, a deep and hearty voice, the looks as striking in person as on stage. He stands back to look Teethadore over.

"My God, they were right about you! A breathtaking resemblance."

Teethadore has the spectacles on, of course, and has ventured to buy, at considerable expense, something very like the suit the new Vice President has been wearing for his campaign appearances.

"I'm not sure what you—"

"A few characteristic remarks should do it. The fellows are down there lubricating themselves—we'll see how long it takes them to smell a rat."

The imagery stings a bit, but trusting him to improvise implies a certain professional respect. "My entrance?"

"I'll go down now and herd them into the Grill Room, announcing that we'll soon have a special surprise guest." Drew smiles, shaking his head and looking him over anew.

"If I didn't know it wasn't you—him—"

"The theater is full of assumed identities."

"Which wouldn't fool the biggest hayseed in the rear of the third balcony, much less the characters in the play. But you—my word!"

They go down then and he can hear conversations moving away from the stairwell. He has never been much for nerves before a performance, the public so—so easily *fooled*, so willing to believe that what passes above the footlights is what is meant to be happening. But this is not his usual house, full of shop clerks and newsboys and free-lunch despoilers, is not even an audience of his peers, these are—

Mr. Oettel is back to tell him that it is time.

He follows down the stairs into the reading room. He has seen such places on the stage but never actually been in one. Leather chairs that could swallow a man, a handsome Persian on the floor, the smell of tobacco, and the great marble mantelpiece flanked by Sargent portraits, one of Booth and one of Joseph Jefferson in character as Peter Pangloss in *The Heir-in-Law*.

And then he is waved through the Great Hall, Drew's much larger frame shielding him from the view of the luminaries in the Grill Room.

"Gentlemen!" booms the actor, and the room immediately quiets. "We have with us, in light of recent occurrence, an extremely distinguished and very surprising guest."

He steps away and Teethadore is on, strutting through the doorway with choppers ablaze, every man not already upright jumping to his feet to applaud. It is a strange business, accepting another man's kudos, the warmth sincere but unearned. He uses it, though, fills himself with it, puffing his barrel chest out a little further, clasping his hands and shaking them over his head like a victorious prize-fighter—the Little Champion. It is difficult not to linger on their faces as he turns to acknowledge them all. These are, if not gods, at least royalty—a Richard III here, a Prince Hal there, a Cardinal Richelieu looming in the rear. Only one bear of a man—is it not Frederick Remington?—smiles slyly and whispers to the fellow beside him.

"I thank you for that reception," he enthuses as the applause finally dies. "And I thank you for your support in the recent contest, though I believe I recognize a few Bryan men skulking on the fringe—here, no doubt, to settle their wagers."

Laughter then, these famous players and men of influence so flattered by his presence that they are blind to the deception.

"The Vice-Presidency," he continues, "though a great honor, is merely an understudy role—" chuckles here, "—waiting in the wings and hoping never to be pressed into service. I imagine I will serve the President as I did during the campaign—as his rather more mobile, and considerably more vocal—" good laugh here, "—rooting section. And in that capacity I come with a charge for you gentlemen of the stage."

They are buying it, rapt. If he asked them at this moment to march on Tammany and tear it from its foundation they would follow him *en masse*.

"Our quest is to be a great—a *greater* nation. A great nation must have a great, a committed *the*ater!"

"Hear, hear!" says somebody in the gathering. He can see Belasco, the master of froth, begin to frown.

"Must our stage be only the purview of fools, the playground of children? Can it not deal honestly with the pressing issues of our day? Where are the works about labor unrest, about the crushing power of the trusts, the shows that address our desperate situation in the Philippine Islands—shows like the estimable *Florodora*—"

Stanford White's booming laugh breaks the spell, and with that, the illusion.

"You're a fraud!" cries William Faversham, who he so admired in the Wilde farce.

"A fraud?!" he cries back. "Does the public cry fraud when you don your tattered buskins and feign nobility? No, sir, they laud you to the heavens!"

Men are laughing now, though eyeing their compatriots to be certain it is allowable to be so fooled.

"If a near-sighted, less-than-statuesque politician can steam to Cuba and impersonate a military man—" a big, knowing laugh at this, "—why, then, may not an honest vaudevillian impersonate a politician, and to equal acclaim?"

Actual applause then, mixed with the laughter. He has touched a nerve.

"Yes, I am an imposter, a pro*fess*ional imposter, but if such illusion had no fascination with the public, think of how many of you gentlemen would not be here!"

"And if you'd been born looking like Eugene Debs," calls James K. Hackett, "*you* wouldn't be here either!"

That caps it, enormous laughter from all and Teethadore spreading his arms to accept the truth of the observation. Drew is the first to slap his back and pump his hand.

"Excellent work, my friend! Very well played!"

Others crowd around with more of the same. His head is buzzing from the energy of the performance and the idea that the leading man of the great Lyceum Company, whose lips have so often touched those of the divine Maude Adams, has complimented him upon his acting.

John Drew leads him to the bar and orders him a Scotch whisky. There is Faversham of course, of the curly locks and British comportment, and Hackett, another Lyceum standout, at least two of the powerful producing Frohman brothers, along with the playwright Bronson Howard, Maurice Barrymore with his boxer's physique and flashing eyes, Otis Skinner, E. H. Sothern, like Hackett the son of a legend, young Tyrone Power who captured so many hearts in *Becky Sharp* a season ago, William Gillette, lean and keen, and, holding himself somewhat above the crowd despite his lack of physical stature, the incomparable Richard Mansfield.

"The Filipinos will surrender within days," he hears Gillette opine. "Bryan was their last hope."

"Perhaps." It is Mayo Hazeltine, the voluminous reviewer from the *Sun*. "But our real concern should be what has been going on in China—"

It is all he can do not to join in—in character of course. He has taken to reading the more serious journals, to formulating opinions on weighty matters, to feeling as if he is on top of world affairs. He can name at least six of the contested islands.

White and Barrymore flank him at the bar then, and Teethadore finds himself a jockey among fullbacks. Both men appear to be well-oiled.

"So glad you mentioned *Florodora*," says the thespian. "Stanny is something of an expert on it."

The architect laughs. "Not the height of dramaturgy by any means, but it has its assets."

"And those assets," grins Barrymore, "have *their* assets."

The gossip sheets spill gallons of ink each week chronicling the mating rituals of the six uniformly winsome Florodora Girls, wreaking havoc upon the affections and bank balances of stage-door Johnnies young and old. Each time one snags her millionaire and leaves the show the Winter Garden is overflowing with sports eager to judge the charms of her replacement. Heavyweight champions and Cabinet ministers come and go with less excitement.

White points a finger at Teethadore. "The last time I saw you, you were slated between Harrigan and Hart and Professor Pembert's dogs."

"You have quite a memory, sir. That was at the Folly, a good number of years ago."

"I recall a barrel-jumper being injured—"

"Amazing! One of the Deonzo Brothers, on opening night."

"Stanny is a first-nighter," says Barrymore, "an every-nighter, and an all-nighter."

Teethadore sees Mansfield passing near, and wonders would he prefer to be extolled for his Dick Dudgeon in the Shaw play or for the sensation he made with the first American *Cyrano*.

"Mansfield!" Barrymore calls out. "What do you think of our Teddy here?"

The man is, in fact, not a hair taller than Teethadore, stopping to appraise him with raised eyebrow.

"'Honest vaudevillian' is, I believe, an oxymoron. As for Roosevelt—inviting the original to visit has always struck me as questionable, and here we have a fac*si*mile. What will be next, bicycling chimpanzees?"

With that he makes for the exit. Teethadore declines to call out that he has in fact appeared several times with bicycling chimpanzees, an act so popular that not a performer on the bill is willing to follow them.

"He's rather more Mr. Hyde than Dr. Jekyll, our Dickie," Barrymore apologizes.

"Arrogant little prick," concurs the architect. "But a marvel on the boards."

David Warfield approaches then, Warfield who he knew as a fixture at Weber and Fields's Music Hall, with whom he has shared many an alleged "dressing room," moving toward him with David Belasco in tow.

"Briz!" he smiles, employing Teethadore's erstwhile nickname. "You fooled even me!"

They clasp hands. He resists the urge to ask the comedian how he snuck in the door.

"This is David Belasco."

"Of course. An honor, sir."

"Wonderfully done," enthuses the Bishop of Broadway. "You had us all going."

"Mr. Belasco is going to make an honest man of me."

The producer smiles. "A small enough penance, as I shall never make an honest woman of anyone."

Teethadore allows himself a smile. Belasco's "casting couch" is notorious.

"There's a play called *The Auctioneer* and I'm to be the lead in it," beams Warfield.

"You'll be a smash," beams Teethadore. They make an odd pair, the writer-director-producer, dressed always in clerical black, some sort of a Spanish Jew, and the resolutely Christian comic noted for his portrayal of East Side shy-locks, sporting a false nose even larger than Cyrano's.

"I agree wholeheartedly," says Belasco. "There is no reason David's talents cannot shine in the legitimate theater."

"As they have in the illegitimate."

Both men laugh, but Teethadore regrets saying it. He is a guest in their club and understands that though distinctions are adhered to, they must not be mentioned.

"If you ever have a role that requires someone of my—of my *abil*ities—" he adds, feeling suddenly very small among the giants of the theater, "I do hope you will think of me."

"I will keep you in mind," smiles Belasco, and they drift away. So many company managers, so many directors in New York are presently keeping him in mind it is a wonder he doesn't burst into flame from the concentrated mental energy. But if it has happened to Warfield, who is a deserving fellow after all, perhaps—

He finds himself unattended for a moment and strolls through the lumi-naries with drink in hand. It is still difficult to accept that he has penetrated this sanctum. The Grill Room is another long enclosure, with pewter drink-ing mugs, those not presently employed by the members, hanging from hooks at his eye level all around the rectangle. Old playbills decorate the walls, deer antlers hang on the chandeliers and heads with horns are mounted over the mantels of the delft-tiled fireplaces set at either end of the room. It is against one of these that he is pinned by the illustrators.

He recognizes some by sight—Remington, of course, wider now than any three of his leathery cow-punchers, Gibson of the haughty, long-necked beauties and square-chinned swains, young Howard Christy, Gibson's rival in defining feminine allure, whose rendering of TR at Siboney and the San Juan Hill were surely a factor in the feisty politician's present success—and once introduced to the others, knows and admires their work. There is Reginald Birch, whose drawings for *Little Lord Fauntleroy* condemn small boys to velveteen torture, Howard Pyle, King of the Pirate Illustrators, and the cartoonists A. B. Frost and Fred Opper, all of them studying his face as if it is a first effort in a sculpture class.

"You must be rather pleased with the election results," ventures Gibson, a gin-soaked pearl onion floating in his glass.

"Yes and no." It is damned hard to keep still with them all peering at his physiognomy. "Though I would have been chagrined had my lookalike lost by a single vote."

"You didn't go for him?"

The irony of it did strike him in the booth, his career, so to speak, at a crossroad. But, son of a fervent Populist, he pulled the bar for the straight Democratic ticket and stepped out through the curtain feeling absolved of sin.

"Some men vote from their pocketbook," he answers, "others from their heart."

"A Bryan man," laughs Gibson. "Astounding."

"At this distance it's still disturbing," frowns Christy, angling his head to look behind Teethadore's prop spectacles. "I mean I've drawn the man from *life*!"

"A good, solid likeness," observes Fred Opper with the tiniest hint of a German accent. "But not *ob*vious enough to be funny."

"They flashed a good deal of your work up on the *Journal* building last night," says Teethadore, feeling as if even the stuffed buck on the wall is staring at his face. "The crowd loved Teddy as an eager beaver."

"The man is a walking caricature," says Frost. "He's more fun to draw than a mule kicking an aristocrat."

"A shame to have him buried in the second spot," muses Remington, who immortalized TR back in his Montana ranching days. "I imagine they'll be keeping our boy on a very short leash."

The illustrators restrain themselves from actually taking his flesh in hand and eventually the crowd in the Grill Room starts to thin. The event began at five, actors' dinner hour, and no doubt many here have shows to perform or attend. Teethadore will not, he knows, be invited to become a member. Their class, despised by polite society though it may be, is nevertheless several stations above his own. This is but a fleeting glimpse, a visit to a mountaintop he shall never dwell upon. He is planning his exit when he takes note of the lanky older gentleman ensconced in a chair in the far corner.

It is Joseph Jefferson, no other. Jefferson who trod the boards with Junius Brutus Booth, whose adopted daughter was the great Edwin's first beloved wife, who breathed life into *Our American Cousin*, associated more now with the Lincoln murder than with its phenomenal success, veteran of hundreds, perhaps thousands of performances of *Rip van Winkle*, a breathing reliquary of American theater history—

Teethadore gathers his nerve and sits beside the legend.

"Sir—"

"That was very entertaining, young fellow. You kept your head."

"Why thank you, sir."

"An interesting character. Rather exhausting to portray him for any length of time, I should imagine."

"He keeps me on my toes."

"If you weren't on your toes," says the old man, "the patrons in the rear would not be able to see you."

Teethadore smiles his own, less dentally revealing smile. Jefferson's admonition that "there are no small roles, only small actors" has been applied often to him, appended with further comments regarding his lack of altitude.

"My father took me to see you play the Dutchman when I was ten years old," he says, attempting not to gush forth. "I thought that they'd hired a young actor and his grandfather to handle the transition."

"You were a very suspicious young man."

"Raised in a steamer trunk. My father toured with Mrs. Stowe's melodrama."

"Such a modest little lady," muses Jefferson, "to cause such a big war."

"I saw you do it again in my twenties. I was transfixed."

"At the beginning they marveled at my ability to play the ancient Rip," says Jefferson. "Now they are amazed that I can portray the young one."

"Does it ever trouble you? Being so—so *iden*tified with one role?"

The old man looks at Teethadore, thinks for a moment. He points across the room to William Gillette.

"He may not know it yet, but that fellow will grow old playing his Sherlock Holmes. And the man he is speaking with—"

It is James O'Neill, waving his arms to tell a story—

"You mean the Count of Monte Cristo?"

"My point precisely. Mansfield has managed to transcend his Jekyll and Hyde, poor Edwin was a man of many faces, but for most of us, if we are fortunate, there is one defining role, a character the public cannot get enough of, who not only pays the rent but becomes something of an extension to our own less vibrant personalities. Mine, fortunately," the old man winks, "affords me the opportunity to do some napping on stage."

"But Rip van Winkle is fictional," says Teethadore, hoping to get at the root of his misgiving. "He is *finite*, trapped within the strictures of the play. My fellow is still breathing, and, I must say, extremely unpredictable."

The aged player's face lights up. He places a hand on Teethadore's shoulder.

"Then Fortune has provided you a spirited mount. *Ride* him, my good friend! Ride him to glory!"

GARRISON

It must be noon by now but they've taken all the clappers out of the church bells. The bells in the little *baryos* ring out every time a patrol is sighted nearby and the ones fighting have time to hide themselves, so the colonel always says "Cut their tongues out!" even here in Las Ciegas when they came back to garrison. Most of the day the googoo mamas are out hulling rice, pounding down with their clubs on the couple handfuls they've tossed into the hollow on top of the belly-high wood stumps that stand in front of each hut, hooking into a rhythm that Kid Mabley will sometimes try to play his horn to. But it must be noon now because even they are out of sight, unhusked rice waiting, spread out to dry on wide bedrolls of woven bamboo and the dogs lying flat on the dirt of the plaza, still as death, baked by the sun. There is only the woman, Nilda, hanging the soldiers' wet clothing on a bamboo rack to dry and Coop at her elbow with a can of goldfish and a fistful of hardtack, pestering.

Nothing else moves.

"This here is good to eat, see?" he says. "Yum-yum. All you got to do is pop inside for a little bit, give Uncle Coop some jiggy-jiggy."

It is none of Royal's business, really, that is the unspoken agreement between all of them, but the sun is boiling the blood in the angry part of his brain and it vexes him. He slowly crosses the plaza, weaving around the prostrated dogs.

"This is hardtack—like crackers, see?" Coop has a tough time breaking off a piece. "See? Won't go soft, even in the jungle. Like me."

The woman, moving as if she can't hear, lifts clothes from the huge woven-reed basket, shakes them out, and goes up on her toes to hang them so the ends don't drag in the dirt.

"And inside this here is goldfish—"

"That stuff is poison," says Royal, stepping over as casual-looking as he can manage. "Even the coolies won't eat it." There is a Chinese who sneaks up once a week to sell the men *beeno*, and canned salmon is the one thing he won't take in trade.

"She get a taste of me, she won't worry about no food."

"She's not interested in you."

"Get your own damn squaw, Roy." Coop, a bit taller, harder, turns back to the woman and wiggles the can inches from her face as if she needs to smell it. "You aint never had nothin like this, darlin."

"If she needs food just give it to her."

Coop turns to step back close to Royal. They are both in their undershirts, pouring sweat from the heat. When the clothes are washed and dried they feel good on your skin for a few minutes and then you are soaked through again.

"You triflin with me?"

"There's plenty of jiggy-jiggy girls in Manila."

"We aint in fuckin Manila."

"Then you're gonna have to try someone else."

Coop smiles. "You know I can whup your ass."

"Most likely."

Coop half turns as if to say something to the woman, who still hasn't looked at him, then pivots to smash Royal on the side of the head with the can, knocking him off his feet.

The woman freezes, bent over the clothes basket.

The nearest of the dogs gets up with some effort, watching the men warily as it slinks several feet farther away, then pancakes itself to the ground again. A few of the men peek groggily out of the huts they are billeted in. A few natives look out too, but see it might be a fight and duck back inside.

Royal gets halfway up, decides, and bullrushes Coop, catching him around the hips and driving him into the bamboo clothestree which collapses into the dust with them.

He has a chunk of Coop's cheek in his fingers, trying to rip it off while Coop thumps him on the back and neck and ribs with the fist that isn't pinned down. He wants some distance so he can really hit but Royal is strong

and won't let loose, their boots scraping the dirt for purchase, the two writhing crookedly across the plaza like a half-stomped cinch bug that just won't
die and the men come out now, the ones not on outpost or patrol, most just
in their underclothes and barefoot forming a shifting ring around the pum-
meling men on the ground.

"What they scufflin about?"

"Don't matter much, do it?"

"Got that woman's wash all dirtied up again."

"Too damn hot to fight."

"Yeah—ought to just shoot each other and be done with it."

Royal is underneath, his forearm wedged under Coop's throat, trying to
feel out a way to break his neck but if he moves anything Coop will be able
to pound him again in the ribs where they feel broken. The thumb in his
eye might be his own. There is a little bit of shade from the men closed in
around them and then it is gone and a bucketful of warm water smacks down
on them and it is Lieutenant Drum's voice.

"You men get on your feet."

The lieutenant has dressed himself in a hurry, the buttons on his tunic
out of line with their holes. The bridge of his nose has been blistered by the
sun. He seems more weary than furious.

"Since you obviously don't appreciate your rest time," says the white
man, "we'll have to find a way to make use of it."

Royal can't tell if he's bleeding or not. The water cooking away on his
skin and hair feels good, and he is glad that Sergeant Jacks is out on patrol.
It has been all marching and guard duty and aimless patrols—Las Ciegas to
Bamban, Bamban to Iba, Iba down to Subig to San Pedro and Botolan and
Angeles and Castillejos and the place they never learned the name of and now
stuck back here in Las Ciegas, their lives dragged out between bugle calls,
sunup and sundown the same every day. Junior says it's because they're on the
Equator. Royal stands at attention, eyes forward, as the lieutenant announces
their punishment. Behind, the woman stoops to lift wet, dirt-dragged uniforms from the ground.

It is the outpost they hate the most, no shade, no cover, just perched on
an outcropping of limestone rocks with a long view in three directions.
Hardaway and Gamble and Corporal Pickney are out of sight but within
shouting distance. There is a finger-sized lizard in a shaded crevice of rock a

few yards from him, and except for the little orange bubble working in and out on the side of its neck it hasn't twitched for hours. How many hours Royal doesn't know because he doesn't have a watch and they've taken all the clappers out of the bells, even in Las Ciegas, and today there will be no relief, not after two, not after four, just Sergeant Jacks coming by to be sure he is still awake and remind him whose ass he has also put in the sling and Coop is out on the other side of the village doing the same thing. The side of his head is swollen, pounding, and his ribs hurt with every breath. He saw the can of salmon lying on the ground as he left, a huge dent in it.

The lizard doesn't move.

The lizard understands how to be in this country. Royal's stomach isn't right and he can't sleep, troops of monkeys screaming all night in the forest just west of town and something, rats or maybe a snake, rustling around in the thatch of the hut. Royal tries to touch only the wooden parts of his rifle as he shifts it from shoulder to shoulder. If Jacks or any of the other officers catch him sitting or just not at attention like a damn tin soldier it will be more punishment under the sun.

She comes from behind over the rocks, so silent that if she was a rebel his throat would be cut. She offers him water in a stoppered length of bamboo and something folded in a banana leaf. When he pulls the leaf open there is a yellow-orange rice ball with bits of chicken and onion and peppers in it. It smells of cocoanut and is still warm from the pot. She sits on a rock near the lizard, which does not move, and watches him eat.

Royal points at her. "Nilda."

She nods. She is short, sturdier than Jessie, her face maybe a little flat but with that good long hair and her eyes—

"*Bringhe*," she says, pointing to the rice ball, then to herself. "Nilda."

CORRESPONDENCE

They have a new hero. And, the Humorist supposes, he is fitting for the age. Not a Washington, stoic, patriarchal, erect upon a towering steed on a hilltop surveying the conflict; not a Lincoln, haunted by carnage, magnanimous, no, positively be*reft* in victory, understanding that too harsh a palliative may vanquish not only the disease but also its host; not even a Grant, steadfast, straightforward, implacable—it is a Funston.

A banty rooster that crows at the opening of a news scavenger's notebook, a bully boy on the field of battle whose idea of sport is to take no prisoners, a Kansan Custer who leaves caution (and humility and compassion and, that antiquated notion, honor) to the wind, and whose biography, when inevitably published, can bear no title more apt that *Pluck and Luck*.

The subterfuge is nothing new. Homer is chock full of it, the wily Odysseus time after time proving to be more a confidence man than a warrior. Intercept the messenger, yes, decipher the code, forge documents—such intrigues are all accepted in the Great Game. Aguinaldo, in his jungle retreat, believes he is to be reinforced, General Lacuna writing to confirm he has sent a company of his men, along with five yankee prisoners. A bold plan, and admirable in that aspect, with an element of risk. Funston himself, with his chosen officers, dressed in rags of uniforms, marched through the hostile wilderness by loyal Macabebes disguised as Filipino insurrectionists. Ninety miles of pain and privation, through enemy territory, lost at times, hunger and thirst a constant, fearing discovery, or, perhaps worse, mutiny. Finally, exhausted and starving, unable to go farther.

"Only eight miles from the enemy stronghold," he boasts, "and *too weak to move.*"

This is where the story diverges from the parable of the Trojan Horse.

Emissaries, Macabebe scouts able to pass as Tagalos, are sent ahead *to beg for food.* Sustenance is delivered to their camp, the ruse maintained. Nourished, their fighting spirit restored, the party marches triumphantly into Aguinaldo's bailiwick, his much smaller compliment of soldiers turning out in parade dress to welcome them, and then—

The Humorist imagines himself a man at the prow of a lifeboat, peering over a restless sea. Perhaps it is in time of War. He spies a figure tossed on the waves, desperately swimming, survivor of some maritime calamity, each stroke more feeble than the last and about to go under. He bids the oarsman put his back to it, the lifeboat plowing through murderous swells, till he can lean forward and stretch his arm out to that solitary victim, reaching, reaching, and finally the exhausted wretch able to clasp his wrist with one hand—and plunge a dagger into his heart with the other.

Funston is the man with the dagger.

He is the toast of the Nation.

"Villia, shot in the shoulder," Funston says of Aguinaldo's chief of staff, "leapt out the window and into the river, but the Macabebes fished him out, and kicked him all the way up the bank, and asked him how he liked it."

Not only intrepid and fearless, but a wag of the first order. This proud jokester is the new model, his name and deeds on every tongue, the paragon of Patriotism, the unbashful subject of glowing editorials and stentorian orations, the centerpiece of an overnight industry of hagiography and boy-admiration. Here is a man, say the politicians, say the churchmen and the public-school teachers, to be proud of. A man to emulate. He has captured Aguinaldo and thus ended the war (the war that was declared over a full year ago, that somehow continues to claim, despite the surrender of its putative instigator, hundreds of new victims each week).

The Humorist once proposed, as a jest, a statue of Adam, the First Man, only to have one civic booster take the idea literally and mount a campaign to construct the thing. Perhaps, with his wide celebrity, he can now arouse interest in a suitable monument to Funston—the doughty colonel on his knees, in tatters, raising a trembling hand in supplication to the diminutive but haughty Tagalo *generalissimo*—while craftily concealing the blade, gilt-edged for glory, behind his back.

Enough to stir the pride of the dullest American schoolboy.

But no, this might be misunderstood. *He has discarded the grin of the funny man*, chided the *Times* after his first mildly satiric writings on the Philippine disgrace, *for the sour visage of the austere moralist*. For what place do morals have in the National Business? His merest whisper, not of reproach, but of frank disillusionment with the feisty Funston's exploit, has brought the Humorist a veritable flood-tide of correspondence from all corners of the Republic, impressive in its profusion, inspiring in the forthrightness of its sentiment, no finer example than the missive that now lies unsheathed on his desk.

Dear Traitor, it begins—

QUANDARY

There is no telling which one they'll run until the Chief comes in. The Cartoonist pins them to the wall side-by-side. He prefers the first as a drawing, a contrite Aggy in short pants writing *I Promise To Stop Fighting* on the blackboard as his new teacher, Miss Liberty, confiscated slingshot in hand, looks on benignly. The other sepia-tinted ragamuffins—Hawaii, Guam, Porto Rico—sit obediently in their labeled chairs, hands folded on desktops, a tiny American flag propped in each inkwell. The focus of the drawing, however, is the lad's mother, a jowly Hoar in a calico dress and straw bonnet, sympathetic tears pouring down his cheeks. The Cartoonist has lettered ANTI-IMPERIALIST LEAGUE on the hem of the frock, unsure if enough readers will recognize the Senator. He's tried Carnegie, but the Scotsman never looks right unless seated on a pile of money bags or the stooped back of a beleaguered ironworker. By now he can draw Bryan with his eyes closed, but the Chief has kept a candle lit for the old warhorse despite his lackluster account in November, and Twain remains beyond the pale.

HIS FIRST DAY AT SCHOOL

—says the caption, condescending but not vindictive, a nod to the elation felt by most citizens at the daring capture of the little *supremo*.

The other sketch keeps the heat on McKinley and the jingoes. A runty, demented TR in his outsized Rough Rider togs and an equally diminutive Colonel Funston (whose mug has been plastered all over the dailies in the last week) shoulder a pole from which they've slung scrawny, bedraggled Aguinaldo like a slaughtered hind.

WE'VE BROUGHT YOU AN APPETIZER

—proclaim the boys as they rush toward the President and Mark Hannah, bibs tucked into their collars, knife and fork poised in hand, greedily surveying the map of the world laid out on their table. A sobering thought that transcends the moment's euphoria, muses the Cartoonist, but not one likely to satisfy the man on the street.

The Chief, when he stampedes in from whatever theatrical event or soirée he has escorted his young ladies to this evening, will not ask the Cartoonist's opinion. He will frown at the drawings, the frown turning to a scowl when he spies the hated Roosevelt, eventually grunt, and, hopefully, jab his finger into the center of one of them. "Print it," he will say, a newsman's newsman, charging uphill as heedlessly as the toothy Vice President during his "crowded hour" on San Juan Hill.

Or maybe he'll ask the Cartoonist if plucky Funston couldn't appear to be just a few inches taller than TR.

PATROL

There are ten of them, with Junior, a buck sergeant now, in charge. The days have been getting cooler since the end of the year but they have been off the road for most of the patrol, up and over the rice-field dikes, working their way through prickerbush and scrub, chasing another rumor of a rebel build-up. The two collections of huts they've walked through, not big enough to be on the lieutenant's map, were deserted, but that might only be for one of the endless religious marches, people here with more saints to celebrate than days to do it on, or else they've heard the rumor too and don't want to be around for reprisals from the losers. Royal sees one man the whole morning, standing thigh-deep in the muck of a flooded rice field whipping a switch on the butt of a sweat-lathered carabao, itself mired to the chest, trying to get it to drag a wooden harrow through the mess and neither of them going anywhere. He feels more like the water buff than the man, hard to say if it is really trying to pull itself forward or just satisfied to sink deeper and ignore what's happening to its hind end.

The men march on, walking in a loose rectangle through a banana plantation, Royal and Willie Mills in the van, carrying their rifles port-arms. The trees are strange, nearly twice as tall as Royal, with each trunk supporting a single massive bunch of fat green fingers, like a man in a bulky overcoat hung by his heels. And the rows of banana fingers all pointing up to the sky—it seems wrong, like a lot of the things that grow here, like something a little boy might draw. Royal keeps an eye out for the spiders he has seen crawling on the bunches. He doesn't like spiders.

They walk, talk for a while, then lapse into silence. There are men among them who would make better sergeants, older men who deserve it, but Junior is the lightest of them and educated and Royal figures that is what the officers were thinking when they had to move somebody up. Junior has been tight since he got the stripe, knowing there is some resentment, and trying to be firm but not lean on his rank too heavy. It is usually Hardaway who starts the talking.

"You member Fagen?"

"Big ole Tampa boy with the 24th."

"That's the one. Word is he run out."

"Run out to where?"

"Loaded up every sidearm he could carry and walked into the boondocks."

"Where the googoos kilt him."

"Naw, man—made him a *cap*tain."

"Captain of the googoos is like King of the Niggers."

"General is king in the Army."

"Then captain is what? Duke? His Royalty, Duke Fagen."

"Story is he been leadin ambushes, and they caught some of them volunteers from Ohio, left em alone with Fagen—"

Too Tall aims a pretend pistol downward.

"Told em to kneel and say their prayers, then *pop! pop! pop! pop!*"

They are quiet for a while, passing from the bananas into a stubbly cane field, considering Fagen.

"Ohio Vols," says Coop.

"Yeah. White boys."

"Well—as long as he don't teach the googoos to *aim*."

They laugh then, even Royal who can go a week without cracking a smile. Junior is heard at the rear.

"Treason is treason. When he's captured they'll hang him."

"Not gonna capture that ole boy. He stepped out that far, he cut his own throat before they take him."

They ponder this, the dead-end nerve of it. Royal can hear the river ahead, see the tops of the trees that line both banks. The patrol is meant to reach the river, work north along it for a few miles, then loop back to the garrison before dark.

"If all he wanted to do was kill crackers," says Gamble, "he could have stayed in Tampa."

The river is not so wide here, but swift-moving from the months of rain.

They keep it on their right and march till they come to a sandy beach piled with driftwood in the crook of an elbow bend. There is none of the usual comment when Junior orders them to fall out.

The men have taken to carrying fruit or boiled eggs they've bargained for in Las Ciegas as well as their rations, and Sims gets a little driftwood fire going to cook coffee.

"How they do it," says Coop, "is they just keeps *mov*in. Them little shit-holes we run through this morning? Full up with googoos five minutes after we leave, havin them a party."

"They aint gonna win no war that way."

"Long as they not where *we* are, they doin fine. Most alla them U.S. volunteers gone home by now, right? And how many ignant niggers like us you think they can fool into coming here?"

"Speak for yourself," says Junior.

"I'm doin that. I been vaccinated twice already, bit by every kind of bug that crawls or flies, had googoos shoot at my head and knock a cocoanut off a tree and the sun done cook me to a whole new shade of dark, and yet I aint put nary a one of these little monkeys in the ground. They just playin with us, is all, cause they don't want to fight no more."

"They've switched to guerilla tactics," says Junior. "Like the Boers in South Africa."

"They've switched to hidin out and laughin at us poor donkeys runnin around in the heat," says Coop. "Aint no *tac*tics to it."

Royal eats to get it over with, staring dully out at the river and the long wall of jagged mountains beyond it. Junior has been drilling him about the importance of a positive state of mind, and every new day he tries to will himself into one, but it never lasts much past Kid Mabley blowing Assembly. Mingo Sanders from B Company and some of the others from the Indian wars say get used to it, this is what regular soldiering is, living out your routines, working your details, keeping yourself razor-sharp so that when the redskins do attack you're more than a match for them, ambushed or not. The fights, if they come, are flash floods in a life of drought.

"Two of you will post up and down the river," says Junior suddenly, standing up from the sand, "while the rest of us bathe."

"I'm staying out of there," says Hardaway. "Might be snakes."

"Man got snakes on the brain."

"All right, Hardaway and Gamble set up as pickets—"

"Why me?"

Junior gives Gamble a long look.

"Because those are your orders. When someone comes out they can relieve you and you can come in."

Coop is up and unhitching his ammunition belt. "I'm getting in that water before you niggers start takin them boots off."

"River look cold."

"Cold sound fine to me."

Every other day the woman, Nilda, walks a mile from Las Ciegas with their clothes and scours them with pumice rock and lye soap in what is more a puddle than a spring, white cattle egrets stepping into the wet grass to search for snails and crayfish as she works. Royal sat to watch her there once, and helped her carry the water-heavy clothes basket back until just before the first outpost. She washes their clothes, but the men themselves stay dirty, dust and dried sweat staying on their skin for weeks. You don't miss a chance to wash yourself.

The water is cold but the current isn't much on this side of the bend, weak enough so you can even swim out a few strokes without worrying. The men shout and splash and duck each other under, most of them fully naked. Junior has his yellow soap and works his way upstream for a little privacy, his desperation to be clean an open joke within the company.

"Junior think if he scrub it hard enough," Too Tall will say, "it might just come off."

"He right too. That boy was born black as me, an lookit him *now*."

The bottom is silted and easy to walk on. Royal steps out up to his arm-pits and can feel it change there, the backwater eddy giving way to the full current. He reaches over the surface and dips his fingers into the water as it rushes by. It will just *take* you.

He stands there, at the edge, for a long time and then turns back to see who's got the soap.

There is still coffee hot when he comes out, skin tingling, and he drinks some from his cup and takes his time dressing, being sure to brush all the sand from between his toes before he pulls his socks on, to stretch the wrinkles out of his pants before he puts them on. The others dress beside him, calling out insults as Hardaway comes back and decides to go in alone.

"See why the man afraid of snakes. Think one is gonna catch a look at what he got hangin there and fall in love."

"Don't let them big ole catfish in there catch holt of it, now!"

Hardaway pays them no mind, bending to duck his head under the water and blowing loud bubbles.

"Where I come up," says Willie Mills, "the catfish gets long as a tall man's leg, and they hole up in the roots under the river bank. We used to go down there, reach in—"

He mimes the action, closing his eyes and probing with an arm—

"—and when you feel one you just stick your hand down his gullet, halfway up the elbow, and yank him out of there."

"Big cat like that will bite on you."

"Oh, you see some blood, but them big ones fry up nice, feed the whole family."

"*Dans le bayou*," says Achille, "we hunt the snapper turtle with our bare foot. Walk in the mud of the bank till you feel a shell, then reach in and pull him up."

"Good way to lose some fingers."

"On the snapper shell he has a *ridge*," he explains. "You feel those ridge with your toe, you know which end is beak and which end is tail."

"Feel em with what toes you got *left*."

You had to go a ways up the river from Wilmington before the turpentine and creosote smell was gone, and Royal and Jubal would fish for bass using crickets they had caught, Jubal making up wild stories about what the Cape Fears and the Waccamaws were up to when they owned the river. Jubal never told the same story twice.

Hardaway screams and they turn to make jokes about snakes in the water but he is naked, scrambling out of the water and behind him there is another thing, light-skinned, floating slowly face-down in a rosy cloud.

It is a lazy kind of floating, peaceful, and it takes a moment to know what has happened.

The others are up with their rifles then and shouting, staying low as they spread and move up the bank, none of them fully dressed. Royal watches it float, turning a half-circle as it drifts away, then hurries out in all his clothes to grab an ankle before the current can take it. He turns and hauls it back through the running water, drags it onto the sand without looking. It is Junior, he knows. Junior is the only one of them that light. Royal is wet and shaking with the cold, still squatting by the body without looking at it when the others come back around, having found nothing upriver but the chunk of yellow soap placed carefully on a rock.

"Must have only been a few of them or we'd all be cooked."

"Aw, damn, lookit what they done—"

"We got to carry him back. Here, spread his clothes out—"

"Got to wrap him careful or his arm's gonna come off."

"They be waiting out there to ambush."

"We don't go back the same way we come, stay in the open. Hell, *let* em show their damn faces—"

"That bolo cut right through a man, don't it?"

There is a buzzing in Royal's ears now, and the river louder than it should be, and the fact of Junior that can't be real, can't be real. Ponder, the corporal and in charge now, kneels beside Royal, hand on his shoulder.

"This aint no different than Cuba, Roy. Pick up your dead and keep moving."

Royal nods.

"So you best get them boots on."

They cover Junior as well as they can with his own clothes and work up a kind of stretcher from driftwood poles and men's shirts tied to it that Gamble and Willie Mills carry, Junior's hat, boots, and canteen sitting on top of the body. Royal insists on carrying the butchered man's Krag and ammo belt as well as his own, able to bear the weight but only dimly aware of the ground they cover as he follows after Pickney and Coop in the lead.

Junior is why he is here, and now he is gone.

Royal sees himself, sees them all, from very high and very far, a tiny procession of nine dark men carrying a dead soldier across the sun-beaten flatlands of somebody else's country.

Junior is why he is here. Junior is why he is anywhere besides breathing cotton chaff at Sprunt's in Wilmington, Junior the doctor's son who watched him in the stable and in the yard and one day invited him inside when Mrs. Lunceford was not home, who said he was smart and ought to stay in school some more and become one of the Talented Tenth. And here he is instead in the Colored 25th, somewhere between Bacolor and Las Ciegas without an idea why.

"They don't know it, but it's a war," Junior used to say, even back when they were still throwing pinecones at trees pretending to be base-ball pitchers. "Only not a war where one side beats the other, but where one side figures out we should be right there marching next to them, that that's where we should have always been."

"I steer clear of white folks," Royal would always remind him, "and hope they does likewise for me."

"You mean you hide."

"I'm right here."

"You hide your talent."

"I got no talent. Less it's throwing a in-shoot. Watch this—"

Pinecones will do all kind of tricks and so will a baseball if you hold it right and throw it fast enough. Junior couldn't throw much but was light-footed and could bunt the ball just where he wanted and beat it to first.

"It's not an oppor*tun*ity to do something for the race," he would say, dead serious, "it is our duty."

Junior got most of this from Dr. Lunceford probably, who was in tight with all the big colored men in town, who got a new-model carriage every couple years and spoke even better than a white man, even if it was only to Uncle Wicklow. Junior was going to be a man just like him, though not a doctor, and his sister Jessie was the most beautiful girl in Wilmington.

The extra belt of ammunition is digging into the side of his neck. They pass through a cornfield, the stalks up to his top button, Gamble and Mills hoisting the stretcher poles on their shoulders to get it over.

Junior was here to impress the white folks. I am here, Royal thinks, to impress Junior's sister. Or that's how it started. But Captain Parker, when they bring the body in, will not be impressed. And Jessie Lunceford is lost to him forever.

They hear the conversation of rifle fire, Krags and Mausers trading compliments, about three miles out. The sun is low in the sky, off to their right. Ponder holds the squad up. Royal tries not to look at the pile on the stretcher. He can hear the flies that have been worrying it all afternoon, following them.

"We gone have to leave Junior back," says Ponder. "No tellin what we got on our hands up there."

"There's at least twenty with rifles," says Coop, listening. "Mausers and Springfields. That usually mean two, three times more with bolos."

"I'll keep with him," offers Royal.

"Can't spare you, Roy. He be all right."

They leave the body in a dry gulch parallel to the east-west road, covered with cornstalks, and Coop ties the laces of Junior's boots together and tosses to snag them, first try, on a cleat high up on a telegraph pole so they have a marker. Not far down the road they find the wire cut, at the same spot they always do it, almost a courtesy by now. The men double-time in two rows, three paces apart. They don't carry bayonets on patrol. When they can see black powder smoke on the horizon Ponder waves them off the road.

"Swing on around behind," he says, "and come at em with the sun behind our backs like they done to the boys."

There is nobody at the western outpost, dead or alive. They hide their canteens and the extra rifle in the rocks and share out Junior's ammunition, pressing the rounds nose-down into their hatbands, then take the slings off their weapons, spreading out into a firing line. Royal realizes it is Junior's Krag he has kept, no nick on the forestock.

"You know what to do," says Ponder and they set off at a trot. When they get to the rice they take the irrigation ditches two at a stride, the Filipinos in sight now, little men, crouching behind the dike at the end of the field, firing into the village. The regulars run twice as close as Royal thinks they should before one of the bolomen sees and points and shouts and then they all flop on their bellies and begin to fire. The rebels can't see how many they are because of the setting sun in their eyes and panic, the ones not hit in the first volley running along the dike but too high, exposed to the soldiers dug in in the village, and falling, falling, wet mud sounds and water splattering up into Royal's face from the ditch in front of him, probably fire from the boys in Las Ciegas and then the rebels scatter in every direction like a startled flock of birds and Ponder yells to run them down.

Royal is up running after, the others whooping beside him and the first one he shoots is wounded already, kneeling, the round passing through his throat and spatting against the wet bank beyond and Royal running past, working the bolt as he goes, dropping one and then two from behind and seeing a third go down, just falling in the uneven paddy with his bolo flying away and Royal is over him before he can rise. The man, not young, clutches a cross hanging from a cord on his neck and says words, sides heaving from the run, and Royal waits till they meet eyes to thrust the barrel inches away and put one through his chest. He sits then on the wet ground then and listens to the man's last wet gasping as the others splash past and the rest of the garrison steps out from the huts on the other side of the irrigation dike, cheering.

PAN AMERICAN

The Assassin begins at the Filipino Village. The tops of thatched huts are visible as he skirts along the fence, smoke rising from a breakfast cookfire inside. Roast-pork smell. He hasn't eaten since yesterday noon. He turns right between the cyclorama dramatizing the Battle of Missionary Ridge, a limping old man in yankee blue shouting the names of dead generals to drum up interest, and the Cineograph exhibit, slowing to mingle with the crowd that flows in and out of the Pabst Pavillion. Nobody is watching him.

Nobody knows.

Across the Midway is an enormous, beautiful woman's face, chin slightly lifted, her eyes closed in sweet reverie while people stroll through the wide entrance portal at the base of her neck. DREAMLAND say the letters on the rim of the corona set in her luscious, wind-blown hair. Only moments after the gates open there are thousands of spectators at the Exposition, sleep-walking, hazily grazing past amusement and advertisement to ponder which exotic world they will surrender the quarters clutched in their fists to.

Only I am awake, thinks the Assassin, and turns away to walk toward the thick brown Bavarian turrets of Alt Nurnberg.

A German brass band thumps away inside the courtyard, tuba grunting rhythmically, and a man outside in lederhosen and a feathered hat does a hopping, knee-slapping dance. The Assassin turns left at the biergarten, passing the Johnstown Flood exhibit and then the tall wood-pole fence that protects the festgoers from Darkest Africa. He hooks south along the

Canal, turning his head away when a motor-gondola passes bearing two men, one cranking the lever of some kind of large camera. He turns again at the Mall, plunging into the crowd between the Electricity building and the Machinery and Transportation complex. If the monster is Capital, as the books and pamphlets have it, then this is its lair. He holds the site map, carefully marked and folded, under his arm. Mines, Railroads, Manufacturing, Agriculture and Government, Standard Oil, Quaker Oats, Aunt Jemima, Horlicks Malted Milk, and Baker's Chocolate, all glorified in plaster and stone. There is no escaping the message-barkers and street bands hammering the air from every side, young girls in strange costumes passing out samples, concession signs boasting that their prices beat any at the Pan. The Assassin squirms through the press of bodies and emerges to face the sparkling blue-green of the Grand Basin, pausing to stare up for a moment at the massive Electric Tower that dominates the fairgrounds. It is an ivory tower with gold trimming and lustrous blue-green panels, a steadfast white sentinel over the riotous reds, yellows, and oranges of the South American buildings, with the gilded Goddess of Light herself sparkling four hundred feet above them.

I will bring this down.

The Assassin turns and walks past the Cascades, each towering plume of water a different color of the rainbow, then takes a seat on the wall of the Fountain of Abundance to wait.

The Kodak fiends are hiding them in their wicker baskets. Or shoeboxes, if less prepared. Word has gone out about the extra charge at the gate, a squad of sharp-eyed boys collecting fifty cents per camera, but with so many visitors blithely carrying their own food onto the grounds for bench picnics it only makes sense to smuggle your Brownie or Bull's-Eye past them. Harry sees the devices everywhere, pulled out to snap the family grouping in front of one of the Exposition juggernauts or immortalize a comrade with his arm around some Midway exotic or a sweetheart precariously astride a dromedary's back, then quickly nestled back into their hiding places. There is no hiding Mr. Edison's apparatus of course, and immediately upon hauling it from the gondola Daddy Paley is surrounded by shutter bugs and small boys wanting to examine it. Ensconced in Luchow's Nurnberg restaurant with the machine at his feet, a platter of steaming wursts and a nickel draught before him, he gives Harry leave to explore until the President comes at noon.

A MOMENT IN THE SUN

"Find us some good views," he says, flicking excess foam off the beer with a finger. "But I don't want to lug this thing up any stairs."

The mirror maze at Dreamland is no good, of course, not enough light and the problem of seeing the camera itself in reflection. Sig Lubin's Cineograph parlor is next door, peddling their copycat views and counterpart boxing dodges, a bold venture considering Lubin himself has fled Philadelphia for foreign climes, avoiding indictment for patent infringement. Or perhaps he is only hiding out in the Gypsy Camp or the Streets of Mexico or sweltering with the sled dogs in the Esquimaux Village. Their own Mutoscope parlor is doing lackluster business so far, what with a live Fatima undulating her torso only one door over in the Cairo Bazaar.

Even here, in the mildly salacious Midway, there are twice as many women as men. Young and old, rich and relatively modest of means, in pairs and groups, a few dowagers squired about on wicker-seated roller chairs, women with picture hats and rented parasols strolling, observing, judging. "The American Girl," as the periodicals like to label her, is here in abundance, and Harry can't help but think of the fun it would be for Brigid and her sisters to do the Pan. He casts a professional eye up at the Aero-Cycle, a kind of giant teeter-totter with a revolving wheel full of screaming enthusiasts at either end. Perhaps a view from a distance, then the dizzied, excited passengers dismounting—but to film on the ride itself seems pointless, too many axes of motion for a viewer to keep a handle on. Those roller chairs, though—remove the old biddy and replace her with a camera operator, the device rigged just above his lap somehow, with a trained man to push him, and they could approximate a long moving shot on land similar to what they just filmed on the Canal—

Something to consider. Harry hurries under the wildly swinging armature and pays fifty cents for a Trip to the Moon.

Several dozen spectators gather in the darkened Theater of the Planets, their guide, a basso-voiced gentleman with riding goggles perched on his forehead, lit dramatically from below while the screen behind him glows with the whorls of the Milky Way.

"We are about to embark on a journey," he intones, "to a landscape on which no human foot has ever trod."

At least not since the last twenty-minute tour, thinks Harry, as they are led into the *Airship Luna* by the crew members. It is a beautifully designed fantasy, with multiple wings and propellers and large open portholes to see out from.

"Please steady yourselves, ladies and gentlemen," suggests the guide, wearing a fancifully adorned football helmet and with his goggles pulled down over his eyes now. "We have some inclement weather reported over the Buffalo area this evening."

It is not evening outside, of course, but as the wings begin to flap madly and the body of the Airship tilts and shakes, rear propeller buzzing as it picks up speed, what they see below them outside the wind-blasted portholes is the Pan-American Exposition at night, lit up in all its electric glory, surrounded by the city of Buffalo and yes, that must be it—

"Those are the Niagara Falls down to your left, ladies and gentlemen," announces their guide from his pilot's seat. "One of the Great Wonders of our own dear Earth, to which we bid a fond adieu—" and here a sudden swift upwrenching that causes the ladies to gasp and grab out for their men, Harry with a sudden pang, missing her here, his Brigid, not so much on this Midway as anywhere on the grounds, pointing things out to her, listening to her beautiful laugh, sitting quietly, perhaps, in the Botanical Gardens, float-ing in a gondola with his hand in hers—

"We're going to fall!" cries the matron sitting beside him, hugging her bag tightly to her chest. "We're going to fall and smash to the ground!"

"Mind yourselves, fellow adventurers, we're passing through a storm!"

And a storm it is, the wind moaning past, a cloud bank enveloping the *Luna*, lightning flashes and the boom of present thunder, even a few drops of precipitation whipping in through the portholes and then—

The passengers sigh as one. Through the front panel, beyond the guide at his controls, the full moon sits like a giant pearl in the suddenly clear night sky, sparkling stars beyond it.

"There she is, dead ahead," calls out the guide. "Our destination, ladies and gentlemen. The Queen of the Heavens."

It grows larger and larger as they approach, a wonderful illusion, thinks Harry, looking around at the delighted, awe-stricken faces of his fellow passen-gers. Méliès knew it from the beginning—the viewer will soon tire of what he can already see, with all its color and immediacy, in the world. Even our actu-alities with the original fighters instead of Lubin's counterparts, our rushing trains and fire wagons, our scenes of exotic or everyday wonder, are illusions, are a series of still photographs, devoid of color, flashed rapidly on a screen to fool the human eye. But treat that eye to something that could never exist—

The light in front of them grows blindingly white as the moon's surface fills the panel.

"Shield your eyes, earth beings, for the intensity of the Lunar Rays may damage them!"

The Airship makes a sudden sweeping turn and there is a thump and scrape as they toboggan along the rough terrain, the faintly lit, cratered surface rushing past the portholes. Some of it is electricity, Harry decides, powered by the Falls not so many miles away, driving the Airship along some sort of rail past sets that have been artfully created. Some is only lantern projections, a horizontal strip, perhaps, or a turret revolved to give the sense of motion. Whether the ship moves past the landscape or the landscape past the ship, it is, with the rocking and buffeting and blasting of air, enormously effective.

"The inhabitants of the realm we have intruded upon are known as the Selenites," says the guide, turning to them and deepening his voice in sober warning. "They are thought to be friendly to visitors, but please, if we should encounter any members of the race, be careful not to provoke them."

The crew members help the voyagers out of the Airship and onto the moon's craggy surface then, Harry refusing the proffered hand. The ground feels spongy underfoot, and his walking stick leaves tiny dents in it as they head away from the craft.

Above their heads hangs a carpet of stars. They are led around the raised lip of a large crater, stepping carefully, till they reach a small hill with a large cavern opening at the base of it.

"This is the Grotto of the City of the Moon. I must plead that we be allowed egress." The guide steps ahead and cups his hands around his mouth, calling into the dark abyss. "Hello! We hail from Buffalo, on the planet Earth! May we enter?"

A gasp of surprise then, as a large-headed, spiky-backed creature in a green and red outfit and sharply pointed slippers appears at the mouth of the grotto. Harry estimates that the fellow barely comes up to his hip. He looks the passengers and crew over for a long moment, then holds a tiny hand straight out to them in greeting.

"Hail, Erse-Dwellairs!" he calls in a strange, high-pitched voice. "I welcome you to ze City of ze Moon."

If Harry is not mistaken the Selenite has a touch of a French accent.

There are more little Selenites inside as they descend into the twisting, turning grotto, weaving through eerily glowing stalactites and stalagmites on a green concrete floor, past towering columns carved with the faces of fierce and unearthly creatures, some of the little inhabitants toiling away with miniature picks and crowbars, revealing veins of glistening gold or jewels gleaming in unimaginable colors. Among them glide lovely Moon-Maids of more human stature, dark-haired beauties dressed in diaphanous robes who stare at the visitors shyly with their huge eyes. They are led into a large chamber, and suddenly there is music, the liquid rippling of a harp, a sweet mandolin, and voices now, as the tiny Selenites and ghostly Moon-Maids join in a melody—

My sweetheart's the Man in the Moon
I'm going to marry him soon
T'would fill me with bliss just to give him one kiss
But I know that a dozen I never would miss!

Harry and the other visitors, slightly embarrassed, look to the dozen or so children in their party, the only ones still rapt in the illusion now that they have left the realms of Galactic Flight for that of Music Hall. There are adults, he knows, who will only visit the movie parlors if they bring their children with them, some lingering unease at giving themselves up to the gossamer images on the screen.

I'll go up in a great big balloon
And see my sweetheart in the moon
Then behind some dark cloud, where no one's allowed
I'll make love to the Man in the Moon!

They lose Harry in the Palace. It is only a proscenium, however elaborately decorated, the giants seemingly bored, the tumbling dwarves no better than circus performers, the Moon Pageant replete with shifting scenery and flashing colored lights but without dramatic tension, the greenish gorgonzola offered by beaming Moon-Maids more than he can stomach this early in the day. Moving, projected views, he thinks, to replace the lantern slides. They can only be tinted, of course, till the color problem is solved, but think of the illusion, think of the impact, if while you are being moved forward in a vehicle all that you see from the front and side portals has been filmed in some foreign capital or natural vista! You could tour the streets of Mexico from any city in the States, and never step out of the carriage.

The show ends with a promise of friendship between peoples. "Just as the nations of North and South America have come together at this great Exposition," says the Man in the Moon, "thus shall the citizens of my realm be ever bonded with those of your planet Earth."

They exit through the shadowy gorge and jaws of a dragon-like creature called a Moon Calf onto the raucous, steaming Midway. Just one entrance down is the Old Plantation, a glimpse, as the brochure describes it, of the sunny South before the War. Sweat begins to run down Harry's forehead from his hat brim. He wonders how they keep it so cool on the moon. Dozens of spectators, yankees, are flowing through the doorway of the "mansion" that fronts the exhibit. Harry checks his pocket watch, digs out a quarter, and follows them in.

Pretty, ringletted girls in stiff pastel dresses greet the visitors, all smiles and coquetry. Harry has been to gala occasions something like the one presented in the chandeliered ballroom they pass into, Sally's coming out for one, though never with a colored band playing *Dixie*, and certainly never with so many colorful fans fluttering in ladies' hands. There are unpainted slave quarters out back, along with log cabins claimed to have been occupied by Abraham Lincoln and Jeff Davis, and a swarm of negroes unlike any he's ever encountered, even in South Carolina. Cotton-headed old uncles, pipe-smoking aunties doing wash and spinning yarn, clean but raggedy children running everywhere. Men and women stoop and pick cotton in several rows planted at the far end of the compound, several pale women with parasols watching intently. One knot of white visitors gathers around two little boys doing a frantic, barefoot buck-and-wing to the ministrations of a grinning banjo player, while others ring an old man sitting on a porch chuckling and giggling and slapping his knee with every response to their queries. Harry drifts over by a young fellow filling buckets of water from a hand pump.

"Good morning."

"Mornin to you, Cap'm," replies the young man, touching two fingers to his forehead in salute but continuing to pump.

"Where you folks from?"

"Oh," he sighs, straightening to look around at his fellow Plantation dwellers, "mostly it's Georgia, Alabama, M'ssippi. Me, I'm fum Valdosta."

"You stay here at night?"

"Mostly, yassuh."

Harry looks over toward the pickers. "That cotton," he says, "what happens when it's all been harvested?"

The hint of a smile tugs at the water boy's mouth. "Well, Mr. Skip who run the Plantation, he bring in another patch by'an'by, but most mornins we gots to get up an stick them bolls back in the plants fore they open up the fair."

"That seems like an awful lot of trouble."

"Yessuh, an that's why he got him some per*fess*ional niggers like us. You see them what's wanderin around the Midway, fum this yere Buffalo? That ain but *am*aters."

"I see." They both turn as the toothless old man on the porch emits a particularly high-pitched cackle, rocking back and forth in mirth as he entertains a growing crowd of yankees.

"That Laughin' Ben. He ain right," says the water boy, touching his temple with a finger. "But the white fokes sure love him."

"I can see that."

"You not fum up here neither, is you, Cap'n?"

"North Carolina."

The boy nods. "Thas one of them in-between states. We run through it on the train."

Harry bids him good day and manages to reach the exit just as the pickers and spinners and tale-tellers all drop what they're doing to join the eleven o'clock cakewalk. His leg is hurting him, sharp pains running from ankle to hip, and he has perspired through to his vest.

At least, he thinks, pushing hard with his cane to make time through the crowded Mall, they haven't included an Irish Pavillion.

He finds Paley still in the restaurant, comparing the apple and cherry pie selections.

"Anything good?"

"The Trip to the Moon—"

"It's on my list," says Daddy, extricating himself from the table. "But Skip Dundy wants a fortune to shoot it."

"I had another idea. What if we were to stage a battle in the Filipino Village? They've got huts, palms trees, a lagoon with canoes, real Filipinos—"

"And who's going to ask the Boss for the money to do that? There's woods in Jersey, right near the shop."

"If we're going to stay competitive—"

"When Mr. Edison's lawyers finish their business," says the cameraman, helping arrange the apparatus and tripod on Harry's shoulder, "we won't *have* any competition."

"But think of the excitement it would add, the verisimilitude." Harry has pictured the view in his mind. A young captain, maybe even Niles himself, leading a desperate charge into the village as *insurrectos* leap from the huts to fire at them. And then a shot—the roller chair could be employed here—as if the viewer himself was running through the melee, native rebels firing directly at him—

"We've nabbed Aggy, my friend. That war's over." Paley stabs a last forkful of pie and snaps it down. "We'd better get over to the Esplanade."

The Assassin watches him approach, preceded by marching bands and squadrons of cavalry, snug in his open victoria pulled by four glistening steeds, waving affably to the cheering citizens who line the Causeway. The Assassin leans on one of the piers till the carriage has passed, then joins the throng across the flag-draped Triumphal Bridge in pursuit.

Idolatry. The word has been pressed in his mind since his entrance this morning. The dreaming woman's massive face, the Sphinx over the Beautiful Orient, Cleopatra, the Baker's Chocolate maiden, the Goddess of Light perched on the Electric Tower, the kindly President in his silk top hat and frock coat—this is the Pantheon of false gods, and these poor, deluded sleepwalkers have come to worship them.

Applause as he climbs down from his carriage, is led onto the platform that has been set up in the Esplanade. The Assassin tries to move forward through the multitude as the Expostion head introduces the President. People are hot, ladies have their parasols open against the noonday sun, all are pressing forward to see closer, hear better. More applause as he rises, begins to speak. The words are unclear at this distance. The Assassin passes the men he saw in the gondola, now with their tripod mounted on what look like apple boxes to see over the crowd, the fat one with his eye pressed tight to it, cranking all the while. A man in a suit silently moving his lips on a platform decked with bunting that will be without color. Pointless idolatry. Men glare as the Assassin pushes between them. He can make out words now, but still they make no sense. He comes to a wall of policemen, standing face to the crowd, hands folded behind their backs, immobile. Expressionless. More statues. The grounds are full of statues, heroic statues, allegorical groupings, Indians in wax and wood, massive bear and buffalo and moose and elk, statues representing Labor and Capital and Motherhood and Bounty. The Shield of Despotism, this grouping could be called, or The Blue Wall of Tyranny.

The Assassin pushes up to look between their shoulders. If he is lucky it might work from here. But no, one of the statues is staring at him.

"Take a step back, Bud," says the policeman. "Yer crowdin me."

Rapturous applause as the President finishes his address, as hands are shaken on the platform, as bemedaled John Philip Sousa himself leads his band in *The Stars and Stripes Forever*. The President starts down from the platform and the crowd behind pushes the Assassin toward him. He reaches into his pocket, closing his hand around the little pistol. Maybe, maybe—but the Blue Wall holds fast, pushing back as McKinley is escorted away in a phalanx of security agents for his tour of the Exposition.

"Easy, folks," calls the burly copper. "He'll be back tomorrow to shake hands."

The Assassin drifts away then, throwing looks back over his shoulder at the official party, counting bodyguards. A man seems to be watching him, following. A blue-eyed man with a moustache and a bowler tilted on his head, a gold-headed walking stick resting casually on his shoulder. The Assassin hurries through the dispersing crowd, pulling his watch out to look at it as if he is late for an appointment, bathed in sweat now, the rubbing bodies of the multitude, the noon sun, the fate of the future in his pocket. He struggles back down the Mall, past the little Acetylene Exhibit, a man shouting the praises of the Wonder Gas even as hundreds turn into the massive Electricity Building across the way, flicking a look back to see that the watcher is still there, closer now, feigning inattention but definitely following. How can they know? How can they know? And the Assassin cuts sharply left and trots into the welcoming coolness of the Infant Incubators.

It is mostly women in the building. The nurses, of course, in their white uniforms, and then a dozen female spectators of various ages, cooing and whispering over the babies in their steel and glass ovens.

"Poor, dear things," says one in a dress of black crepelike material. "I can't imagine they'll be normal."

"Our graduates do very well," responds a nurse, transferring one of the tiny, monkey-face creatures from incubator to a basket in a dumbwaiter shaft. "Those that survive."

"You've lost some, then?"

"A few. Less than one out of ten."

"God wanted them."

"God is in no hurry," says the nurse. "They just died, and their mothers were distraught." She presses a button and waits while the basket is drawn out of sight, then turns to the watching women. "Every two hours each child is changed and fed."

The Assassin walks along the machines, peering in at the infants, mindful of the entrance door. The man has not followed him in.

"No matter what their weight, Dr. Couney believes that a warm, clean environment is the key to these babies' survival. Until the hospitals in this country accept his findings," the nurse spreads her arms to indicate the exhibit, "here we are."

"I don't think I could bear having my child in a side-show hatchery," says a young woman making a pained face as she stares in through a porthole.

The nurse smiles politely. "Let's hope you never have to, then. Please tell your friends who visit the Exposition about us," she says brightly to the others in the room. "Your quarters make our efforts possible."

America, thinks the Assassin, watching a discolored, pint-sized creature struggle for breath, translucent eyelids fluttering but never quite opening. Even the infants have to earn their keep.

Harry spends the afternoon touring the more educational exhibits. Graphic Arts, Ethnology, Machinery and Transportation, the state and foreign buildings. All very informative but nothing active enough for the camera lens. They'll do the Indian Congress tomorrow, maybe get the President with Red Cloud or Geronimo, and film the mock battle with the cavalry in the Stadium. Evening brings more young couples to the Pan, strolling hand-in-hand to Venice in America and taking the boat ride, swaying together by the many bandstands listening to waltzes, sitting in the Plaza by the Sunken Garden. There is a casual anonymity here, an escape from judgment. Not that he is ever ashamed to be seen with Brigid, but—

As the sun sets most of those still strolling the grounds make their way back to the Esplanade. The speakers' platform is now serving as a reviewing stand for the President and his entourage, gazing with thousands of his constituents across the Court of the Fountains toward the Electric Tower, waiting for the Illumination.

It begins at the very edge of dusk.

The doors of the Temple of Music have been thrown open and the Great Organ within, joined outside by Sousa's band, begins to play *The Star-Spangled Banner*, slowly building power and volume. The lamps set low around the fountains dim, as do the streetlamps. Then, starting with the Electric Tower and the larger structures, lights begin to glow, faint and pink at first, just a few of them, then more, outlining the buildings, outlining the fountains, edging the heroic statues, growing in number and intensity as the crowd sighs as one, and then as the last blush of sun fades from the sky the whole Exposition blazes forth in golden effulgence as the organist strikes a mighty chord and the people are cheering and applauding and thrilled to be here for this wonder, light all around them, a city of light, and if the Airship could indeed make the voyage Harry has no doubt you would see this beautiful light from the moon.

It isn't over, though, not tonight. As the organ's last note echoes away there is another mass sigh—spitting, sparkling fires of green, red, blue, and gold flame up at the four corners of the fairgrounds, and then hundreds of balloons, somehow glowing from within, are released at once and float above the light-adorned buildings of the Pan, followed by a barrage of rockets, a hundred of them streaking and screaming up from all sides and then larger rockets exploding, shrieking horizontal to the ground with silver and gold comet tails streaming after and *BOOM! BOOM! BOOM! BOOM! BOOM!* rainbow starbursts in the air and Harry almost breathless with it, the crowd gasping and oohing and aahing like a great enraptured creature and he aches to have her with him at this moment, Brigid beside him, longs to see her face lit by these colors, to feel her pulse quicken, the radiance of her unstudied delight. Fireworks are exploding now to form the colorful flags of the South American nations taking part in the Exposition and he wonders what the Judge would think, can feel the tone of Niles's dismissive banter like a twinge down his spine and *BOOM! BOOM! BOOM! BOOM!* each bombardment more spectacular than the last, shells bursting into flowering patterns and beginning to fade just as *BOOM! BOOM!* the next barrage begins, raining parachutes now that swing down slowly toward the earth with ruby globes sizzling beneath them, pouring multi-hued lightning over the Rainbow City from the black sky and he vows to himself, Harry Manigault vows that he will come back to this place with her, that they will see the Falls as man and wife like so many of these beaming, cheering Americans around him have done before and a band begins to play, Sousa's band again and *BOOM! BOOM! BOOM! BOOM!* the ground trembles as four mighty bombs explode, one forming an outline of the United States, one forming the outline of Cuba, one of Porto Rico, and the last spattering into smaller shells that pop into a myriad of Philippine islands. We should have the camera here, thinks Harry, something of this would register on the nitrate. *KABOOM!* a last, earth-shaking explosion, directly above the Tower, and then a gunfire crackling as a thousand tiny balls ignite while they hang in the air to make a portrait of their beloved leader, the one who has brought them to prosperity, to victory, to this glorious new century, and Harry wonders if they are watching in the Filipino Village and the Indian Congress and in the red-dirt courtyard of the Old Plantation, wonders what those dusky, vanquished peoples feel as they gaze upon this majesty—

WELCOME, PRESIDENT McKINLEY

—announce the sparkling silver letters below the portrait—

CHIEF OF OUR NATION AND OUR EMPIRE!

The Assassin sits drinking beer in Pascek's saloon on Broadway, thinking about the stacking game. There are amusements of the cheaper sort just outside the Exposition grounds and he lingered at one after leaving today, watching to see if he was being followed. The sharper had built an elaborate house of tiles on his little table, balancing one upon the other till the structure was almost up to his chin. A spectator bet him a quarter against a five-dollar bill that he couldn't place another without the toppling the whole edifice, and this he did. The next bet had to be fifty cents—only fair, as it was now an even more impossible feat—and then seventy-five cents and then a silver dollar to see another tile balanced, the structure beginning to wobble slightly even when he wasn't touching it. The circle of spectators grew as the amount of the wagers rose, till one gent in a checked suit stepped forward and plunked down two dollars and fifty cents to beat the master architect. The sharper put on a long face, then, holding a tile with the very tips of the fingers of his two hands, lowered it gingerly toward the top of his mansion.

This is my bullet, thought the Assassin, *this is my gift to the world.*

And yes, that was the last straw, the tile that brought it all crashing down, spectators yowling with a mix of disappointment and glee depending on the direction of their side bets. It was a sign. Yes, the system had not fallen after the Habsburg Empress was eliminated, or the French President or even King Umberto. But the weight of each killing upset the balance of the edifice, undermined its foundations. One more, the right one, and there will be blessed release. If not, he will have done his duty, bringing the inevitable day that much closer.

The working men at the end of the bar begin to curse each other in Polish. "You filthy pig," shouts one, "you filthy lying pig!" Stools are toppled. Only a moment ago they were quietly drinking themselves unconscious. "I'll kill you!" cries the other man, the shorter one. The Assassin stands and backs away from the working men. The shorter one draws a knife and suddenly he is stabbing the other, again and again in the head and neck, shrieking all the while "I'll kill you, I'll kill you, I'll kill you!" The bartender leaps over the counter and tries to pull him away, the taller man sliding silently to the floor, blood spurting from him like an obscene fountain.

"Get help!" yells the bartender to the Assassin in English. "Go get help!"

The Assassin runs out onto Broadway, turning to hurry back to his hotel. Two beefy patrolmen sprint past him, heading for Pascek's. He slips his hand into his pocket to make sure the pistol doesn't swing as he picks up his pace. It will be quick and clean, not like the hapless Berkman's botched *attentat* on Henry Clay Frick, no, quick and clean and irreversible. The Assassin hears fireworks above, but keeps his gaze fixed straight ahead.

LADY IN THE FOREST

Nobody can drink that much *vino* and not have to urinate. Crouching hidden on the slope above the town, Diosdado has watched the fiesta of Ina Poon Bato, watched the headmen celebrating noisily afterward at the table set up in the plaza, banners of Nuestra Señora de la Paz y Buen Viaje still hanging overhead. It was not hard to follow the movements of the *alcalde*, the best-dressed of all in his *barong* with the crimson embroidery, the one with the braying laugh and the surprisingly beautiful tenor voice when they sang. He is a *fanfarrón*, this mayor, Ignacio Yambao by name, bragging of his good *amigos* the *yanquis* and all they have offered for his cooperation, bragging of his disregard for whatever deluded bandits may still be hiding in the moun-tains. Which is why Colonel San Miguel has ordered Diosdado to cause his disappearance.

Other men have staggered out of their houses, a few only pausing to irrigate from the rear platforms, most making the trip to the *letrina* on the other side of the bamboo stockade. One fellow veered far enough off the path that he was unable to find the gate and decided to *orinar* through the fence slats into a cassava patch. But so far no Ignacio Yambao, who, though *alcalde* of Taugtod, surely has no modern receptacle within his house of nipa and bamboo. It will be light soon, cocks already voicing their impatience with the night, and Diosdado has to wiggle his bare toes to keep his feet from fall-ing asleep. He is dressed in the simple, soiled cotton of the *kasama*, his story if discovered that he has fled his mountain town because a band of *insurrectos* have taken it over. The *yanquis* are easier to fool than Zambal villagers, of course, having no local knowledge, and more than one of his boys when spotted has strolled grinningly up to the foreigners, rifle held useless at arm's length, and thanked *el Dios en el Cielo* that the Americans are finally here to accept his surrender. Most have returned within the month, with many a story to tell and occasionally a better weapon than the one they turned in.

"*The* yanquis *recognize only two kinds of Filipinos*," Bayani is fond of saying. "*The living and the dead.*"

Bayani offered to do tonight's business, naturally, insisted on it, but Diosdado is the *teniente* still, despite having left his uniform under a rock on a hillside near Bacolor, and it is not something he will order another man to bloody his hands with.

"Who have you ever killed?" demanded the sargento.

"I shoot when the rest shoot," Diosdado answered. "Sometimes an enemy falls."

"But close, close enough so you can look into his eyes?"

Diosdado did not ask if Bayani had killed men in this way.

"If I don't come back in two days," he told the sargento, "move the band to the *escondite* north of Iba."

He has always been suspicious that it was the friars who made up the story of the Ina Poon Bato. A negrito man, years before the arrival of the first Spaniard, meets a beautiful, glowing lady in the forest. "Take me home with you," she says. He protests that he already has a wife, and a jealous one at that, so she gives him a carved image of herself, a small wooden statue. As he walks back to his village he hears her voice, over and over, saying "You must take me home with you." When he arrives his wife is immediately suspicious of the statue, and when he is not looking she hurls it into the fire. Their entire hut is immediately engulfed in flames, the couple barely escaping. But when they sift through the ashes later, the one thing that has not even been charred is that wooden statue, now stone, the Ina Poon Bato. It becomes a sacred object of their tribe, carried from place to place as they migrate through the mountains, bringing them peace and good fortune in their travels. But somehow the statue is lost, and food grows scarce, diseases strike their children, their enemies grow in power. The story of the lost statue remains in their minds, though, and so when the men with beards wearing long robes arrive from across the sea carrying their statue of the same beautiful lady, their Virgin Mary, it is cause for celebration, for the renewal of hope.

A fabricated legend maybe, but an enormously popular one in these mountains, and Diosdado has tried to use it to explain the war to the Zambals. "This fight will cause great destruction," he tells them, "but at the end when we sift through the ashes, something will remain untouched, something pure and miraculous and as permanent as stone—a Filipino Republic."

It is perhaps too distant a metaphor. In Nacolcol the consensus was that the problems all sprang from that ancient negrito's wife, who should have known better than to throw enchanted statues into a fire.

There is a dog, rat-tailed and underfed, making its way up the slope with its nose up, alert, and Diosdado notes that the air has shifted, a cold wind rolling down off the *monte* behind him. The dog slows a few meters away and sniffs at the edge of the *copita* bushes, stepping cautiously now, till it sees him. The cur's head goes down, ears back, and a warning growl vibrates its scrawny chest. Diosdado tightens his grip on the bolo but does not move. The dog investigates, body stiff, bumping its wet muzzle twice against Diosdado's face before stepping aside to lift its leg on a *macaranda* and trot back down to the village.

Only the *alcalde* has not yet taken a piss.

He lost a few men, deserters, when the news came that the silver-voiced Bryan had not won his election, that the Americans would be staying. And then they caught the *supremo* on the day before his birthday. Funston of Kansas and a handful of his junior officers marched as prisoners through the wilderness by Macabebes disguised as rebels, stumbling half-dead into Aguinaldo's mountain retreat, and after being revived by the food and water and the respect due to captured warriors, able to pounce on the General in an unguarded moment. And the General, delivered back aboard the great ship of the White Admiral like a penitent schoolboy, called immediately for his followers to join him in compliance. Now even people like Scipio Castellano have become *americanistas*, declaring that anyone still in the field is no more than a bandit.

"This is not an insurrection," Diosdado lectured his men, "it is not a revolution. It is all of us, *patriotas humildes de las Filipinas*, defending our homelands, our families. If the General is in their hands, so be it. Until the last man lays down his rifle, our cause is alive."

It has been nearly three years since he took the head of Colón off with a blacksmith's hammer. "Columbus" as the *yanquis* call him, the first European to claim their continent, another mercenary for the Spanish crown. When the Assimilation decree was posted, before the shooting war began, Diosdado was the one chosen to go to Cavite and wait until night and desecrate the Americans' favorite statue. He felt more like a student on a prank than the avenging arm of the revolution.

The ground and the buildings have begun to take on color by the time Ignacio Yambao steps down the ladder from the platform of his house, walking in a surprisingly steady line toward the path to the *letrina*. He is singing very softly to himself, a *kundiman* from the party, in his beautiful tenor. Diosdado rises slowly from his crouch, legs burning with the sudden rush of blood, and angles down the slope with the bolo swinging loose from the thong around his wrist. If the *alcalde* turns to see him he will smile and keep coming and tell his story.

But no story comes to Diosdado as his bare feet, still tender, suffer over the jagged ground. *Señor mio, Padre y Redento*, he thinks, *me pesa de todo corazón haberte ofendido porque me puedes castigarme con las penas del Infierno—*

The Act of Contrition must come after the sin. The *alcalde*, Ignacio Yambao, is squatting with his pants around his ankles when Diosdado steps up behind him. The smell is awful.

He has practiced the stroke on the way to the village, a chopping backhand through green saplings and thick poles of bamboo, careful to resharpen the blade with his whetstone afterward, and knows he needs to use both hands. *I studied anatomy with the Jesuits* he thinks as he fixes on the back of the squatting man's neck and raises the heavy *itak* to strike.

There is light now, enough to see details of the slaughter, but it will be a full hour before the sun peeks over the tip of the *monte*. Diosdado strides away from the trench, first carefully wiping the bolo clean on the man's *barong*, leaving a dark stain behind.

Halfway up he comes upon a negrito man, naked but for a loincloth of pounded bark and a curved knife stuck in the drawstring, walking down. They always make him nervous, even the ones when he was a boy who lived in the *rancherías* and obeyed the priest. The man's eyes are yellowish, as if he may be suffering from one of their mountain diseases, and he has patterns scarred onto his arms and chest. *Un cortacabeza verdadero*, as his father used to say, a real headhunter.

The men nod silently to each other, and go their separate ways.

They are moving again, marching out from Las Ciegas as part of a flying column, the sky behind them filled with smoke. Royal is sick, sick like at the end of Cuba, a little less fever in the hot spells and a little less bone-aching chill in the cold. The doctor in Long Island had said it might catch up with him, that there might be rough spells, and the men reporting queasy or fevered this morning have been told they have to march with the rest, that there will be no treatment or conveyance back to Manila till they reach Subig.

Right now he is burning, walking at the rear of the company with everything too bright and loud and even with the others warned not to talk there is the sound of them creaking, jiggling, breathing, the stampede of their footsteps on the hard-baked road, the sloshing of water in the canteens. Nobody noticed till it was too late, they said, but all the villagers, all the *muy, muy amigos*, disappeared from Las Ciegas just before the attack. Not a word, not a warning, just gone. They have not returned, and orders were to burn the village and move out to garrison another area the rebels are supposed to be operating in. At first he thought it was the flames making him burn but then the chills started in the middle of it, Royal in a cold sweat torching the off-kilter little hut where Nilda had been staying, where she must have gotten word and left with the others without warning them. Before starting the blaze the lieutenant had them round up what animals were left, the pigs herded screaming into the thorn-branch corral and butchered. The pigs were out on the Filipino dead the night after the attack and Royal wanted to shoot them then but the lieutenant said no more firing.

They walk up and down a series of hills through a forest of hemp, the towering plants seeming to provide no shade. The white fiber is hung out on long lines to dry, making a kind of fence, and if there are any workers meant to be out here they have all gone and hid.

The land flattens out then and Royal keeps his eyes fixed on Corporal Ponder's back and puts one foot in front of the other, all of them wary of straggling now after Junior. It feels like his head is cooking under his hat but he knows he can't take it off. The worst was last night with the fever dreams again and Jessie in them, calling to him from across a swift river too loud in its rushing to hear her voice. It feels like he couldn't lift his arms if his life depended on it, that marching is possible only if he leans enough to fall forward and then manages to keep his feet in front of him. Hardaway alongside has something wrong with his stomach and is the wrong color. Sergeant Jacks drops back every now and again to look over the sick men and Gamble, who was hit in the arm in the attack, and tell them with his eyes that they need to keep up.

Maybe they were in with the rebels, some of them, the people in Las

Ciegas, or maybe they weren't. Just got wind of it and they didn't want to be there when whatever happened started up.

"Make yourself scarce," they always said at home, like when he was little and a colored man had cut a white man down on Dock Street. Make yourself scarce tonight, cause anyone colored and out on the street was an insult, was temptation for the rope and the torch, and even the tough sports at the Manhattan Dance Hall kept the lights low and didn't play their music. You almost didn't need words, just get a feel on the street and hurry to get behind a door somewhere. This is their country, the Filipinos, and they have that kind of feeling for it. They know where to go and wait till it is safe to come back again.

The lieutenant said to leave the church alone. No sense in being disrespectful.

They veer off the road and march through a section of what they called *chaparral* at Huachuca, Gamble moaning a bit now and holding his shattered arm tight to his side. Royal has Junior's Krag still, the artificer having taken his own to use it for parts. With the marching orders there was no way to send the body back, but the boys pitched in and dug a good deep hole and borrowed a cross from the church. There is no chaplain with either H or L, so they stood uncovered around the hole and the lieutenant said some words and told Royal he would write to the Luncefords in New York and then they filled it in. Royal would write, too, only they might blame him for it. It doesn't seem possible that anything, much less one little piece of paper, could start from this hot island in the middle of the sea and find its way to some colored people lost in a great city in the north of America.

Royal moves ahead with the column, all his joints aching now with the fever, flushed with a liquid heat that seems to flow up across the back of his neck to his cheeks and to his temples and everything so bright it is hard to tell what is near and what is far as they reach the river, the same one, he thinks, but a different spot, and the column bends alongside it for nearly a mile before the lieutenant says it is a place they can ford.

The banks look high here but when it is Royal's turn he sees there is a section that has caved in and the head of the column has already reached the far side, men holding their rifles over their heads and wading up to their chests, moving slowly on what looks like slippery footing, the double line bent in the middle by the current. The water is cold and feels good on his legs, tugging. It is all a jumble of rocks below and the Krag seems to weigh as much as a man when he lifts it overhead, Hardaway making little noises in front of him, afraid of his snakes like always in the water and the current is even stronger than it looks, making you brace yourself and push one leg forward and get a foothold before you dare swing ahead. There are no shoals but the sound of the water rushing between the soldiers is insistent, deafening, and it is Too Tall just next to him upstream who falls and knocks him loose, off his feet in the water and swept away and the bottom is gone, can't find it, his head under once, hat gone, men's shouting voices growing distant so quickly and he thrashes his free hand and his feet searching for something, anything and then finally thinks *let it go* and lets Junior's Krag slip from his hands so he can try to swim. But the banks are so high here, the river deeper, swifter, and his arms are so weary, the fever taking all the starch out of him and Royal gulps air and puts his head in the cold water and just lets it take him away. Away. Make himself scarce. He is getting scarcer and scarcer, the cold passing into him, and it is an annoyance that he has to raise his head to take a breath.

There is a tree downed partway across the river ahead and if he had the strength he might paddle around it and let the river keep him. A branch cuts his cheek as he is driven into it by the current and his legs are swept under and then he is struggling with the tree, wrestling branches and ducking under and then there are rocks, some of them sharp on his hands, and he pulls himself half out of the water like a mudpuppy, legs still tugged by the current behind, and lies on his face with nothing left to spend. He doesn't think they'll bother to send anybody after him.

The heat is gone out of him and the chills come, running up the backs of his legs and out his arms like ripples before a fast wind. The rushing river sounds hollow and far away, all sound dull till the snap of the rifle bolt above.

Royal manages to roll onto his side. A boy stands on the thick trunk of the upended tree, bare toes dug into the bark, his skinny arms leveling a battle-scarred Model 93 Mauser at Royal's head. He looks scared or excited or both. He says something and jerks the barrel of the rifle up and down.

Royal closes his eyes and lays an arm over his face.

Kalaw whistles the warning and Diosdado slows, raises his arms over his head so they can see that it is him. The sentry waves him on gravely, no question as to whether his mission in Taugtod was successful or not. When he approaches the camp he sees them all gathered around somebody, men barely glancing at him as he steps to the center to find out what has happened.

It is little Fulanito with a big, black American. The American looks more exhausted than scared. Bayani comes up the hill then and tells them to break camp, that one *yanqui* in the river means more are near, then goes to explain to the refugees who have joined them what may happen next.

"Sit down here," Diosdado says to the American, who he can see is surprised to be addressed in his own language. The man, who is big but not so big as some of them, has to support himself with one arm to stay upright, even sitting.

"You are of the 25th Infantry."

The man nods.

"And you have burned Las Ciegas."

When Colonel San Miguel ordered the attack on the garrison, Diosdado told Bayani to stall enough getting there that they were not part of it. Since Aguinaldo's capture the Republic has ceased to exist as such, only groups of independent raiders left, striking when they have the advantage. Why attack the enemy where he is dug in with an ample supply of ammunition?

"The people are all gone there," says the American.

"Yes. Some have come to us." He points to the dozen they have met on the way, sitting anxiously with the things they have carried piled around them. "And where is your column going?"

The man hesitates. "They don't tell us the names till after we took it over."

Subig will be next. The column must have crossed some distance upriver. Nothing to be done, and he needs to get his people to San Marcelino before the *yanquis* arrive.

"What is your name?"

"Royal Scott," says the *americano negro*. "Private."

Diosdado looks the man in the eye and sees only someone waiting, resigned, for what happens next. This close, their faces are only human, not like the stories from Manila or the cartoons in the newspapers. But he finds himself speaking very slowly, as if to a child.

"I must tell you, Private Scott, that you have only two courses open. Either you will come with us in silence as a prisoner and a *cargador*—a carrier of things—or we must shoot you now."

Fulanito stands with his rifle aimed, unwavering, waiting for the American's response.

The rebels hang their heaviest supplies on a pole they lift onto the American's shoulders. Most of the Pampanganos want to return to the burned village and rebuild, but Nilda lifts her own burden and begins to walk. The American, Roy, gives her only a quick glance and does not smile at her. The rebels are going north to Zambales, they say, and that is where she wants to be. He looks like he is wounded or sick, Roy, staggering under the load, struggling to keep up with the swiftly moving band. She walks behind, and once when he seems about to topple she puts a hand to his back and gently pushes forward. She asks the Virgin, in the familiar but respectful way that Padre Praxides taught her in Candelaria, to intercede.

Mother of God, she prays, *do not let them shoot this man.*

TEMPLE OF MUSIC

The Temple of Music belongs on the head of a Byzantine despot. Its sides, anchored by statues of bards and Bacchae, are a deep Chinese red with trimmings in gold and yellow, the panels of its massive dome an aquatic blue-green, facing its slightly less gaudy sister, the Ethnology Building, across the Esplanade. Today it is even hotter inside the Temple than out, many of the patient citizens dabbing the sweat from their faces with handkerchiefs as they wait to greet the President. The line begins outside, where a pretty girl strolls along it selling samples of cool Lithia Water from a tray, then hooks into the southeast entrance. Inside there are soldiers and Exposition police forming a chute between their human chain and the curving row of seats, to guide the well-wishers in single file toward their destination. A soloist is playing Bach's *Toccata and Fugue in D Minor* on the immense organ that takes up much of the eastern wall of the structure. There is a slight blue-green cast to everything touched by the afternoon sun slanting through the dome panels. The President is flanked by his secretary, Cortelyou, and the Exposition director, who introduces any prominent Buffalonians as the line comes from the left. A pair of Secret Service men stand across from them, watching the crowd.

The Assassin has his handkerchief wrapped around his right hand, as if it has been injured, the pistol wet and hot in his palm beneath it. There is a very large colored man behind him. He realizes he should have eaten, but the stabbing he witnessed the night before has driven all thoughts of food from his mind. "Keep moving," says a policeman, though it is clear everybody in the line is eager to get to the President.

He is a bland pudge of a man, thinks the Assassin on seeing him so closely, a willing tool of the Monopolists and money-riggers, a smug prattler of Christian bromides. The President smiles and shakes hands in the line ahead. "A pleasure to meet you," the Assassin hears him say. A bland pudge of a man with a massive, self-satisfied belly who scratches a pen on paper and men lose their farms or are thrown out of work or sent to foreign jungles to kill and die. I will do this thing, thinks the Assassin—there is no turning back. Easy as standing in front of a train. Two more people.

"I spent a long, sleepless night," he hears the President explain to the man who lingers in front of him, "but in the morning I found that the Lord had spoken. We could not abandon the Philippines to paganism and anarchy."

The Assassin is the pebble under the iron heel of the Rulers. He is the Voice drowned out by their machinery. He is invisible. He sees the eyes of the bodyguard shift from him, uninterested, to the negro giant next in line. The Assassin is No Man. In '93 when they cut wages at the rolling mill he went out with the others, walked the picket line, was fired and put on their blacklist. Nieman, he said after the strike had failed and they were rehiring and the new foreman asked his name, Fred Nieman. No Man. The foreman did not speak German, did not see the smirks of the other workers as banished Leon Czolgosz strolled back onto the factory floor. He had been cool-headed on that day, had waited in line for his interview, had done what was necessary. He steps past the Exposition man. The President holds his hand out. The Assassin pushes it away.

The soloist pauses then, or perhaps the piece is over, the last great organ note echoing in the Temple.

The Assassin stares into the great, self-satisfied belly of the man and squeezes the trigger.

Harry is helping to set up for the Parade when the shots and the shouting begin. The Temple is behind them. He helps Paley reposition the apparatus, helps him up onto the apple boxes they have nailed together to make a shooting platform. They asked to be inside but the Exposition organizers said no, even the still photographer would have to step out before the greeting process began. The word of the deed crackles around them like static electricity, the line of well-wishers dissolving into an ever-growing mob. The

President has been shot, that much is for certain, and the assailant has been made captive. Exposition police have rushed out of the Temple and from other parts of the fair to guard the four entrances, enraged citizens pushing at them, men who have come to stroll the grounds with their loved ones now red-faced and hysterical.

"Lynch him! Lynch him!" they shout.

"Bring the son of a bitch out here and burn him!"

Harry takes his hat off and mops his brow with his handkerchief.

"That's just talk, kid," Daddy Paley calls down to him. "We don't usually go for the rope up here."

"What should we do?"

"Shoot," says the cameraman, trying to crank steadily despite his excitement. "Shoot till we run out of film."

"It's just a crowd. The backs of people's heads."

"The backs of people's heads trying to get into the building where their President has just been shot. And we're the only camera outfit on the grounds." With that he begins to slowly pan the apparatus left to right on the swivel-joint Harry has been trying to perfect.

Harry turns as an electric ambulance pushes its way through the mass of people, siren wailing. Beyond it he sees the denizens of the Midway approaching, cautious, looking stunned and awkward outside of their native habitats. Arabs, Turks, and Armenians, Egyptian dancing girls, Mexican vaqueros, Filipinos of various shades and sizes, Esquimaux, Hawaiians, feathered Indians from the Congress, Japanese in their colorful robes, the Baker's Chocolate Dutch girl in her wooden shoes, tiny Selenite Moon-Men, tribal chieftans from Darkest Africa and cotton pickers from the Old Plantation. They hang back a ways from the throng of Americans angrily surrounding the Temple of Music, not sure of their place here but knowing something important has occurred.

If there was a way, thinks Harry, to begin with the whole motley gathering of them, wide enough to hold the camel's head in the frame, then slowly lose all the others so only one face fills the shot, the buckskinned beauty from the Five Nations gift shop perhaps, twisting her braids and crying. And then, turning back as the police raise their clubs to quell a murderous rush on the main entrance, he prays that the assassin is at the least a white man.

TELEGRAPH

They all want to be put wise and expect Shoe to come up with the dope.
The rumpus out front has barely settled down when the six o'clock from
Syracuse pulls through, factory whistles screaming and the bell gonging at
the tractor works. Shoe rolls off his rack, feeling the cold concrete through
his socks, steps to the basin and splashes his face with the tiny bit of water
left standing, no light yet but everything in the cell within the arm's reach
of an amputee. He wrestles into his pants, shirt, vest and jacket, then jams
his feet into the prison-issue gunboats and laces them up. By the time the
lights are switched on in the tier, his own bare bulb flickering overhead,
he is dressed and combed, ready to peel another day off his sentence. Shoe
hooks the rack up flush to the wall, rolls the thin mattress, folds the blanket
and lays the sorry excuse for a pillow on top. He does his morning set-up
routine, facing the door and pressing hard against the concrete on either
side with his arms, straining as if to push the walls apart, then reaching up
to touch the ceiling, followed by a dozen squats, knees popping each time
he bends them.

"Give him to us!" they shouted. "Hand the filthy bastard over!" That
size crowd in the dead of night, police whistles shrilling and every one of
the night bulls clomping out to the front gate, it must be some holy terror
they've brought in, some spitting, unrepentant menace to society hustled
past the warden's desk and flung directly into a punishment cell. Wife-killer
maybe, local enough to draw a mob, or maybe a chickenhawk caught with

his beak where it shouldn't be. Whatever the beef, it's the first flash of novelty at Warden Mead's hotel for months, and the boys will want to know the particulars.

Time for bolts and bars now, as Grogan, with his heavy tread, clangs up the stairs with Pete Driscoll gimping behind him. The long bar is sprung and Shoe stands with his hands on the grated iron, the levers clunking as the Captain and the trustee approach from the right—*chunk! chank!* and when his door is free Shoe pushes hard to swing it open, then grabs his shitbucket by the handle and steps out onto the wooden gallery walk. He stands at attention, face forward, shooting his eyes to Pete. But the trustee only raises his eyebrows, in the know but unable to pass it on, and follows Grogan unlatching the cells. The faintest light sneaks through the barred windows of the outside wall across from him now as the company forms up con by con, each with bucket in left hand and wearing their joint faces, indifferent to the day, waiting for permission to breathe. Grogan reaches the end of the tier, every man accounted for, and raps his metal-tipped stick once on the floor. The men half-turn left. Grogan raps twice and they begin to still-march in rhythm with each other, till he raps a third time and they short-step forward, single file along the gallery walk, right hand laid flat on the guardrail where it can be seen, and down the narrow iron stairs to the bottom, crossing the stone floor till the lead man reaches the wing door where they stop and wait in silence till all the tiers are in formation and then Grogan double-raps again and they head out past Captain Flynn counting at the door and into the damp, cold shock of the yard.

The line short-steps out from the north wing building then bends sharp to the right at the center walk, forming up double file now and waiting for Grogan, who lets them cool a moment, the breath of two hundred men visible in the yard, leaves just beginning to turn on the birches along the walk, a yellow-tinted canopy for the line of gray men with black stripes. They stand with eyes front, swindlers and pete-men, gashouse pugs and forgers, sneaks and stalls, smash-and-grab artists, pennyweights, till-tappers, boarding-house thieves and moll-buzzers, each one willing himself invisible, hoping to be passed over by Grogan's bloodshot eyes. The Captain, satisfied for the moment, raps twice against the stone of the walk and the double line moves, full-stepping the length of the great rectangle back to the brick shithouse.

It is still the Rule of Silence in line and at meals, though they nixed the Lockstep just last year. No more chugging along with your right on the shoulder and your left on the hip of the con in front, no more tripping on the new fish, no more easy slipping of kites into your front man's waistband. It took Shoe three weeks to remember how to swing his arms.

It is cold in the yard as they march down the center walk, crows flapping down into the birches, the first frost of the season sitting pale on the grass, and cold in the shithouse as each line enters a door, Shoe flipping the bucket lid up, dumping last night's business into a large stone hopper, scooping water into it at the next basin, shaking it to rinse before dumping it into the final basin and the Owasco River beyond on the way out, then adding it to the pile at the disinfecting station before forming up again. This will be the only exercise most of the cons get all day. Captain Grogan raps and they full-step back, past the punishment cells and the new brick shock shop on the south wing to the mess. Sergeant Kelso, looking more exhausted than usual, stands at the door counting as they enter in single file, shooting a look to Shoe as he passes. Shoe slaps his right hand to his left breast in salute as he marches by the Principal Keeper, the PK peeping each con with equal disinterest till they have filed down into their rows and stand, row after row after row after row, all facing the same direction, waiting at the long chow shelves. The PK turns, ganders that all is in order, raps his skull-cracker on the floor and a thousand men pull their stools from under the shelf, then step back to attention. He raps again and they sit as one, food already laid out in front of them, oatmeal sludge, two slabs of punk and a cup of lukewarm bullpiss which Shoe puts away mechanically, shying one of the bread slices back into the basket when the mess con passes, no food wasted at Auburn, no, anything you leave on the table you finish in the cooler. They are given only minutes to stoke up, though how many is not clear as there are no clocks or watches in the joint, at least none that a con can get a rubber at. The screws own not only your time, good and bad, easy and hard, but Time itself. The PK raps twice and they stand and exit by rows, spoon held out in the left hand and dropped into the washbin as they short-step out, Sergeant Kelso counting and giving Shoe another look, widening his eyes to indicate it is big news.

Daylight then, slanting through the bars of the high windows as Grogan's company enters the north wing again, and the crows, more crows than cons in the yard some mornings, ganging in the trees outside mocking the Rule of Silence. The men stand in formation till the Captain raps and they climb the iron stairs to their tiers, Shoe facing the cell at attention till the double rap and then stepping into his stone coffin, turning and pulling the grated door just short of closed. He waits till the footsteps come near and then gives the door a shake to prove the hinges are still good, and steps back. *Chank! Chunk!*

the levers go down and he is double locked, standing with a checkerboard of light coming through the iron lattice and onto his body, waiting till *whump!* the long-bar falls into its brackets and seals the whole row before turning to check the mail. There is a kite, folded smaller than a dime and left between his pillow and blanket, written in haste with the char of a used matchhead, scrawled by Pete Driscoll and left by the other gallery boy, the Jew kid with the harelip. It is one short, shaky word and only that.

MACK, it says.

There is time for a coffin nail before First Work, and Shoe lights one from his boodle and stands blowing the smoke out through the grated iron. They say how Sitting Bull's outfit and the rest of the horse Indians can write a telegram with a woodfire and a wet blanket, and Shoe wishes he could do the same when Grogan's footsteps have faded and the tapping starts up. Tin cups on iron grating, nothing subtle, and all of them want to know the same thing. He uses his stool against the door to answer, *thump, thump, thump,* yeah, yeah, yeah to let them know he'll find out what the rumpus was, what it meant, is there going to be a party in the shock shop, and then the bullpen door screeks open and it is Grogan back below them calling up.

"If I have to climb those feckin stairs an extra time," he warns, "one of yez will pay for sure."

And then even the crows are quiet.

There is Mack Crawford on the south wing and Mack something or other who works in the basket shop and any number of Irish and Scots cons, MacThis and MacThat, and there is Sergeant McCurran on the graveyard shift and Captain McManus who supervises the laundry. Pete's message is like most prison dope, one-third bullshit and two-thirds speculation.

Shoe stabs out the cig and saves the butt in his boodle, never know when hard times will hit, and then the screws clomp up into the tiers again to make their music on the metal and it is First Work. Shoe jams his cap on this time and short-steps with the others to the iron stairs and down and out into the yard where the details are separated and marched away to their shops. Sergeant Kelso fingers him.

"Shoemaker."

"Sir."

"With me. Carpentry."

Shoe falls out from his line and begins to full-step, slowly, toward the woodshop. Kelso strolls two steps behind him, waiting till none of the other bulls can see their faces before speaking.

"Opening day."

It is Saturday, Shoe remembers, and the college boys will be knocking heads.

"They're not giving anything on Princeton till they reach twenty-four fecking points. Can ye imagine that?"

Kelso smuggles Shoe the sporting pages from the Rochester rag and pumps him for advice on his wagers.

"Against Villanova?" says Shoe, eyes forward as he walks. "Take it."

"Their first game of the season?"

"First game for Villanova too. They don't belong on the same grass with the Tigers."

"Same odds with Pennsylvania and Lehigh."

"Take it. These are just warmup games for the big squads."

"Harvard and Williams?"

Shoe considers for a moment. "Harvard takes their time on the field—"

"But Harry Graydon is fullback again."

"I say they win by two, maybe three touchdowns. Be careful there."

They pass the punishment cells and Shoe is aching to ask but that's not how you play it with Kelso.

"I've got Cornell over Colgate—"

Kelso is a hopeless gambler, a pigeon born to be plucked. Shoe can only try to steer him away from his worst hunches.

"By a few maybe," he cautions. "Starbuck is on the sidelines this year."

"Then Yale, my God, they've only got three men coming back—"

"But their scrubs last year could lick most of the teams in the country, and this Chadwicke is the real article. Who's the victim?"

"Trinity."

"Trinity, right—they go down by at least three scores."

They reach the carpentry building and wait at the door for the work detail to pass inside.

"I've got Army over Georgetown by four," says Kelso when the gang has cleared.

"I'd steer clear of that. Georgetown is turning out a real eleven this year."

"But Army—"

"—can't bring their artillery onto the field."

"Yer wrong about that, laddy."

Shoe shrugs. "It's your funeral, Sergeant. Personally, I'd run away like it was on fire."

Lachman, the contractor, has the shop already banging away when they step in, cons at their benches sawing and staining, hammering together crates and coffins. Shoe worked here for a year, after they'd run him through the baskets and the horse collars, and he always loved the smell and having something to pound. Nose DiNucci is waiting by the chair on the keeper's platform, his metal basin on a stool and his tools in a box on the floor. Kelso eyes the basin as he steps up.

"Is that water hot?"

"Hot as I can get it, Sergeant," says the Dago, dipping a thin towel into the basin.

Kelso sits and leans back in the chair, sighing with pleasure as DiNucci wraps the hot, wet cloth around his beezer. Shoe stands on the floor next to the platform, by Kelso's right hand, waiting. Runner duty is the beans— no heavy lifting, a chance to roam around the joint and poke your sniffer into things—but a lot of standing and waiting goes with it. Kelso starts to talk with the towel over his face while DiNucci makes with the brush and cup, working up a lather.

"I'm already under the blankets with the Missus," he sighs, "when the fecking telephone rings. We've got the service now, the Warden insists on it—and they tell me there's a passenger car been put on the night run from Buffalo and we'll be getting a special delivery around three o'clock. 'It's the middle of the cold dark night,' says I. 'What could you possibly need me there for?' Unawares as I was of the tragic events at the Pan."

Shoe has been following stories of the great Exposition in the scraps of rag he's been able to glom on to. Every watchpocket cannon and con artist not wearing stripes must be in Buffalo, working the herd.

"I don't read the evening editions," Kelso confides to the Dago as he carefully peels the towel off, "as I don't find it conducive to sleep. A stroll around the block after your meal, says I, a friendly hand of pinochle with the neighbors, but nothing to tax the mind."

"So—big news at the Exposition," Shoe offers casually. The keeper's train of thought is prone to frequent derailment, and Shoe has learned to steer him back on track.

"A terrible business. A national shame."

DiNucci, who is bending down with razor in hand to scrutinize the Sergeant's lathered neck, looks to Shoe, who nods for him to get busy.

"'Just get yourself down here on the double,' says the PK, and an order is an order, so I climb into the uniform and I says to Margaret, says I, 'This will be a great deal of effort about *noth*ing when it comes out in the wash.'"

The Sergeant points his chin toward the ceiling to help DiNucci with his scraping.

"And so you can imagine my bestonishment when I arrive to find several hundred extremely agitated citizens, many of them strangers to our town, camped across the street at the station." Kelso raises his voice to be heard over the whine of an electric table saw. "'Michael,' I says to myself, 'this is not the new policy of the New York Central Railway, these are not passengers awaiting transport in the wee hours, but an unlawful assembly determined to obstruct the orderly machinations of our judicial system.'"

"All these years on the job," muses Shoe, "have sharpened your powers of deduction."

Kelso raises an eyebrow at Shoe.

"And who, might I ask, is the one of us with STATE PRISON stamped on all his buttons?"

"You got me there, Sergeant. So—there was a crowd—"

"A mob, it was, with the bloodlust in their eye, refusing our instructions to peacefully disperse themselves. Captain Singleton was in the process of reading them the Riot Act—"

"That's a real thing?" interrupts the barber. "The Riot Act?"

"Real as rain. There's a copy in Warden Mead's office."

DiNucci shakes his head. "Live and learn."

"So this mob—" prompts Shoe.

"Disrespectful is the least of it. Halfway through the Captain's declamation the train pulls in and all hell breaks loose. The boys in Buffalo have been all over this Goulash fella, you can see that the minute they drag him off the car, he's been through the wringer backwards and forwards, and he takes one look at his reception committee and his knees give way, the detectives on either side holdin him up by the bracelets, and then the crowd rushes forward—careful of that bit there, it can be tricky—"

Nose carefully shaves the cleft in Kelso's chin.

"Goulash," says Shoe.

"Some sort of Hunkie appellation," frowns the Sergeant. "I heard him say it in the Warden's office when we took his information, but it's Goulash to me. Oh, the mob went after that lad hammer and tong they did, and they had him on the ground more than once before we could drag him up the steps and into Administration. I split a few heads with my stick, I can tell you, and there was others got a rifle butt in the chops for their trouble. Twas like one of your lynching events in Old Dixie, only instead of a blackie on the rope it's an alien assassin that's insinuated himself onto our fair shores to strike a blow at liberty."

"It sounded like a hell of a donnybrook out there."

"I tell you, Shoe, if it hadn't been for the bravery of our boys in blue they'd have cheated the State for sure."

"An assassin." Shoe muses. If you show too much interest they start to think it's dope you shouldn't be in on.

"A sniveling little hop o' me thumb that's laid a great man low."

And sometimes you just have to pop the query. "Who did he kill?" asks Shoe.

The Sergeant turns his head to glare. "And where in God's name have you been?"

"Cell 43," says Shoe. "Third tier, north wing."

Kelso raises a brow. "Not so easy to follow the game when you're incarcerated, is it? That'll teach you a lesson." He closes his eyes and settles back, as if the subject is closed.

DiNucci begins on the Sergeant's cheeks, stretching the skin with his thumb and shaving with long, careful strokes. Shoes gives him the nod to pitch in.

"Sergeant," asks the Dago, idly curious, "have you ever seen a moving picture?"

It isn't what Shoe had in mind. DiNucci is in for thirty, having settled his unfaithful wife, as it happens, with a razor, and when asked why by the judge was reported to answer "Cause I didn't own a gun."

"Indeed I have," answers the keeper.

"And what is it, exactly?"

"Just what the words say. A picture that moves. Say you had one of their cameras pointed at us right here. Once the fillum was developed, an audience in New York or Buffalo would be able to see every flick of your blade, every snip of the scissors."

DiNucci frowns. "Why would they want to see that?"

"It's the novelty, isn't it? Seeing it projected on a wall rather than in actual life."

"There's plenty things I'd rather see than a shave and a haircut."

"As would we all. But could you get the camera apparatus close enough to photograph them?"

The Dago ponders this, wiping foam from his blade onto his apron.

"This Goulash character," says Shoe, casually stepping in to the lull, "did you run him through the usual reception?"

Kelso shifts in the chair. "Nothing usual about it. The Buffalo dicks drag the boy up the stairs like a rag doll and unlock the bracelets and throw him down onto the floor in the Warden's office, where he begins to froth at the mouth and cry out like a banshee. 'You're going to kill me!' says he. 'I know you're going to kill me!'"

"And where would he get that idea?"

Kelso opens one eye to search Shoe's face for irony.

"If you had shot the President," he says, "you might expect a bit of rough treatment."

DiNucci gasps. "The President of the United States?"

"No—the President of the Skaneatles Culinary and Debating Society. You think if he'd shot any simple fecking rubberneck at the fair he'd rate a hemp brigade the like of what we saw here last night?"

"So he's foaming at the mouth," Shoe prompts, "this Goulash—"

"Doctor Gerin is there and he slaps the lad and yells, straight into his face, 'Drop the theatricals,' says he, 'we know yer faking it!'" Kelso shakes his head. "Can you imagine that, making a show that he's insane when he's only a fecking little anarchist."

Shoe rubs elbows with murderers on a daily basis, men who have killed for money or passion or survival, and most of them seem pretty well organized upstairs. To kill somebody for a hinky-dink idea of how the world ought to work, and to do it in broad daylight in front of ten thousand witnesses—this, he thinks, would qualify you as a serious candidate for the bughouse.

"That what he copped to?" he asks. "Being an anarchist?"

"Words to that effect," the screw answers nasally as DiNucci pinches and lifts his honker to get at his upper lip. "Anarchist, anti-Christ, something along those lines. He knew what he was about and said as much between all his blubbering. So we just pulled his clothes off and yanked a cooler suit onto him and chucked the murdering little bastard into isolation."

"They had me down there in the nut-hatch for a couple years," says DiNucci, a troubled look on his face. "Right after the trial."

"Matteawan."

"I had to beg them to send me here. That place'll drive you crazy."

Crazy. Unless, thinks Shoe, Goulash was only following orders, was the worst kind of sap, buying into some load of malarkey he heard in a speech. Like these ginks who can't wait to climb into Uncle's uniform, think they're fighting for Old Glory and instead get sent to some monkey patch in the Pacific to snatch the goods for the ones who got the whole game rigged, the ones who'd sic the bulls on a sorefoot private soldier if he dared to call at their back door for a drop of water.

"So they'll burn this character for sure," says Shoe.

Kelso shakes his head. "The President has only been wounded, and he is a solid, fleshy man. Girth is Nature's strategy for protecting the vital organs. No, Mac will come through like a champion. And our little friend in the punishment corridor," he nods toward the south wing, "will be with us indefinitely."

Shoe tries to wrap his mind around it. "Shooting the President."

"Some are born to greatness," declaims the Sergeant as DiNucci gently pats astringent on his face, "and some seek notoriety through its de*struc*tion. Now go get me the paper, and be quick about it."

Shoe leaves the noisy woodshop and full-steps down the center path, crows solemn above him, filling the birches, as he heads for the administration building. There are bulls strolling the tops of the walls, bulls on the parapets, peeping him all the way across the yard. He sees Lester Gorcey on all fours with the rest of the grounds detail, frowning at the grass as if daring it to grow. Shoe slows, then stops a few yards away and kneels to pretend to deal with his laces. At least one of the bulls up top, probably that wildass Thompson, must have him in the sights by now.

"New guest on the Row," he says softly, keeping his eyes fixed on his gunboats. "Shot the President in Buffalo."

Gorcey reaches out to clip a single blade that has dared to rise above its neighbors. Stick your head up in Auburn and they'll cut it off. "Cleveland is dead?"

Not so easy at all, thinks Shoe, to keep track of the game in here.

"McKinley," he hisses. "Hanging by a thread."

He stands and continues down the path. Gorcey will share it with the grounds detail and they'll clue in the whole south wing. Shoe slows as he passes the punishment cells and the shock shop, and though there is nothing to see but brick, can't help running his eyes over it.

He'd been young when they transferred him up from Blackwell's on his first jolt, young and stupid. Pilsbury wasn't running the Island then and it had been a free-for-all, hard to tell the cons from the poverty cases from the derelicts they passed off as prison guards. You could buy a tumble with a whore for a half-dozen cigarettes. Pick up a nail too, since it was the diseased ones they sent to die there. He'd been out and about there, running with a gang, and then all of a sudden transferred to Auburn and forced to walk in lockstep like a fucking caterpillar's ass and not a word past your gizzard from lights on to lights out and he kicked, told a keeper where he could put his stick but instead the screw put it hard over his head, more than once, and he woke up in the dark in a metal box on the Row.

First there was the sound, the steady deep thrumming of the prison dynamo through the wall, and then the sting of the rivets sticking up from the metal floor into his flesh. He was wearing a filthy uniform a size too large and shoes made of felt. He crawled to the nearest wall, rivets digging into his knees, and used it to pull himself shakily to his feet. His head was throbbing and there was dried blood on his face. The walls were all sheet metal, a little farther apart than in the cells upstairs. He felt his way around to a narrow, barred slit, head-high in a solid iron door, dizzy, grabbing the bars to steady himself, his mouth like dusty carpet as he began to shout.

"What happened? Where the fuck am I?"

"Where the fuck you think you are?" called a voice from over to the left. "And you don't have to shout."

It was true, everything they said echoing in whatever space lay beyond the iron door.

"What time is it?"

The laughter came from both sides, echoing. "You gotta be kiddin me."

"How many of you down here?"

"Eight cells, half of em full now that you come. The fella in Number Three don't talk."

"Then how you know he's there?"

"How you know I'm here?"

"I can hear you."

"I might just be your imagination. You could be buried in a coffin somewhere, havin a dream."

"Stiffs don't dream."

"How do you know?"

Whoever it was in the cell to the left, he didn't like him.

"Relax, kid," said a different voice from the right. "Whatever they got in mind for you, aint nothin you can do about it."

"Who's that?"

"That's Number Eight."

"He don't have a name?"

"My name is Kemmler," said the voice from the right.

Shoe knew that Kemmler was the gink they were going to hook up to their new electrical contraption at the end of the week.

"Oh. Sorry."

"It don't matter now."

"Number Eight," says the first voice, "is three steps from the door to the chamber. So's the Long Walk won't be so long."

Shoe gripped the bars harder, little sense of what was up or down in the total blackness. "I need to see a doctor."

"Yeah, and I need a steak and some spuds and a jug of Scotch."

"How bout water?"

More laughter then, echoing.

"When do they come?"

"They come when they want to and don't when they don't. You'll get used to it."

"For how long?"

"Depends on what you done."

"Mouthed off to a keeper."

"Which one?"

"Freidlander."

There was no response but the grinding of the dynamo.

"Hey! You still there? Jesus, don't leave me in the dark—"

"Don't worry, son," said Kemmler then. "We aint goin nowheres."

He went back down on the floor then, scuffing along on his keister till he found the papier-mâché bucket, no lid, to throw up in. His head hurt like hell, and was still hurting like hell when there was a scrape and a clang and then light, enough light for him to see the four walls, nothing but sheet metal and rivets and the stinking bucket on the floor and some torn strips of newspaper left to wipe himself with and the little barred slit in the iron door that he rose and stumbled over to. On the other side of the door was a vaulted stone dungeon, maybe fifty feet long, and a screw he'd never seen before walking toward his cell, footsteps echoing in the cavern, holding a bullseye lantern hung from the ceiling by a very long chain.

"You," said the screw when he shined the bullseye in through the window slit, "step back from there and get your cup."

Shoe took two steps back, then located a tin cup on the floor by the door. The narrow spout of an oil can was poked through the bars, waggled.

"Come get it."

Shoe brought the cup under the spout and the screw tilted the can for a moment before pulling it out, leaving less than a finger's thickness of water in the cup.

"What's this?"

"What's it look like?"

"That's all I get?"

"One gill," said the screw, "twice a day."

"Can't nobody live on that."

"Do your best," said the screw, and moved on to the next cell.

The water barely wet his mouth, not enough to work up a full swallow. He pressed his face against the window bars, just able to see the screw shining the bullseye lamp into the last cell in the dungeon corridor, then turning to head back his way.

"How long I got to be here?" he asked, trying to push the desperation from his voice.

"Keep count of your water," said the keeper as he opened the door to the south wing, then extinguished the lantern and let it swing back into the dungeon. "One gill twice a day, you keep count. When we let you back into the population you can figure the time."

The door to the wing slammed shut, the key grinding in the lock, then darkness again and the rumble of the dynamo and Shoe smelling his own puke in the tiny cell. He threw his cup hard and listened to it ping off the wall and rattle on the metal floor and then he lay down, rivets digging into his hide, stripping his filthy jacket off to roll into a cushion for his head. He lay for some time, probably awake cause who could dream such a monotonous hell and then there was a new voice, deep and echoing, singing in what he thought might be Yiddish.

"Who the fuck is that?" he called out from the floor.

"Number Three," answered the con in the cell to his left.

"I thought he didn't talk."

"Singin aint talkin."

The song was strange and mournful, full of quick risings and fallings and things that sounded more like moans than words.

"How long does he go at it?"

"No saying." The echo from the vaulted chamber made it sound like the singer was everywhere, like the cell was Shoe's head and the con was inside of it, wailing. "But when he stops you kind of miss it."

Shoe was there long enough to learn to sleep through the singing, or to work it into his constant nightmare, was there when Number Two got pulled out and sent back to the tiers, a little gimpy con he later got to know was Pete Driscoll, was still in stir the day they came for Kemmler and made history with their electric death chair. A regular crowd come into the vault that day, four screws for an escort and a holy joe mumbling from his Bible, Shoe only getting a glimpse of the condemned man's back as they led him out through the other door, the one that led to the shock shop.

It was the last he ever pulled cooler time. If he could con college-educated pigeons out of their pocket stuffing he could convince a bunch of dimwit screws he was a square egg, a new man. It was still your life, zebra suit or no, and you had to make the best of it.

The crows are restless in the afternoon, shifting from tree to tree, scolding each other, bending the branches with their weight. Shoe reaches the administration building and halts in front of Riordan.

"Shoemaker, sir. On an errand for Sergeant Kelso. Second floor."

The keeper nods and he enters, climbs the stairs. There are no more than a half dozen runners assigned on First Work, and the day-shift turnkeys are used to seeing him loose. He knocks before entering and then stands just inside the bullpen door, waiting, with eyes locked on nothing, for them to cop to his presence. Dortmunder has his jacket unbuttoned, straddling the bench by his locker, his huge belly resting on the pine.

"It took us some time to perfect the procedure," he says, "but now they come from all over the country, all over the world to observe it. You'll get a go at it soon enough."

Flanagan is there, and Gratz who the cons call Der Captain after the guy with the walrus moustache in the comic panels and a new one nobody has a nickname for yet.

"When we did our first it hadn't been used on anything bigger than a dog."

"There was that trolley worker in Rochester," offers Flanagan.

"Oh, there was no doubt the juice would do for the job, no doubt at all. But the trolley fella was an accident, left smoking on the cobblestones with his hair stuck out like a scalded cat. A stray bolt from a thundercloud would have done the same to him. But an execution is a solemn business, a state function, and we had no idea if the contraption they'd rigged together down there was capable of completing the task in a dignified manner."

"Ax-murderer, as I recall," says Gratz.

"A brute of a man. You were here then, weren't you, Shoe?" Flanagan somehow knowing he is there without turning to look.

"Two cells down from him on the Row."

Dortmunder squints his eyes. "You? In the punishment block?"

Shoe shows them a wistful smile. "Before I got wise to how the joint operates."

"It was just at sunrise," Flanagan recalls. "'Take your time, boys,' says he, 'and do it right.' He even asked us to snug up the electrode on his head."

"This is before we knew to stuff a bit of wet sponge in there," says Dortmunder to the rookie screw. "To improve your connectivity."

"Then we dropped a hood over his face, so as not to upset the witnesses present—"

"A full house that morning, two dozen at least. Novelty will always pack them in."

"And as soon as we had him squared away they yanked the lever for the first jolt."

"It took more than one?" asks the new man.

Dortmunder sighs. "We didn't have our own dynamo then, and a belt came loose on the one they'd borrowed. Kemmler only got a prick of the devil's tail and it stopped."

"He must have been scared."

"One might suppose so," says Gratz. "But we stuck a scrap of shoe leather between his teeth before the hood went on, and he was unable to share his observations."

"So they fixed the generator—"

"In a flash. And the second helping—well, there were members of the press observing and the effectiveness of the device to be established—"

"It must have been at least four minutes."

"Full power?"

"Oh, he yanked the lever all the way down, all right."

"Just to be certain. It was 'Molly, ye've burnt the roast' in there."

"The whole body stiffens," says Gratz, tensing his muscles and arching his head and shoulders backward, "and if it wasn't for the straps fastened tight it would fly clear across the room."

"And the smoke—"

"That's your resistance," says Dortmunder. "I've discussed it at length with the electrician fella—"

"Davis."

"Him. And he explained to me that different bodies present different resistance to the electrical current. For instance, electricity will pass through copper wire—"

"Like shit through a tin horn."

"So to speak—"

"What I don't understand," says Flanagan, squeezing his brow into a frown, "is why a tin horn would have shit in it in the first place?"

"We're getting off the subject here, gentlemen." Dortmunder heaves a thick leg over the bench and pulls himself to his feet. "The greater the resistance the electricity has to pass through, the greater the heat generated. So if a great deal of electrical current—*vol*tage is the word for it—attempts to pass through a body of great resistance—an ax-murderer, let us say—you can imagine the heat that might result."

"So a stouter man—"

"—will burn hotter than a little wisp like this Goulash fella, should it come to that. It's scientific fact."

"Is McKinley on his way out?"

They all turn then and look at Shoe.

"And to what do we owe your presence here, Shoemaker?"

Shoe straightens slightly. "Sergeant Kelso requests that I bring him the newspaper, sir."

Dortmunder jerks his head toward the jumble of early edition lying on the end of the bench. "And when did Kelso learn to read?"

Shoe steps forward to gather up the entire pile. "Thank you, sir."

"Now, green corn through a goose, I understand," says Flanagan, brow still knitted. "It paints a lively picture. But shit in a horn, or any other musical instrument for that matter—"

Dortmunder rolls his eyes to Shoe and jerks his head toward Flanagan. "And you cons complain about the Rule of Silence."

In the anteroom Shoe nicks a stub of a pencil, slipping it through the string dangling by the roster sheet on the wall. He stops on the stairway landing halfway down, out of sight but able to hear any movement from the bulls, and makes his kites, scribbling on scraps torn from the newspaper and folding them a dozen ways before slipping them into his jacket pocket. He sees that there is both the Auburn paper and the *Buffalo News* and quickly separates the local rag and stuffs it under his shirt.

He drops one of the kites, without breaking stride, only inches from Lester Gorcey's grass snippers as he passes.

"I sent you for the newspaper," Kelso complains when Shoe steps back into the shop, "not for an Easter egg hunt."

"Your brothers in blue were shooting the breeze." He hands Kelso the *News*. "It took a while to get their attention."

"Like a bunch of old hens." The keeper disappears behind the unfolded sporting pages. "It's a wonder the lot of yez don't scarper over the wall some day while they're up in the bullpen floggin their gums."

DiNucci is finished with his work, putting his equipment away. He raises his chin to Shoe, who flicks a kite into the Dago's box. Nose will be cutting at the broom shop next and can whisper the news to the boys there. Shoe takes a quick peek at the *News* headlines about the assassination attempt.

"Jeffries versus Ruhlin," muses Sergeant Kelso from behind his wall of paper. "What d'ye make of it, Shoe?"

First Work ends and Shoe heads up Kelso's company, full-stepping to the shithouse to retrieve their cleaned buckets and full-stepping back to the north wing to be counted and single file up the iron stairs to the tier and waiting, counted again, till they step into their cells and are locked down. There is a half-hour before dinner and Shoe carefully works the stub of pencil into the lining of his cap just behind the bill where it won't show and reads through the Auburn paper he's smuggled. He'll need to lay that off during Second Work. They search the cells while you're out, picking one or two at random and going over them with a jeweler's loupe, even his own. There is no trust in trustee anymore, not enough confidence left in the world to work a paying dodge.

The bulls on the outside, in the old days, understood the game. Oh, they'd give you a whack on the noggin if they caught you below the Deadline south of Fulton without a pass from the Chief, or if you were late with your contribution, but they understood that if the marks were on the square there was no way to beat them. Green goods, the glimmer drop, gold bricks—if they got no larceny in their hearts they'll walk straight away from you. And if you trimmed the wrong bird, somebody connected, the word came down and an envelope appeared on the desk of the local Tammany chief, every cent accounted for, the offended party reimbursed, minus handling, and then it was back to business. Byrnes ran the detectives then, and was as square as you could ask for, insisting on solid evidence before he beat a confession out of you. But once the Lexow Report come out and they put that little four-eyes Roosevelt in charge it was every man for himself. No order left in the game, no sense of proportion. Like the play that bought him this bit.

The high hat from Philly and his midget sidekick are practically begging to be taken, three rows ahead in the swells' box and piping Shoe and Al's conversation, till finally the high hat turns and hoists an eyebrow at them. "I gather that you gentlemen are searching for an investor?"

Al Garvin playing sore and thumping Shoe on the chest. "I told you to keep your voice down, you mutt."

And Shoe, feigning sly and stupid at the same time. "Look, Mister, it'd be better if you didn't hear nothin, see?"

The high-rollers all gathered for the Stakes at Saratoga and every dip and swindler on the East Coast gathered to take a swipe at them. Fred Taral was favored riding Archduke but the suckers were leaning toward Willie Sims up on Ben Brush—the little goat could fly on a dry track—and him and Al discussing a proposition about buying the race, just loud enough to be overheard by Mr. Silk Drawers and the one who keeps braying that he's the Gold King of the Yukon.

"What he said, Mister," echoes Al. "Forget you heard it."

"I didn't hear an amount mentioned," says the sidekick.

You set the hook right and they practically choke trying to swallow it.

He and Al trade another look, like now that they been caught at it there's no use lying.

"Too rich for our blood," says Al.

"Perhaps we could be of service," the high hat says, winking to show it's only a lark, a trick that naughty boys might play. "But of course we'd need to be assured of the outcome."

"We can't guarantee you Ben Brush wins," Shoe cuts in. "Only that Archduke don't."

"It's four grand," says Al. They have moved up a couple rows and lean on the divider behind the swells now. "But we only got three-fifty, maybe four hundred between us."

If you can get them adding and subtracting, working percentages, you're more than halfway home.

"And if we were to make up the deficit—?"

"Then the Archduke gets assassinated in the backstretch."

The tall one and the runt trade a look.

"We'll need to witness the transaction," says the swell.

Garvin stands then, swiveling around like he's peeping the stands for

Pinkertons. "I'll go square it with Taral. Catch up with me in ten."

Shoe is left to hold the pigeon's wings.

"Woman troubles," he explains. "Alla these jockeys they're crazy for women. Get used to all that power between their legs, if you know what I mean."

The sawed-off character, who has informed them and everybody within shouting distance that he is Flapjack Fredericks and that he made a pile in the gold fields, winks then, digging an elbow into the high hat. "Women can be an expensive hobby."

"You're telling me," Shoe returns, and then the fourth race ends, Taral picking his nag up by the tail and dragging it into third.

"Money problems or no," muses Shoe, "he's a hell of a horse-pilot."

Shoe takes them on the fox hunt then, in and out of doors, under the stands for a while, lots of nosing out to peep both ways and then wave them ahead. Give the ginks a thrill. They come out by the far end of the paddocks and there is Garvin with little Sammy Chase dressed like Fred Taral—the green silks from the last race splattered with turf, whip resting over his shoulder—deep in conversation. Shoe whistles low and Al pricks his ears up and hustles over, mopping sweat off his dome with a rag. Nobody could sweat on cue like Al Garvin.

"The guy is impossible," he sighs. "He wants another two beans."

Shoe is steamed at Al for upping the ante without squaring it before-hand. He'd done it once before, playing the nag-doctor who'd lost his license and was willing to dope the favorite for a modest sum, and almost queered the grift.

"From each of youse," adds Al.

"Greedy little midget," hisses Shoe.

"I don't think that should pose any difficulty," says the high hat, hold-ing up a hand. If there was anything else quicker than a glacier in the race it would be a tough sell, but everybody agrees it's strictly Ben Brush and Archduke, with the rest of the tailbangers left back at the gate.

"Also he worries you might be a pair of plainclothes bulls," says Al. "So he don't want to meet you."

The high hat pulls out a card, presents it. "This should allay his fears." Like a Pinkerton couldn't print up a phony greeter.

Shoe is able to peep that it says YARDLEY ENTWHISTLE JR. with a Philly location and then something about legal services. Shysters make good pigeons cause they think they know all the angles.

"I don't carry a card," Fredericks admits, not to the manor born. "But where sporting men gather to match their greenbacks, I am *leg*endary."

Al nearly chokes on this one, but keeps up his game. "I'll see what I can do," he says, "but I'd bet my mother he don't act so suspicious if we let him sniff the kale up close."

Garvin can turn on the color if that's what they're looking for, give them a story to tell back at the club.

So Yardley surrenders a thin stack of hundreds that look like they been ironed and the Gold King peels off his green from a wad that could choke an alderman and Al scampers back with that and the calling card. There's a little back and forth and then Sammy snatches the bills, looks over, and raises his whip. A nice touch, the jockey salute to seal the deal.

"The thing is," confides Shoe as he leads the swells, lighter by several grand, back to the stands, "we don't any of us want to lay our action with the same book. They get wise and the odds are gonna tumble."

"I have a personal wager in mind," winks the high hat, in very high spirits. "A gentleman of my acquaintance who merits a good fleecing."

Shoe seconds the high hat's grin. "I'd like to see his face when Taral puts the collar on that oat-burner in the stretch," he says. "That boy can make a horse run backwards."

Shoe shakes hands then and thanks them for being so white about the whole deal. He and Garvin and Sammy Chase are at the station waiting for the westbound by the time the post horn blows for the Stakes.

There is always the chance with the Lovesick Jockey that the pigeon will make out, that whatever gluepot he's put his cheese on will have its best day ever and outrun the favorite to the wire. Ben Brush was small and ugly but nobody's dog, all heart and flying hooves, and with the Dueling Dinge up on his back he had a shot. As it happened, though, Archduke not only took him but took him from behind in the stretch, Fred Taral driving him through a crowd with the whip and the Duke kicking turf in everybody's faces by the finish. The Gold King just laughs it off, says We been skinned, buddy, but Mr. Yardley Entwhistle Jr. is honor-bound to fork over another grand or two to the gink he'd planned on trimming. A man without humor, he calls a judge he happened to go to a high-toned diploma mill with and makes noise about heading up a commission to probe and castigate and the judge tells his pals in Albany who get a healthy rake-off from Saratoga and immediately passes on not only a verbal description of the three of them but a drawing—seems Yardley is a wizard with the pen and ink—all so quick that no word goes out, no warning, no Send back the take and we're square, just they all get pinched stepping out of a Pullman in Poughkeepsie and run before that very same judge.

Not so bad, fixable even, only Al Garvin tends to unwind with a couple shots of the hard stuff after a good score, nerve tonic he calls it, and is so tight he don't remember Yardley Entwhistle Jr.'s card still sitting in his coat pocket.

"Three years for this?" Shoe complained when Tammany had thrown their hands up and the mouthpieces had said Cop a plea and scarpered with their pay and the judge, Yardley Jr.'s old classmate, settled his hash.

"One year for this," said the judge, "and the other two for all the things you've done we never caught you at."

Which, strange as it might seem, is some consolation.

Footsteps on the stairway again and the long bar clunking, the litany of cell doors opened till it is his own and Shoe steps out. Dinner is mutton stew today, one of his favorites. Monday is bean soup, ham, and potatoes, Tuesday pork and beans, beef stew on Wednesday, Thursday hash and cornbread, Friday chicken and gravy, Saturday mutton and Sunday just the oatmeal porridge in the morning, chapel, and the long day alone in your cell to think about how hungry you are. Captain Grogan leaves them standing for a long count. Goulash will be getting his two ounces of bread about now, and the gill of water to tease his gullet with. Grogan taps and Shoe half-turns with the others. Double tap and the cons short-step down the gallery.

The mutton is hard to swallow today, tougher than usual. Shoe has grown to hate the back of the head of the second-tier con who sits at the shelf in front of him. Keepers stroll up and down the rows, making sure you keep your jaws working and your glimmers fixed on nothing. They could march you straight from First Work to dinner if they wanted, and save everybody a lot of routine. But routine is the point, to make you feel like a cog in the world's slowest gristmill, grinding, always grinding, instead of a person with enough left upstairs to have an idea of your own.

He scored an apple last week, first of the fall, traded for a word in Grogan's ear about who should fill Wiley Wilson's spot on the bottom row. Wiley had been in since two days before Lincoln was shot. "Or else," he liked to say, "they would of pinned that on me too." Wiley locked up in the next cell during Shoe's first jolt here, and he'd been at Auburn through the yoke and the paddles and the shower-bath torture and finally been made gallery boy on the bottom so he wouldn't have to deal with stairs anymore. On Wednesday he didn't step out with the rest in the morning and when Captain Lenahan went in to rap him on the shins with the stick he didn't twitch. Shoe was on the detail, holding a corner of the blanket they carried him out in, the old man dried out and weighing next to nothing. He'd lived past all his kin, so a couple of the mokes from the south-wing coal gang dug him a hole in the little prison patch and they dropped the body into it.

Pete Driscoll had left the apple in the fold of Shoe's mattress. Shoe took most of the evening to finish it.

Second Work he is running for Dudley in clerical, who likes to keep you hopping. Get me some water, get me some chewing gum, pull down the shade, pull it back up, run this note here, run that note there, run down to the kitchen and get me some java.

"More when I know it," Shoe whispers as he doles the kites out in the shops, cons hissing questions at him when their supervisor isn't looking.

"Shoal-gosh," says Stan Zabriski in the ironworks. "That's how you say it."

"The Hunkie."

"He's Polish. You say the *c-z* like a *s-h*."

"You people expect to get ahead in this country," Shoe tells him, "you better straighten that out."

He is less than surprised, proud even, that the scrap of newspaper he left at the broom shop has beat him to the ironworks.

"Telling jokes, he is," says Sergeant Kelso when he stops by clerical to check on his pay slip. "Sitting up with his hand firm on the tiller of the ship of state. That's our Mac."

"You've heard more?"

"The wop who drives the breadwagon got it straight from the special edition. They've dug out all but one of the bullets and he's as right as rain."

"Thank God," says Dudley, scribbling in his ledger. "If that damn cowboy gets in we're all cooked."

Kelso sits on the edge of the desk. "Oh, Teddy's all right. A bit impetuous is all. The boys on Capitol Hill will cure him of that soon enough."

Shoe stands by the blackboard memorizing the shift assignments for the next month. Never know what you might earn with that sort of dope to pass out. "So they left a slug in him?"

"Let sleeping dogs lie, says I. If Mac's not squawking it's best to leave it sit there."

"Sit where?"

"If they knew," says the keeper, giving Shoe an exasperated look, "d'ye think they wouldn't have yanked it out of him by now?"

As you come in from Second Work there is a bin full of bread and Shoe grabs two slices to take up to his cell, thinking of Shoal-gosh down there sitting on the rivets, pondering his future with an empty stomach. His future that sits only three steps away, on the other side of the barred oaken door. Shoe pulls his rack down and lays out the mattress and blankets and sits on the edge of it, slowly eating the bread and draining the tin cup of warm coffee left on his shelf. They come through twice a night down in the punishment cells, shining the bullseye lantern in on your face and calling your name and if you don't repeat it right away they come in and kick you where it hurts. What surprised him was how there could be bedbugs when there was no bed, by the third day a lively nest of crotch crickets in his pants. Scratching their bites and finding and killing them became his only enter- tainment. The Yiddish singer fell apart a week after they fried Kemmler, screaming how his brains were leaking out through his ears and pressing his shit through the narrow slit in his door till the bulls got arm-weary from slugging him and wrote him a ticket to Matteawan.

"What have you got to say for yourself?" Grogan asked Shoe when he finally wobbled back out into the yard, pale and squinting, his teeth loose with scurvy.

"You win."

"We always do," smiled the keeper.

There are worse things, he muses, than doing a three-spot in Auburn. It could be your home, like old Wiley, in the slammer so long that everybody outside forgets you. Or you could be stuck on the Row like this Shoal-gosh, listening to the dynamo grind.

A little before lights-out Pete Driscoll gimps down the gallery, pausing by Shoe's door.

"Garvin says he'll give you three-to-two the President lives."

They've planted Al in the south wing, but he and Shoe manage to keep a few wagers running—Al lost a bundle to him on Bryan in the last election, everything he'd won on the Gans–McGovern scrap. It helps to pass the time.

"He's betting on Mac?"

"Says he'll serve his full jolt in the White House and waltz on back to Canton."

According to the papers every two-bit croaker in Buffalo stuck their fin- gers in the guy, searching for the missing slug. Shoe's own father walked out of the hospital with a clean bill of health from the docs, only to be kayoed by an infection a week later.

"Tell him I'll take it for fifty."

Pete limps away, going down the iron steps one at a time. The bulb hanging overhead flickers, then goes out with the light in the rest of the wing as the seven o'clock from Syracuse rattles past outside. Shoe lies on his back in his prison-issue union suit and listens to the prison telegraph. Tapping from above, tapping from below, tapping from all sides, the bars singing with questions. They all want to know, but Shoe has no answer.

He dreams of crows.

LAZARUS

The men don't want to leave the caves. It is cool inside during the day and there is water running, cold water, in one of them. The American is fevered, mumbling, and sleeps through the first day inside. Fulanito is strutting, proud of his capture, for even if the American is a *negro* he might be worth somebody in a trade. There was trading in the early days of the campaign, when they were still an army, a half-dozen *insurgentes descalzos* equal to one American captain. Orestes comes back to report the American column has in fact marched on over the mountains toward Subig and there seem to be no more behind them. The woman from Las Ciegas brings the American water twice without being told to.

The fever of the *negro* breaks on the afternoon of the second day. Diosdado goes to sit by him.

"Do you understand your situation?" he asks, speaking slowly.

"I got to carry or you gone shoot me."

Diosdado smiles. "We do not wish to do this. We should be fighting on the same side, you and I."

"We're not."

The man is not stupid. Diosdado asks the woman from Las Ciegas, who speaks Zambal and Tagalog, to bring some of the broiled *kamote* left from the morning meal, then watches him eat.

"Do you like these?"

"Like eatin em more than carryin em," says the American. "You a general?"

"Teniente. A lieutenant—in name only. As we have disbanded the army, rank is no longer so formal."

"Where you learn to talk?"

"In Hongkong. From the British."

He resembles the mountain *negritos* in the nap of his hair and the shade of his skin, but his features are what Diosdado guesses is a combination of the African and the European. The man cocks his head as he looks back, calculating.

"How you mix?"

"In Zambales many of us are partly Chinese. And I have a Spanish grandfather on my mother's side of the family," he explains. "You, on the other hand, are a Royal Scot."

The man almost smiles. "They call me Roy in the company."

"And why do you fight for them?"

It is what he has been wanting to ask, what truly puzzles him, but suddenly out loud it sounds rude.

Royal Scott considers, shrugs slightly. "S'what I signed up to do."

"But why?"

"Best job they offerin."

"A job killing people you know nothing about."

"All I got to know is they shoot at me and I shoot back." The man softens his voice. "I'm a p'fessional soldier, Regular Army," he says, face growing blank with belief. "You fight who they say to fight."

"A mercenary."

"Pay aint bad, when it comes."

"Did you ever think," asks Diosdado, trying to make it sound offhand, "of doing what we have done? Defying your oppressors?"

"You mean the white folks?"

"Of course."

"Quick way to get yourself hung."

"But your comrades here, men of color, are trained soldiers, they have arms—"

"Back home they got eight, nine white folks for every one of us. Got more guns than anybody can count, got a navy, got cannons. You seen em, seen what they can do—"

"Somebody is fighting back. They shot your president."

The American's face reveals very little, the information seeming to confuse more than to shock or upset him.

"Colored man do it?"

"No."

"That's good, then. Colored man shoot the President, there be hell to pay."

"If you join with us," says Diosdado, "fight with us, you would be a free man."

"Free to go home?"

Diosdado can think of nothing to counter this. No, the man is not stupid.

He looks at his soldiers, most of them sitting at the mouth of the cave, moving as little as possible, making grim jokes with each other in soft voices. He is not certain that a one of them could articulate a vision of the future they are fighting for, but each, he knows, would risk his life unthinkingly for any of the others.

"Mule don't care which side is loadin weight on his back, and a mule don't kill nobody," says the American. "Just think bout me like I'm a mule."

SCRUBWOMEN

The townhouse is almost bigger than the Eden Musee, and nothing here is faked in wax. They are working their way down through the stories under the supervision of Mrs. Coldcroft, who becomes distant and red-cheeked by the late afternoon.

"She's been rearranging that liquor cabinet again," Molly will say after the housemistress has made her way, chin elevated but gripping the balustrade tightly, down the grand staircase. "No dust on them bottles."

It is Brigid and Molly and the colored girl with a week's labor in the palace, dusting and scrubbing and scraping and polishing and scrubbing some more. Molly talks as much as she scrubs, maybe more, and the colored girl seems unsure of the work, as if she has never done a great deal of it.

"It's criminal, if ye ask me," says Molly from her knees on the massive parquet floor of the ballroom. "One family with all of this. Ye could shelter half of Kilkenny in here."

"Thank Jaysus that's not who we're cleaning up after," says Brigid.

"Greedy people," says Molly, looking around disapprovingly at the huge room, dozens of chairs pushed together in one corner, a balcony large enough for a small orchestra over her head.

"Fortunate," Brigid corrects, head down, digging into where the baseboard meets the floor with her rag. "They're fortunate people."

"Fortune—yer right, that's what it is. Fortune has smiled upon them.

Fortune has emptied its bloody pockets into their laps, is what it's done. Railroad money, if I'm not mistaken."

"I wouldn't know."

Molly sniffs the air. "To me it smells like railroad money."

"And to me," says Brigid, wringing the cloth into the bucket, "it smells like Sapolio and vinegar."

The colored girl works steadily, silently, by the heavy velvet drapes, now and then stealing a glance at Brigid to take note of how she is doing it. Not that there's any mystery.

"Hot water, brown soap, and elbow grease," her Ma used to say. "And plenty of the latter."

The family has left "for the season" as Mrs. Coldcroft put it, though what that season might be Brigid has no idea. She wonders if Harry comes from a house like this down in the South, with its gas lighting in every room, its entrance hall and staircases, its beautiful stained-glass windows in the parlor and delicate gilded tea tables in the salon, canopied bed in the lady's room and wallpaper with huntsmen on it in the gentleman's, with a dining room that will seat a hundred, four chandeliers required to light them all, its marble floors and skylights and domed ceilings and fireplaces and dark-wood library that smells like the inside of a humidor. Did he grow up with servants, colored girls perhaps more robust than their working partner, to see to his every whim? When Brigid asks about it he tries to divert her to another subject, revealing only that his father is a judge of some sort.

"Darlin, ye've got to put some muscle into it," Molly calls to the colored girl, who shyly told them her name was Jessie. "Just pushin the soap around won't get it clean. Have ye never washed a floor before?"

"Why don't ye demonstrate it for her?" says Brigid, lightly. "Bein an expert at the trade."

Molly gives her a narrow look but does go back to her scrubbing. The only way to deal with it is to concentrate on what is within your arm's reach and not think about the vast areas yet to come. The best bedroom was more detail work—putting camphor gum in the linen chests, replacing the sachets in the emptied drawers of the vanity, polishing the beautifully carved rosewood posts and headboard of the bed with beeswax, hauling the Oriental rugs out back to be beaten and aired. Mrs. Coldcroft was there all the while, of course, to be sure none of them pocketed a souvenir or curled up for a nap on the plump, inviting mattress, but the light, filtered through damask curtains, was lovely in the morning and the smell of the room was like a spring garden. It is the hallways and the stairs, carpets pulled up for their ministrations, and this football pitch of a ballroom where it took an hour just to wipe the dust off the top of the dado rail all around, that are apt to break your spirit.

Brigid finds it all so beautiful, and wonders if the lady, whoever she is, does not merely move from room to room during the day, looking upon each finely crafted detail with awe and admiration. Or is the society life so engaging that you barely have time to notice your surroundings? She doesn't worry much about how the family came by their fortune, only that such a place exists, exists on a block of similar houses in the very same city that she herself resides in, a palace that puts the one moldy-stone Irish castle she's seen to shame. If only it were available for everyone to enjoy, like the Musee—

"It's about time to change, wouldn't ye say?" calls Molly, looking into her bucket.

Mrs. Coldcroft insists that they get their water in the scullery, which is three floors down.

Brigid sighs. "So yer hungry."

Molly is a strapping Kilkenny girl with an appetite to match her size. "Ye've read me mind," she smiles. "I was just feelin a bit light-headed, I was."

The colored girl follows them down, careful not to spill on the stairs. The idea is to go from top to bottom, cleaning backward out of every room, so as never to foul their own handiwork.

Mrs. Coldcroft is in the kitchen, slumped over the baking table, sleeping with her head resting on her arms.

"They probably run her ragged when they're here, poor thing," whispers Molly as they pass through. "I'd crave a drop or two meself."

They lift stools into the butler's pantry to eat at the shelf where the meals are arranged before going up to table in the dumbwaiter. Molly crosses herself, bows her head over her bulging ham sandwich.

"May the good Lord and all the saints above bestow their blessing upon us," she says, "and kape our poor Mr. McKinley on the road to recovery."

"Did ye vote for him then?" asks Brigid, who knows that Molly has family, mostly coppers, in the Tammany machine.

"I did not," she snorts, indignant. "But I'd sooner have *him* at the top than that little Roosevelt. He tossed me cousin Hughie off the force, fer nothin more than a little tit-fer-tat."

"He's a reformer—"

"Let him reform the bankers and the coal barons as rubs elbows with him in his fancy clubs, then," says Molly, attacking her sandwich, "and lave our byes in blue alone."

The colored girl has only a poppyseed roll without butter.

"And where d'ye hail from, darlin?" asks Molly, who has not a mean bone in her body nor a sharp thought in her head, as she attacks her sandwich. "Somewheres in the South, is it?"

"North Carolina," says Jessie.

"And what brung ye up here to the cold and the crowd?"

The girl thinks for a long moment before answering. "It was time to leave," she says.

Molly accepts it for an answer. "Can ye imagine this lot here," she sniffs, nodding her head toward the upstairs as she eats, "houses scattered all over Creation, luggin their entire mob of servin people, except poor Mrs. Coldcroft, from pillar to post every time they want a change of scenery? A dozen staff for only the two of em and a set of wee twins. There's a photograph of em in the gentleman's library."

"It's a lot to manage," Brigid agrees.

"And d'ye have children yerself?" Molly asks the colored girl.

"I have a baby daughter," says the girl. "Her name is Minnie."

"Well, it's a start," Molly approves. "I've got five meself, and I believe they'll be the death of me. They say there's war in this Philippines—ye should see the slaughter I've got to face every night when I come into our rooms. A mob of heathen savages, that's what they've become, with me out workin every day."

"Who looks after them?"

"Fiona is the oldest, but she's only ten and no match for her brothers when they join hands against her. They say she's threatened to brain em with a sashweight."

The girl only picks at her roll and has the good manners not to inquire about Molly's husband, who is a lout and a tippler as likely to be sleeping in a cell in the Tombs as in her bed. The girl makes Brigid uneasy, though she has worked with colored many times before. The Irish boys and the colored boys are always fighting on the streets of her Hell's Kitchen, of course, sometimes with their hands and sometimes with sticks and rocks or worse and their language is a scandal. But when there are no colored handy the Irish boys fight each other or go hunting for Italians. Harry is much more comfortable with them, able to engage a strange colored man on the street to ask a question or offer a comment, but he is from the South with all its twisted history, and she from a scrap of turf that rarely saw a Protestant, much less a black man.

"D'ye think," asks Molly, peering in at the stacks of gleaming chinaware in the glass-paneled cabinet before them, "that somewhere there is a gentleman and a lady livin off the fruits of our labor? I've heard tell of the Rail Trust and the Coal Trust and the Steel Trust and Wheat Trust—there must be a debutante somewheres who when she passes in her carriage, lookin like a gleamin pearl on an oyster shell, they all whisper 'Here she is now, heiress to the great Scrubwoman Fortune.'"

"Mr. Burke at the employment agency takes out his percentage, I know," Brigid answers, "but he hasn't changed that vest he wears, or washed it, in the five years I've worked for him."

"The money goes further up," says Molly. "It *rises*. Like smoke."

If her father were alive and here, Brigid knows, he would be grumbling about how to burn the townhouse to the ground.

There is a gas heater in the scullery just for the deep basin used to wash dishes, where they refill their buckets. When they walk into the ballroom again Brigid can see a difference, very faint, between where they've scrubbed and where they haven't.

"A pity they didn't leave the orchestra," says Molly, "to coax us through the afternoon."

The trick is to keep your weight balanced between your knees and the heels of your hands. Patsy Finnegan's father would have her brothers kneel on marbles when they were wicked, and Brigid thinks of that often when it feels like she can't bear another moment. She only stands to refill the bucket or when the backs of her legs begin to cramp. There are venerated saints, she thinks, whose road to glory was paved by little more than what I'm doing now. But then they were rich men's daughters, promised a life of ease but scrubbing the floors of lepers or other unfortunates without pay.

"Self-abnegation," Sister Gonzaga always told them, waggling her finger with the huge Bride-of-Christ ring on it, "is the quickest way to Heaven."

They have worked their way almost to the tall sliding doors when Brigid realizes the colored girl is no longer with them. Then she hears the music.

It is not religious music, exactly, but it gives her the feeling she has now and then at a High Mass, with the singing, when she thinks if God pays attention to us at all it is this he listens to. Brigid stands, wincing, and steps straight across the hall to the doorway of the music room.

Jessie sits at the piano nearly in the dark, the late-afternoon sun slanting through the skylight to spill only on her long fingers at the keys. And the music, angry then sad then romantic then brooding—who could believe it is one small person filling the air with this war of emotions? The music seems to grow larger, to possess the entire house, and Brigid imagines it entering each of the countless, empty rooms like a warm liquid, bringing a glow of life back into them. Brigid feels Molly at her elbow and for once the woman has nothing to say, only watching and listening. They stand for a long while, till Jessie ends the piece, last note hanging in the air—

The girl rests her elbows on the keys and puts her head in her hands.

Brigid and Molly walk softly back to the ballroom and kneel at their buckets.

"Would ye believe it?" says Molly, shaking her head.

The colored girl comes back then, not a word, and puts her little bit of weight into scouring away the scuff marks just inside the sliding doors. The sun deserts the floor and Brigid has to turn on the gas lamps. They are finished with the ballroom and have done the back half of the hallway when it is time to quit.

The colored girl says thank you, quietly, when she takes her pay and puts her coat on, a worn-looking item not nearly up to the weather outside, and leaves with a small nod of goodbye.

"I'll expect you to have reached the reception room by tomorrow," says Mrs. Coldcroft, a mite bleary-eyed, face creased on one side from where she's slept. "Which means the fireplace will have to be dealt with. And how is the—" she nods, frowning, toward the deliveries door that Jessie has just left through. "How is *she* making out?"

"Oh, she's a crackerjack, she is," says Molly, beating Brigid to it. "Not much for conversation, but she's a terror on the floors."

Jessie's legs are aching by the time she reaches the third-story landing, and she can hear little Minnie crying inside. The heat is on again, but unbearable now, either none at all or an inferno, and Minnie is wrapped tight in a blanket lying in the cradle Father made from a dresser drawer he found on the street, wailing her strange little cry that sounds as if it comes from a tiny spirit inside of her. Jessie wrestles the kitchen window open and props it with a can of beans, then unwraps her daughter and lifts her into her arms. She is overheated, which Father says is just as dangerous as her being too cold. Jessie is about to call angrily for her mother when she sees the opened envelope on the little kitchen table. It is stamped just the same as the letters that come from the Philippines, but it is not her brother's writing on the front, the words squarish and thick and filling her with dread. Minnie has stopped crying.

Mother is sitting on the bed, staring out into the air shaft, the letter lying folded beside her.

"They've killed him," she says wearily, not turning to look at Jessie. "They've killed my son."

UNDERSTUDY

"He's gone," says the messenger. "We need you now."

Alexander must have had a similar moment, ungirded in his tent at the news of his father's murder, or Marcus Antonius on the stabbing of Caesar, even poor hapless Andrew Johnson when word sped back from Ford's Theatre. *Some are born Great, but others*—

But there is no time for reflection when a nation has been orphaned. The coach awaits below, the steeds restless in their traces as if they sense the urgency of their mission. The jehu flicks his persuader and they are off, careening pellmell through the labyrinthine passages of Greenwich Village, citizens clustered on each corner reacting to the announcement with shock and mourning. The tidings had been so propitious at first, medical experts present at the calamity, speedy intervention, clear sailing expected for the President. Then the first grudging qualifications—the bullet left imbedded, the rise in temperature, the threat of dreaded infection. But this—this was not to be imagined, it was unthinkable that he, of all men, should be hoisted so precipitously to the summit, that his hand should rest upon the tiller of the Ship of State—

"What will you say?" asks the messenger. The boy is pale, goose-necked, sweating, no doubt unnerved to play even a supporting role in history's great drama.

"Words are of minor importance in times like these," he replies. "What is paramount now is a display of strength and continuity, a reassurance that though their beloved captain has passed, we are not without rudder in the storm."

The messenger looks out the window of the coach. "There's going to be a storm?"

They considered him a joke at first, no better than fifth business. A buck-toothed little runt, an asthmatic four-eyes with a grating voice, the sort who came on after the sword-swallower or the skating chimpanzee. A meddler and a blue-nose, an overgrown boy playing with his toy boats in the bathtub. And then Cuba and his crowded hour and the public reassessed him. There was laughter still, yes, but with a tinge of respect. What will the little man do next?

On to the White House—but as an appendage. Second billing, a court jester employed to fill out the bill for the veterans and the crowd in the cheap seats, or worse, a "chaser," meant to aid the ushers in clearing the auditorium. But he bore it with fortitude, as a man must, taking the national stage with the same brio that had made him a byword in New York. The campaign hat was somewhat battered, true, the uniform no longer *à la mode*, but they still cheered him in the hinterlands, some wag inevitably shouting "Take that blockhouse!" from the throng and the merriment that ensued was fond enough. That alone would have been career enough for some men, but to scale the heights yet never stand at the pinnacle—

The coach jolts to a stop and the doors are thrown open. Attendants are waiting, hustling him into the building, husky bodies shielding him from solace-seeking eyes.

There is a full house out front, he can sense it. Keith himself is waiting in the wings.

"The uniform!" the theater magnate exclaims, panic tightening his voice. "You're not wearing the uniform!"

"The moment demands a statesman," he demurs, "not a warrior."

"One minute!" hisses the wizened caliph of the curtain. "Get him out there!"

As he steps out to his platform in the dark, as he has done so many times before, Goldoni is onstage massaging his tonsils. But tonight is different. Tonight is Destiny—

God of our fathers, known of old—

—sings Goldoni—

Lord of our far-flung battle line—

—singing with his hand over his heart, facing a bier with a coffin draped in the Flag upon it, a diapositive of the martyred McKinley's profile shining on the flat behind him—

Beneath whose awful hand we hold
Dominion over palm and pine—

Behind, in the dark, he pulls the spectacles, clear glass, out from his vest pocket and adjusts them on his nose. The moustache, affixed with spirit gum in the early years, has grown with the man. And now for the role of a lifetime—

Lord God of Hosts, be with us yet
Lest we forget—lest we forget!

—Goldoni finishes and there is muted applause, sniffling from the stricken multitude.

"And so," the tenor intones to the fervent throng, their yearning almost palpable, "we bid adieu to our trusted steward, our stalwart in peace and in war. O where, where shall we find a man to replace him?"

And then the spotlight rises on a stoic five feet and two inches of muscular Christianity, eyes fixed on glory—

Teethadore Resplendent.

And some, he thinks as the applause spreads like his lock-jawed grin, first one, then a dozen, then the entire house rising to their feet in thunderous ovation, *some have Greatness thrust upon them.*

HOSTAGE

They don't have a shovel. Royal hacks and jabs at the rocky soil with a rusted bayonet, then tosses what comes loose out with his hands. The fever has passed but he is running with sweat and finally Bayani, the one who does most of the bossing, gets disgusted and jumps down with him, digging with his own knife. One of the rebels, who had been falling a lot as they climbed, didn't wake up this morning. A couple of the other men are laid out and moaning, Royal surprised that they get just as sick as imported troops do.

When the hole is deep enough, about the size of a small bathtub, Bayani taps him and Royal crawls out, his hands bleeding. At first he just sits out of the way as they lay the body down, but then when the leader of the rebels, who speaks English and says to call him Teniente, starts to say what sounds like religion over it he stands to be respectful. One of them, the one with the beak of a nose, is crying as he holds his hat over his heart and looks down at his dead friend. There is some praying of the men together and then most of them help Royal cover the body with dirt and rocks. Somebody has made a cross from bolo-cut branches bound with a piece of harness and it takes a while to get it to stand straight. When they buried Junior in Las Ciegas, Kid Mabley played his bugle after, but these people are afraid to make noise.

"These mountains are full of danger," says the Teniente, sitting beside Royal as he washes his hands clean. They've made a camp in a little bowl on the side of the mountain, a place where rainwater pools up and there are some trees high enough for shade. The Teniente won't leave off him with the "*colored American soldier*" business, how he should be on their side against the white folks. But there's nobody else he can understand, and the more they know you the harder you are to shoot.

"There are the Igorot who will cut off your head and maybe eat you after, and the *Negrito*, who are of your color but very small and will kill you with a dart that they blow from a tube, and a group of very religious people, the Guardians of the Virgin, *santones*, who you cannot predict what they will do. That is if you are not stung by a viper or die of hunger before they find you."

Royal has no thoughts of trying to escape. The fever has passed and the rebels have very little to carry and he has no idea where he is. Nilda is still with them, helping to gather firewood and to cook when that is possible.

"It is dangerous even for us."

"So why you want to be here?"

The Teniente waves a hand at his dozen sorry-looking *insurrectos*. "Most of my men were born in these mountains. And I lived here, on the other side near the sea, when I was very young."

"You think you can beat them?"

He isn't dressed any different but the way they treat him he must really be a lieutenant or maybe just rich before the war or what they have instead of white people. It is hard to tell the differences just by eye, specially with all them looking so raggedy and underfed and no coolies to truck their goods but him. They don't joke with Teniente like they do with each other and a couple even take their hats off when they talk to him. Bayani, who they call *sargento*, looks at Royal the way you look at a brood hen that might be ready for the pot. If the time comes for killing the dark-skin American, he will be the one to do it.

"Are they willing to follow us all the way up here?" asks the lieutenant. "To send men to every island, to fight the *moros* whose god tells them it is beautiful to die in battle and who were never broken by the Spanish army?"

Up here, hungry, cold now, and if the Teniente is telling the truth, surrounded by all these wild people, it seems crazy to think you could ever bring it all under control. But the people who make the decisions, who send the Army to do their business, are not up here and never will be.

"They run the flag up," he tells the Filipino. "And once they done that they won't leave off, no matter what. I been to where they chased old Geronimo, there aint enough in that country to keep a snake alive, and still they went and chased him down and thrown the irons on him and drug him back to the reservation. Once they run that flag up, the story is over."

He can tell it is not what the Teniente wants to hear. He seems to ponder something for a moment. "What do you know of Roosevelt?"

"Teddy? He was in Cuba. Got up the hill without they shot him, so he's a hero now."

"He is your new President."

"That dog sink his teeth in," Royal tells him, "he aint letting go."

The Teniente nods, looks over to where the little boy, who the others call Fulanito, sits staring at the pile of rocks and wooden cross.

"Nicanor, the man who has fallen, was not meant to be a soldier," he says. "He was a breeder of the male birds."

"For rooster fights."

"You have this?"

"Sure. I seen a bunch of em."

"It is very popular among my people. Wagering—"

"Hell, my people bet on whether the sun come up."

"And music. You are also great musicians."

"Some of us are. I can't hardly sing."

"You won't try to escape," says the Teniente, more a statement than a question. "Will you?"

It is so many years since he has prayed. Diosdado was a firm believer as a child, the star pupil of the *cura parroco*, wearing the subaltern's vestments for special masses, thrilling his poor, God-intoxicated mother with his ability to parrot the Latin phrases. He sits alone on a knob of limestone looking eastward down at the valley they've run from, straining to muster the faith to tell his men what must be done next. If the Father in Heaven who Diosdado was taught to adore—remote, wise, looking very much like a Spanish don—is a fabrication, a mere projection of men's fears and desires, then what of this mythical Republic? The men who personified it, Bonifacio and Luna murdered, Aguinaldo captured and tamed, San Miguel and *la Víbora* Ricarte grown less rational with each doomed engagement, have all failed them. *Our Father Who art in—*

He prayed, pretended to pray, over Nicanor, over the other fallen who they've had time to bury. The men expect it, need it, sometimes demanding that hostage friars be dragged from their confinement to mutter phrases in languages the men do not understand, to make their holy signs. A breeze climbs up the side of the mountain, carrying the smell of canefields burning over, sugar rising up into the stalks. The Igorots have an older god, one they never speak of to the *curas españoles*, a god who makes the spears fly true and the arrows find blood, a god of severed heads and fire. It is a terrible god to have to pray to, thinks Diosdado, dreading whatever decision comes next, but the only one left who will listen to him.

Royal hears banging and sees the little boy, Fulanito, slamming the barrel of his rifle against a rock.

"What you doing that for?"

Royal squats next to the boy. Fulanito snags the fixed sight of the rifle on his shirt front and says something. Royal has seen Mausers abandoned in the field or in the arms of dead rebels with the sight filed off. These are the people who hacked Junior to death, not the very ones maybe, but on the same side. Up close, though, they only seem scared and confused, running and hiding and running again the way a rabbit will if you've filled up all its holes. He holds a hand out. "Lemme show you what that's for."

The boy has only one 7-mil round, carried in a small pouch hung around his neck. After he brought Royal in he jacked it out of the magazine and stuffed it back in the pouch. He does the same now before letting Royal touch the rifle.

Royal flips the rear sight ladder up, then pushes the elevation button and slides the marker up and down the calibrated numbers.

"You got to guess at how far your target is and set the number here, then you line it up with the tip of your front sight there—which is why you don't want to go knocking it *off*. And if they close to you—" he indicates Bayani standing forty yards away, looking back down the mountain, "you slap this down and just use that front one. Otherwise you might's well just grab it by the barrel and try to club em on the head."

Fulanito takes the Mauser back and Royal leaves him playing with the sight ladder. The Teniente says the boy, no telling where he came from, walked into their camp carrying the Mauser one day, doing a dumb-show about how he stole it from a Spaniard. Since it is old and crooked-looking and there is only the one round they let him keep it. This bunch seems mostly to want to move as fast and as far from the shooting war as they can, and Fulanito can run with any of them.

* * *

Nilda is shelling corn, piling the dry kernels on a banana leaf, when the American sits to talk at her again. The men don't seem to care. Fecundo talked at her like this when they were still in Las Ciegas and he wanted to leave, only Fecundo was always nervous and waved his hands and talked loud like making a speech. The American, Roy, has a soft voice and is sad and sometimes helps her with whatever work is simple enough for a man to understand. Fecundo hit her once because he thought she wasn't listening. There was nowhere to go. She had run away from Candelaria at fifteen to be with Fecundo even though her parents said he was a gambler and a *bassi* drinker, even though they had chosen Ciriaco Kangleón who was the *cabeza de barangay* and had two boys nearly her age from his wife who died of the coughing. They sent word that she was no longer their daughter. In Las Ciegas she had to live with Fecundo's mother who had wanted him to marry a different girl and called her a *puta*, even when Fecundo was in the room. When Padre Praxides finally came to marry them and end the scandal he said she had offended Our Father. But she decided that Our Father had surely gotten a look at *el viejo* Kangleón and his two lazy sons and would understand.

"Nobody who is intelligent can live like this," Fecundo would say. "The people here are ignorant and jealous and they cheat at cards."

She would keep weeding or digging or chopping or cooking or washing or feeding what few chickens the wild dogs hadn't eaten and usually he didn't need her to speak. Fecundo was sure that the people in town were all against him, telling lies and spreading rumors, maybe even poisoning the crops though he had given up caring for them already.

"Any man with sense would be in Manila by now, where there are jobs that pay a real wage, where you don't have to scratch in the dirt to eat and there are things to do besides listen to our pile of shit neighbor brag about his Hercules."

Hercules had killed Fecundo's last fighting bird, Relámpagos, and Fecundo did not have enough money to cover his bet so all the men were making jokes about what he would have to give up to settle it. They passed the house and if Fecundo's mother was not outside they made noises at Nilda.

"All I need is a little something in my pocket to get started," he would say. "And then we will live a real life."

What he turned out to need wasn't in his pocket but in a sack that Fecundo would not let her touch or look into, leaving in the dead of night and saying if she did something to wake the dogs he'd leave her behind.

They made Iba by the next day and he sold what was in the sack for the boat fare.

"When we get to Manila," he told Nilda, who hadn't spoken since they stepped on board, "don't talk to anybody. You don't want to give yourself away as a *boba*."

Tondo was full of *bobos*, and when they opened their mouths they revealed it in Zambal and Pampangano and Ilocano and Pangasinense and Tagalog. Nilda walked to the *cuartel* every day hoping for uniforms to wash while Fecundo carried bales of hemp at the port with the Chinese. When they met at the end of the long day in the tiny room they were renting he would pace, four steps between walls, and wave his arms and talk loud as if making a speech about how the *españoles malditos* had fixed it so an honest Filipino couldn't rise to his proper station. If she had money that day he would take it and look for a *pangingi* game in which to change their fortune.

The men who came to search the room for *filibustero* papers wouldn't tell her what had happened or where Fecundo was, but the neighbors knew, and spoke of others who had been strapped to the chair and strangled. She went to the *cuartel* then and asked the soldiers what she should do, and they said forget him, find yourself another man to take care of you. A few volunteered. She took their dirty uniforms, then, and washed them to earn enough to rent the oxcart for the body.

Nilda does not speak as she shells the corn, does not respond or look at the American when he pauses in what he is saying with his soft voice. He has eyes that are not afraid, a captive here among his enemies, but sad. He says a word again and again, and the way he says it she thinks it must be a woman's name. She folds the leaf into an envelope to hold the pile of corn and then starts on another. The American, not really paying attention to it, takes up an ear of the corn and starts to worry the kernels off with his thumbs. She steals a look at the skin of his arm, dark and glossy with sweat, and wonders if he feels like a normal man.

REQUIEM

It appears that they will have to make their own electric chair. Despite Mr. Edison's intercession the Warden has not been moved. They may film the prison's exterior walls from a distance and nothing more, not even the arrival of the state's witnesses. A dozen illustrators and news photographers wait under umbrellas farther down State Street in front of the institution, hoping that somebody of note will venture outside. A pair of uniformed guards stand before the front gate to keep them at bay.

It is very early, cold and starting to rain, and Harry has had the device out before sunup to be sure the lens won't fog, rigging a tarp overhead to keep the wet off it. Rain this sparse won't register on film, which is a shame given the circumstances. Harry pulls his watch from his pocket. If the authorities have kept to their schedule the Assassin within must already be dead. Ed Porter, come over from the Eden Musee to work in the film department at Edison, steps over blowing on his hands.

"I don't think the light will get any better today."

Harry holds his watch up high and swings it from the chain. "If we wait ten minutes more we'll have the 8:19."

"And so—?"

Harry stands in front of the camera and makes an arc from left to right with his hand. "We follow the locomotive coming in to begin the move, not quite matching its speed, so when it passes out of the frame it brings us along the wall to the rows of elms out front. Otherwise we have only stationary boxcars sitting idle in front of a mass of stone."

"But the prison is the subject," says Porter.

"If we're going to bother with a panoramic, something should *move*."

As if to support him a whistle sounds in the distance, three times, approaching.

Porter grins. "You know I love a train." He steps behind the camera and loosens the pan head. "After this we'll make a shot of the front from the roof over there, looking down in. Maybe we'll see a convict moving."

The New York Central is rumbling past when Grogan taps Shoe for the detail. Five cons in all, and more shields than you can shake a billy at—prison screws, state bulls, Doc Gern scowling and Warden Mead himself to escort them out with the box, Mead hunching in the light rain and peeping up on the walls like there might be snipers lurking. Most of the cons who croak in the joint go to the state lot at the Fort Hill boneyard, but then there are special cases who end up in the shadow of the back wall. Shoe has planted cons in the Warden's garden before, and the wrinkle this time is there's no lid on the crate, only a sheet thrown over the fried remains of the former Mr. Goulash. There's a con on each corner of the stained-black crate and one of the colored they call Scrap Iron following, pulling a hand trolley with a big slab of concrete on it.

Father Costello is waiting, his Book open and getting wet. Shoe and the other trustees let it down easy into the hole, then pull the ropes up. There is a funny smell, like eggs left too long in the skillet. They say it cooks your insides, the jolt, that your blood boils and your brains go to hot mush and run out your ears. They say a lot of crazy things, but nobody's come back from the hot seat with the straight dope.

They usually shoot the juice before daylight, get it done with and move on with life as usual on the yard. The Warden is very big on routine, only he calls it Discipline.

"You men are here, principally, because you lack Discipline in your daily lives," he tells them every time there's a big Sunday powwow. "This will not be a problem at Auburn, as we will provide it for you."

Father Costello mutters a quick one, ashes to ashes, dust to dust, while Shoe and the other cons stand with their eyes down and their hats in their hands. The bulls all keep their lids on. Captain Grogan says to step back and then a pair of the troopers lug up a huge glass carboy like they use at the brewery and the smell hits him big time. The troopers got their riding gloves on, bending and shutting their eyes tight while they tip the carboy into the hole and a steaming liquid dumps out and sizzles loud when it hits Goulash down below, smoke coming up and the smell really godaw- ful, makes your eyes tear up. There is a half-dozen guys on the north wing wouldn't be inside if they'd been this thorough disposing of their victims. Shoe is wise to the play now—the Warden don't want nobody pestering him later to dig up the deceased and poke around in his skull for clues as to why a gink would want to pop the President. There was a bird come through during Shoe's first bit on Blackwell's Island who they let stick calipers on the noggins of all the cons and old poxy parlor girls and write down the results and he never seen the point of it—what are you going to do, toss some guy into the slam on account of his hat size? The sizzling and smoke keep on for a while, Father Costello turning his back on it, and then it's over.

It takes all five of them to get the slab centered over the crate and drop it, the dinge having to jump down on one corner to get it level in the hole. All the bulls but Sergeant Kelso and Stuttering Steinway go back then, the Warden watching the walls as he walks like he's still expecting company, leaving the detail with a pile of dirt turning to mud and five shovels.

"Fill her in quick, lads," says Kelso, lighting up a coffin nail when the Warden is out of sight. "I don't like the look of this sky."

The heart tries to compensate. At first she just said her chest was sore, but they'd only just received the news about Junior and she was weeping so much, waking him with it, and he'd hold her then but she seemed to take no comfort in him. Then the headaches, and finally she couldn't lie on her left side.

You can only tell so much listening to it. There was a clink just to the right of the apex beat, a metallic clink, then a murmur. The heart tries to compensate. There is a lesion, or a valve collapses, some insult to the system, and one of the ventricles, usually the left, has to do twice the work and it starts to grow, like any muscle. It is trying to keep you breathing, to keep you alive. But it thickens and becomes too strong, too strong—

It was clear she shouldn't be climbing the stairs anymore, but she didn't want to be a prisoner.

"Minnie and I can't stay inside all day," Yolanda said. "She needs fresh air to grow."

So they moved again, to a place even worse, which he had not thought possible, but the apartment was on the ground floor in the back. There was a bulge then, just below her sternum on the left. He tried bleeding. He tried ammonia and digitalis. Yolanda stopped eating. She slept badly, jolted awake by nightmares that white men had come to kill them with a Gatling gun, that Minnie was burning in the oven. He resorted to spirits of chloroform with a little camphor, dissolved in hot whiskey, just before bedtime. She slept so soundly that he worried she would not wake, and spent the whole night laying his ear against her chest.

Dr. Lunceford had planned their redemption. They would build a new fortune in the North, would ascend to their former heights and someday return, preferably with a federal marshal and several armed officials, to reclaim what was theirs.

At the end, when her blood pressure was so high and her spirits so low, he could only try a pill that combined digitalis, squill, and black oxide of mercury.

"No more medicine," Yolanda said. "I am in the Lord's hands now."

It is hard, still, for him to accept. Dr. Osler thought that severe fright or grief could induce a failure of compensation, and he himself has seen patients, older people mostly, seem to will themselves to die. But the look on her face, even after the letter sometimes, when she would walk with Minnie, alive, loving, joyful—

"You wouldn't catch me dead in Brooklyn," she used to say, but that was the neighborhood in Wilmington, where the idlers and the fallen women congregated, where the colored people seemed happy to live for the moment. This Brooklyn is a tentative green, the very first stirring of spring showing on the hillsides, and there is ground not profaned by tenements or commercial buildings and here she will lie forever.

It is all the money he has saved to bury her, the carriage fare across the Bridge alone more than he can scrape together in a week. There will be no redemption for the Luncefords, even if his license to practice is finally awarded. Without her—

"You have to take care of them, Aaron," she said on the last day. "They have no one else in this terrible place."

The baby, against all his expectations, is thriving. The human organism, that can be so fragile, that contains an organ capable of exploding itself, can also prove indestructible under the most inauspicious conditions. And Jessie, who has become a mystery to him, barely speaking these days, is now a toiler, the sort of woman they used to employ to keep the house clean. After this is ended, the phrases uttered, the earth piled over, it will only be him and Jessie and the baby in the miserable rooms across the river, across the island, in a building that looks like a tomb.

His wife is dead of a heavy heart and he cannot bear to live so far away from her.

Jubal stays at the edge. The turnout is not so bad when you think about how far it is from home, Reverend Endicott come up from where he's staying in Philadelphia to say the words and Felix Birdsong there, and Dr. Mask and Mrs. Knights and Ned Motherwell who used to work at Sprunt's and Dr. Lunceford up front with Jessie and what folks are sposed to think is Dorsey Love's baby. It is nice to see some faces he knows here in the City, but Jubal stays at the edge because he didn't know Mrs. Lunceford so well, just Yes M'am, thank you M'am delivering goods to their big house and because of how it went with Jessie and Royal.

It is a middling-sized cemetery, not nearly so pretty as the Oak Grove in Wilmington, but there are some old dates on the stones in the colored section. People been resting here for a long time. It brings Mama to mind, and Royal, who nobody has heard from for so long.

"*As I pass through the Valley of the Shadow of Death,*" says Reverend Endicott, "*I shall fear no evil—*"

Jubal wonders how he would do, passing through the Valley of Death like his brother done in Cuba, where you don't know is it you they gone to kill or the man next to you and it's not for the moving pictures. The closest he ever come was the riot and there it was just busting out all around you with no sense to it and nobody expecting you to act brave. *If we had guns*, all the men said afterward, but the ones who did have guns ended up shot dead and sunk to the bottom of the Cape Fear River.

The Reverend finishes his words and then Miss Alma who used to work for the Luncefords steps out to sing.

Even though he stands back at the edge Jubal can see tears shining on her cheeks, all dressed in black and singing like to pull your heart out—

Just a closer walk with Thee
Grant it Jesus is my plea
Daily walking close to Thee
Let it be, dear Lord, let it be—

He has always admired Miss Alma, love the way she smile, how she carry herself, but never known she had a voice like this—

When my worldly life is oer
Time will be for me no more

Something melts in Jubal and he wants to cry for all of them—Mrs. Lunceford and the Doctor and Jessie and poor Junior buried so far across the ocean and Royal lost in the Valley of the Shadow and all of them wandering here in what the Jamaica man who hollers on the corner call Babylon, all of them run out from their homes and their lives and lost in this City—

Guide me safely, safely oer
To Thy shore, Thy kingdom
To Thy shore

What kind of woman carry a voice like that in her? She is tall and handsome and wide-shouldered and Jubal didn't even know she come up here like the rest till now. Miss Alma ends the song and it is quiet but for the rolling of the carriage wheels over on Bushwick Avenue, never gets all the way quiet in the City, even out here. Dr. Lunceford drops a handful of dirt in the hole and then Jessie, who is older now but still look like an angel cut in butter, does the same and the people start away. If this was home it would be a hundred or more to pay their respects, but up here Jubal only counts nine and then him who maybe doesn't even belong there.

Dr. Lunceford carries himself heavy when he step by. He set Jubal's arm back when he break it falling off Jingles and was as polite with Mama as if she was a white lady.

"*That is a man of* stature," Mama would always say when his doctor buggy pass by. Only he don't appear so high right now, hair gone to gray, lost his wife and son one right after the other.

Jessie comes past next with the baby in her arms and if she sees him she doesn't let on. It is a girl baby, not enough hair yet to put a twist in. Jubal nods to the ones he knows and to the Reverend and waits for Miss Alma, who is lingering, reading off the headstones.

"Miss Alma?"

She smiles just a little bit. "Jubal Scott."

"Yes, M'am." He nods after the mourners. "You still doin for the Luncefords?"

"They can't keep nobody now. Doctor lost everything he had."

"He have some money if they sell that house."

"They took the house."

"How they do that?"

Miss Alma shakes her head like he is a fool. "Same way they took the city. How you think?"

He frowns and falls into step beside her, still carrying his hat.

"How you keepin, then?"

"I got on with some Jewish people, mind their little boys. Ira and Reuben. They had a German girl, but she gone moody and set their place on fire."

"You a nursemaid."

"They too old for nursing."

"Jewish people."

She raises her eyebrows. "I aint seen no horns, if that's what you wonderin."

He laughs. "May I offer you a ride, Miss Alma? I got a wagon."

She looks him over. She is maybe five, six years older than him, and nearly a inch taller. "What you haul in it?"

"Cameras," he says. Mr. Harry give it to him to have the springs changed out but the shop don't open till Monday. "For the moving pictures."

Miss Alma laughs. Her laugh is just as good as her singing. "You always been a lucky one. Jubal Scott fall in the creek, he come out with a catfish in both pockets."

"You member Mr. Harry Manigault? Mr. Harry is who I'm working for."

She look like she just swallow something bad. "That other one aint up here, is he?"

"No, M'am. Mr. Harry say he went over fightin Filipinos, just like my brother, and now he gone missin."

She is still frowning. "Well let him *stay* missin."

She stops to ponder the writing on the side of the panel wagon, looking struck by it. "Cameras, huh. What they take pictures of?"

"Mostly people act out stories and they take pictures of that."

She nods. "I heard of it, but I aint never seen one."

"Maybe I take you to see it sometime. They put the stories up and then there's singing and dancing and whatnot."

Miss Alma looks the wagon over like she doesn't know if it's safe to get on it. "You carry a lot of gals around on this?"

"No, M'am," he says. "You the first one I ast."

She smiles at him then—Lord, that smile—and he unties Hooker and climbs quick into the seat and pulls her up after. People walk by and stare at the writing on the panel and he gathers the reins and the horse's ears go up.

"That up there is Hooker," he says, pointing. "She been through a lot, but she got plenty good years left."

"Her and me both," says Miss Alma Moultrie.

AMBUSH

Royal is loaded with the rest of the food, with sticks for the fire, with the cookpot and ground mats and the empty Winchester of Joselito, who has come up lame, when they are surrounded by the other band. He counts about thirty of them, just as hungry-looking as his own outfit, many of them stepping close to look him over. He puts only the cookpot down, meeting their stares evenly as the Teniente palavers with the head man, who is staring at him suspiciously. It isn't an argument exactly, but the Teniente is tight and frowning when he comes back to talk to Royal.

"I told them you are with us. If I don't say this they will take you as a prisoner with the others."

"Others."

"Act as if you are not afraid."

The new band escorts them up a rocky, zigzag trail to the saddle of the mountain. They've seen *yanquis* patrolling the area, says the Teniente, and an ambush is planned.

There are three American prisoners in the camp.

Two of them are Colorado Volunteers in uniform, a lieutenant and a private, and the other a man in civilian clothes, sitting with their hands tied, backs to the trunk of a stunted acacia tree, with a single rope around their necks that holds them tight to it. They look even more starved than the rebels, and the private is only half-conscious, eyes swimming.

"Oh, Jesus," says the lieutenant when Royal passes, "it's *him*. It's Fagen, come to murder us."

They are allowed to unload and start a cookfire, the rebels around them watching Nilda as she moves. There is no joking. Royal's legs are knotted from the climb, his back sore. The Teniente squats beside the head man, who is taller than most of them and bearded, some kind of a Spanish mix, scratching in the dirt with a stick. Bayani steps by Royal on his way to join them, catching his eye and putting a finger to his lips.

There is nothing he can do for the prisoners. He is in his underwear shirt, his uniform blouse sewed up by Nilda to make a carrying pack, the arms serving as straps, and he hasn't shaved or had his hair cut since the river. Look like some nigger gone wild, he thinks as he steals a look over to the hostages. The private's head is lolling, rope cutting into his neck.

"They want us to join the ambush with them in an hour," says the Teniente when he returns. "You will have to attend."

"What they gonna do with those three?"

"Perhaps they will able to trade them for some of our own people," he says. He doesn't sound hopeful about it.

The new band has not been resupplied for a week, so Royal's bunch shares their food—handfuls of corn, the sweet-potato-looking thing they dug up on the way, some bananas. There is not much for anybody once it is all divvied out. The prisoners are not fed. Nilda sits by Royal while they eat, which she has never done before. A couple times she has done for the chigger bites on his legs without him asking, spitting tobacco juice on them and rubbing it in, and the welts have gone down some. There is no taste to the food, but it is gone quickly and then they are preparing for battle.

The Filipinos have rituals. Some kneel and pray and make a cross—head, heart, and shoulders—with their right hand. Others of them have charms they wear around their necks or wrists or put in their hats or in their mouths and some do the kind of witchy business his mother used to, like they're putting some kind of spell on their rifles and bolos.

The Teniente gives him Fulanito's Mauser and its one round. The boy sits sulking by the dying cookfire.

"They'll be watching you."

"They can watch all they want," says Royal. "I aint shootin nobody."

The men from Teniente's band, Bayani, Kalaw, Legaspi, Pelaez, Ontoy, El Guapo, Puyat, and Katapang, seem to take no notice of him as he joins them filing back down the mountain. They walk for nearly an hour, silent, then deploy in the pass at the bottom, some in the sharp rocks jumbled at the base of the slope and some in the trees a bit ahead and on the other side where the pass makes a bend, offset so they don't shoot into each other when the smoker begins. They are supposed to wait for the head man, whose name is Gallego, to fire before they open up on whoever walks into the trap.

If it is the 25th or one of the other colored outfits he supposes he will have to try to switch sides. If it is white soldiers he doesn't know. There are a couple of Gallego's rebels in the rocks just above and behind him and when he looks back one has him sighted.

It is hot again and the shade is on the other side of Royal's boulder. The one round for the Mauser is still in his pocket. He tries to work his way into a position where nothing is digging into him, then closes his eyes.

The first gunshot wakes him. Regulars, white men, one hit and writhing on the ground and the others forming up, kneeling or flopping down in a rectangle to return fire. Royal stands and works the bolt a couple times, pretending to shoot, and hears one of them shout "Get the nigger!" before he ducks and the rocks before him are blasted into chips by a concentrated volley. The firing is wild on all sides then and Royal keeps his head down till he hears whooping and looks out to see the white boys charge the woods, shooting as they run, and take the position in a moment. The two sides, dug in, trade shots and insults for a while, the engagement hot at first and then cooling down to an on-and-off, harrying fire. Royal does not bother to pretend to shoot again. If they try to retreat back up the mountain now they'll be exposed, so he has to hope the regulars won't make another charge before it gets dark.

"Come on out you yellow-footed, back-shootin nigger," drawls a voice across the pass. "We seen you, you goddam turncoat. Come on out and die like a man."

Gallego's man is still there and if Royal answers he will likely be shot from behind. If he managed somehow to cross over, the regulars would probably kill him on the spot instead of dragging him back to Manila to be tried and hanged.

In that land of dopey dreams
Happy peaceful Philippines—

—the regulars sing from behind the trees now—

Where the bolo-man is hiking night and day
Where Tagalos steal and lie
Where Americanos die
There you hear the soldiers sing this evening lay—

Royal knows the words and sings along softly, thinking about Junior and the boys in the 25th—

Damn, damn, damn the Filipinos!
Slant-eyed khakiac ladrones
Underneath the starry flag, civilize em with a Krag
And return us to our own beloved homes!

It is not nearly dark yet when one of the rebels signals by shooting a chunk out of the rock not far from his ear. Or maybe trying to kill him. The man jerks his rifle for Royal to come up, then draws a bead on him again. There is cover here and there but wide spaces between it and he is scrambling uphill on loose rock with the Americans whooping in joy and trying to nail him and by the time he dives behind the first outcroppping he has been grazed on the arm and is soaked with sweat. He catches his breath and on his second run there is some covering fire and he can see other rebels climbing around him so he is not the only target. His next dash is sideways across the base of the mountain to where the footpath starts and there behind a tangle of uprooted trees he finds the Teniente with Bayani, who has been shot up bad.

"We have spotted another patrol on the way," says the Teniente. "We must retreat."

Bayani is shot in the hip and through one side under his arm, having a tough time breathing. Got a lung, thinks Royal, and hands the Mauser to the Teniente, who has his own rifle and Bayani's captured Krag as well. Royal turtles down and the Teniente helps Bayani, surprisingly light, onto his back. They wait until there are others climbing and being shot at before they move, Royal almost running uphill with the wounded Filipino till they are behind cover again and he can get his wind back. Bayani clenches his grip tight a couple times but doesn't make a sound and the Teniente hurries behind them, the rifles rattling on their slings.

"It hurts when we move," Bayani reports, "and it hurts when we stop."

When they get back to the camp the American drops to all fours, exhausted, and Diosdado helps the woman from Las Ciegas pull Bayani off his back and lay him out on a mat.

"The other time I was shot," says Bayani, "it didn't hurt like this."

There is not much to do without a doctor. One bullet has passed through his chest and out his back but the one in his hip is embedded. Another wounded man, hit in the jaw, is already there drooling blood on the ground. Diosdado waits for his own men to arrive—Legaspi, then Ontoy, then El Guapo, then Kalaw, then Katapang and Pelaez and Puyat, then Gallego stomping into the camp, furious.

"We have them outnumbered and your *maldito africano* doesn't shoot."

"He ran out of ammunition," Diosdado says to him. "He never had a chance."

"I'll give him a chance."

The American has caused him no trouble and in time might even join their cause, but now Bayani is hurt and they need to get him down to help, so when Gallego has his men drag the *negro* forward, hands him a bolo, and demands that he execute the prisoners, Diosdado does nothing.

The *negro*, Royal Scott, raises the bolo over his head. The prisoner who is a lieutenant of volunteers cries out "No, don't do it, boy, don't do it! I got land here, plenty of land and I'll give you some!" and the other man who is not in uniform tells him to shut his mouth. Royal throws the bolo down so it sticks in the ground.

"Hell with it," he says. "Yall want em dead you can do it yourself."

The Colorado lieutenant starts to weep.

There isn't room for him on the tree, so the *negro* is tied hand and foot and thrown on the ground next to the man with the shattered jaw.

"*He saw his father's nakedness.*"

The Correspondent only groans.

"*Noah drank of the wine,*" Niles whispers feverishly, "*and was drunken; and he was uncovered within his tent. And Ham, the father of Canaan, saw the nakedness of his father, and told his two brethren without. And Shem and Japheth took a garment, and laid it upon both their shoulders, and went backward, and covered the nakedness of their father; and their faces were backward, and they saw not their father's nakedness. And Noah awoke from his wine, and knew what his younger son had done unto him. And he said, Cursed be Canaan; a servant of servants shall he be unto his brethren.*"

The Correspondent, dullard, does not stir.

"It is more than Genesis, though," hisses Niles. This is important, this is so very important. "There is Leviticus 20:11—*If a man has sexual intercourse with his father's wife, he has exposed his father's nakedness.*"

"Lunatic," mutters the Correspondent.

"He must have been a lunatic, no doubt, to do such a thing and at such a time. *For there were three that copulated on the ark, and all punished—the dog was doomed to be tied, the raven to spew his seed into the mouth of his mate, and Ham, Ham was smitten in his skin, and thus was darkened the face of Mankind.* They are the sons of Ham, the descendants of Canaan."

None of the tormentors are awake. It is only Niles, Niles ever vigilant, beyond sleep—

"Their blackness comes not from their time in the sun, but the dark source from whence the degraded race sprang." If his hands were free to gesture he would indicate all of those sleeping about them. "These are the children of vile incest, and thus have been cursed with darkness. Darkness of the skin, of the mind, of the soul. That nigger—it was Fagen, the demon. He was going to smite us but I fixed him with my eye. They cannot abide that. As long as we are steadfast, as long as we do not sleep, they cannot slay us, for we are the children of God. It is written on our faces."

This is a test. Noah was tested, and Abraham, and poor sweet Jesus on the cross, and now Niles Manigault. He will not falter. He will not fail. He will not pray or plead, for God loves a forthright man, a self-reliant man, a manly man. The nigger with the sword was only a test, a creature from Hell, and I stared it in the eye and it was vanquished. The Hamites are our servants, it is written in the Book and they know it within their hearts. When they rise up, when they rebel, they know in their hearts that He will not let them succeed, for they are the spawn of filth and wickedness.

"On the Ark," Niles sighs, his heart racing, all his senses open, alive to epiphany. "With his father's wife. Can you imagine such evil, such bestiality? On the *Ark*."

"Stark, raving mad," mutters the Correspondent.

They have men waiting down the pathway to shoot if the Americans decide to climb up after them, but nobody above and nobody on the other side of the mountain. Everybody left in camp is asleep but Roy and the man who was shot in the jaw, who has his eyes closed and is crying. Even the other American prisoners sleep now, heads nodded forward and to the side, the rope binding them to the tree digging into their necks. Nilda takes a small sack of the corn and an American canteen that is almost full of water. Her knife is dull from splitting bamboo and it takes a long time to saw through the hemp around his wrists and ankles. They soaked it before tying so the knots can't be untied. Roy says nothing and watches her face, which makes her cheeks burn. They have left him at the edge of the camp, far away from the fire, and his hands are cold to the touch. He shouldn't have to die. None of them should have to die, but they are set on their war and haven't decided to stop fighting yet.

When he is free, they stay low and walk as silently as possible. There are fireflies dancing all around them, and it feels like magic, like the other men will not wake up as long as the spell continues. In the village there would be dogs but the dogs here in the *monte* have been eaten. She leads when they start to climb, careful not to pull any rocks loose. She can hear his breath behind her. When they are over the crest and starting down the other side she is less worried. The men won't bother to come after once they're out of sight.

Once, on the far side when it is very steep, he holds her arm to help her down and it is a strange feeling. She has been inside herself, alone, since Fecundo left her for the last time, saying she was his problem, that you couldn't bring a village girl to Manila and expect to become wealthy.

Nilda doesn't know if her parents are still living or not. If they are, seeing her with the dark American will not make them think any worse of her. If she is truly dead to them they will give her what she needs to move on. Nobody wants to live with ghosts.

VARIETY ARTS

The way it works is you got to fill in between one picture and the next. The Yellow Kid is feeling about as bum as a newsie can without he's croaked on the pavement but the yarn on the screen takes him away for as long as it lasts. A girl in a green dress stands in a spotlight next to it, singing along with a violin, one of those weepers about she misses her Dear One who's across the sea. Not much of a canary but she's easy on the glimmers.

It starts out how they always do when it's a war story, with the soldier boy in his outfit kissing off the old folks and his girl, who is another looker. His old lady don't stop honking into her snotrag the whole time and his old man who is one of those Mr. Whiskers like they trot out for parades all the time is pounding the soldier on the back and probly saying Go over there, boy, an give em hell. It's like when you look in through the window displays at one of the swell shops on Broadway and there's people inside jawing and waving their paws around and you try to suss out what they're saying. The first picture in the story ends when the soldier marches out the door and the looker throws herself down on the ottoman and hides her head under her arms. These people got such a big room, fit a whole floor of apartments from East 5th Street in it, so you wonder how she's got anything to kick about.

The canary gives her pipes a rest and the screen goes dark for a second the way it does and then they're in the jungle, big tall palm trees all around and the soldier boy with a bunch of his pals blasting away with their rifles at something you can't see. There is lots of smoke from the rifles and they shoot off some firecrackers in the Hall so the pair of old babes sitting right by the Kid with their big hats on blocking the view cover their ears and make with the Oh my oh dearie me and then the soldier boy tells the others to scarper, that he'll stay back and cover their keisters. So they run off the screen and drums start pounding at the back of the Hall and on the screen this bunch of darkies run in wearing skirts made of palm leafs and nothing else only a couple got a bone in their nose, waving their spears and swords and the soldier boy uses his last shot to plug one of them dead and then they're all over the guy, grabbing his rifle and one stabs him with a sword and they got him down on his back and start to do the googoo dance while the biggest darky stands over him with a spear ready to finish him off. The Yellow Kid is sweating and his head feels hot, maybe cause it's the jungle or he's worried about the geezer gonna get croaked or cause there's so many people crowded in the seats here even on a Tuesday or maybe he's just down with the crud. It don't even help when this doll wearing not much more than the darkies runs in and throws herself on top of the soldier. She isn't so dark as the other characters, but you can tell she aint white. Still she's a doll and for some reason she's telling the one with the spear to hold his water. The Kid wonders if he missed something or if the other paying customers have read about this deal in one of the rags he peddles. Even if she seen him fighting in the jungle at some point a doll, even a Filipino doll if that's what she's sposed to be, wouldn't tumble for a guy that quick. Dolls take some heating up is what Specs and everybody behind the *Journal* building says, you got to blow them to a good feed or do the candy-and-flowers routine before you can lay the first digit on em.

Only this one must be bughouse for the soldier boy, cause even when the big geezer puts the spear to her throat she don't leave off begging for him to be spared. Then the pit band plays *Hot Time in the Old Town* and there's more fireworks and the pals who scrammed come blasting back onto the screen, bagging the big one and chasing the rest away. When their smoke clears somehow there's the looker from back home kneeling by the wounded soldier boy and the pals have got the drop on the native doll. Only then the wounded guy does a lot of palavering and pointing and finally the girl from home falls wise and gives the doll her necklace as thanks for saving his bacon and the soldiers lay off of her. She seems pretty gaga about the necklace, clutching it to her melons and falling on her knees in front of the white girl. The looker from home and the soldier grab hands then and the two old babes start to blubber and the spotlight comes back on the canary in green only now she's with a geezer decked out like a soldier only you can glim that he's not the same one, the pair of them looking lovey-dovey and warbling at each other and the Yellow Kid can't take no more.

He stomps over the old babes' trotters on his way out of the aisle and makes a beeline for the exit. There is more on the bill, Wheezer and Spats and then The Great Bendo and then Professor Poodle which is what he really come to see but right now he needs air.

14th Street never smelled so good. He feels dizzy but the sun is out and the cabbies are trotting their nags up and down and the moll-buzzers are shuffling by the box office and some old wop with an accordion is wheezing away and the only thing that don't seem right on the block is maybe the monkey dancing on the sidewalk, and even he is wearing a fedora.

The Yellow Kid sits on the curb and watches the carriage wheels roll past and waits for his head to clear. The evening edition will hit the bricks pretty soon and he's got to get hisself down to Park Row. When he holds his head in his mitts it is still cooking, which makes it hard to think and is maybe why he missed how the looker gets herself all the way to Googooland just in time to save her boyfriend.

And how did she know to wear her pearls?

It goes by so fast. People shooting and smoke and soldiers with the flag and everybody in the theater cheering and then him flopping round so the horse don't stomp him. People laughing in the theater when he run off, the white folks like that, and then it is over. He wants to say to Miss Alma that there was more to it, that if they had more cameras looking from different spots they'd of got the whole story. But Miss Alma grabbed his arm when the volunteers charged and he fell down, Jubal sitting with her back where the colored are supposed to, or at least where they always do sit in the theater. They don't have it marked off up here. It goes by so fast and then they are in Auburn.

Buzzing from the folks when they see the title. When the train runs across the screen in front of the prison wall Miss Alma gasps. It's her first time seeing a moving-picture show and Jubal is feeling proud he is the one to take her.

There is another view of the front of the prison from high up, nothing moving but the camera, the way you'd swing your head from left to right to look for something, and then they are in the hallway.

"Assassin!" cries somebody sitting up with the white folks. "There's the assassin!" and sure enough there he is behind the iron bars of the door to the left while the prison guards wait on the right for their orders.

"Murderer!" hollers somebody else, standing up from his seat and pointing, and for a moment it is so real Jubal thinks maybe they will rush the screen and hang the man themselves.

But then the guards, four of them, march to the cell and one unlocks it and goes in to bring the killer out. He is not in the striped suit but in dark pants and a gray jacket and there is one guard on each side of him and two behind as they walk off to the right.

Next the picture kind of goes hazy and then comes clear and they are in the Chamber itself. Jubal leans over to Miss Alma. "I help build that," he says, and she looks impressed and squeezes his arm.

There is the Edison man who got a board filled with light bulbs laid across the arms of the Chair and when they turn the juice on to test it in front of the Warden and the doctors all the bulbs flash on. The Edison man takes the board off to the left then and the guards march the Assassin on from the right and put him in the Chair and are all over him tying straps—straps on his wrists and on his ankles rolling up one leg of his pants and straps over his thighs and chest and even one across his forehead. Then the Edison man come out and check that they're all fixed tight and nods to the Warden that it is ready to go.

Jubal can feel Miss Alma holding her breath beside him. There are three different times they put the juice through, the Assassin trying to rise up but the straps keep him down—Miss Alma like to crawl in his lap when they make sparks crackle up on both sides of the screen and people cheer.

"Kill him!" hollers the man who stood up. "Fry the sorry son of a bitch!"

Jubal looks over and Miss Alma is crying. Got a soft heart, even for a white man shot Mr. McKinley.

"That's only the actor," Jubal says to her, quiet. "I seen him get paid afterwards."

One doctor puts the heart button against the Assassin's chest and listens and then hands the earpieces to another doctor who has been feeling the man's wrist for life and he listens and they nod to the Warden who is a long drink of water, and he turns to look right at them in their seats like they are the witnesses and if you watch his lips he say "The Assassin is dead."

Big cheering then, lots of the white men and even some of the colored standing up to clap their hands. Then the lights come on and the band starts playing and it is the next act, Moke and Smoke.

Moke and Smoke are two colored men who tell jokes and act funny but they got the cork ash rubbed all on their face to make them even blacker and wear suits that is green and yellow with big square checks and Miss Alma is not laughing. The more folks in the theater laugh, even the colored around them, the less she think it's funny. They go on rolling their eyes and saying their jokes and end with singing a song about Old Alabamy but she is crying again. Miss Alma always seem like one who could go through the Fire and not drop a tear so Jubal ask does she want to go and she says yes.

Another time he would worry about people staring at him, leaving down the aisle while the show is still running, but Miss Alma still got hold of his arm and he can't help but smile.

Look who I got.

He takes a look back right before they step out into the lobby room. Teethadore the Great who is a friend of Mr. Harry is coming out, dressed up like Mr. President, which is what he is now, and right away people start up clapping.

Teethadore does not run onto the stage anymore. The strut is slow, confident. Presidential. There is a full minute of applause and he lets it fill him up, chest out, grin locked in place. He puts one foot slightly in front of the other, squares his shoulders. The diapositive flashes on the screen behind him.

AMERICA AND THE PHILIPPINES

—it says in bold letters.

Take up the White Man's burden—

—he says, and there is another wave of applause from those familiar with the verse—

Send forth the best ye breed
Go bind your sons to exile
To serve your captives' need
To wait in heavy harness
On fluttered folk and wild—
Your new-caught, sullen peoples
Half-devil and half-child—

PRODIGAL

Nilda hangs the Bleeding Jesus over him in the morning.

"*Para los santones,*" she says.

It is two squares of cloth connected by red shoestrings, one hung down on your chest and the other in back between your shoulders, both with Christ on the cross sewed on them and some words Royal can't read, Catholic words probably, and He is bloodied up something awful. There is a tiny stitching of blood from the thorns and from the spikes in His hands and feet and the spear in His side and little red dots of blood-tears down His cheeks. It is more of their hoodoo that doesn't work as far as Royal can tell, meant to protect you from bullets, but he doesn't fuss when she hangs it on him any more than he did when Mama put herbs and bird bones in a little sack round his neck. She, Nilda, cut him loose and is leading him, he hopes, away from folks who want to shoot him or cut him up, so why kick about it?

The sun is on their right the whole morning, the two of them heading north, following a foot trail that runs just below the mountain ridge. She knows where she is going, slowing to turn and look at him a few times, stopping once to share the last potato. Royal tries not to think any further ahead than he can see and not to think behind at all. It is not so bad except he's thirsty. Royal's undershirt is torn and his leggings stolen and his boots still on his feet only because they didn't fit none of the rebels who tied him down. He wishes he had his hat and some wet banana leaf under it the way he's seen them do. The sun isn't high but already it is cooking his skull.

There is a man walking toward them on the path. Barefoot, his hair longer and wilder than any of the rebels. When the man steps aside to let them by, his eyes burning, Royal sees that his shirt is hanging open to show off a dozen of the cloth squares, different colors and pictures and words on each. Nilda keeps walking like it's nothing so Royal follows. They come to a swaying bridge made of *bejuco* rope and bamboo slats suspended over a little gorge, and halfway across he feels it shudder behind him. The man is following, maybe twenty yards behind, and is muttering something to himself.

The footpath picks up on the other side and there is a little bamboo shack next to it, and then another a little farther along, the houses here roofed with grass instead of palm, and then as the path widens there are men walking alongside them, men wearing the religious squares and medals and crosses on the outside of their shirts and all of them with eyes red and burning, muttering, like a humming prayer, as they walk. These men have bolos dangling from a thong around their wrist or some gripping tight to the handle. An older man, wild hair touched with gray, stands blocking the way in the center of the little group of huts that make up the town. The old man has dozens of pictures hung on him, Bleeding Jesuses and red crosses and lots of the Holy Mother and he has a flaming cross painted or maybe even tattooed on his forehead.

Mama wear some things, some homemade and some boughten, but not like these people. There was a crazy man at home, called himself Percy of Domenica, who jingled and clacked with all sorts of hanging charms and grew his hair down long and woolly, but he never had a follower. The man with the cross on his head starts to bark at Nilda and she answers back steady while the mumbling men surround them and other people, women among them, step out from the huts to watch. Sometimes Mama go off at the Pentecostal. The first time it scared the living Jesus out of him and Jubal, Mama hollering in the tongues and her body twitching and the sisters in white not able to get down the aisle before she could knock her head on the floor a couple times. The flaming-cross man pushes past Nilda and fixes his hot eyes onto Royal's and yanks the Bleeding Jesus out from under his shirt.

"*Your Mama been saved,*" the righteous sisters would say over their shoulders. "*She give up on her evil ways.*"

At least one of those sisters come to Mama later for a root cure to lose a baby, but that first time it felt better to know the twitches and hollers were about Salvation and not some sickness that come on her.

The mumbling men are very close, hot breath on his neck from behind and all of them gripping hard on their bolos, make him think of Junior all cut apart, think of the man he shot with the gun barrel almost touching his body and there is a desperate note in Nilda's voice now and the flaming-cross man is shouting questions Royal can't answer right into his face.

"*You don't call Him,*" Mama always say. "*You just open all the way up an in He come.*"

He sees Junior at the river, hacked apart like a side of bully beef.

"*Kasheeebobobobobobobobobobosheegowanda*!" Royal cries out, eyes rolling back in his head. "*Kwasheeedavasagavasagachooogondadada*!'" He sinks to his knees and the Spirit, or whatever it is his fear has called up, rattles through his body like a runaway freight train, his right arm curling up to his chest and his left shooting straight up over his head, fingers splayed out wide. The bolomen back away. Royal jerks forward, his forehead rapping hard against the ground and his stomach begin to heave, spasming his body like when he got the fever in Cuba though nothing but a taste of bile comes up and then for a little while he loses himself to it and doesn't know what he is doing exactly. Finally he is able to right himself and sees through eyes streaming with water that Nilda is kneeling and rocking and praying and making the Sign, head, heart, shoulder, shoulder and he makes it too, again and again, the Spirit or whatever it was run through him and gone now, so he sings, as holy as he can sound, rocking back and forth—

Life is like—a mountain railway—

—being the only song he can think of at the moment—

With an engineer that's brave
We must make the run successful
From the cradle to the grave

—rocking and singing, never the voice that poor Little Earl had, but nothing to be ashamed of—

Watch the curves, the fills and tunnels
Never falter, never fail
Keep your hand upon the throttle
And your eye upon the rail

The cross man barks something and a woman steps into a hut and then comes out with a piece of pork wrapped in a leaf and some cooking bananas and lays them beside Nilda—

Blessed Savior, wilt Thou guide us
Till we reach that blissful shore?

—Nilda gently guiding him to his feet and the cross man stepping aside and her leading him, still singing, through the sorry little village—

Where the angels wait to join us
In God's grace forevermore!

—on down the path and away from them, Nilda carrying the food, safe now but singing because it feels good, because it puts him in mind of Mama and Jubal and himself before he ever killed anybody—

There you'll meet the Superintendent
God the Father, God the Son
With a hearty, joyous greeting
Weary pilgrim, welcome Home

When he finishes singing Nilda stops and takes the cloth of the bleeding Jesus hung on his front in her hand and kisses it in thanks. Royal wants to kiss her back.

They leave Gallego's band and take only what they came with, food all gone, Legaspi and El Guapo lifting each end of Bayani's *camilla* and Kalaw shouldering the extra ammunition and the iron cookpot. "Every time I lift something heavy," says Kalaw, "I'm going to miss that *negro*."

"Without us he won't survive," says Diosdado. Pelaez leads the way down the mountain on the far side, raising his arm in warning when the slope grows treacherous. It is a clear morning, clear enough to see all the way across the misty coastal plain to the distant horizon-line of sea. "If the headhunters don't get him the *cristeros* will."

"No—if he's with that woman he'll be safe. I wouldn't want to cross her. A real *Zambala*." Kalaw shakes his head. "The ones still tied to that tree though—"

Diosdado shrugs. He had avoided talking to the three tied by their necks. "That is their problem."

It is hard going down the pathway, Bayani having to clutch the sides of the litter, cursing, to keep from being pitched off it. Diosdado gives him the last of their medicine, black poppy tar they bought in Pampanga, and he chews on it grimly as they descend. They reach the bottom at noon and stop to replenish their water at the stream that crosses Don Humberto Salazar's property, crossing fields of *petsay* till they come to the north road and hear the loud *chok chok chok* of a *karatong* ahead of them, someone beating the bamboo gong to announce that strangers have arrived. Diosdado waits for Fulanito to shinny up the telegraph pole and cut the line, then puts his pistol in a sack and sends the boy ahead, telling him to fire a warning shot if he sees any sign of the Americans, then run as fast as he can. Fulanito hurries away, excited as always to have a mission.

"He's your best soldier," says Bayani. The wounded sargento's eyes are all pupil now as the narcotic takes effect.

"He doesn't even know what he's fighting for."

"The war is his home. He fights to keep it alive."

Diosdado looks across the familiar fields. "But one day we're going to win," he hears himself say, "and it will end. You're going to live to see a Filipino Republic."

Bayani holds a hand over the wound in his side as he laughs silently. "Is this a promise or a threat?"

The men spread out around them at the side of the road.

"Let me tell you a story, *hermano*," says Bayani.

"Are there women in the story?" asks Kalaw.

"Not the kind you like," the sargento answers. "These are the kind that will cut your *pinga* off."

"Then I'm not listening."

"When I left San Epifanio," says Bayani, turning his head to the side to stare at the countryside, "I fell in with a group of *tulisanes*, not so different from our glorious Filipino army today—only when we robbed and kidnapped we had no great cause to excuse it."

Diosdado's men are expressionless, exhausted as they listen. They have all heard the rumors, legends almost, about their sargento, but he has never spoken of his past to them before.

"We told ourselves at first that we would only take from the rich, because we hated them and because they have more to steal. But it is always less dangerous to steal from the poor. One of our band was captured by the *guardia civil*, and he betrayed me. I would have done the same to him, I suppose, because when I was given the choice of swinging from the hemp or fighting for the Spanish, I made the coward's decision.

"They treated the *disciplinarios* like the scum that we were. I don't know how they treat their own men, the *jóvenes pobres* who join or are conscripted back in Spain, but five of our company were shot during the first week. One of them complained too loudly about an order to march when we were tired and the capitán stepped up and put a pistol bullet through his brain, which stayed on all of us, in small pieces, for the rest of the march. Many of us were killers already and by the end of our training we were organized, disciplined killers. They called us their *tigres*, and somehow I felt proud to be a member of this brigade.

"We were sent to Mindinao and barracked at Fort Pilar in Zamboanga. There were no women, of course, the *moro* girls afraid to even meet our eyes in public lest they be beaten or even killed by their men, and the *vino* we brewed there was very bad.

"'*Muchachos*,' said our alferez, because he always called us his *muchachos indios*, 'we are here for one purpose only. To kill *moros*.'

"There was an old *datu* in the interior, Datu Paiburong, who was the devil's own servant. The tribes along the coast were afraid of him and the ones who spoke *chabacano* and had come to Christ were terrified of him and it was he and his people we were sent to destroy. You know how once their *kris* is drawn from their belt in anger it must not be replaced before blood has been spilled? Datu Paiburong drew his when he was a young man and never put it away.

"For almost a year we raided the stockades his people lived in, but whenever we came the men would be gone. Some of our own were ambushed and some fell into the man-traps the *moros* dug and were killed or lost a leg, so we began to tear the stockades apart, to burn them to the ground. But they would rebuild almost overnight. The next time we raided and there were no men the alferez looked the other way and some of the women were violated. There were men among us who had done these things before. We knew that this was the same as murdering the women, that even if their lives were spared and they did not kill themselves they would be filth in the eyes of their people until the day they died. And after these violations one of our men was captured and tortured and when we found him his intestines had been pulled out of his stomach and tied to a tree and he had been forced to walk around it many times, wrapping his insides around the trunk and then left for the tree ants to eat him. They wrote on his chest in his blood—they wrote *Each of you shall die like this*.

"'There you have it, *muchachos*,' said our alferez. 'It is a Holy War that we are fighting.'

"The order came down then to herd all the people who followed

Paiburong—this is the time of General Weyler—into one guarded area where we could keep them under control. But they knew. Sometimes we thought the birds of the forest were in league with them, because whenever a new campaign was ordered they knew almost before we common *soldados* did, and this time when we came to the stockades they were deserted. Not a hen living, not a mouthful of food left. So we began to track them, farther and farther in from the coast, deep into the jungle, and by the time we started to climb we were exhausted and short on supplies, eating nothing each day but a tiny *puñal* of rice and beans mashed together and cooked in our own drinking cans and a man was bitten by a *víbora* and died screaming. The capitán and the teniente and the alferez no longer called us their boys, they called us *indios hijos de puta* or *malditos criminales* and kept their weapons ready all the time, afraid we would mutiny.

"Datu Paiburong's men laid ambushes for us on the way up the old volcano. They are excellent shots, the *moros*, even with those ancient muskets they use, and our men who were hit in the first volley almost always died. And then they would be gone, and it was time to climb again. We could not pause to bury our dead, so we wrapped them in ponchos and tied them with *mil leguas* vines into the branches of trees and hoped to be back before the ants and the *jaguares* got to them."

The men all sit close to Bayani now, listening. When he breathes in there is a wheezing sound, but his voice is calm, steady.

"The colonel broke us into three parties, each climbing from a different direction. We were to meet at the top in the evening.

"When we reached the part of the mountain where there were no more trees our buglers signaled and the *moros* fired at us from the rim and we had to charge up over the bare ground. We had started with a half-dozen field pieces but they'd been left behind so we could keep up with the chase. So we had only our rifles and they killed many of us as we charged up the slope, hating them, hating them for murdering our friends and for the jungle and the heat and for the *oficiales* cursing at our backs and because they were *moros*, though we were not, in fact, the truest of Christians.

"By the time we reached the top they had retreated down into the old crater. The crater was deep and so old that a ways down inside it there started to be trees again, and soil, a little round valley within the mountain.

"We had suffered many *bajas*, but it was the whole battalion and we had them outnumbered and had better rifles and knew they must be nearly out of ammunition. We had no fires that night, but they did, two huge fires where they cooked and sang and chanted and then, very late, the women began to shriek. It drilled into your soul, the noise they made. One of our guides said the singing was to their god, telling him they would soon be at his side, but he had never heard the women shriek like that. You could see their shadows, moving around the fires, but the colonel said to save our bullets for the morning.

"'They're halfway to Hell down there,' said our alferez. 'Tomorrow we send them the rest of the way.'

"The women came in the front. The sun rose and we heard them all making that noise with their tongues, high, like when the cicadas in the trees are singing their last notes because the day is dying, and then they came running up the side of the crater toward our positions, their faces painted and a dagger or a sword or some only with a sharp rock in hand and the men right behind, some with muskets and the rest with their *kris* drawn for the last time. They are beautiful people, the *moros*, their long hair, the colors they wear—beautiful. Beautiful targets as they ran up the side of the crater to us and we fired in volleys and then at will, hardly needing to aim, the men climbing over the bodies of the women as they fell and we were told to fix bayonets as they kept coming, muskets fired and thrown aside, screaming as they climbed up the steepest part where there was no cover and tumbling backward. Only a few survived for us to run the steel through. One of these was the old *datu*, who had some bullets in him and eyes like a cat and managed to hack one man in the arm before he was killed. We lifted him up on bayonets and marched around and all the men left in the battalion cheered till the colonel said to lay him down, we were taking the body back to Zamboanga for display.

"I was among the men who were ordered to go down into the volcano. On the way we finished the ones who were wounded. I finished a girl, a beautiful young girl, who was shot in both legs. She looked into my soul and cursed it and I shot her in the heart. At the bottom we found the children, the ones they thought were too little to fight, with their throats cut like lambs. The women had been shrieking by the fires while the men killed their children. They were laid out on flat stones, stuck to them with blood. I was afraid that the mountain would wake when it understood what had been done in its heart, that God or Satan would melt the rock and drown us in fire.

"The *moros* had thrown the last of their food into the fires so we would not get any of it. We pulled the jewelry off all the dead except for the *datu* and started back for the coast. All the men who had been wounded became infected and died. A man in our company who had worked in a bank in Manila and stole money from it went crazy and said he would walk no more and was left behind without his rifle. We took turns carrying the body of the *datu*, who was sewn up inside the canvas of a tent, two men at a time. He didn't weigh much but he smelled like something from Hell. There were mosquitoes everywhere and no water left that was drinkable and nobody spoke except to abuse the Lord's name or give an order. We knew we had been cursed.

"'At least,' said our teniente, 'we left all that heavy ammunition behind in the *moros*.'

"When we came to the field pieces, there were lizards living in the barrels. None of the bodies of the ambushed men were where we had left them, or else we weren't on the same path. The officers would compare their compasses to be sure we were heading in the right direction, but it took two days longer to come down from the mountain than it took to get up it, and a third of our battalion was gone.

"They hanged the body of the *datu* from a crane arm in the port, with his beautiful clothes and jewelry still on him, but the *moros* there, even the ones who had hated and feared him in life, only came to kneel and touch their foreheads to the ground. Honoring him. After a few days of this the *gobernadorcillo* had him taken down and stripped and thrown into the harbor for the fishes to eat."

Bayani closes his eyes. The men are silent. A flock of birds twists over the cassava field across the road, changing shape, threatening to break apart and then flowing together.

"If we had that kind of unity," says Diosdado after a while. "If we believed like the *moros*—"

"You miss the point of the story," says Bayani from his stretcher. "You always miss the point. They believed. They believed so much that they slaughtered their own children. But they were outnumbered and outgunned and so they all died."

Diosdado scowls. The valley is very lush now, crops growing as if there is no war. "It doesn't matter how you die, or when," he says. "It matters how you live."

Bayani sighs and there is a rattle in his chest. "Say that when you are down inside the mountain, *hermano*. Say that when you are where I am now."

* * *

They walk through the valley, crossing *petsay* bean and corn fields, and then come to his father's vast *huerta*, mango trees as far as the eye can travel. These first ones are the *abuelos*, a hundred feet to the crown, the dark green spear-shaped leaves nearly a foot long, the trees full and round-topped and laden with hundreds of *carabaos*, fat and green and just about to turn. The smell, sweet and resinous, makes Diosdado's mouth water. His mother would chop the young leaves for salad with tomatoes and onions, would shred the unripe fruits and serve them with *bagoong*, the salt of the shrimp paste cutting the sour of the green mango, and him out climbing the sturdy branches with the sons of the *trabajadores* till it was time for his lessons.

They are halfway through the orchard, in the section where the *picos* and the tiny *señoritas* are mixed in with the *carabaos*, when his father's workers surround them. Diosdado is suddenly aware that he is dressed in rags like the rest of his men. He recognizes a few of the dozen *trabajadores* but not their leader, who points a shotgun at his belly.

"What are you doing here?" asks the man in Zambal.

"We are soldiers of the nation," answers Diosdado. His men are ready to fight, even at such a disadvantage, but there should be no need to. "We have a wounded man."

"This land belongs to Don Nicasio," says the foreman. "You are not welcome here."

A few of the workers have rifles, the rest bolos. One clutches a rusted cavalry saber. They are better dressed and better fed than Diosdado's men, and know loyalty only to their *patrón*.

"We will walk with you back to where his lands begin," says the foreman.

"Put your fucking weapons down," snaps Bayani, whose fists are clenched against the pain once more, "and go tell Don Nicasio that his son is home."

The plantation house is, like his father, solid and implacable, built of stone on both stories and buttressed for an earthquake that has not yet come. Don Nicasio does not embrace Diosdado when he receives him in the *despacho*. Nothing has changed in the room, the smell of leather and ink, the map from the shipping company displaying its myriad routes still covering the wall behind his father's desk. The desk was Diosdado's favorite forbidden playground when he was small, its dozens of cubbyholes and sliding panels and secret drawers revealing their treasures—a magnifying glass, a flask of Scotch whisky, the heavy pistol he was afraid to even touch.

"While you were busy running from the Americans," his father informs him, still seated, regarding his son's torn *kasama* clothing and sun-weathered face with weary condescension, "your mother, *Dios le protige*, has passed away."

Diosdado feels unsteady on his feet, but that may only be hunger and the long journey over the mountains. He has guessed the sorry news already, noting the ribbon of black crepe stretched diagonally across her portrait, chrysanthemums abundant throughout the house.

"I am sorry."

"She was a good woman. Too good for this world."

Don Nicasio's face is more lined than he remembers, yellowish, but his eyes burn as they always did.

"I suppose you're here to demand tribute."

"One of my men is wounded and needs a doctor," he says flatly. "And an offering of food would be considered patriotic."

Don Nicasio snorts, pushes himself up from his chair and steps past Diosdado. "Let's see what we're dealing with here."

The men are in the rear garden, by his mother's shrine to the Virgin of Antipolo. The statue is of a young, beautiful woman with her head tilted to one side, as if trying to hear something far away.

"She is listening for an infant's cry," his mother explained to Diosdado when he was little. "She is the Mother of us all."

Beyond the stone bench where they have laid Bayani out Diosdado can see the *panteón familiar*, a tiny alabaster tomb with a cross upon it marking the grave of Adelfonso, his brother who did not thrive in the School of Survival, and his parents' mausoleum, recently garlanded with wreaths of carnations.

That was her name—Encarnación.

The *segundo* with the shotgun and several of the other workers stand nearby, watching Don Nicasio's face for instruction.

It takes the old man a moment to recognize Bayani, studying the wounds first before looking at the man's face. Don Nicasio's body stiffens. He turns away to confront Diosdado.

"Why have you brought him here?"

"He needs a doctor."

"Dr. Estero is in Palauig."

"That is ten miles farther on."

"You have no right."

"But here we are."

Bayani raises an arm with some difficulty. "Don't you recognize me, Don Nicasio?" he asks in Zambal.

Diosdado's father does not speak. Bayani raises his voice, speaking to the old man's back.

"Both of your boys home and this is your reception?"

The other men, Diosdado's *guerilleros*, look away. Don Nicasio tells his *segundo* to send a carriage for Dr. Estero and to have Trini bring some food for these beggars, and then strides back into the house.

"I'm sorry, *hermano*," Bayani says to his brother. "I was never taught proper manners."

It was somewhere back in Pampanga that Diosdado guessed, but he has not found the words to acknowledge it.

"Why didn't you tell me?"

"I did," Bayani shrugs. "Not in so many words, but I did. You people only hear what you want to."

Trini comes out then, bent with age, tears in her eyes.

"God has spared you," says his old *ama*, embracing Diosdado and then setting up a table for the men to eat. When the food comes there is more than enough to fill their shrunken bellies.

"We had better finish this," says Kalaw through a mouthful of *lechón*, "before the Americans take it all."

Diosdado is certain his father will have no trouble with the Americans, even if his son—sons—are *insurrectos* with a price on their heads. Men like his father are making their accommodations all over the Philippines, coming to an understanding, waiting in line for the positions that will be handed down by the new masters of the land. The *americanistas* will not look so different than those who did the bidding of the Spanish—businessmen, the wealthier politicians, the owners of plantations. *Ilustrados*, even many of the scribblers, especially the ones who can write in English, have begun to campaign for "wiser heads to prevail" and "the gradualist approach" to independence. He has heard of a masquerade party in Manila with an *adobo* prepared, quite purposely, with American tinned pork obtained from their quartermaster corps.

"I've never set foot in that house," says Bayani when they try to move him into the *zaguán*, "and I'm not going to now."

Finally Diosdado sends the others to sleep on the palm mats Trini has laid out, and stays outside with Bayani in the garden, covering him with a blanket. It is very difficult for the sargento to breathe now, as if he had to strain through a quart of water to find the bubble of air within it.

"The doctor will be here soon," Diosdado tells him.

"The doctor isn't coming."

It grows darker in the garden, the shadow of the Virgin lengthening toward them. Bayani fights to keep his eyes open.

"I hated you," he says after some time. "I hated your clothes and I hated your shoes and I hated seeing you in your *carroza* on the way to church and the times I heard you speak I hated your voice. I hated Don Nicasio too, though my mother said he was a great man, great and proud and very intelligent. But I hated you more because you were where I should have been. You wore my shoes and ate at my table, the one with the cloth covering it, with a separate plate for every dish, while I was out sneaking chickenshit from your yard to spread on our potato patch. I tried to get the Baluyut brothers to beat you up because I was too shy, too ashamed, to do it myself."

Diosdado smiles. "I always wondered what I did to upset the Baluyut brothers."

"When you went away to school I was already in the world, stealing from people, killing *moros* for the Spanish, and I forgot about you. I thought I did. But when I joined the *sublevo* my first thought was to come to Zambales, to evict Don Nicasio from this house in the name of the Revolution and live here, rule here, myself. And when you came back one day, looking like a *maricón* in your white suit with your hair full of brilliantine and speaking Spanish like a *peninsular*, I would say 'Go away, boy, you are not welcome on this land.'"

Talking costs Bayani, and he pauses to catch his breath.

"Then you ruined my dream," he says when he can speak again, a slight smile on his lips. "You ruined my sweet dream of revenge. 'We have a young lieutenant from Zambales,' they told me, 'and we want you to look out for him.'"

"I am sorry," Diosdado tells him. For confession, carefully choosing one of the friars who didn't know his voice to unburden to, he said the words but never felt the remorse. He feels it now. "I am sorry for what was done to you and your mother."

"She didn't want money. She only wanted him to look at her when he passed on his horse, passed in his carriage. To look at her as if she was there, as if he had loved her. But he is not corrupt enough, our father, to love two women and be just to them both."

"My mother must have known about you."

"We called her *La Rezadora*, whenever we'd see her coming back from morning mass, muttering her novenas. The One Who Prays. Maybe she was praying for our father's soul."

"And you still hate me."

Bayani laughs, coughs wetly. "Take a look at us now. We could be twins, except I have more holes in me than you do. How can you hate your twin?"

Diosdado feels himself crying now. Maybe for his mother. The shadow of the Virgin covers Bayani's face.

"The doctor will be here soon," he says. "We'll regroup and make a stand here in Zambales and on some of the other islands—"

"They're paying fifteen American dollars if you hand in your rifle. How many of our men have ever had that much in their pocket? No—the *yanquis* will win and all of your friends will learn their language, your children will learn their language and priests of the American religion, if they have one, will take the place of the friars."

"Maybe." Diosdado has had to wrestle with the possibility. Being steadfast does not mean you have to be stupid. "But one day they will leave—"

"But one day they'll leave," says Bayani, "just like the Spanish are leaving, and then we'll be able to kill each other in peace, the Christians against the *moros*, the Tagalos against the Ilocanos, the rich against the poor, men like me against men like our father. A true Republic of the Philippines."

One of the workers returns then, a young man Diosdado remembers climbing trees with when they were boys, the kind of young man who should be bearing arms for his country. He steps forward shyly, deferential.

"Señor," he says, "I am very sorry to report that Dr. Estero cannot be persuaded to come. He says that he is afraid that when the Americans arrive people will tell stories. He sends this."

The young man, Joaquín is his name, Diosdado thinks, holds out a hand to reveal a small black ball of opium.

"No more," Bayani growls. "If it hurts enough, I won't regret leaving."

Diosdado sits with him into the night, the *tuko* lizards chirping, the moon rising slowly over the grave markers in the *panteón*. Diosdado is cold but does not move.

"Bury me with my mother," says Bayani at the end. "May God forgive us all."

PROMETHEUS

It is the filth he can't abide. Niles has come, in the last few days, to pray that
they will kill him.

"They live like beasts, like hunted beasts," he remarks to the Correspondent, who he knows is still alive because of the occasional tightening of
the tether around his neck. "And we are less than beasts to them."

It has been some time since the Correspondent has acknowledged his
complaints or observations, the man going mute this morning after they cut
poor Private Moss, dead from his wound and their appalling treatment, loose
from the tree and tossed him into the ravine. Niles worries his teeth with his
tongue to see how loose they have gotten. He tried once, maybe yesterday, to
asphyxiate himself with the rope around his neck but was only able to slump
enough to make himself less comfortable. He has witnessed two hangings in
his life, one a formal and somewhat legal execution that ended with a hard
snap and twitching legs, and the other an amateur affair meant to prolong
the agony of the miscreant, a white man vile enough in his predations to
merit the attentions of Dr. Lynch. There will be no public obloquy attendant
on his own passing, the wretched niggers barely glancing in their direction
anymore, moving them from camp to camp like necessary but annoyingly
unwieldy baggage.

Niles has been recalling his Bulfinch of late, the Judge's voice intoning
Olympian exploits to him and Harry when they were boys, Niles perking
up at the naughty bits and staring longingly, whenever the Judge was not

present, at the gauze-caressed bosoms of violated maidens in the wonderful illustrations. Lately it has been the fate of Prometheus weighing on him, bound to a rock for his transgression, the giant golden Eagle of Zeus sent each day to tear his still-beating heart from its cavity. How the screech of the feathered terror, how the breeze from the waft of its enormous wings must have quickened that heart with apprehension! And then, after the wrenching pain—what? Was he made whole immediately or left pouring blood from his violated innards, life ebbing from him, thinking this is the last, the end, till darkness—and then a sharp jolt of consciousness, sun bleeding onto the ocean horizon and the heart pumping life again? He imagines that the groan emitted from Promethean lips is not unlike his own when coming to, still knotted to a tree, and realizing that nothing has changed.

He has begun to envy the Titan. Bound, yes, but with the healthful sea air in his lungs, the magnificent blue waters, joyous with dolphins, stretched below him, and the song of cliff-nesting birds in his ear. Wind in the hair. What of a few sharp moments with a razor-beaked demon, a gory, if inconclusive death? Niles is being consumed by insects while still breathing. Lice cavort in his scalp, ants, beetles, many-legged crawling vermin he cannot imagine inhabit the rags of his clothing and every sweat-sticky fold of his body—biting, nesting, breeding. Flies have burrowed into his face and left their eggs, the lumps on his tortured countenance growing larger and more tender each day, filling him with terrible thoughts of what will come with their spawning, what manner of squirming pupae unleashed to feed on him. There is no place on the surface of him that does not itch or sting or prickle with the traffic of tiny legs and he has taken to cursing the niggers in the crudest and most detailed manner whenever they wander near, hoping one will understand and take enough umbrage to send a quick bullet through his worm-infested skull. He feels not so much Prometheus as Caliban, styed in a crevice and bent with ague, victim to sorcerers without wit or pity.

"The Anglo-Saxon," he informs the Correspondent, "has the ability to amuse himself without cruelty. However, even among those considered, academically, as members of the white race, there is a great deal of variation in this attribute. Take the Dago and his *corrida*, for instance, or the slaughter in your typical Italian *musicale*. And these miserable buggers," he jerks his head, though the Correspondent cannot see him, toward the rebels, who have stirred from their midday torpor and seem to be breaking camp, "these mongrelized Asiatics practice cruelty as a matter of course, barely taking any pleasure in it."

There was one for a while who spoke English and would share a few words, but he is gone. The *jefe* of this pack, a degenerate Spaniard of some sort, has a hateful, impatient disposition and rules his cretinous minions through fear.

There is gunfire lower on the mountain.

"Another of their hapless ambushes. We'll be moving soon."

If he refuses to go, feigns unwillingness or inability to move his legs, surely they will kill him. Quickly, dispassionately, but not with a bullet. There's the rub. He has seen them butcher a captured mule with their bolos, the animal dismembered before someone thought to silence its bellowing with a chop to the neck, eyes still large and sentient after its larynx was cut. They fed Niles bits of the half-charred, purplish meat for a week. No, when they come to make him move he will clench his toes to force some blood into his numbed leg, will try to hold the mewling woman of a Correspondent he is yoked to upright and drag him down the pathway after their captors. If they haven't been killed yet, burdensome as they are, there may yet be an exchange, something already in the works.

The rifle fire is closer now, closer than he's ever heard it.

"Buck up, my friend," he calls to the man tied to the other side of the tree. "Our salvation may be at hand."

The rebels are running now, this way and that way to gather their paltry belongings, and the *jefe*, whose name he knows is Gallego, is walking toward them with the brute who has been charged with their security ever since the colored renegade was untied, the brute who yanks the knots so tight that both Niles's wrists are chafed and infected, so tight that he has lost feeling in the discolored fingers of his left hand.

Gallego barks an order to the brute and stalks away. The others are nearly all gone now, fled in panic. The man has only a bolo, one of the long ones they use for killing, tight in his hand. He scowls down at them for a long moment.

"If you're not going to kill us," says the Correspondent flatly, breaking his long silence, "at least cut this cracker bastard's tongue out."

The pain is worse than Niles has imagined, the first blow snapping his collarbone close to the neck and twisting as it rends him apart, and he hears something like the bellowing of a mule before the white light—

* * *

He wakes anew, still bound, heart pounding, but far from whole. The pain is like a scream tearing at every fiber of him and there is another scream, audible, something like a baby's constant wail, only from a grown man on the other side of the tree. When his eyes clear, Niles sees the googoo lying several yards away, a huge stain of blood spreading on his back, bolo still clutched in his outstretched hand. He goes away again, pain still there. He is only pain. And then he feels a hand take his chin and lift it up. It is a nigger staring him in the eyes, not one of theirs but one of the back-home variety, in a Regular Army uniform.

"This one still breathin, too, Lieutenant," the man calls. "But the googoos done hack him up to pieces."

MONSOON

It is raining again today. Nilda is already cooking when Royal wakes and sits up on the *banig*. The mosquitoes have been at him again in spite of the netting they sleep under, sneaking up through the cracks in the split-palm flooring. The thatch above makes a raspy sound as the rain hits it, and he can hear the surf, waves breaking steadily. Unless there is a storm he figures that four waves tumble in and sweep away for every minute in the long day. Maybe sometime he will get out there and count them, sunup to sunup, and do the sums and it would be like a clock. Though nobody here needs a clock.

Nilda looks at him when he stands but she doesn't say anything. He has learned some of the words, like *lalo* which is "more," and learned "yes" and "no," but she is not much of a talker, Nilda. You don't need so much talking here on the coast to get by, only the men when they sit after the fishing is done and drink palm *beeno* and tell stories or the women when they play cards and chew all that business that makes their teeth go red. Nilda doesn't chew and doesn't seem to be invited for cards. He wonders if that makes her sorry. It is the kind of thing they don't have the language for. And the love-words, when they're doing it, which is often on the long rainy days, he would like to know some of her love-words but all she'll say is *lalo* sometimes, at least make him feel she wants it. He can say whatever he wants but hearing himself say things she doesn't understand makes him disbelieve them, so now it is mostly just noises.

He takes the bamboo tubes and steps out onto the narrow platform, barefoot. His boots are too hot and the soles starting to pull away from all the wet, the leather with a green mold on it, and he's only bothered with the sandals Nilda made him the few times they've walked in to her mother's village. The rain is cool on his bare shoulders and when he is wet enough he rubs himself down to get the night-sweat off. He hops off the platform onto the dirt, startling one of Bung's half-wild pigs sleeping underneath, and heads for the beach.

It's not a village, really, eight of the bamboo and palm-thatch huts scattered along the ocean and another half-dozen, like the one he and Nilda have taken over, on the banks of the little stream that runs into it. A couple of the men are already out in the stream, thigh-deep, checking their fish weirs. They see him but don't say good morning. A couple of the men are runaways like him, dodging something or other, and except for Bung, folks pretty much ignore him. A low mist comes up off the water as the rain hits it and Royal thinks again how pretty, in its dopey, dreamy, slow-ass way, it is in this country.

The beach is wide with a gentle slope to it, yellow-brown sand leading back to a thin strip of cocoanut palms before the thick brush begins. The stream cuts a different channel through the sand to the ocean every day, and this morning it is deep and swift-moving, churning at its wide mouth where the waves roll in over the freshwater pushing out. There are stick-legged birds skittering along the surfline and ghost crabs popping in and out of their holes, but it is too cool and rainy for the big lizards, lizards as long as Royal if you count their tails, to be out on the sand. Royal sees the pigs first, snuffling around some fallen, rotting cocoanuts, and then spots Bung way up in one of his palms. Bung waves and shouts a greeting, always cheerful.

Bung cut the notches for Royal's first tree, somehow able to get enough mustard on the bolo while he's clinging halfway up the trunk and not chop his own fingers off, taught him the whole routine. Royal stuffs the bamboo tubes in his belt and starts up. Bung cut the notches to fit his own legs which are shorter, but Royal is glad for so many hand- and footholds as he wrestles his way up the slippery-sided palm. They are so damn high, swaying mightily at the top on windy days, and he tries to never look down. In Cuba the little *muchachos* had a way of tying a short cord between their ankles and gripping the trunk with that but they were just skin and bone and had been doing it their whole life. It is a long hard climb for Royal, nothing like getting up in the spreading sycamores back home, and he has to rest his arms and legs a bit when he reaches the top. He pulls off a few ripe-looking cocoanuts and drops them to the sand, the time between letting them go and the soft smack reminding him how high he is.

He's tapping just three of the flower stems, like Bung showed him, rattan strips tied to bind them over so the sap drips down into the bamboo tubes. The sap will run for half a day before the cut heals up and clogs, and then you have to climb again. Royal unhooks the bamboo tubes he's left there, all three full with the whitish sap, carefully slipping them into his belt. He cuts a finger-long section off the end of each of the stems with Nilda's little curved knife, then binds them down with the rattan strips and fixes the new collector tubes underneath. He licks his fingers off, sweet and sticky, clamps the knife between his teeth and begins to feel his way down the trunk.

The stems give less in this rainy season than before, but with two trees it is enough. Bung works six of them, but Bung does it as a living, selling some as frothy *tuba* in the village of Nilda's mother and letting some pass into vinegar which he spices with hot peppers and once a week cooks down in the still he's built to make *lambanog* which is even stronger than the *beeno* locals used to peddle to the boys in the garrison. Lift the top of your skull right off. Royal trades whatever he doesn't drink himself to Bung for a little pigmeat.

Bung's little herd is mostly out on the beach now, rooting for crabs, and Bung is waiting at the base of the palm, grinning, offering Royal a strip of the mangrove tanbark he crumbles into the *tuba* for color and to give it more punch. Bung talks at him, laughing and dancing around in the sand the way he does, waving his hands. He is bowlegged and keeps his hair short and bristly, rubbing the back of his head whenever he laughs. He is ripe-cocoanut colored, like when the bark first turns from green to tan, and lives with a very short, very round woman whose teeth are so red from the betel nut that when she smiles it looks like she doesn't have any. At first Royal thought Bung was so happy because of his home brew, but has never seen him take a drop of it. Bung and his wife speak a different lingo than the other folks here, and even Nilda who has been other places doesn't always understand them.

Royal is soaked through from the drizzle by the time he is done tapping his second tree, wearing only his pants which Nilda has cut and hemmed above his knees. He has gotten used to being wet all day. He leaves the tubes of palm sap on the bank of the stream and wades in, picking his way over the ankle-breakers on the bottom to the fish trap he has set up. There are three caught in the hemp, foot-long, bass-looking things, and he bends to snake his arm in and pull them out. He cracks their heads against a hardwood stump on the bank and strings them through the gills to carry. Food, at least enough to keep you going, pretty much just comes to you here. Fruit falls, root crops bump up from the dirt, fish are flushed down the river or swim in close to the beach to be caught. Before the rain started some of the beach men went in to work in the fields for the people in the village of Nilda's mother, but none of them would hire Royal. They are poor, what people back home call catfish poor, having enough to eat and a roof overhead but not much else.

Their *bahay* has a steep-pitched roof for all the rain, hinged thatch shutters propped open and a little rough hemp mat on the platform to wipe your feet on. Nilda dries his hair with a cloth and has fish and rice hot for him when he comes in from the rain, pulling it off the indoor stove that is nothing but a hollowed section of log lined with mortar. It tastes like geechie food, only hotter when it is hot and sweeter from the cocoanut when it is sweet. They eat with their hands from the same bowl, sitting cross-legged on the woven sea-grass *banig* with their shoulders touching. Everything she fixes tastes fine but it is always the same things mixed in different ways.

Better than Army food.

When they are finished Royal sticks his hands out in the rain to wash them and then drinks some of yesterday's *tuba* juice, already tangy with alcohol, from a gourd. Nilda will take some with food when it is maybe a half day old and still sweet, calling it *lina*, but Royal needs the extra kick.

He sits in the opening and watches the rain come off the thatch, watches the stream roll by, taking another sip now and then. The *tuba* softens the sound of the water hitting the roof, dulls the sound of the waves pounding the sand, smooths the edges off any thoughts that try to force their way into his mind. After a while he will lie out on the mat, not so much tired as waiting out the long day, and if she wants it Nilda will be lying next to him when he wakes. She is careful never to wake him, explaining in a complicated pantomime that when you sleep your soul wanders away, and that a person startled from sleep might lose it. Royal doesn't have the words to tell her he left his behind long ago, in a cactus patch outside Bisbee.

In the early evening, hard to be exact in this season where you never see clear sky, he will climb to tap the palms again. Bung has a store of rice and he will trade some sap for it and then maybe sit and listen to the sea fishermen when they come in with whatever they've netted and drink and tell their long stories, eyes and voices growing soft with liquor, talking along with the slow rhythm of the waves. If there is news from the war, or if the war is still going on, nobody is trying to tell him about it. He feels his eyelids growing heavy. He senses Nilda moving around behind him, always with her hands busy, sewing mostly. She can make all kinds of pictures and patterns with the thread, and other women, the ones who don't ask her to play cards and the ones in her mama's village who won't hardly look her in the eye, pay her in goods or sometimes in Mex money to put fancy borders on their clothes. Sometimes she will get up and step over to just touch him, like she needs to check that he is still there, that he is real. He knows she is there, always. This is where she is from, where she belongs, and he is just something that has washed up and doesn't really fit. It is not so bad, a dreamy sort of life, the waters he has given himself up to warm and gently flowing. Royal drifts on the palm wine, barely able to hear the drops hit anymore, the air just a kind of water that is not so thick as what is in the slow, meandering stream outside, the sky is water and the earth soaked and overflowing with it and he lies on his side right where he is. A little *chacón* lizard is scuttling across the wall, hunting for insects. He can't hear the waves but knows they haven't stopped rolling. It will rain again tomorrow.

REAPER

The boy has been following him for two blocks, eyeing the bag, undoubtedly seeking the perfect moment in which to spirit it away. Dr. Lunceford has never been this far south, below Canal Street, and is unfamiliar with the neighborhood. It is his last day in Manhattan, the apartment across the river arranged for, and he has exhausted the appetite for Dr. Bonkers' elixir in the tenements farther north. There is alleged to be a settlement of colored people down here, but thus far he has not discovered it.

"Hey Mister!" calls the boy.

Dr. Lunceford stops and turns to face him. The boy is perhaps eleven or twelve, though it is difficult to be certain with the more undernourished of the street Arabs. The boy glances down to the bag.

"You a croaker?"

The license has been promised, but given the vicissitudes of state bureaucracy there is no telling when it will be delivered.

"Are you in need of a doctor?"

"It's me pal," explains the urchin. "He's awful sick."

The boy leads him to Duane Street, then toward the West River. Dr. Lunceford is wary, not discounting the possibility that the boy has older confederates in waiting. He has been waylaid twice uptown, once losing several bottles of Dr. Bonkers' to a gang, boys who were not, surprisingly, interested in the more valuable leather bag or the rest of its contents. He assumes they were disappointed upon drinking the nostrum. In the other incident he merely fled, prudently if not with dignity.

The boy, who offers his name as Ikey Katz, stands at the head of an alleyway a block from the pier and waves him in.

"He's down here at the end, Doc," he says. And noticing the doctor's suspicious demeanor, adds, "On the level."

The spill from the streetlamps does not completely penetrate the narrow passage. A trio of eating establishments of the lower echelon back onto the alley and the smell is not pleasant.

He notes rat droppings as he walks, and trash bins that have not been emptied in some while. At the end there is a hodge-podge of discarded wooden pallets, and lying on one of these, muttering in a language Dr. Lunceford has no inkling of, is a semi-comatose young boy.

"We figgered somethin was crook wid him when he don't show at the Newsies' Home yesterday night," says Ikey. "Thursdays they wash your drawers for free, and he don't ever miss out on that. So we been checking all the spots where he flops at night, an I found him here."

The boy is moaning and muttering, his forehead damp and hot, his pulse racing.

"He's been like off his nut lately, the Kid, and—you know—getting *dark*er."

"What is his name?"

Ikey shrugs. "We call him the Yella Kid."

He is not yellow now, despite his mop of blond hair, but more of an angry bronze. Dr. Lunceford presses lightly on the swollen abdomen and the boy cries out, his eyes popping open to stare at the stranger in fright.

"Aw Jeez, not yet!" he cries. "I ain ready to go!"

"Calm yourself, son. I'm here to help you—"

"Shit you are! You're here to stick me on the boat!"

"I don't understand—"

"He thinks you're the Reaper, Doc," says Ikey. "The character that takes you unnerground."

Dr. Lunceford removes his black homberg, forces what he hopes is a reassuring smile.

"I'm here to help you."

The boy's terrified eyes swing to his friend. "You member the one I showed you, Ikey? Right in the front winda at Altgeld's. It's all white—"

Ikey turns to Dr. Lunceford. "See? He's been like that all week. Bughouse."

"You got the meatwagon here, right?" says the boy. His voice is hoarse, unsteady, his eyes burning feverishly.

"I am not Death," says Dr. Lunceford. "I am neither a butcher nor an undertaker. I am a doctor and I'm going to take you somewhere you can be treated."

The boy's eyes grow wider. "I aint goin to no croaker shop! They slip you the black bottle or you end up on one of them Orphan Trains—"

"Those are just stories—"

"The Orphan Trains is *real*," says Ikey Katz. "They got their paws on Jinx McGonigal and shipped him out to some farm where there's nothin but squareheads. Made him work like a dog and kneel on a wooden pew every Sunday. Took him most of a year to scarper and bum his way back here."

"He won't be going anywhere for a long time," says Dr. Lunceford, realizing how little reassurance the phrase offers. "Do you know where the Hudson Street Hospital is?"

"Sure."

"You run there as fast as you can, straight to the ambulance barn, tell them that it is an emergency and bring them back here."

"You got it, Doc."

Ikey runs off down the alley. The sick boy's breathing is rapid, shallow. A late-phase cholestatic jaundice, the bile ducts obstructed by a tumor or, less likely in one so young, gallstones, growing steadily. Nothing to be done till he is on an operating table.

The boy squints his eyes at him, as if his features are hard to make out in the weak half-light from the street. "You gotta tell em about the funeral crate," he pleads. "It's right up front in the winda. I got enough saved to cover it."

With a good surgeon, thinks Dr. Lunceford, and the helping hand of Providence—

"I'll be sure to let them know," he tells the boy.

The boy clutches his middle, tears streaming down his cheeks. "It hurts somethin awful," he says. "It hurts awful."

"I know," says Dr. Lunceford. "I know it does."

The boy begins to convulse then, eyes rolling up into his skull, slender limbs thrashing against the pallet until Dr. Lunceford is able to take hold of him. The doctor hugs the boy's head against his chest, wrapping his arms around him tightly till the spasms stop, muscles exhausted. His eyes clear slowly.

"I'm scared as hell, Doc," he says, grimly lucid now, turning his head to look up to Dr. Lunceford. "I never figgered on that."

"Don't you worry," says Dr. Lunceford. "It won't be long now."

The doctor sits on the pallet holding the Yellow Kid, waiting and thinking. Thinking about his life and what has happened to it, thinking about where he should be now, with Yolanda, instead of down this filthy alley in a city of orphans. Junior was about this size the one time they thought they were going to lose him to scarlet fever, Yolanda furious at him for being a doctor and not being able to do more, only hold him and rock him and talk to him while Yolanda pressed the ice packs to his forehead. He felt it in his fingertips when the fever broke and his son was able to sleep, past all danger.

The street boy, shaking weakly, manages to lay his hand over the back of Dr. Lunceford's.

"Lookit that," he says in a small voice. "We're the same color, you an me."

RESCUE

Jacks watches the sand. The rebels are keeping close to the crashing waves but it isn't high tide yet and they'll have to leave track on dry sand to get into the trees. The tip was on the level for a change, some *amigo* earning himself a couple gold eagles or a pass out of the hoosegow, and if they'd gotten there a few minutes earlier they would have had the rebels boxed in. For some of the terrain here it would be good to have horses, ride down fast on the little shack towns before anybody has a chance to holler, run down whoever tries to light out. This humping around on foot won't get it done.

"Got to be something *wrong* with these people," says Coop. "Don't know when they been beat."

"Or maybe they know it, but got nothin better to do," calls Hardaway from the rear of the squad. "Vex us with sniper fire and make us haul our narrow asses down this damn beach chasin em."

"Army's not paying you to eat beans and sleep, Private." Jacks turns and walks backward for a few steps, making sure his men aren't strung out too much. There is a good thirty yards of open sand before the tree line here, perfect for a googoo ambush.

"I forgot," says Hardaway. "We all making a fortune here."

Coop walks like he's on a Sunday picnic, rifle held casually in one hand. "We ought to send the ones we caught back home," he says. "Let them be the niggers for a spell."

*   *   *

Even on a flat beach the surf can kill you. The wind is moving one way and the current another today, something like a storm collecting out over the water, and the waves are high as Royal's shoulder with the out-sucking fierce enough that they seem to hang in the air for a moment before slamming down on the hard, bare sand. Bung maneuvers his little *banca* out beyond the breaker line, looking for an opening, turning the boat out to face the biggest of the swells, now and then raising his oar to be seen when he slides into the steep troughs. He is riding low, like he has a big haul of fish or has taken on water. The outrigger is about the only thing Bung owns in the world and Royal knows he will risk his life to save it.

Bung makes no signal when he starts in, just paddling hard, one side and then the other, trying to ride a medium-high swell in without getting too far down its slope, no reason to think this one is any easier than the others so he must be at the end of his strength. Royal stands up on the beach where the spent waves race around his calves and then hurry away, the front line of the ocean booming, churning white, and wishes Nilda was here. But it is too late to run for her and the surf too loud for him to shout and everyone else is in Candelaria for the festival of Saint Somebody. Bung is moving fast in the *banca* now, flying like a spear, and on some days when the waves aren't high and undercut Royal has seen him glide ashore, effortlessly disengaging from the boat to grab the painter at the bow and run it up another ten feet without breaking speed. But today the water comes apart before you can get to the sand, the sea violent against itself, and Royal pulls a deep breath into his lungs before rushing in.

He stands sideways to the first wave and is almost torn off his feet by it, then runs three long steps forward to dive into the base of the next breaker the way he's seen the boldest of the local boys do, swimming hard to push out the other side of it, and feels right away that he's never been in anything this powerful, stronger than the water that swept him away from the company, fighting hard just to keep himself pointed out to sea. Three strides and dive, two strides and dive, not making any ground but surviving each wave and not at all sure how he's going to help but he can't just watch a man drown. He digs in, chest-deep and able only to duck under the next rumbling wall of water. He pops up to see Bung still coming, looking sideways and back over his shoulder as he paddles, as if trying to outrace the swell he is on. They meet eyes before it happens, Bung indicating with a flick of his oar that Royal needs to get out of the way, and then the next wave is bigger than all the others and Royal is wrenched off his feet as it breaks early and he is tumbled, the bottom smacking him in the shoulder, back, head, knee, head again, a rag doll in the churning white, saltwater driven up his nose and then lying sideways in outrushing foam being pulled back toward the next breaker till Bung, it must be Bung, grabs him by an ankle and pulls him out of the surf.

Royal snorts out water and sand. The *banca* flips and tumbles down the breaker line, both outriggers snapped off, and Bung is frantically running, bowlegged, to toss flopping fish higher onto the sand before the sea can take them back.

Royal stands. One knee has been twisted, his shoulder scraped, his jaw sore. There is sand in between his teeth. Bung is pointing at Royal, giggling now but with his arms and legs trembling from the struggle and fish, dead and dying, scattered all around him. He sees something beyond and the smile dies on his face. Royal turns to look.

They are coming up from the south, moving fast like something is behind them, with the Teniente in front. He hasn't shaved or cut his hair for a long time and looks skinnier than ever. Kalaw is still with him, and Locsin and Pelaez and Ontoy and the little boy Fulanito. The *segundo*, Bayani, is missing. All of them have rifles.

The Teniente speaks to Bung first, but the man is frozen, too terrified to answer. Royal steps in front of him.

"Yall people still running?"

The Teniente does not smile at him. "We need the road to Candelaria."

"I take you there."

The men all stare at Bung as they step past him, eyeballing a warning, and Kalaw quickly gathers some fish to stuff in his *mochila*. Though nobody is pointing a rifle at him Royal feels like a hostage again.

"The war gone come up here?"

The Teniente looks back as they wade across the mouth of the stream where it hits the beach. "It has already arrived. Your men are behind us."

They squeeze through the stand of nipa palm that lines the far bank, then step carefully over the gnarled, guano-spattered roots of the mangroves, branches laden with sleeping fruit bats hung upside-down, the only thing Nilda ever cooked for him that he wouldn't eat. Royal leads the band through a maze of boulders then, turning inland when the dunes begin, sandy, palm-studded mounds that lead to the Candelaria road without taking you past any of the fishermen's huts. The Teniente pauses at the top of the first one, giving Fulanito an order, then waves for the others to keep going.

The boy lays on his belly at the top of the dune, facing the beach, rifle by his side.

"Fulanito will fire when they come into view." The Teniente's face is grim. He looks as if he hasn't slept for a long time. "If they believe they are attacked they will delay their pursuit."

"They aint gonna care he's so little," says Royal as they hurry away. "They kill him anyways."

There are a few shacks up by the tree line and a broken dugout boat tumbling in the surf and Coop finds a fish lying in the dry sand, gills still pumping.

"This got to be a googoofish," he shouts before flinging it over the breakers and into the sea. "Don't know where it suppose to be."

"We could of ate that."

"I aint eatin no more fish in this lifetime." Coop has been the one most eager to believe the rumor that they will all be replaced by Texas Vols and sent back home. "Rice neither. I get back it's gone be steak and potatoes or nothin."

There is a woman, youngish, eyeing them from up the bank of a little stream that empties out into the ocean, standing motionless. There are still a lot of them up here never seen an American, colored or not. A number of the palm trees have bolo slashes on their sides, footholds, and Jacks looks into the tops for snipers. It has become that kind of fight, like a handful of wasps worrying a water buffalo. No way they can bring you down, but now and then you get stung.

The tracks of the band, six of them now, appear on the far side of the stream past the nipa fronds, cutting away from the roaring surf and into a jumble of boulders. The new one is bigger, barefoot. Jacks holds his arm up and Gamble and Ponder scoot ahead into the rocks, ducking low as they run. The rest of the patrol squats or takes a knee. There is no shade here, and Jacks has his midday headache, the rhythmic pounding from the shore working on him all morning long. Huachuca and Bliss would cook you but it never made you wet like this, like you been steamed through. He wonders how Lupe would make out here. He misses her.

Gamble and Ponder pop out and wave them up.

"Single file," he says, and they head into the boulders.

The rocks are near shoulder-high, no reason they should be there, just something God didn't have noplace else to put. The men walk silently, rifles held high and ready. Jacks doesn't have to do much sergeanting with this bunch, all of them experienced soldiers now, turning quick but holding fire when the rustling off to the left turns out to be only a monitor lizard, one of the big long ones that all start to sing when the sun drops out of sight.

They come out at the base of a low dune with a few crooked palms sticking out from the top. The rebels have climbed it.

"These boys never learnt to cover they tracks," says Coop and then his head makes a snapping sound, a wet clot of it hitting Jacks on the shoulder and they are all down on their bellies firing at the top of the dune at the spot between two palms where there was a flash of metal. Gamble and Ponder split wide from each other, lizard-crawling up the slope while the others continue to pour it on to cover them. They hold fire when the boys wave.

Coop is gone, laid backward in the sand with a hole between his eyes and his head in a puddle.

"Cover him up with something," says Jacks and trudges up the side of the dune, slinging his rifle and dropping onto his hands for the steep part. It is only a boy at the top between the palms, shot four or five times, a Mauser lying next to him. Ponder picks up the rifle to put another in him, but the chamber is empty.

"Hit the man when he didn't have but one shot," says the corporal. "What's the odds on that?"

Diosdado has given up trying to read the gunfire. It was Fulanito and then a lot of Krags and then silence.

"Road just up over the top of this hill," the American says, pointing. "You head east on it. But that boy, if they didn't get him, he gone get lost."

"You could join us."

"And yall could give up. You give them rifles over, I bet they still payin out."

There are Americans, white men, living in his father's *hacienda* now. Americans hold the railroad all the way up to Bayambang. When he gets the men to Candelaria they will bury the rifles and split up, each going to a *baryo* where they have friends, and pass as Juan Tamad. See their families, maybe raise a crop until it is time to strike again. The *yanquis* are impatient people, and if they think this war is a disease they can never shake, persistant and painful, maybe they will go home.

His men are waiting for an order. There is no firing now and they feel the enemy closing in.

"Go back and find the boy if you can," he says to Royal Scott, "and lead him to the road when it is safe. We aren't finished yet."

He starts over the hill and the others hurry after.

Royal backtracks a ways and then sits out in the open just over the crest of a dune. Fulanito should find his way at least this far, and if it is the others they will at least see he is unarmed. He rubs the flea bites on his legs softly with the palm of his hand, soothing not scratching like Mama taught him, and waits. Bung will have told everybody left near the shore by now and they will make themselves scarce. It seems like the end of the earth, but the flag has followed him even here.

He recognizes them before the faces take detail, the way they move on patrol, their shapes. Sergeant Jacks spreads them out in a defensive position and climbs the dune alone.

"You not supposed to be here, Private."

"That aint a lie."

Jacks steps past him to the top, looks down the other side, then comes back to sit beside Royal in the sand.

"Where they gone to?"

"Up the road. There's a village."

"That boy killed Cooper. We come into any village, somebody's dyin."

"Cooper."

"Uh-huh."

The waves seem very far away, rolling now, and the sky has gone clean of bad weather. Royal is wearing only a wrapped cloth like Bung does and feels naked next to the sergeant. Jacks stands.

"You better get your story together, son."

The other men nod and Too Tall mutters a hello when he comes back down with the sergeant, but they keep their eyes away like he might be a ghost. Corporal Ponder is carrying Fulanito's Mauser.

"Those people long gone," Jacks tells them. "So we just liberate this prisoner and head back to the garrison."

They follow their own tracks back over the dunes to the boy's body. They have rolled him onto his side and except for the blood he could be napping in the sand. Coop's body is stretched out way down the slope, a palm leaf covering his head. It wasn't an easy shot.

Nobody offers to help when Royal squats and puts Coop's body over his shoulder to carry. He feels the head sticky against the small of his back as they walk, over and through the dunes to the beach, making their way around the boulders, squeezing through the nipa and crossing the stream knee-high where it spreads out. The tide is up now, only a little strip of sand left uncovered. Royal kneels and lays Coop down on it.

"I get something we can carry him in the rest of the way."

"You go with him, Hardaway," says Jacks, looking into Royal's eyes. "Might be some of them googoos still about."

He leads Hardaway to Bung's hut, better built than most, and unties the hammock stretched between the deck post and the cocoanut palm growing next to it. He speaks softly, searching hard for the words in Tagalog. Bung won't be far away.

"What you say there?" Hardaway asks when they are coming back with the hammock.

"Told where that boy is. Maybe somebody will do for him before the crabs get busy."

The others have stripped most of Coop's clothes off.

"I tell the lieutenant you got lost in the river, got caught, run away and spent you some time in the sun out here," says Sergeant Jacks, tossing Coop's pants at him. "But you best walk in there looking like a soldier and not some wildass golliwog been shacked up with a native gal."

The other men busy themselves wrapping the body in the hammock, satisfied with the story. You sign up to fight for the flag but at the end it's only each other you risk yourself for. Coop's clothes fit Royal fine except for the hat, which slips down over his eyes, and the boots. His feet have gone wide from walking barefoot so long and they pinch like a son of a bitch.

Nilda stands back from the beach, watching from behind the trunk of a big *dapdap* tree as they file past. Even in the uniform and at this distance she can tell which one is him by the way he moves. And by the way he moves, she knows it is no use following.

ARRIVISTE

Uncle has put on some muscle. Sleeves rolled up, the biceps of his powerful arms bulging as he holds the squalling, ragged pickaninny labeled PHILIP-PINES over his knee and administers the medicine, a shoe with AMERICAN MILITARY printed on the sole raised in the other hand. Other urchins in their native costumes—a dark-haired little Spaniard, a big-lipped Hawaiian, a Mexican in a sombrero, a yellow Chinaman, an Indian in breechclout and feathers—nurse their throbbing backsides while kindly Lady Liberty deals out schoolbooks to each and indicates the bench on which they are to sit quietly. An unruly gang of onlookers, German, Jap, Colombian, Russian, even a portly John Bull, observe the thrashing with wide eyes, duly impressed. Uncle fixes them with eyebrows raised and chin thrust forward—

WHO'S NEXT?

WHISTLE STOP

They are all colored, the ones who come in, which makes it simple. Hod doesn't care, it's all business, but some of the white soldiers and the leftover Spanish do and they are the customer, who is always right. The locals, whatever their color, tend to wait for the time in between trains to come in and he has decided not to put up a sign or make a policy. Let them work it out on their own. He catches the sergeant looking between him and Mei while they handle orders at opposite ends of the counter, the troop with maybe a half hour before their transport is serviced.

"This place has gone through some changes since we last come through," says the sergeant. It's clear he means San Fernando, not the lunch room, which has been open just two weeks.

"Earthquakes, Spaniards, American gunboats—" says Hod, "not the first time it all come down." The sergeant has ordered a hamburger sandwich like most of the others, like most of the Americans who come in off the train. The carabao beef is a might stringy so he has Chow mix a little duck fat into the grind. "But you can't leave it just sit. Hell—I heard them folks back in Galveston already built their downtown back."

"Never understood why people want to stay there," says the sergeant. "I'm from El Paso—the river don't flood and the earth don't shake."

"On your way home?"

There is a looseness to these men, a lightness, that he remembers from when the Colorados got pulled off the line for good. Had your chance to kill

933

me and now it's gone.

"They send us to some fort," says the sergeant, looking down the counter at his laughing, shouting soldiers, "and we'll sort it out from there. Not like you vols, walk off the boat and that's the end of it."

Mei touches his arm and tells him she's going back to help Chow fix the orders. He can feel the sergeant watching them.

"Where you been garrisoned?" he asks. It is no skin off his ass what people think, it really isn't, but some of them act like if you married a Chinese it's their business to say something.

"Zambales."

"Sittin on the beach."

"Ever walk ten miles over loose sand with your full kit on?"

Hod grins. "Wasn't any picnic where we was either. How the people up there?"

"Not so different than here. Got some different languages, some folks up in the mountains still carryin spears."

"I heard about them."

The sergeant swivels around in his seat to look out the front window. The window cost more than anything else, that much glass a rare item in earthquake country, but the swivel seats were a steal after Hod told the work- men what he wanted, the head fella having seen the real thing on a visit to Manila and able to copy it.

"It's no wonder my boys just give up and called em all googoos," says the sergeant. "So many kinds to keep track of."

"I suppose."

"The Mexicans, they got names for every kind of mix. *Mestizo, castizo, mulato, morisco.* Even got something called a *salta-atrás*—a jump backwards."

"Which is—?"

"Chinese man and an Indian woman." The sergeant shrugs. "You figure these folks have their own words for all of it." He points out the window. "Like what would you call that?"

He is pointing at Bo, who stands on the porch holding himself up by the bamboo roof support watching the other boys hustle their peanuts and cigarettes and bananas next to the steaming locomotive. Mei has scared him enough about the tracks that he will stay there for hours, following the action in the station like it is all a show put on for his enjoyment. He doesn't look like the other boys here, who could all go for twins, and Hod has never thought before about what name to give. He told the major he'd applied to be British so they'd let him stay, but has let it slide and once the ship sailed with the regiment nobody has questioned him. Bo turns to look inside, and, seeing Hod, lights up with the smile he does with his whole body.

"That," says Hod, reaching for the water jug to serve the colored infantry, "would be a Filipino."

FAVORITE SON

If it wasn't so damned blue. The band is playing *When Johnny Comes Marching Home* as his son requested and Sally is weeping prettily and half the folks who matter in Wilmington are on the platform waiting. But the first thing the Judge's eye falls on is the blasted yankee outfit Niles is got up in, and it makes his blood boil same as always. Niles pauses in the doorway of the Pullman, showing his brilliant teeth and waving his arm at them and all the ladies crying now and the men clapping their hands, he looks so heroic, and then there is the sleeve pinned up on the other side and what they've done to his face and the Judge has to breathe deep to hold himself together. He steps forward and takes his son's hand, the right, thank you Lord, and they embrace. The band rushes into *There'll Be a Hot Time in the Old Town Tonight*, people clapping and stomping as Sally hugs Niles and the people cheer and then he is led to the little platform they've set up where Tom Clawson and Mayor Waddell are waiting, the other instruments dropping out to leave just the boy on the trap drum rattling a quiet tattoo to reclaim the military theme of the proceedings and the redcaps stop and set their burdens down, watching respectfully at the edge of the crowd.

"My fellow citizens," intones the old Colonel, "it is my great honor to welcome home a son of our soil, a young man who has risked his life and sacrificed his health that the light of Freedom might shine on one of the darkest corners of our world. Lieutenant Niles Manigault, our prayers have been with you, you have done us proud, and we offer you our everlasting gratitude and esteem!"

The boy on the trap is joined by three more drummers now and a color guard from the Wilmington Light Infantry steps forward, the master-at-arms presenting Niles with a yankee flag folded in a triangle. He's paid a damned arm to protect it, thinks the Judge, they might as well give him one for a souvenir. There is more clapping and folks calling for a speech and the drumroll cuts off sharp.

Niles looks around at the gathering. The engineer has stepped out to watch, his locomotive wheezing hot water up the track, waiting for the ceremony to end before he pulls out of the station.

"It has been my honor," says Niles finally, "to represent you good people, to represent our fine city and the great state of North Carolina, in this desperate and glorious conflict."

Cheers and exhortations. Whatever the Judge's apprehensions about his son serving in a Colorado unit with a troop of illiterate miners, the experience may well have made a man of him.

"As Colonel Waddell has so eloquently stated, our mission in Asia is not one of conquest, but no less than the struggle of Christianity and enlightenment against the forces of darkness and ignorance. I believe that in my absence you folks have triumphed in a similar crusade."

Laughter and applause at this. There has been some grumbling, concern that the best of the niggers were driven out with the worst of them, Sprunt even sending recruiters up North to bring some back and fill out his shifts. But on the whole, white Wilmington is pretty pleased to have recaptured the city.

"I believe that our success on both of these fronts is evidence that our cause is just and that Almighty God is with us. I have returned not only to reunite with those dear to my heart—" turning to nod fondly at Sally and the Judge, "—but to offer my support, in whatever form proves most useful, to the revitalization of our city and the ascent of our section to its rightful prominence in national affairs."

More cheering. The Judge gives a nod to Clawson, who steps forward to stand beside Niles.

"We'd all like to know," grins the editor, quieting the crowd, "if that support might include a run for public office?"

Niles puts his hand over his heart and smiles modestly. The saber scars on his face temper his good looks—even with the gap cut into his moustache he seems more trustworthy than before. War has carved him into something finer.

"I believe Colonel Waddell would concur," he says, "that if the times demand it, a man must step forward to meet his responsibilities."

A cheer then and the Judge nods to the band leader, who drops his baton and it is *Dixie* with the Stars and Bars unfurled from the roof of the station and confetti tossed into the air and stomps and yells and the Judge is not the only man with his heart in his throat. The whistle blows then and all move away from the blasts of steam as the train starts to roll and Niles steps down for what seems like an hour of handshaking and backslapping, the yankee flag wedged under the stump of his left arm and the band shifting into *The Volunteer* to serenade the folks heading home.

"I thought that went rather well," says Niles when they are just family and on the way to the carriage.

"The state ought to have a regiment in this fight. With you as commander."

Niles smiles faintly. "I believe I've seen enough of that hellhole for the present, thank you."

The Judge is glad to see Niles swing himself up into the barouche on his own and then reach back to help Sally. Coleman, the third driver the Judge has hired since the city was liberated, does not think to come down from his seat. Decent government is restored, but the impudence lingers.

"Clawson and I have spoken with Josephus Daniels," says the Judge, hauling himself on board and facing backward. "There's a position in the state senate about to open up, and he says he'll run a campaign in the *News and Observer* to draft you. With your approval, of course."

Niles leans his head back against the seat as Coleman sets the team in motion. The journey has tired his son, or else he is just looking older.

"Until I learn to deal poker with one hand," he says with his new, saber-slashed grin, "I might as well give politics a go."

NAGASAKI

They won't step ashore in Nagasaki. Just a coaling stop before the long leg to Honolulu and then to the States. Royal wonders if the white troops going home get to go in and stretch their legs. Except for the crew it is only colored on the *A. T. Crook*, sitting out in the long protected anchorage with low mountains on both sides, the harbor ending with the little man-made island of stone warehouses where the chaplain says they kept the Dutch traders operating after they crucified all the Catholics, a short bridge connecting it to the small city that spreads by the river's mouth. The Japs have their navy training here, thick fortress walls near the water's edge and warships maneuvering all around them for what looks like practice.

Royal sits up on the forecastle deck and watches the first of the barges come alongside. The loaders squat on the mounded coal till the lines have been secured, then clamber up the webbing, one man and more than three dozen women forming their line from the port gangway across to the coal bunker, four men left on the barge to shovel. The sun is straight down on them, harbor surface dead flat and most of the soldiers lolling on deck wasted from the heat. The women chatter with each other as they get into position, gabbling like a flock of wild turkey hens, and then go silent the moment they are in place and the coal starts moving, big bamboo baskets loaded with forty, maybe fifty pounds hoisted hand-to-hand up the side of the ship and then passed down the line by the women, the hems of their short robes tucked up into waistbands, baskets never slowing for a moment till the man at the end dumps the coal into the bunker opening and flings the basket toward the rail, where a woman catches it in two hands and drops it over the side to another woman feeding baskets to the shovelers below.

Ants, thinks Royal, ants like he's seen in the jungle, filing into their anthill with their loads and filing back out to carry more, blind to everything but the task. Some of the other men come out to the edge to watch with him, mute with the heat, five more gangs feeding the bunkers now and then more as the other barges and lighters swarm both sides of the ship and it is all women doing the passing, the webbing and decks overrun with them, hundreds of women passing baskets of coal toward the bunkers. No shouting, no talking, only the crunch of the shovels in the coal and the hollow crashing as it tumbles into the bunker and the occasional *thunk* of a barge against the big ship's hull.

They are short, sturdy women, from fifteen to fifty, many of them wearing straw hats with very long bills against the noonday sun, keeping their legs slightly bent as they turn their hips to take a load, turn to pass it on and then turn back to take the next, their faces and arms glistening with sweat, clothes sticking wet to their bodies, long black hair, where it hangs loose, dripping with sweat. A few of them are as brown as Nilda. He was starting to have more of her words just before the Army came to bring him back, words for things you could point to, for water and fire and wood and the names of things to eat. The other ones, words between a man and a woman that aren't things you can point to, those he can barely remember in American. They don't look like people right now, these coal-passing women, only like part of a machine that is feeding the ship. He can't imagine Jessie here, can barely even bring back her face. She is a little girl he used to look at through window glass, wearing a velvet dress and gloves that she only pull off to play white people's music on the piano.

But she is not there behind the glass anymore, and Junior cut to pieces and Coop laying in the dirt up in Zambales and Jubal run north, all of them dead or scattered and Royal is cooking under the sun in the middle of a harbor on a hot metal ship crawling with ant-women.

The last basket makes its way down the first of the lines and as each loader unhands it she sits or lies on the deck to recover till the next barge is in place, hands black with coal from the baskets and faces darkened with it now as they wipe the sweat away, a trail of exhausted women laid out with their eyes shut tight against the sun and their tiny ribs moving up and down.

A coal-smudged young woman with no hat but a red band around her forehead looks up to the forecastle before she sits on the frypan of a deck, locking eyes with Royal. There are another two ships, a German and an English, waiting behind them to be serviced. She cocks her head sideways as if considering something she has never seen before, then smiles at him, face glistening black as a minstrel. Royal feels tears running down his cheeks and suddenly aches, aches all over to be somewhere he can call home.

AMNESTY

Diosdado searches along the edge till there is nothing but reflection. The pond is filled with weeds, their ragged tops poking through the surface, but he finally finds a smooth patch and sees himself looking down with the open sky behind him. When he empties his eyes of comprehension there is nothing about the unshaven, shabbily dressed man to suggest he is more than an illiterate *tao*. He hides his *alpargatas* under the roots of a flowering *narra* tree, sinks his bare feet into the pond to coat them with muck, then heads down the acacia-lined road to Tautog.

He won't be the last patriot to surrender his rifle, not even in Zambales. Luciano San Miguel will fight on, and some of Tinio's people who have crossed over from the Ilocos, and Toque Rosales, who was a *tulisan* before the war and will become one again. But they will not win. If dying could drive the *yanquis* back across the sea he would find a way to die.

The sentry calls halt and he stops on the path with the rifle held in both hands high over his head. There is a rumor that the Americans have been shooting men who try to surrender, tired of paying the amnesty fee for rifles, angry and hot and bored and claiming their victims were ambushers or bandits. It is a rumor Diosdado helped to start when the men were weary of fighting, weary of running. Two soldiers step out at him, white men, each with a Krag aimed at his heart.

"Lay that piece down, *amigo*. Real slow."

He remains with frightened eyes and the crooked-barreled Remington overhead. He traded his Mauser to Pelaez for it, a piece of his soul left in the fight.

"Lookit here, nigger," says the other, and broadly mimes laying a rifle in the dirt. Diosdado puts the Remington down and steps back from it.

"There's a good boy. Now march."

The other Americans in Taugtod barely look at him as he is led in with his hands behind his neck. Two of them are chasing a flapping rooster around the plaza, cursing it, and another is shaving himself in a tiny mirror hung by a cord from the branch of a barren *santol*. The villagers seem resigned to the *yanquis* among them, as they were resigned to the Spanish before. Little boys are throwing a white ball back and forth with one of the soldiers who wears a leather glove on the hand he catches with. A lieutenant steps down from the house of Ignacio Yambao, the *alcalde* with the beautiful singing voice who was assassinated after the fiesta of the Ina Poon Bato.

The lieutenant has very green eyes and a blond moustache. The interpreter is a Macabebe, dressed in the *yanqui* uniform but for gray trousers and a red band around his hat. The Macabebe pokes Diosdado with a stick and indicates a stool placed in front of the lieutenant, who sits on a dusty friar chair and glares at him. Diosdado sits stiffly and looks at the ground like any terrified peasant, twisting his battered straw hat in his fingers, answering the questions in a respectful monotone.

"Who were you fighting with?" barks the Macabebe, first in Pampangano and then in heavily accented Tagalog.

"I was taken from my village, *jefe*. They tore up my *cédula* and forced me to go away with them," he answers, in Tagalog. "They called the leader El Porvenir."

"That is a lie."

"As you say, *jefe*. They told me I was fighting for our nation—"

"You are a bandit and you should be hanged from a tree. Where were you born?"

"I was born in Moncada, in Tarlac, but we moved to San Felipe when I was small. I made my First Communion there."

"You are a liar and a heathen."

"As you say, *jefe*."

Behind them, next to the little chapel, he sees the cemetery. He wonders if the tall marker with the angel on top belongs to the *alcalde*. He turns to the lieutenant and tries to grin as idiotically as possible.

"*Americano mucho* boom-boom," he says. "*Filipino mucho vamos.*"

If things get really ugly he will tell them where the head of Columbus is buried.

"What is this one's name?" growls the lieutenant, pen poised over a ledger book held in his lap.

"How were you baptized?" asks the Macabebe.

There is a price on his head throughout the province, even a picture of his face, badly drawn, tacked to the telegraph poles.

"My mother named me Bayani," he says in Tagalog, raising his eyes to meet the unsettling gaze of the American officer. There is no way to trust a man whose eyes are so green. "Bayani Pandoc."

There are bats gathering in the acacias in the evening as he heads back to reclaim his sandals, screeching, squirming, the branches bending with the weight of them. Diosdado pauses to wrap the thirty pieces of Mexican silver they gave him for the rifle tightly in a handkerchief, making sure the packet doesn't jingle, and stuffs it down the front of his shirt. The *yanquis* cannot be everywhere, and there are bandits on the road.

FORT GREENE

There are too many trains. Royal takes the Ninth Avenue elevated all the way down to Park Row and then transfers to the Myrtle Avenue line that crosses the bridge to Brooklyn. They have moved three times since the last address Junior wrote them at, no trace in those sorry buildings but Jubal able to come up with another possibility through Alma Moultrie. It has been too long. Dragging his feet after mustering out at Fort Reno, sick again, feeling like it was hopeless, something gone forever. The bridge makes him sweat, so high over the water, the train wobbling as it speeds across, passing wagons and carriages and even some people walking beside the tracks. San Francisco was enough of a mare's nest, but this city, spread across rivers, looming over your head, even tunneling under your feet—the idea of finding anybody in it seems impossible, the kind of lucky accident that never happens to him. People here move all the time, says Jubal, move up, move down, move out, Jubal himself just resettled to the far north of the main island.

That any city can have two hundred streets all in a row, and more without numbers below those, is more than he wants to think about.

One day at a time, the doctor at the military hospital told him. You're still carrying the worst of the tropics in that body.

Royal gets out at Navy Street, climbs down the stairs, and walks to a large park a block away. He needs more time to think. If they haven't moved, if she is still there—

He crosses the long, grassy rectangle of a park to a bench that faces a large stone crypt and sits.

TO THE VICTIMS OF THE PRISON SHIPS

—is inscribed on the side of the crypt. Royal wonders who the victims were, whose ships they were on.

There are women pushing babies in perambulators, and there are children running free, some making a hoop roll with a stick, and people sitting on the other benches alongside the path that snakes down the terraced hill to a large circular walk. It is a relief, this green after the brick maze of the island, but he doesn't feel any more sure of what he is here for.

"Somethin for the kiddies?"

It is a small man, maybe forty, white, with a crate strapped around his neck. WORLD OF FUN say the red letters painted on the front and sides. The man steps up and drops one knee onto the grass so Royal can see into the box.

"Got a little bit of everything here, dirt cheap."

There are tops and jacks and small wooden horses and rubber balls and throwing rings and a paddle-whacker and five metal soldiers, regular infantry. One of them, only one, is a tan color, something like Junior's shading. Royal points to it.

"Aint that the nuts?" says the man. "A one-of-a-kind item."

Royal lifts it out of the crate to study the face. It is surprisingly heavy for a toy. The eyes are not bugged, the lips not bloated like the golliwogs sold on almost every street corner here. Just a colored soldier.

"How much?"

"Fitty cents," says the older man. Royal gives him a look.

"Hey, like I said, it's one-of-a-kind."

Royal pays the man and sets the soldier on the bench. He sits. The other people in the park, who know why they are here, go about their business.

Royal sits and watches the carefree people on the green. The sun feels good against his skin as it dips lower and lower in the sky. They are all different colors up here, sometimes all jammed together in the same trolley car, and there must be rules about it but not so clear as back home. What was home. The shadow of the prisoners' crypt is very long when he stands to go back to the elevated train. It was never in the cards and time passing doesn't change anything. Spend the night with Jubal, tell him they've moved on, gone who knows where, say goodbye the next morning and then—what?

Royal realizes he's left the iron soldier on the bench. He goes back and when he picks it up he is suddenly ashamed. He can't leave it here, and riding back over the river with it sitting beside him—

A bullet in the head will only kill you, Sergeant Jacks used to say, but cowardice in the field will hound you into the grave and beyond.

It is a street of three-story brownstone buildings with front stoops leading down to the sidewalk. There are children everywhere, mostly colored, running and playing and talking in groups, ignoring Royal as he searches for the number Jubal told him.

There is a middling-sized girl at the top of the steps, minding a very tiny girl with her hair twisted into braids and red ribbons tied at the ends.

"The Luncefords live here?"

The girl looks at him sideways, suspicious.

"They aint in."

"But they do live here?" The tiny girl is staring at the iron figure in his hand.

"Doctor out with his bag. An Miz Jessie workin."

It would be easier, better probably, if they had moved on.

"You mind if I sit?"

"S'a free country."

Royal sits a couple steps below them. The tiny one is pointing at the soldier now, making sounds, so he sets it in front of her. She smiles and grabs around its body, maybe not strong enough to lift it, and begins to talk to it. Not words, really, but with the music of a conversation.

"Miss Jessie has a job?"

"Right now she learnin to be a typewriter girl."

Royal looks into the tiny one's face and counts the time. She seems too little to be three, but her eyes are old.

"If you sick," says the big girl, "Doctor don't usually get back till dinner."

She is halfway down the street before he knows it's her. She is wearing spectacles and no gloves and doesn't look like a girl anymore. Jessie slows as she sees him, then comes forward. She looks up to the top of the stoop.

"Thank you, Berenice."

"Night, Miz Jessie."

The girl goes inside. Jessie steps up past him and lifts the tiny one into her arms.

"Hope you don't mind," says Royal. "I was visiting my brother—"

"This is Minnie," Jessie tells him, holding his eye and placing the tiny girl in his lap. "We have been waiting so *long* for you."

ALTERNATING CURRENT

They are putting her feet in the shoes while Harry sets up the camera. The crowd in Luna Park is growing, held back at what the policemen think is a safe distance. Harry helps lift the instrument onto the tripod and levels it. A trainer with a wooden crook taps the huge beast on her rear leg. She shifts it and a pair of nervous-looking roustabouts quickly strap on the copper-lined shoe. She seems impassive, obeying each new tap from the trainer until all the shoes are secured, a thick hawser rope around her neck running taut to a donkey engine on one side and a telegraph pole on the other. If the cyanide carrots have affected her at all she doesn't show it.

They petted her, Topsy, only last summer, Brigid commenting on the bristles on the top of her trunk, on the incredible heat coming up through her skin. Technicians step in warily to attach cables to each of the shoes, cables leading back to the electrical plant that powers the million lights of Coney every evening. Harry was there in the stadium on the last day of the Pan when they tried to shock Jumbo II, another man-killer. There for the smoke and the sparks and the horrible trumpeting of the beast and then the laughter of the crowd when the giant animal remained standing, angrier than ever. The price of admission was refunded.

"I hope they do a better job of it on Czolgosz," quipped the wag in the next seat.

Jubal is ready at the wagon with another roll of film in case the first jolt fails and they choose to try again. Harry feels his stomach flutter, nervous, unsure if it is because of the fiasco in Buffalo last year or because this is his first time as operator. Ed Porter is supervising, having him roll a few feet as the mammoth was led up to the shoes. Porter is watching for the signal from the technicians.

The owners of Luna Park wanted to hang Topsy, but there were protests that hanging is barbaric, a relic of a bygone age, so Mr. Edison has stepped in to volunteer his expertise.

The eyes are so tiny for the bulk of it, as if a smaller and very intelligent creature is trapped within the monstrous body. The eyes of the people in the crowd, wide with anticipation, seem enormous by comparison. If there was a second camera Harry would love to do a panoramic of them—begin on Topsy's tiny, disinterested eye, then use the pan-head to circle slowly, registering the face of every human witness in the front ranks of the throng, holding on this woman in the purple velvet hat, or perhaps that worried little boy clutching his father's massive hand, holding on a human face as it contemplates the world's largest land mammal felled by George Westinghouse's alternating current.

Or pan a little farther to show Jubal at the wagon, back turned to the event, holding his horse by the bridle and covering its eyes with his hat.

"Get ready," says Porter. The technician by the cable-join relays a signal from the dynamo, windmilling his arm. Harry begins to turn the crank, steady, the rhythm of it like breathing now, trying not to let his nerves push him faster. The camera operator is the God of Time, Porter always says, the power to speed or slow events resting in the palm of his hand. Topsy begins to tap the ground with her trunk, as if searching for something, and Harry remembers the song—

You absent-minded beggar—

The young men on the ferry were singing it and he was worried it would offend his Brigid, but she sang along. They have been back here just once, Brigid attracted to novelty but even more delighted to witness the joy of others. On their trip to the Falls she was constantly looking out for other honeymooning couples.

"Do ye think," she'd shout to him, over the roar of the great waters, each time she spotted a likely pair, "they could possibly be as happy as we are?"

He doesn't see the second signal.

He is cranking steadily and there is a noise from the crowd around him, a thousand gasping at once as smoke billows up from all four shoes, white

smoke and burned-flesh odor and then Topsy buckling without a cry, collaps-
ing in a pile like a condemned tenement building.

Shouts and some cheers and somebody crying, but Harry cranks through
it, strangely shaken by the end of this breathtaking, murderous creature, the
song in his head running to the rhythm of his cranking, as if it is a hurdy-
gurdy and not a motion-picture camera—

> *You absent-minded beggar*
> *Be you city-sport or jay—*

The roll runs out and Harry calls to Jubal for another. The veterinarian
is there to proclaim that the beast has been executed and a trio of grounds-
keepers, colored men, wait to dispose of the gargantuan carcass. It is a heroic
task, much more difficult than throwing a switch, and he wants to record the
process on film. But Porter is already taking the instrument off the tripod.

"People have seen what they came for, Harry," he says. "Show's over."

But it won't leave his head, the song the young men were singing inces-
santly on that first boat trip to Coney Island with Brigid McCool—

> *You absent-minded beggar*
> *Be you city-sport or jay*
> *If you want to see the Elephant*
> *You must pay, pay, pay!*

John Sayles's previous novels include *Pride of the Bimbos*, *Los Gusanos*, and the National Book Award–nominated *Union Dues*. He has directed seventeen feature films, including *Matewan*, *Eight Men Out*, and *Lone Star*, and received a John Cassavetes Award, a John Steinbeck Award, and two Academy Award nominations. His latest film, *Amigo*, was completed in 2010.